Disney · PIXAR

TOY STORY

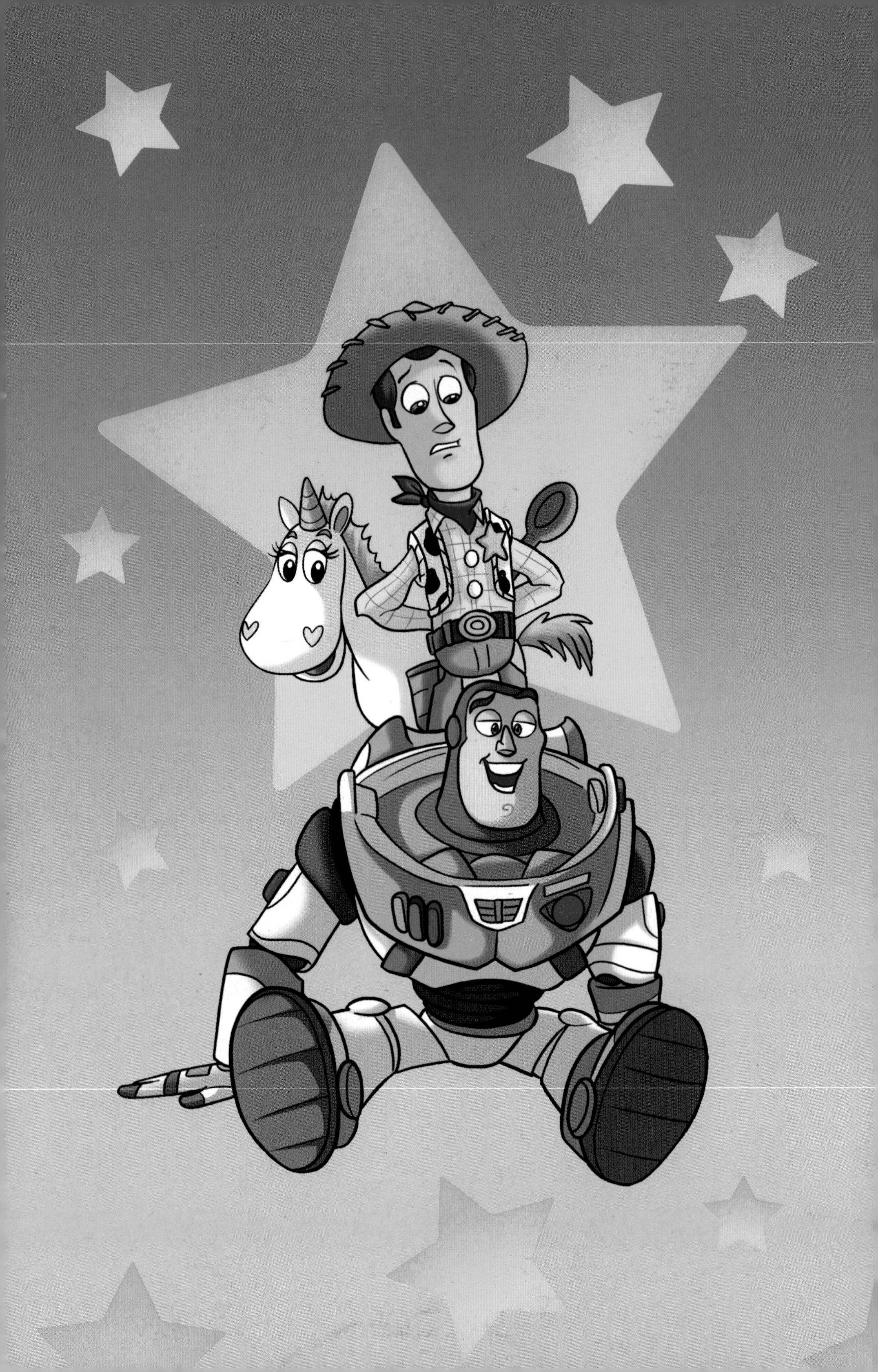

Disney · PIXAR

TOY STORY

ADVENTURES

VOLUME 2

Dark Horse Books

DARK HORSE BOOKS

PRESIDENT AND PUBLISHER Mike Richardson

EDITOR Shantel LaRocque

ASSISTANT EDITOR Brett Israel

DESIGNER Anita Magaña

DIGITAL ART TECHNICIAN Christianne Gillenardo-Goudreau

Neil Hankerson (Executive Vice President), Tom Weddle (Chief Financial Officer), Randy Stradley (Vice President of Publishing), Nick McWhorter (Chief Business Development Officer), Dale LaFountain (Chief Information Officer), Matt Parkinson (Vice President of Marketing), Cara Niece (Vice President of Production and Scheduling), Mark Bernardi (Vice President of Book Trade and Digital Sales), Ken Lizzi (General Counsel), Dave Marshall (Editor in Chief), Davey Estrada (Editorial Director), Chris Warner (Senior Books Editor), Cary Grazzini (Director of Specialty Projects), Lia Ribacchi (Art Director), Vanessa Todd-Holmes (Director of Print Purchasing), Matt Dryer (Director of Digital Art and Prepress), Michael Gombos (Senior Director of Licensed Publications), Kari Yadro (Director of Custom Programs), Kari Torson (Director of International Licensing), Sean Brice (Director of Trade Sales)

DISNEY PUBLISHING WORLDWIDE GLOBAL MAGAZINES, COMICS AND PARTWORKS
PUBLISHER Lynn Waggoner · **EDITORIAL TEAM** Bianca Coletti (Director, Magazines), Guido Frazzini (Director, Comics), Carlotta Quattrocolo (Executive Editor), Stefano Ambrosio (Executive Editor, New IP), Camilla Vedove (Senior Manager, Editorial Development), Behnoosh Khalili (Senior Editor), Julie Dorris (Senior Editor), Mina Riazi (Assistant Editor), Jonathan Manning (Assistant Editor) · **DESIGN** Enrico Soave (Senior Designer) · **ART** Ken Shue (VP, Global Art), Manny Mederos (Senior Illustration Manager, Comics and Magazines), Roberto Santillo (Creative Director), Marco Ghiglione (Creative Manager), Stefano Attardi (Computer Art Designer) · **PORTFOLIO MANAGEMENT** Olivia Ciancarelli (Director) · **BUSINESS & MARKETING** Mariantonietta Galla (Marketing Manager), Virpi Korhonen (Editorial Manager)

Published by Dark Horse Books
A division of Dark Horse Comics LLC.
10956 SE Main Street
Milwaukie, OR 97222

DarkHorse.com
To find a comics shop in your area,
visit comicshoplocator.com

First edition: September 2019
ISBN 978-1-50671-451-6
Digital ISBN 978-1-50671-452-3

10 9 8 7 6 5 4 3 2 1
Printed in China

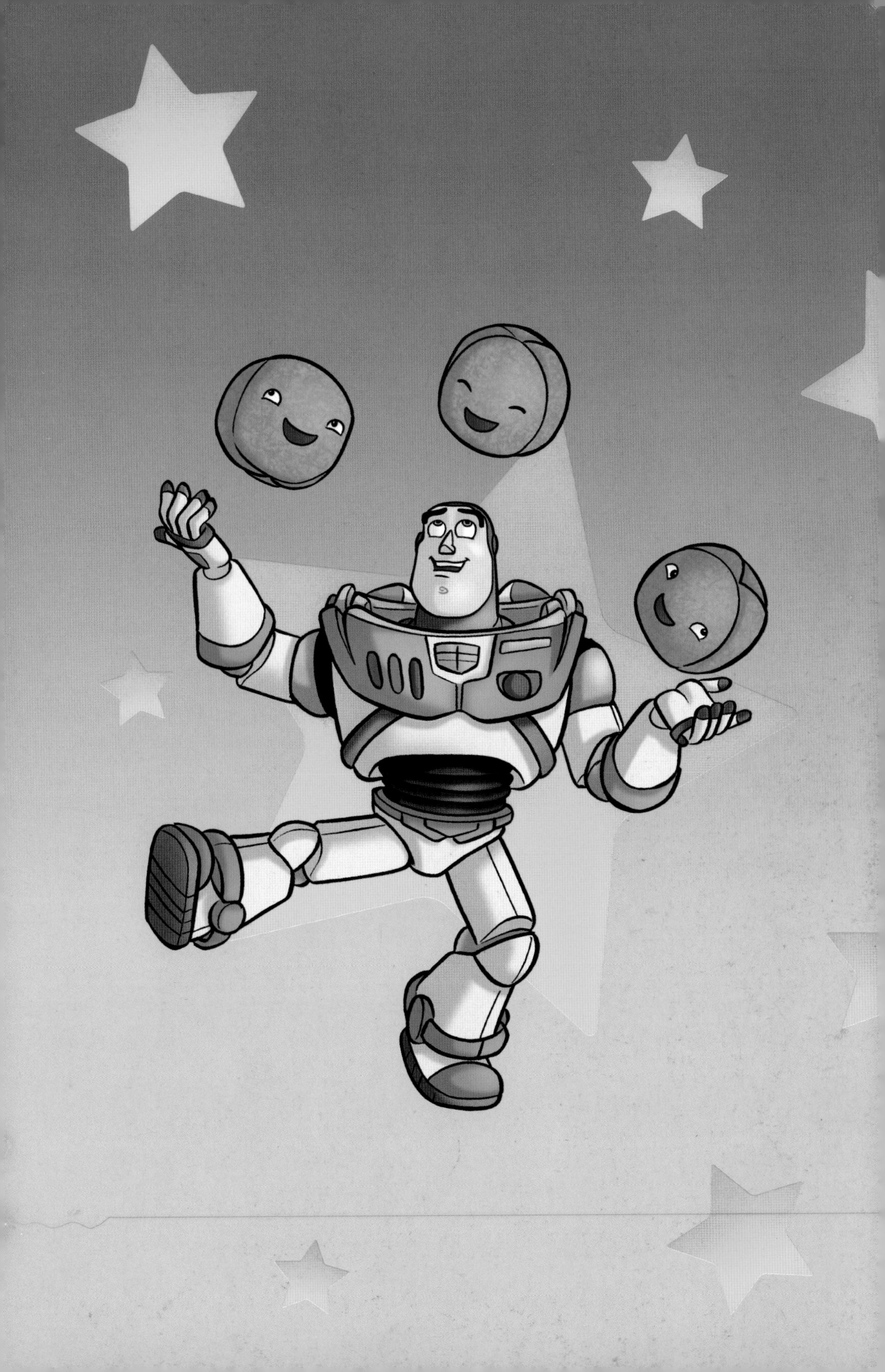

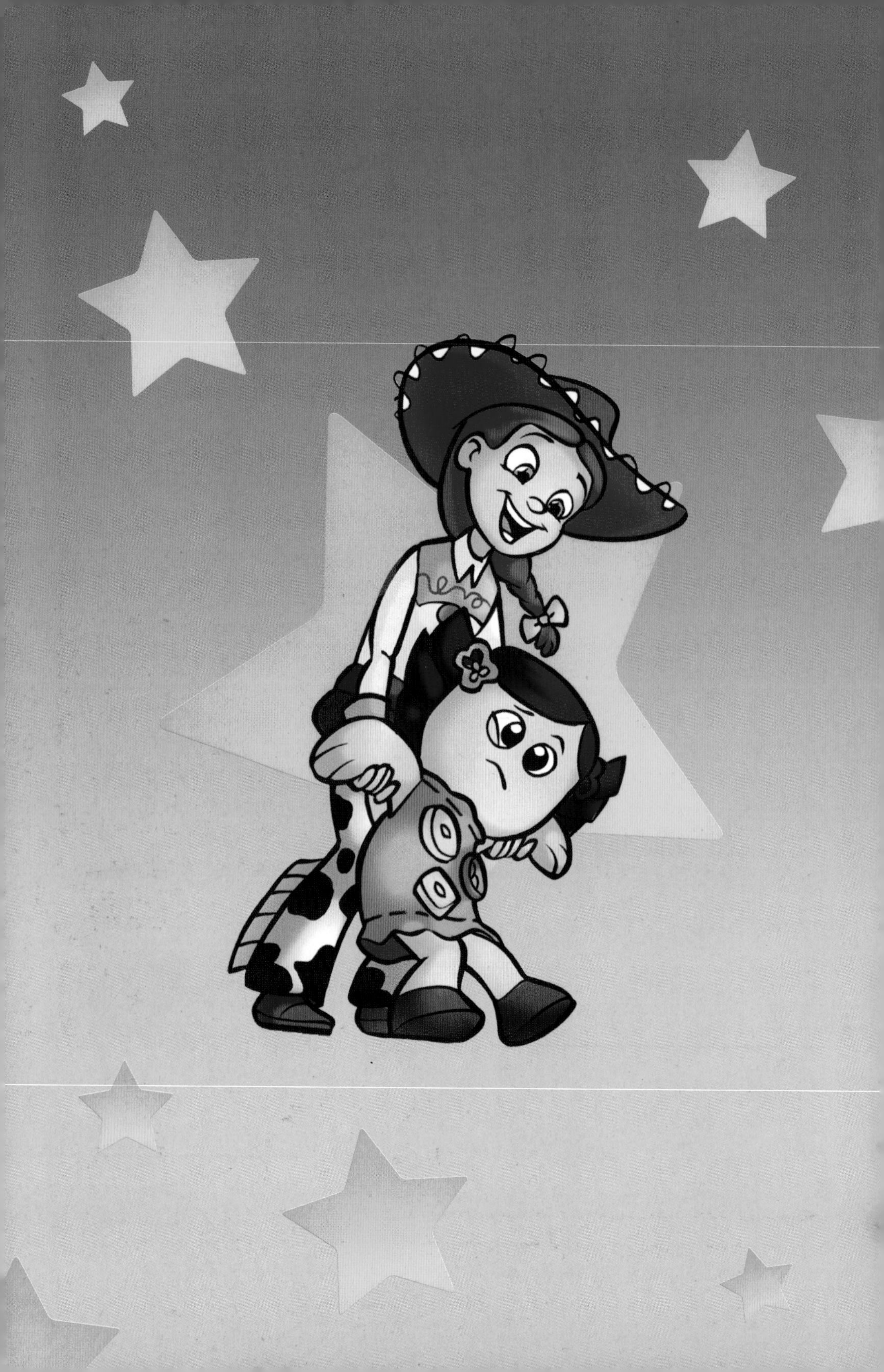

THE HAUNTED CLOSET

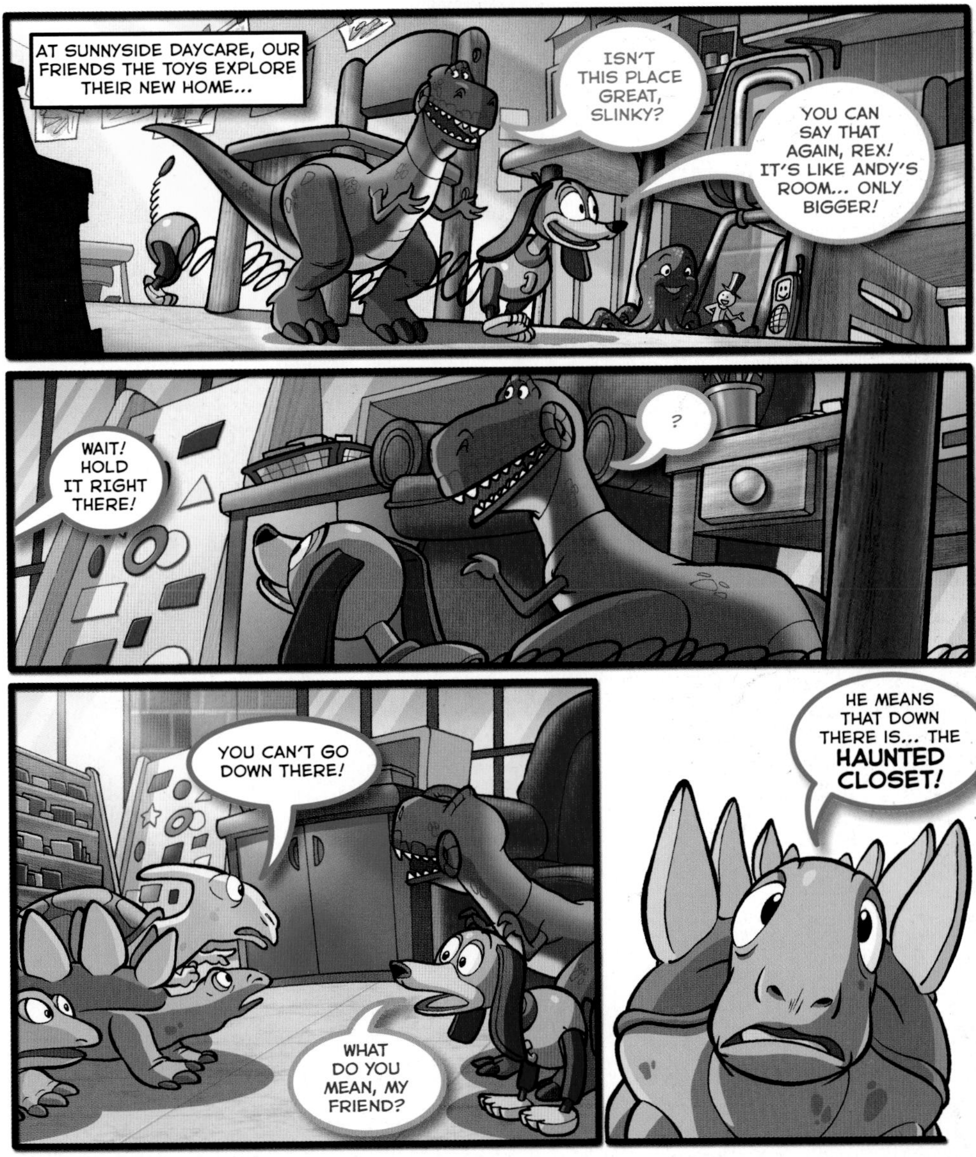
AT SUNNYSIDE DAYCARE, OUR FRIENDS THE TOYS EXPLORE THEIR NEW HOME...
ISN'T THIS PLACE GREAT, SLINKY?
YOU CAN SAY THAT AGAIN, REX! IT'S LIKE ANDY'S ROOM... ONLY BIGGER!
WAIT! HOLD IT RIGHT THERE!
?
YOU CAN'T GO DOWN THERE!
WHAT DO YOU MEAN, MY FRIEND?
HE MEANS THAT DOWN THERE IS... THE **HAUNTED CLOSET!**

SCRIPT: ALESSANDRO FERRARI; PENCILS: VALENTINO FORLINI; INK: FEDERICA SALFO; PAINT: GIANLUCA BARONE

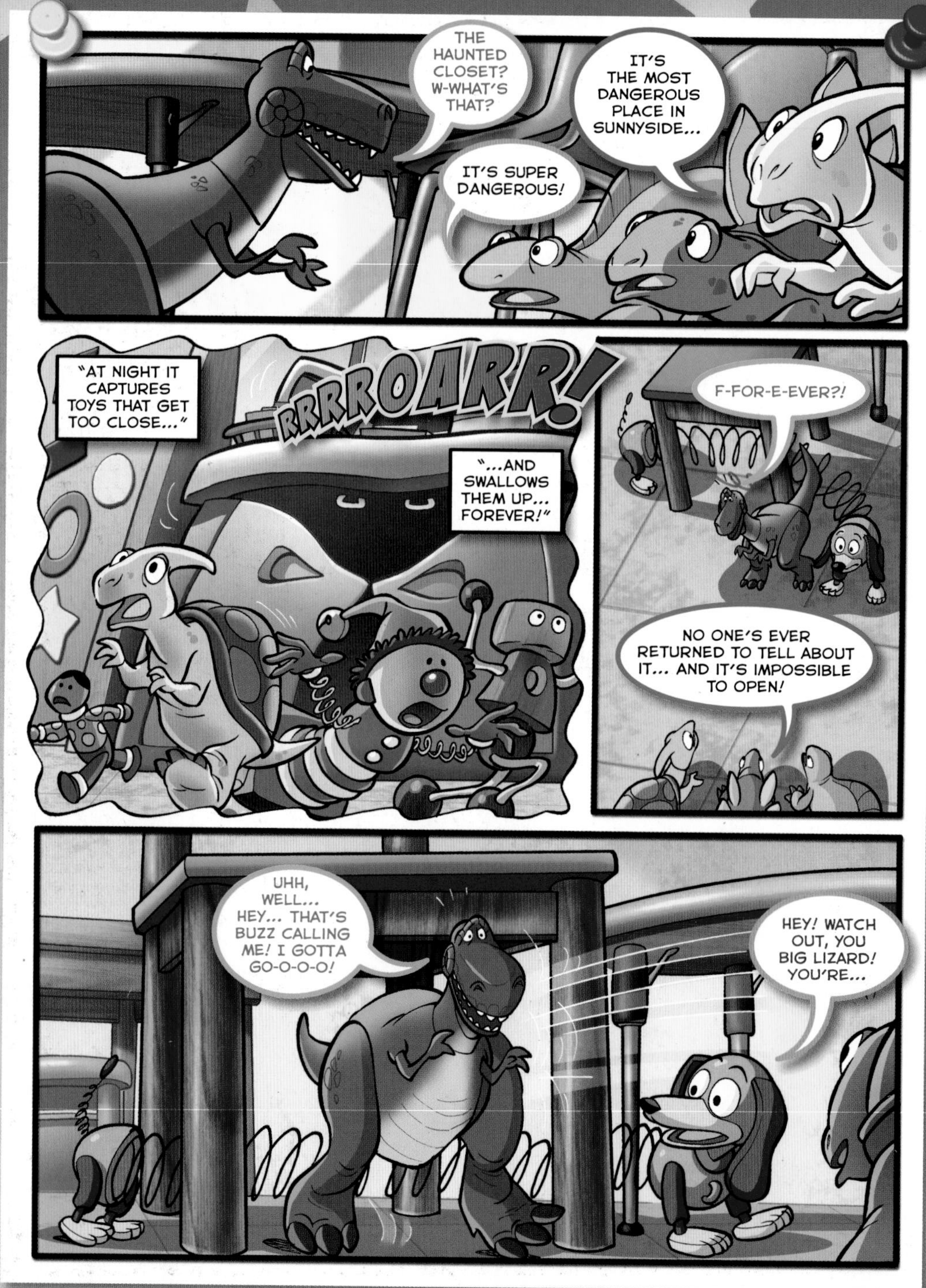
THE HAUNTED CLOSET? W-WHAT'S THAT?
IT'S THE MOST DANGEROUS PLACE IN SUNNYSIDE...
IT'S SUPER DANGEROUS!
"AT NIGHT IT CAPTURES TOYS THAT GET TOO CLOSE..."
RRRROARR!
"...AND SWALLOWS THEM UP... FOREVER!"
F-FOR-E-EVER?!
NO ONE'S EVER RETURNED TO TELL ABOUT IT... AND IT'S IMPOSSIBLE TO OPEN!
UHH, WELL... HEY... THAT'S BUZZ CALLING ME! I GOTTA GO-O-O-O!
HEY! WATCH OUT, YOU BIG LIZARD! YOU'RE...

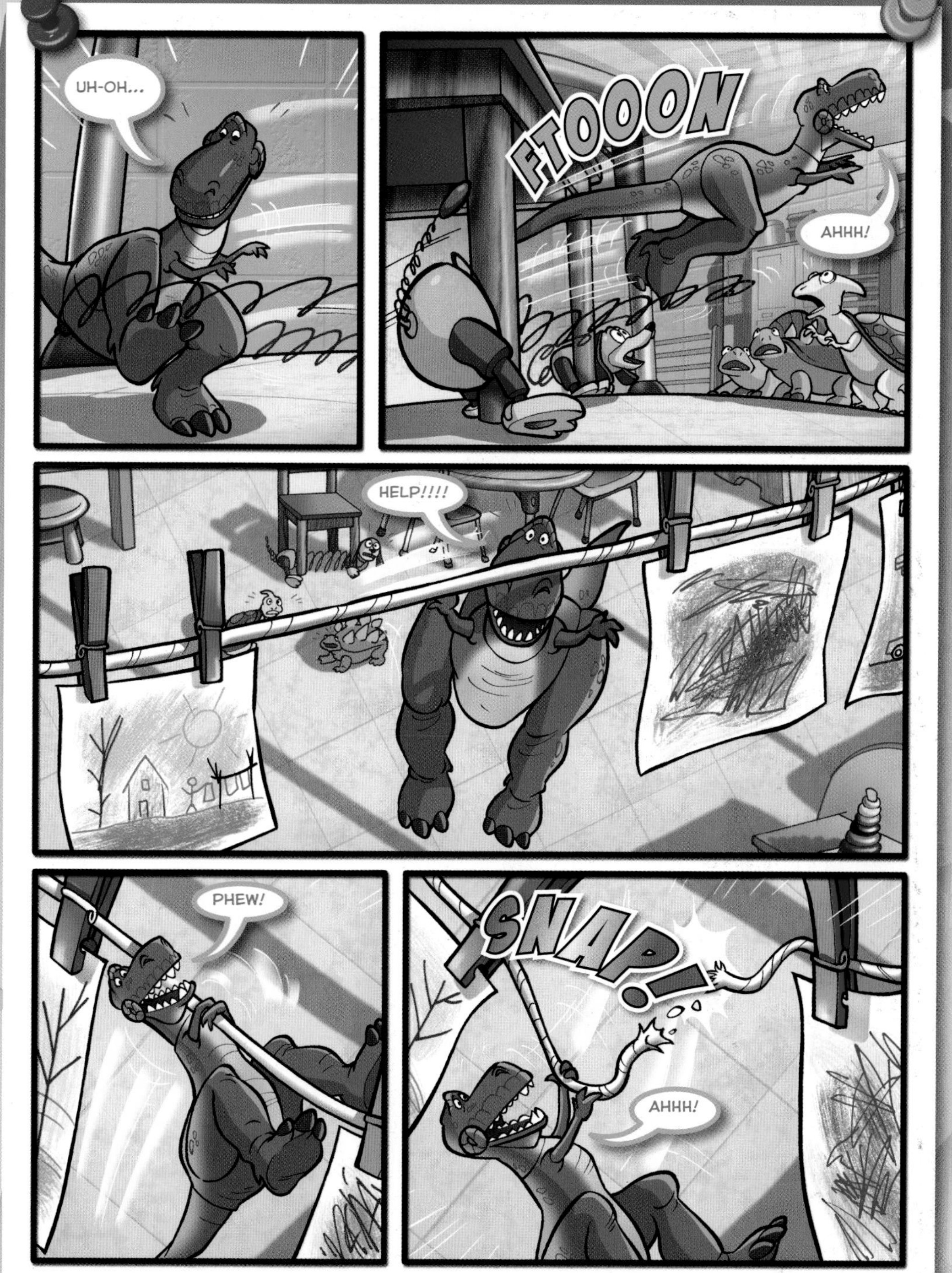
UH-OH...
FTOOON
AHHH!
HELP!!!!
PHEW!
SNAP!
AHHH!

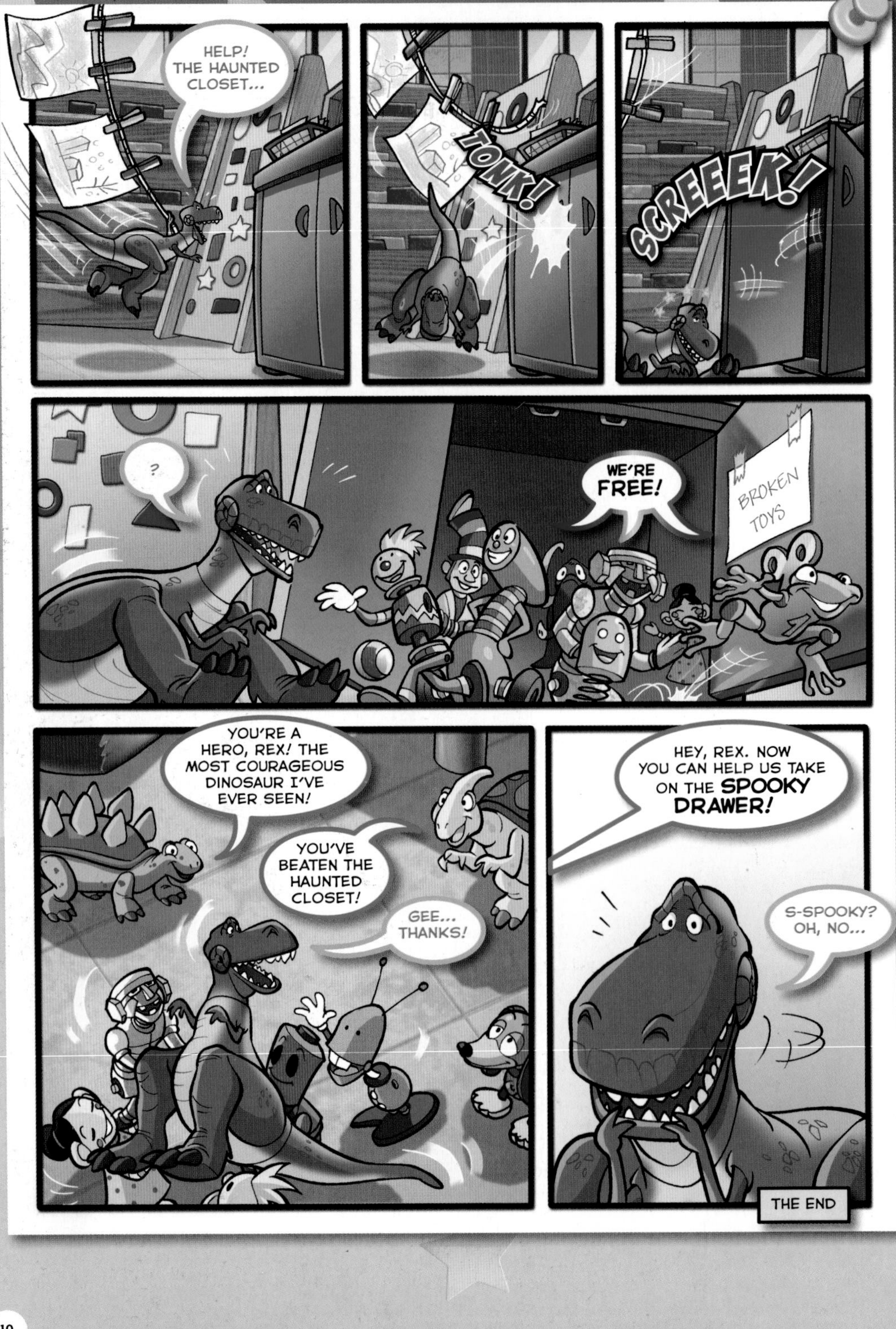
HELP! THE HAUNTED CLOSET...
TONK!
SCREEEEK!
?
WE'RE FREE!
BROKEN TOYS
YOU'RE A HERO, REX! THE MOST COURAGEOUS DINOSAUR I'VE EVER SEEN!
YOU'VE BEATEN THE HAUNTED CLOSET!
GEE... THANKS!
HEY, REX. NOW YOU CAN HELP US TAKE ON THE SPOOKY DRAWER!
S-SPOOKY? OH, NO...
THE END

TOY GHOSTS

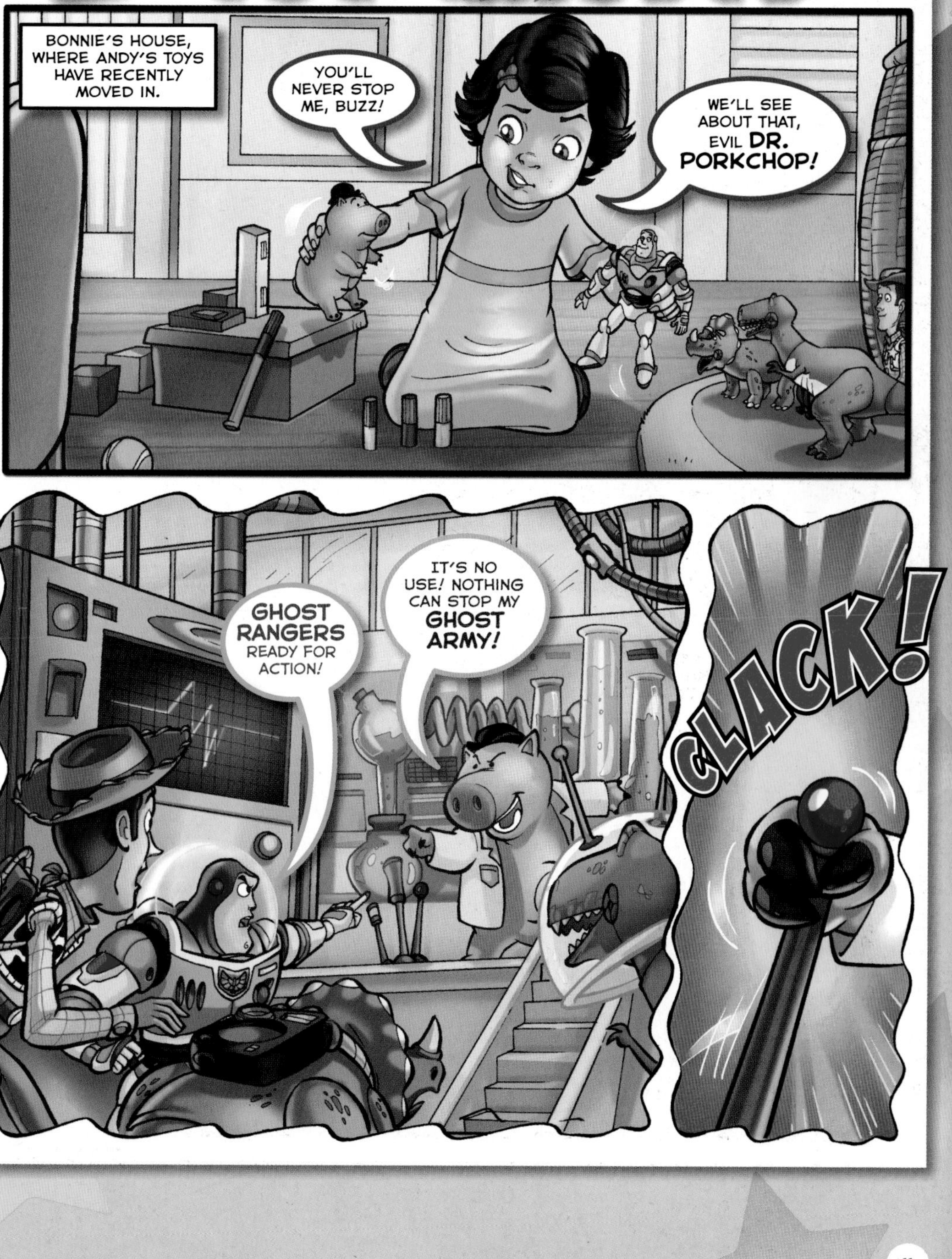

BONNIE'S HOUSE, WHERE ANDY'S TOYS HAVE RECENTLY MOVED IN.
YOU'LL NEVER STOP ME, BUZZ!
WE'LL SEE ABOUT THAT, EVIL **DR. PORKCHOP!**
GHOST RANGERS READY FOR ACTION!
IT'S NO USE! NOTHING CAN STOP MY **GHOST ARMY!**
CLACK!

SCRIPT: ALESSANDRO FERRARI; PENCILS: VALENTINO FORLINI; INK: FEDERICA SALFO; PAINT: KAWAII CREATIVE STUDIO

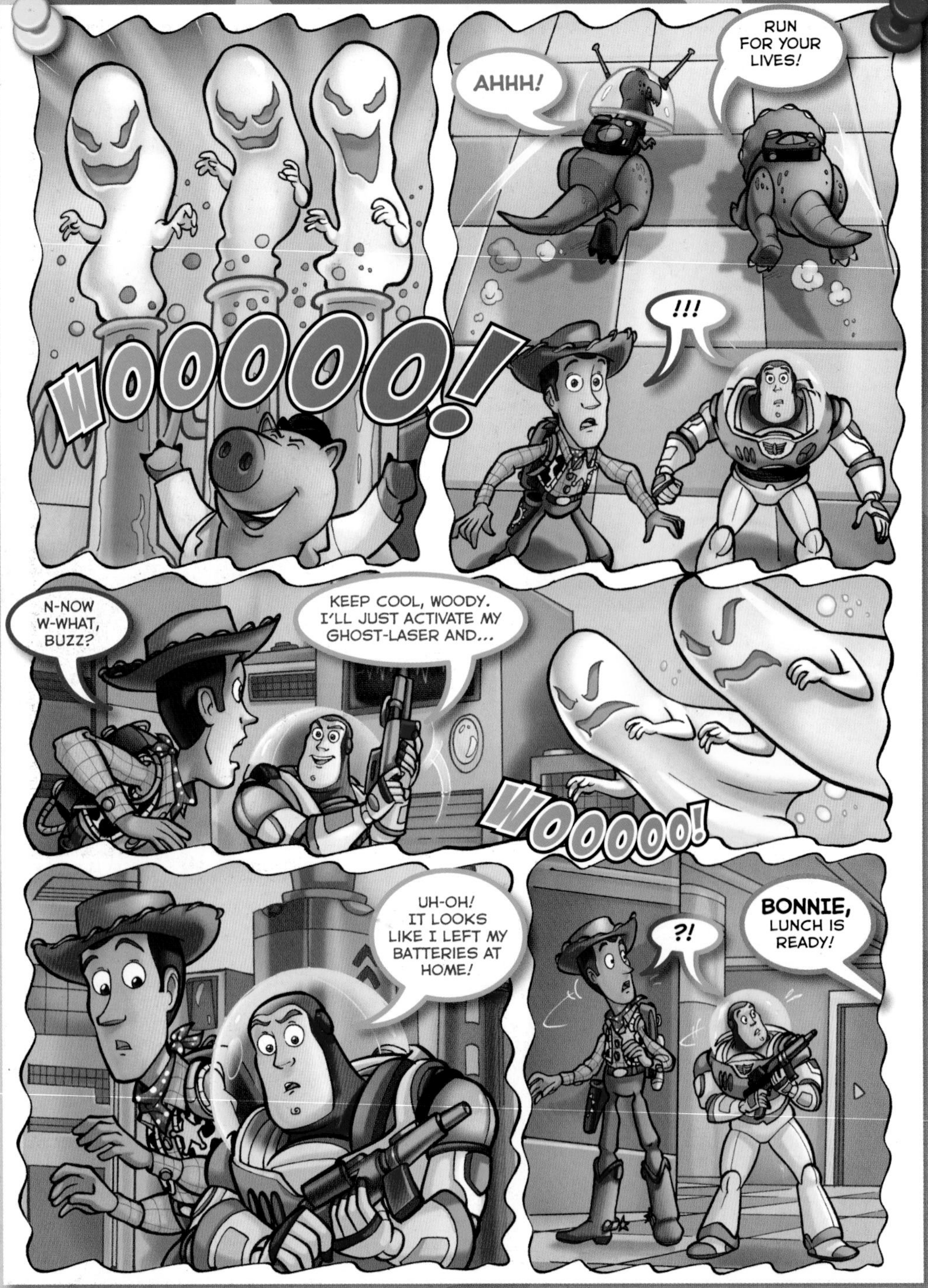
WOOOOO!
AHHH!
RUN FOR YOUR LIVES!
!!!
N-NOW W-WHAT, BUZZ?
KEEP COOL, WOODY. I'LL JUST ACTIVATE MY GHOST-LASER AND...
WOOOOO!
UH-OH! IT LOOKS LIKE I LEFT MY BATTERIES AT HOME!
?!
BONNIE, LUNCH IS READY!

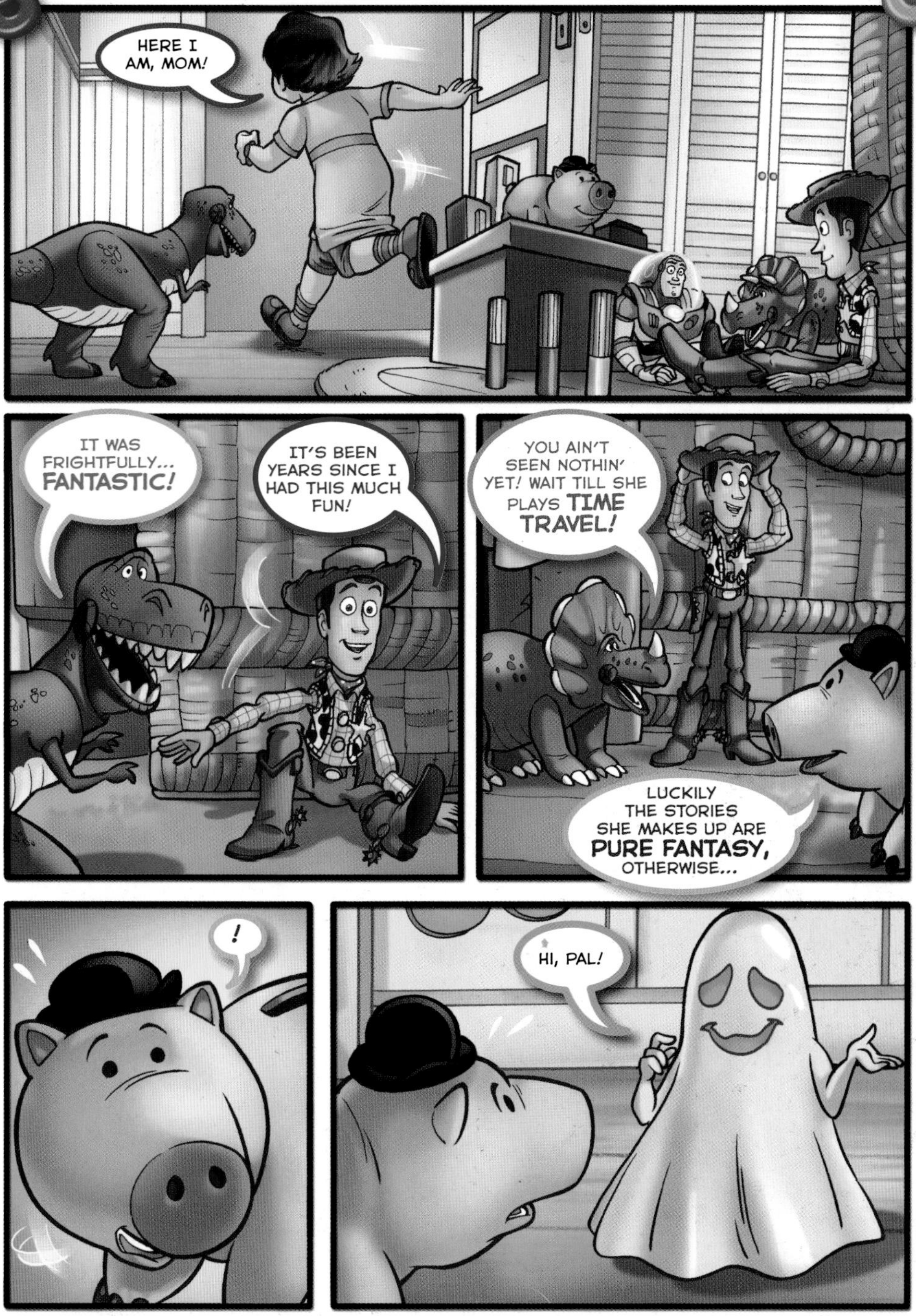

HERE I AM, MOM!
IT WAS FRIGHTFULLY... FANTASTIC!
IT'S BEEN YEARS SINCE I HAD THIS MUCH FUN!
YOU AIN'T SEEN NOTHIN' YET! WAIT TILL SHE PLAYS TIME TRAVEL!
LUCKILY THE STORIES SHE MAKES UP ARE PURE FANTASY, OTHERWISE...
!
HI, PAL!

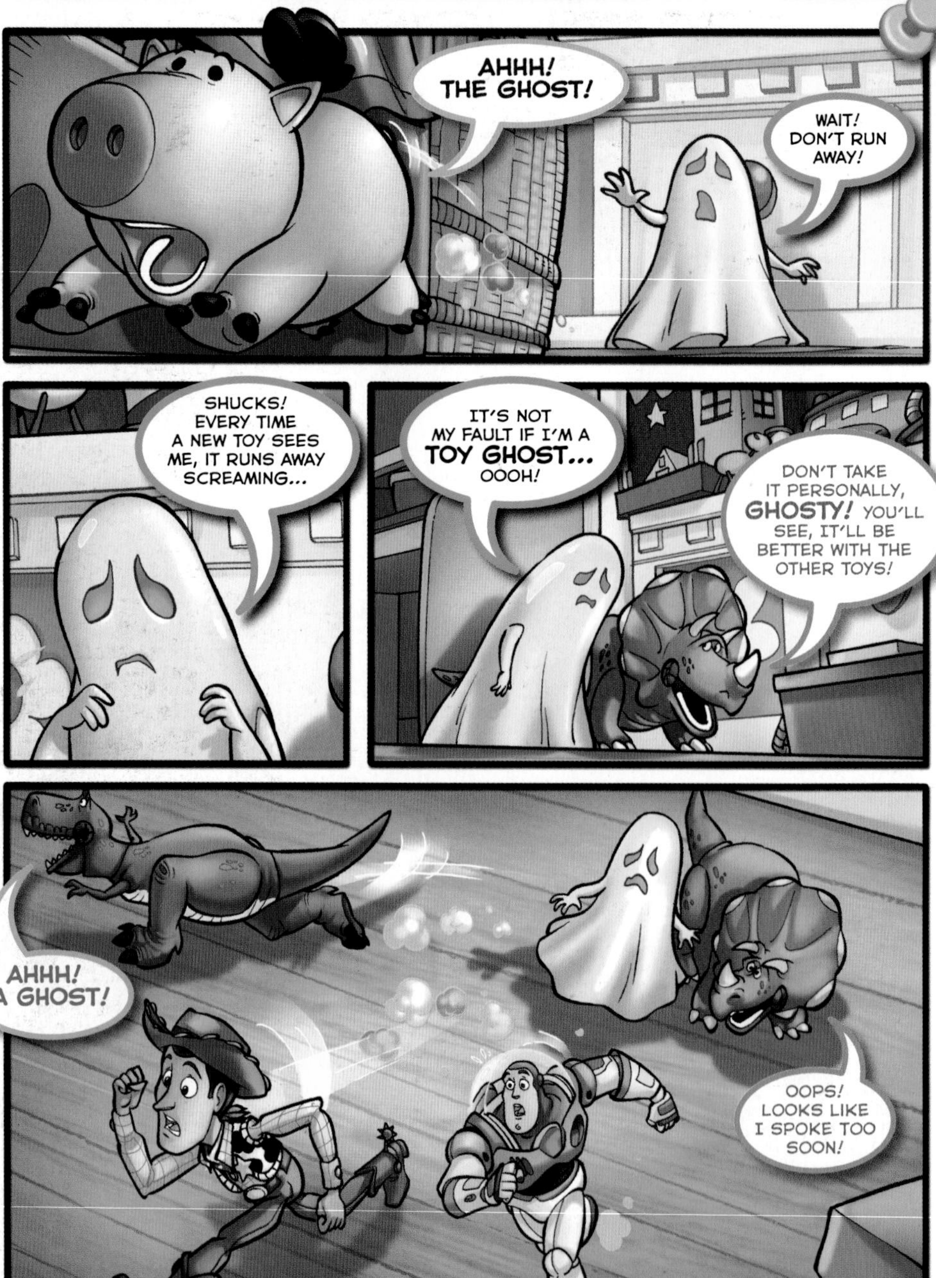
AHHH! THE GHOST!
WAIT! DON'T RUN AWAY!
SHUCKS! EVERY TIME A NEW TOY SEES ME, IT RUNS AWAY SCREAMING...
IT'S NOT MY FAULT IF I'M A TOY GHOST... OOOH!
DON'T TAKE IT PERSONALLY, GHOSTY! YOU'LL SEE, IT'LL BE BETTER WITH THE OTHER TOYS!
AHHH! A GHOST!
OOPS! LOOKS LIKE I SPOKE TOO SOON!
THE END

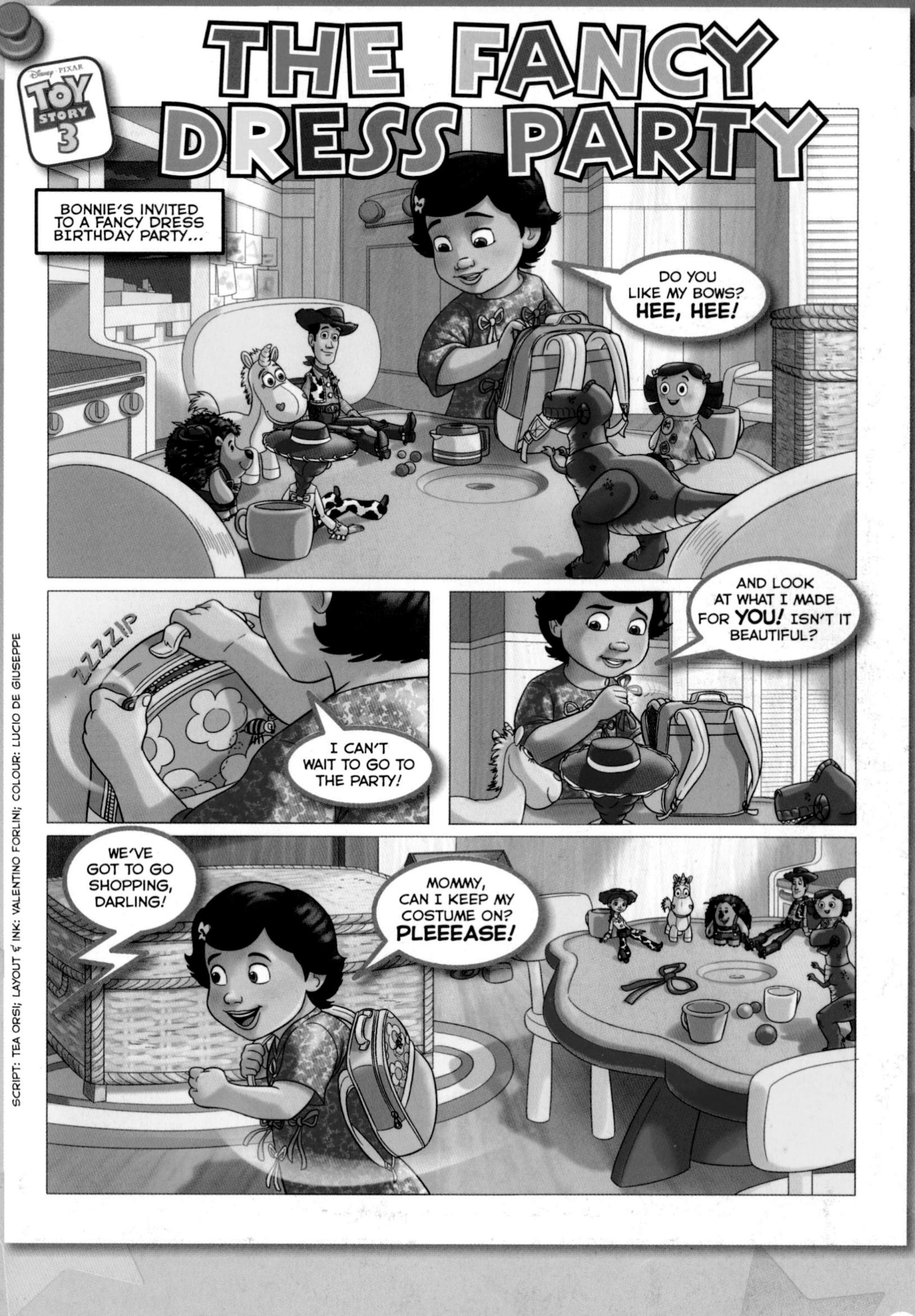
DISNEY · PIXAR
TOY STORY 3
THE FANCY DRESS PARTY
BONNIE'S INVITED TO A FANCY DRESS BIRTHDAY PARTY...
DO YOU LIKE MY BOWS? HEE, HEE!
ZZZZIP
I CAN'T WAIT TO GO TO THE PARTY!
AND LOOK AT WHAT I MADE FOR YOU! ISN'T IT BEAUTIFUL?
WE'VE GOT TO GO SHOPPING, DARLING!
MOMMY, CAN I KEEP MY COSTUME ON? PLEEEASE!
SCRIPT: TEA ORSI; LAYOUT & INK: VALENTINO FORLINI; COLOUR: LUCIO DE GIUSEPPE

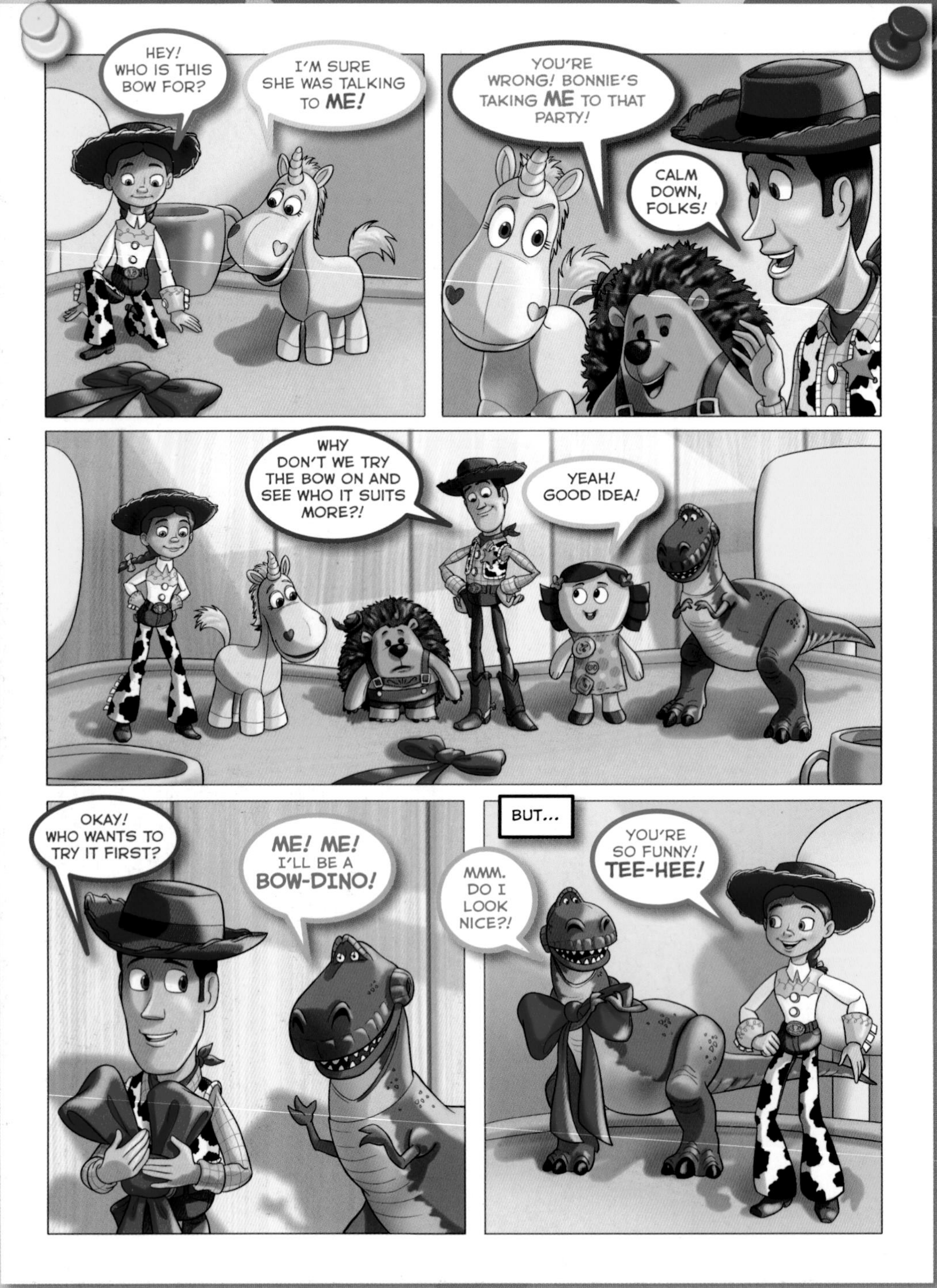
HEY! WHO IS THIS BOW FOR?
I'M SURE SHE WAS TALKING TO ME!
YOU'RE WRONG! BONNIE'S TAKING ME TO THAT PARTY!
CALM DOWN, FOLKS!
WHY DON'T WE TRY THE BOW ON AND SEE WHO IT SUITS MORE?!
YEAH! GOOD IDEA!
OKAY! WHO WANTS TO TRY IT FIRST?
ME! ME! I'LL BE A BOW-DINO!
BUT...
MMM. DO I LOOK NICE?!
YOU'RE SO FUNNY! TEE-HEE!

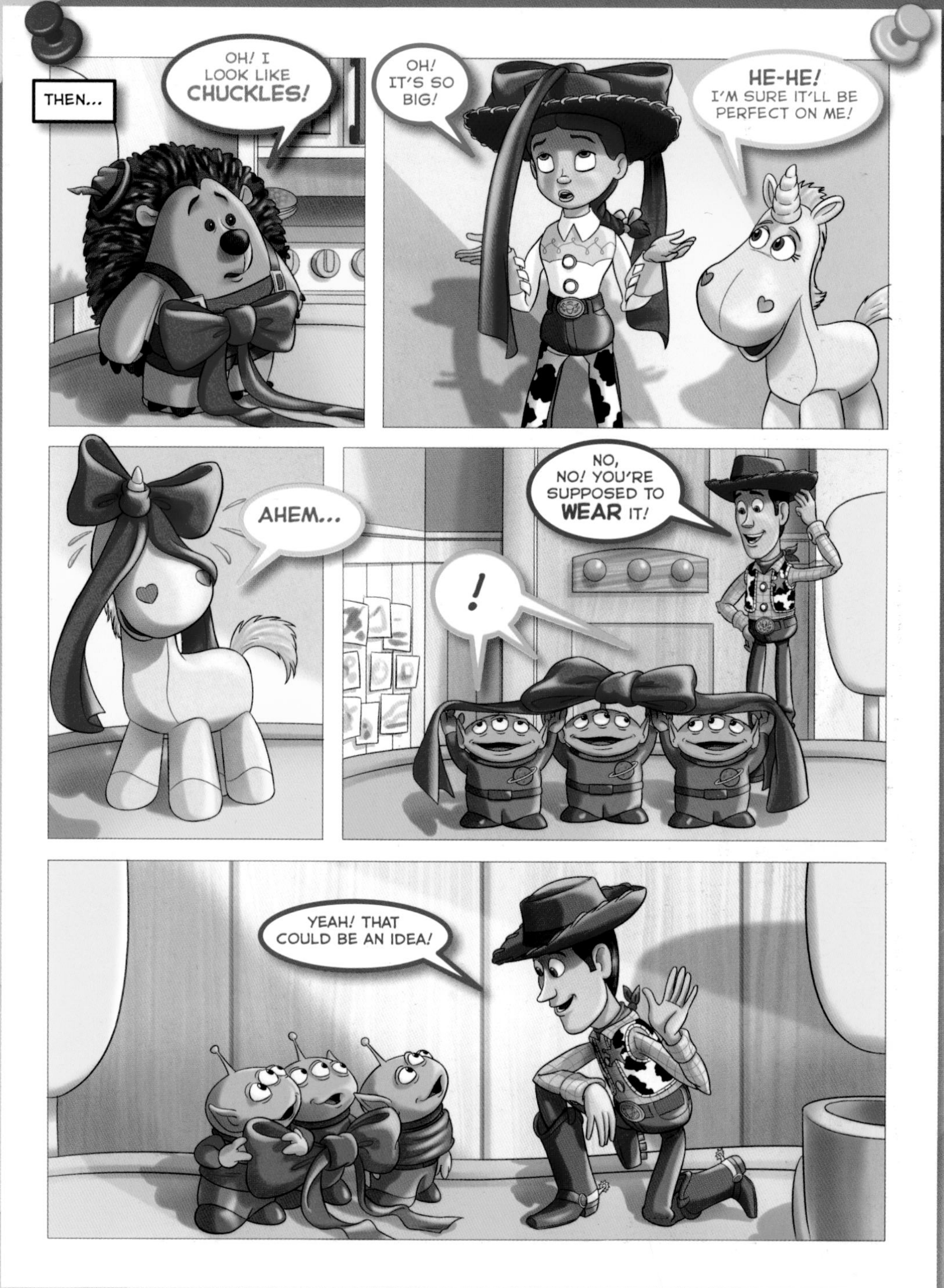
THEN...
OH! I LOOK LIKE CHUCKLES!
OH! IT'S SO BIG!
HE-HE! I'M SURE IT'LL BE PERFECT ON ME!
AHEM...
NO, NO! YOU'RE SUPPOSED TO WEAR IT!
!
YEAH! THAT COULD BE AN IDEA!

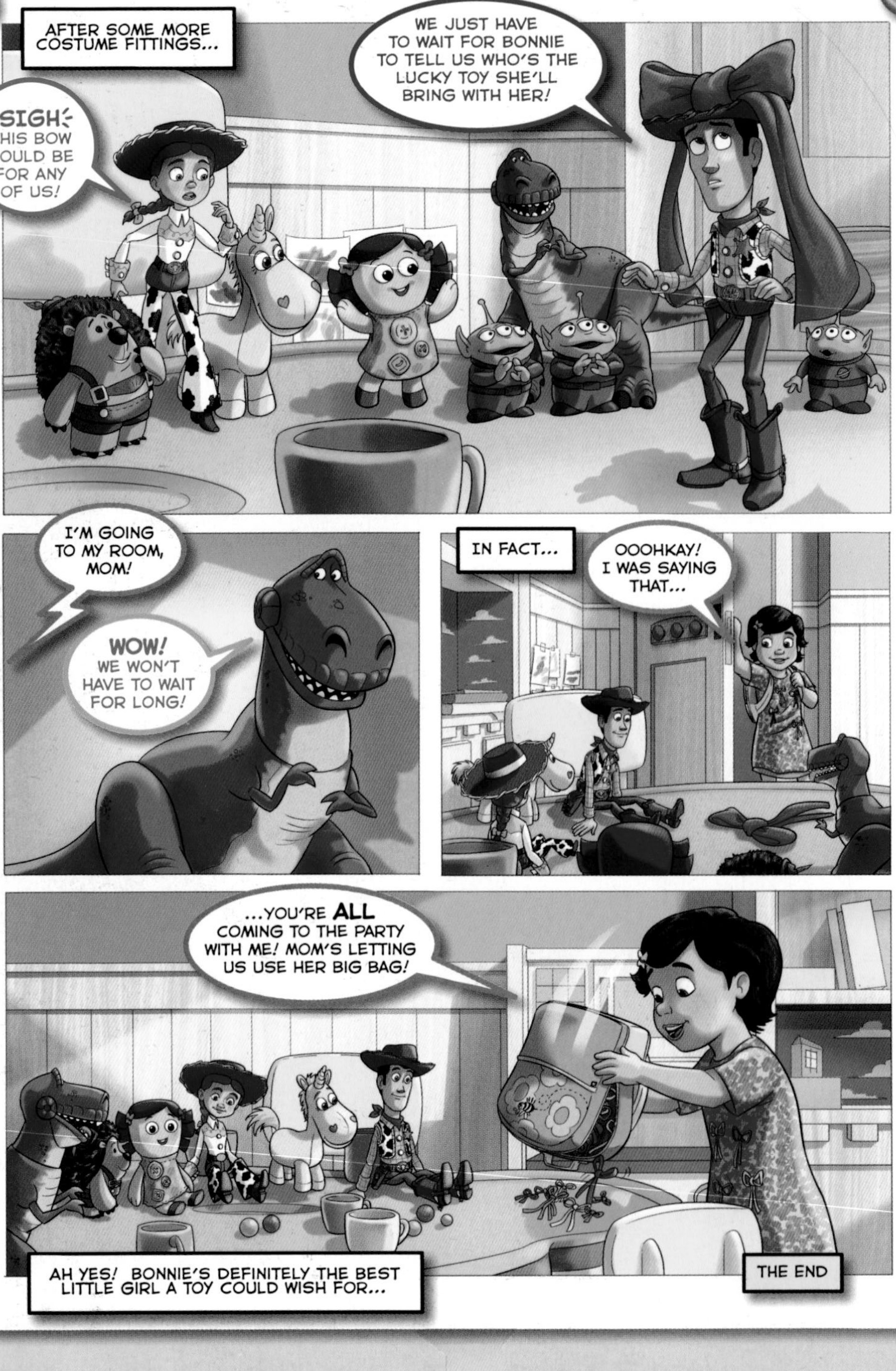
AFTER SOME MORE COSTUME FITTINGS...
SIGH THIS BOW COULD BE FOR ANY OF US!
WE JUST HAVE TO WAIT FOR BONNIE TO TELL US WHO'S THE LUCKY TOY SHE'LL BRING WITH HER!
I'M GOING TO MY ROOM, MOM!
WOW! WE WON'T HAVE TO WAIT FOR LONG!
IN FACT...
OOOHKAY! I WAS SAYING THAT...
...YOU'RE ALL COMING TO THE PARTY WITH ME! MOM'S LETTING US USE HER BIG BAG!
AH YES! BONNIE'S DEFINITELY THE BEST LITTLE GIRL A TOY COULD WISH FOR...
THE END

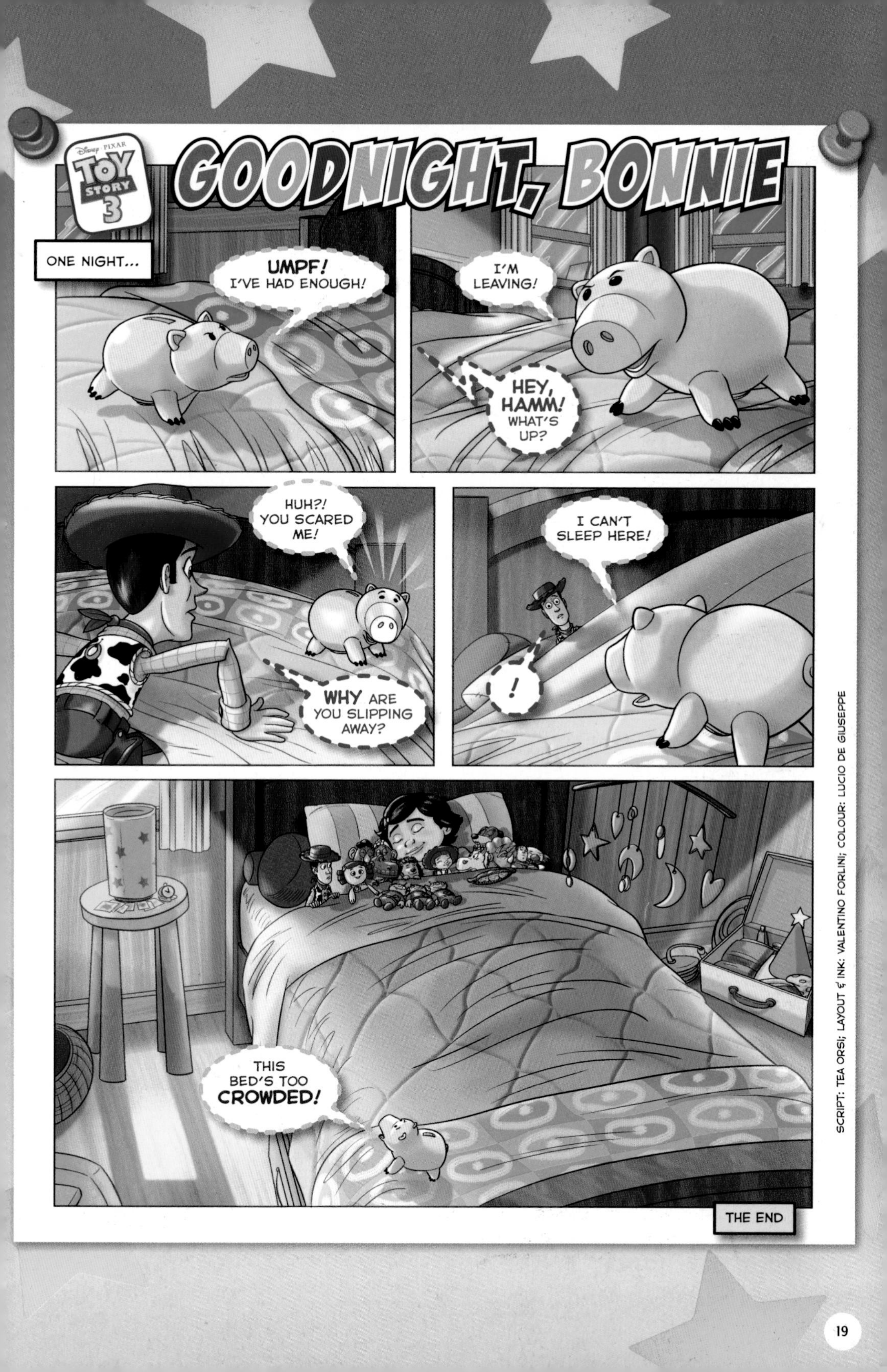
DISNEY PIXAR
TOY STORY 3
GOODNIGHT, BONNIE
ONE NIGHT...
UMPF! I'VE HAD ENOUGH!
I'M LEAVING!
HEY, HAMM! WHAT'S UP?
HUH?! YOU SCARED ME!
WHY ARE YOU SLIPPING AWAY?
I CAN'T SLEEP HERE!
!
THIS BED'S TOO CROWDED!
THE END

SCRIPT: TEA ORSI; LAYOUT & INK: VALENTINO FORLINI; COLOUR: LUCIO DE GIUSEPPE

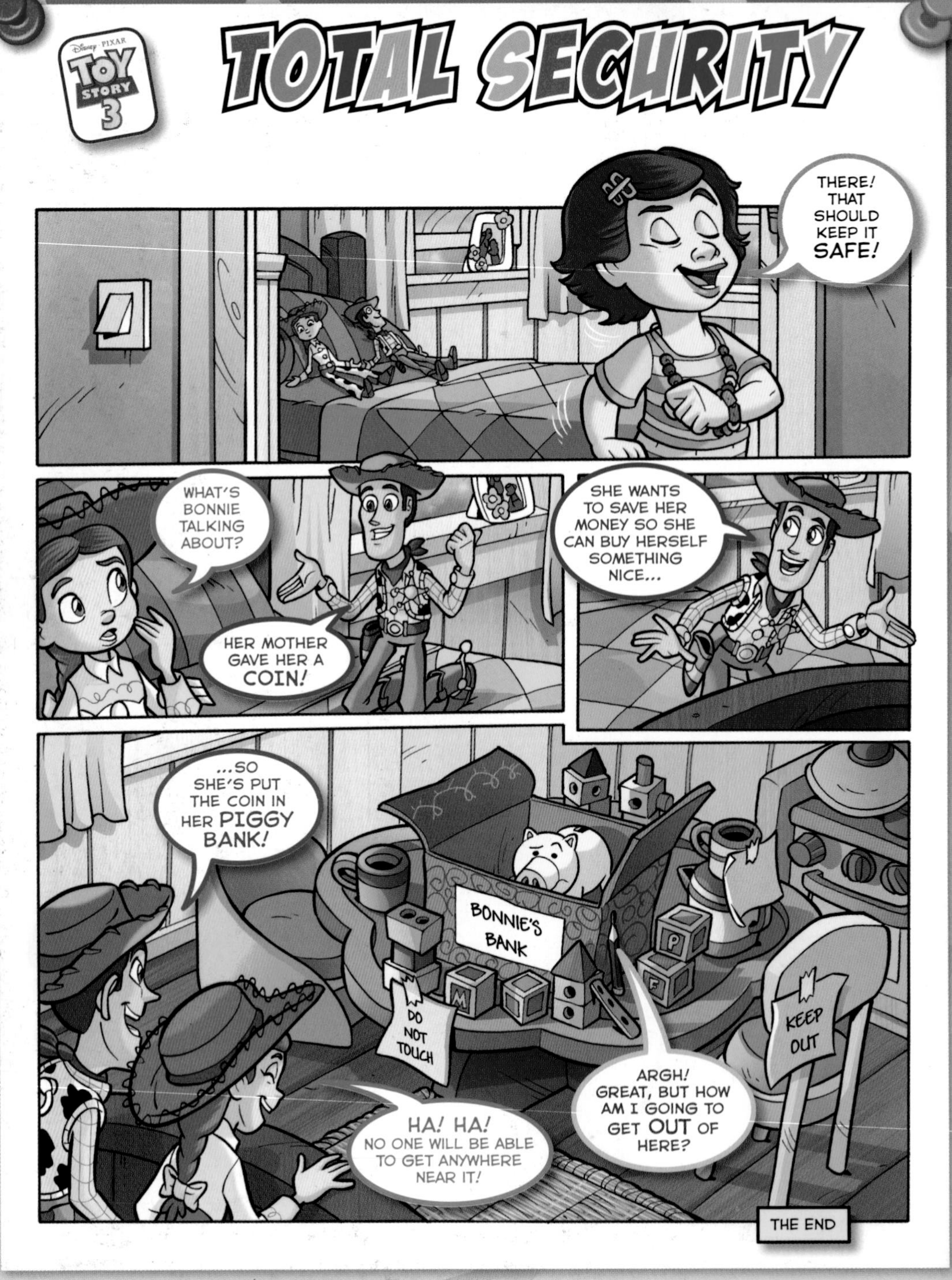
TOY STORY 3
TOTAL SECURITY
THERE! THAT SHOULD KEEP IT SAFE!
WHAT'S BONNIE TALKING ABOUT?
HER MOTHER GAVE HER A COIN!
SHE WANTS TO SAVE HER MONEY SO SHE CAN BUY HERSELF SOMETHING NICE...
...SO SHE'S PUT THE COIN IN HER PIGGY BANK!
BONNIE'S BANK
DO NOT TOUCH
KEEP OUT
ARGH! GREAT, BUT HOW AM I GOING TO GET OUT OF HERE?
HA! HA! NO ONE WILL BE ABLE TO GET ANYWHERE NEAR IT!
THE END

SCRIPT: ALESSANDRO SISTI; PENCILS&INK: LUCA USAI; COLOUR: MARA DAMIANI

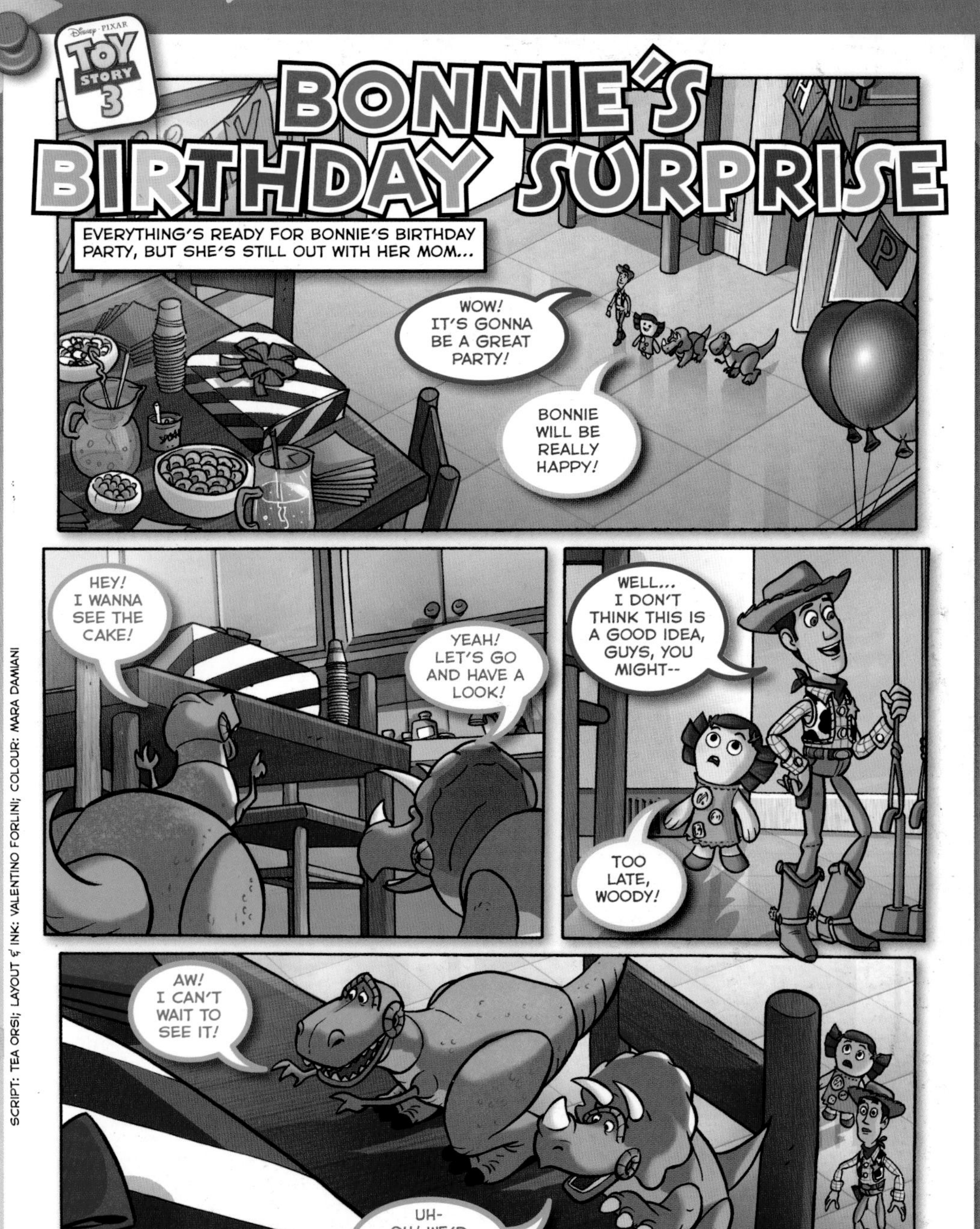
DISNEY · PIXAR
TOY STORY 3
BONNIE'S BIRTHDAY SURPRISE
EVERYTHING'S READY FOR BONNIE'S BIRTHDAY PARTY, BUT SHE'S STILL OUT WITH HER MOM...
WOW! IT'S GONNA BE A GREAT PARTY!
BONNIE WILL BE REALLY HAPPY!
HEY! I WANNA SEE THE CAKE!
YEAH! LET'S GO AND HAVE A LOOK!
WELL... I DON'T THINK THIS IS A GOOD IDEA, GUYS, YOU MIGHT--
TOO LATE, WOODY!
AW! I CAN'T WAIT TO SEE IT!
UH-OH! WE'D BETTER REACH THEM!

SCRIPT: TEA ORSI; LAYOUT & INK: VALENTINO FORLINI; COLOUR: MARA DAMIANI

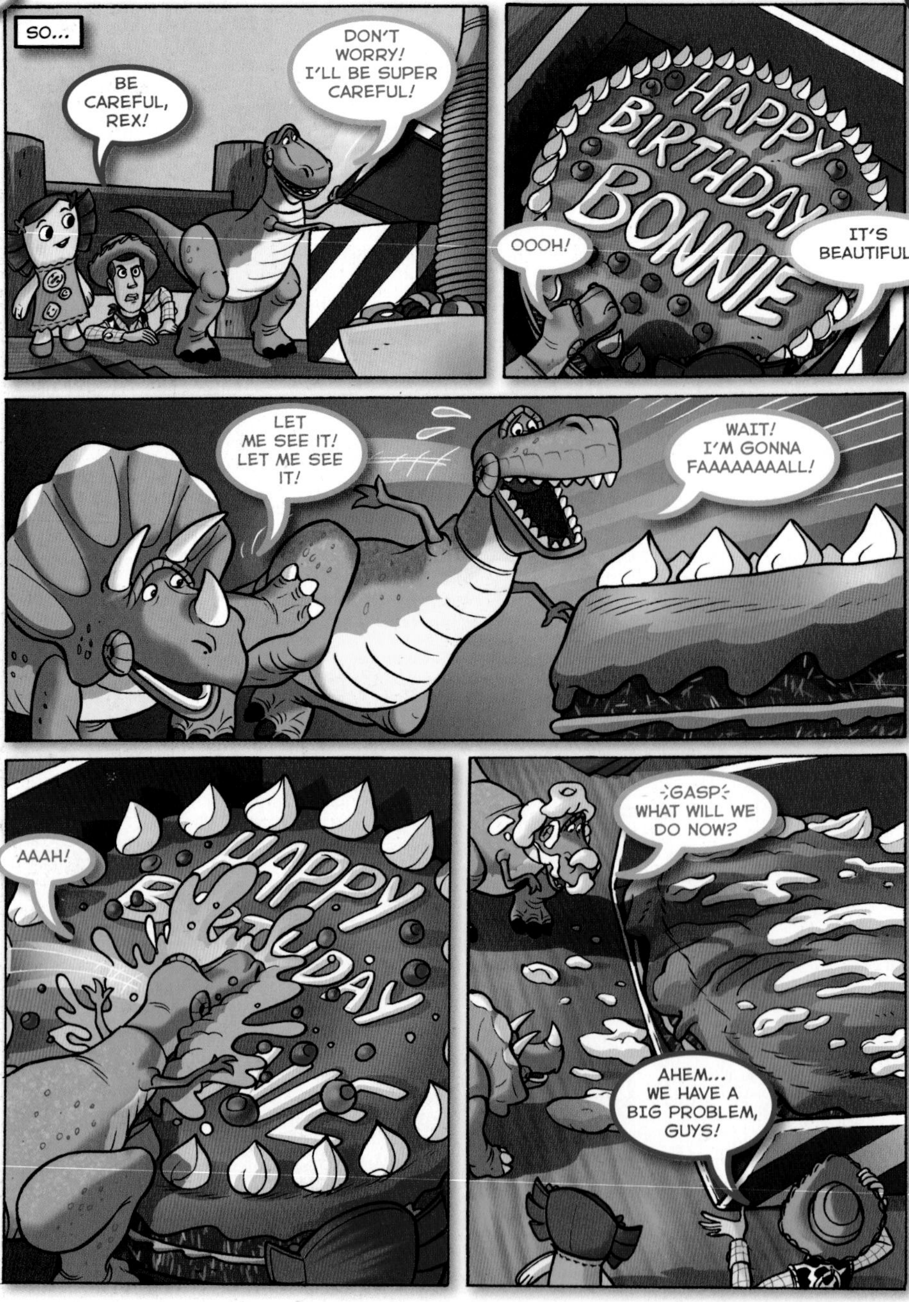
SO...
BE CAREFUL, REX!
DON'T WORRY! I'LL BE SUPER CAREFUL!
HAPPY BIRTHDAY BONNIE
OOOH!
IT'S BEAUTIFUL!
LET ME SEE IT! LET ME SEE IT!
WAIT! I'M GONNA FAAAAAAAALL!
AAAH!
HAPPY BIRTHDAY
GASP WHAT WILL WE DO NOW?
AHEM... WE HAVE A BIG PROBLEM, GUYS!

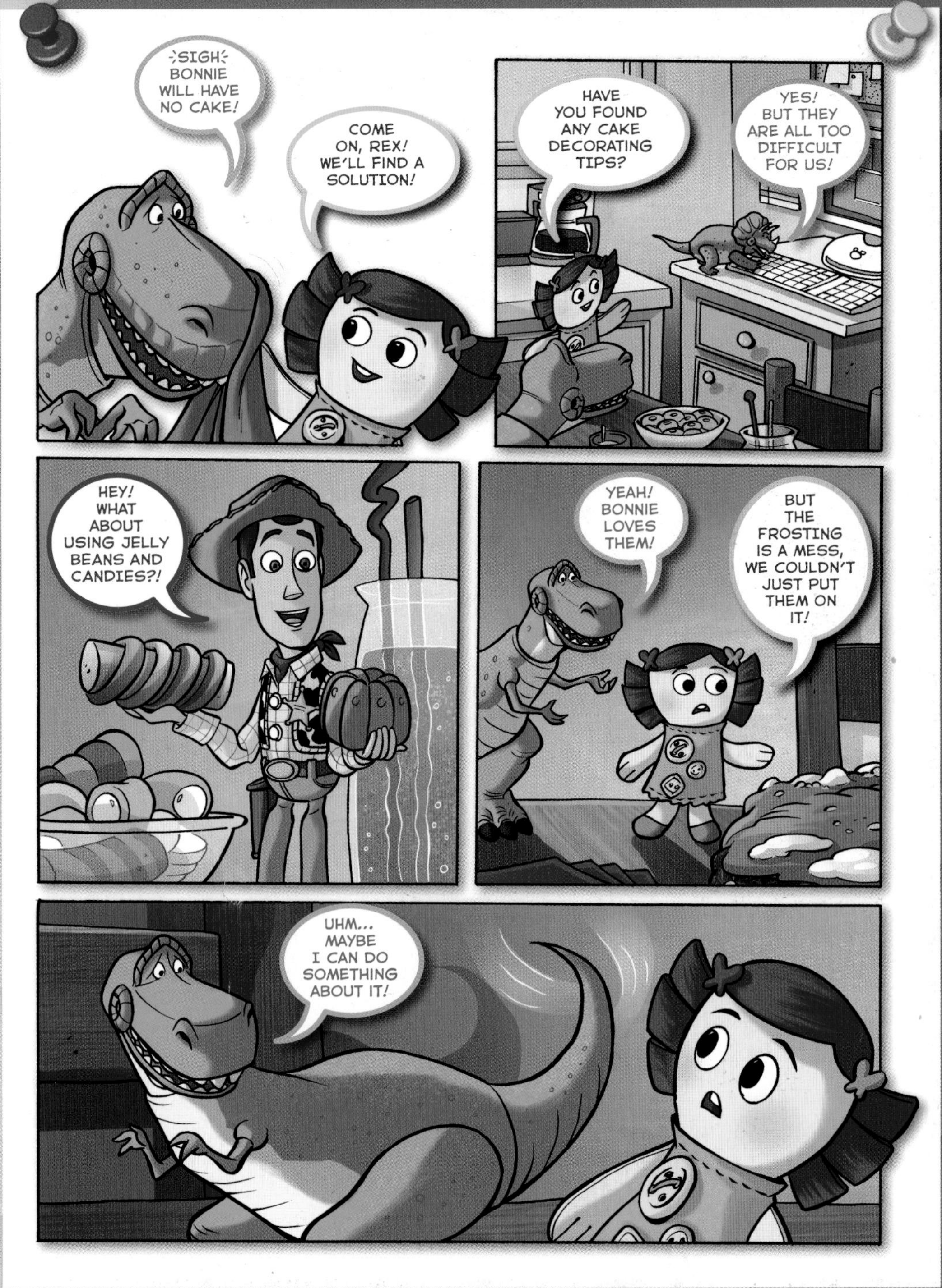

SIGH BONNIE WILL HAVE NO CAKE!
COME ON, REX! WE'LL FIND A SOLUTION!
HAVE YOU FOUND ANY CAKE DECORATING TIPS?
YES! BUT THEY ARE ALL TOO DIFFICULT FOR US!
HEY! WHAT ABOUT USING JELLY BEANS AND CANDIES?!
YEAH! BONNIE LOVES THEM!
BUT THE FROSTING IS A MESS, WE COULDN'T JUST PUT THEM ON IT!
UHM... MAYBE I CAN DO SOMETHING ABOUT IT!

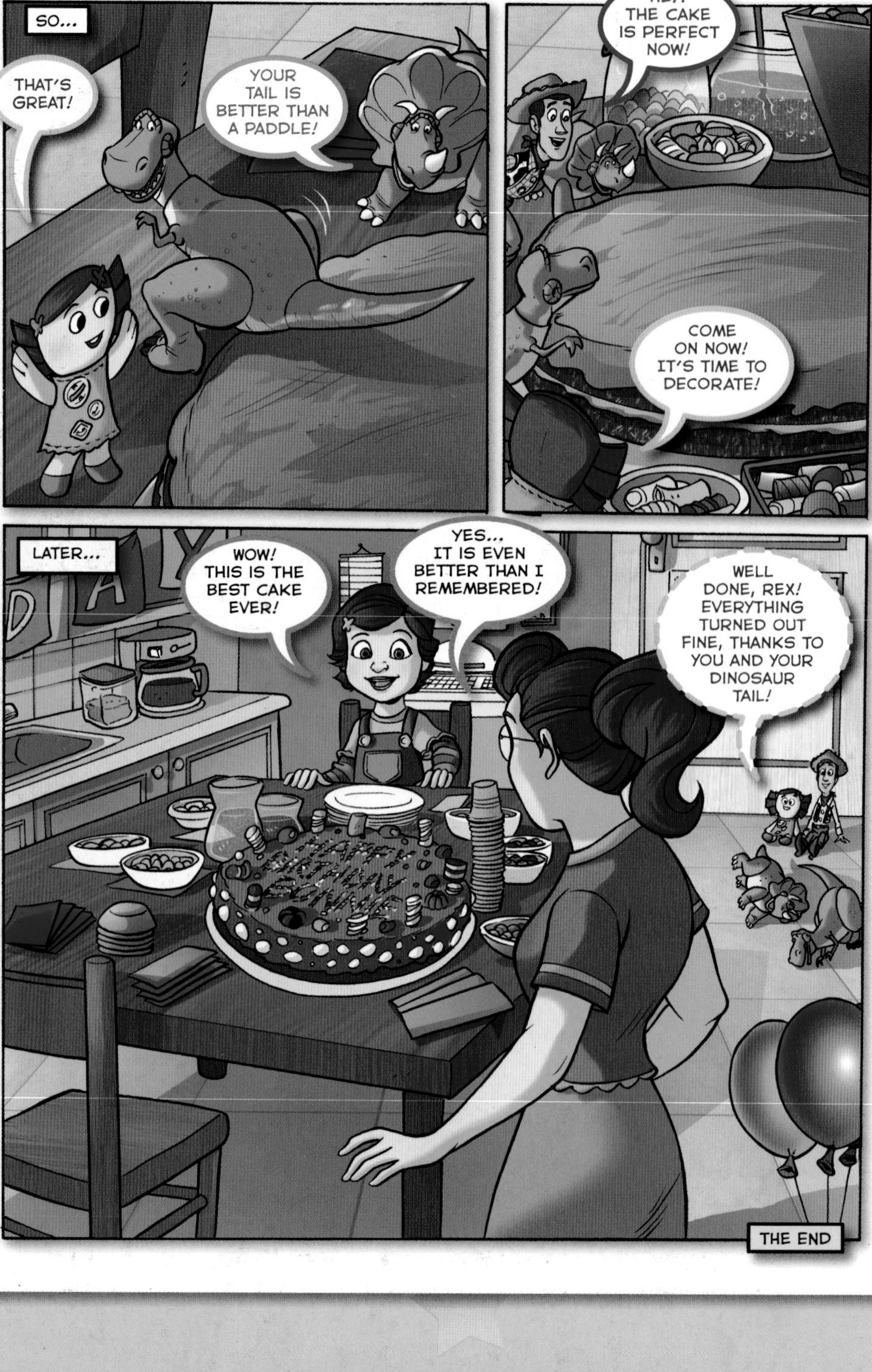
SO...
THAT'S GREAT!
YOUR TAIL IS BETTER THAN A PADDLE!
HEY! THE CAKE IS PERFECT NOW!
COME ON NOW! IT'S TIME TO DECORATE!
LATER...
WOW! THIS IS THE BEST CAKE EVER!
YES... IT IS EVEN BETTER THAN I REMEMBERED!
WELL DONE, REX! EVERYTHING TURNED OUT FINE, THANKS TO YOU AND YOUR DINOSAUR TAIL!
THE END

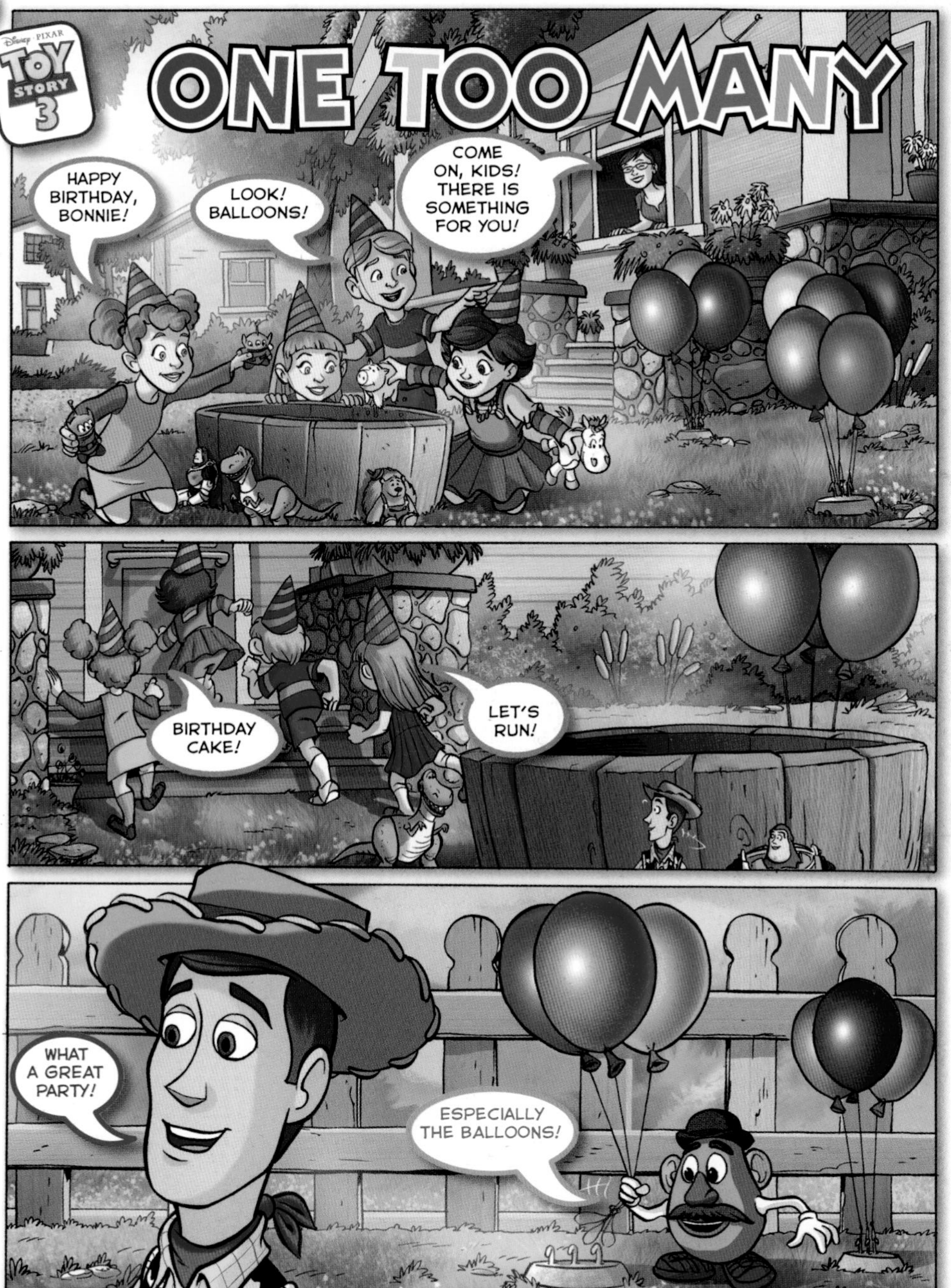
TOY STORY 3
ONE TOO MANY
HAPPY BIRTHDAY, BONNIE!
LOOK! BALLOONS!
COME ON, KIDS! THERE IS SOMETHING FOR YOU!
BIRTHDAY CAKE!
LET'S RUN!
WHAT A GREAT PARTY!
ESPECIALLY THE BALLOONS!

SCRIPT: ALESSANDRO SISTI; LAYOUT & INK: VALENTINO FORLINI; COLOUR: MARA DAMIANI

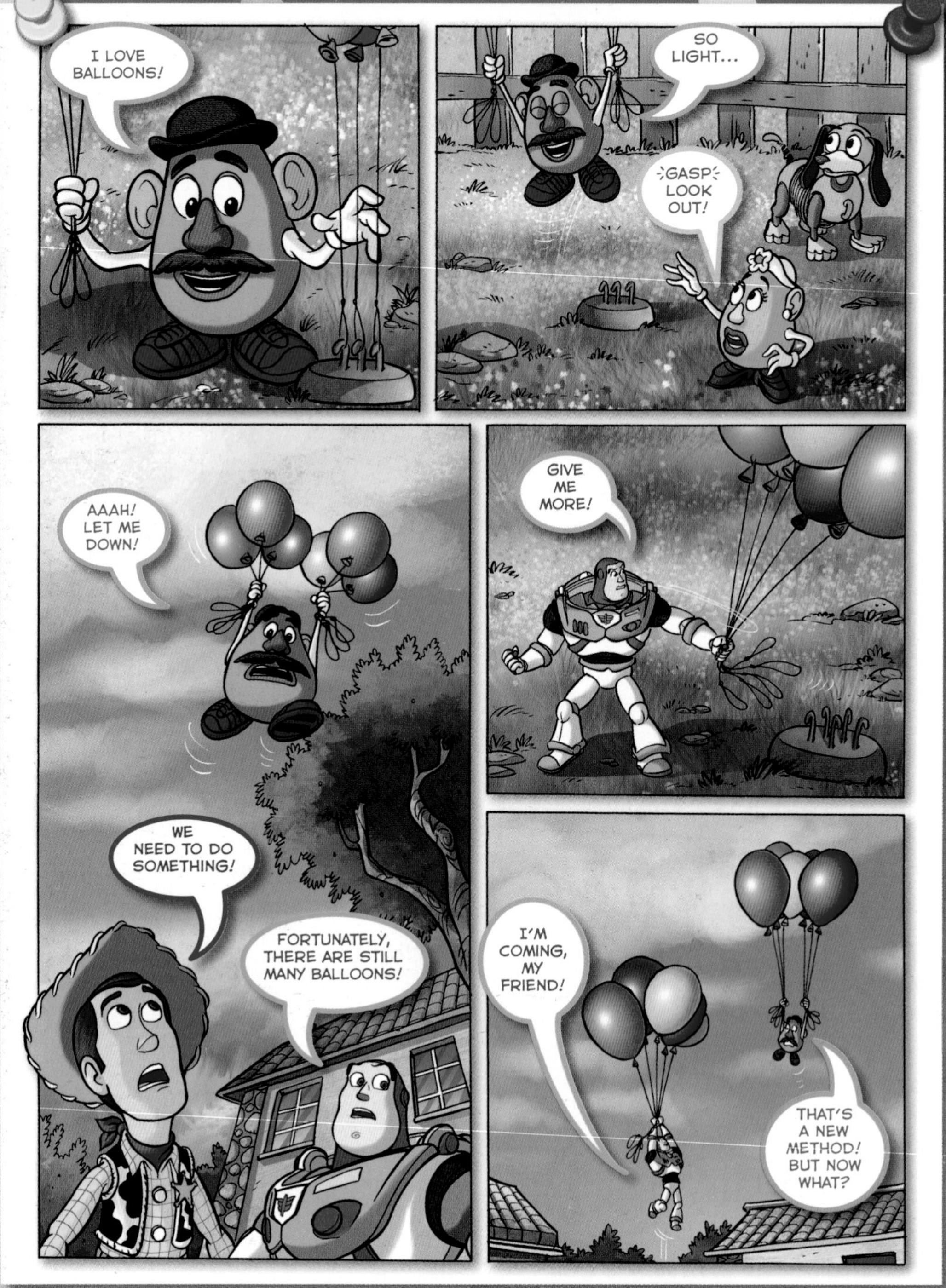
I LOVE BALLOONS!
SO LIGHT...
GASP LOOK OUT!
AAAH! LET ME DOWN!
GIVE ME MORE!
WE NEED TO DO SOMETHING!
FORTUNATELY, THERE ARE STILL MANY BALLOONS!
I'M COMING, MY FRIEND!
THAT'S A NEW METHOD! BUT NOW WHAT?

YOU'LL SEE!
HUH?
TOGETHER WE ARE HEAVIER. THAT WAY WE WILL SOFTLY COME BACK TO THE GROUND!
AGH! WE ARE TOO HEAVYYYYYYYY!
BUZZ! HERE!
ROGER, SHERIFF!
NOOO! WHAT ARE YOU DOING?
YOU CAN'T FLY! NOT REALLY!
PERHAPS NOT TO INFINITY AND BEYOND...

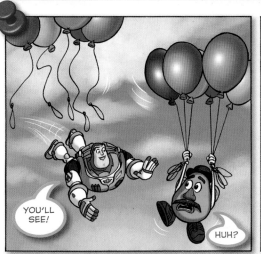

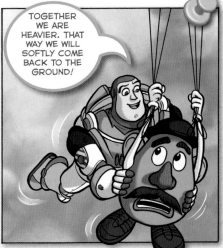

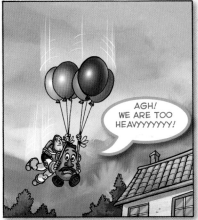

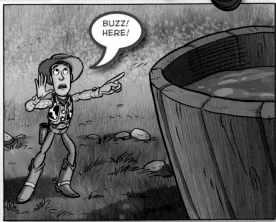

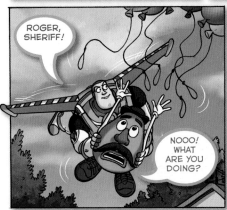

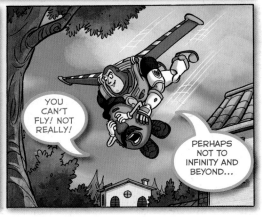

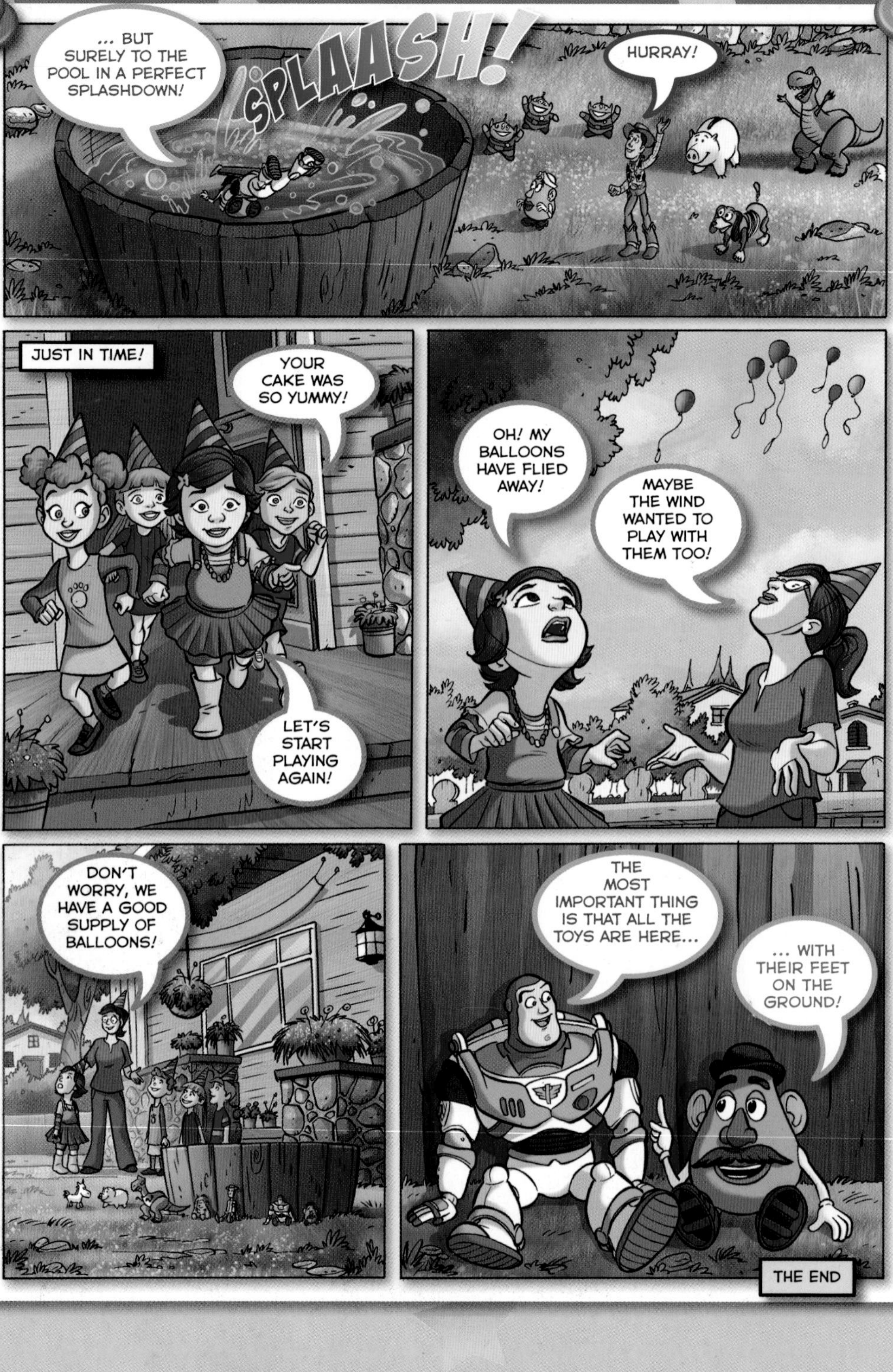
... BUT SURELY TO THE POOL IN A PERFECT SPLASHDOWN!
SPLAAASH!
HURRAY!
JUST IN TIME!
YOUR CAKE WAS SO YUMMY!
LET'S START PLAYING AGAIN!
OH! MY BALLOONS HAVE FLIED AWAY!
MAYBE THE WIND WANTED TO PLAY WITH THEM TOO!
DON'T WORRY, WE HAVE A GOOD SUPPLY OF BALLOONS!
THE MOST IMPORTANT THING IS THAT ALL THE TOYS ARE HERE...
... WITH THEIR FEET ON THE GROUND!
THE END

A BIG SURPRISE

SCRIPT: ALESSANDRO FERRARI; PENCILS & INK: LUCA USAI; COLOUR: MARA DAMIANI

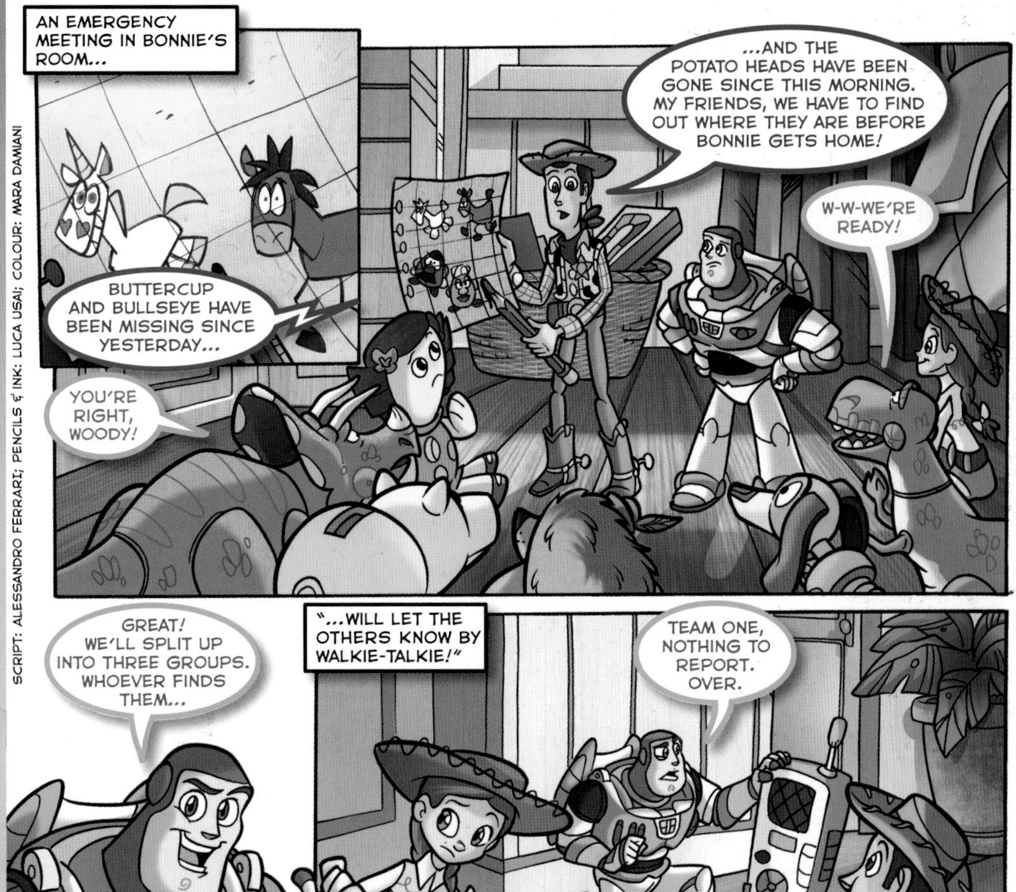
AN EMERGENCY MEETING IN BONNIE'S ROOM...
BUTTERCUP AND BULLSEYE HAVE BEEN MISSING SINCE YESTERDAY...
...AND THE POTATO HEADS HAVE BEEN GONE SINCE THIS MORNING. MY FRIENDS, WE HAVE TO FIND OUT WHERE THEY ARE BEFORE BONNIE GETS HOME!
YOU'RE RIGHT, WOODY!
W-W-WE'RE READY!
GREAT! WE'LL SPLIT UP INTO THREE GROUPS. WHOEVER FINDS THEM...
"...WILL LET THE OTHERS KNOW BY WALKIE-TALKIE!"
TEAM ONE, NOTHING TO REPORT. OVER.

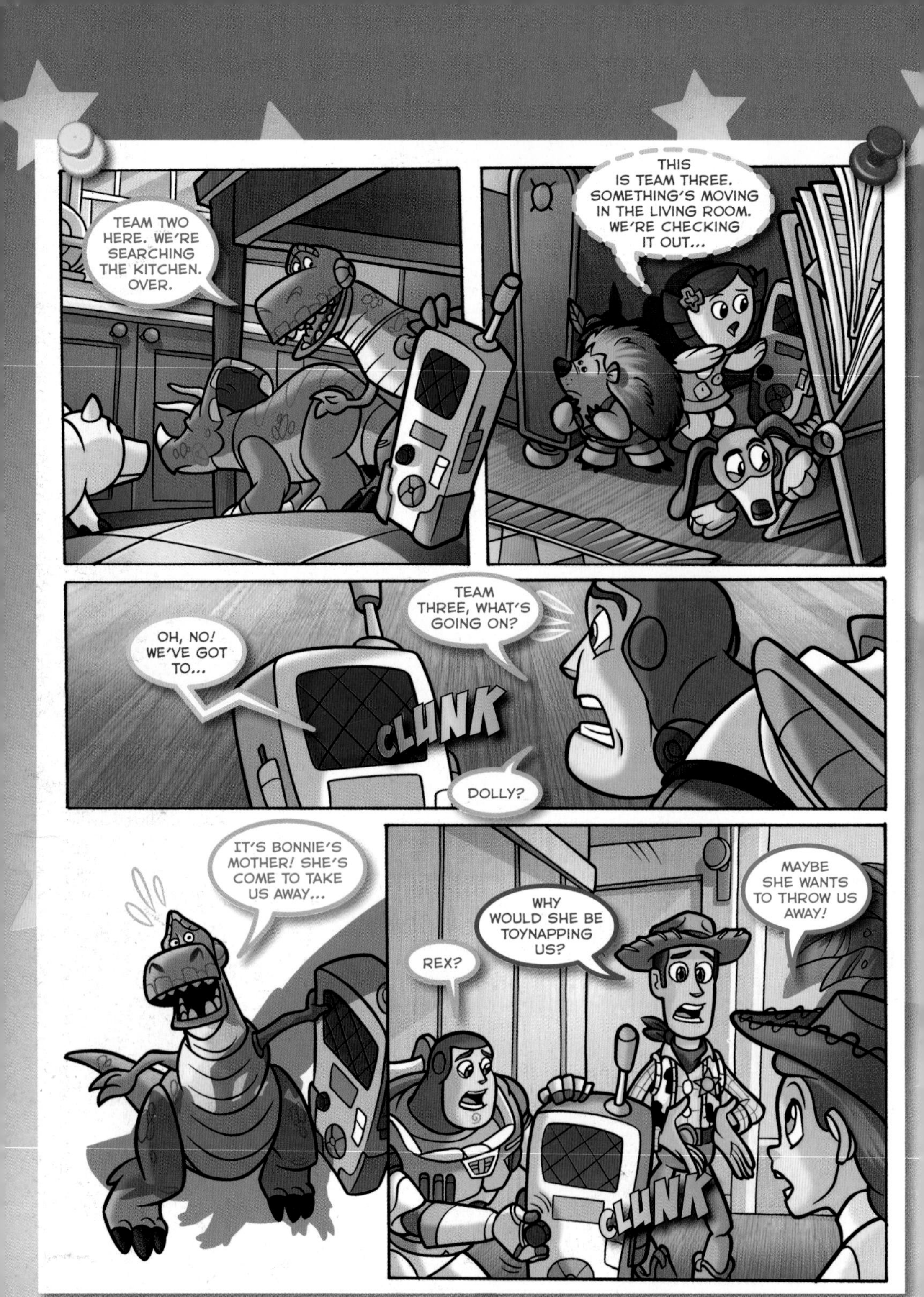

TEAM TWO HERE. WE'RE SEARCHING THE KITCHEN. OVER.
THIS IS TEAM THREE. SOMETHING'S MOVING IN THE LIVING ROOM. WE'RE CHECKING IT OUT...
OH, NO! WE'VE GOT TO...
TEAM THREE, WHAT'S GOING ON?
CLUNK
DOLLY?
IT'S BONNIE'S MOTHER! SHE'S COME TO TAKE US AWAY...
REX?
WHY WOULD SHE BE TOYNAPPING US?
MAYBE SHE WANTS TO THROW US AWAY!
CLUNK

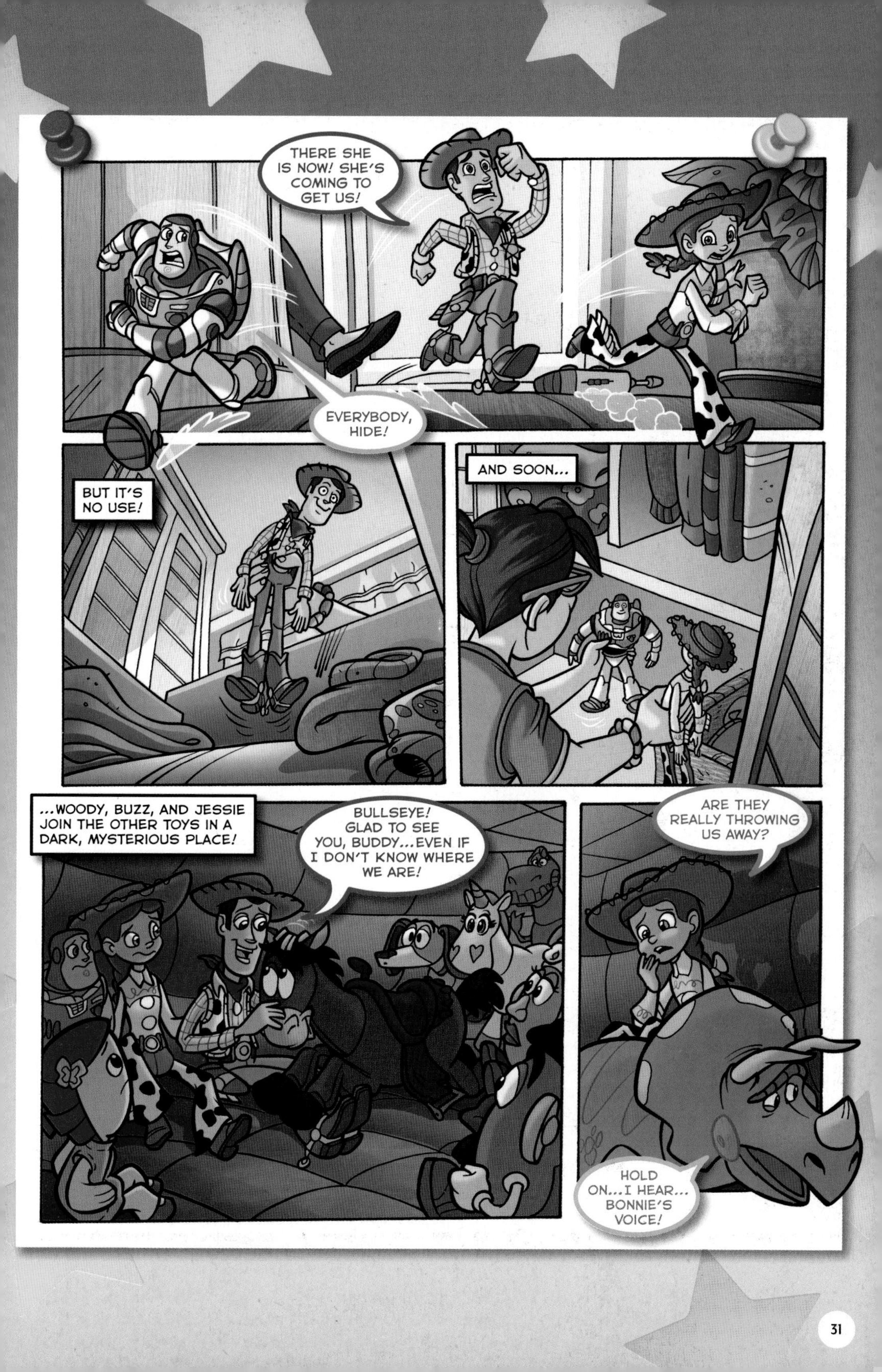
THERE SHE IS NOW! SHE'S COMING TO GET US!
EVERYBODY, HIDE!
BUT IT'S NO USE!
AND SOON...
...WOODY, BUZZ, AND JESSIE JOIN THE OTHER TOYS IN A DARK, MYSTERIOUS PLACE!
BULLSEYE! GLAD TO SEE YOU, BUDDY...EVEN IF I DON'T KNOW WHERE WE ARE!
ARE THEY REALLY THROWING US AWAY?
HOLD ON...I HEAR... BONNIE'S VOICE!

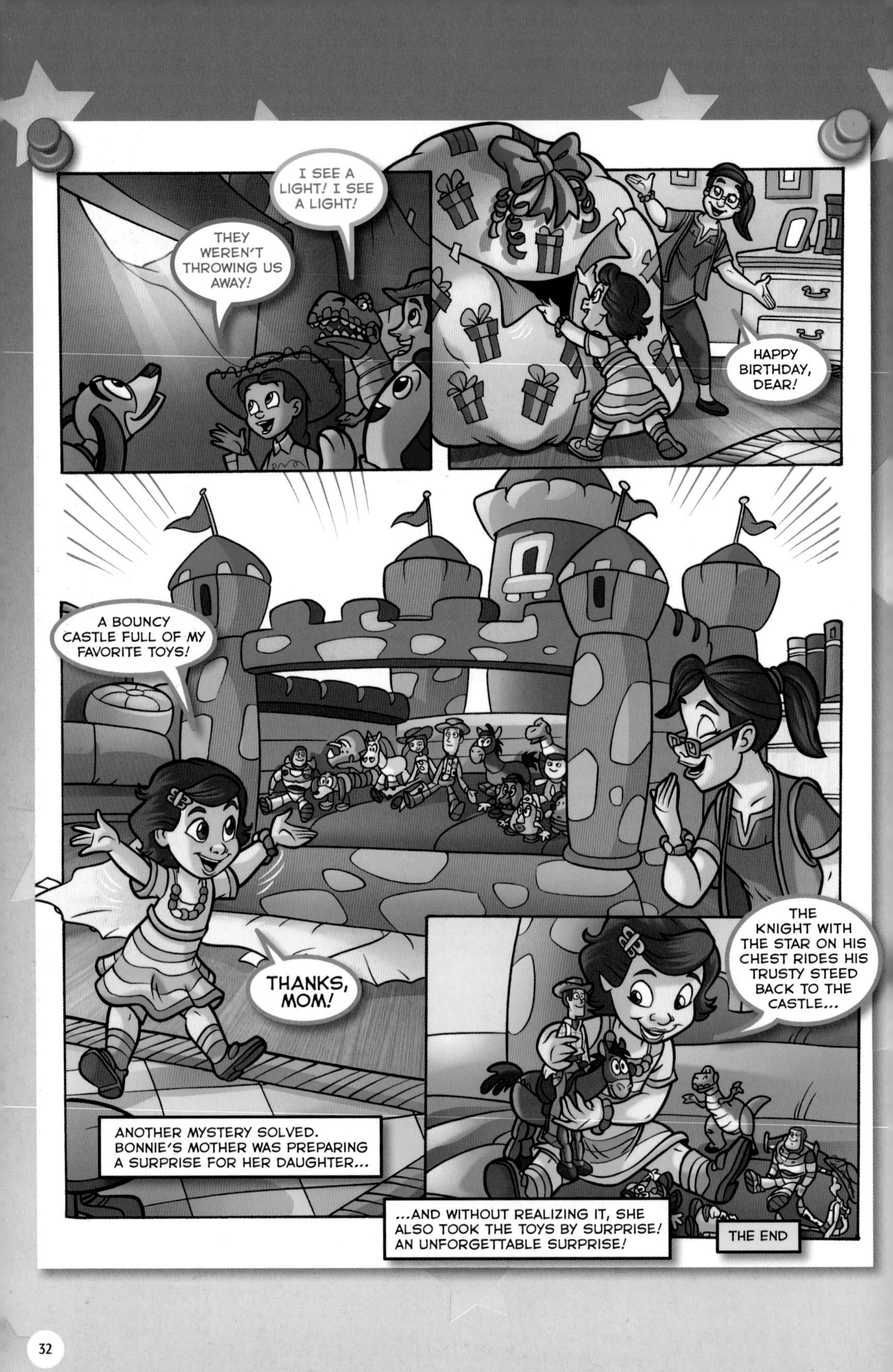
THEY WEREN'T THROWING US AWAY!
I SEE A LIGHT! I SEE A LIGHT!
HAPPY BIRTHDAY, DEAR!
A BOUNCY CASTLE FULL OF MY FAVORITE TOYS!
THANKS, MOM!
ANOTHER MYSTERY SOLVED. BONNIE'S MOTHER WAS PREPARING A SURPRISE FOR HER DAUGHTER...
THE KNIGHT WITH THE STAR ON HIS CHEST RIDES HIS TRUSTY STEED BACK TO THE CASTLE...
...AND WITHOUT REALIZING IT, SHE ALSO TOOK THE TOYS BY SURPRISE! AN UNFORGETTABLE SURPRISE!
THE END

NEW FRIENDS

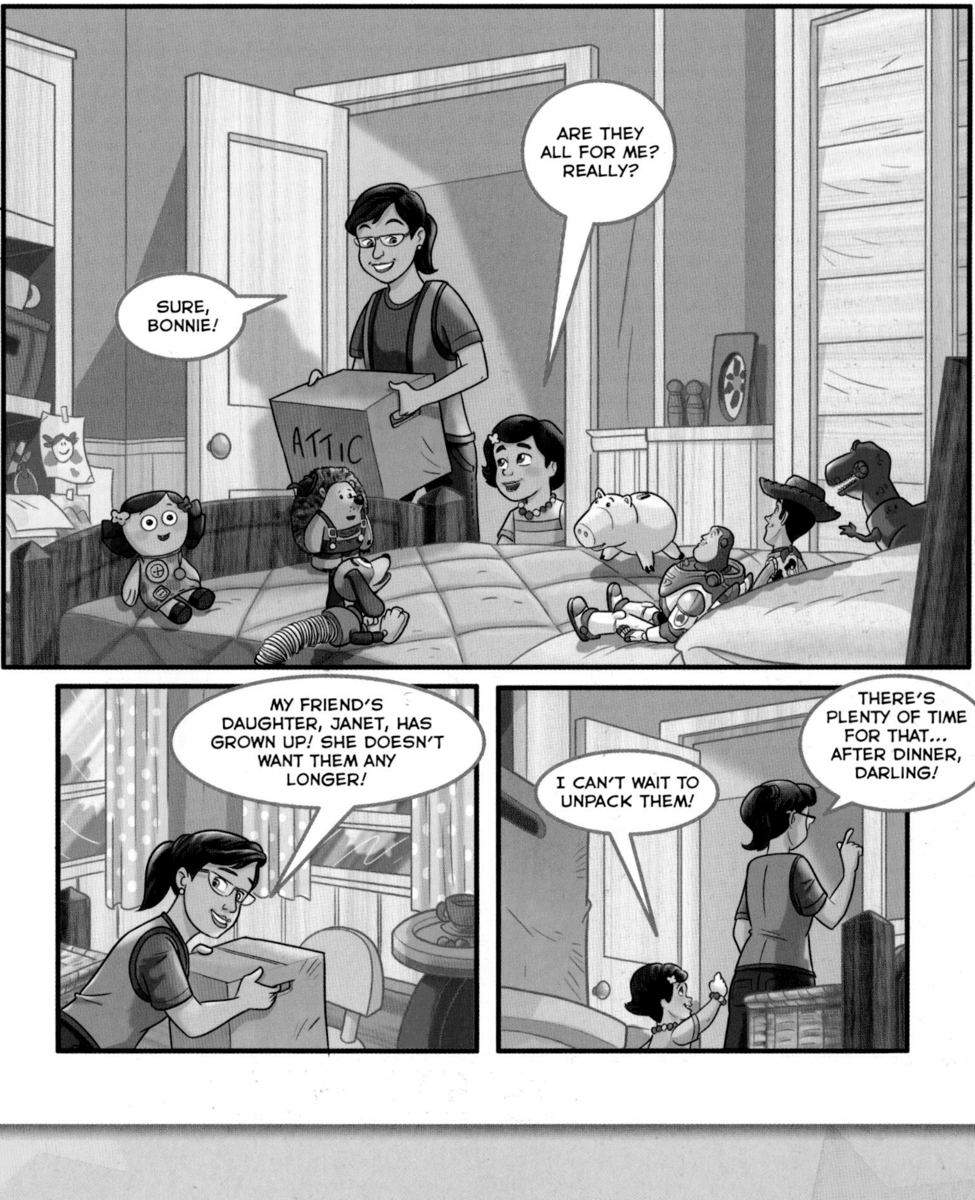
ARE THEY ALL FOR ME? REALLY?
SURE, BONNIE!
ATTIC
MY FRIEND'S DAUGHTER, JANET, HAS GROWN UP! SHE DOESN'T WANT THEM ANY LONGER!
I CAN'T WAIT TO UNPACK THEM!
THERE'S PLENTY OF TIME FOR THAT... AFTER DINNER, DARLING!

SCRIPT: ALESSANDRO SISTI; LAYOUT: LUCA USAI; INK: MICHELA FRARE; COLOUR: LUCIO DE GIUSEPPE

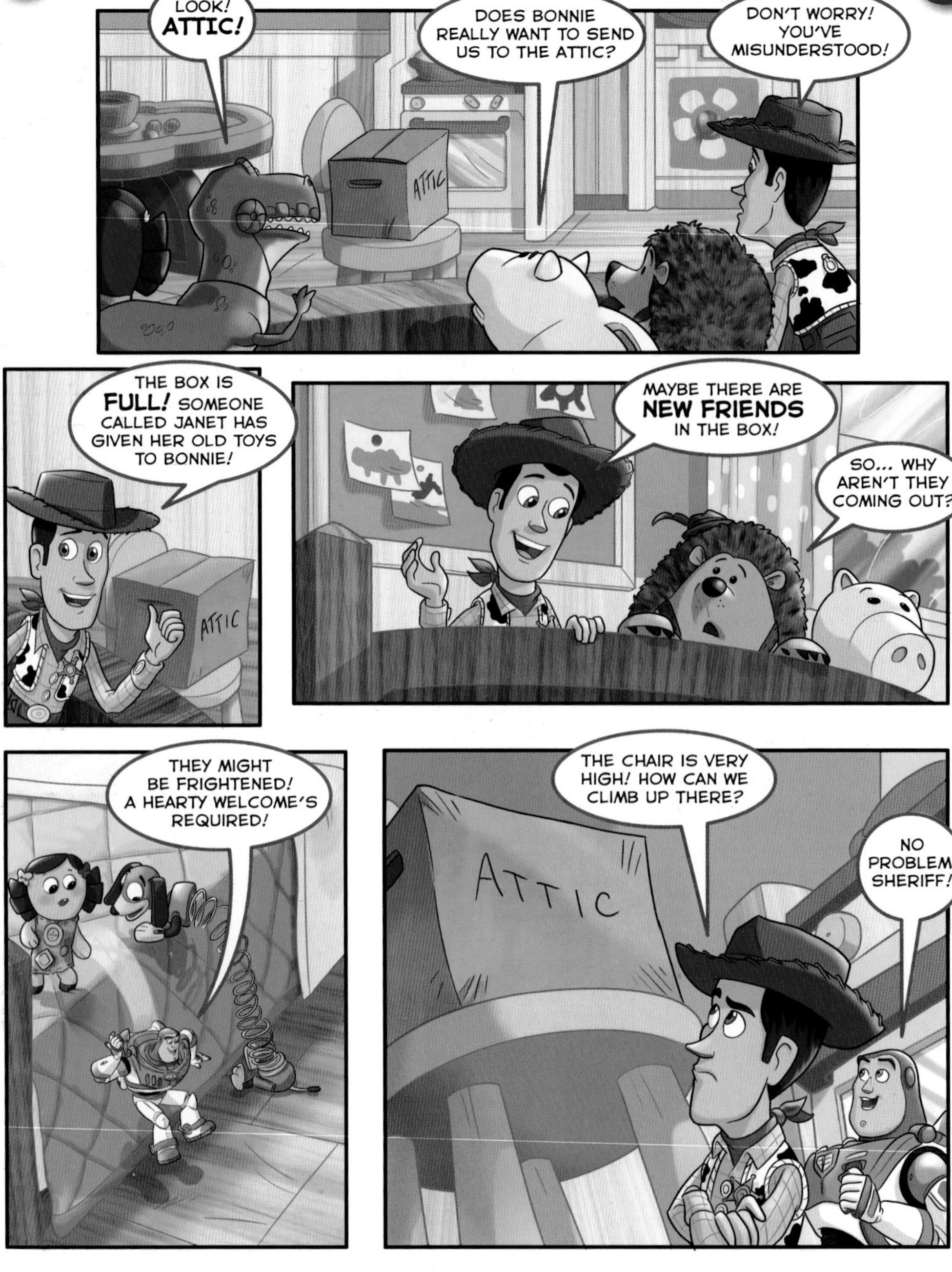
LOOK! ATTIC!
DOES BONNIE REALLY WANT TO SEND US TO THE ATTIC?
DON'T WORRY! YOU'VE MISUNDERSTOOD!
ATTIC
THE BOX IS FULL! SOMEONE CALLED JANET HAS GIVEN HER OLD TOYS TO BONNIE!
ATTIC
MAYBE THERE ARE NEW FRIENDS IN THE BOX!
SO... WHY AREN'T THEY COMING OUT?
THEY MIGHT BE FRIGHTENED! A HEARTY WELCOME'S REQUIRED!
THE CHAIR IS VERY HIGH! HOW CAN WE CLIMB UP THERE?
ATTIC
NO PROBLEM, SHERIFF!

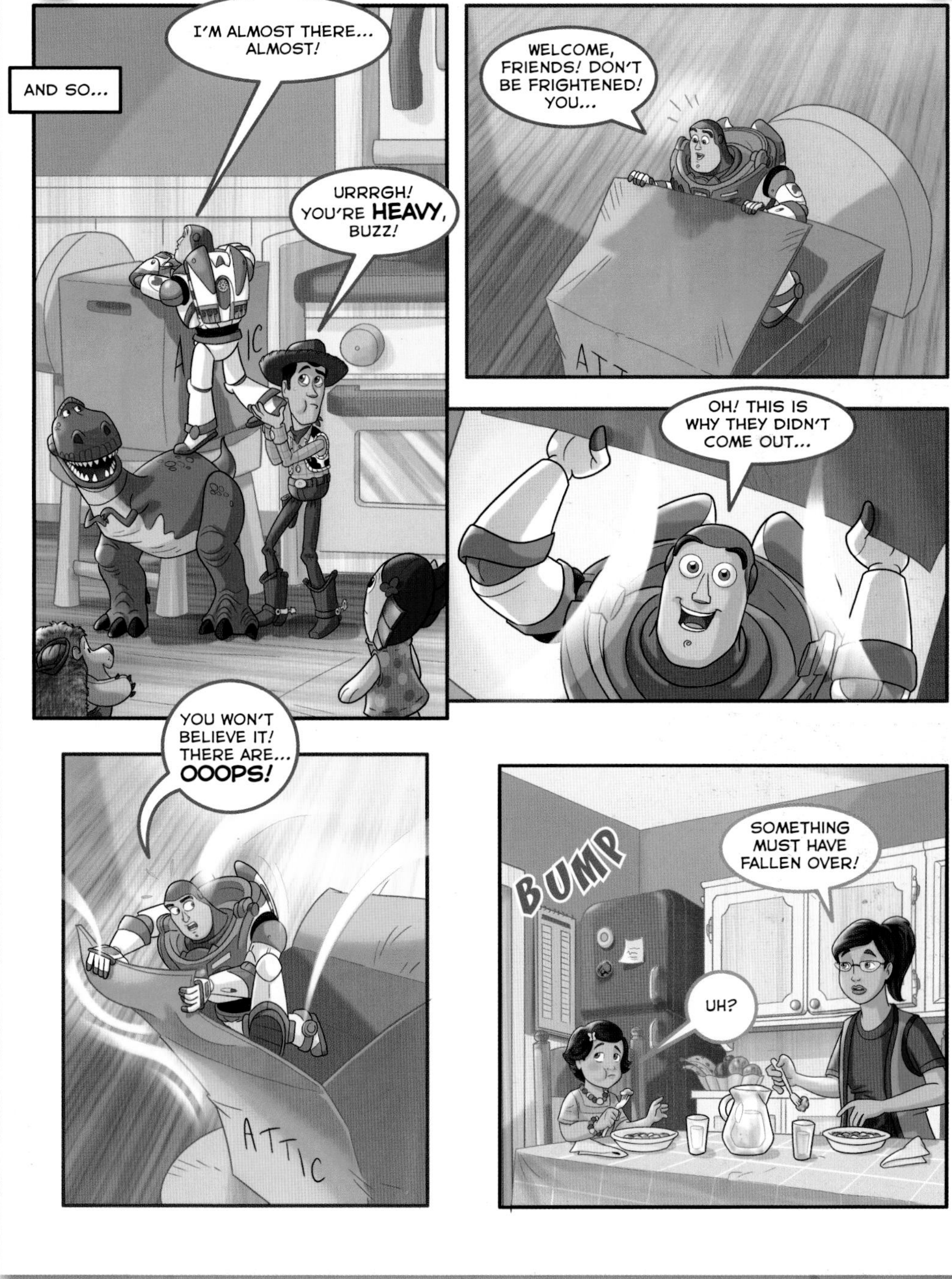
AND SO...
I'M ALMOST THERE... ALMOST!
URRRGH! YOU'RE HEAVY, BUZZ!
ATTIC
WELCOME, FRIENDS! DON'T BE FRIGHTENED! YOU...
OH! THIS IS WHY THEY DIDN'T COME OUT...
YOU WON'T BELIEVE IT! THERE ARE... OOOPS!
ATTIC
BUMP
SOMETHING MUST HAVE FALLEN OVER!
UH?

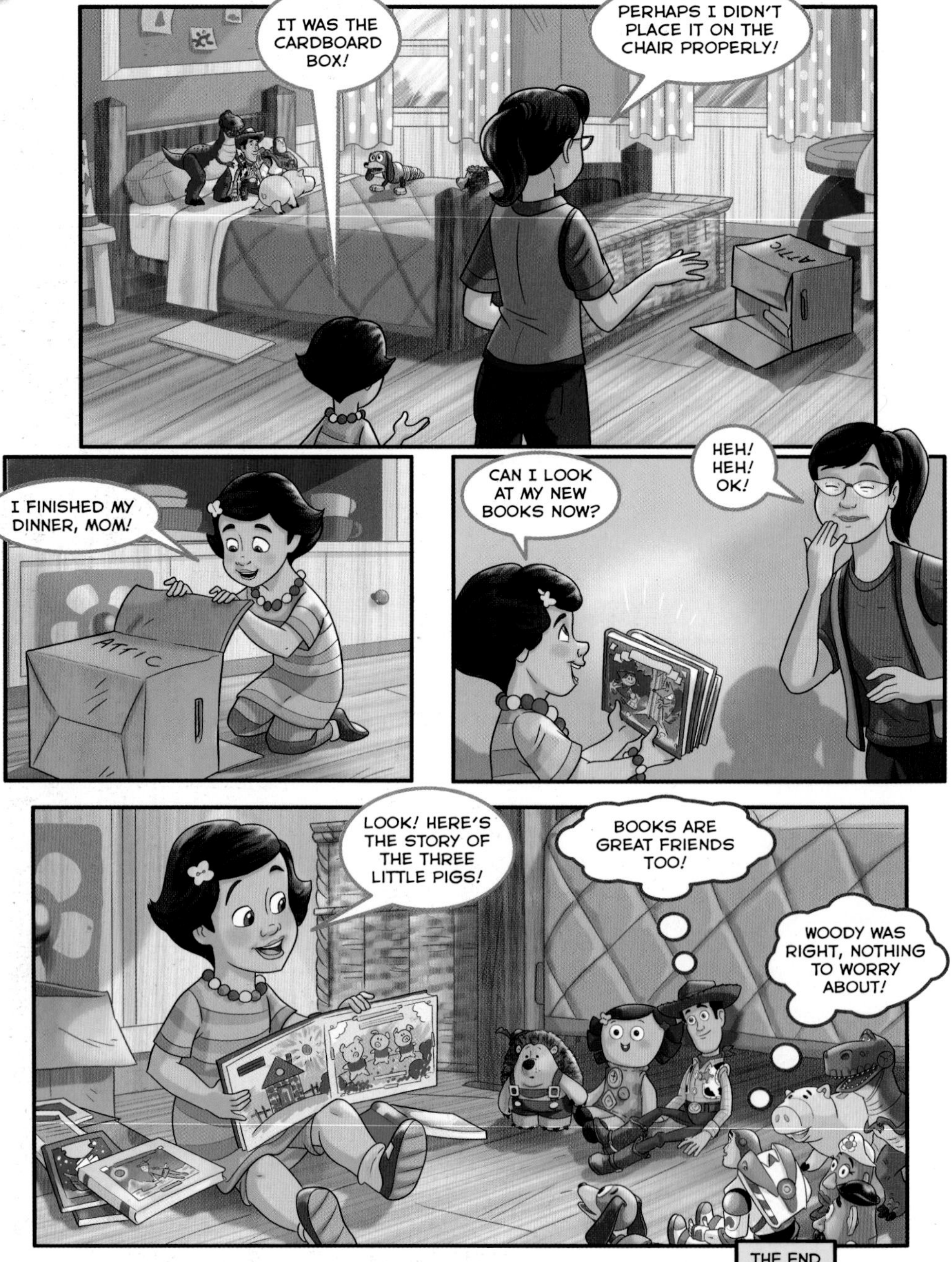
IT WAS THE CARDBOARD BOX!
PERHAPS I DIDN'T PLACE IT ON THE CHAIR PROPERLY!
ATTIC
I FINISHED MY DINNER, MOM!
ATTIC
CAN I LOOK AT MY NEW BOOKS NOW?
HEH! HEH! OK!
LOOK! HERE'S THE STORY OF THE THREE LITTLE PIGS!
BOOKS ARE GREAT FRIENDS TOO!
WOODY WAS RIGHT, NOTHING TO WORRY ABOUT!
THE END

A TRIP TO THE FUNFAIR!

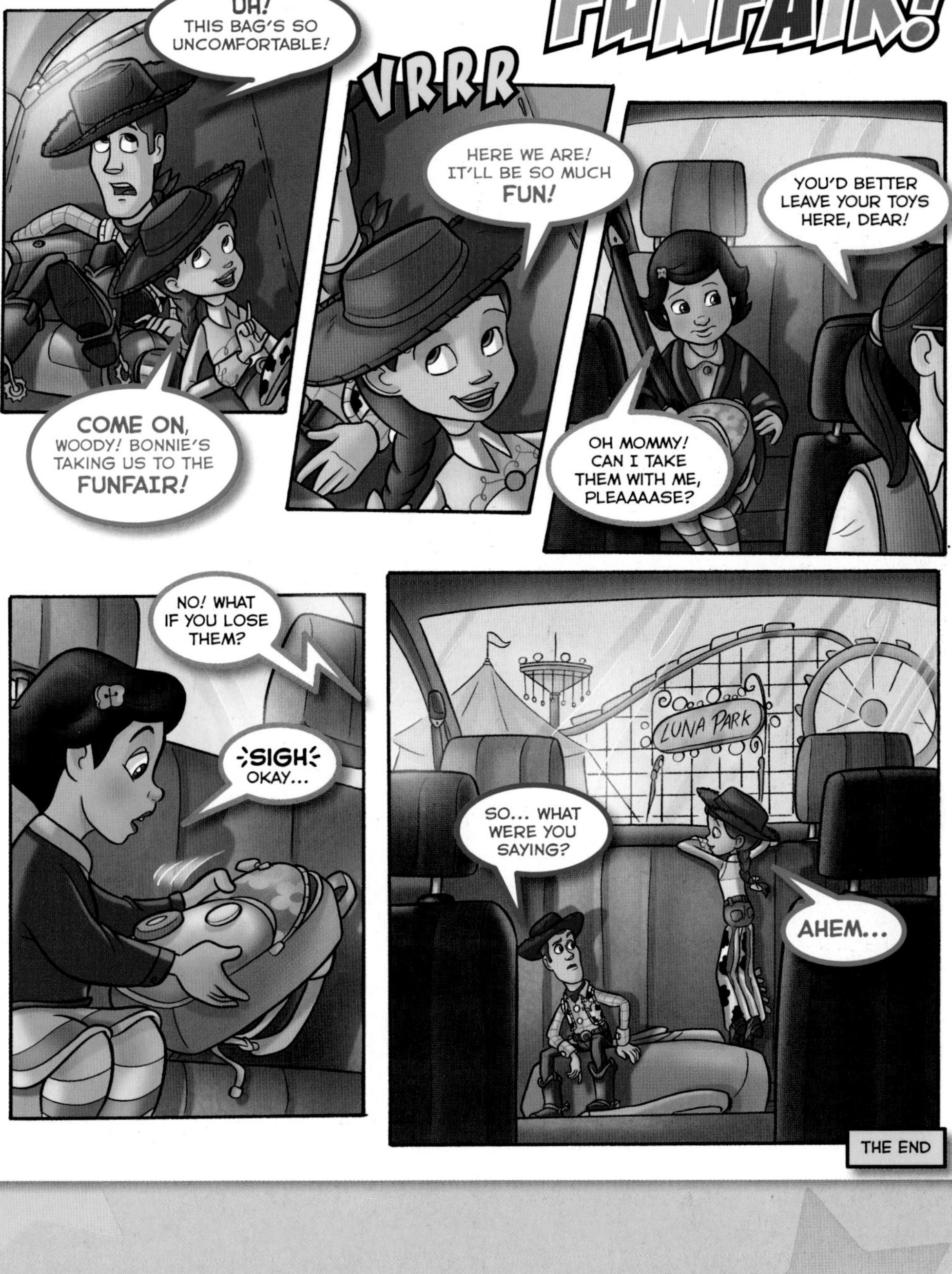

UH! THIS BAG'S SO UNCOMFORTABLE!
COME ON, WOODY! BONNIE'S TAKING US TO THE FUNFAIR!
VRRR
HERE WE ARE! IT'LL BE SO MUCH FUN!
YOU'D BETTER LEAVE YOUR TOYS HERE, DEAR!
OH MOMMY! CAN I TAKE THEM WITH ME, PLEAAAASE?
NO! WHAT IF YOU LOSE THEM?
SIGH
OKAY...
LUNA PARK
AHEM...
SO... WHAT WERE YOU SAYING?
THE END

SCRIPT: TEA ORSI; LAYOUT: LUCA USAI; INK: MICHELA FRARE; COLOUR: ANGELA CAPOLUPO

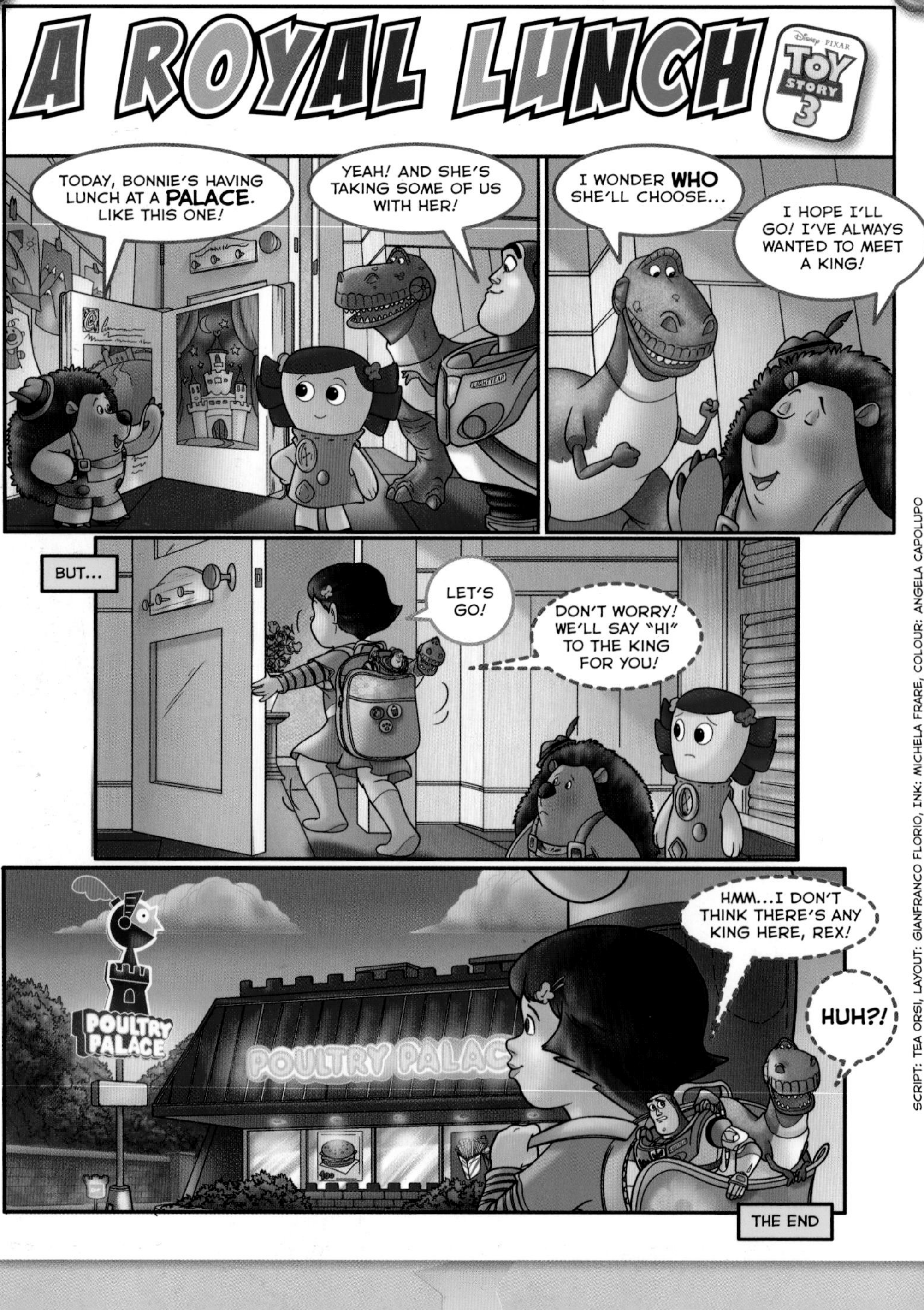
A ROYAL LUNCH
DISNEY PIXAR TOY STORY 3
TODAY, BONNIE'S HAVING LUNCH AT A PALACE. LIKE THIS ONE!
YEAH! AND SHE'S TAKING SOME OF US WITH HER!
I WONDER WHO SHE'LL CHOOSE...
I HOPE I'LL GO! I'VE ALWAYS WANTED TO MEET A KING!
BUT...
LET'S GO!
DON'T WORRY! WE'LL SAY "HI" TO THE KING FOR YOU!
POULTRY PALACE
POULTRY PALAC
HMM...I DON'T THINK THERE'S ANY KING HERE, REX!
HUH?!
THE END
SCRIPT: TEA ORSI, LAYOUT: GIANFRANCO FLORIO, INK: MICHELA FRARE, COLOUR: ANGELA CAPOLUPO

A VERY GOOD IDEA!

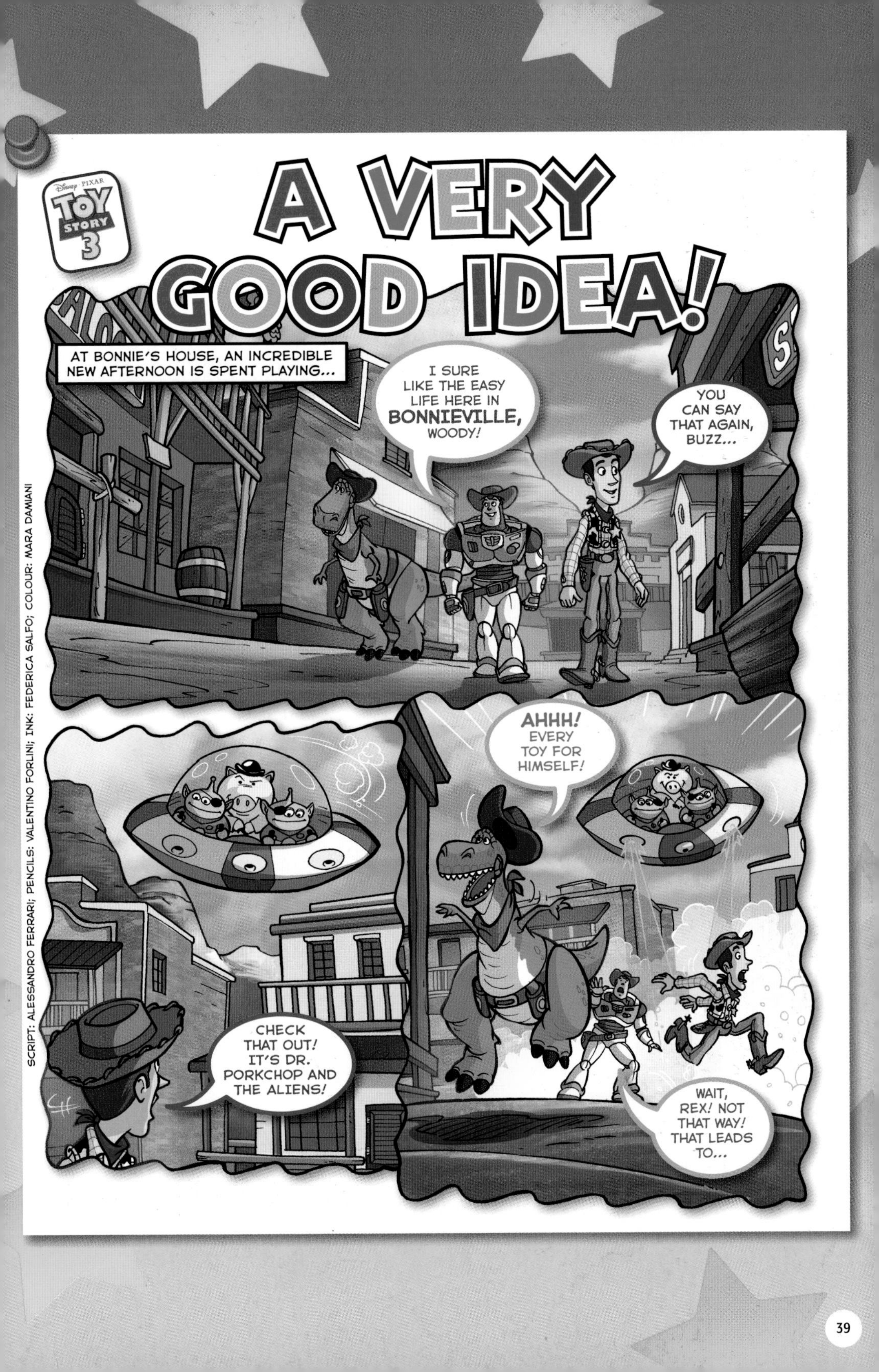
AT BONNIE'S HOUSE, AN INCREDIBLE NEW AFTERNOON IS SPENT PLAYING...
I SURE LIKE THE EASY LIFE HERE IN BONNIEVILLE, WOODY!
YOU CAN SAY THAT AGAIN, BUZZ...
CHECK THAT OUT! IT'S DR. PORKCHOP AND THE ALIENS!
AHHH! EVERY TOY FOR HIMSELF!
WAIT, REX! NOT THAT WAY! THAT LEADS TO...

SCRIPT: ALESSANDRO FERRARI; PENCILS: VALENTINO FORLINI; INK: FEDERICA SALFO; COLOUR: MARA DAMIANI

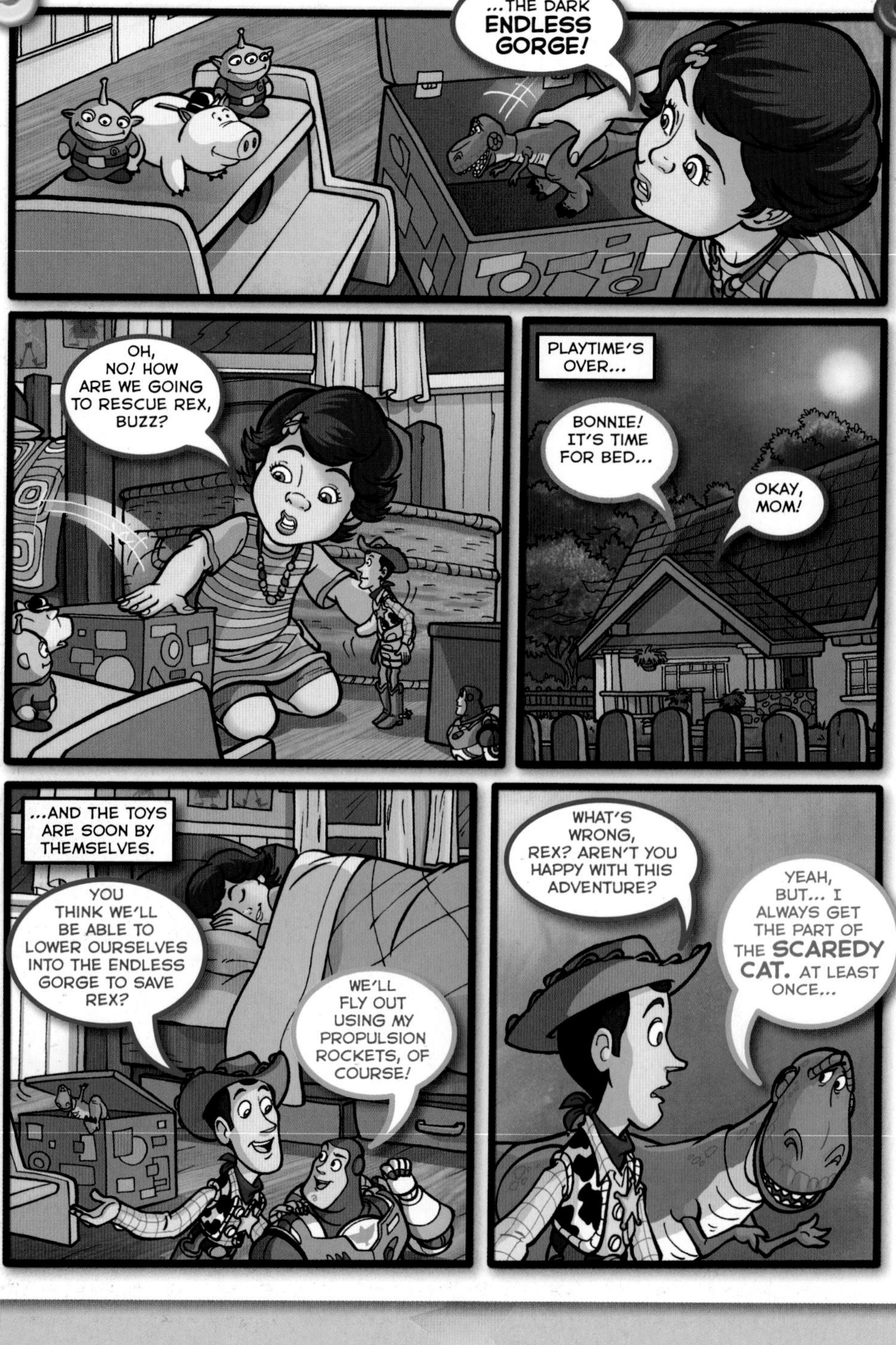
...THE DARK ENDLESS GORGE!
OH, NO! HOW ARE WE GOING TO RESCUE REX, BUZZ?
PLAYTIME'S OVER...
BONNIE! IT'S TIME FOR BED...
OKAY, MOM!
...AND THE TOYS ARE SOON BY THEMSELVES.
YOU THINK WE'LL BE ABLE TO LOWER OURSELVES INTO THE ENDLESS GORGE TO SAVE REX?
WE'LL FLY OUT USING MY PROPULSION ROCKETS, OF COURSE!
WHAT'S WRONG, REX? AREN'T YOU HAPPY WITH THIS ADVENTURE?
YEAH, BUT... I ALWAYS GET THE PART OF THE SCAREDY CAT. AT LEAST ONCE...

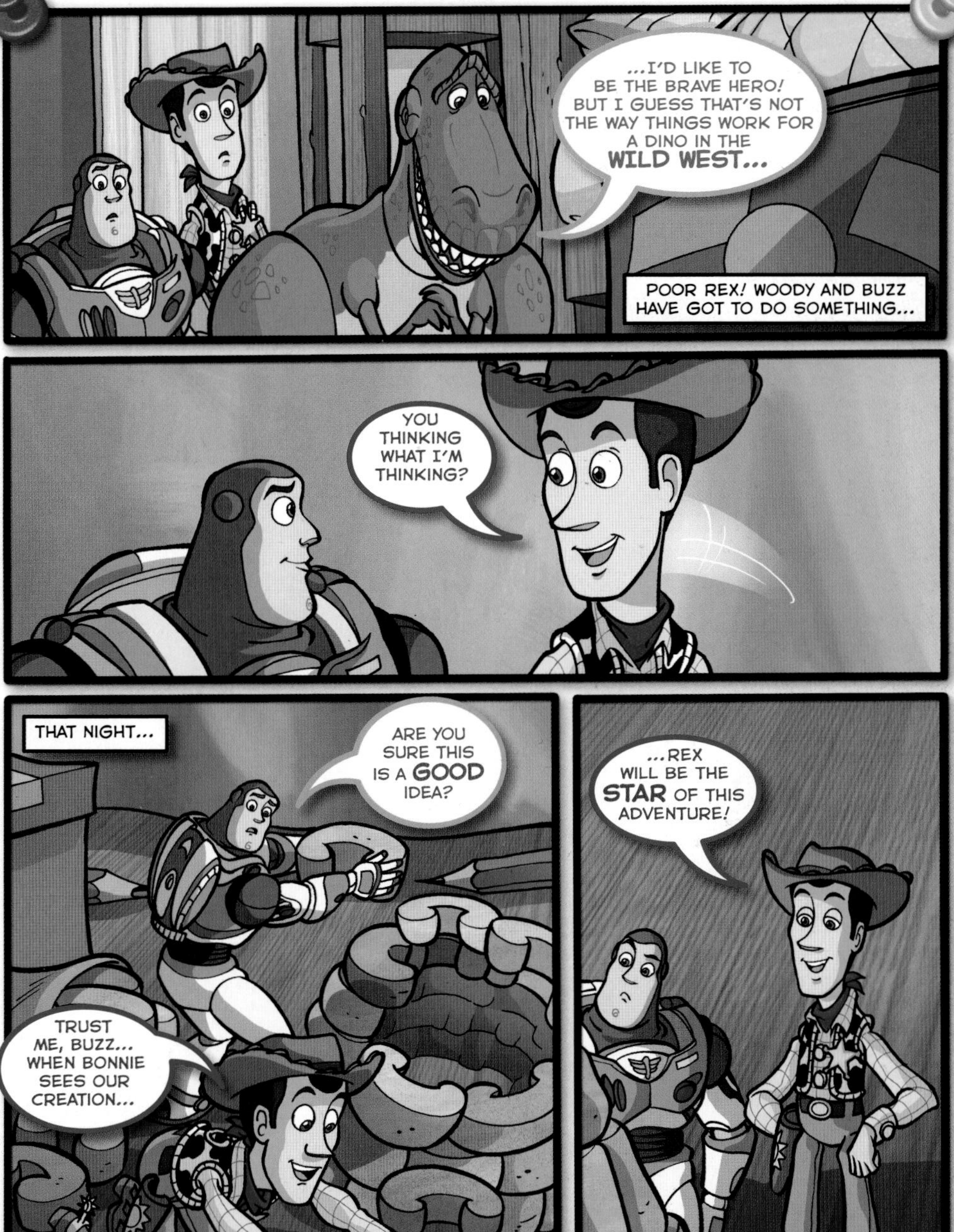
...I'D LIKE TO BE THE BRAVE HERO! BUT I GUESS THAT'S NOT THE WAY THINGS WORK FOR A DINO IN THE WILD WEST...
POOR REX! WOODY AND BUZZ HAVE GOT TO DO SOMETHING...
YOU THINKING WHAT I'M THINKING?
THAT NIGHT...
ARE YOU SURE THIS IS A GOOD IDEA?
TRUST ME, BUZZ... WHEN BONNIE SEES OUR CREATION...
...REX WILL BE THE STAR OF THIS ADVENTURE!

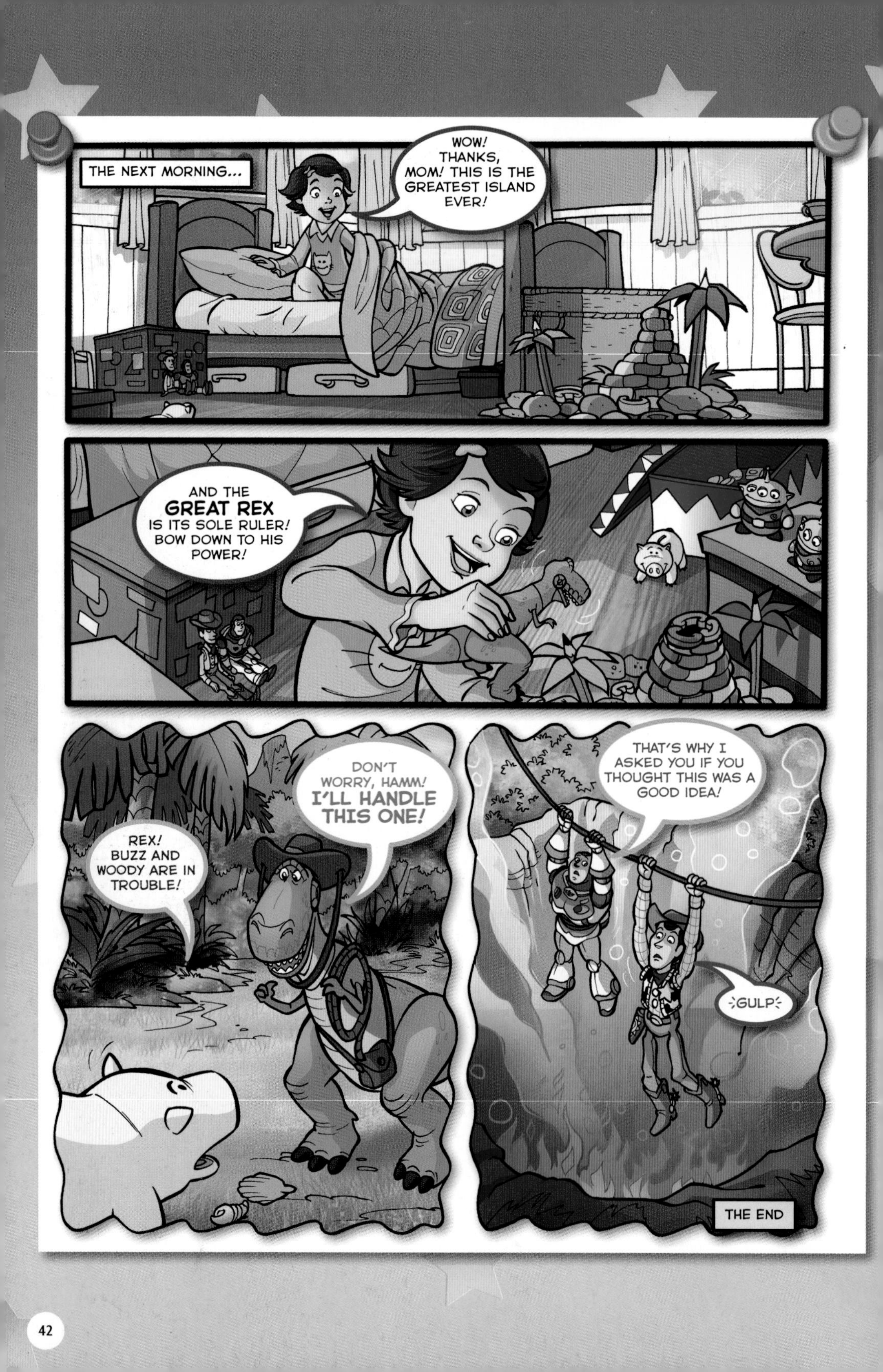
THE NEXT MORNING...
WOW! THANKS, MOM! THIS IS THE GREATEST ISLAND EVER!
AND THE GREAT REX IS ITS SOLE RULER! BOW DOWN TO HIS POWER!
REX! BUZZ AND WOODY ARE IN TROUBLE!
DON'T WORRY, HAMM! I'LL HANDLE THIS ONE!
THAT'S WHY I ASKED YOU IF YOU THOUGHT THIS WAS A GOOD IDEA!
GULP
THE END

A PERFECT METHOD

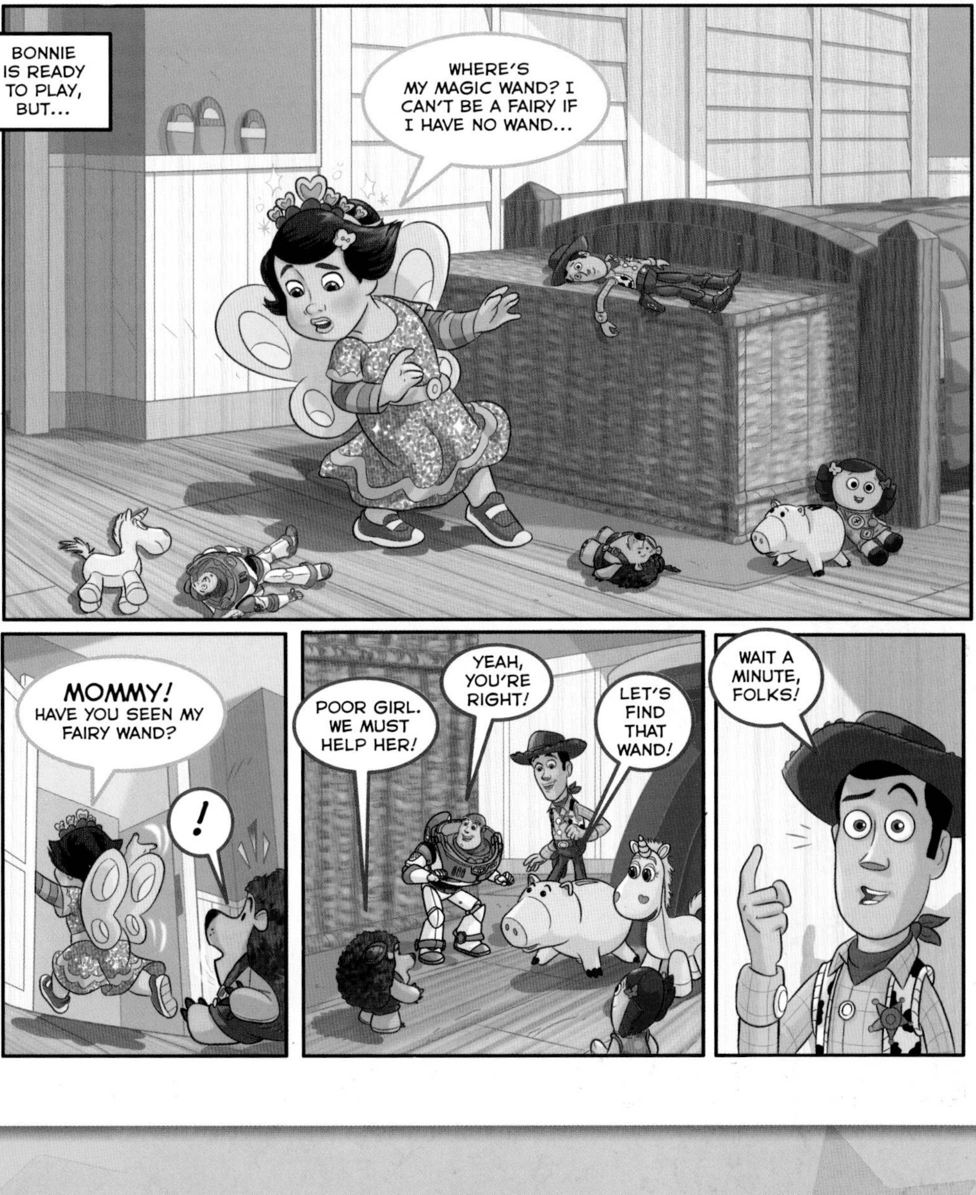
BONNIE IS READY TO PLAY, BUT...
WHERE'S MY MAGIC WAND? I CAN'T BE A FAIRY IF I HAVE NO WAND...
MOMMY! HAVE YOU SEEN MY FAIRY WAND?
!
POOR GIRL. WE MUST HELP HER!
YEAH, YOU'RE RIGHT!
LET'S FIND THAT WAND!
WAIT A MINUTE, FOLKS!

SCRIPT: TEA ORSI, PENCIL: LUCA USAI, INK: MICHELA FRARE, COLOR: LUCIO DE GIUSEPPE

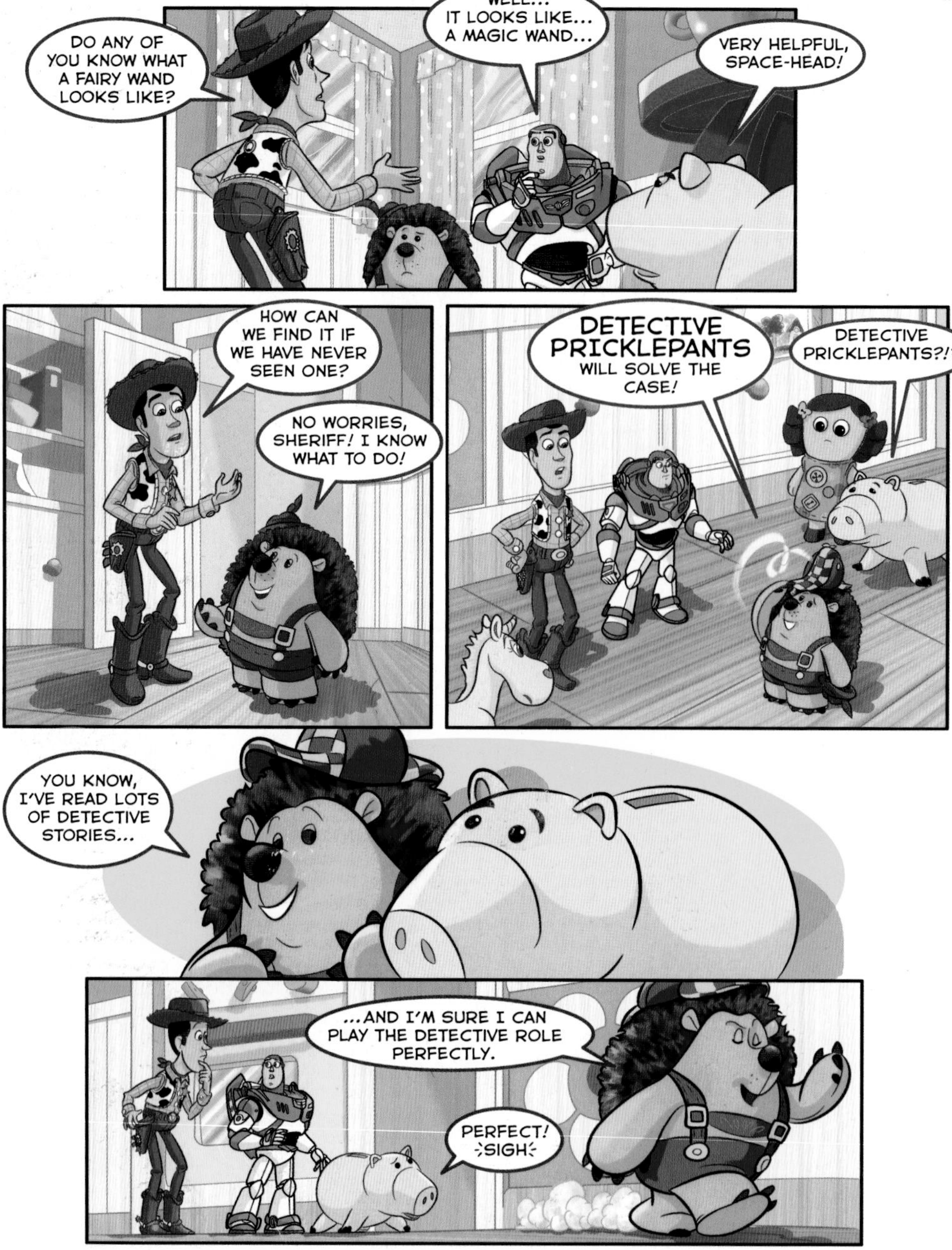
DO ANY OF YOU KNOW WHAT A FAIRY WAND LOOKS LIKE?
WELL... IT LOOKS LIKE... A MAGIC WAND...
VERY HELPFUL, SPACE-HEAD!
HOW CAN WE FIND IT IF WE HAVE NEVER SEEN ONE?
NO WORRIES, SHERIFF! I KNOW WHAT TO DO!
DETECTIVE PRICKLEPANTS WILL SOLVE THE CASE!
DETECTIVE PRICKLEPANTS?!?
YOU KNOW, I'VE READ LOTS OF DETECTIVE STORIES...
...AND I'M SURE I CAN PLAY THE DETECTIVE ROLE PERFECTLY.
PERFECT! SIGH

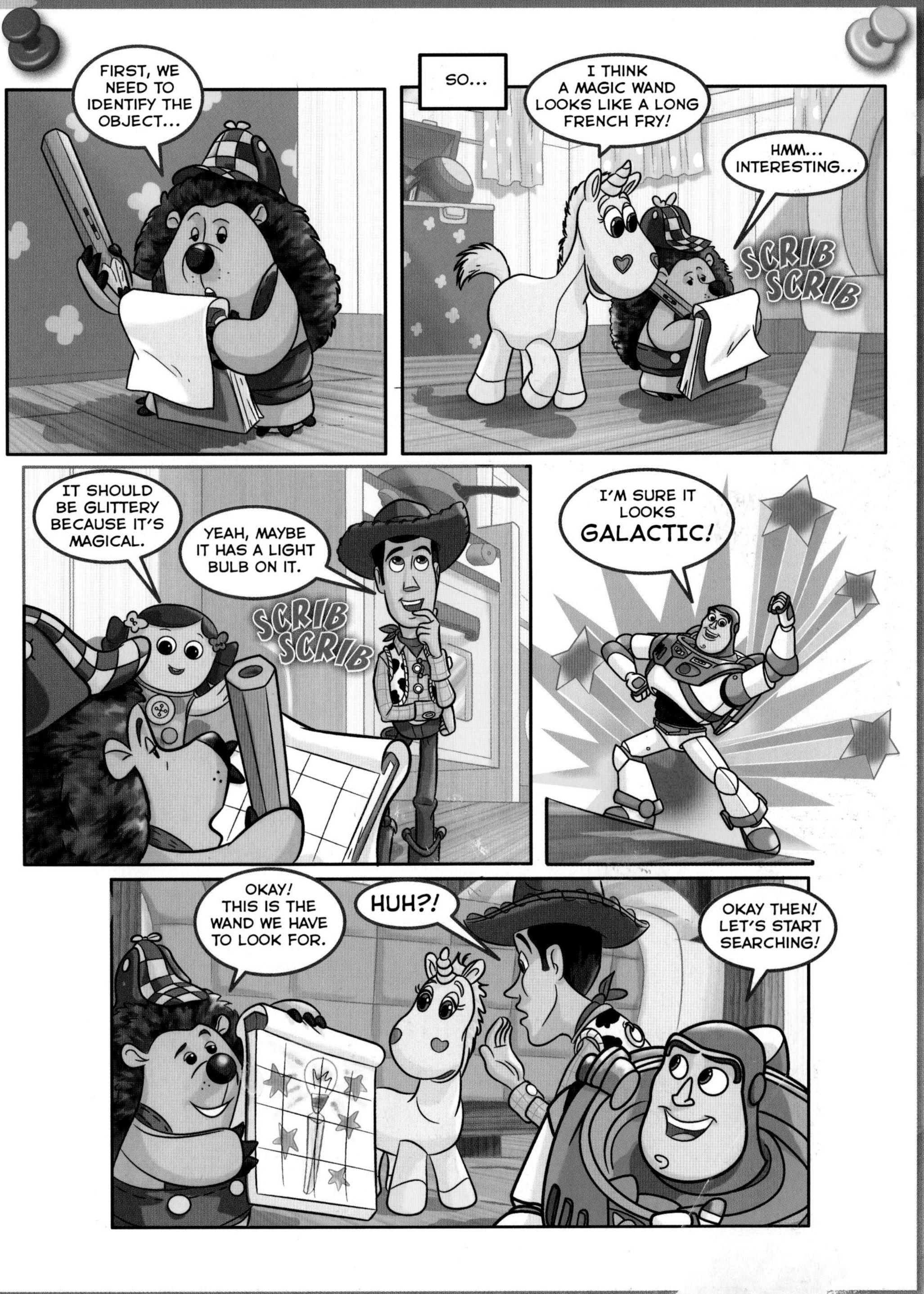
FIRST, WE NEED TO IDENTIFY THE OBJECT...
SO...
I THINK A MAGIC WAND LOOKS LIKE A LONG FRENCH FRY!
HMM... INTERESTING...
SCRIB SCRIB
IT SHOULD BE GLITTERY BECAUSE IT'S MAGICAL.
YEAH, MAYBE IT HAS A LIGHT BULB ON IT.
SCRIB SCRIB
I'M SURE IT LOOKS GALACTIC!
OKAY! THIS IS THE WAND WE HAVE TO LOOK FOR.
HUH?!
OKAY THEN! LET'S START SEARCHING!

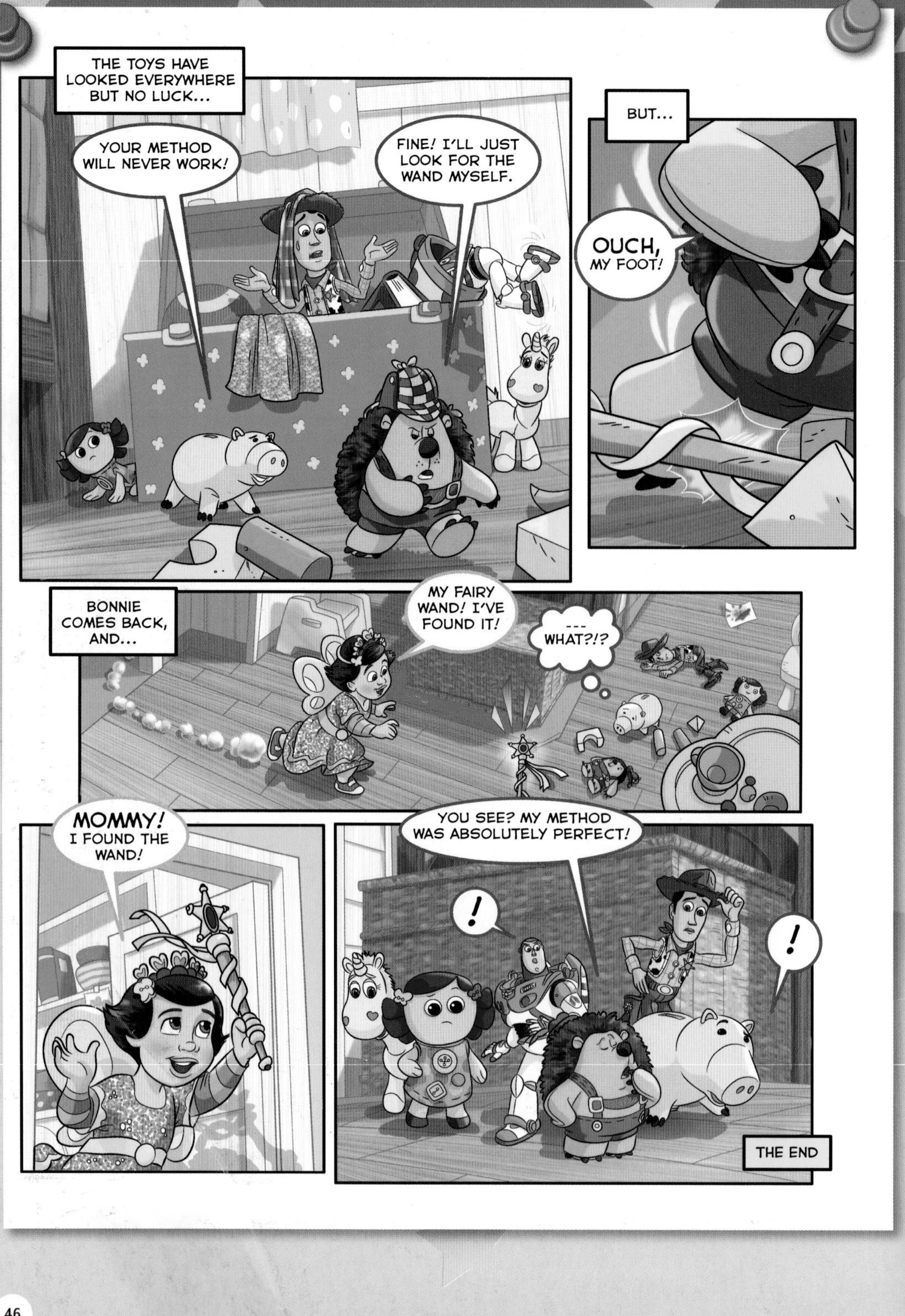

THE TOYS HAVE LOOKED EVERYWHERE BUT NO LUCK...
YOUR METHOD WILL NEVER WORK!
FINE! I'LL JUST LOOK FOR THE WAND MYSELF.
BUT...
OUCH, MY FOOT!
BONNIE COMES BACK, AND...
MY FAIRY WAND! I'VE FOUND IT!
--- WHAT?!?
MOMMY! I FOUND THE WAND!
YOU SEE? MY METHOD WAS ABSOLUTELY PERFECT!
!
!
THE END

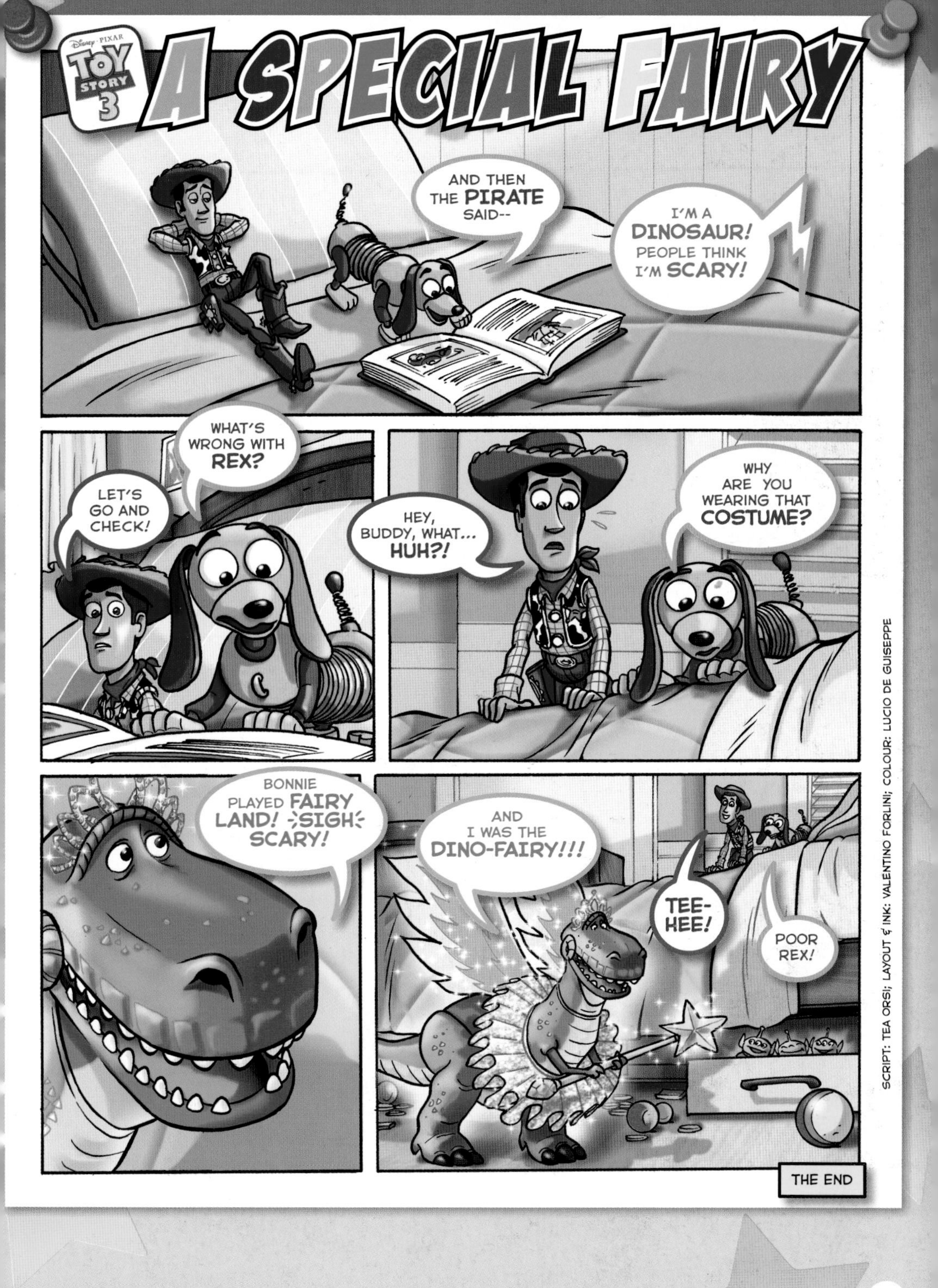

TOY STORY 3
A SPECIAL FAIRY
AND THEN THE PIRATE SAID--
I'M A DINOSAUR! PEOPLE THINK I'M SCARY!
WHAT'S WRONG WITH REX?
LET'S GO AND CHECK!
HEY, BUDDY, WHAT... HUH?!
WHY ARE YOU WEARING THAT COSTUME?
BONNIE PLAYED FAIRY LAND! *SIGH* SCARY!
AND I WAS THE DINO-FAIRY!!!
TEE-HEE!
POOR REX!
THE END
SCRIPT: TEA ORSI; LAYOUT & INK: VALENTINO FORLINI; COLOUR: LUCIO DE GUISEPPE

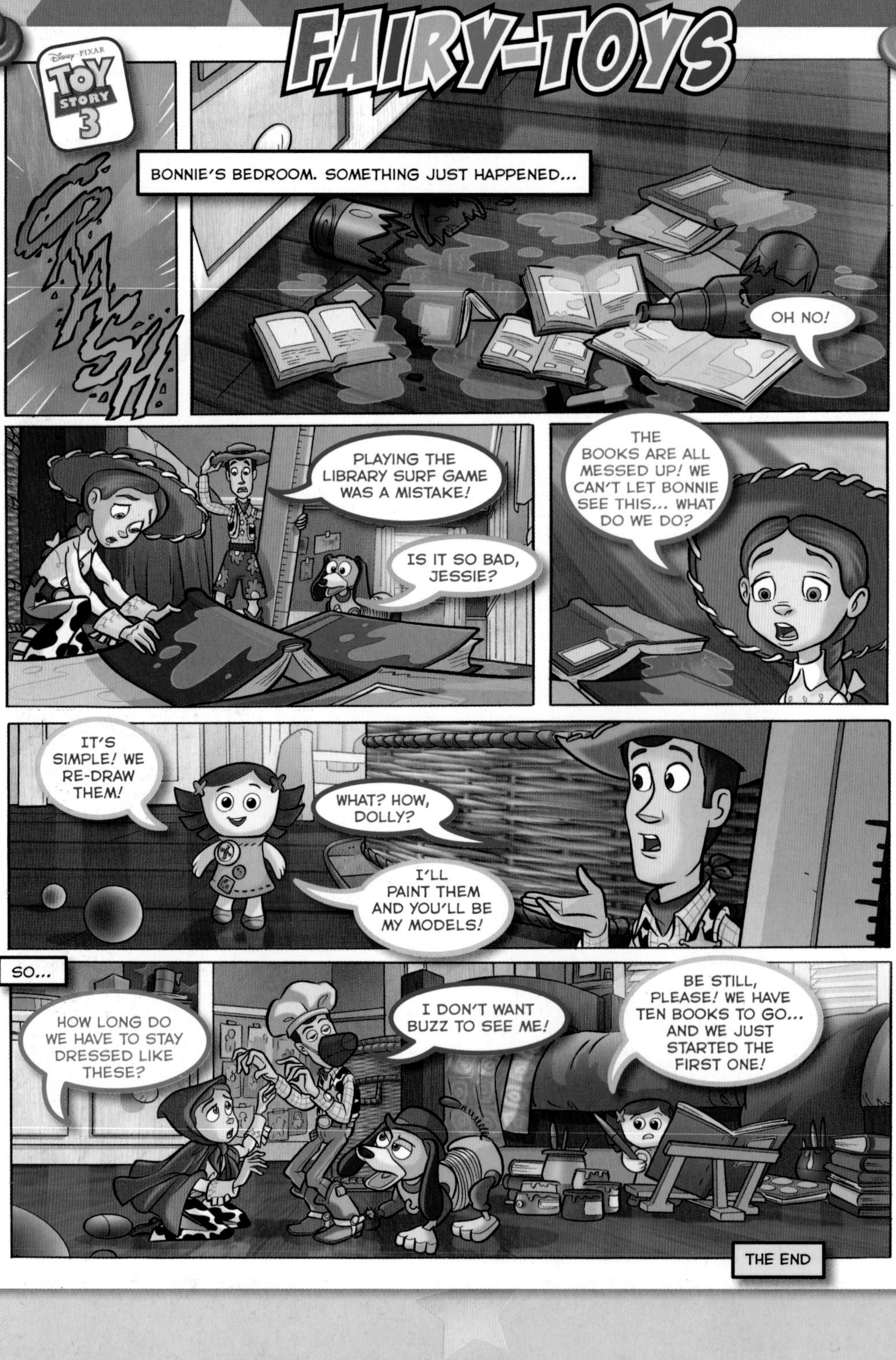
FAIRY-TOYS
DISNEY·PIXAR TOY STORY 3
BONNIE'S BEDROOM. SOMETHING JUST HAPPENED...
CRASH
OH NO!
PLAYING THE LIBRARY SURF GAME WAS A MISTAKE!
IS IT SO BAD, JESSIE?
THE BOOKS ARE ALL MESSED UP! WE CAN'T LET BONNIE SEE THIS... WHAT DO WE DO?
IT'S SIMPLE! WE RE-DRAW THEM!
WHAT? HOW, DOLLY?
I'LL PAINT THEM AND YOU'LL BE MY MODELS!
SO...
HOW LONG DO WE HAVE TO STAY DRESSED LIKE THESE?
I DON'T WANT BUZZ TO SEE ME!
BE STILL, PLEASE! WE HAVE TEN BOOKS TO GO... AND WE JUST STARTED THE FIRST ONE!
THE END

SCRIPT: ALESSANDRO FERRARI; PENCILS: VALENTINO FORLINI; INK: MICHELA FRARE; COLOUR: MARA DAMIANI. SLINKY® DOG. © POOF-SLINKY, INC.

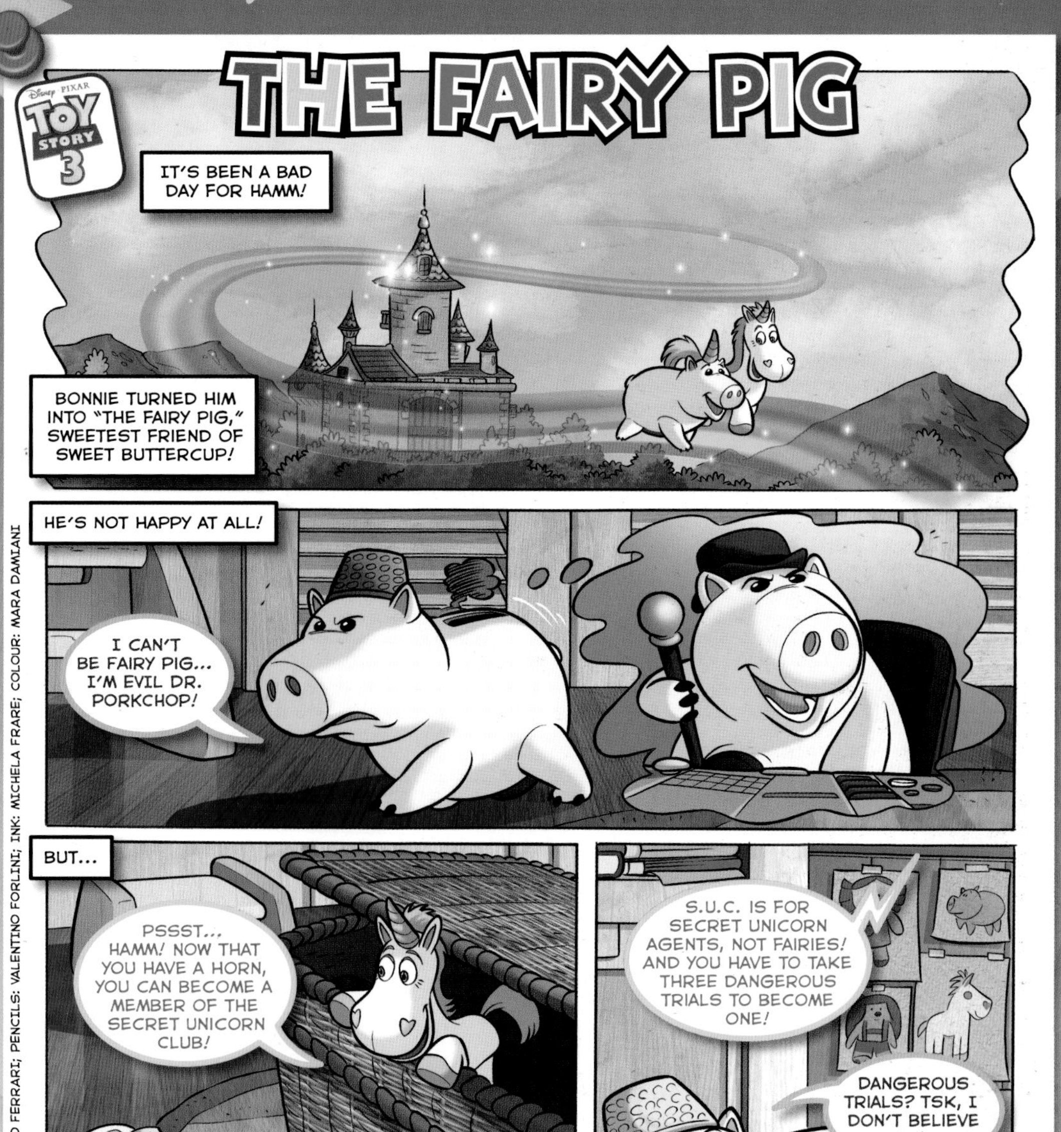
THE FAIRY PIG
DISNEY PIXAR TOY STORY 3
IT'S BEEN A BAD DAY FOR HAMM!
BONNIE TURNED HIM INTO "THE FAIRY PIG," SWEETEST FRIEND OF SWEET BUTTERCUP!
HE'S NOT HAPPY AT ALL!
I CAN'T BE FAIRY PIG... I'M EVIL DR. PORKCHOP!
BUT...
PSSST... HAMM! NOW THAT YOU HAVE A HORN, YOU CAN BECOME A MEMBER OF THE SECRET UNICORN CLUB!
ENOUGH OF YOUR FAIRYTALES FOR TODAY, BUTTERCUP!
S.U.C. IS FOR SECRET UNICORN AGENTS, NOT FAIRIES! AND YOU HAVE TO TAKE THREE DANGEROUS TRIALS TO BECOME ONE!
DANGEROUS TRIALS? TSK, I DON'T BELIEVE IT!
SCRIPT: ALESSANDRO FERRARI; PENCILS: VALENTINO FORLINI; INK: MICHELA FRARE; COLOUR: MARA DAMIANI

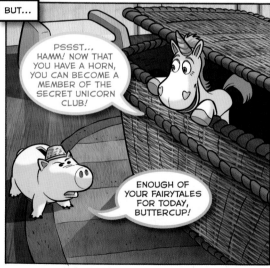

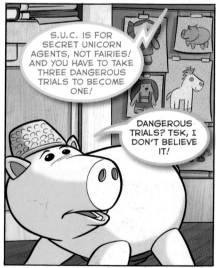

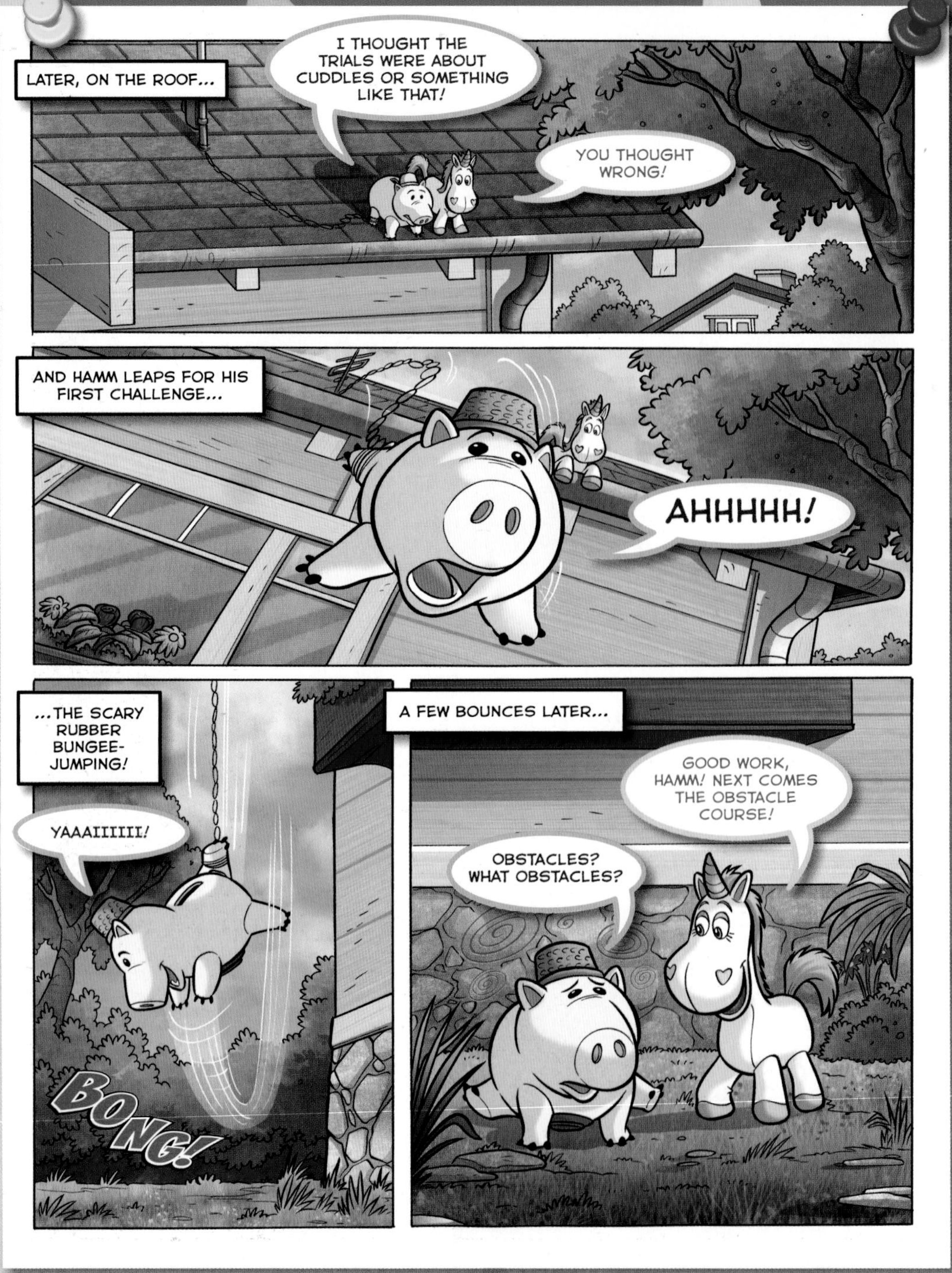
LATER, ON THE ROOF...
I THOUGHT THE TRIALS WERE ABOUT CUDDLES OR SOMETHING LIKE THAT!
YOU THOUGHT WRONG!
AND HAMM LEAPS FOR HIS FIRST CHALLENGE...
AHHHHH!
...THE SCARY RUBBER BUNGEE-JUMPING!
YAAAIIIIII!
BONG!
A FEW BOUNCES LATER...
GOOD WORK, HAMM! NEXT COMES THE OBSTACLE COURSE!
OBSTACLES? WHAT OBSTACLES?

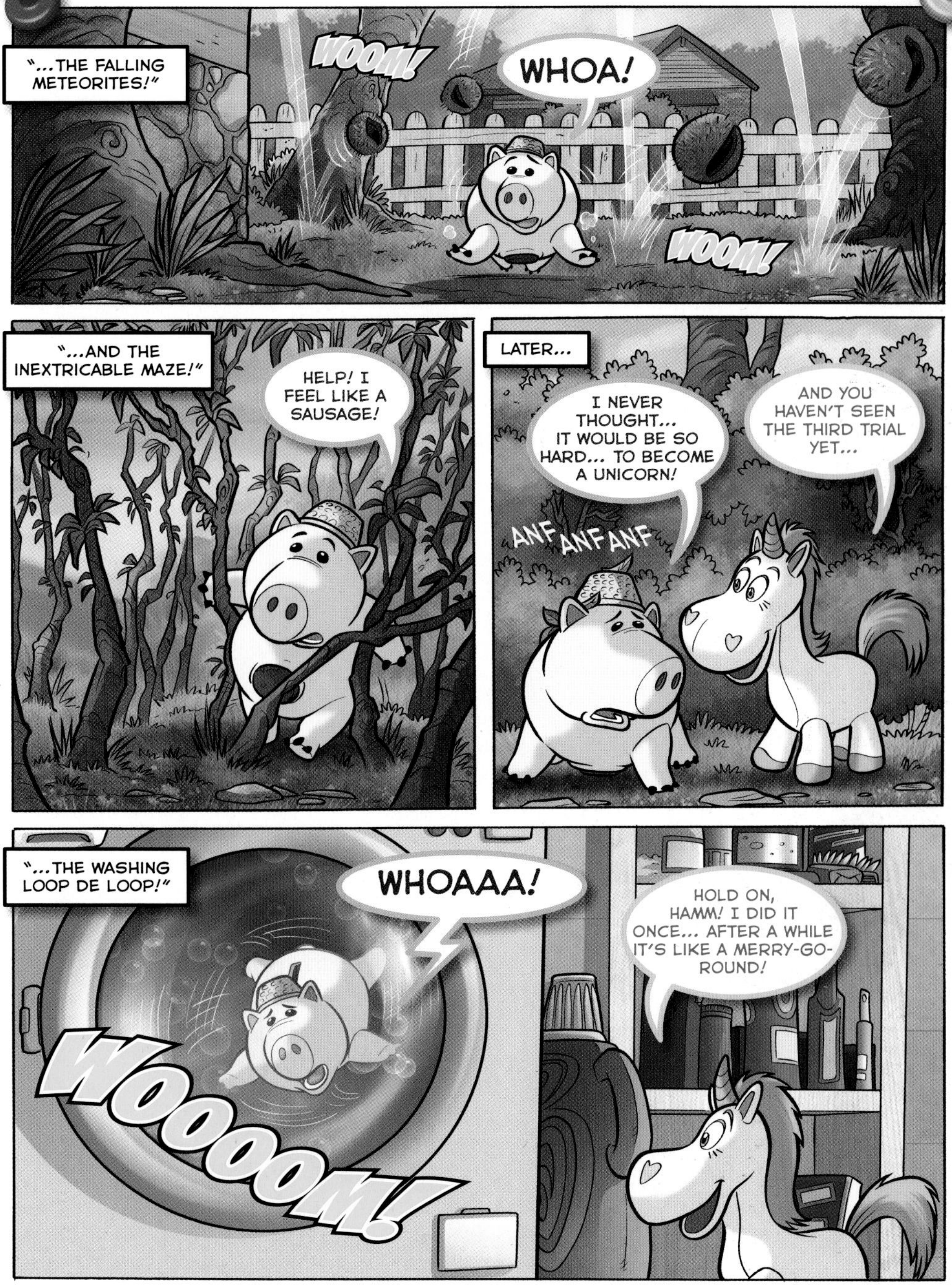
"...THE FALLING METEORITES!"
WOOM!
WHOA!
WOOM!
"...AND THE INEXTRICABLE MAZE!"
HELP! I FEEL LIKE A SAUSAGE!
LATER...
I NEVER THOUGHT... IT WOULD BE SO HARD... TO BECOME A UNICORN!
AND YOU HAVEN'T SEEN THE THIRD TRIAL YET...
ANF ANF ANF
"...THE WASHING LOOP DE LOOP!"
WHOAAA!
WOOOOOM!
HOLD ON, HAMM! I DID IT ONCE... AFTER A WHILE IT'S LIKE A MERRY-GO-ROUND!

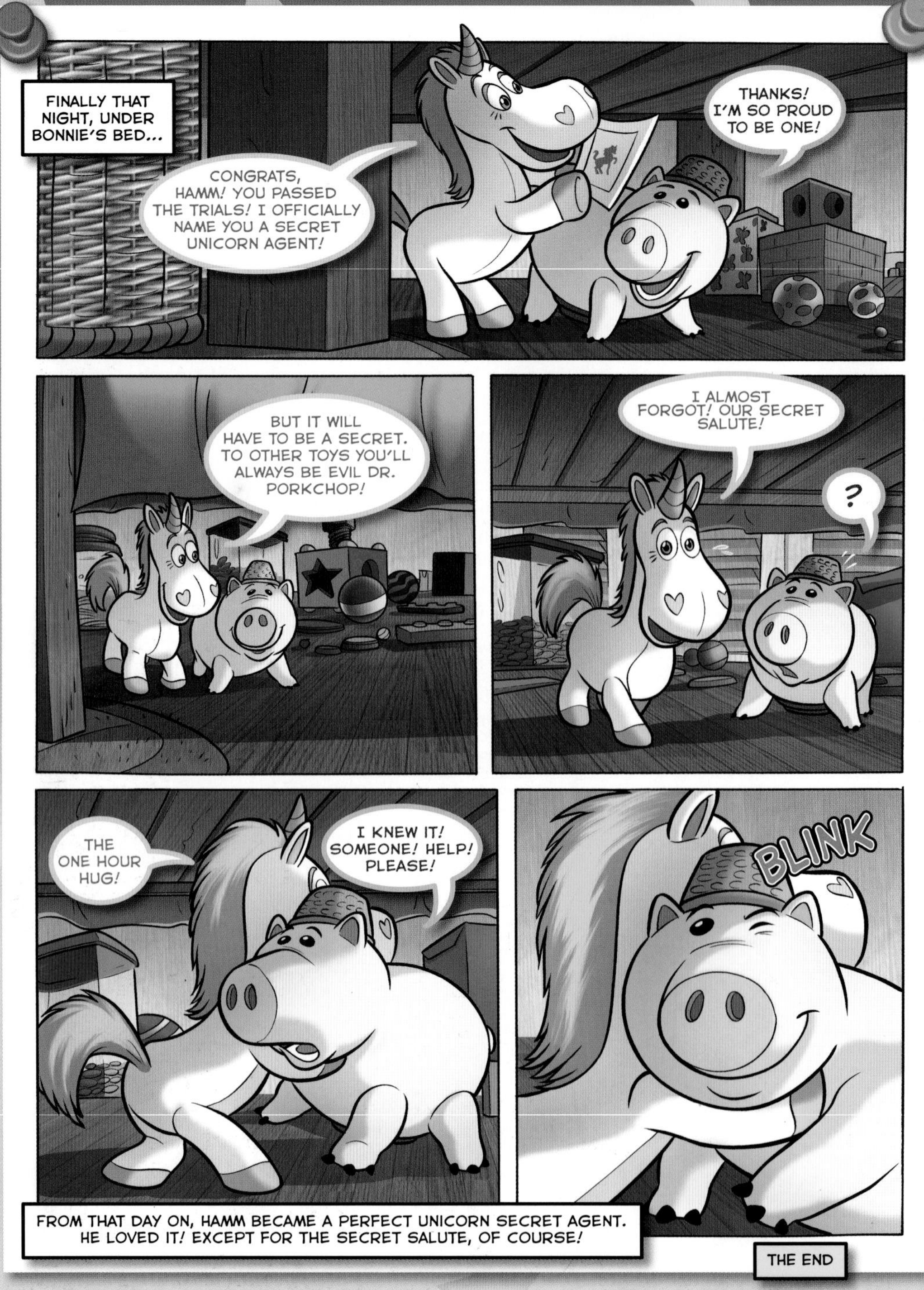
FINALLY THAT NIGHT, UNDER BONNIE'S BED...
CONGRATS, HAMM! YOU PASSED THE TRIALS! I OFFICIALLY NAME YOU A SECRET UNICORN AGENT!
THANKS! I'M SO PROUD TO BE ONE!
BUT IT WILL HAVE TO BE A SECRET. TO OTHER TOYS YOU'LL ALWAYS BE EVIL DR. PORKCHOP!
I ALMOST FORGOT! OUR SECRET SALUTE!
?
THE ONE HOUR HUG!
I KNEW IT! SOMEONE! HELP! PLEASE!
BLINK
FROM THAT DAY ON, HAMM BECAME A PERFECT UNICORN SECRET AGENT. HE LOVED IT! EXCEPT FOR THE SECRET SALUTE, OF COURSE!
THE END

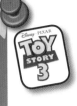

DANGEROUS PEARLS

HEY! HAVE YOU SEEN BONNIE'S NEW GAME?

THEY ARE **PEARLS** TO CREATE **JEWELS!**
THEY ARE SO COLORFUL!
I HAVE ALWAYS LOVED NECKLACES!

SCRIPT: ALESSANDRO SISTI; LAYOUT & INK: LUCA USAI; COLOUR: MARA DAMIANI

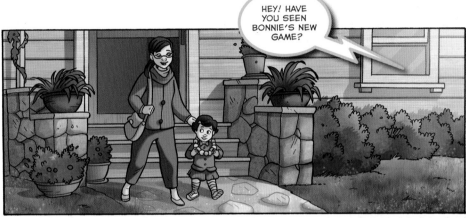

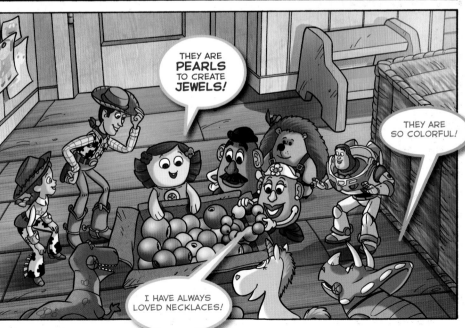

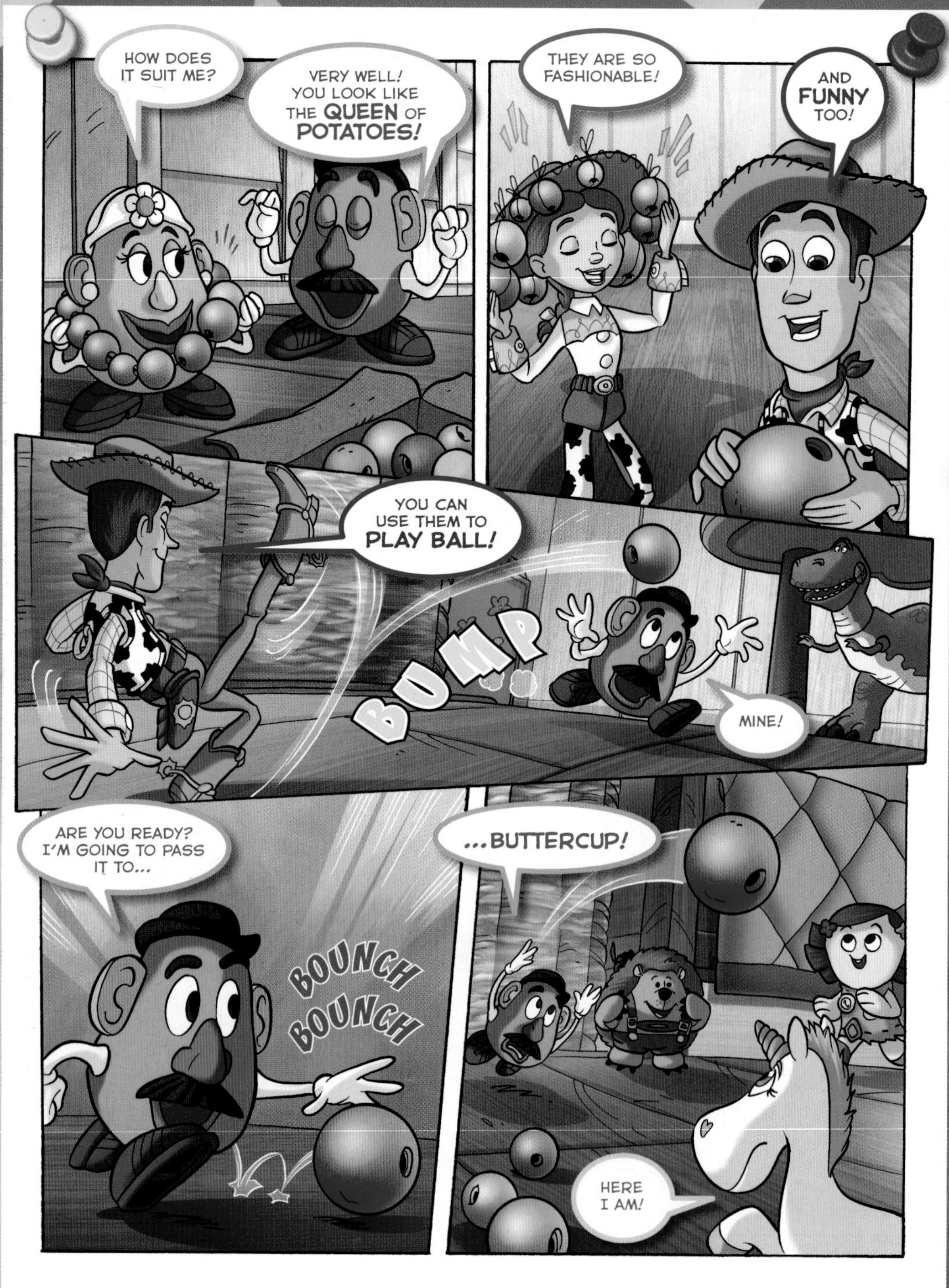
HOW DOES IT SUIT ME?
VERY WELL! YOU LOOK LIKE THE QUEEN OF POTATOES!
THEY ARE SO FASHIONABLE!
AND FUNNY TOO!
YOU CAN USE THEM TO PLAY BALL!
BUMP
MINE!
ARE YOU READY? I'M GOING TO PASS IT TO...
BOUNCH
BOUNCH
...BUTTERCUP!
HERE I AM!

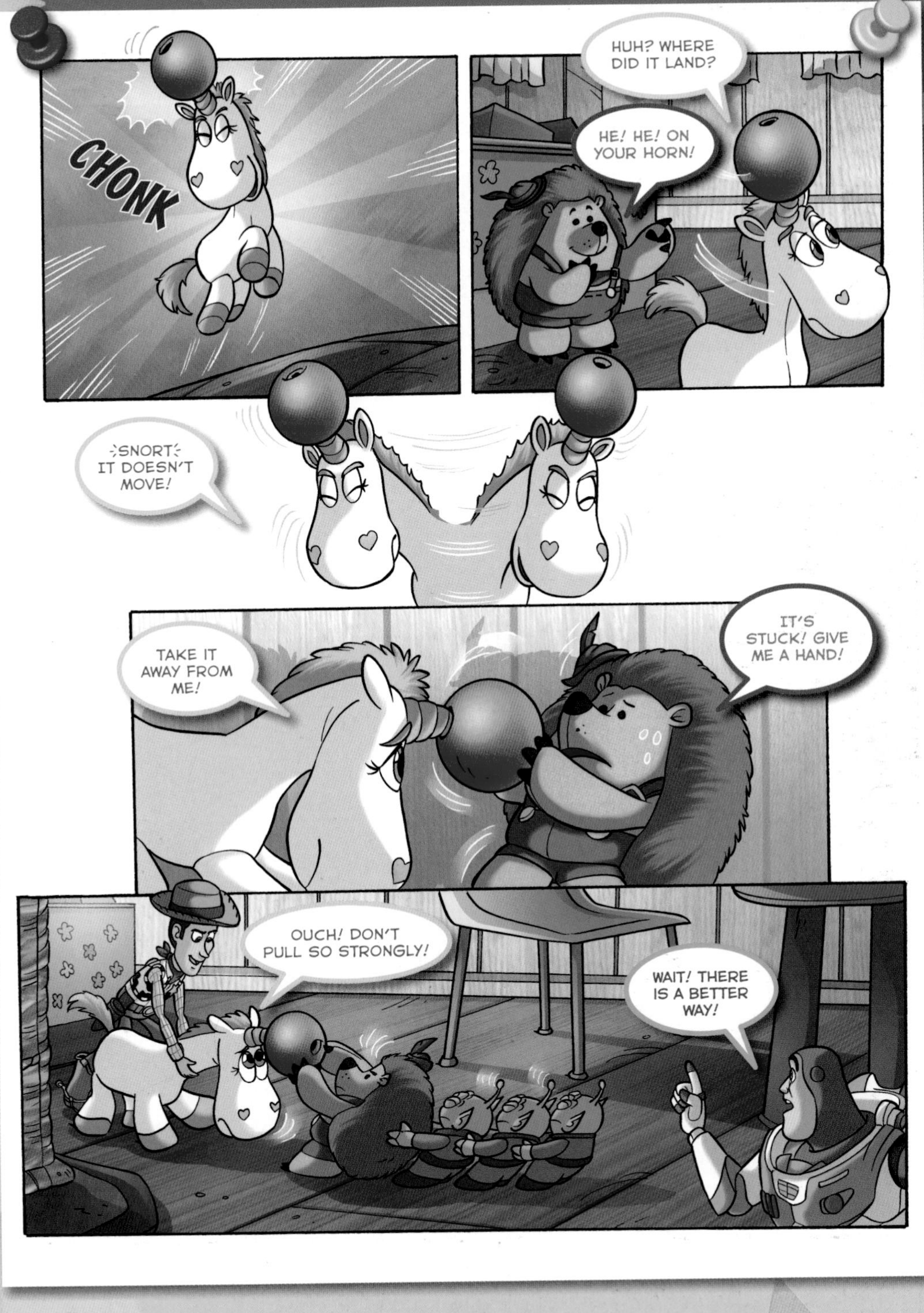
CHONK
HUH? WHERE DID IT LAND?
HE! HE! ON YOUR HORN!
-SNORT- IT DOESN'T MOVE!
TAKE IT AWAY FROM ME!
IT'S STUCK! GIVE ME A HAND!
OUCH! DON'T PULL SO STRONGLY!
WAIT! THERE IS A BETTER WAY!

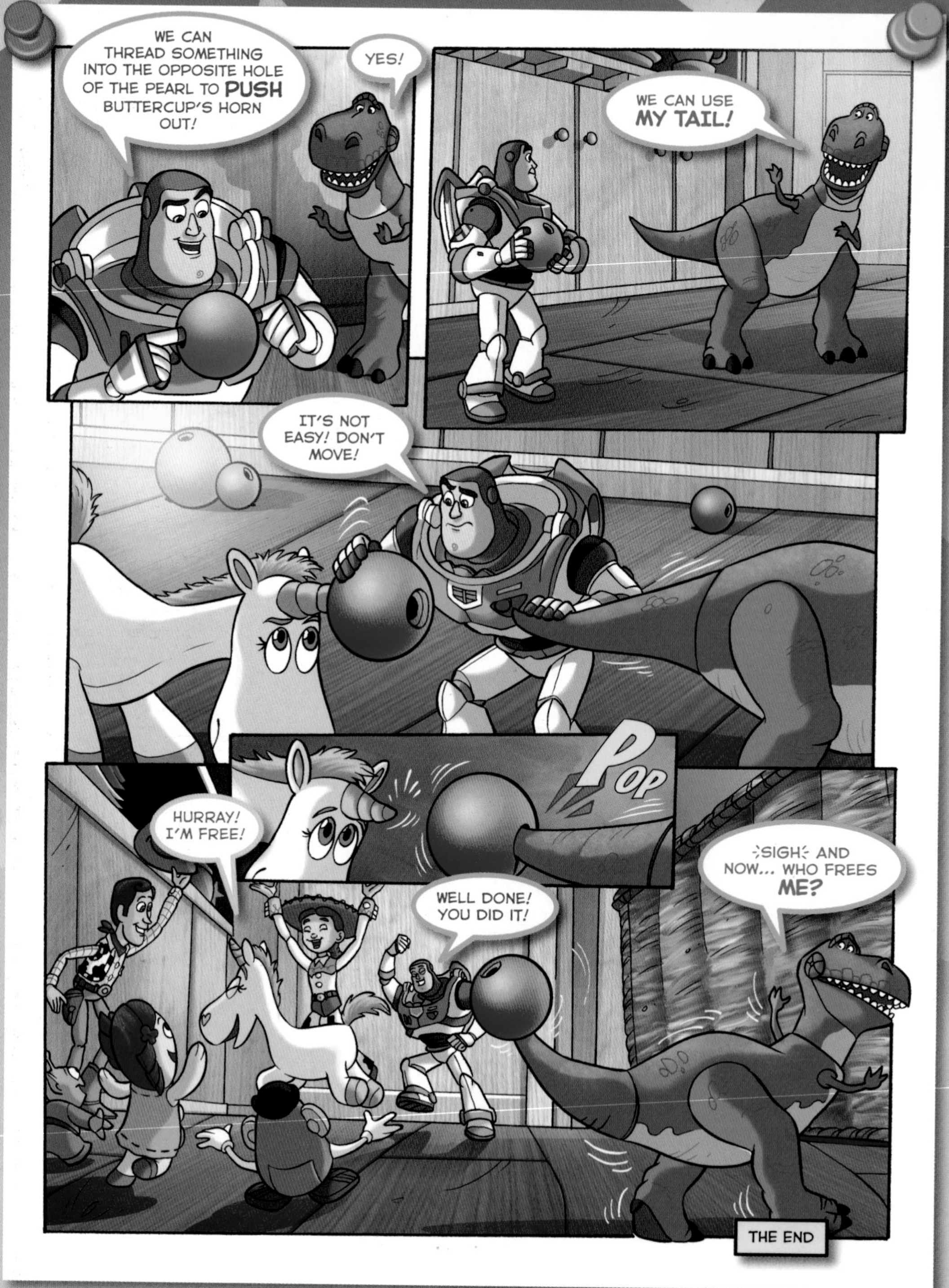
WE CAN THREAD SOMETHING INTO THE OPPOSITE HOLE OF THE PEARL TO PUSH BUTTERCUP'S HORN OUT!
YES!
WE CAN USE MY TAIL!
IT'S NOT EASY! DON'T MOVE!
POP
HURRAY! I'M FREE!
WELL DONE! YOU DID IT!
-SIGH- AND NOW... WHO FREES ME?
THE END

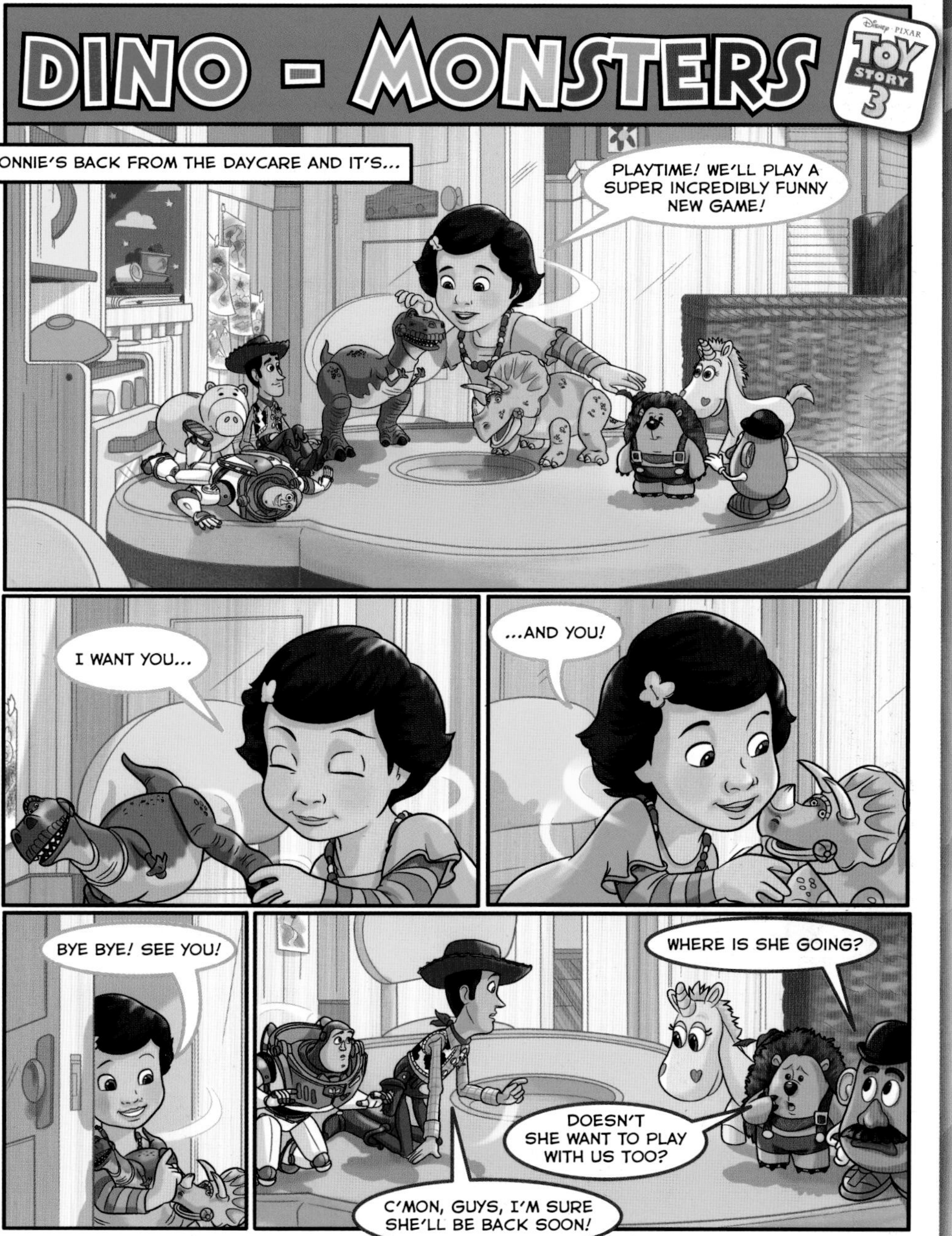
DINO - MONSTERS
DISNEY PIXAR TOY STORY 3
BONNIE'S BACK FROM THE DAYCARE AND IT'S...
PLAYTIME! WE'LL PLAY A SUPER INCREDIBLY FUNNY NEW GAME!
I WANT YOU...
...AND YOU!
BYE BYE! SEE YOU!
WHERE IS SHE GOING?
DOESN'T SHE WANT TO PLAY WITH US TOO?
C'MON, GUYS, I'M SURE SHE'LL BE BACK SOON!

SCRIPT: ALESSANDRO FERRARI, PENCIL: GIANFRANCO FLORIO, INK: MICHELA FRARE, COLOR: LUCIO DE GIUSEPPE

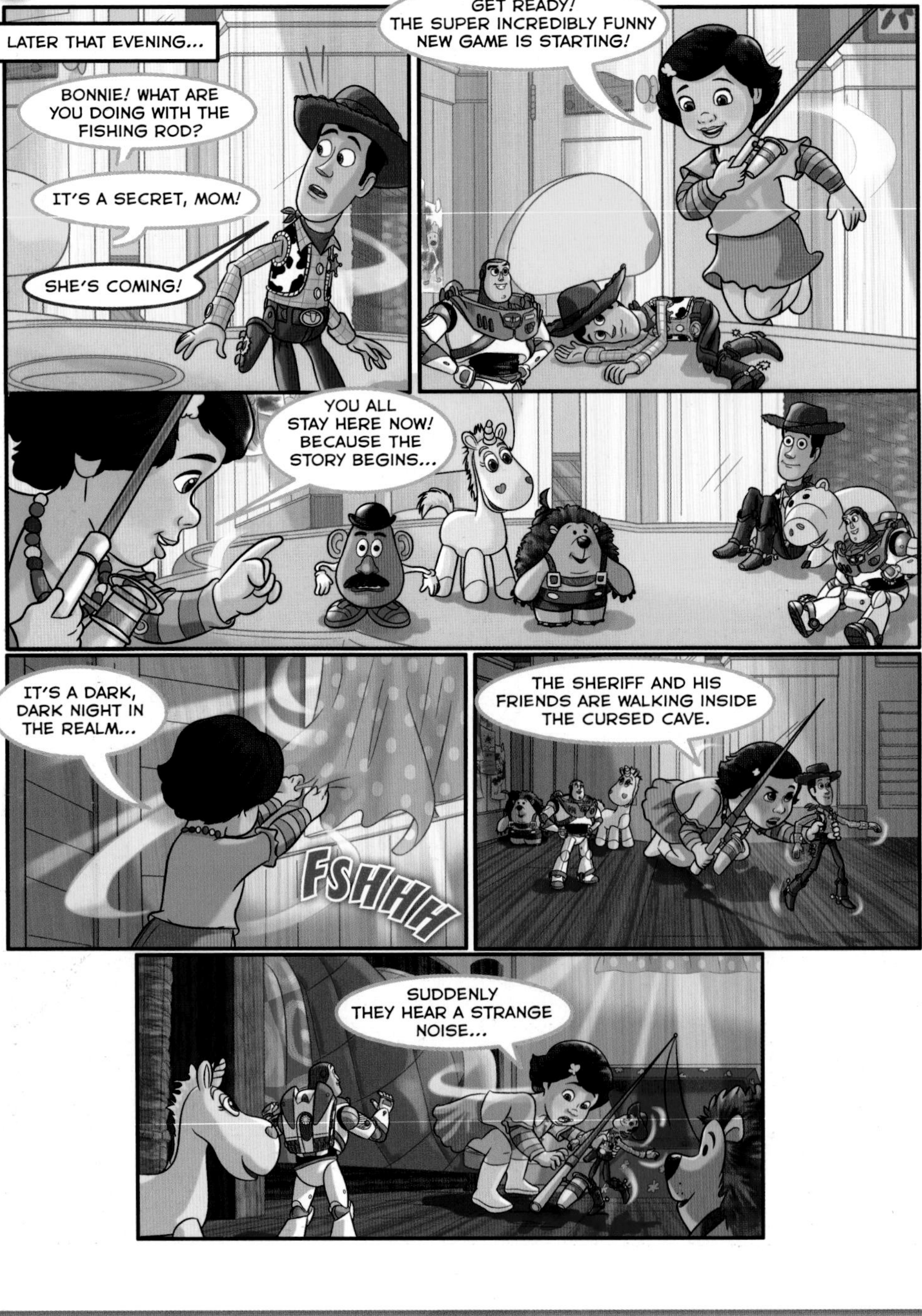
LATER THAT EVENING...
BONNIE! WHAT ARE YOU DOING WITH THE FISHING ROD?
IT'S A SECRET, MOM!
SHE'S COMING!
GET READY! THE SUPER INCREDIBLY FUNNY NEW GAME IS STARTING!
YOU ALL STAY HERE NOW! BECAUSE THE STORY BEGINS...
IT'S A DARK, DARK NIGHT IN THE REALM...
FSHHHH
THE SHERIFF AND HIS FRIENDS ARE WALKING INSIDE THE CURSED CAVE.
SUDDENLY THEY HEAR A STRANGE NOISE...

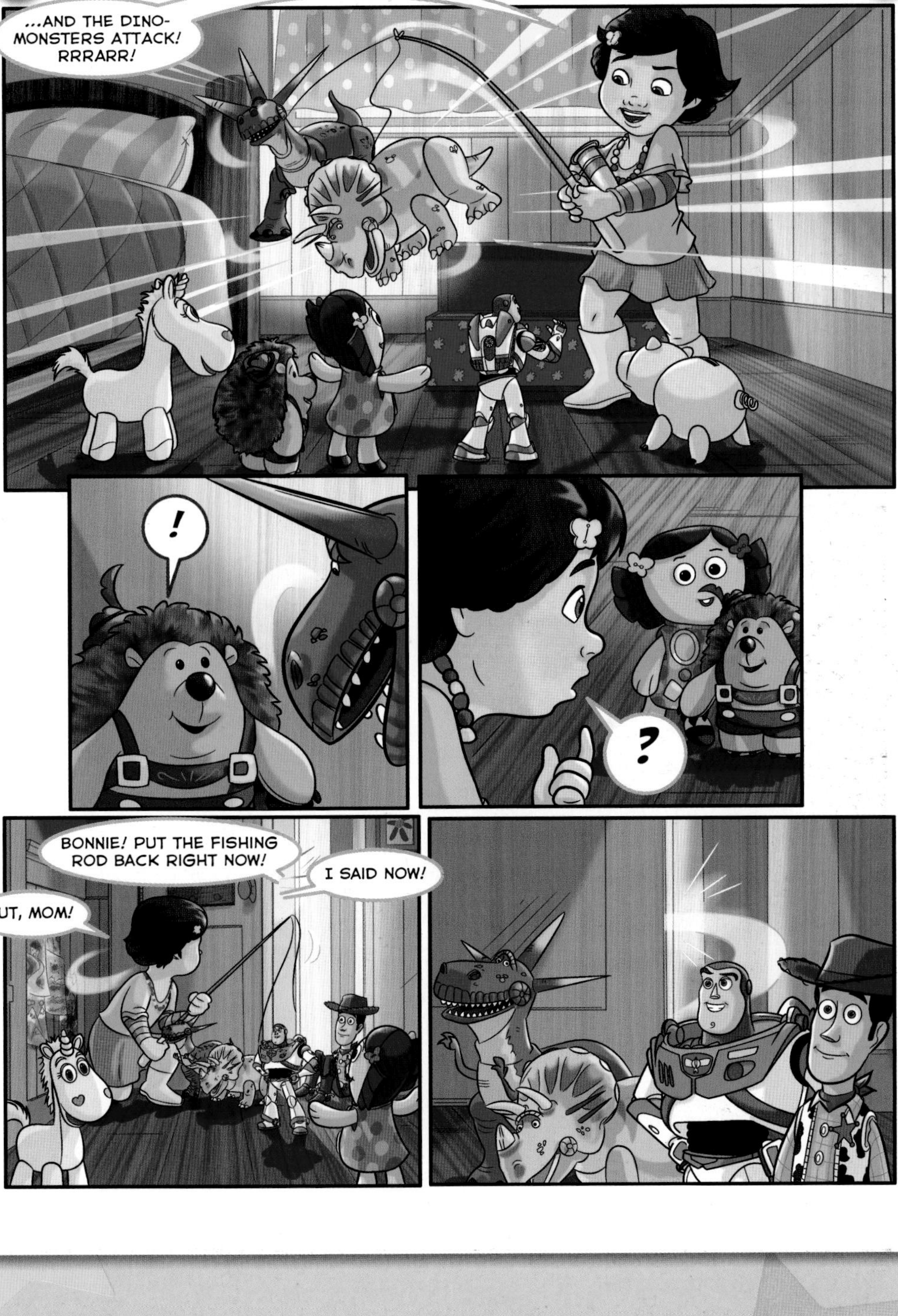
...AND THE DINO-MONSTERS ATTACK! RRRARR!
!
?
BONNIE! PUT THE FISHING ROD BACK RIGHT NOW!
I SAID NOW!
BUT, MOM!

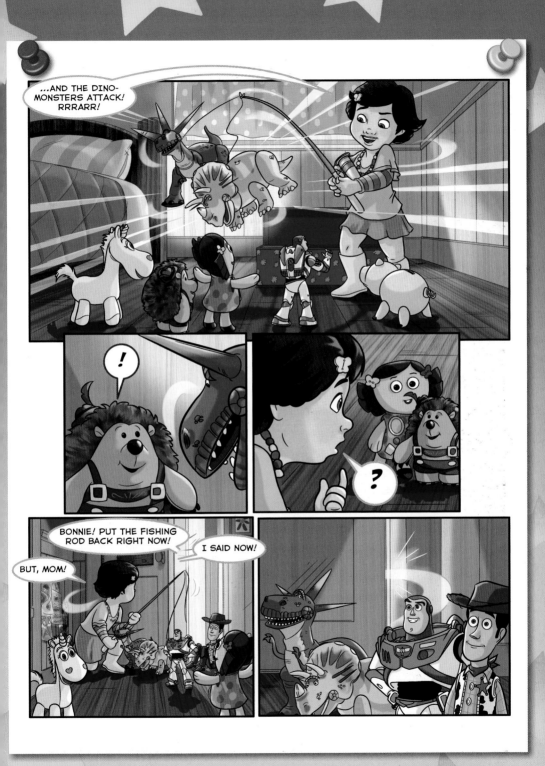

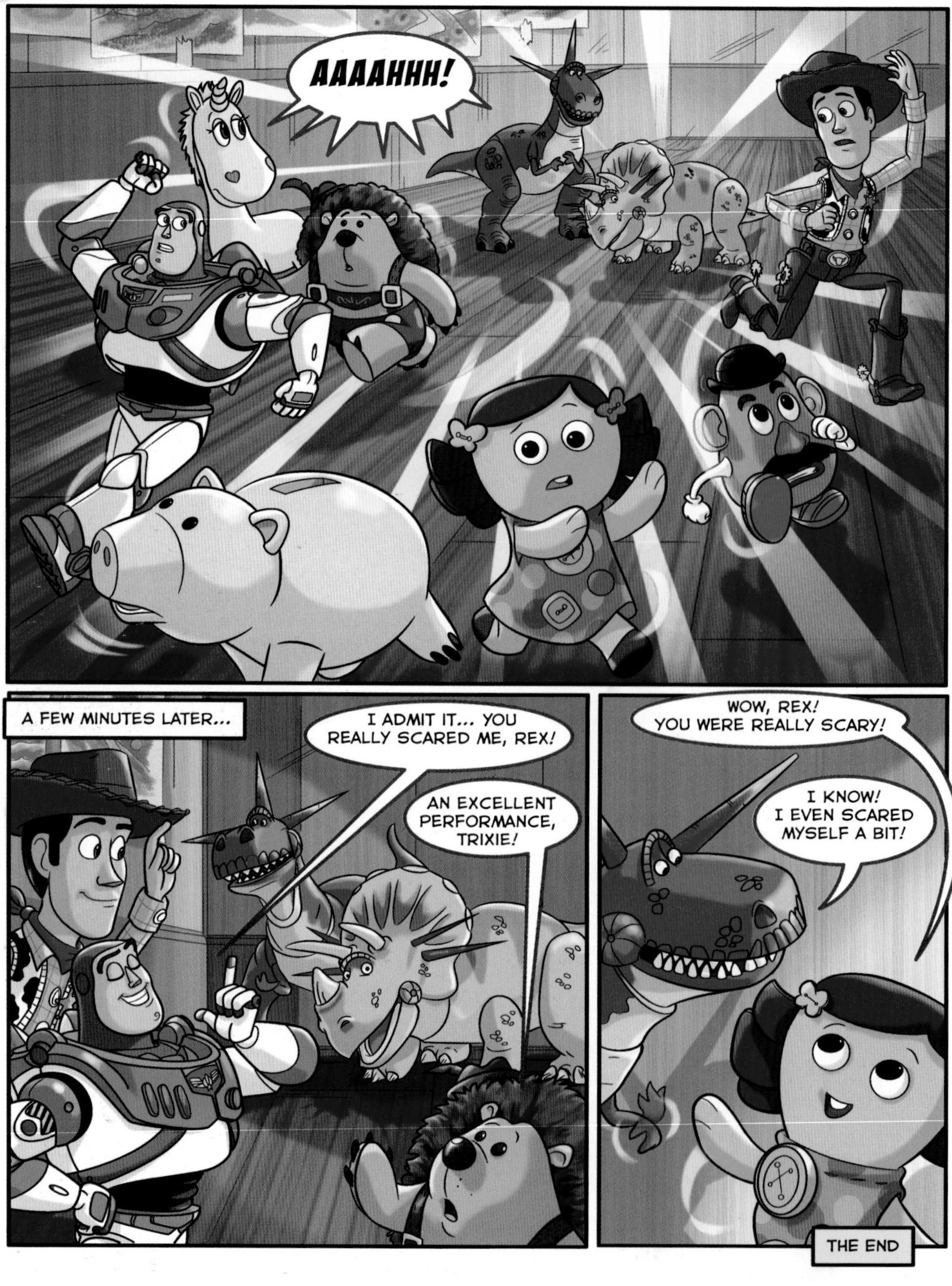
AAAAHHH!
A FEW MINUTES LATER...
I ADMIT IT... YOU REALLY SCARED ME, REX!
AN EXCELLENT PERFORMANCE, TRIXIE!
WOW, REX! YOU WERE REALLY SCARY!
I KNOW! I EVEN SCARED MYSELF A BIT!
THE END

A SPECIAL ASSIGNMENT

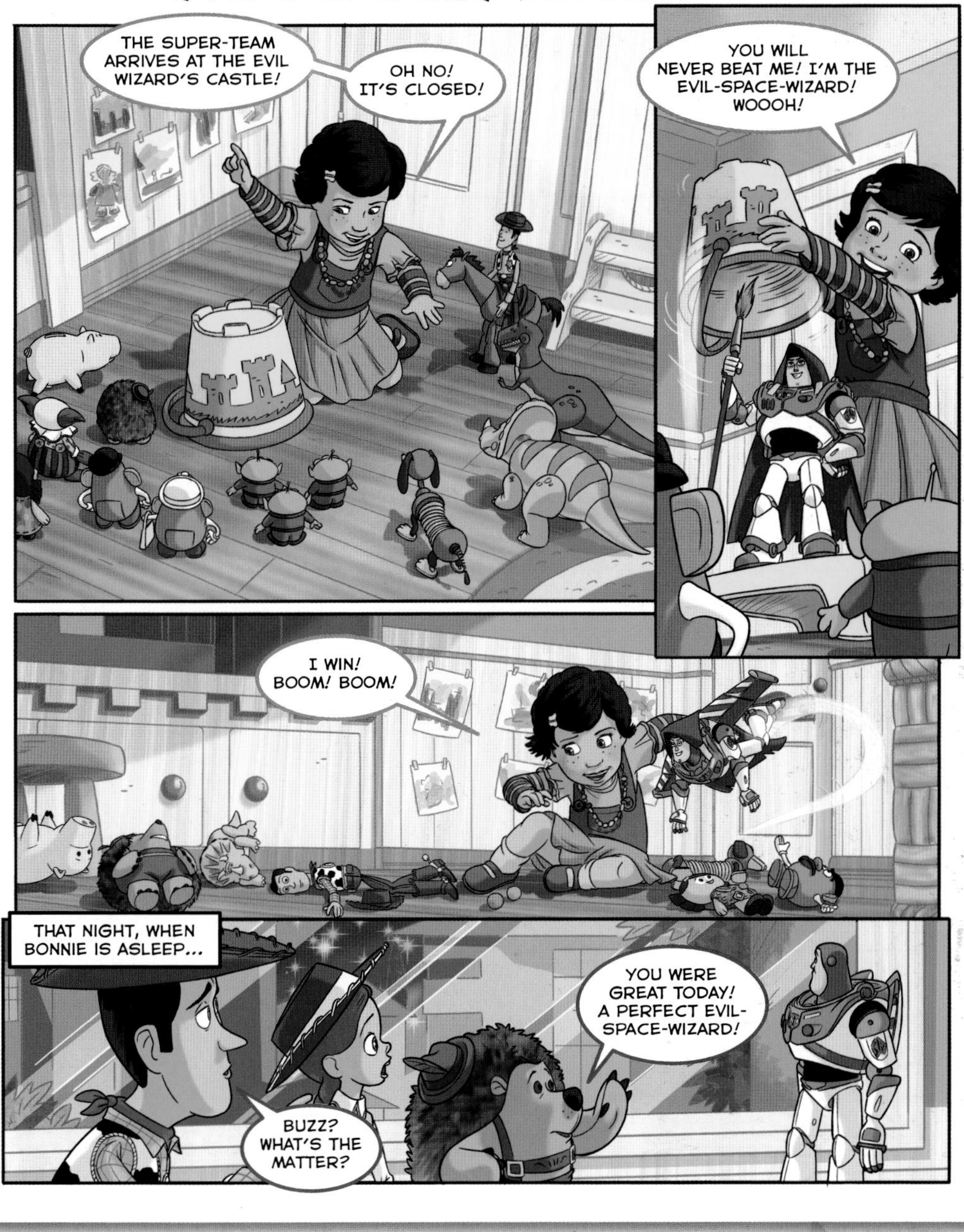

THE SUPER-TEAM ARRIVES AT THE EVIL WIZARD'S CASTLE!
OH NO! IT'S CLOSED!
YOU WILL NEVER BEAT ME! I'M THE EVIL-SPACE-WIZARD! WOOOH!
I WIN! BOOM! BOOM!
THAT NIGHT, WHEN BONNIE IS ASLEEP...
YOU WERE GREAT TODAY! A PERFECT EVIL-SPACE-WIZARD!
BUZZ? WHAT'S THE MATTER?

SCRIPT: ALESSANDRO FERRARI; LAYOUT: ANDREA GREPPI; INK: MICHELA FRARE; COLOUR: LUCIO DE GIUSEPPE

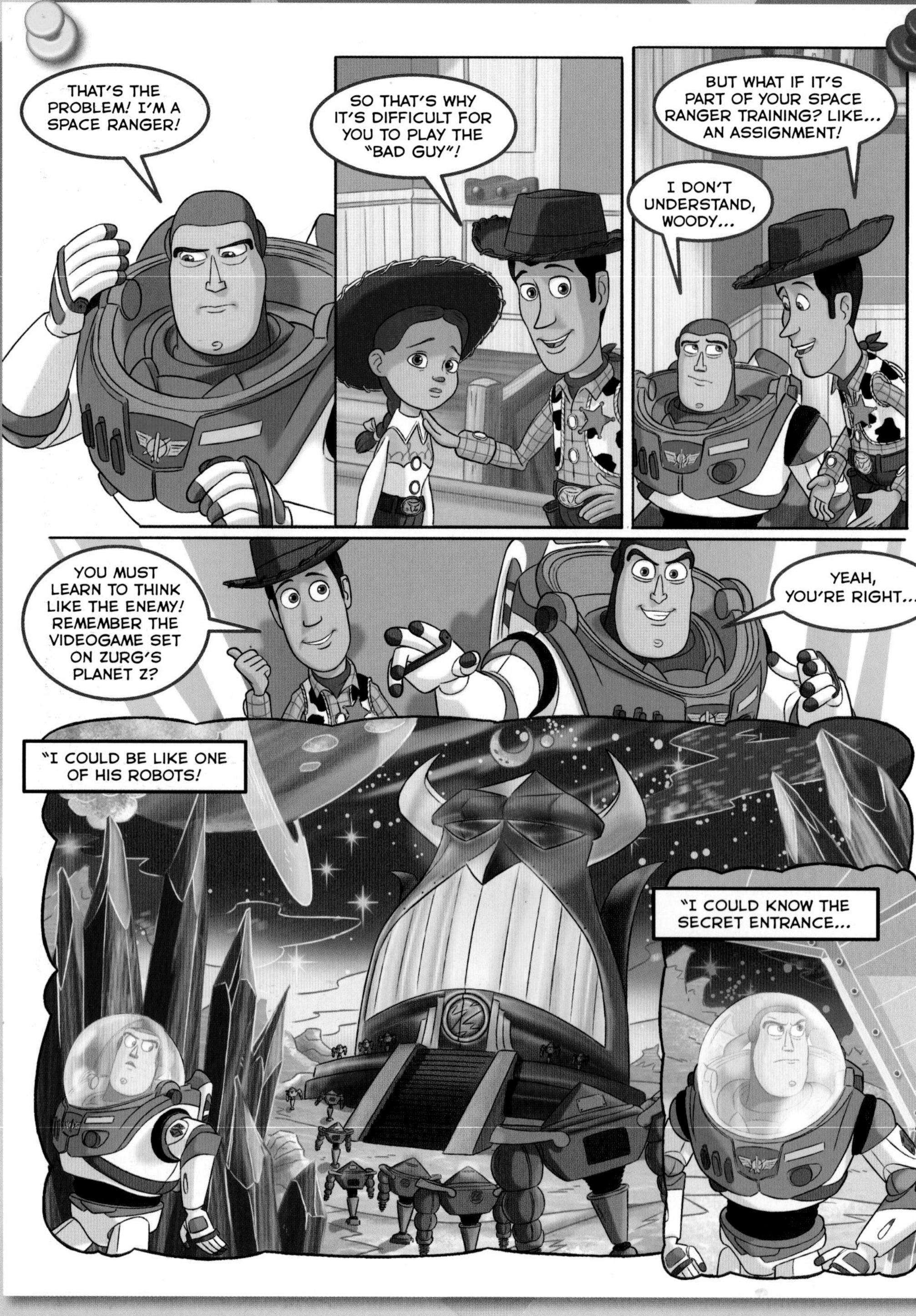
THAT'S THE PROBLEM! I'M A SPACE RANGER!
SO THAT'S WHY IT'S DIFFICULT FOR YOU TO PLAY THE "BAD GUY"!
BUT WHAT IF IT'S PART OF YOUR SPACE RANGER TRAINING? LIKE... AN ASSIGNMENT!
I DON'T UNDERSTAND, WOODY...
YOU MUST LEARN TO THINK LIKE THE ENEMY! REMEMBER THE VIDEOGAME SET ON ZURG'S PLANET Z?
YEAH, YOU'RE RIGHT...
"I COULD BE LIKE ONE OF HIS ROBOTS!
"I COULD KNOW THE SECRET ENTRANCE...

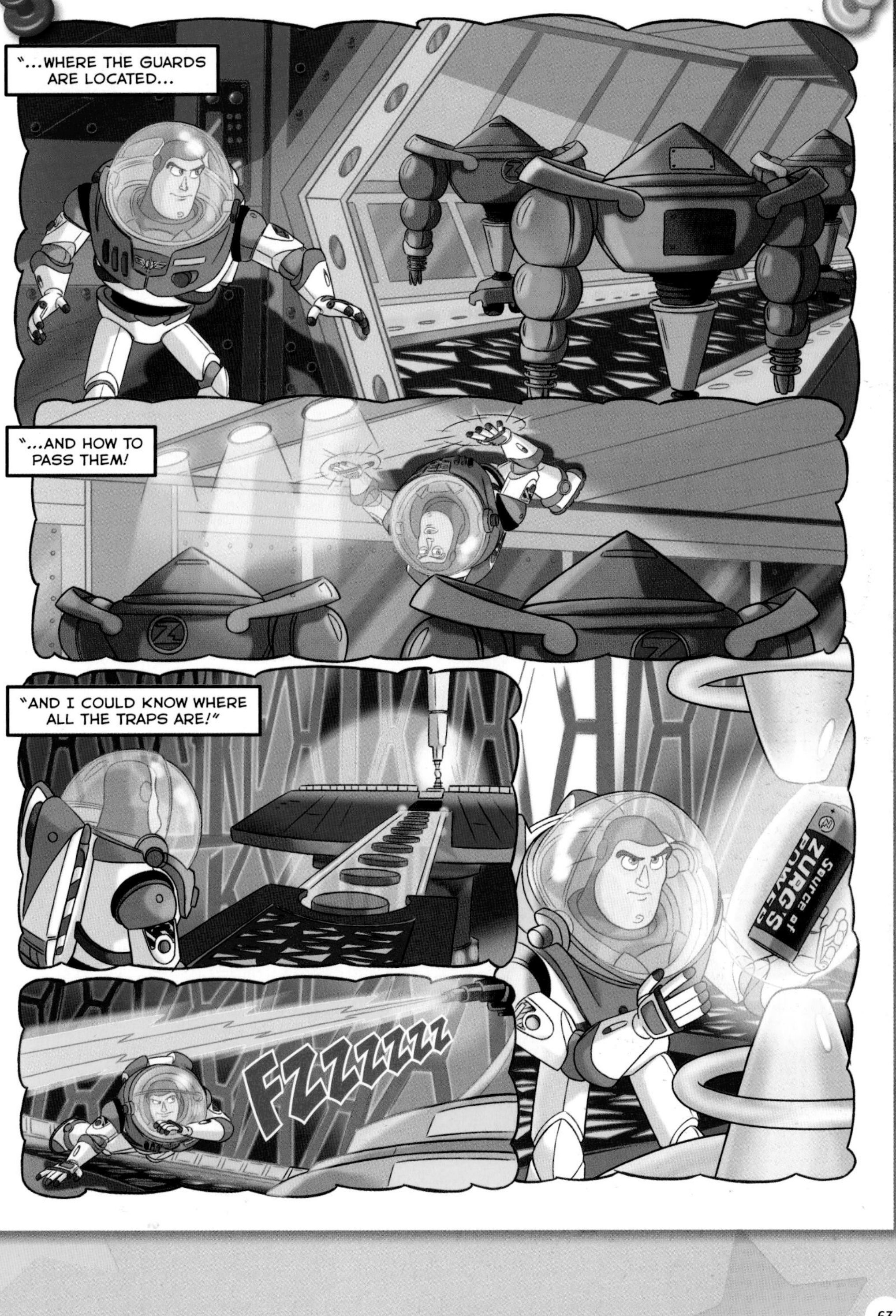
"...WHERE THE GUARDS ARE LOCATED...
"...AND HOW TO PASS THEM!
"AND I COULD KNOW WHERE ALL THE TRAPS ARE!"
SOURCE OF ZURG'S POWER
FZZZZZZZ

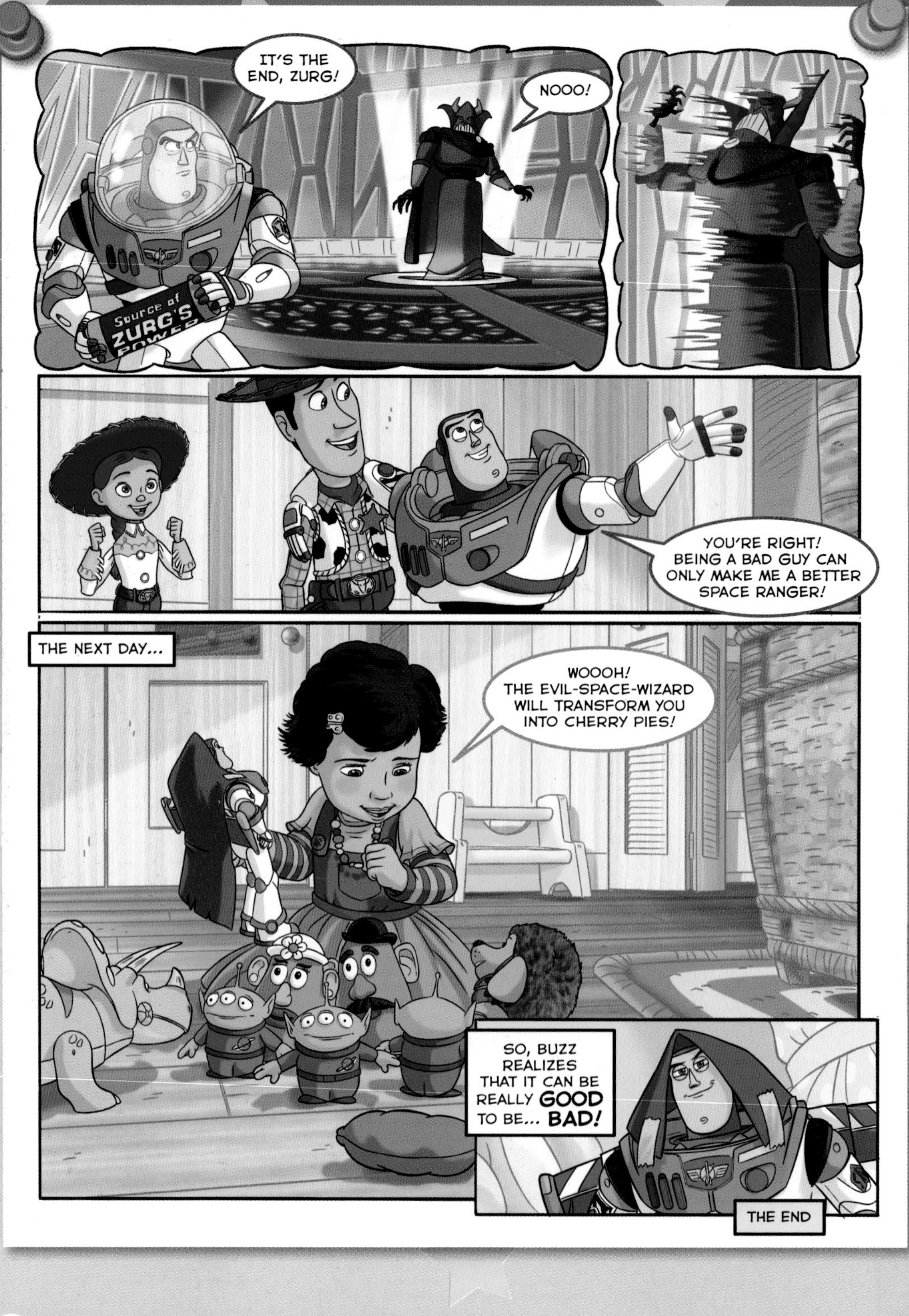
IT'S THE END, ZURG!
Source of ZURG'S POWER
NOOO!
YOU'RE RIGHT! BEING A BAD GUY CAN ONLY MAKE ME A BETTER SPACE RANGER!
THE NEXT DAY...
WOOOH! THE EVIL-SPACE-WIZARD WILL TRANSFORM YOU INTO CHERRY PIES!
SO, BUZZ REALIZES THAT IT CAN BE REALLY **GOOD** TO BE... **BAD!**
THE END

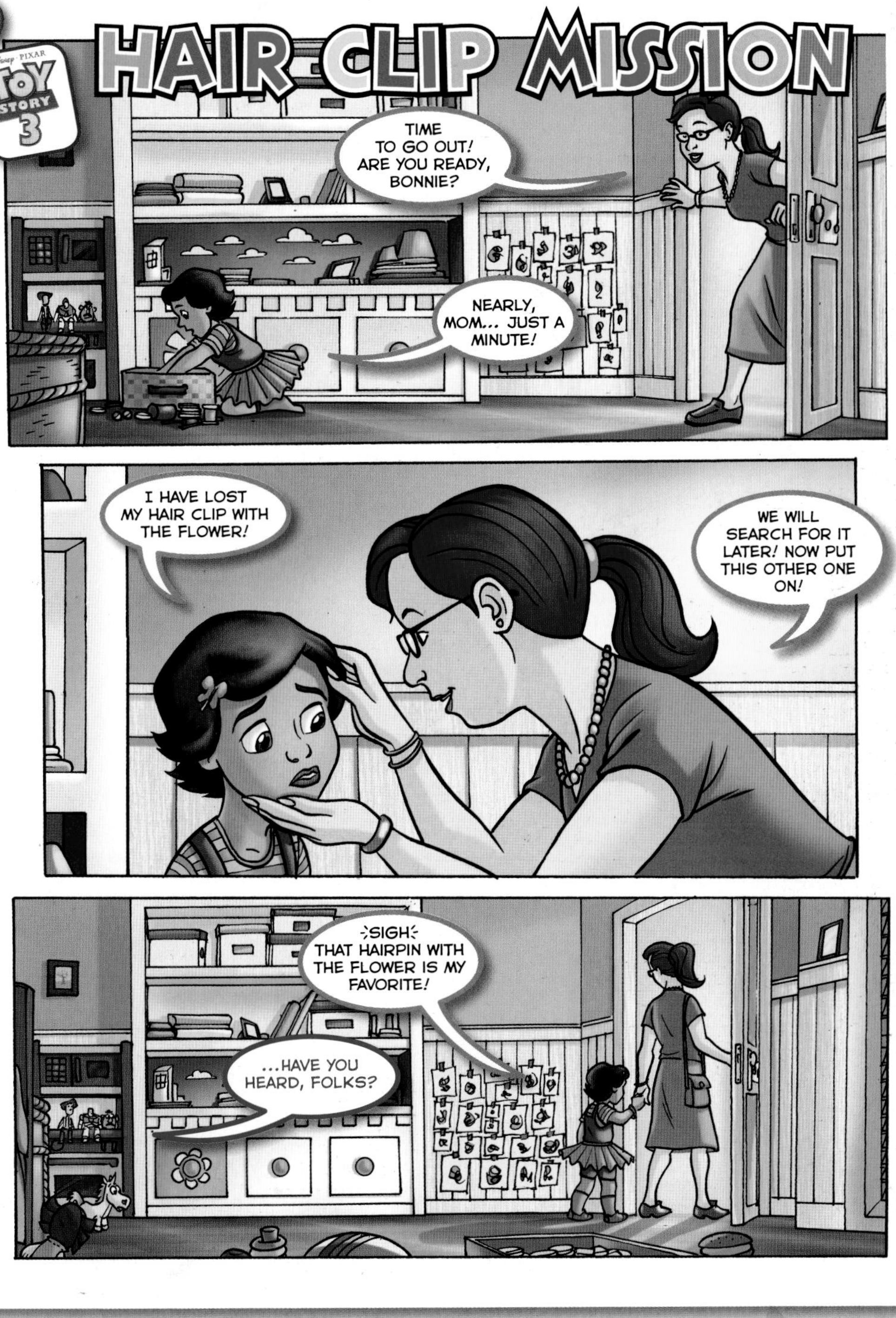
HAIR CLIP MISSION
TOY STORY 3
TIME TO GO OUT! ARE YOU READY, BONNIE?
NEARLY, MOM... JUST A MINUTE!
I HAVE LOST MY HAIR CLIP WITH THE FLOWER!
WE WILL SEARCH FOR IT LATER! NOW PUT THIS OTHER ONE ON!
SIGH
THAT HAIRPIN WITH THE FLOWER IS MY FAVORITE!
...HAVE YOU HEARD, FOLKS?

SCRIPT: ALESSANDRO SISTI; LAYOUT & INK: VALENTINO FORLINI; COLOUR: ANGELA CAPOLUPO

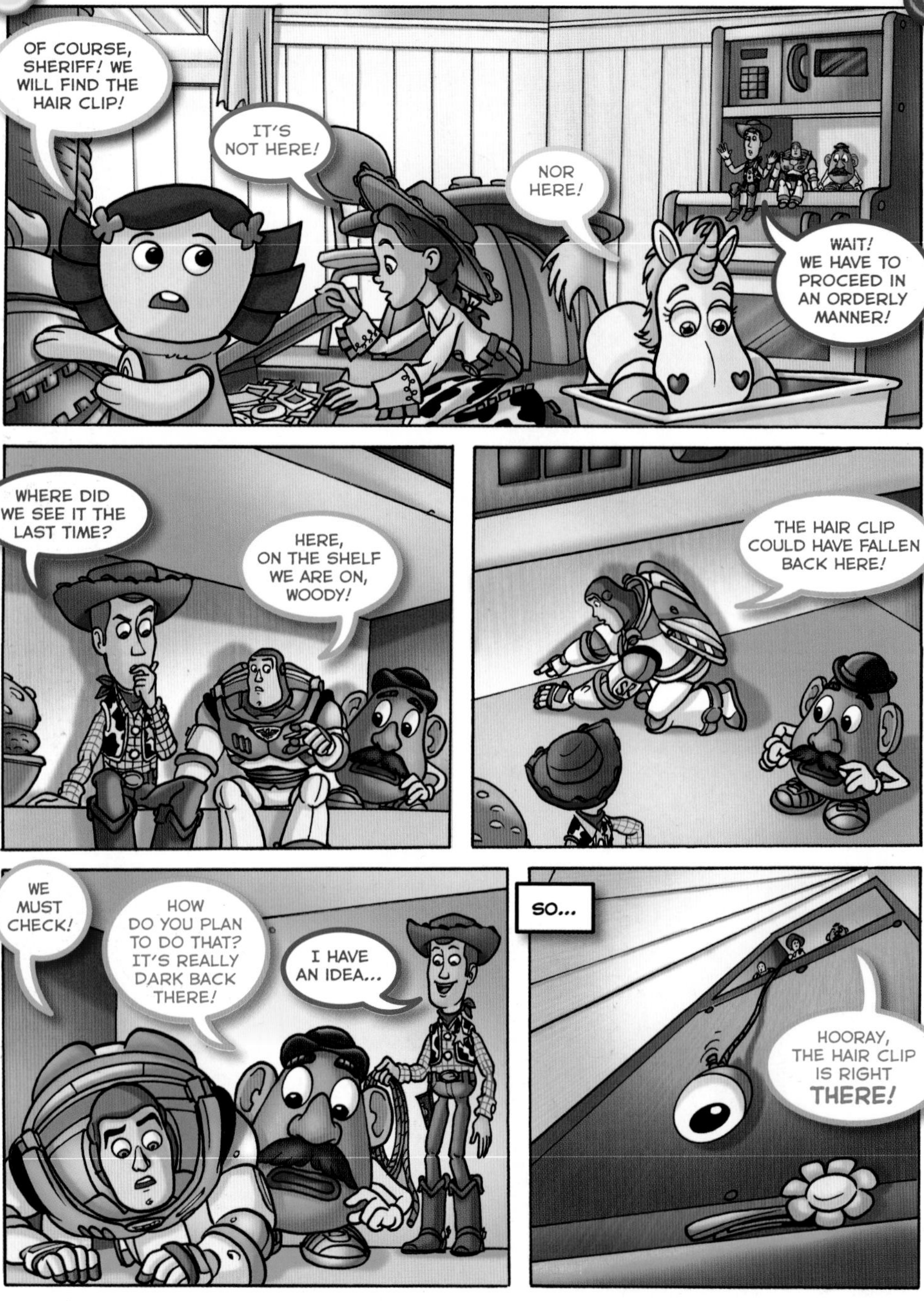
OF COURSE, SHERIFF! WE WILL FIND THE HAIR CLIP!
IT'S NOT HERE!
NOR HERE!
WAIT! WE HAVE TO PROCEED IN AN ORDERLY MANNER!
WHERE DID WE SEE IT THE LAST TIME?
HERE, ON THE SHELF WE ARE ON, WOODY!
THE HAIR CLIP COULD HAVE FALLEN BACK HERE!
WE MUST CHECK!
HOW DO YOU PLAN TO DO THAT? IT'S REALLY DARK BACK THERE!
I HAVE AN IDEA...
SO...
HOORAY, THE HAIR CLIP IS RIGHT THERE!

WELL DONE, SHERIFF!
SLAP
OOPS!
AARGH! MY EYE!
TUNK
THAT'S WONDERFUL! NOW WE HAVE TO RECOVER BOTH THE HAIR CLIP AND MY EYE!
MAYBE I CAN SLIDE DOWN THERE!
URRGH! NO WAY, IT'S TOO NARROW!
WHAT?
NO! NO! TRY AGAIN, YOU MUST...
STOP IT NOW, POTATO HEAD!
-GROAN- I'M STUCK!

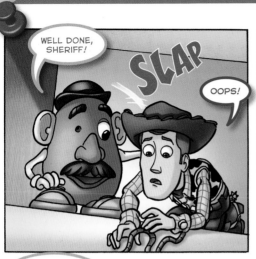

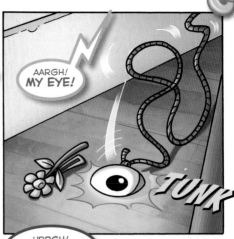

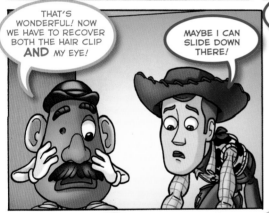

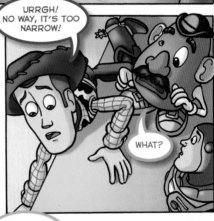

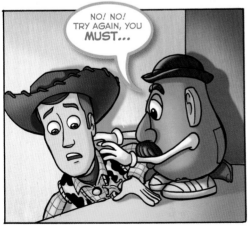

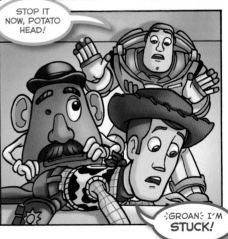

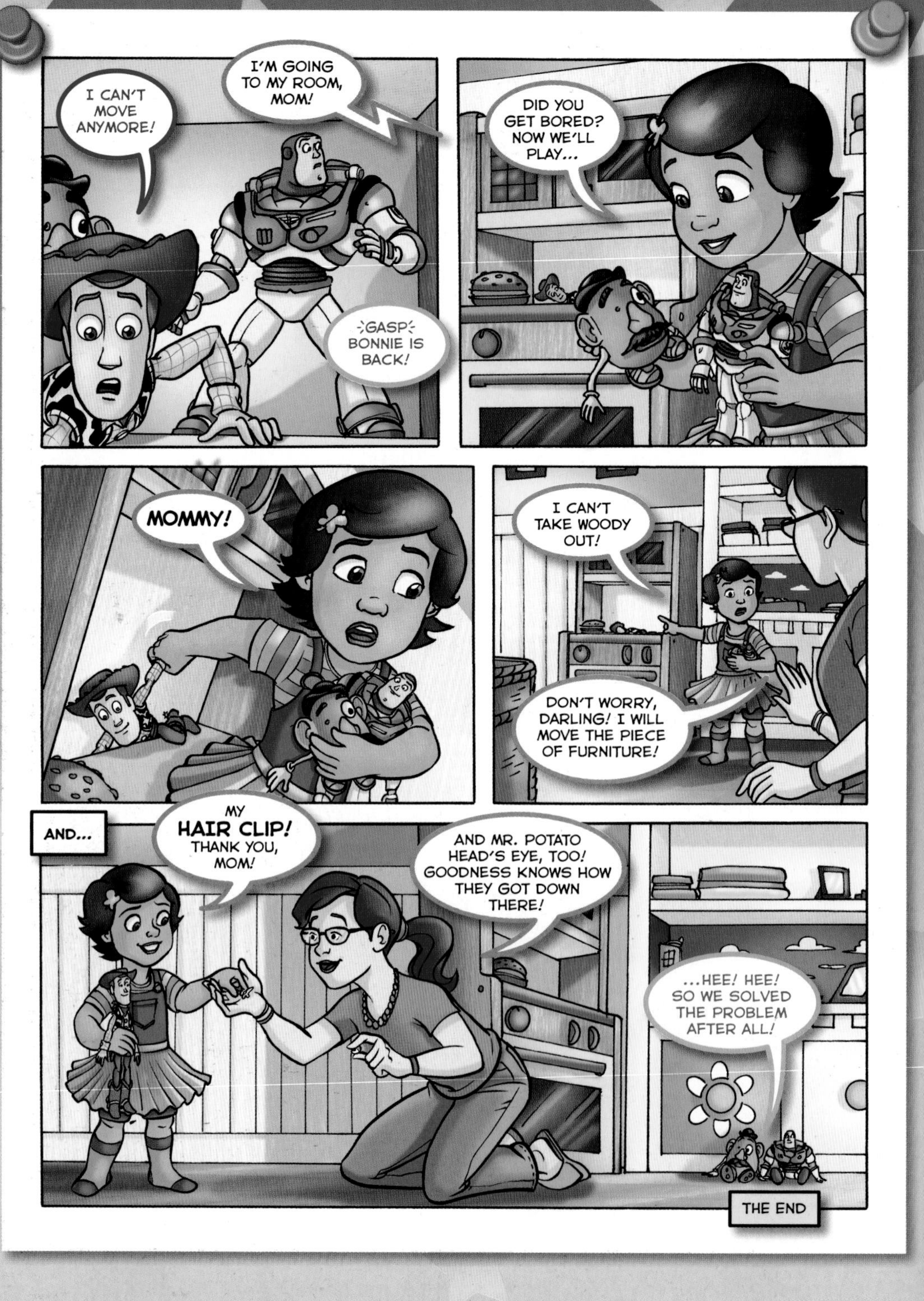
I CAN'T MOVE ANYMORE!
I'M GOING TO MY ROOM, MOM!
GASP BONNIE IS BACK!
DID YOU GET BORED? NOW WE'LL PLAY...
MOMMY!
I CAN'T TAKE WOODY OUT!
DON'T WORRY, DARLING! I WILL MOVE THE PIECE OF FURNITURE!
AND...
MY HAIR CLIP! THANK YOU, MOM!
AND MR. POTATO HEAD'S EYE, TOO! GOODNESS KNOWS HOW THEY GOT DOWN THERE!
...HEE! HEE! SO WE SOLVED THE PROBLEM AFTER ALL!
THE END

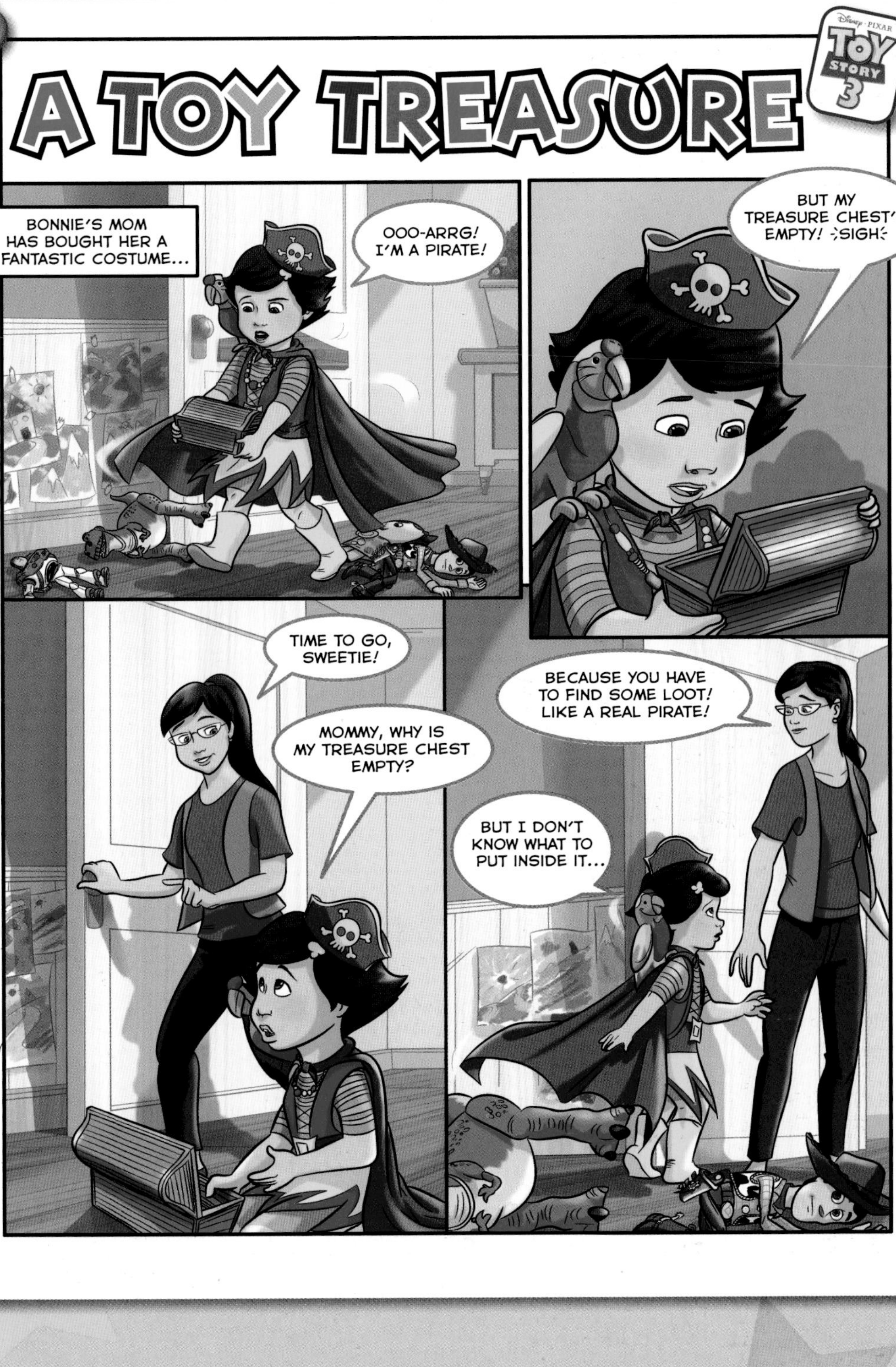

DISNEY · PIXAR
TOY STORY 3
A TOY TREASURE
BONNIE'S MOM HAS BOUGHT HER A FANTASTIC COSTUME...
OOO-ARRG! I'M A PIRATE!
BUT MY TREASURE CHEST'S EMPTY! ⁓SIGH⁓
TIME TO GO, SWEETIE!
MOMMY, WHY IS MY TREASURE CHEST EMPTY?
BECAUSE YOU HAVE TO FIND SOME LOOT! LIKE A REAL PIRATE!
BUT I DON'T KNOW WHAT TO PUT INSIDE IT...

SCRIPT: TEA ORSI; LAYOUT: GIANFRANCO FLORIO; INK: MICHELA FRARE; COLOUR: LUCIO DE GIUSEPPE

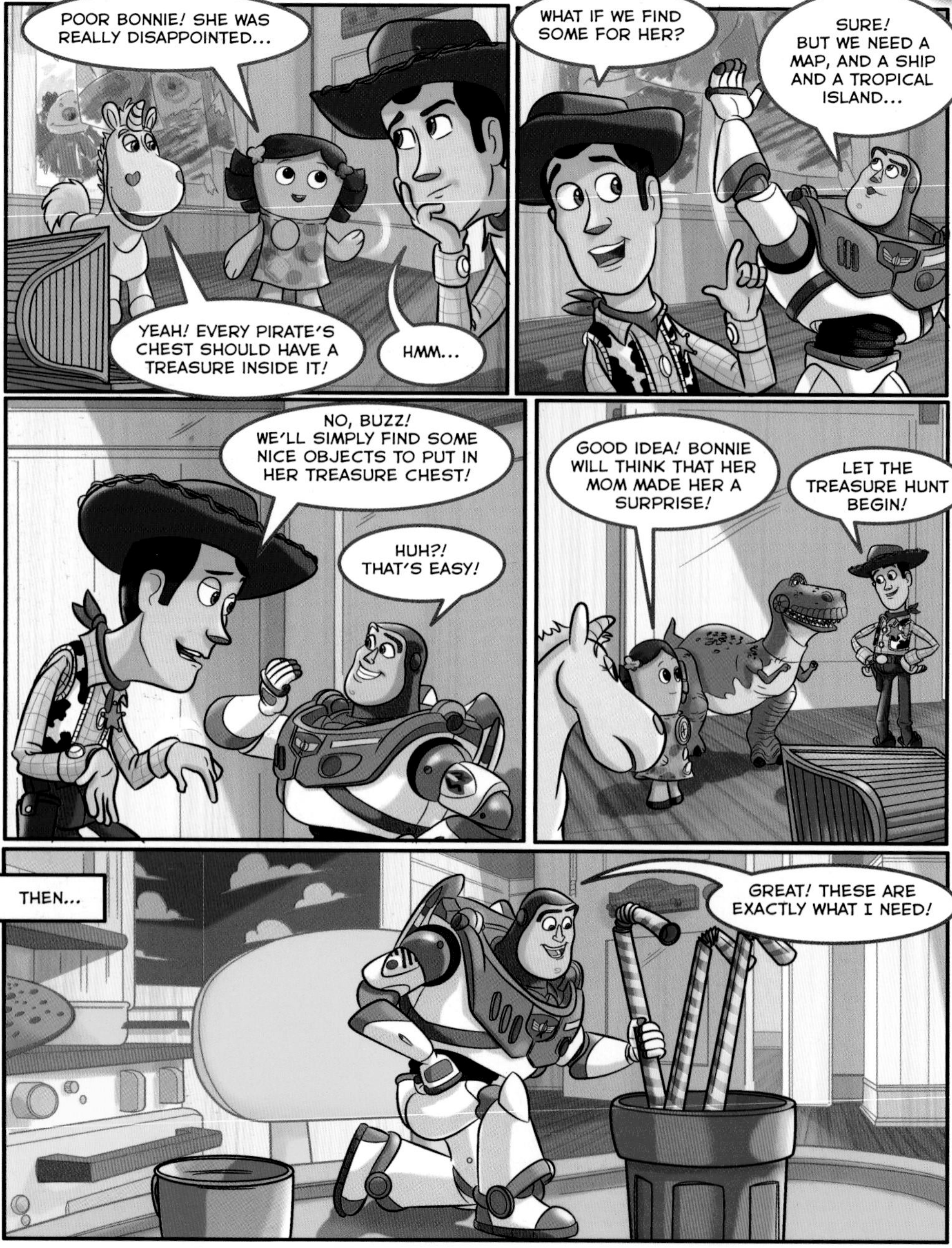
POOR BONNIE! SHE WAS REALLY DISAPPOINTED...
YEAH! EVERY PIRATE'S CHEST SHOULD HAVE A TREASURE INSIDE IT!
HMM...
WHAT IF WE FIND SOME FOR HER?
SURE! BUT WE NEED A MAP, AND A SHIP AND A TROPICAL ISLAND...
NO, BUZZ! WE'LL SIMPLY FIND SOME NICE OBJECTS TO PUT IN HER TREASURE CHEST!
HUH?! THAT'S EASY!
GOOD IDEA! BONNIE WILL THINK THAT HER MOM MADE HER A SURPRISE!
LET THE TREASURE HUNT BEGIN!
THEN...
GREAT! THESE ARE EXACTLY WHAT I NEED!

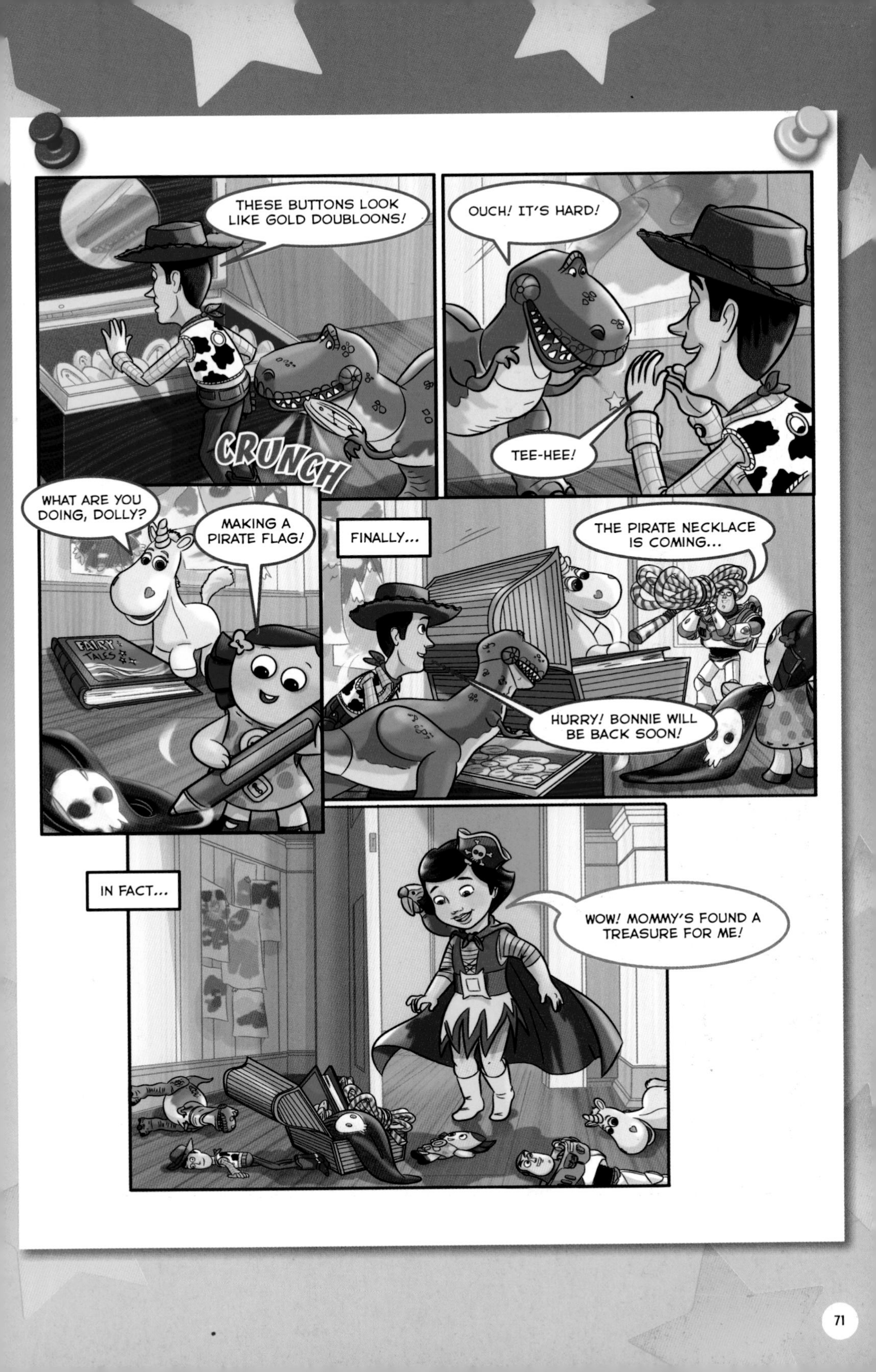
THESE BUTTONS LOOK LIKE GOLD DOUBLOONS!
CRUNCH
OUCH! IT'S HARD!
TEE-HEE!
WHAT ARE YOU DOING, DOLLY?
MAKING A PIRATE FLAG!
FAIRY TALES
FINALLY...
THE PIRATE NECKLACE IS COMING...
HURRY! BONNIE WILL BE BACK SOON!
IN FACT...
WOW! MOMMY'S FOUND A TREASURE FOR ME!

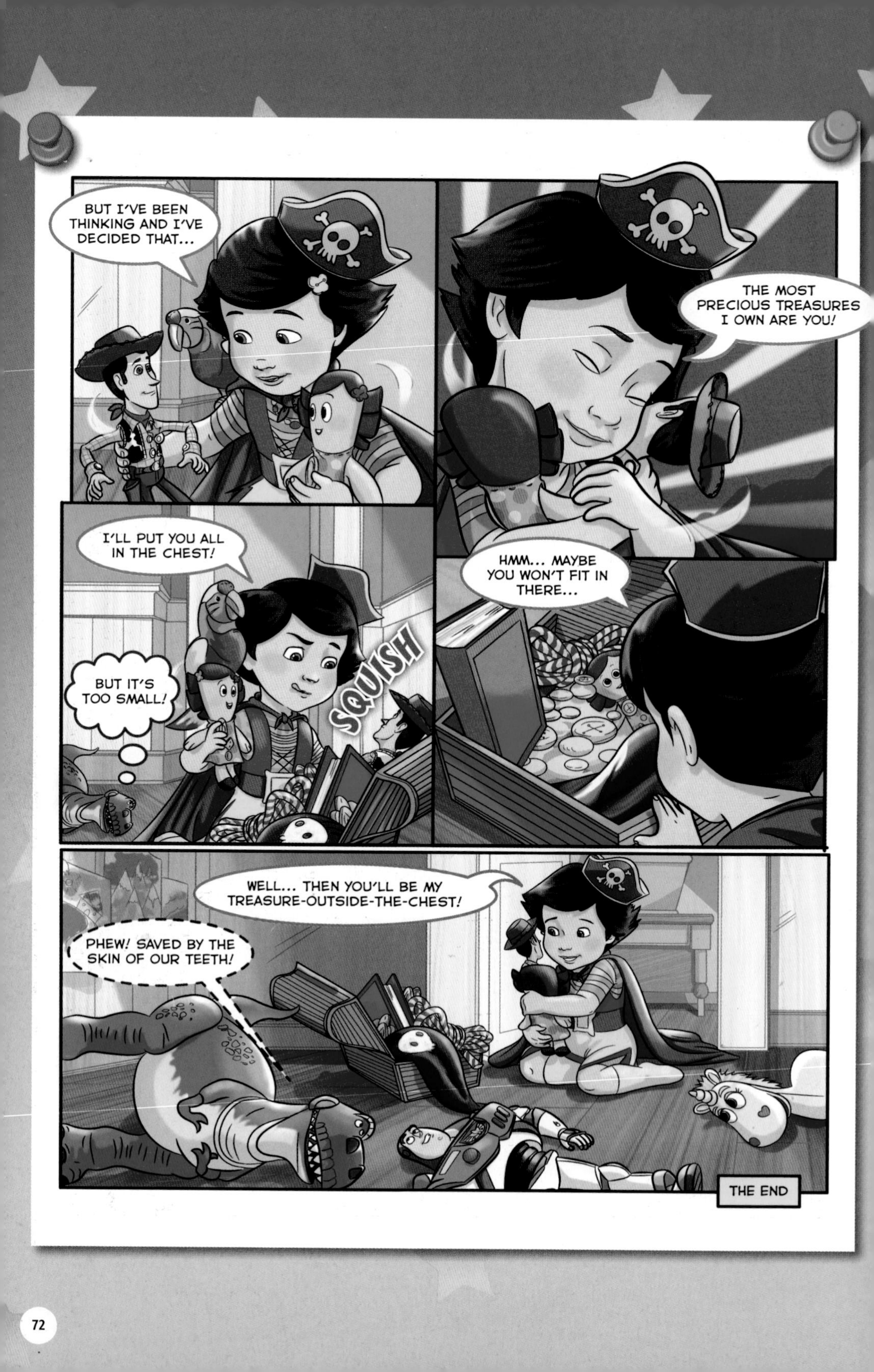
BUT I'VE BEEN THINKING AND I'VE DECIDED THAT...
THE MOST PRECIOUS TREASURES I OWN ARE YOU!
I'LL PUT YOU ALL IN THE CHEST!
BUT IT'S TOO SMALL!
SQUISH
HMM... MAYBE YOU WON'T FIT IN THERE...
WELL... THEN YOU'LL BE MY TREASURE-OUTSIDE-THE-CHEST!
PHEW! SAVED BY THE SKIN OF OUR TEETH!
THE END

DOCTOR BONNIE

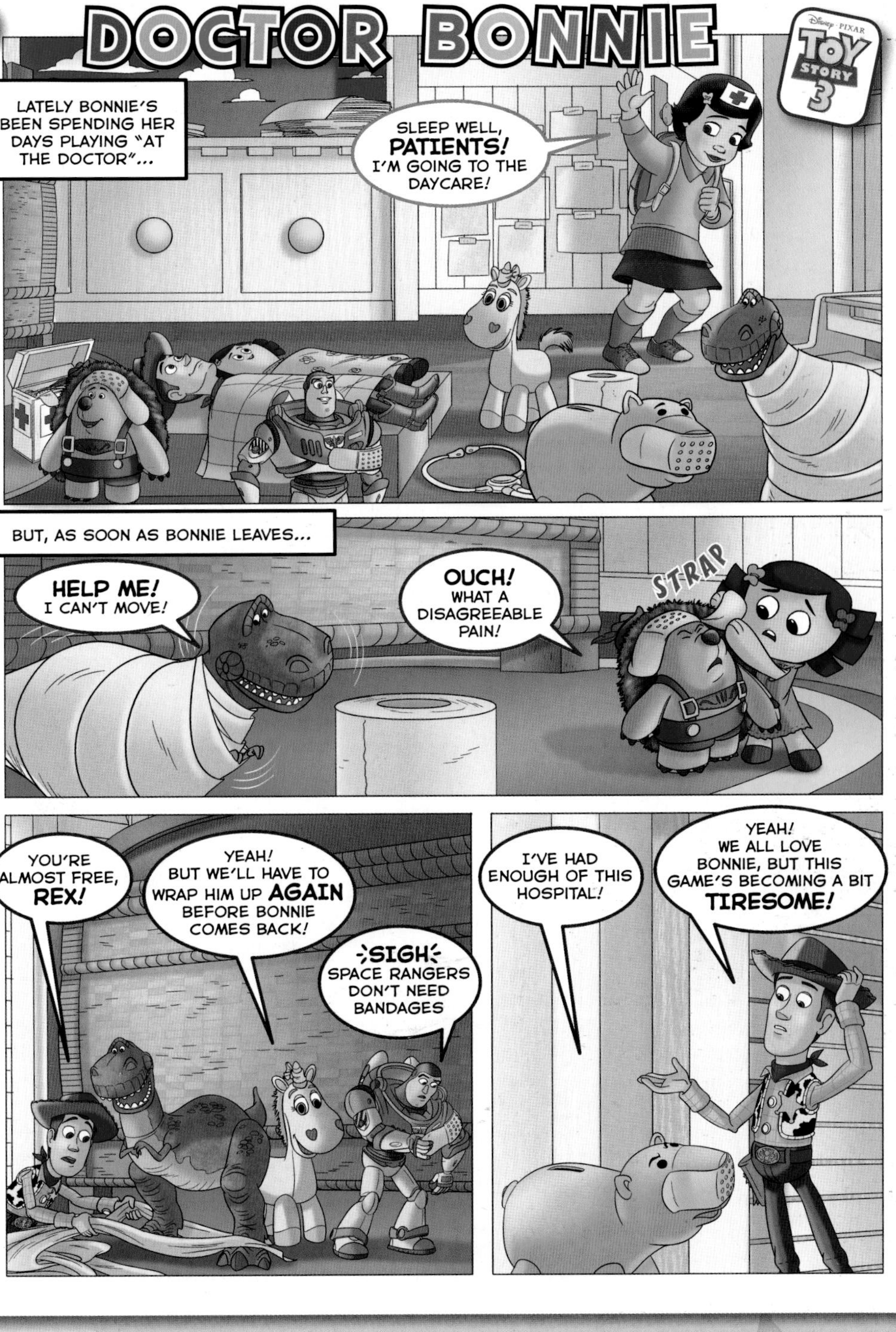

DISNEY · PIXAR TOY STORY 3
LATELY BONNIE'S BEEN SPENDING HER DAYS PLAYING "AT THE DOCTOR"...
SLEEP WELL, PATIENTS! I'M GOING TO THE DAYCARE!
BUT, AS SOON AS BONNIE LEAVES...
HELP ME! I CAN'T MOVE!
OUCH! WHAT A DISAGREEABLE PAIN!
STRAP
YOU'RE ALMOST FREE, REX!
YEAH! BUT WE'LL HAVE TO WRAP HIM UP AGAIN BEFORE BONNIE COMES BACK!
SIGH SPACE RANGERS DON'T NEED BANDAGES
I'VE HAD ENOUGH OF THIS HOSPITAL!
YEAH! WE ALL LOVE BONNIE, BUT THIS GAME'S BECOMING A BIT TIRESOME!

SCRIPT: TEA ORSI; LAYOUT: VALENTINO FORLINI; INK: VALENTINO FORLINI; COLOUR: ANGELA CAPOLUPO

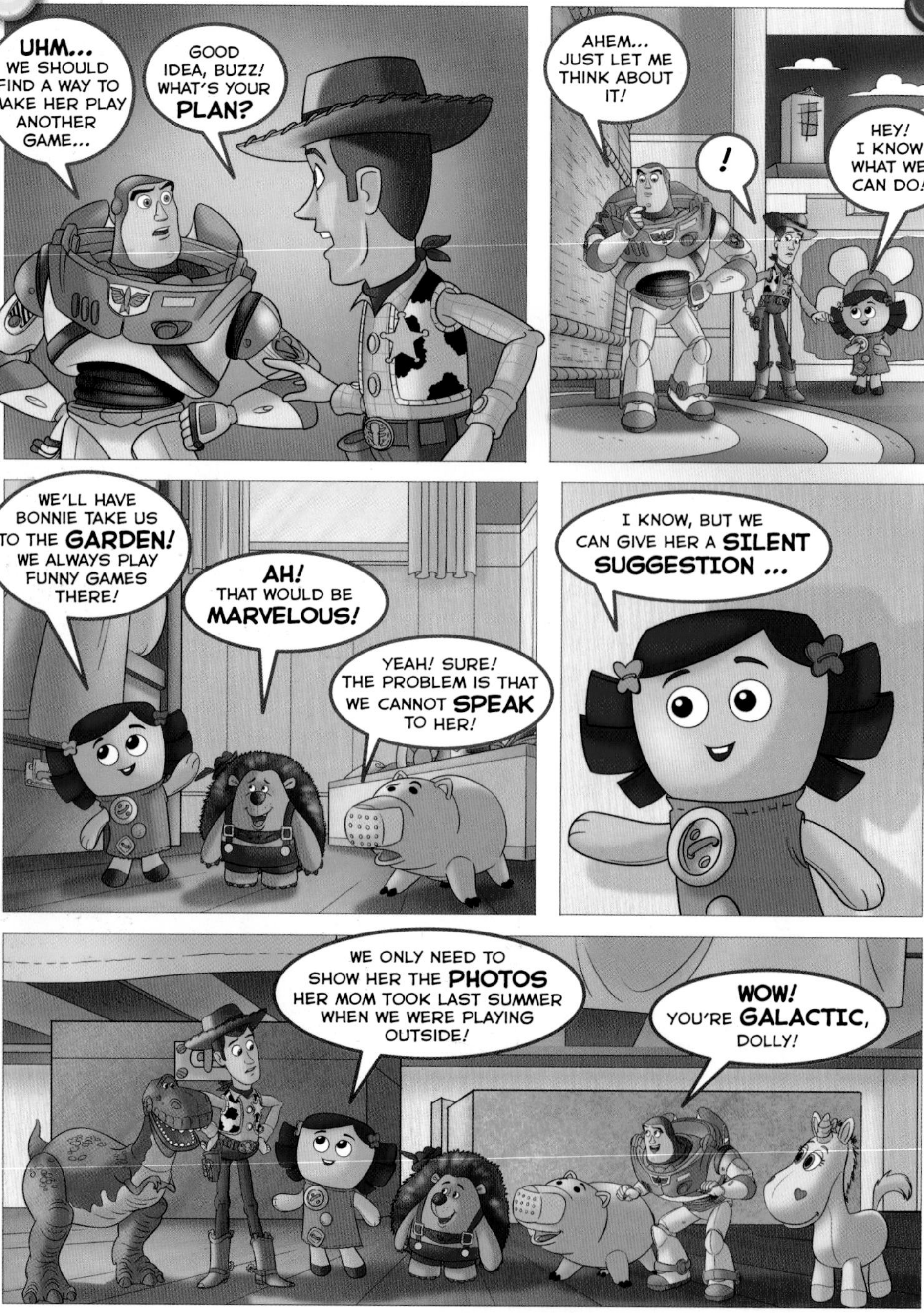
UHM... WE SHOULD FIND A WAY TO MAKE HER PLAY ANOTHER GAME...
GOOD IDEA, BUZZ! WHAT'S YOUR PLAN?
AHEM... JUST LET ME THINK ABOUT IT!
!
HEY! I KNOW WHAT WE CAN DO!
WE'LL HAVE BONNIE TAKE US TO THE GARDEN! WE ALWAYS PLAY FUNNY GAMES THERE!
AH! THAT WOULD BE MARVELOUS!
YEAH! SURE! THE PROBLEM IS THAT WE CANNOT SPEAK TO HER!
I KNOW, BUT WE CAN GIVE HER A SILENT SUGGESTION ...
WE ONLY NEED TO SHOW HER THE PHOTOS HER MOM TOOK LAST SUMMER WHEN WE WERE PLAYING OUTSIDE!
WOW! YOU'RE GALACTIC, DOLLY!

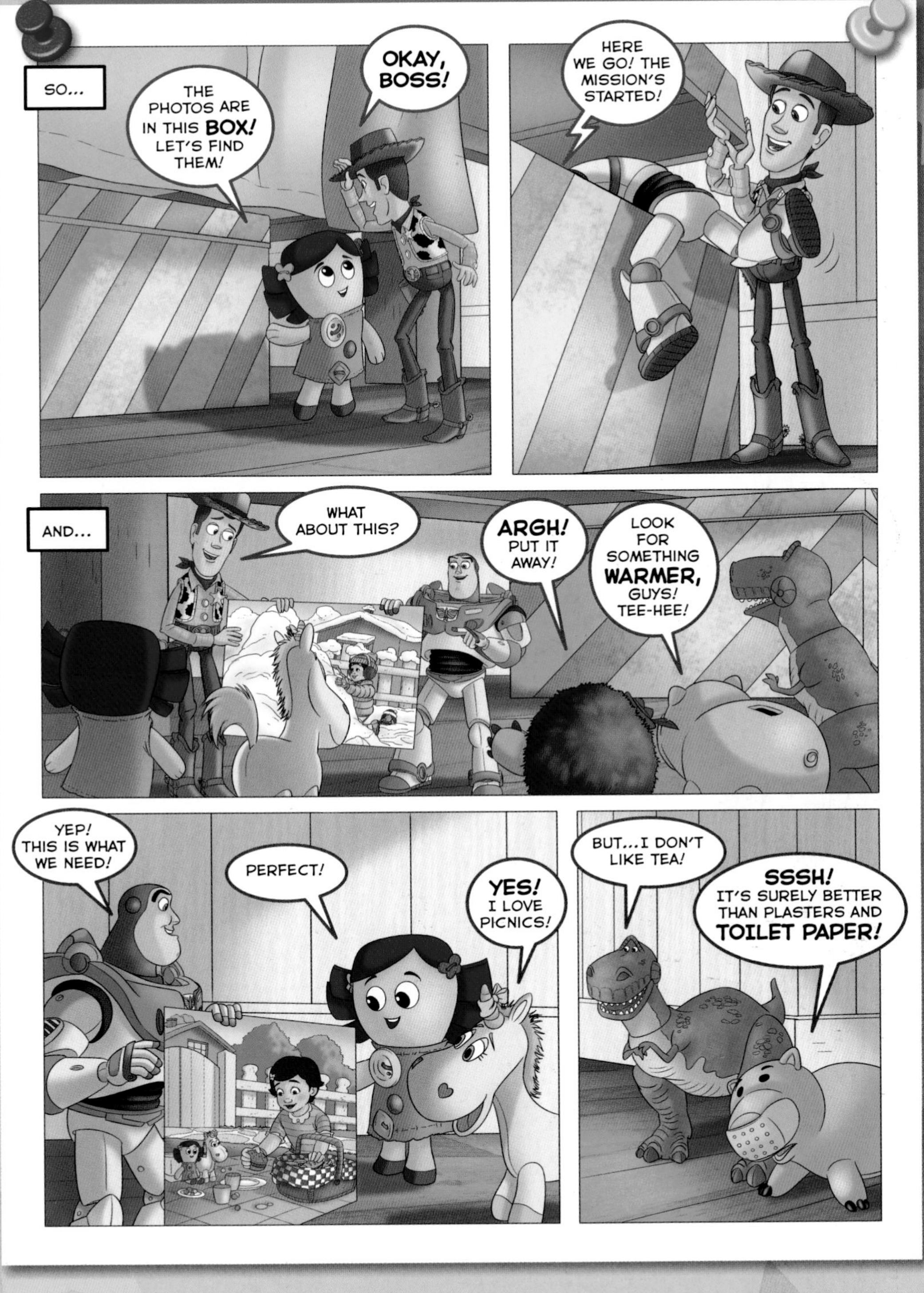
SO...
THE PHOTOS ARE IN THIS BOX! LET'S FIND THEM!
OKAY, BOSS!
HERE WE GO! THE MISSION'S STARTED!
AND...
WHAT ABOUT THIS?
ARGH! PUT IT AWAY!
LOOK FOR SOMETHING WARMER, GUYS! TEE-HEE!
YEP! THIS IS WHAT WE NEED!
PERFECT!
YES! I LOVE PICNICS!
BUT...I DON'T LIKE TEA!
SSSH! IT'S SURELY BETTER THAN PLASTERS AND TOILET PAPER!

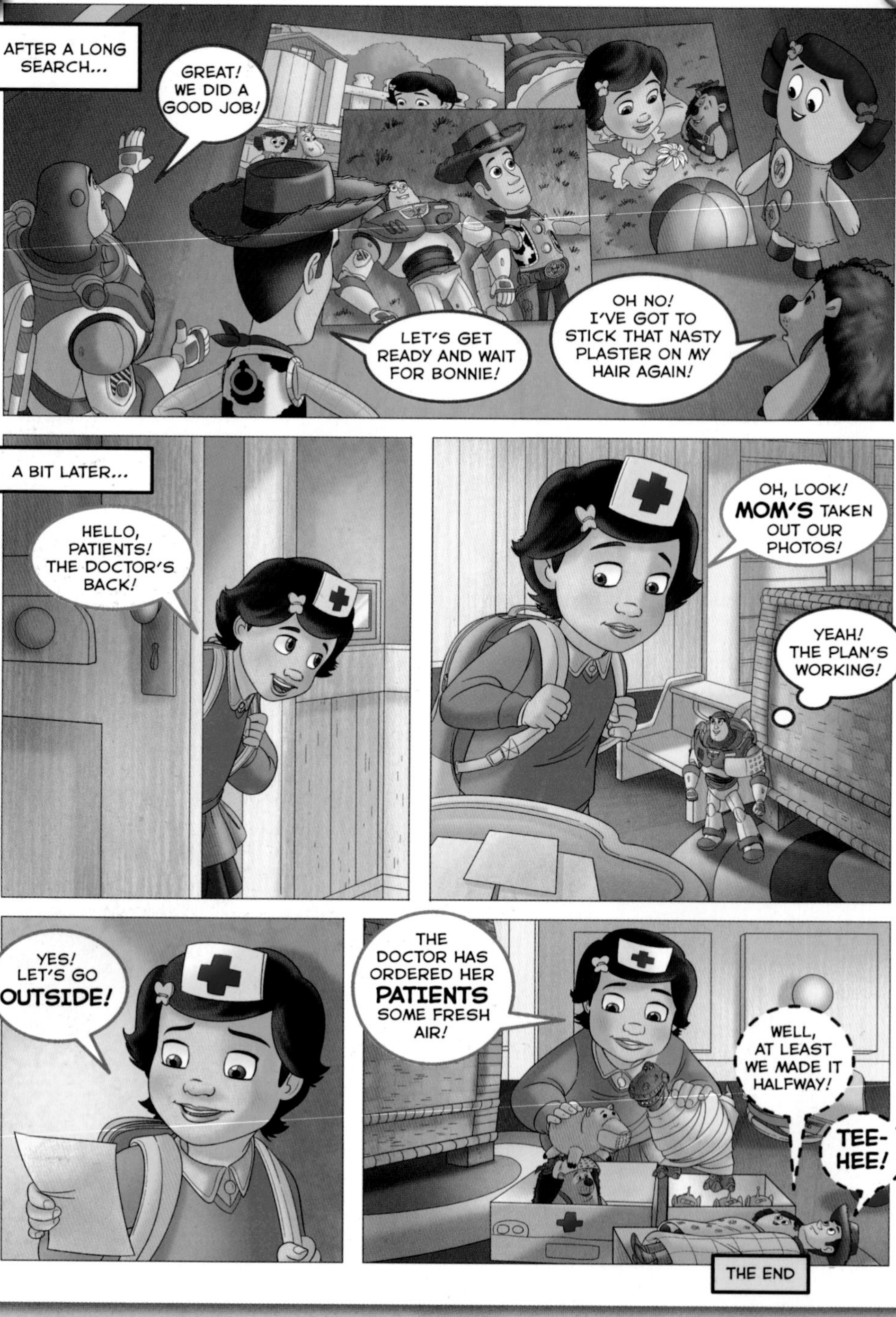
AFTER A LONG SEARCH...
GREAT! WE DID A GOOD JOB!
LET'S GET READY AND WAIT FOR BONNIE!
OH NO! I'VE GOT TO STICK THAT NASTY PLASTER ON MY HAIR AGAIN!
A BIT LATER...
HELLO, PATIENTS! THE DOCTOR'S BACK!
OH, LOOK! MOM'S TAKEN OUT OUR PHOTOS!
YEAH! THE PLAN'S WORKING!
YES! LET'S GO OUTSIDE!
THE DOCTOR HAS ORDERED HER PATIENTS SOME FRESH AIR!
WELL, AT LEAST WE MADE IT HALFWAY!
TEE-HEE!
THE END

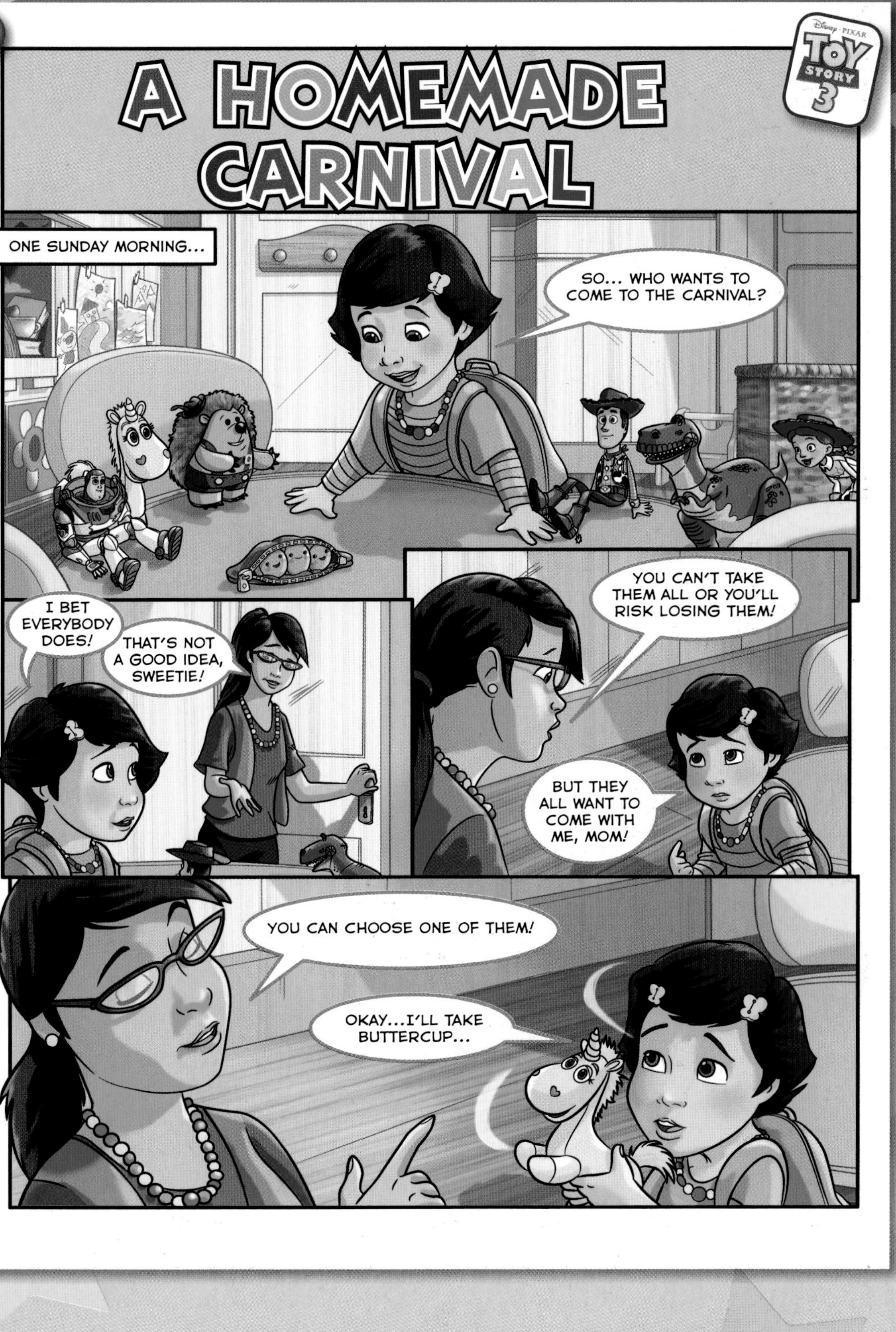
A HOMEMADE CARNIVAL
DISNEY PIXAR TOY STORY 3
ONE SUNDAY MORNING...
SO... WHO WANTS TO COME TO THE CARNIVAL?
I BET EVERYBODY DOES!
THAT'S NOT A GOOD IDEA, SWEETIE!
YOU CAN'T TAKE THEM ALL OR YOU'LL RISK LOSING THEM!
BUT THEY ALL WANT TO COME WITH ME, MOM!
YOU CAN CHOOSE ONE OF THEM!
OKAY...I'LL TAKE BUTTERCUP...
SCRIPT: TEA ORSI, PENCIL: GIANFRANCO FLORIO, INK: MICHELA FRARE, COLOR: LUCIO DE GIUSEPPE

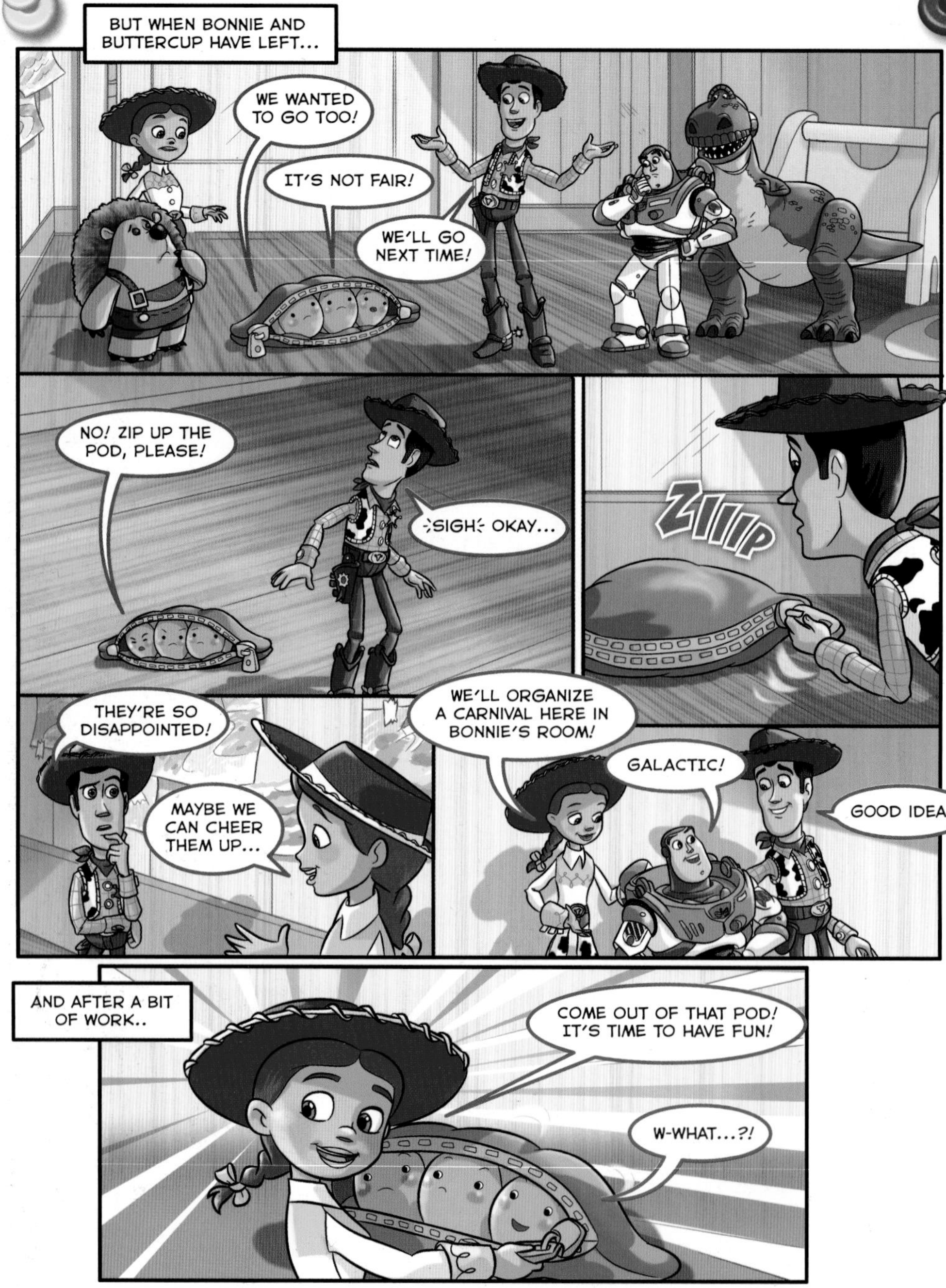
BUT WHEN BONNIE AND BUTTERCUP HAVE LEFT...
WE WANTED TO GO TOO!
IT'S NOT FAIR!
WE'LL GO NEXT TIME!
NO! ZIP UP THE POD, PLEASE!
SIGH OKAY...
ZIIIP
THEY'RE SO DISAPPOINTED!
MAYBE WE CAN CHEER THEM UP...
WE'LL ORGANIZE A CARNIVAL HERE IN BONNIE'S ROOM!
GALACTIC!
GOOD IDEA!
AND AFTER A BIT OF WORK..
COME OUT OF THAT POD! IT'S TIME TO HAVE FUN!
W-WHAT...?!

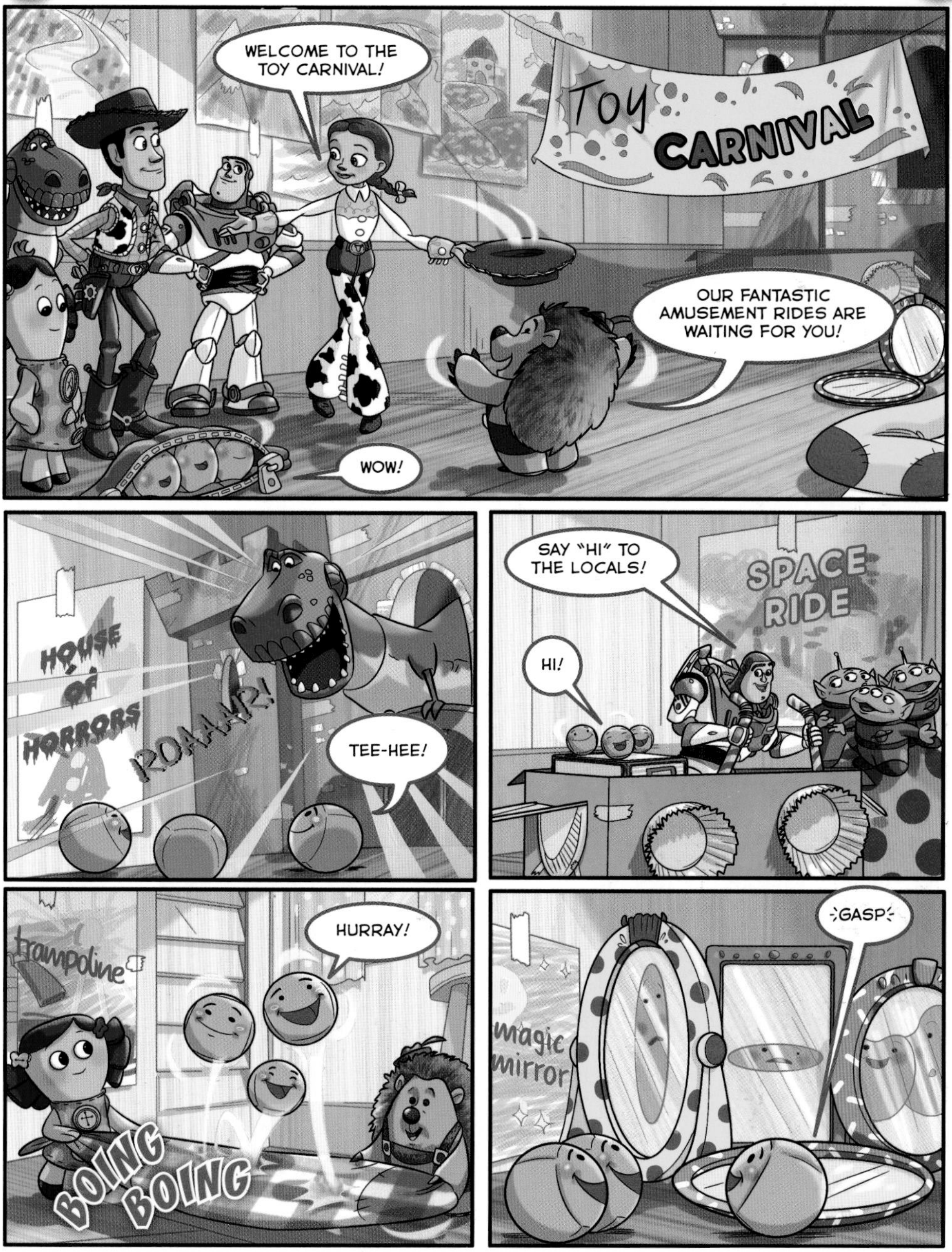
WELCOME TO THE TOY CARNIVAL!
TOY CARNIVAL
OUR FANTASTIC AMUSEMENT RIDES ARE WAITING FOR YOU!
WOW!
HOUSE OF HORRORS
ROAAAR!
TEE-HEE!
SAY "HI" TO THE LOCALS!
SPACE RIDE
HI!
trampoline
HURRAY!
BOING BOING
GASP
magic mirror

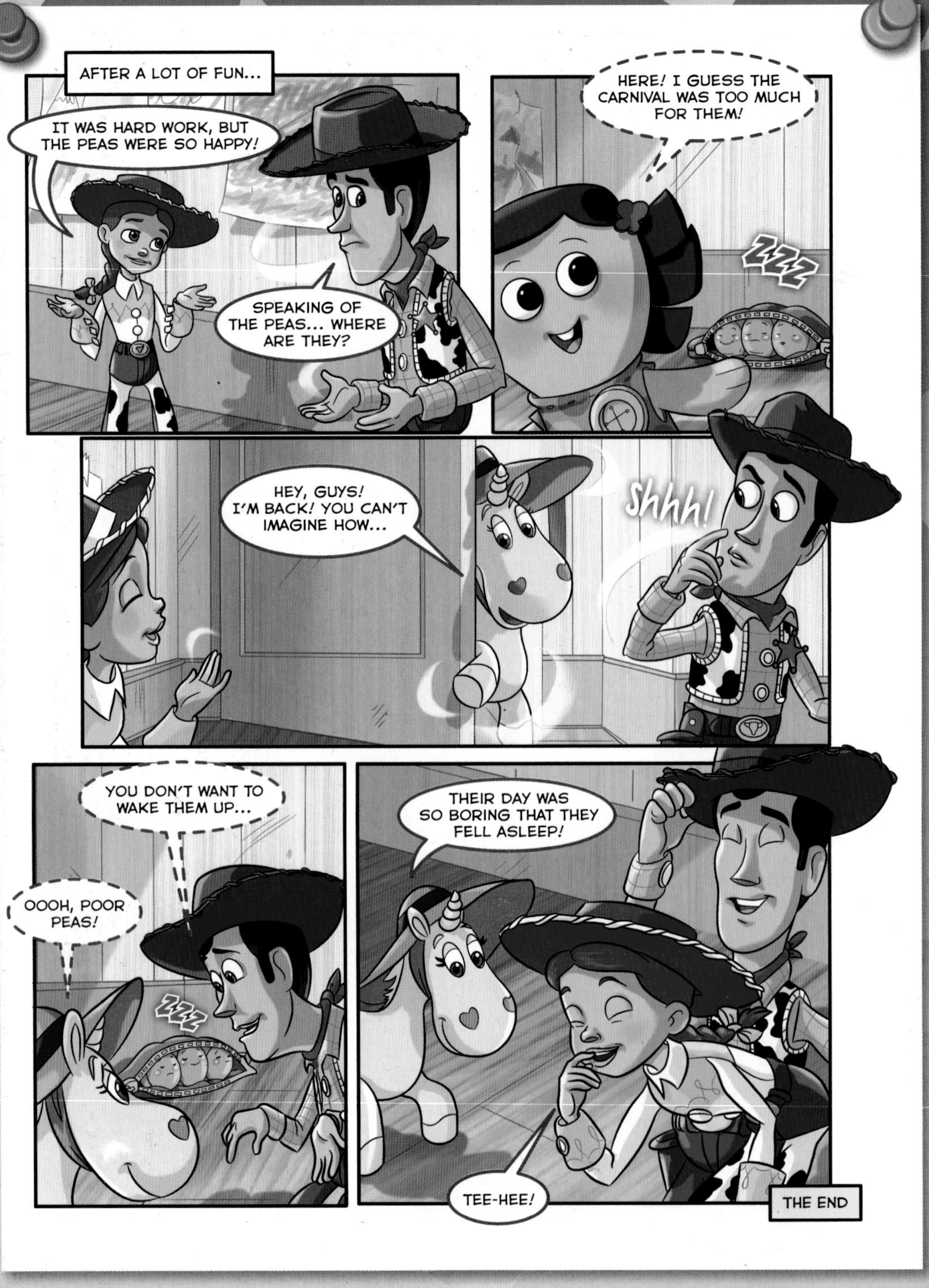
AFTER A LOT OF FUN...
IT WAS HARD WORK, BUT THE PEAS WERE SO HAPPY!
SPEAKING OF THE PEAS... WHERE ARE THEY?
HERE! I GUESS THE CARNIVAL WAS TOO MUCH FOR THEM!
ZZZ
HEY, GUYS! I'M BACK! YOU CAN'T IMAGINE HOW...
Shhh!
YOU DON'T WANT TO WAKE THEM UP...
OOOH, POOR PEAS!
ZZZ
THEIR DAY WAS SO BORING THAT THEY FELL ASLEEP!
TEE-HEE!
THE END

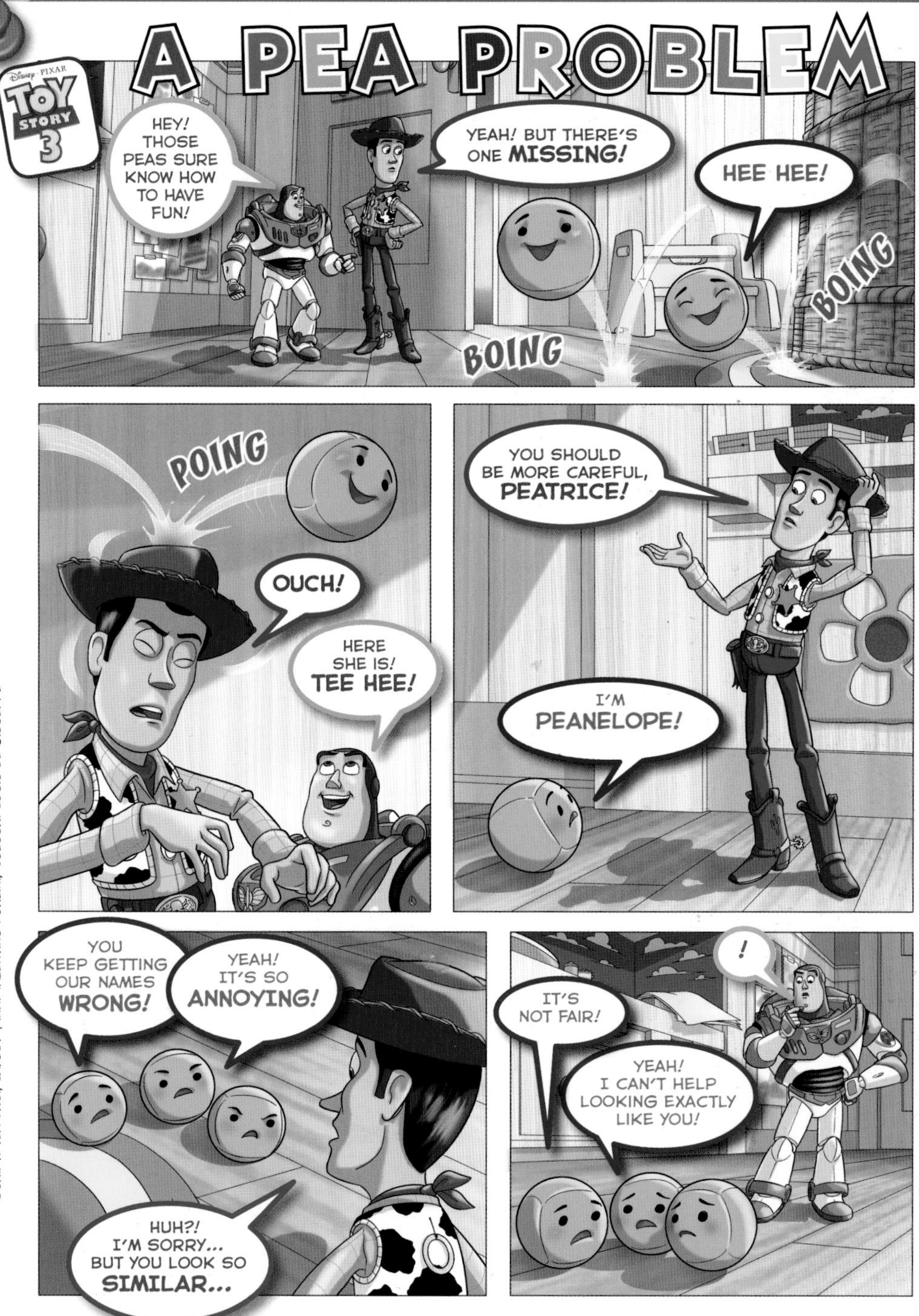
A PEA PROBLEM
DISNEY · PIXAR TOY STORY 3
HEY! THOSE PEAS SURE KNOW HOW TO HAVE FUN!
YEAH! BUT THERE'S ONE MISSING!
HEE HEE!
BOING
BOING
POING
OUCH!
HERE SHE IS! TEE HEE!
YOU SHOULD BE MORE CAREFUL, PEATRICE!
I'M PEANELOPE!
YOU KEEP GETTING OUR NAMES WRONG!
YEAH! IT'S SO ANNOYING!
HUH?! I'M SORRY... BUT YOU LOOK SO SIMILAR...
!
IT'S NOT FAIR!
YEAH! I CAN'T HELP LOOKING EXACTLY LIKE YOU!

SCRIPT: TEA ORSI; LAYOUT & INK: VALENTINO FORLINI; COLOUR: LUCIO DE GIUSEPPE

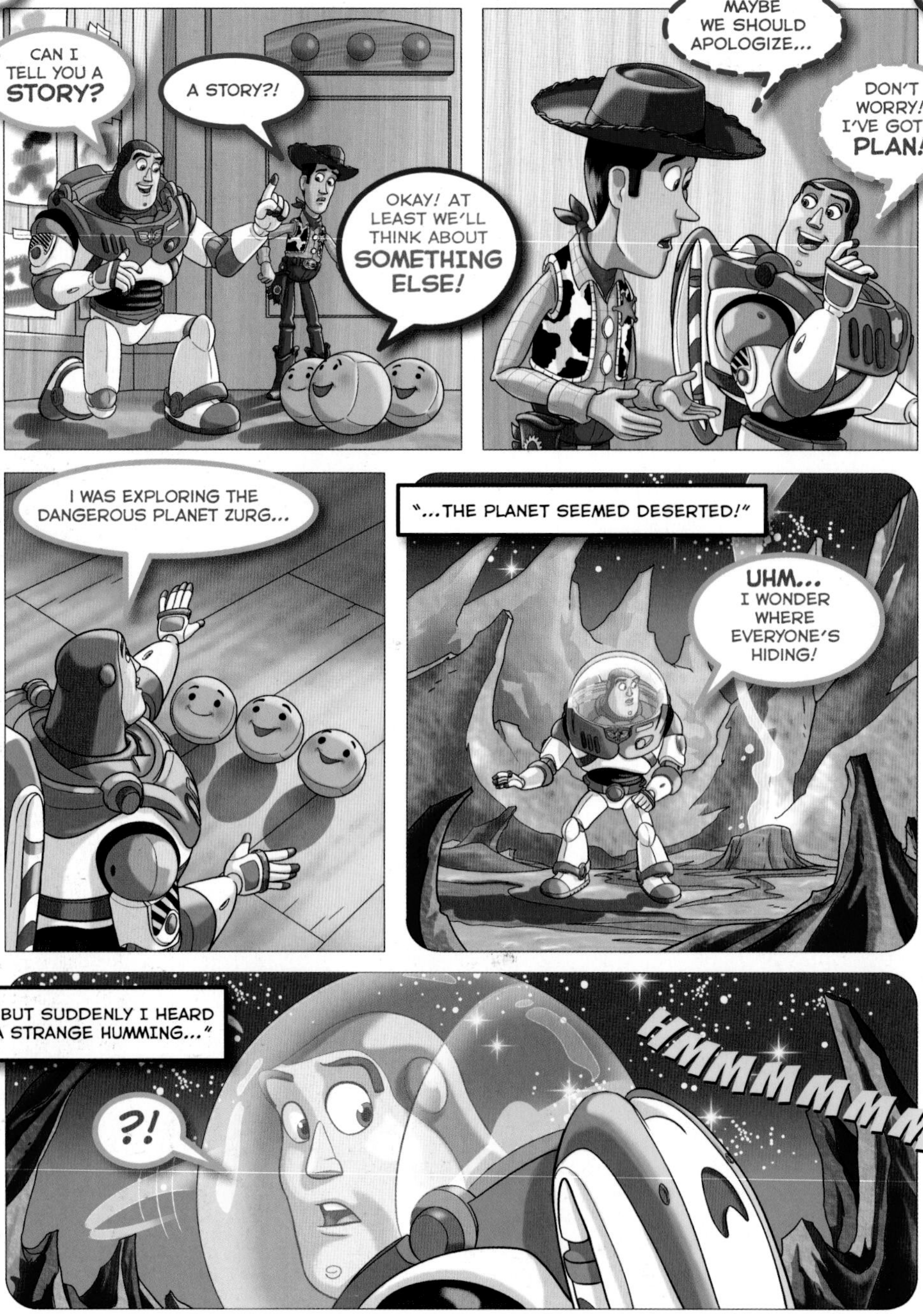
CAN I TELL YOU A STORY?
A STORY?!
OKAY! AT LEAST WE'LL THINK ABOUT SOMETHING ELSE!
MAYBE WE SHOULD APOLOGIZE...
DON'T WORRY! I'VE GOT A PLAN!
I WAS EXPLORING THE DANGEROUS PLANET ZURG...
"...THE PLANET SEEMED DESERTED!"
UHM... I WONDER WHERE EVERYONE'S HIDING!
"BUT SUDDENLY I HEARD A STRANGE HUMMING..."
?!
HMMMMMMM

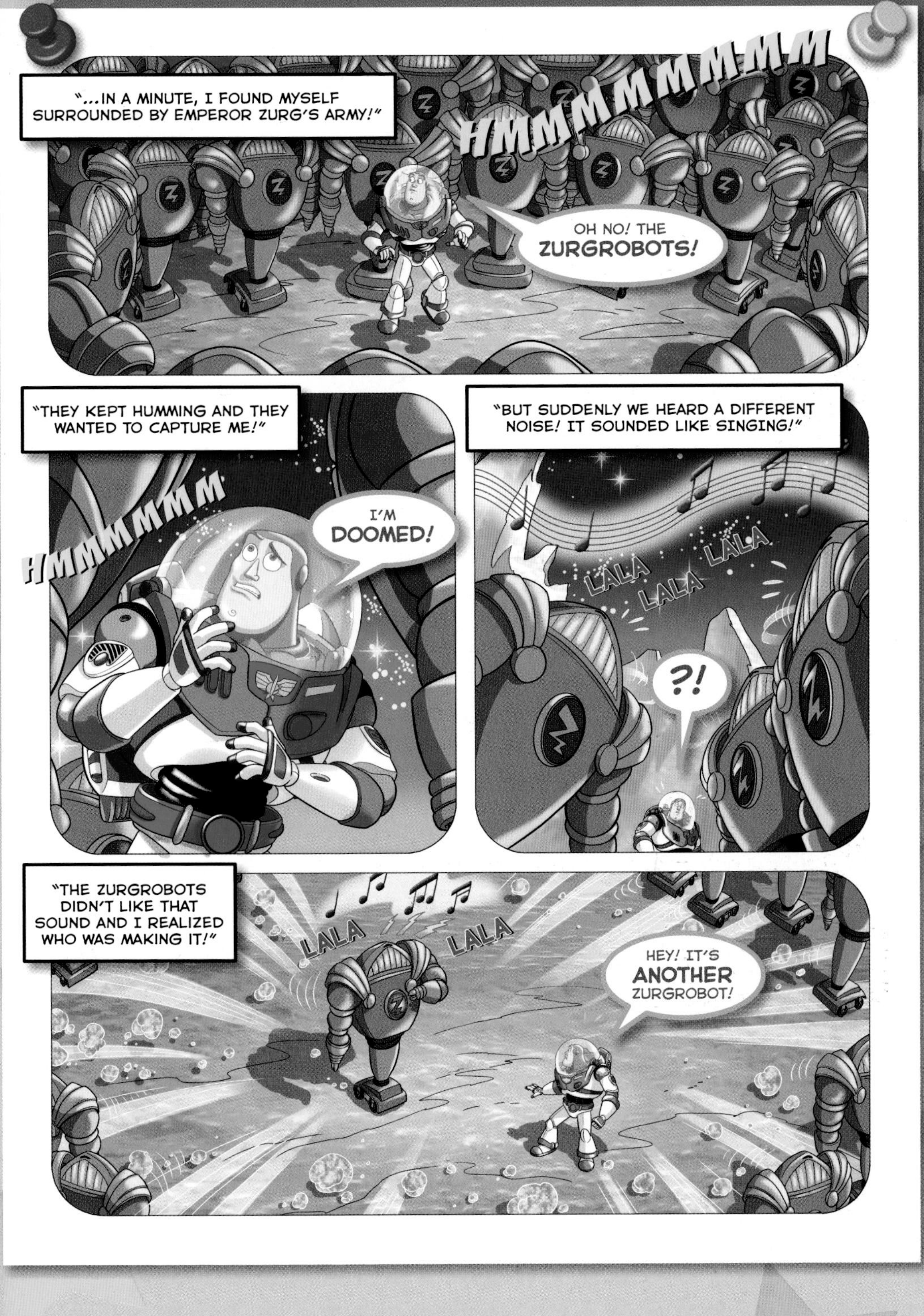
"...IN A MINUTE, I FOUND MYSELF SURROUNDED BY EMPEROR ZURG'S ARMY!"
HMMMMMMMMMM
OH NO! THE ZURGROBOTS!
"THEY KEPT HUMMING AND THEY WANTED TO CAPTURE ME!"
HMMMMMMM
I'M DOOMED!
"BUT SUDDENLY WE HEARD A DIFFERENT NOISE! IT SOUNDED LIKE SINGING!"
LALA
LALA
LALA
?!
"THE ZURGROBOTS DIDN'T LIKE THAT SOUND AND I REALIZED WHO WAS MAKING IT!"
LALA
LALA
HEY! IT'S ANOTHER ZURGROBOT!

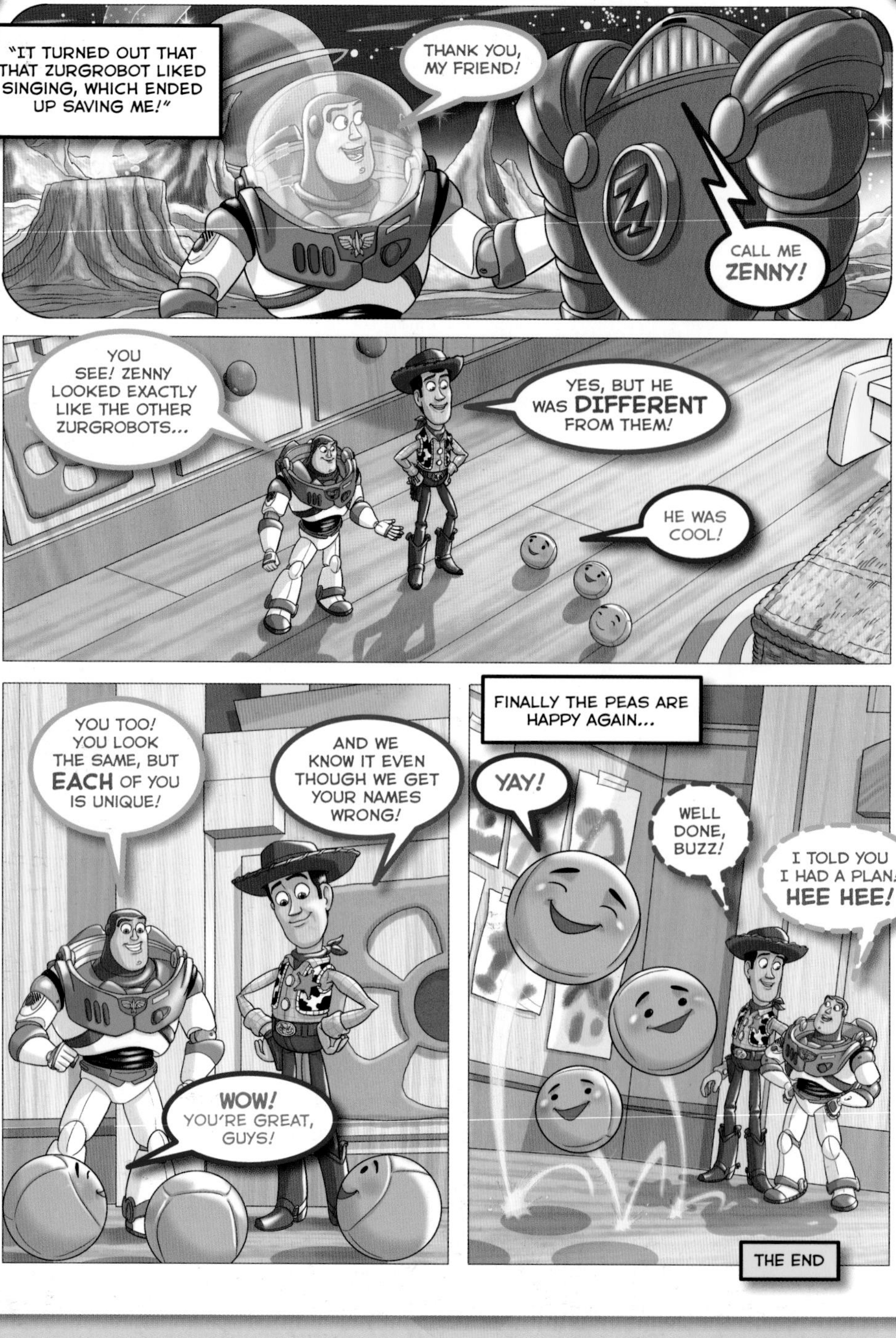
"IT TURNED OUT THAT THAT ZURGROBOT LIKED SINGING, WHICH ENDED UP SAVING ME!"
THANK YOU, MY FRIEND!
CALL ME ZENNY!
YOU SEE! ZENNY LOOKED EXACTLY LIKE THE OTHER ZURGROBOTS...
YES, BUT HE WAS DIFFERENT FROM THEM!
HE WAS COOL!
YOU TOO! YOU LOOK THE SAME, BUT EACH OF YOU IS UNIQUE!
AND WE KNOW IT EVEN THOUGH WE GET YOUR NAMES WRONG!
WOW! YOU'RE GREAT, GUYS!
FINALLY THE PEAS ARE HAPPY AGAIN...
YAY!
WELL DONE, BUZZ!
I TOLD YOU I HAD A PLAN! HEE HEE!
THE END

AN EXCLUSIVE RIDE

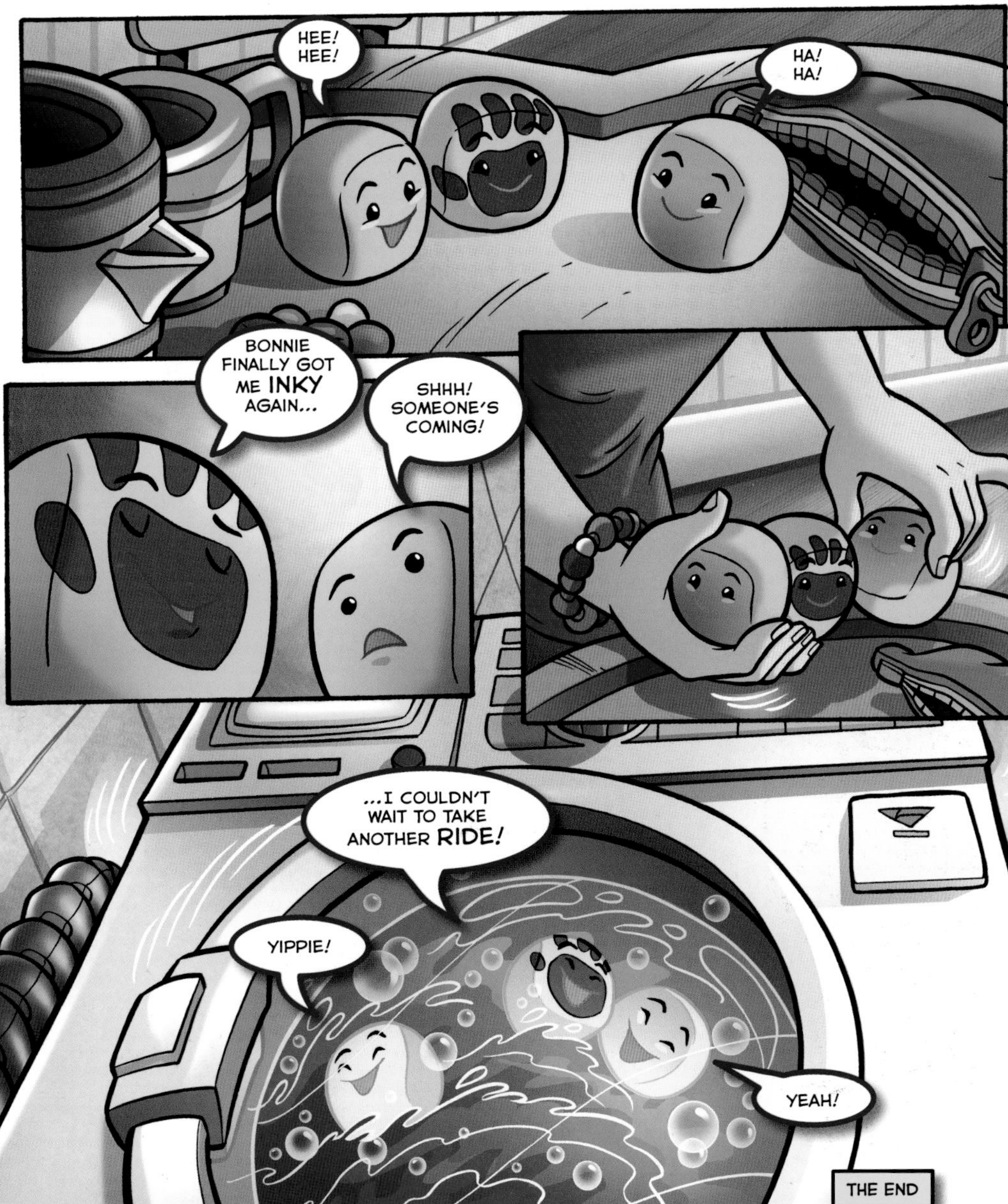

HEE! HEE!
HA! HA!
BONNIE FINALLY GOT ME INKY AGAIN...
SHHH! SOMEONE'S COMING!
...I COULDN'T WAIT TO TAKE ANOTHER RIDE!
YIPPIE!
YEAH!
THE END

SCRIPT: SILVIA MARTINOLI; PENCILS&INK: LUCA USAI; COLOUR: MARA DAMIANI

BACK TO THE POD

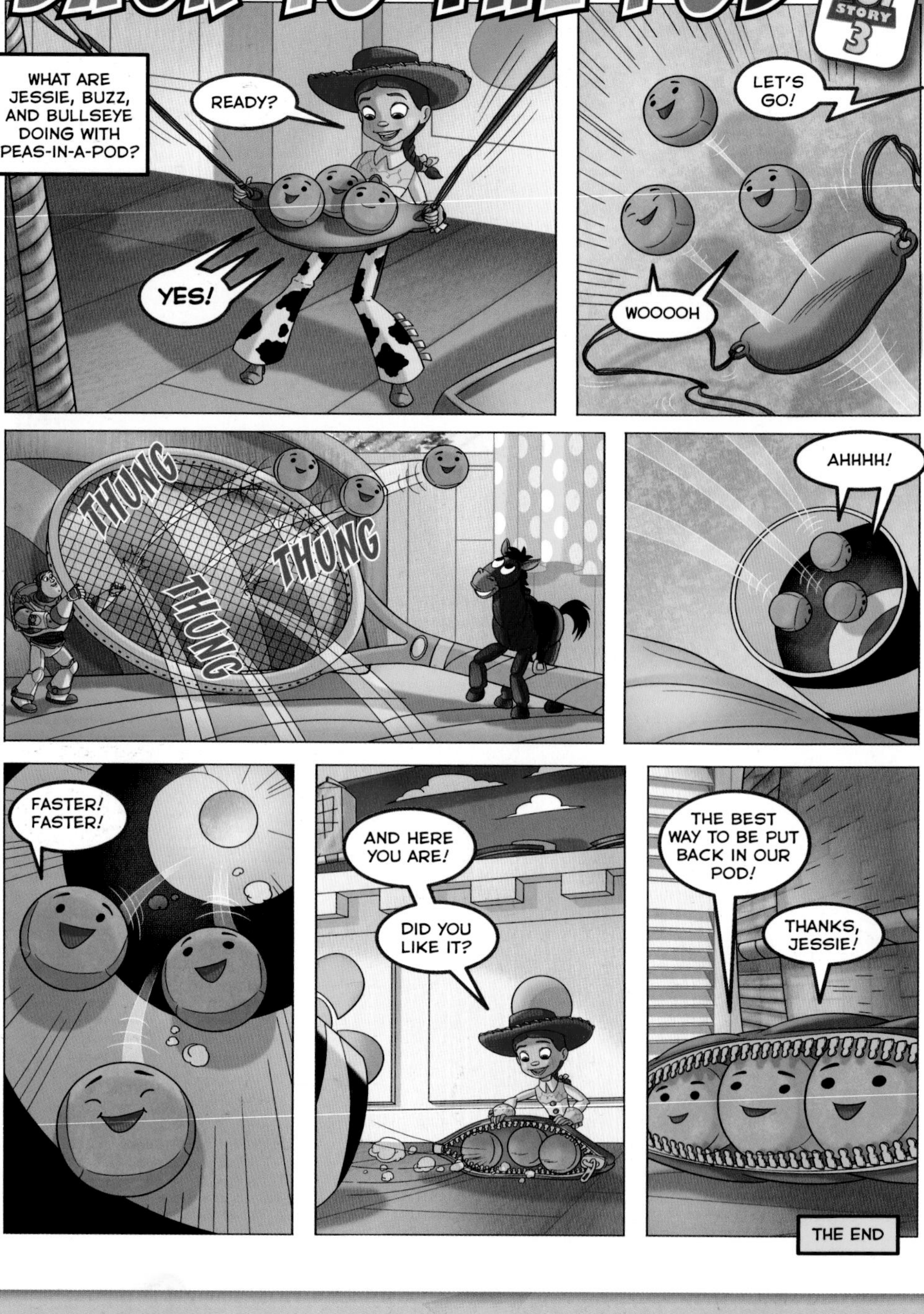
WHAT ARE JESSIE, BUZZ, AND BULLSEYE DOING WITH PEAS-IN-A-POD?
READY?
YES!
LET'S GO!
WOOOOH
THUNG
THUNG
THUNG
AHHHH!
FASTER! FASTER!
AND HERE YOU ARE!
DID YOU LIKE IT?
THE BEST WAY TO BE PUT BACK IN OUR POD!
THANKS, JESSIE!
THE END

SCRIPT: ALESSANDRO FERRARI; LAYOUT: VALENTINO FORLINI; INK: VALENTINO FORLINI; COLOUR: ANGELA CAPOLUPO

THE RUNAWAY PEA

ONE MORNING, WHEN BONNIE'S AT SCHOOL...

HEY, I NEED MORE SPACE!

NO WAY! YOU TWO ARE SQUEEZING ME!

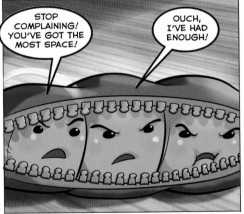

STOP COMPLAINING! YOU'VE GOT THE MOST SPACE!

OUCH, I'VE HAD ENOUGH!

I'D BE MUCH BETTER WITHOUT YOU AND THIS SMALL, SILLY POD!

WHAT? BUT, PEATRICE...

I'M LEAVING!

BOING

?

SCRIPT: TEO ORSI, PENCIL & INK: VALENTINO FORLINI, COLOR: LUCIO DE GIUSEPPE

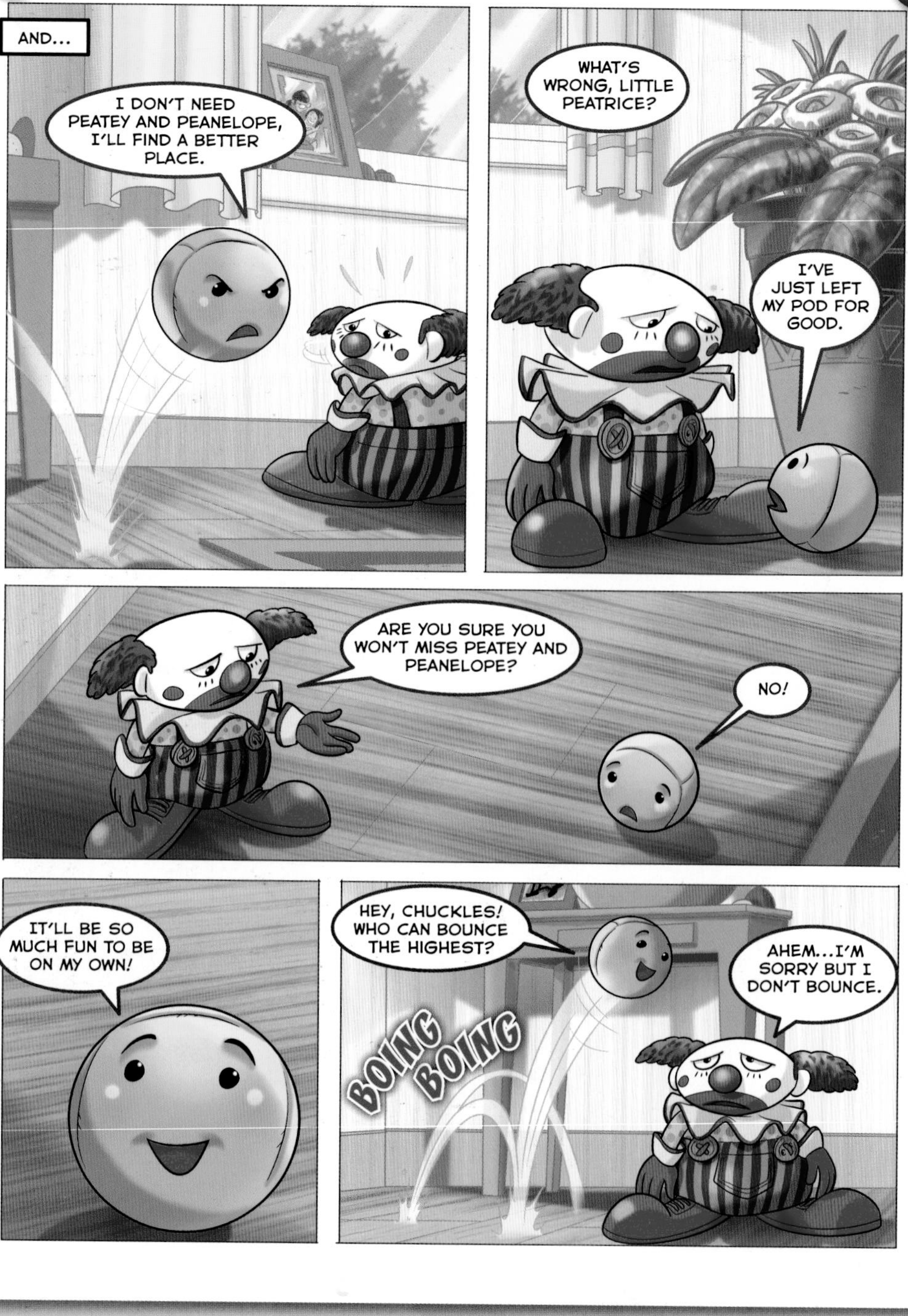
AND...
I DON'T NEED PEATEY AND PEANELOPE, I'LL FIND A BETTER PLACE.
WHAT'S WRONG, LITTLE PEATRICE?
I'VE JUST LEFT MY POD FOR GOOD.
ARE YOU SURE YOU WON'T MISS PEATEY AND PEANELOPE?
NO!
IT'LL BE SO MUCH FUN TO BE ON MY OWN!
HEY, CHUCKLES! WHO CAN BOUNCE THE HIGHEST?
BOING BOING
AHEM...I'M SORRY BUT I DON'T BOUNCE.

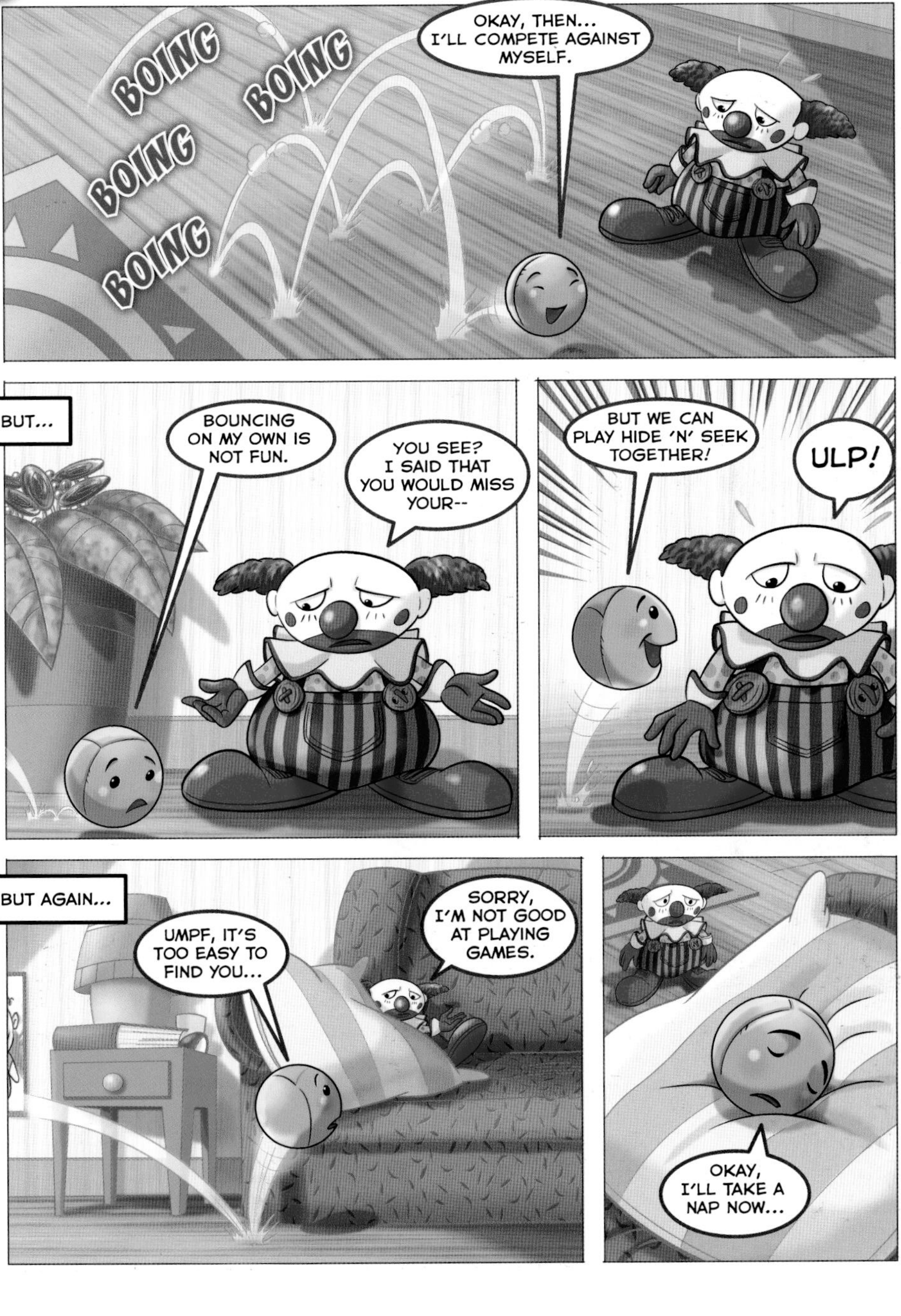
BOING
BOING
BOING
BOING
OKAY, THEN... I'LL COMPETE AGAINST MYSELF.
BUT...
BOUNCING ON MY OWN IS NOT FUN.
YOU SEE? I SAID THAT YOU WOULD MISS YOUR--
BUT WE CAN PLAY HIDE 'N' SEEK TOGETHER!
ULP!
BUT AGAIN...
UMPF, IT'S TOO EASY TO FIND YOU...
SORRY, I'M NOT GOOD AT PLAYING GAMES.
OKAY, I'LL TAKE A NAP NOW...

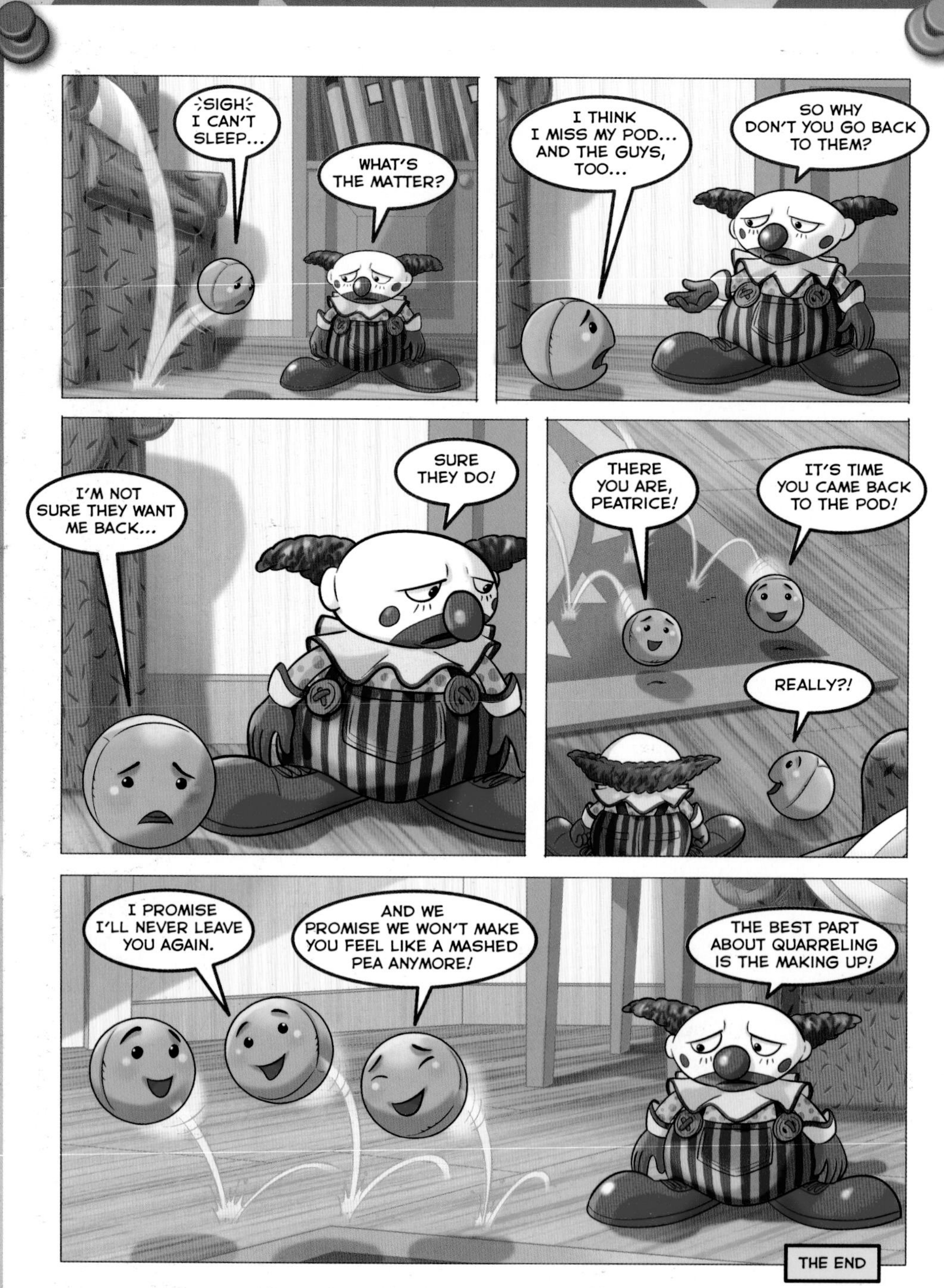

SIGH I CAN'T SLEEP...
WHAT'S THE MATTER?
I THINK I MISS MY POD... AND THE GUYS, TOO...
SO WHY DON'T YOU GO BACK TO THEM?
I'M NOT SURE THEY WANT ME BACK...
SURE THEY DO!
THERE YOU ARE, PEATRICE!
IT'S TIME YOU CAME BACK TO THE POD!
REALLY?!
I PROMISE I'LL NEVER LEAVE YOU AGAIN.
AND WE PROMISE WE WON'T MAKE YOU FEEL LIKE A MASHED PEA ANYMORE!
THE BEST PART ABOUT QUARRELING IS THE MAKING UP!
THE END

PEAS WITHOUT A POD

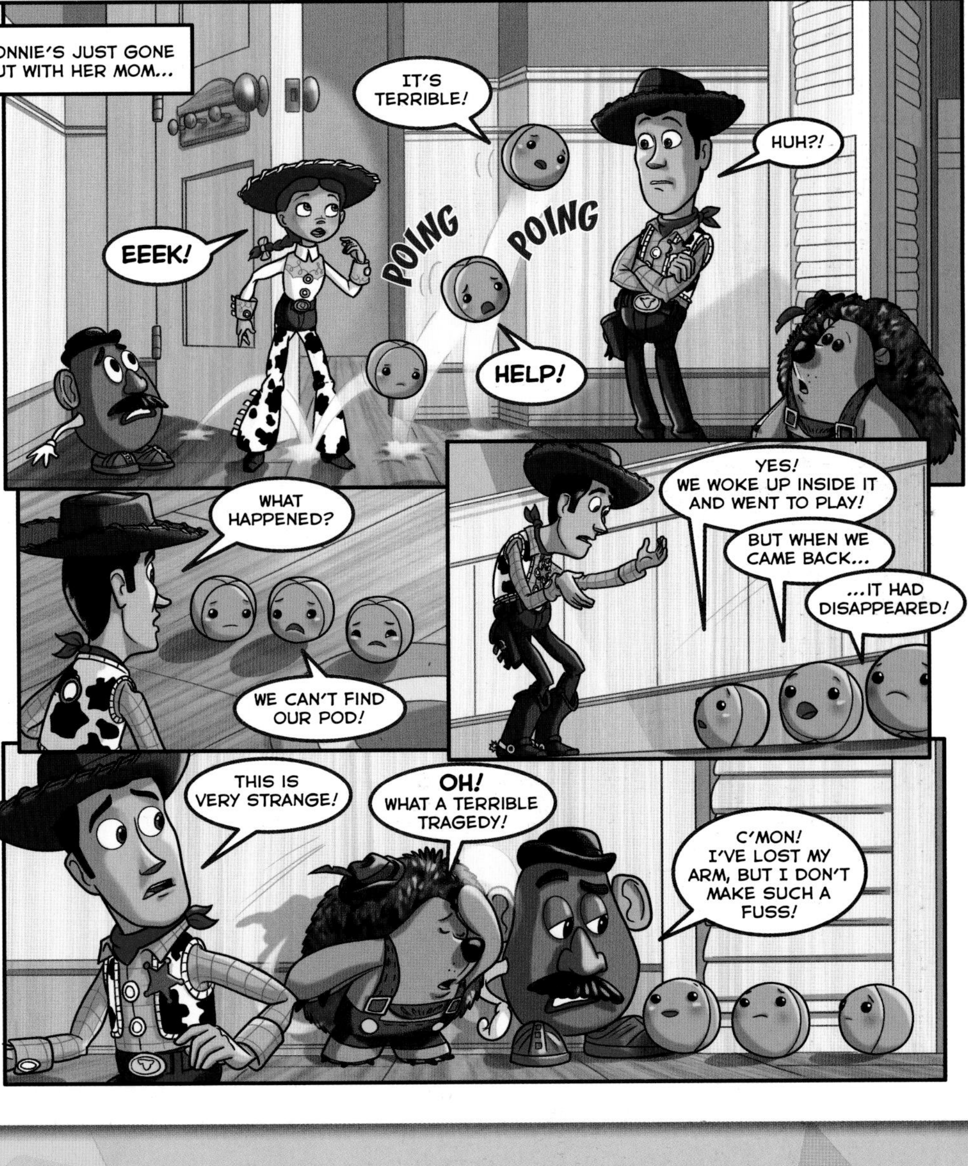
BONNIE'S JUST GONE OUT WITH HER MOM...
IT'S TERRIBLE!
HUH?!
EEEK!
POING
POING
HELP!
WHAT HAPPENED?
WE CAN'T FIND OUR POD!
YES! WE WOKE UP INSIDE IT AND WENT TO PLAY!
BUT WHEN WE CAME BACK...
...IT HAD DISAPPEARED!
THIS IS VERY STRANGE!
OH! WHAT A TERRIBLE TRAGEDY!
C'MON! I'VE LOST MY ARM, BUT I DON'T MAKE SUCH A FUSS!

SCRIPT: TEA ORSI; LAYOUT: GIANFRANCO FLORIO; INK: MICHELA FRARE; COLOUR: LUCIO DE GIUSEPPE

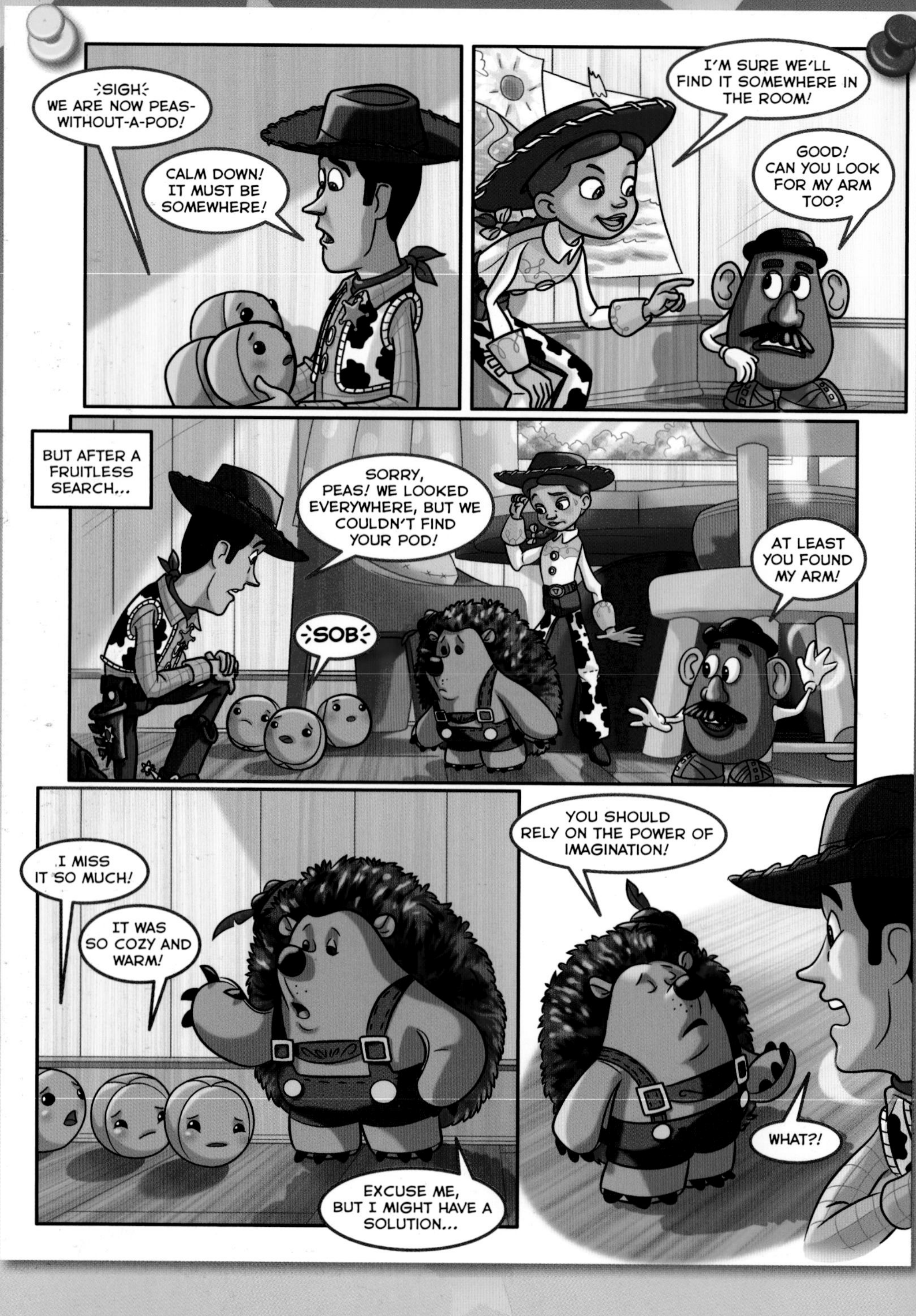

SIGH
WE ARE NOW PEAS-WITHOUT-A-POD!
CALM DOWN! IT MUST BE SOMEWHERE!
I'M SURE WE'LL FIND IT SOMEWHERE IN THE ROOM!
GOOD! CAN YOU LOOK FOR MY ARM TOO?
BUT AFTER A FRUITLESS SEARCH...
SORRY, PEAS! WE LOOKED EVERYWHERE, BUT WE COULDN'T FIND YOUR POD!
SOB
AT LEAST YOU FOUND MY ARM!
I MISS IT SO MUCH!
IT WAS SO COZY AND WARM!
EXCUSE ME, BUT I MIGHT HAVE A SOLUTION...
YOU SHOULD RELY ON THE POWER OF IMAGINATION!
WHAT?!

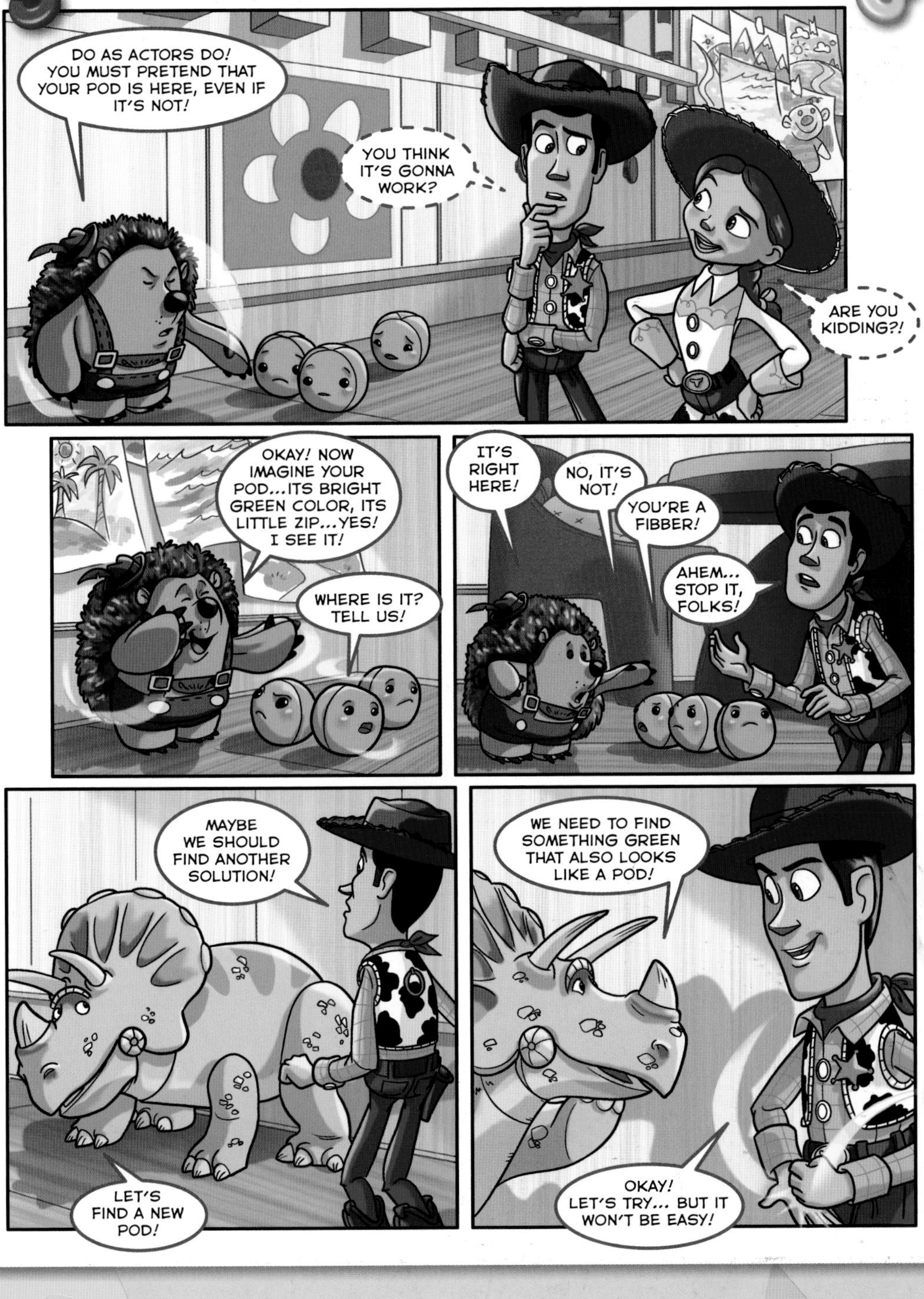
DO AS ACTORS DO! YOU MUST PRETEND THAT YOUR POD IS HERE, EVEN IF IT'S NOT!
YOU THINK IT'S GONNA WORK?
ARE YOU KIDDING?!
OKAY! NOW IMAGINE YOUR POD...ITS BRIGHT GREEN COLOR, ITS LITTLE ZIP...YES! I SEE IT!
WHERE IS IT? TELL US!
IT'S RIGHT HERE!
NO, IT'S NOT!
YOU'RE A FIBBER!
AHEM... STOP IT, FOLKS!
MAYBE WE SHOULD FIND ANOTHER SOLUTION!
LET'S FIND A NEW POD!
WE NEED TO FIND SOMETHING GREEN THAT ALSO LOOKS LIKE A POD!
OKAY! LET'S TRY... BUT IT WON'T BE EASY!

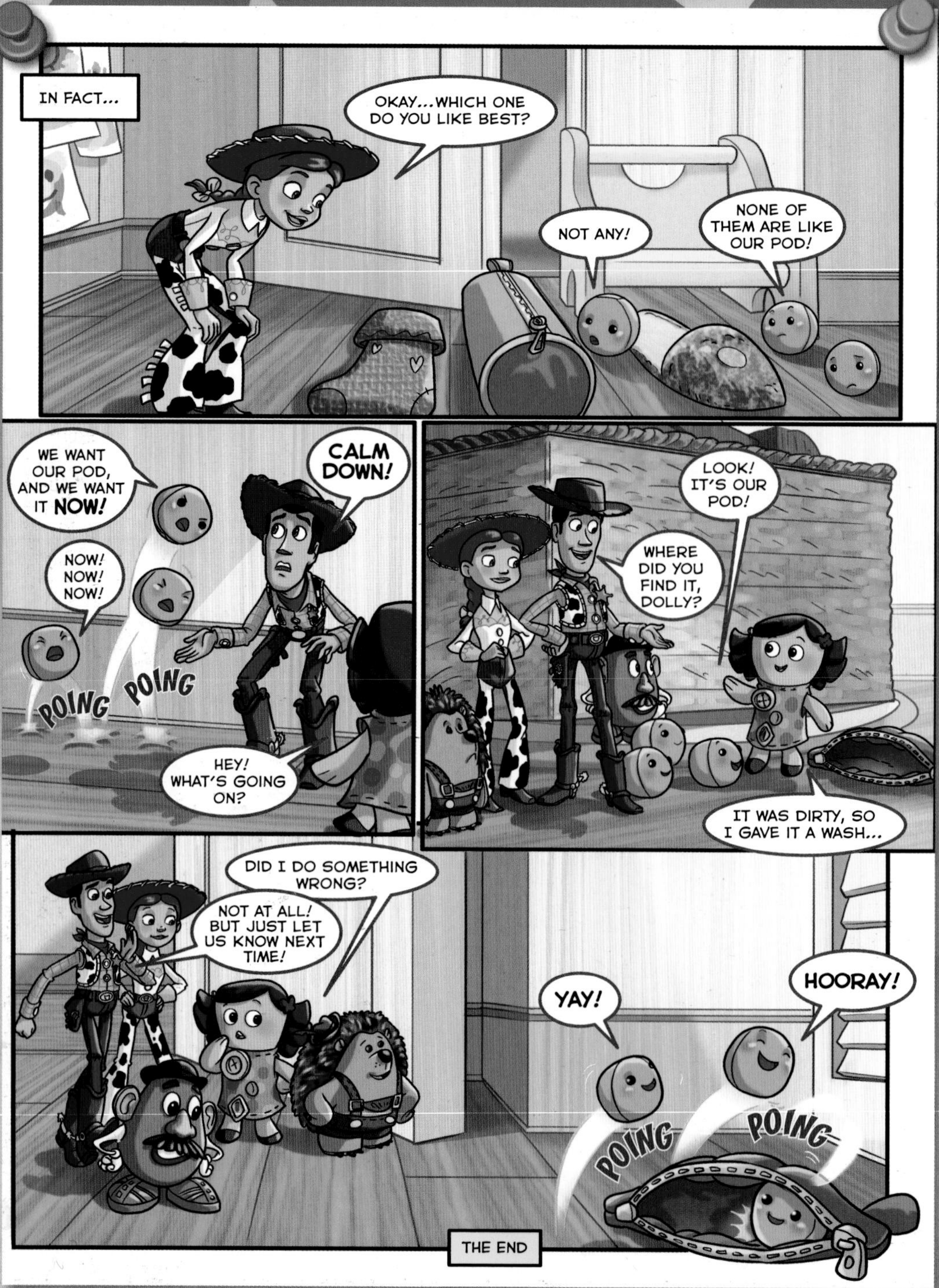

IN FACT...
OKAY...WHICH ONE DO YOU LIKE BEST?
NOT ANY!
NONE OF THEM ARE LIKE OUR POD!
WE WANT OUR POD, AND WE WANT IT NOW!
CALM DOWN!
NOW! NOW! NOW!
POING
POING
HEY! WHAT'S GOING ON?
LOOK! IT'S OUR POD!
WHERE DID YOU FIND IT, DOLLY?
IT WAS DIRTY, SO I GAVE IT A WASH...
DID I DO SOMETHING WRONG?
NOT AT ALL! BUT JUST LET US KNOW NEXT TIME!
YAY!
HOORAY!
POING
POING
THE END

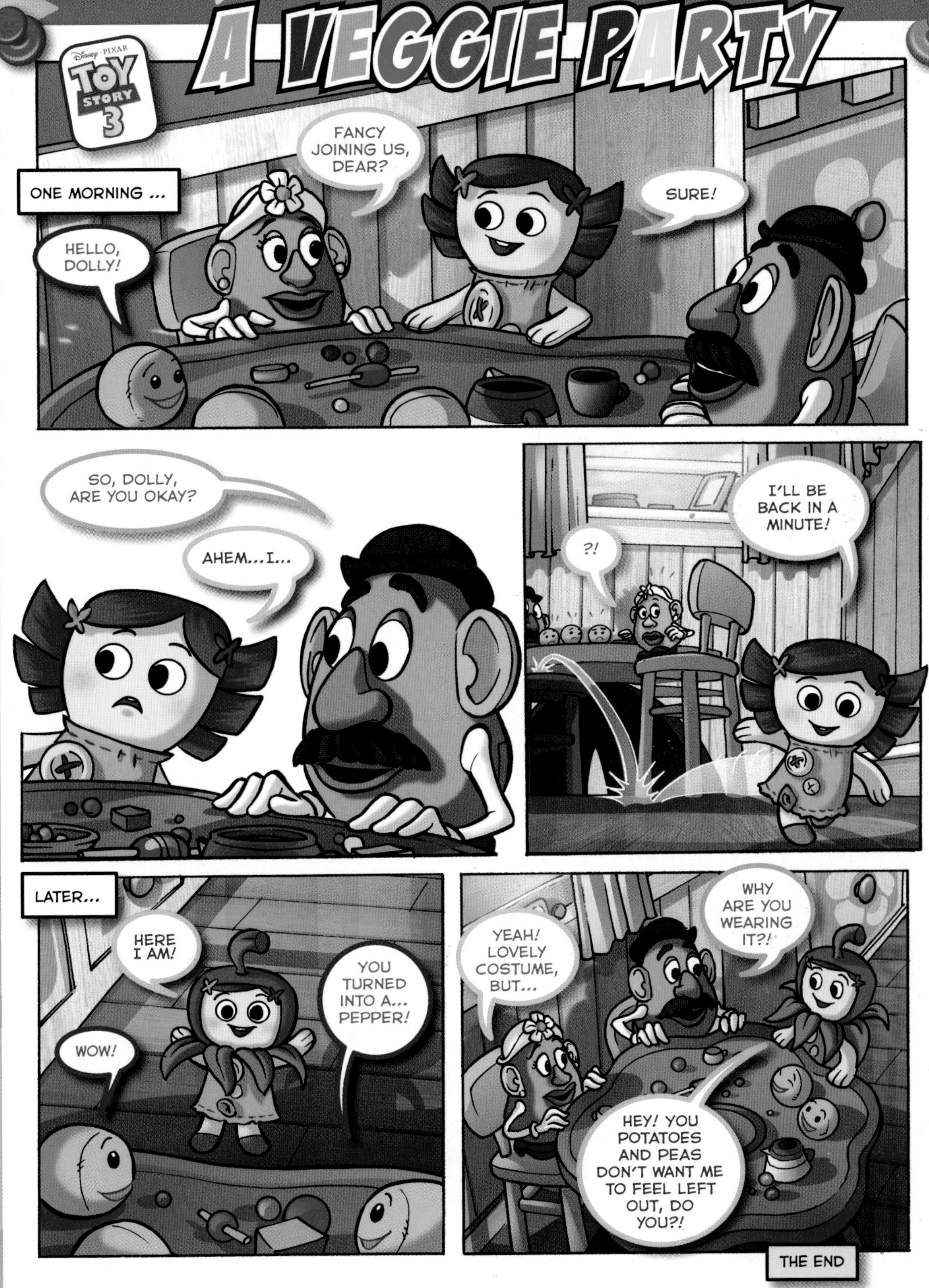
A VEGGIE PARTY
ONE MORNING ...
HELLO, DOLLY!
FANCY JOINING US, DEAR?
SURE!
SO, DOLLY, ARE YOU OKAY?
AHEM...I...
?!
I'LL BE BACK IN A MINUTE!
LATER...
HERE I AM!
WOW!
YOU TURNED INTO A... PEPPER!
YEAH! LOVELY COSTUME, BUT...
WHY ARE YOU WEARING IT?!
HEY! YOU POTATOES AND PEAS DON'T WANT ME TO FEEL LEFT OUT, DO YOU?!
THE END

SCRIPT: TEA ORSI; LAYOUT & INK: VALENTINO FORLINI; COLOUR: MARA DAMIANI

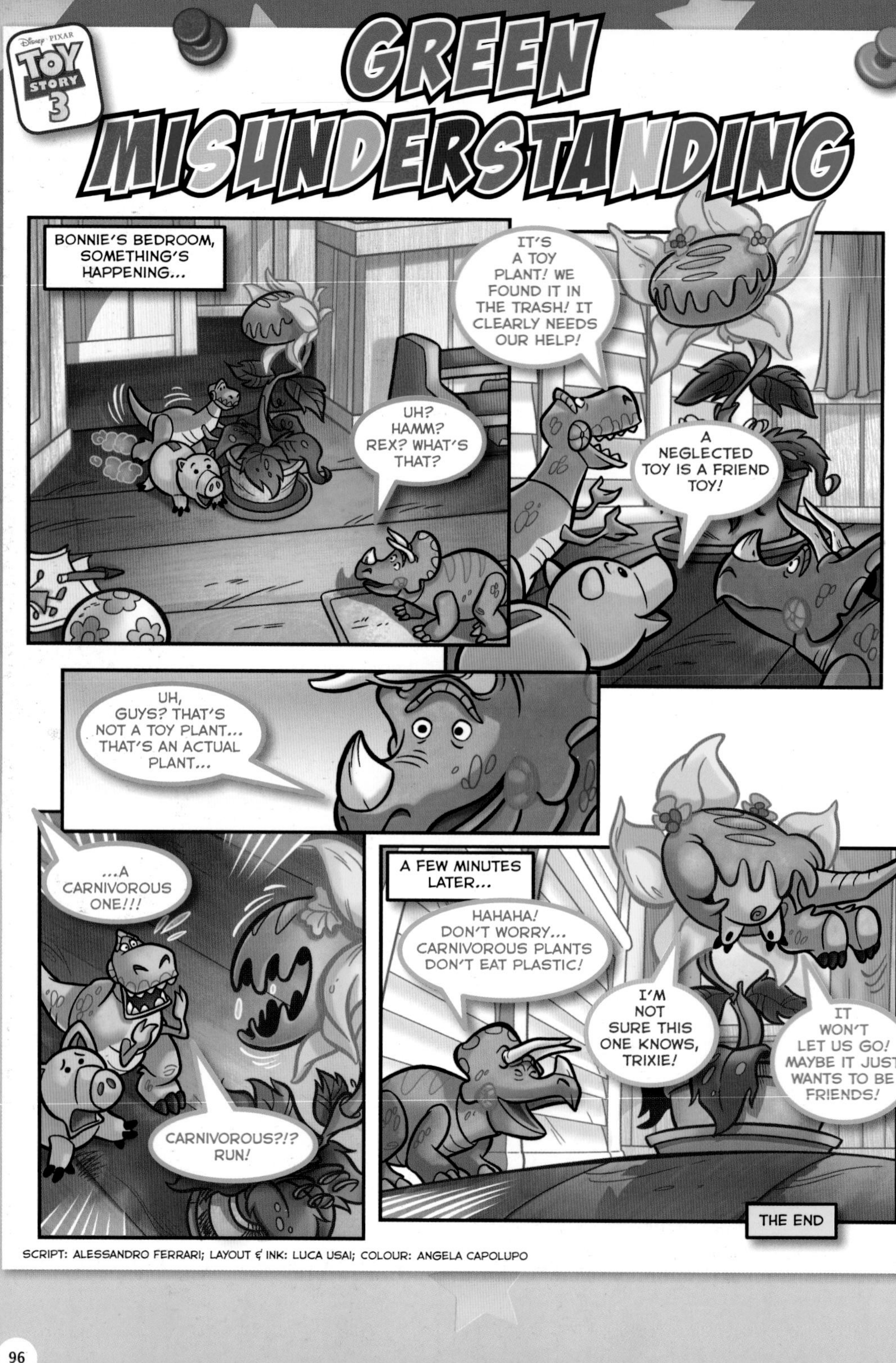

GREEN MISUNDERSTANDING
TOY STORY 3
BONNIE'S BEDROOM, SOMETHING'S HAPPENING...
UH? HAMM? REX? WHAT'S THAT?
IT'S A TOY PLANT! WE FOUND IT IN THE TRASH! IT CLEARLY NEEDS OUR HELP!
A NEGLECTED TOY IS A FRIEND TOY!
UH, GUYS? THAT'S NOT A TOY PLANT... THAT'S AN ACTUAL PLANT...
...A CARNIVOROUS ONE!!!
CARNIVOROUS?!? RUN!
A FEW MINUTES LATER...
HAHAHA! DON'T WORRY... CARNIVOROUS PLANTS DON'T EAT PLASTIC!
I'M NOT SURE THIS ONE KNOWS, TRIXIE!
IT WON'T LET US GO! MAYBE IT JUST WANTS TO BE FRIENDS!
THE END

SCRIPT: ALESSANDRO FERRARI; LAYOUT & INK: LUCA USAI; COLOUR: ANGELA CAPOLUPO

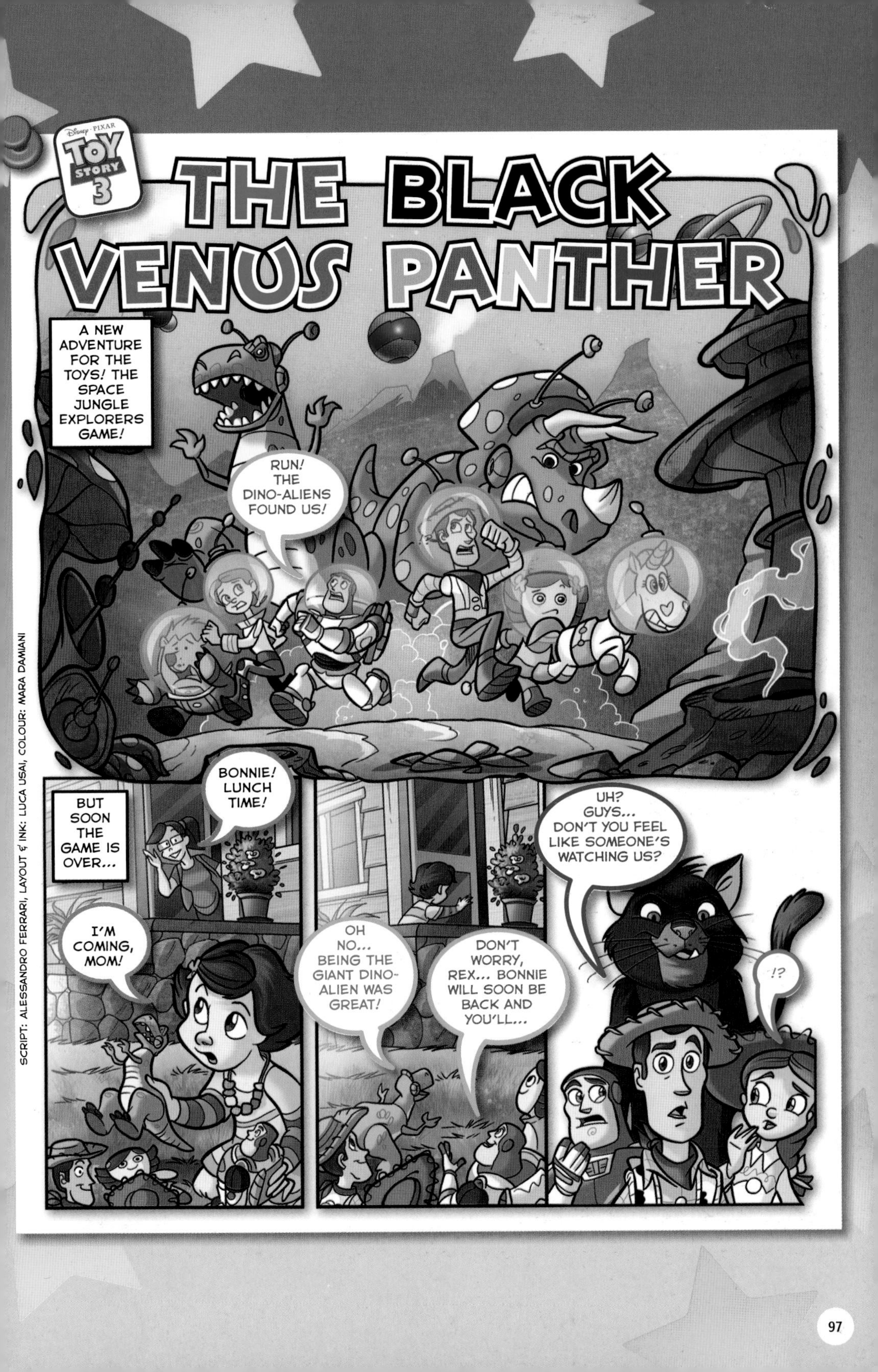
Disney · PIXAR
TOY STORY 3
THE BLACK VENUS PANTHER
A NEW ADVENTURE FOR THE TOYS! THE SPACE JUNGLE EXPLORERS GAME!
RUN! THE DINO-ALIENS FOUND US!
BUT SOON THE GAME IS OVER...
BONNIE! LUNCH TIME!
I'M COMING, MOM!
OH NO... BEING THE GIANT DINO-ALIEN WAS GREAT!
DON'T WORRY, REX... BONNIE WILL SOON BE BACK AND YOU'LL...
UH? GUYS... DON'T YOU FEEL LIKE SOMEONE'S WATCHING US?
!?

SCRIPT: ALESSANDRO FERRARI, LAYOUT & INK: LUCA USAI, COLOUR: MARA DAMIANI

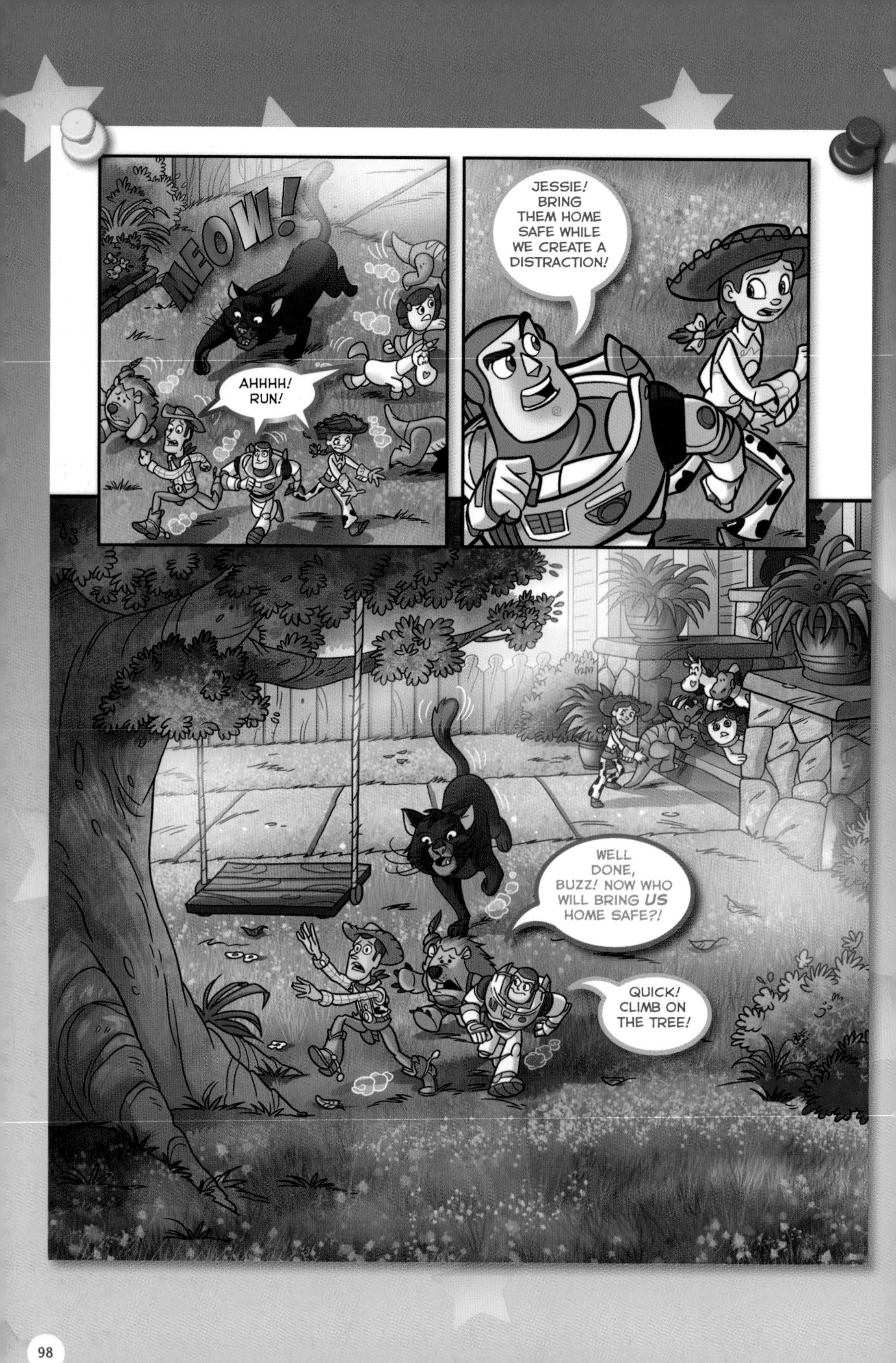
MEOW!
AHHHH! RUN!
JESSIE! BRING THEM HOME SAFE WHILE WE CREATE A DISTRACTION!
WELL DONE, BUZZ! NOW WHO WILL BRING *US* HOME SAFE?!
QUICK! CLIMB ON THE TREE!

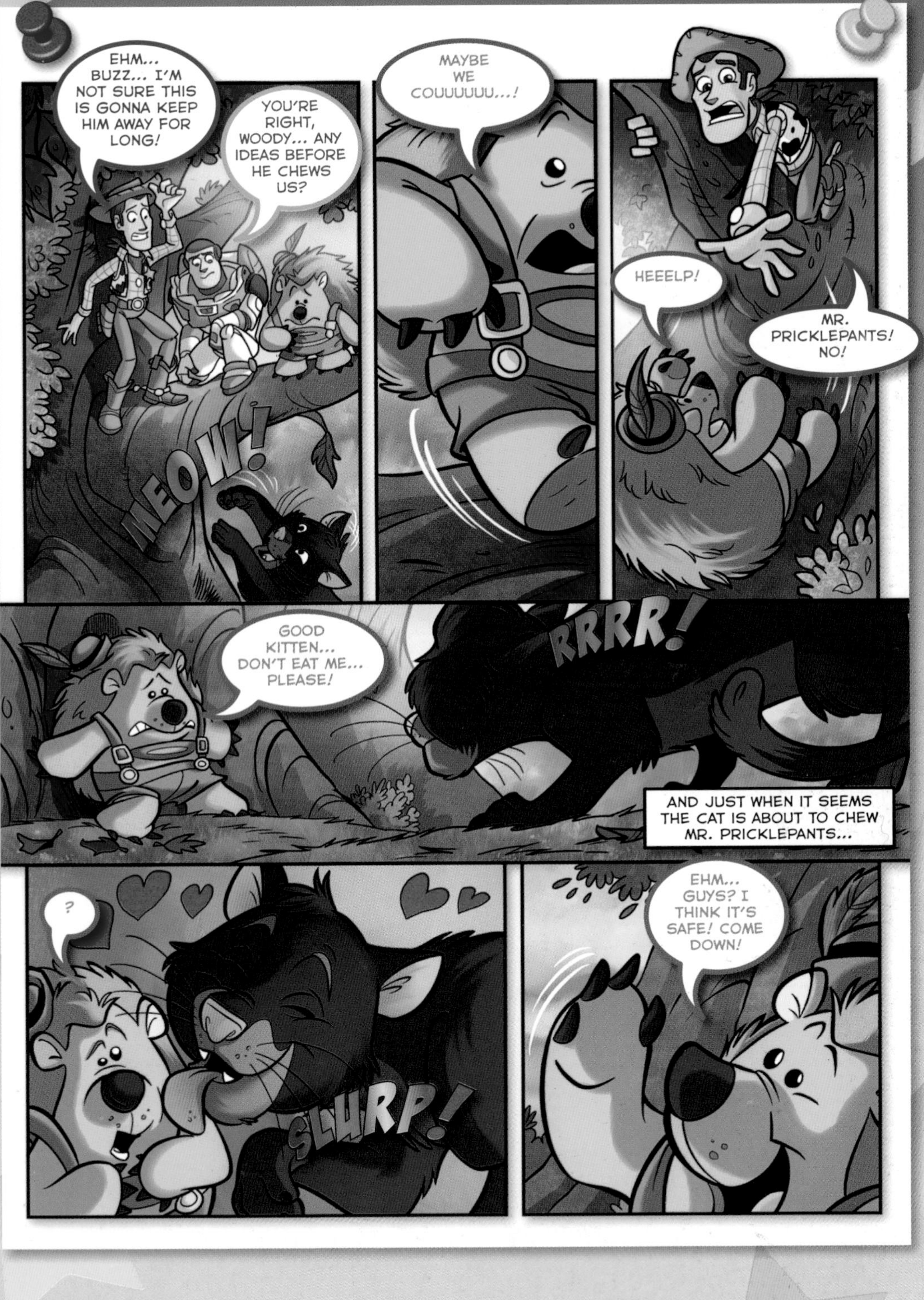

EHM... BUZZ... I'M NOT SURE THIS IS GONNA KEEP HIM AWAY FOR LONG!
YOU'RE RIGHT, WOODY... ANY IDEAS BEFORE HE CHEWS US?
MEOW!
MAYBE WE COUUUUUU...!
HEEELP!
MR. PRICKLEPANTS! NO!
GOOD KITTEN... DON'T EAT ME... PLEASE!
RRRR!
AND JUST WHEN IT SEEMS THE CAT IS ABOUT TO CHEW MR. PRICKLEPANTS...
?
SLURP!
EHM... GUYS? I THINK IT'S SAFE! COME DOWN!

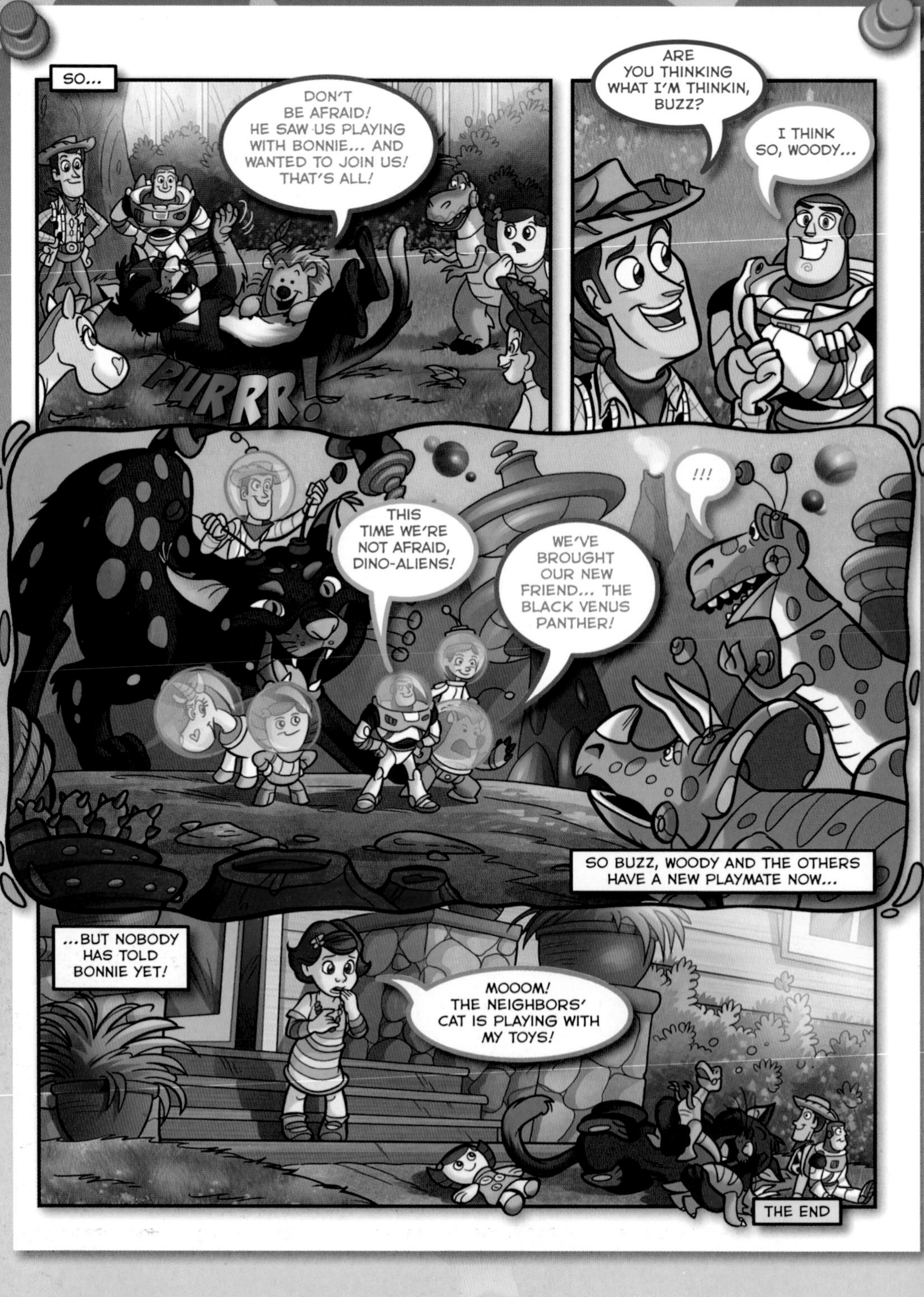
SO...
DON'T BE AFRAID! HE SAW US PLAYING WITH BONNIE... AND WANTED TO JOIN US! THAT'S ALL!
PURRR!
ARE YOU THINKING WHAT I'M THINKIN, BUZZ?
I THINK SO, WOODY...
THIS TIME WE'RE NOT AFRAID, DINO-ALIENS!
WE'VE BROUGHT OUR NEW FRIEND... THE BLACK VENUS PANTHER!
!!!
SO BUZZ, WOODY AND THE OTHERS HAVE A NEW PLAYMATE NOW...
...BUT NOBODY HAS TOLD BONNIE YET!
MOOOM! THE NEIGHBORS' CAT IS PLAYING WITH MY TOYS!
THE END

SPACE MODES

YAY! IT'S FUN TIME!

BONNIE'S JUST GONE TO SCHOOL...

THUD

~YAAAWN~

BONK

UH?!

FINALLY!

ARE YOU OKAY, BUZZ?

OH NO! I BROKE HIM!

AHEM... I THINK YOU DID SOMETHING WORSE!

DÒNDE ESTÀ MI NAVE ESPACIAL?*

YOU ACTIVATED HIS SPANISH MODE!

*WHERE'S MY SPACESHIP?

SCRIPT: TEA ORSI; LAYOUT & INK: LUCA USAI; COLOUR: MARA DAMIANI

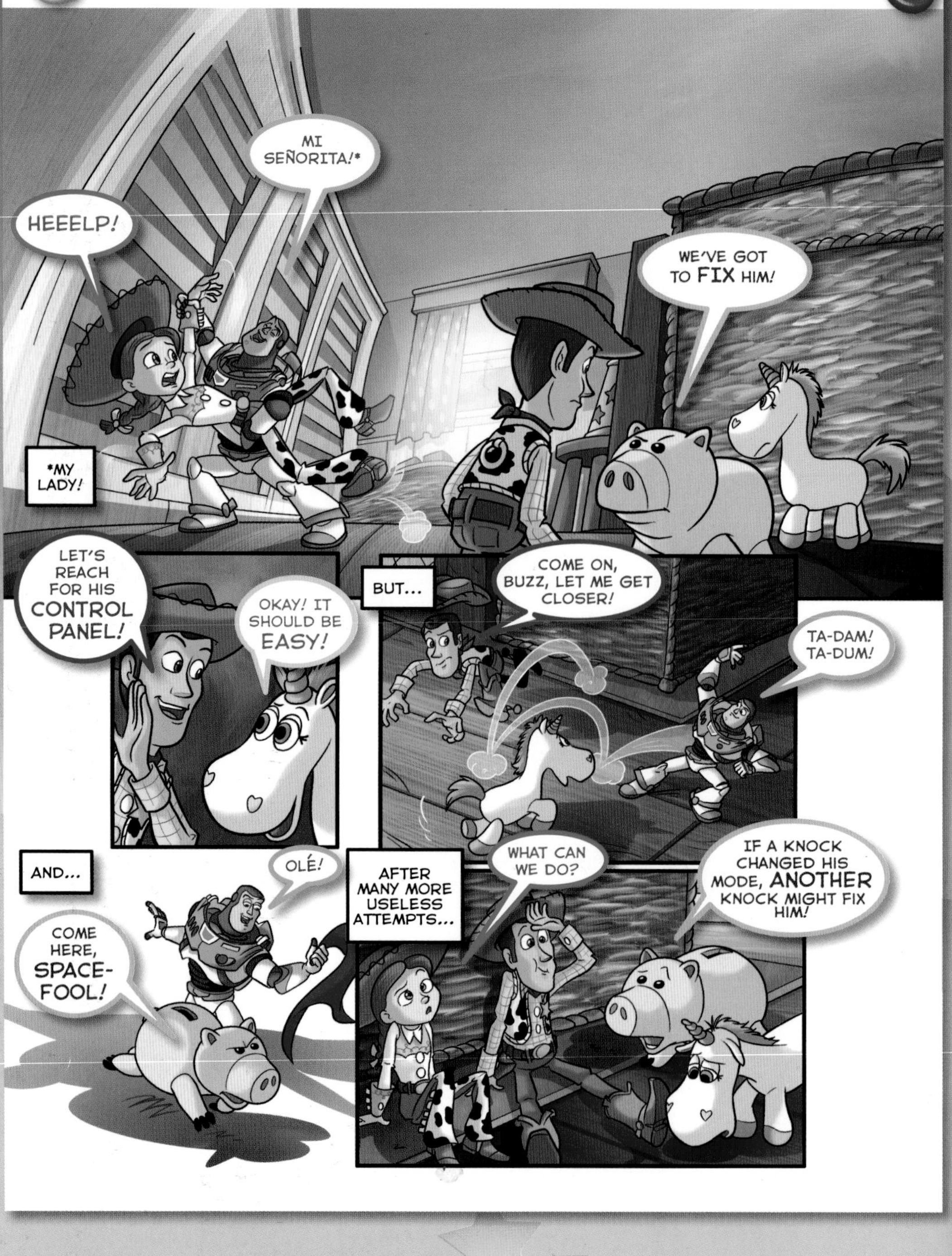
HEEELP!
MI SEÑORITA!*
*MY LADY!
WE'VE GOT TO FIX HIM!
LET'S REACH FOR HIS CONTROL PANEL!
OKAY! IT SHOULD BE EASY!
BUT...
COME ON, BUZZ, LET ME GET CLOSER!
TA-DAM! TA-DUM!
AND...
OLÉ!
COME HERE, SPACE-FOOL!
AFTER MANY MORE USELESS ATTEMPTS...
WHAT CAN WE DO?
IF A KNOCK CHANGED HIS MODE, ANOTHER KNOCK MIGHT FIX HIM!

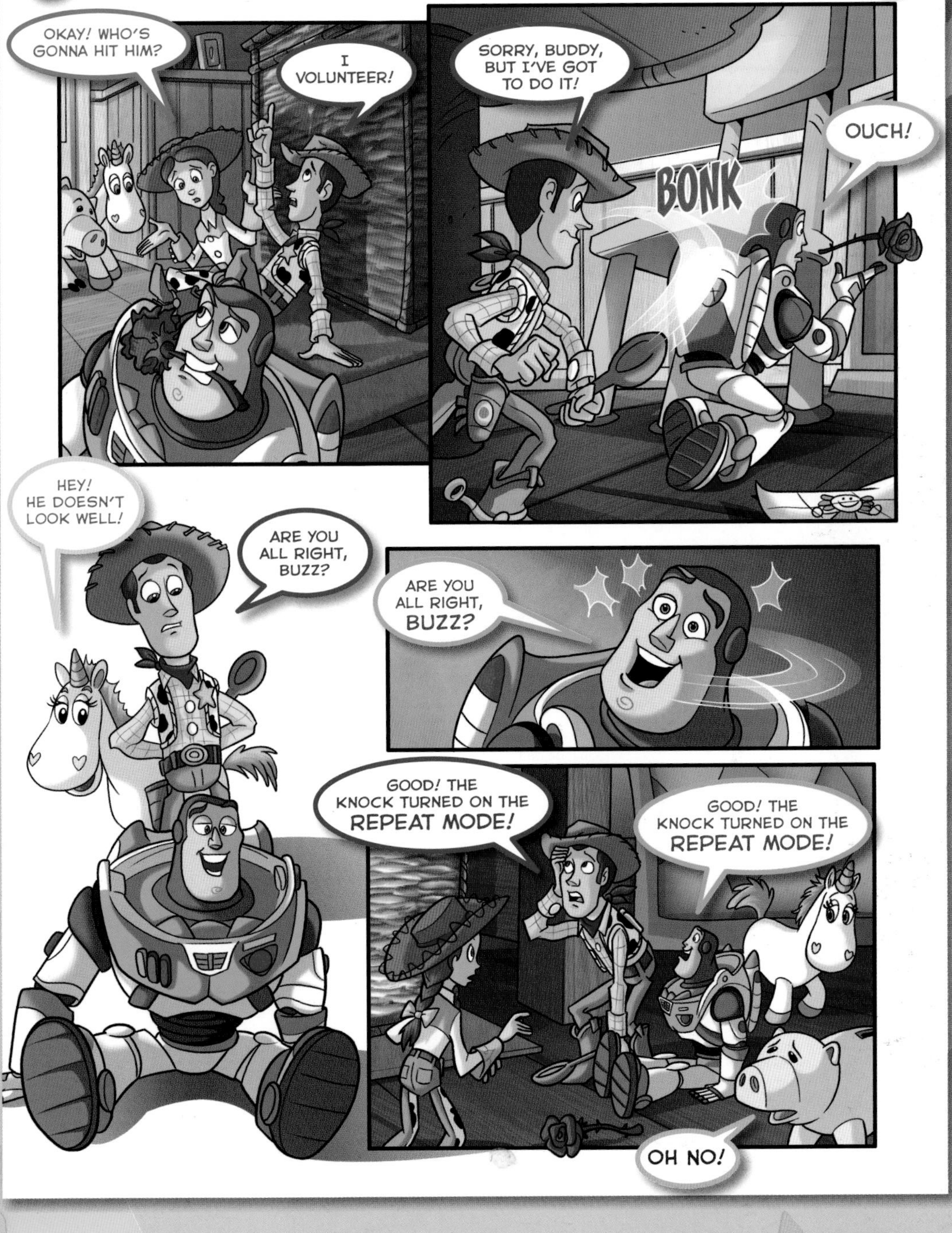

OKAY! WHO'S GONNA HIT HIM?
I VOLUNTEER!
SORRY, BUDDY, BUT I'VE GOT TO DO IT!
BONK
OUCH!
HEY! HE DOESN'T LOOK WELL!
ARE YOU ALL RIGHT, BUZZ?
ARE YOU ALL RIGHT, BUZZ?
GOOD! THE KNOCK TURNED ON THE REPEAT MODE!
GOOD! THE KNOCK TURNED ON THE REPEAT MODE!
OH NO!

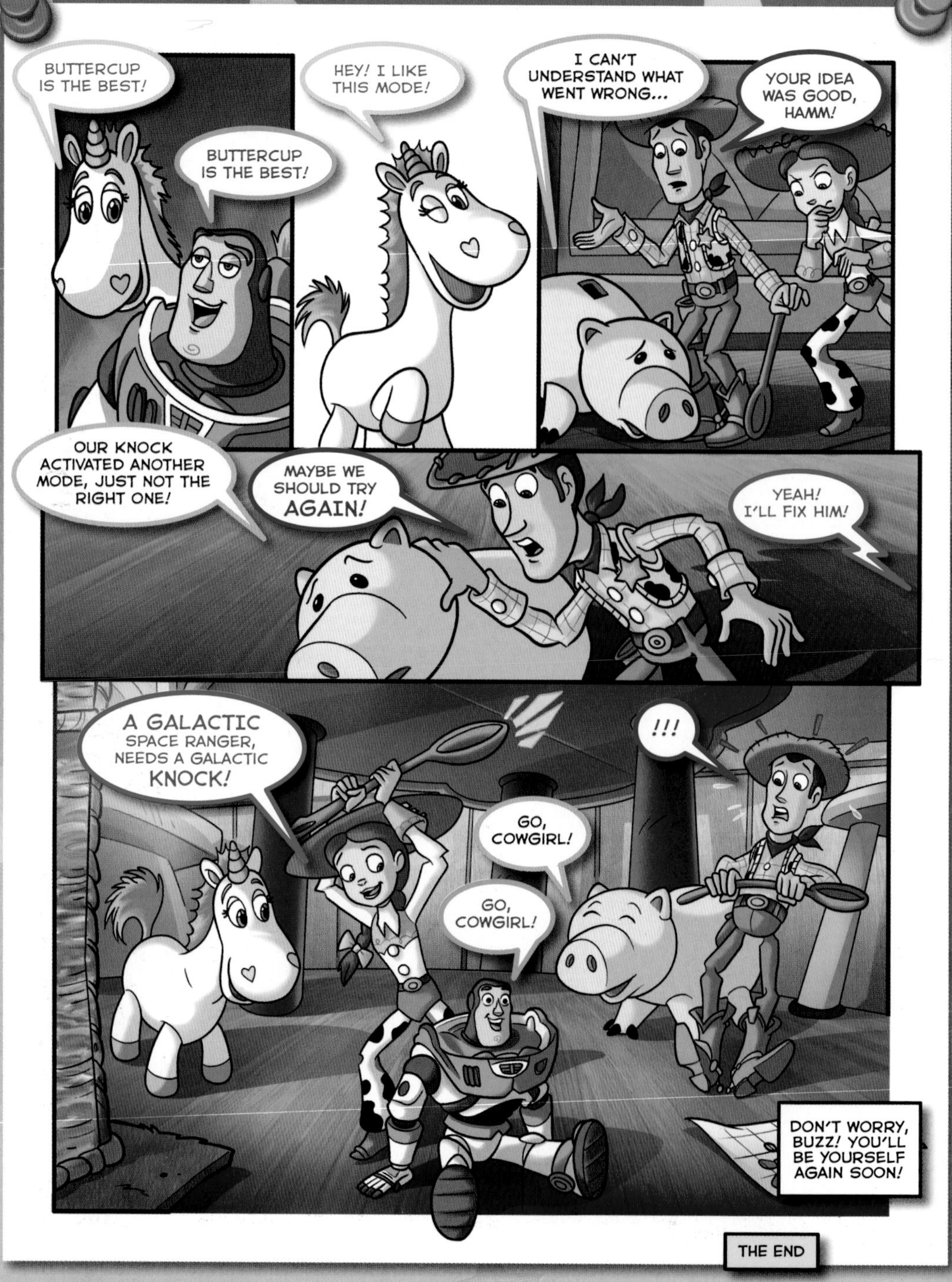
BUTTERCUP IS THE BEST!
BUTTERCUP IS THE BEST!
HEY! I LIKE THIS MODE!
I CAN'T UNDERSTAND WHAT WENT WRONG...
YOUR IDEA WAS GOOD, HAMM!
OUR KNOCK ACTIVATED ANOTHER MODE, JUST NOT THE RIGHT ONE!
MAYBE WE SHOULD TRY AGAIN!
YEAH! I'LL FIX HIM!
A GALACTIC SPACE RANGER, NEEDS A GALACTIC KNOCK!
!!!
GO, COWGIRL!
GO, COWGIRL!
DON'T WORRY, BUZZ! YOU'LL BE YOURSELF AGAIN SOON!
THE END

SPACESHIP EMERGENCY

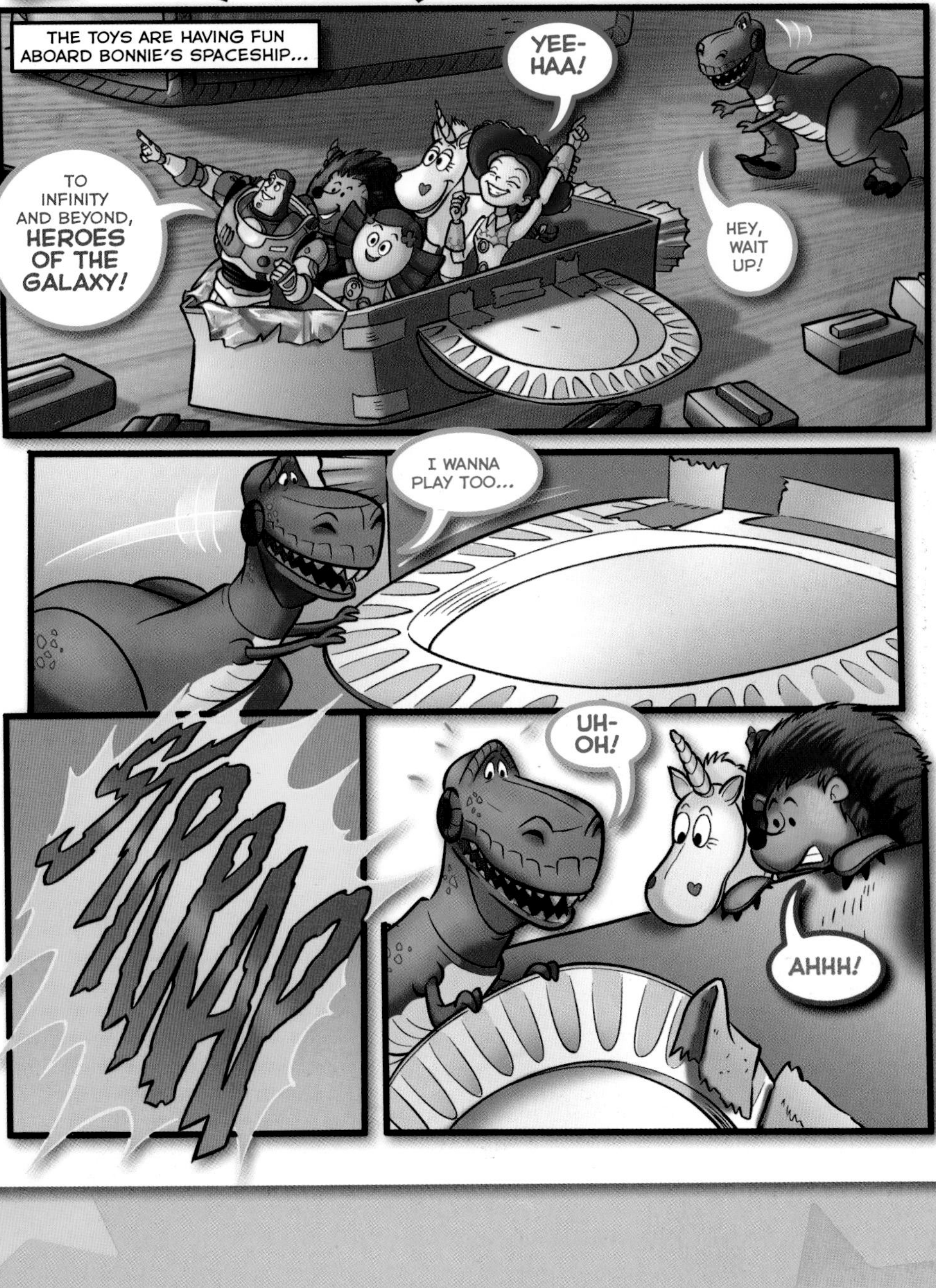
THE TOYS ARE HAVING FUN ABOARD BONNIE'S SPACESHIP...
YEE-HAA!
TO INFINITY AND BEYOND, HEROES OF THE GALAXY!
HEY, WAIT UP!
I WANNA PLAY TOO...
UH-OH!
AHHH!

SCRIPT: TEA ORSI; PENCILS: VALENTINO FORLINI; INK: MICHELA FRARE; COLOUR: KAWAII CREATIVE STUDIO

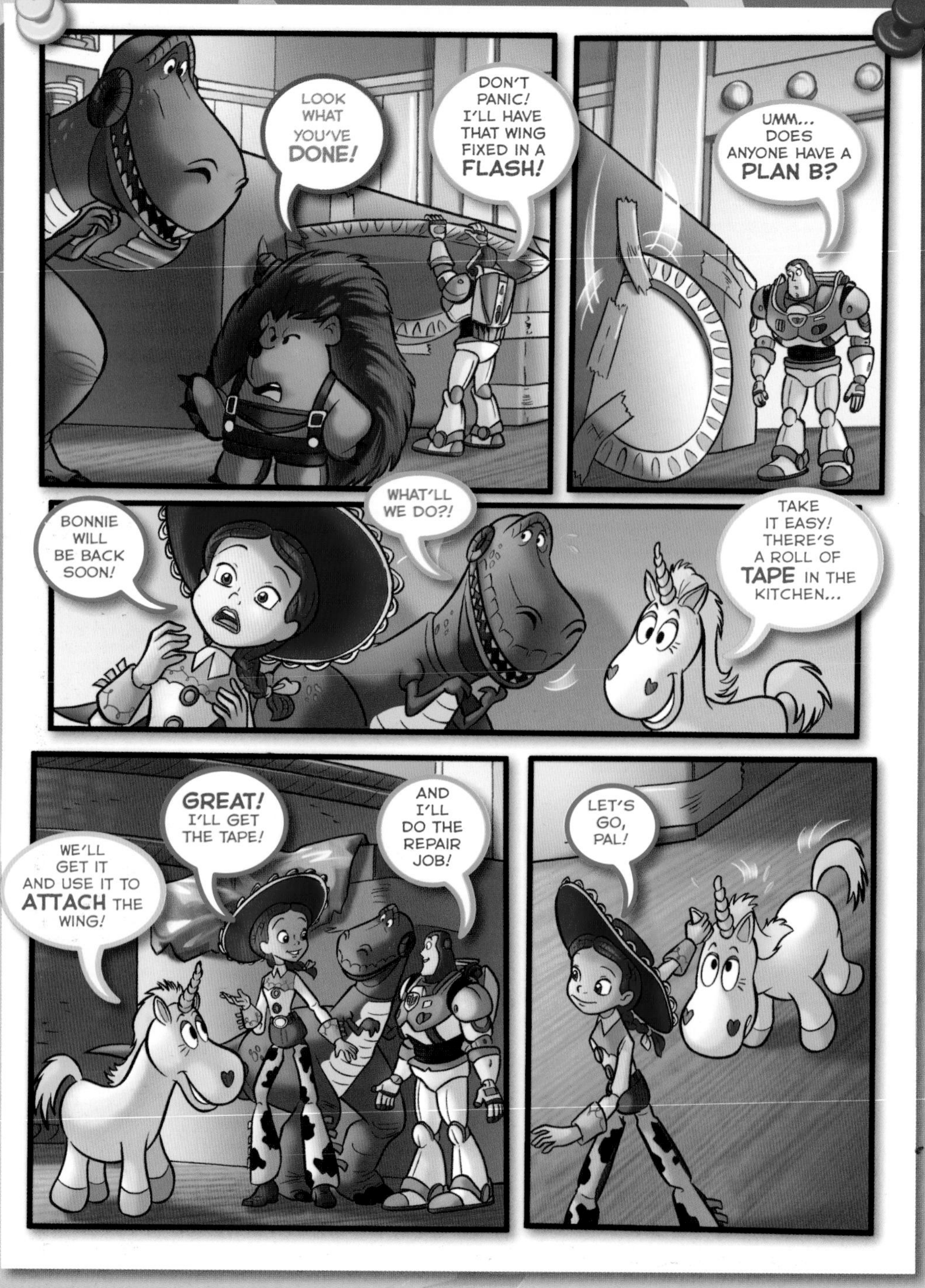
LOOK WHAT YOU'VE DONE!
DON'T PANIC! I'LL HAVE THAT WING FIXED IN A FLASH!
UMM... DOES ANYONE HAVE A PLAN B?
BONNIE WILL BE BACK SOON!
WHAT'LL WE DO?!
TAKE IT EASY! THERE'S A ROLL OF TAPE IN THE KITCHEN...
WE'LL GET IT AND USE IT TO ATTACH THE WING!
GREAT! I'LL GET THE TAPE!
AND I'LL DO THE REPAIR JOB!
LET'S GO, PAL!

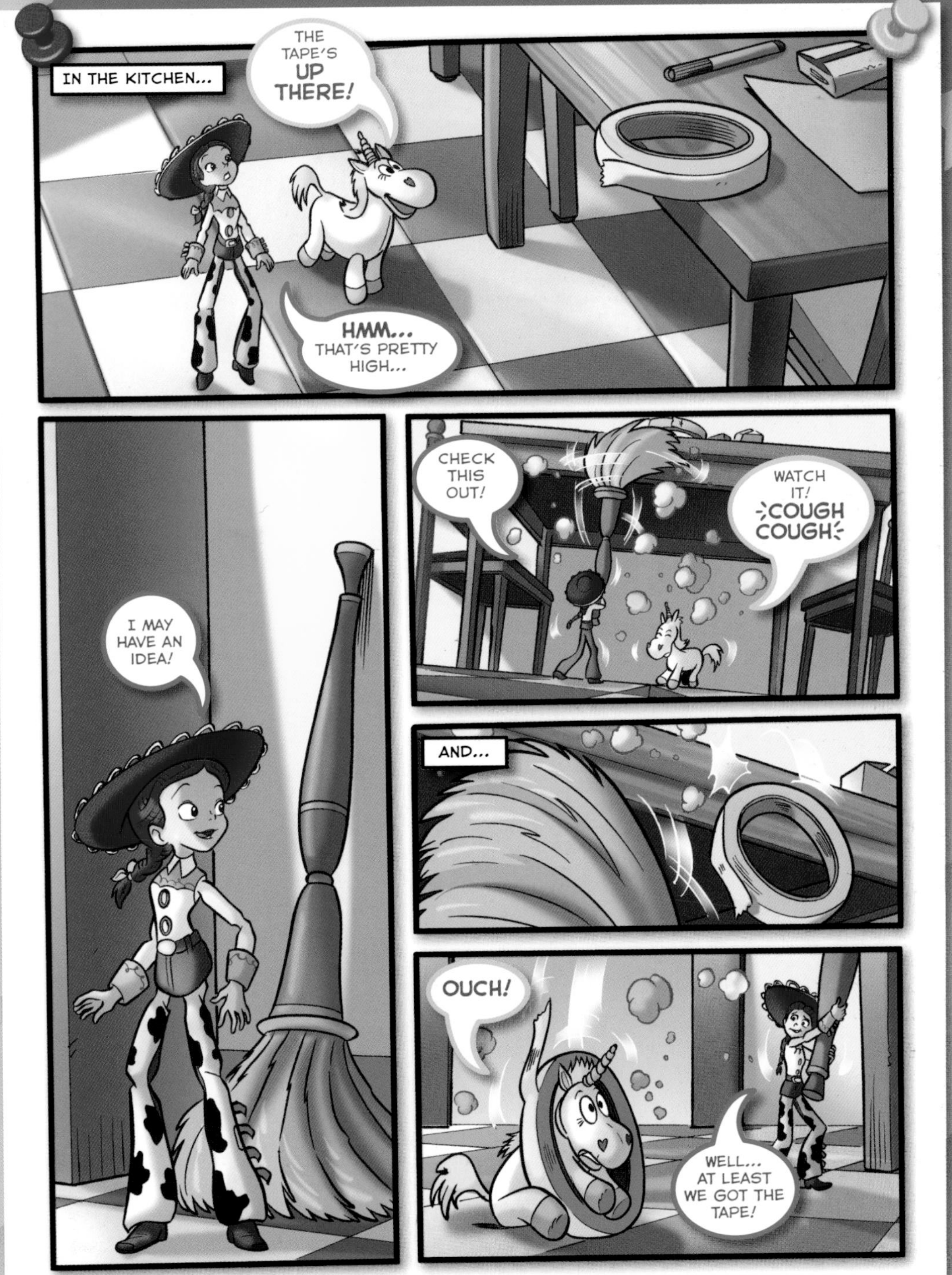
IN THE KITCHEN...
THE TAPE'S UP THERE!
HMM... THAT'S PRETTY HIGH...
I MAY HAVE AN IDEA!
CHECK THIS OUT!
WATCH IT! COUGH COUGH
AND...
OUCH!
WELL... AT LEAST WE GOT THE TAPE!

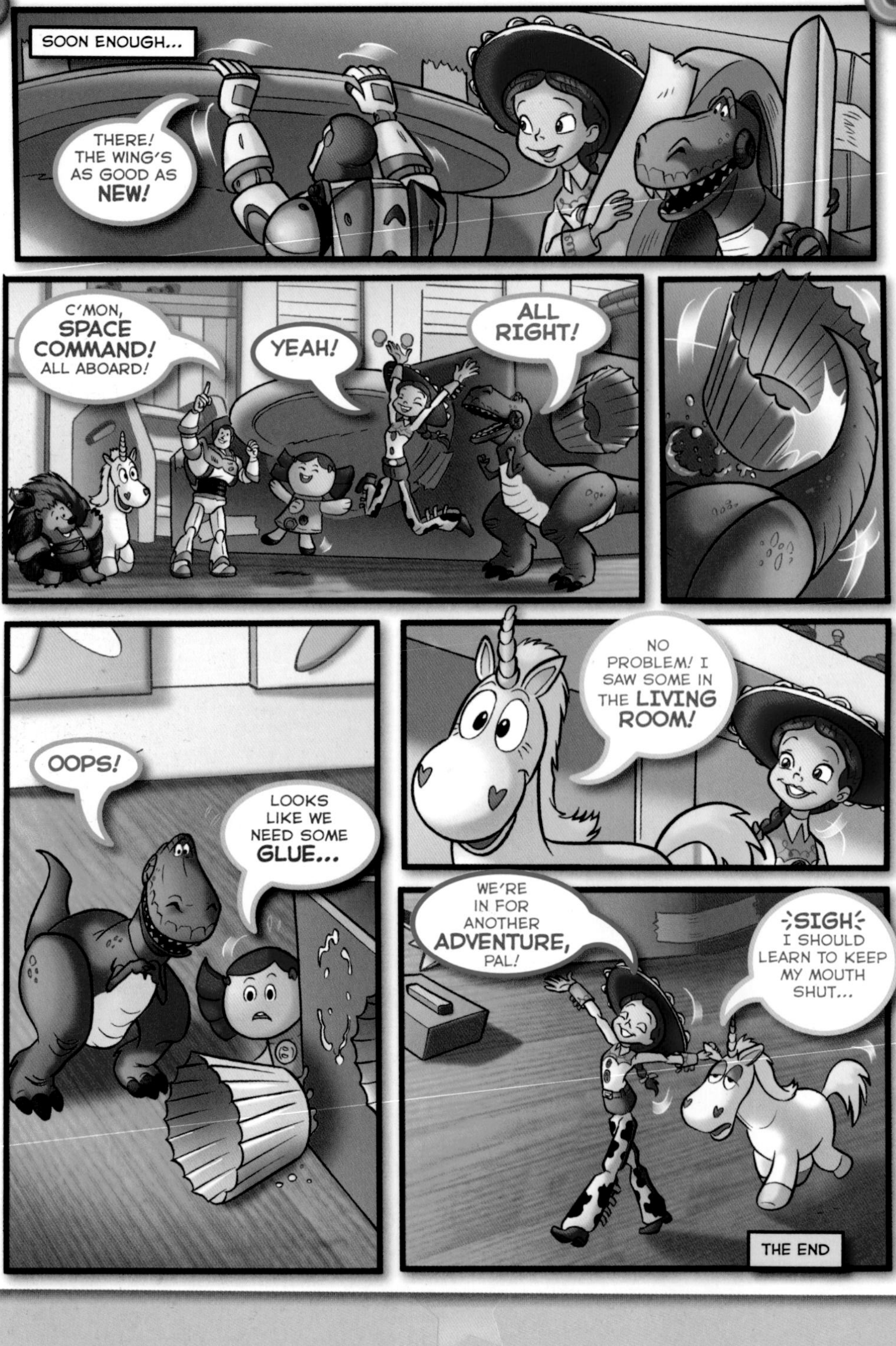
SOON ENOUGH...
THERE! THE WING'S AS GOOD AS NEW!
C'MON, SPACE COMMAND! ALL ABOARD!
YEAH!
ALL RIGHT!
OOPS!
LOOKS LIKE WE NEED SOME GLUE...
NO PROBLEM! I SAW SOME IN THE LIVING ROOM!
WE'RE IN FOR ANOTHER ADVENTURE, PAL!
SIGH I SHOULD LEARN TO KEEP MY MOUTH SHUT...
THE END

SHAMPOO TIME

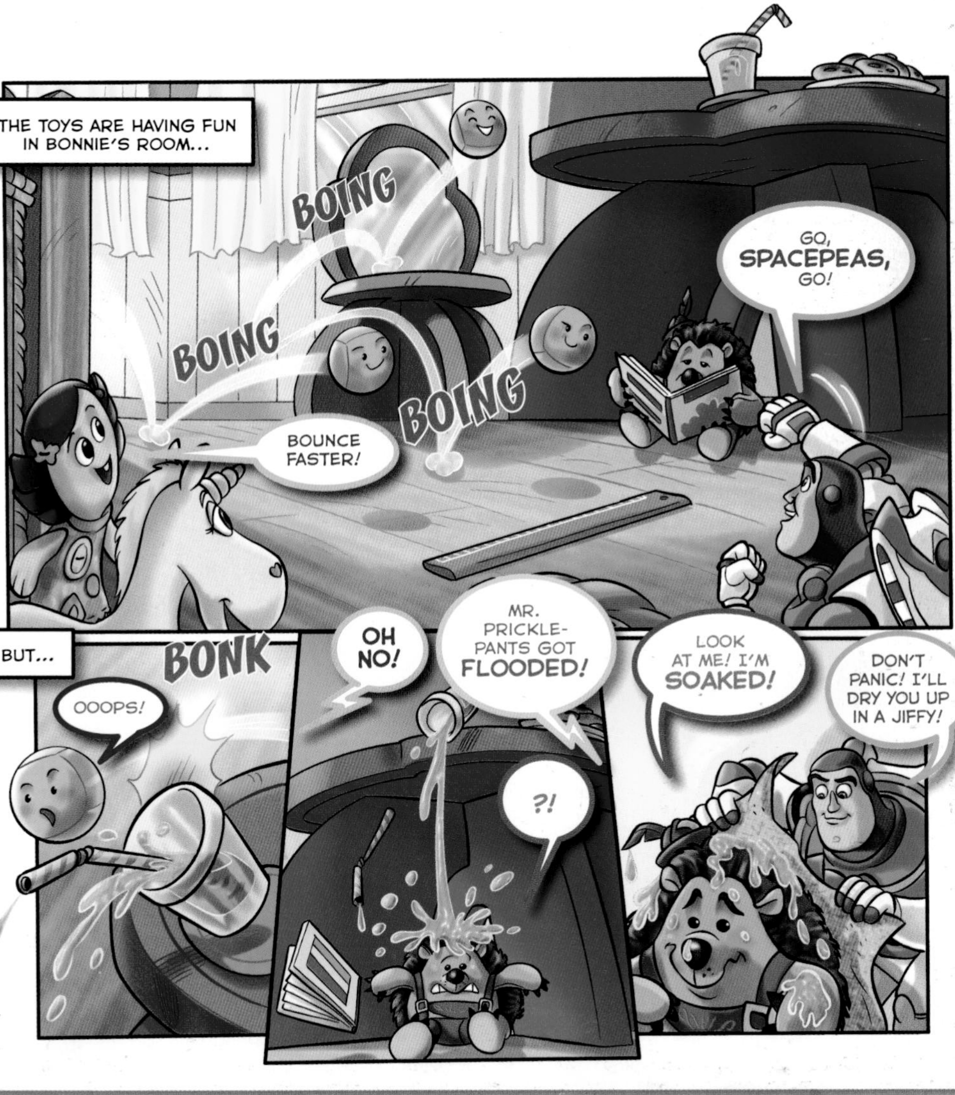

THE TOYS ARE HAVING FUN IN BONNIE'S ROOM...
BOING
BOING
BOING
GO, SPACEPEAS, GO!
BOUNCE FASTER!
BUT...
BONK
OOOPS!
OH NO!
MR. PRICKLEPANTS GOT FLOODED!
?!
LOOK AT ME! I'M SOAKED!
DON'T PANIC! I'LL DRY YOU UP IN A JIFFY!

SCRIPT: TEA ORSI; LAYOUT & INK: LUCA USAI & MICHELA FRARE; COLOUR: LUCIO DE GIUSEPPE

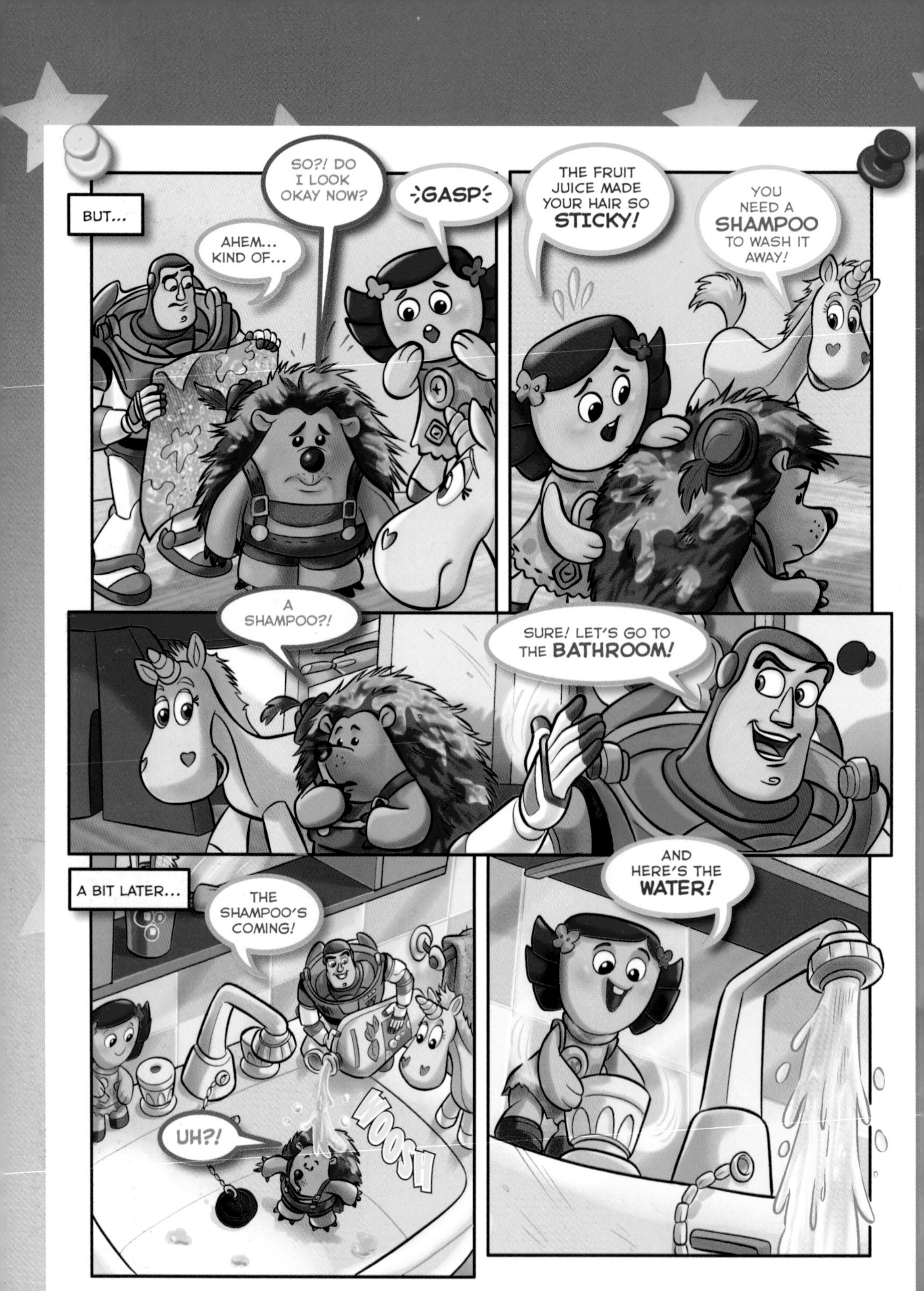
BUT...
SO?! DO I LOOK OKAY NOW?
AHEM... KIND OF...
GASP
THE FRUIT JUICE MADE YOUR HAIR SO STICKY!
YOU NEED A SHAMPOO TO WASH IT AWAY!
A SHAMPOO?!
SURE! LET'S GO TO THE BATHROOM!
A BIT LATER...
THE SHAMPOO'S COMING!
UH?!
WOOSH
AND HERE'S THE WATER!

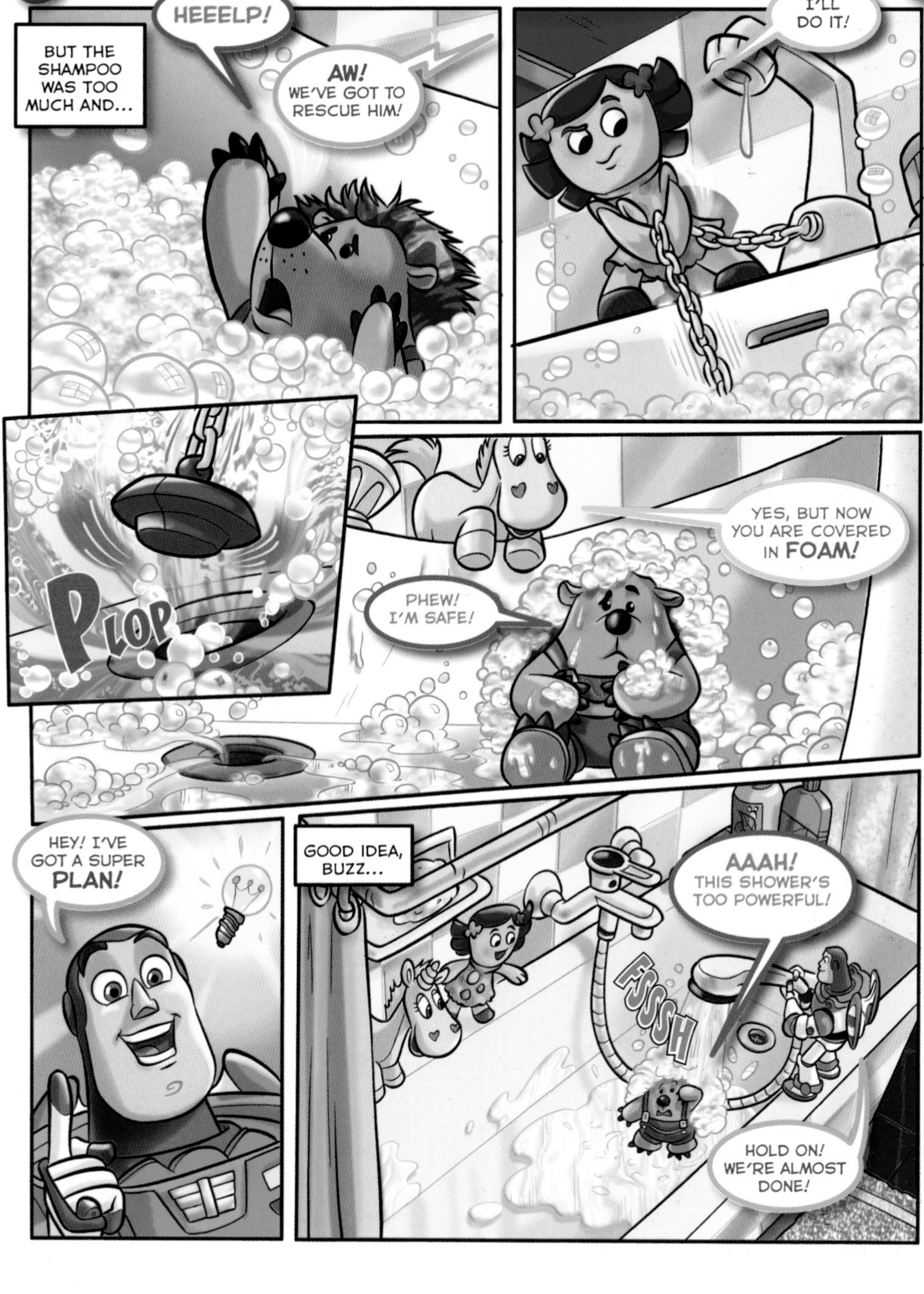
BUT THE SHAMPOO WAS TOO MUCH AND...
HEEELP!
AW! WE'VE GOT TO RESCUE HIM!
I'LL DO IT!
PLOP
YES, BUT NOW YOU ARE COVERED IN FOAM!
PHEW! I'M SAFE!
HEY! I'VE GOT A SUPER PLAN!
GOOD IDEA, BUZZ...
AAAH! THIS SHOWER'S TOO POWERFUL!
FSSSH
HOLD ON! WE'RE ALMOST DONE!

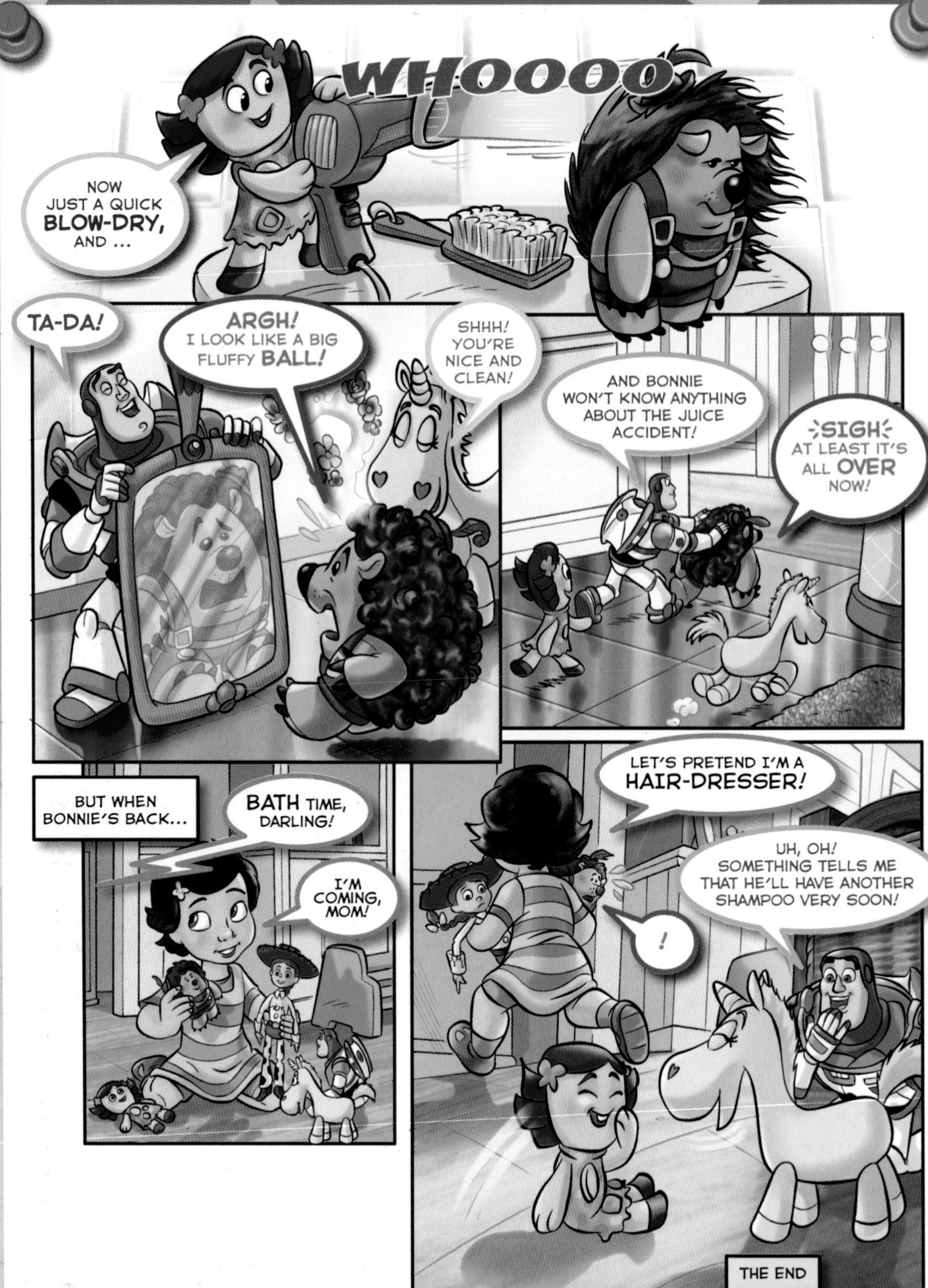
WHOOOO
NOW JUST A QUICK BLOW-DRY, AND ...
TA-DA!
ARGH! I LOOK LIKE A BIG FLUFFY BALL!
SHHH! YOU'RE NICE AND CLEAN!
AND BONNIE WON'T KNOW ANYTHING ABOUT THE JUICE ACCIDENT!
SIGH AT LEAST IT'S ALL OVER NOW!
BUT WHEN BONNIE'S BACK...
BATH TIME, DARLING!
I'M COMING, MOM!
LET'S PRETEND I'M A HAIR-DRESSER!
UH, OH! SOMETHING TELLS ME THAT HE'LL HAVE ANOTHER SHAMPOO VERY SOON!
!
THE END

BATH TIME

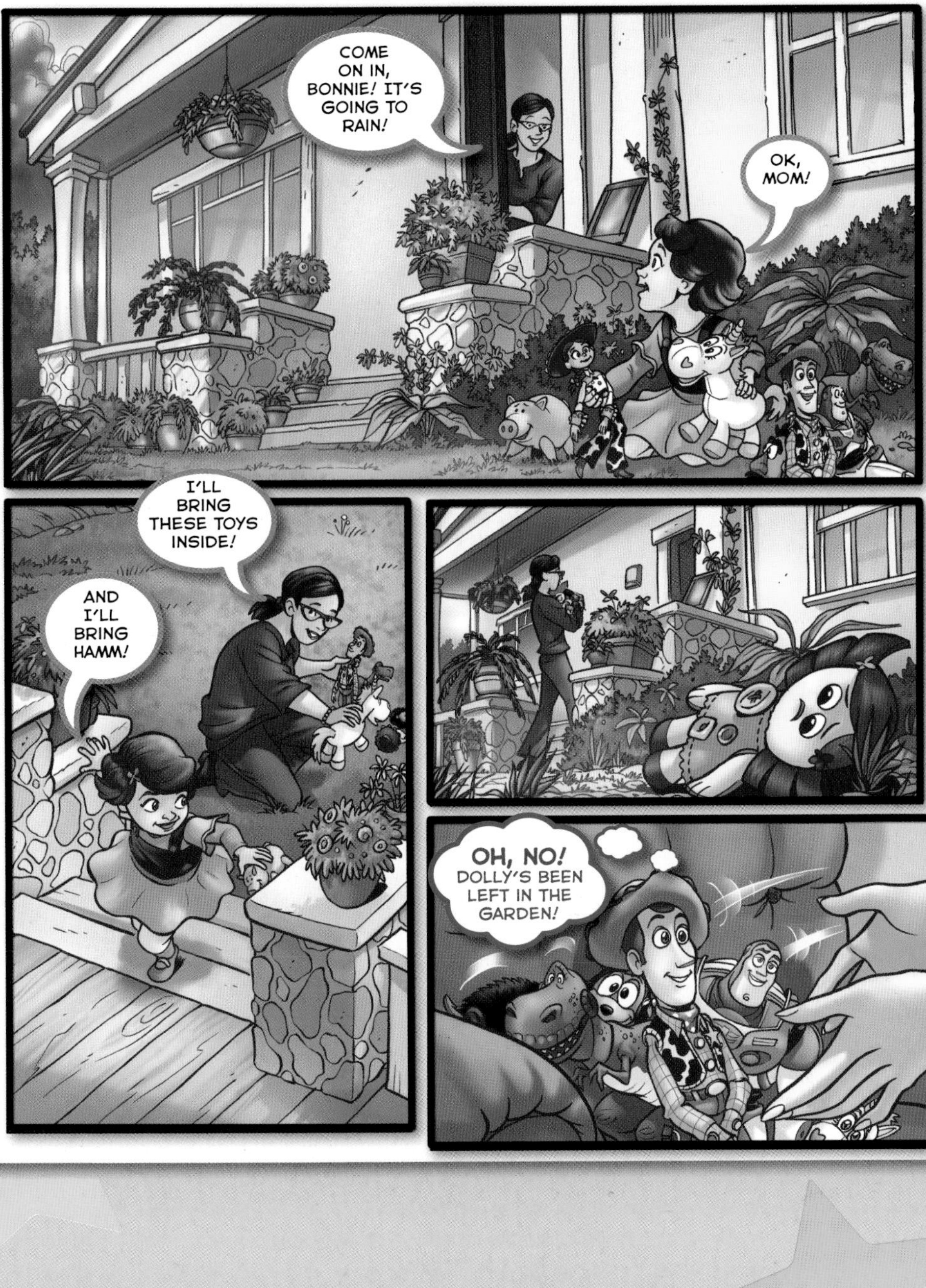
COME ON IN, BONNIE! IT'S GOING TO RAIN!
OK, MOM!
I'LL BRING THESE TOYS INSIDE!
AND I'LL BRING HAMM!
OH, NO! DOLLY'S BEEN LEFT IN THE GARDEN!

SCRIPT: ALESSANDRO SISTI; PENCILS & INK: VALENTINO FORLINI; COLOUR: KAWAII CREATIVE STUDIO

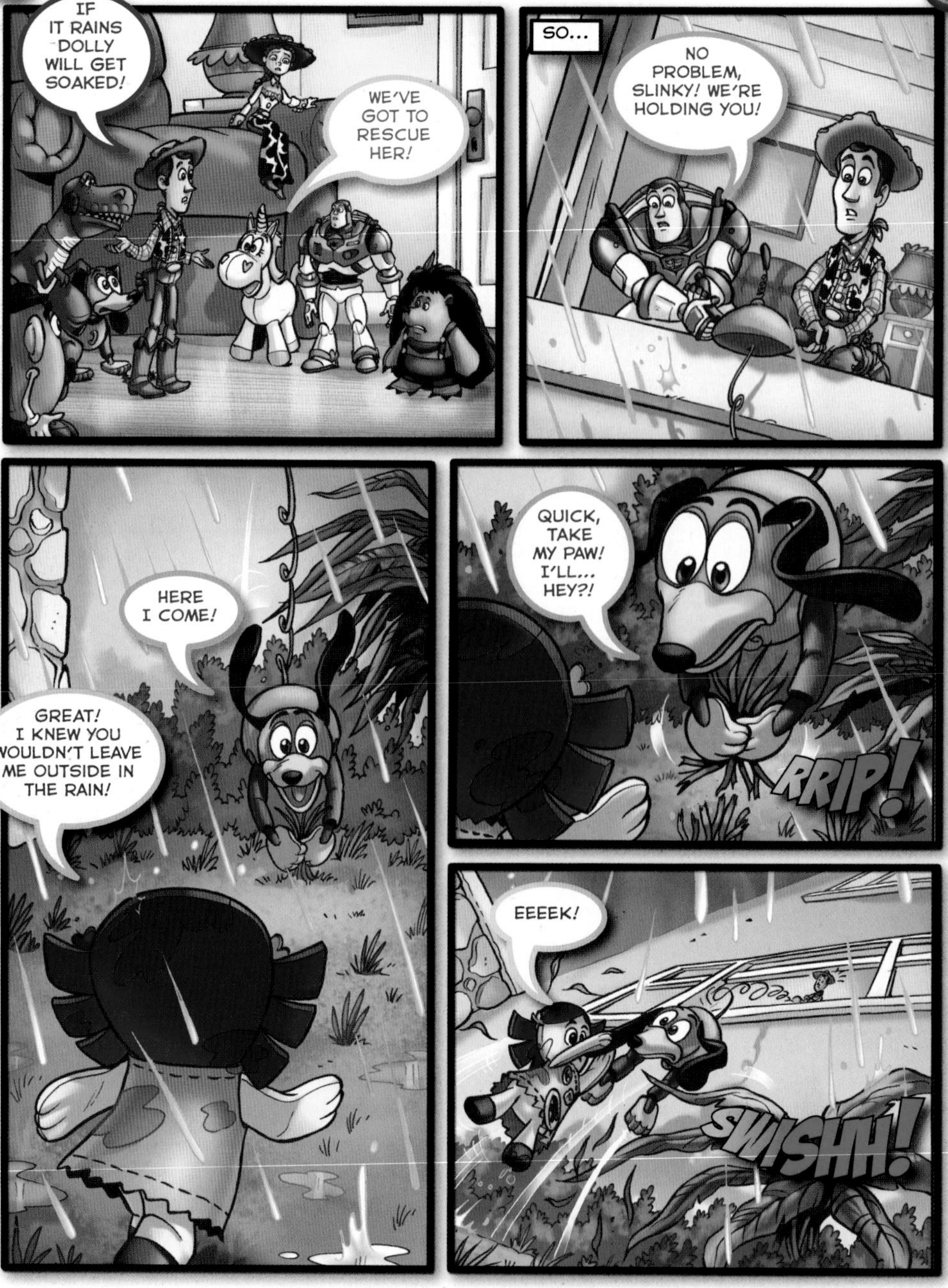
IF IT RAINS DOLLY WILL GET SOAKED!
WE'VE GOT TO RESCUE HER!
SO...
NO PROBLEM, SLINKY! WE'RE HOLDING YOU!
HERE I COME!
GREAT! I KNEW YOU WOULDN'T LEAVE ME OUTSIDE IN THE RAIN!
QUICK, TAKE MY PAW! I'LL... HEY?!
RRIP!
EEEEK!
SWISHH!

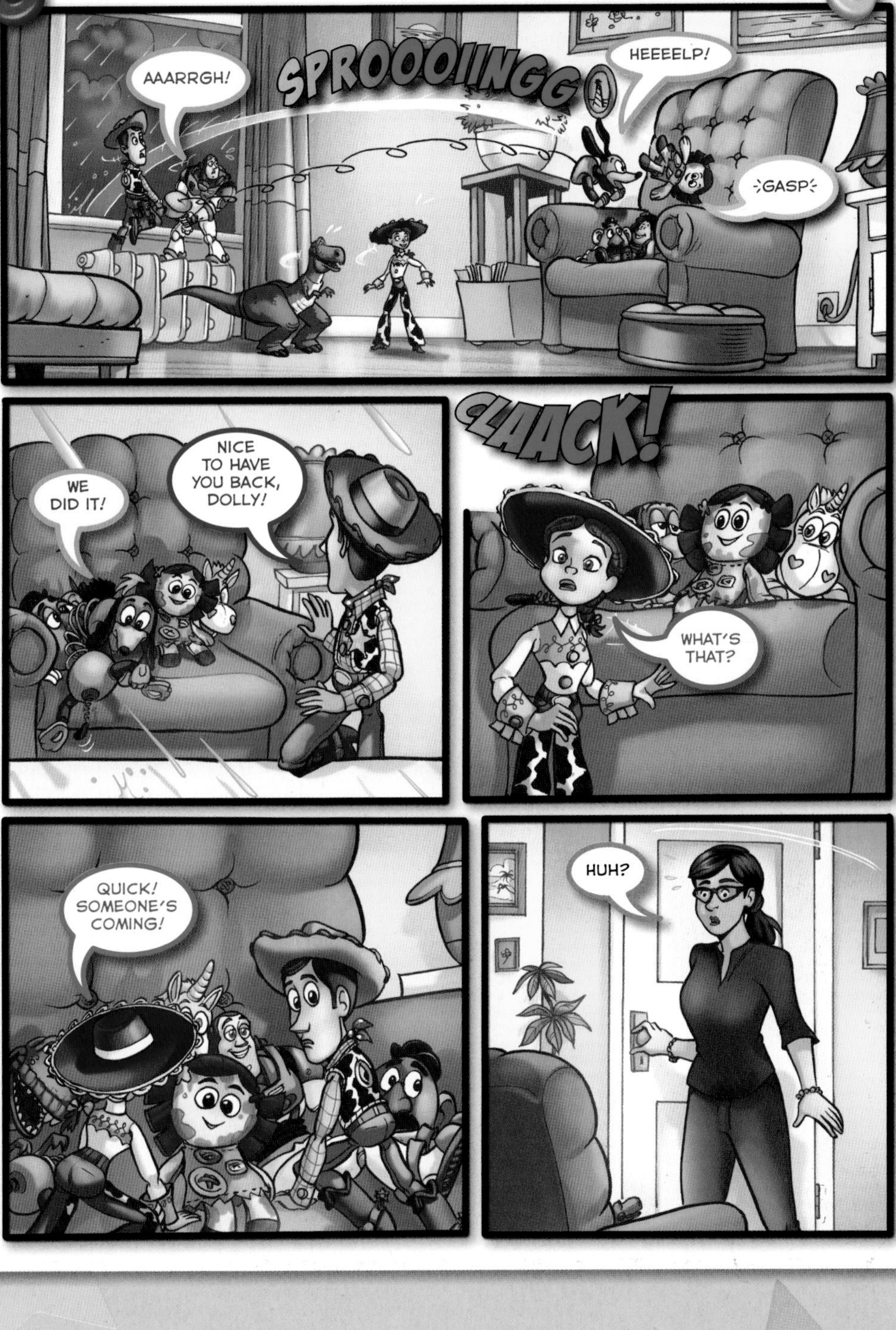
AAARRGH!
SPROOOIINGG
HEEEELP!
GASP
WE DID IT!
NICE TO HAVE YOU BACK, DOLLY!
CLAACK!
WHAT'S THAT?
QUICK! SOMEONE'S COMING!
HUH?

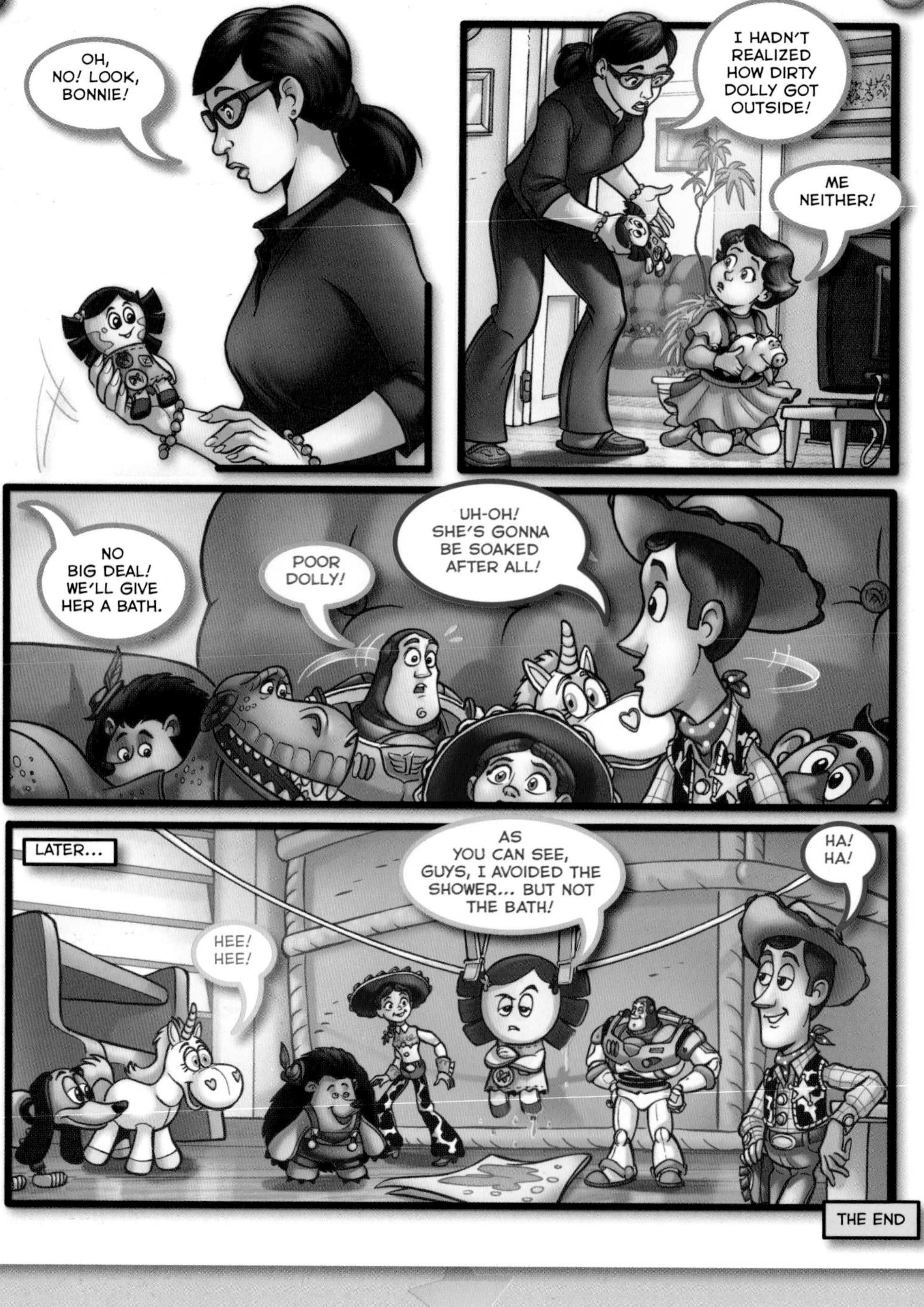
OH, NO! LOOK, BONNIE!
I HADN'T REALIZED HOW DIRTY DOLLY GOT OUTSIDE!
ME NEITHER!
NO BIG DEAL! WE'LL GIVE HER A BATH.
POOR DOLLY!
UH-OH! SHE'S GONNA BE SOAKED AFTER ALL!
LATER...
HEE! HEE!
AS YOU CAN SEE, GUYS, I AVOIDED THE SHOWER... BUT NOT THE BATH!
HA! HA!
THE END

BONNIE'S SPA

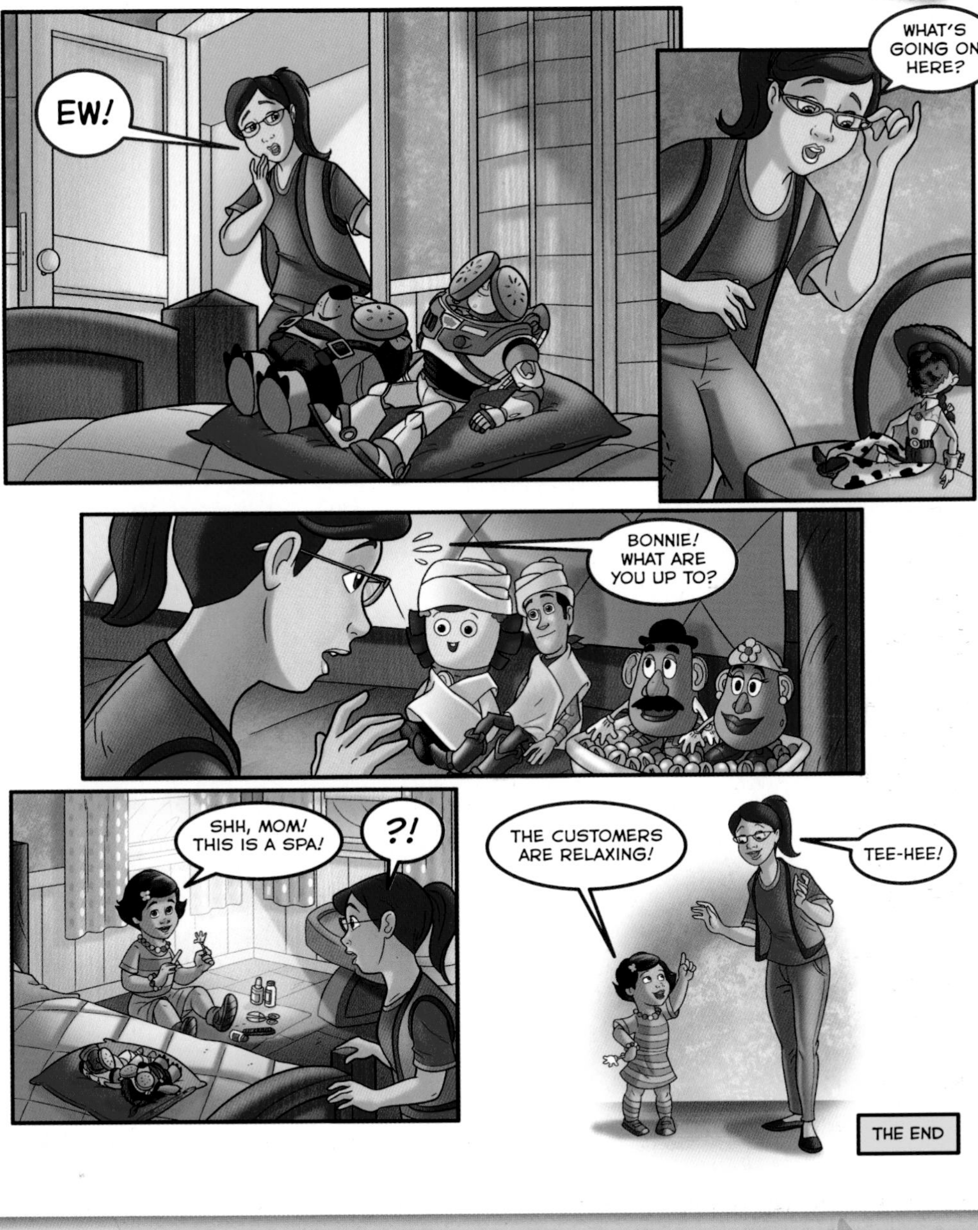
EW!
WHAT'S GOING ON HERE?
BONNIE! WHAT ARE YOU UP TO?
SHH, MOM! THIS IS A SPA!
?!
THE CUSTOMERS ARE RELAXING!
TEE-HEE!
THE END

SCRIPT: TEA ORSI, PENCILS: LUCA USAI, INK: MICHELA FRARE, COLOR: ANGELA CAPOLUPO

A DANGEROUS MISSION

TOY STORY 3

COLOUR: LUCIO DE GIUSEPPE

A DANGEROUS MISSION TO ACCOMPLISH FOR BONNIE'S TOYS... WHO WILL BE BRAVE ENOUGH?

C'MON, GUYS! IT'S IMPORTANT!

S-SORRY, DOLLY... I'M TOO AFRAID!

DON'T LOOK AT ME! I DON'T HAVE ENOUGH SPARE PARTS!

IT'S MORE DANGEROUS THAN A TRIP TO THE DAYCARE!

IT'S A MISSION FOR BUZZ LIGHTYEAR! I'LL HANDLE THIS, DOLLY!

THANK YOU, BUZZ!

SCRIPT: ALESSANDRO FERRARI; LAYOUT: LUCA USAI; INK: MICHELA FRARE;

NO MISSION IS TOO DANGEROUS FOR A RANGER!

AND THERE GOES OUR SPACE FRIEND...

TOO BAD... I LIKED HIM!

A FEW MINUTES LATER...

BE STILL, BUZZ! IT'S MY NEW DRESS YOU'RE MODELING FOR!

MAYBE I WAS WRONG! THIS MISSION IS TOO MUCH FOR ME!

THE END

118

RESCUE MISSION

SCRIPT: ALESSANDRO SISTI; PENCILS & INK: LUCA USAI; COLOUR: DARIO CALABRIA

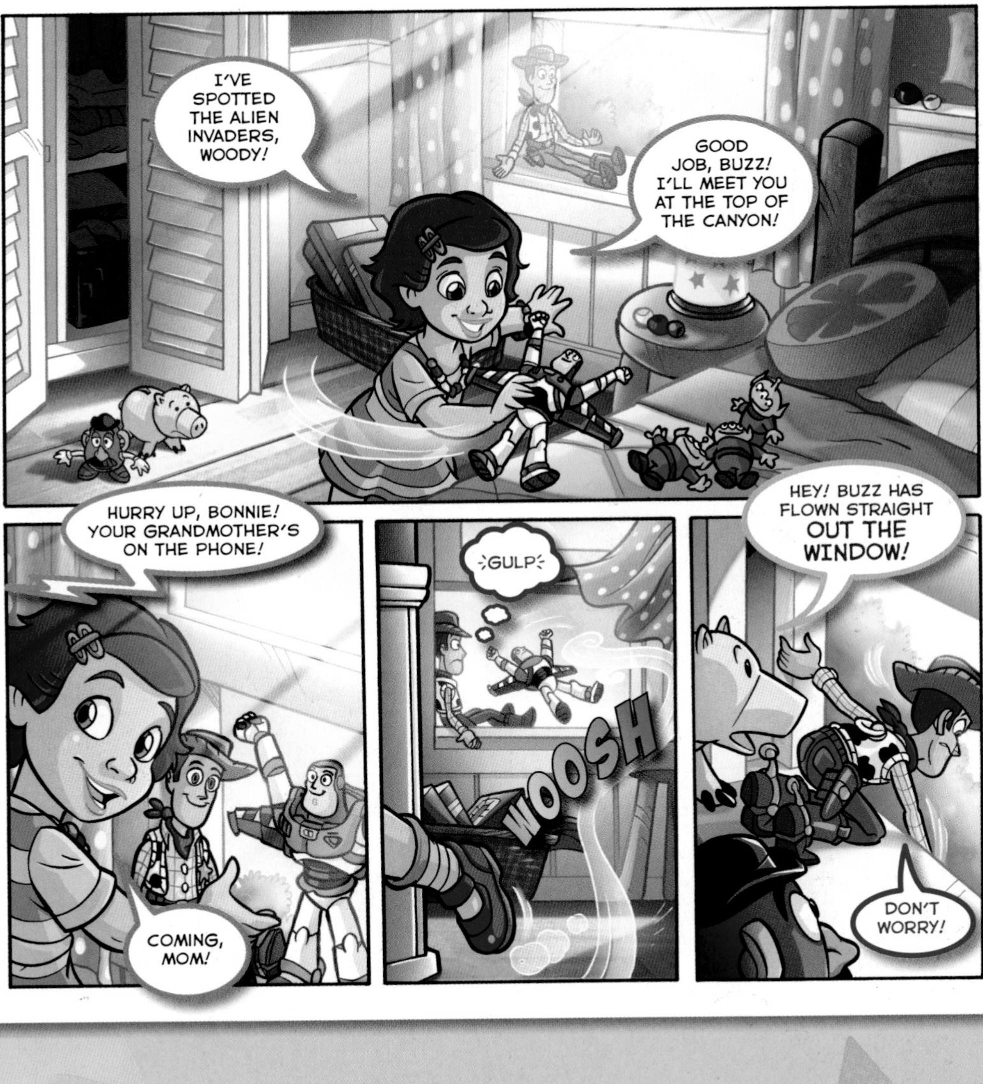

I'VE SPOTTED THE ALIEN INVADERS, WOODY!
GOOD JOB, BUZZ! I'LL MEET YOU AT THE TOP OF THE CANYON!
HURRY UP, BONNIE! YOUR GRANDMOTHER'S ON THE PHONE!
COMING, MOM!
GULP
WOOSH
HEY! BUZZ HAS FLOWN STRAIGHT OUT THE WINDOW!
DON'T WORRY!

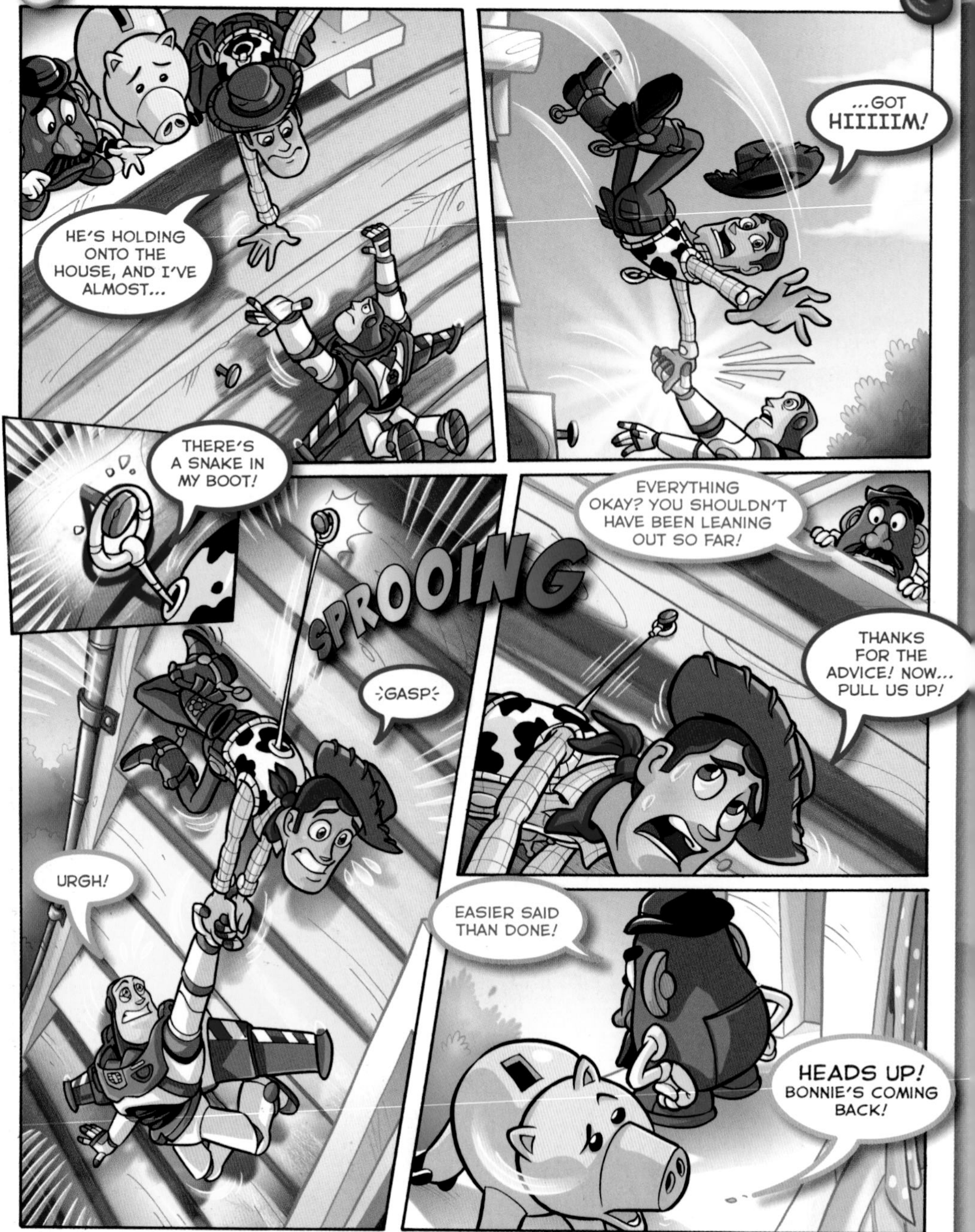
HE'S HOLDING ONTO THE HOUSE, AND I'VE ALMOST...
...GOT HIIIIIM!
THERE'S A SNAKE IN MY BOOT!
SPROOING
GASP
URGH!
EVERYTHING OKAY? YOU SHOULDN'T HAVE BEEN LEANING OUT SO FAR!
THANKS FOR THE ADVICE! NOW... PULL US UP!
EASIER SAID THAN DONE!
HEADS UP! BONNIE'S COMING BACK!

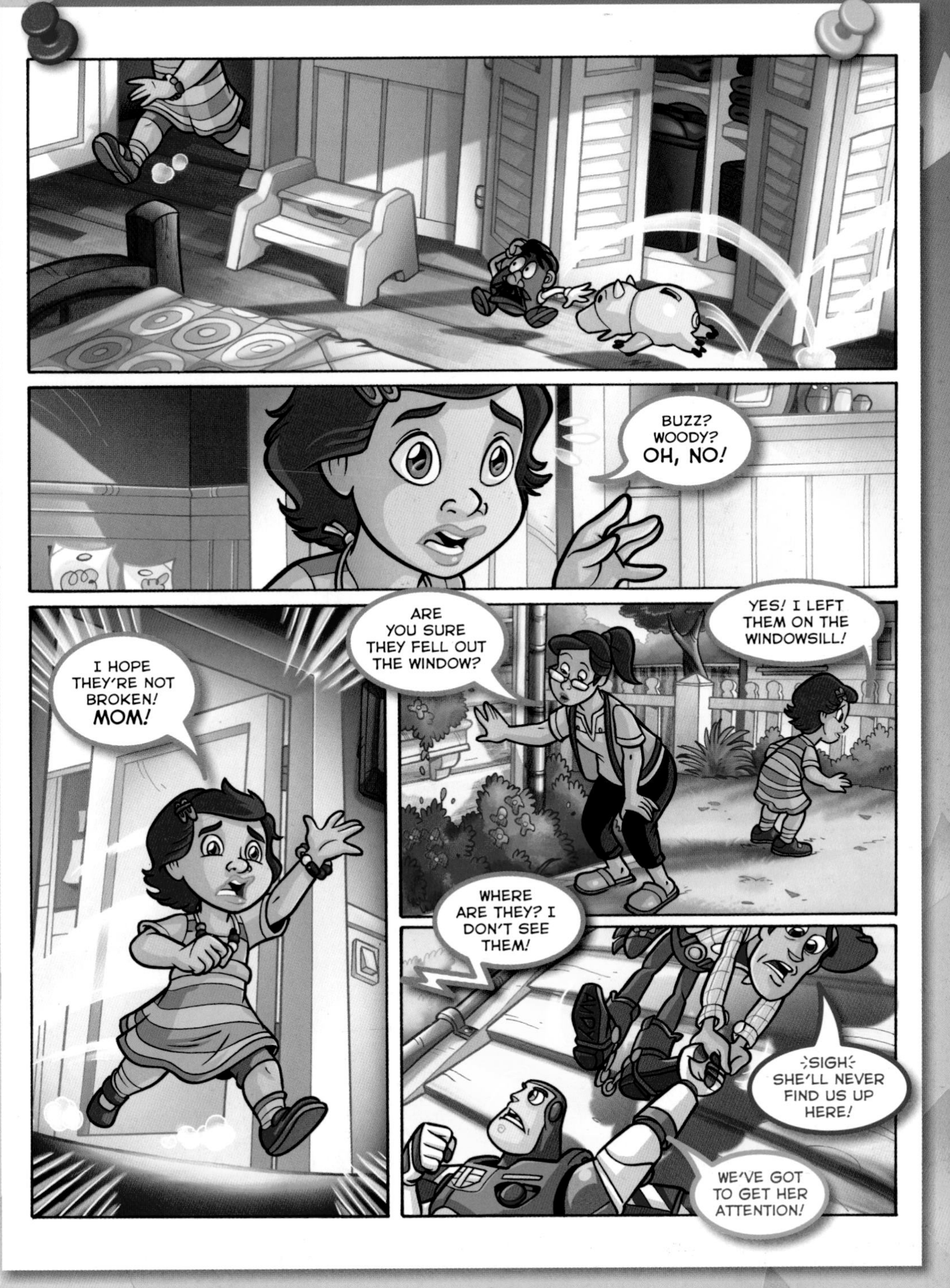
BUZZ? WOODY? OH, NO!
I HOPE THEY'RE NOT BROKEN! MOM!
ARE YOU SURE THEY FELL OUT THE WINDOW?
YES! I LEFT THEM ON THE WINDOWSILL!
WHERE ARE THEY? I DON'T SEE THEM!
SIGH SHE'LL NEVER FIND US UP HERE!
WE'VE GOT TO GET HER ATTENTION!

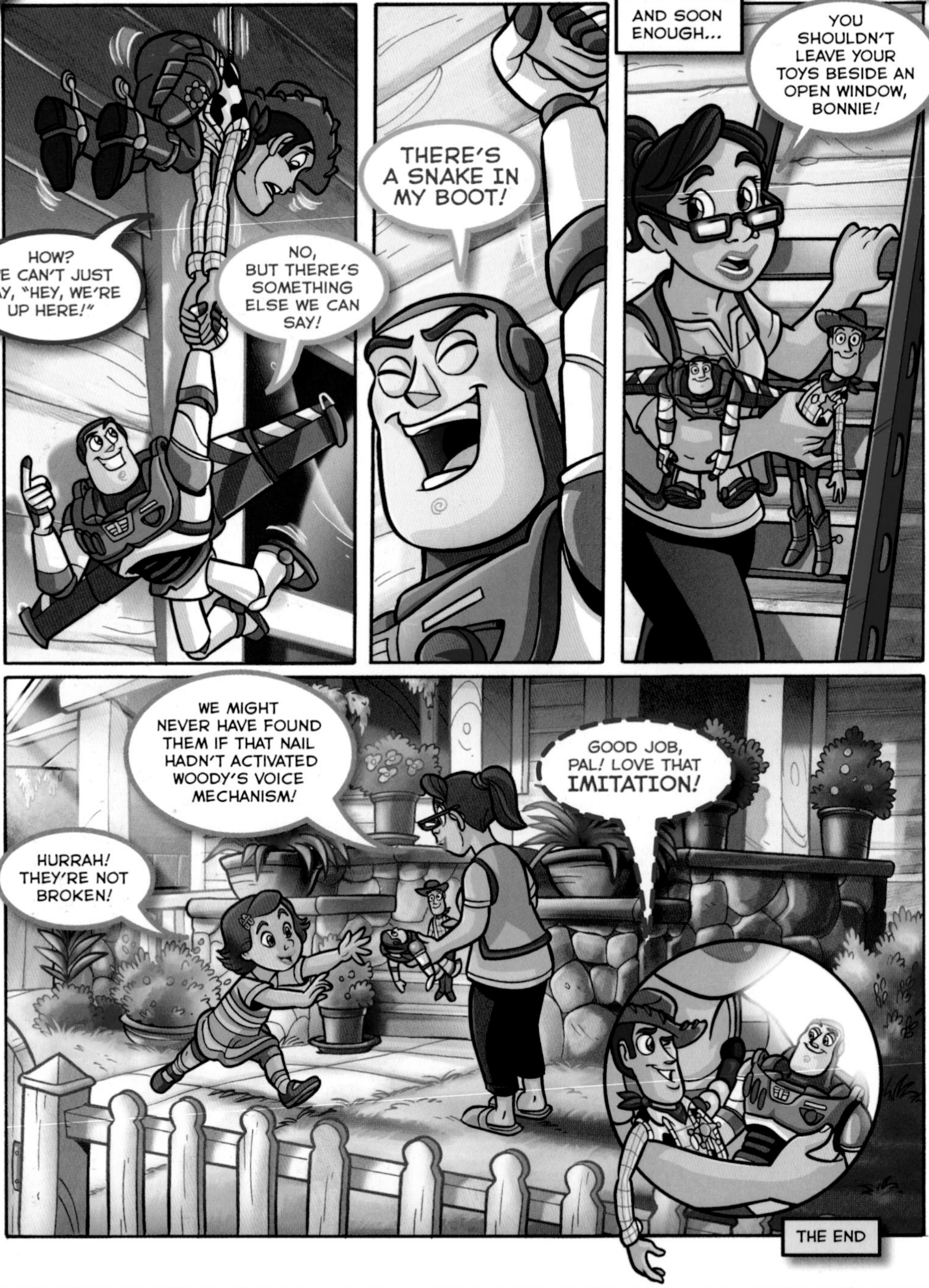
HOW? WE CAN'T JUST SAY, "HEY, WE'RE UP HERE!"
NO, BUT THERE'S SOMETHING ELSE WE CAN SAY!
THERE'S A SNAKE IN MY BOOT!
AND SOON ENOUGH...
YOU SHOULDN'T LEAVE YOUR TOYS BESIDE AN OPEN WINDOW, BONNIE!
WE MIGHT NEVER HAVE FOUND THEM IF THAT NAIL HADN'T ACTIVATED WOODY'S VOICE MECHANISM!
HURRAH! THEY'RE NOT BROKEN!
GOOD JOB, PAL! LOVE THAT IMITATION!
THE END

SUPERMARKET ADVENTURE

SCRIPT: ALESSANDRO SISTI, LAYOUT: LUCA USAI, INK: MICHELA FRARE, COLOUR: ANGELA CAPOLUPO

DON'T WORRY, DOLLY! I'M COMING TO YOUR RESCUE!

LET ME OUT, SHERIFF!

I HAVE TO CUT THE BARS!

CHOOSE YOUR BREAKFAST CEREAL, BONNIE!

YES, MOM!

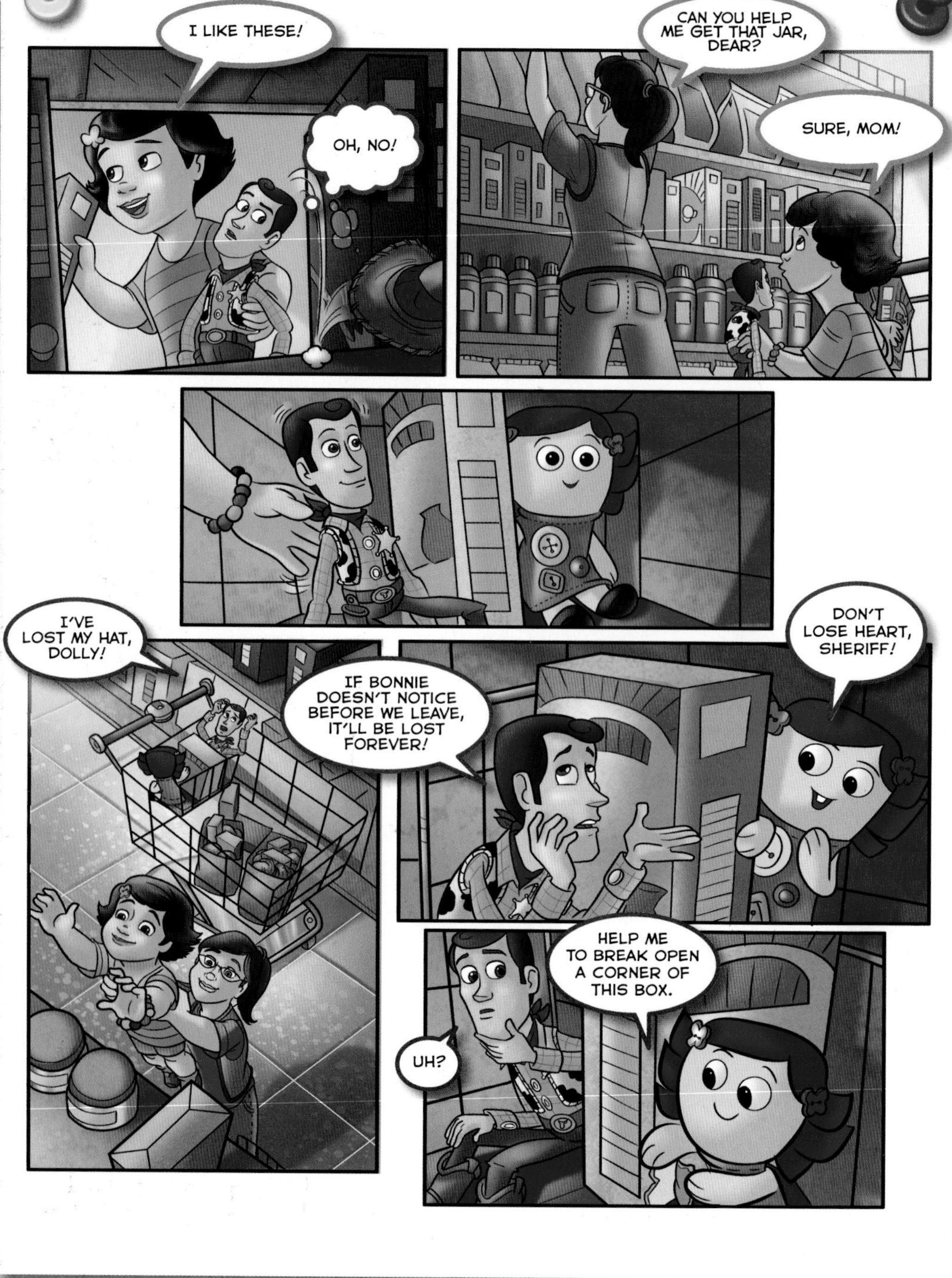
I LIKE THESE!
OH, NO!
CAN YOU HELP ME GET THAT JAR, DEAR?
SURE, MOM!
I'VE LOST MY HAT, DOLLY!
IF BONNIE DOESN'T NOTICE BEFORE WE LEAVE, IT'LL BE LOST FOREVER!
DON'T LOSE HEART, SHERIFF!
HELP ME TO BREAK OPEN A CORNER OF THIS BOX.
UH?

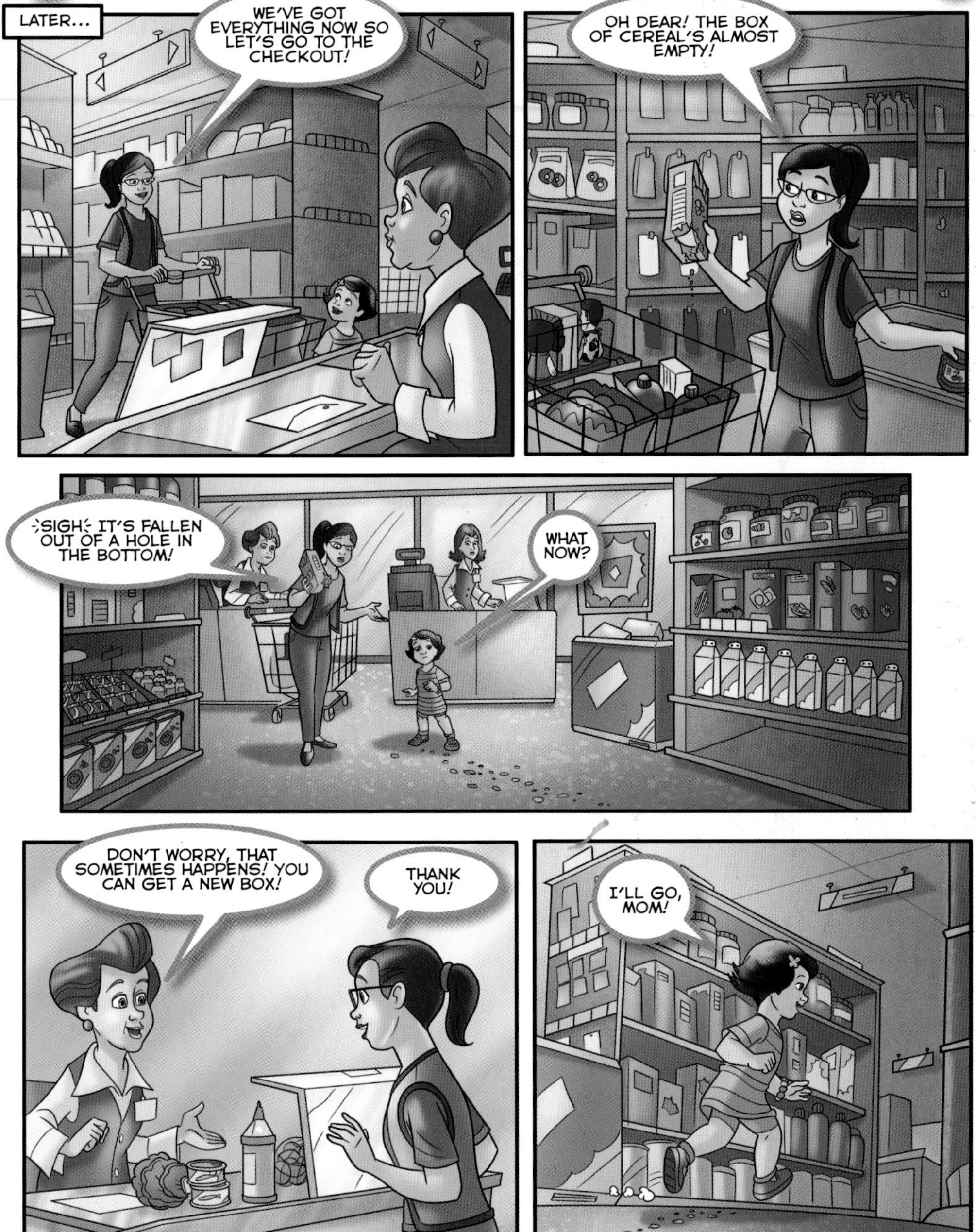
LATER...
WE'VE GOT EVERYTHING NOW SO LET'S GO TO THE CHECKOUT!
OH DEAR! THE BOX OF CEREAL'S ALMOST EMPTY!
SIGH IT'S FALLEN OUT OF A HOLE IN THE BOTTOM!
WHAT NOW?
DON'T WORRY, THAT SOMETIMES HAPPENS! YOU CAN GET A NEW BOX!
THANK YOU!
I'LL GO, MOM!

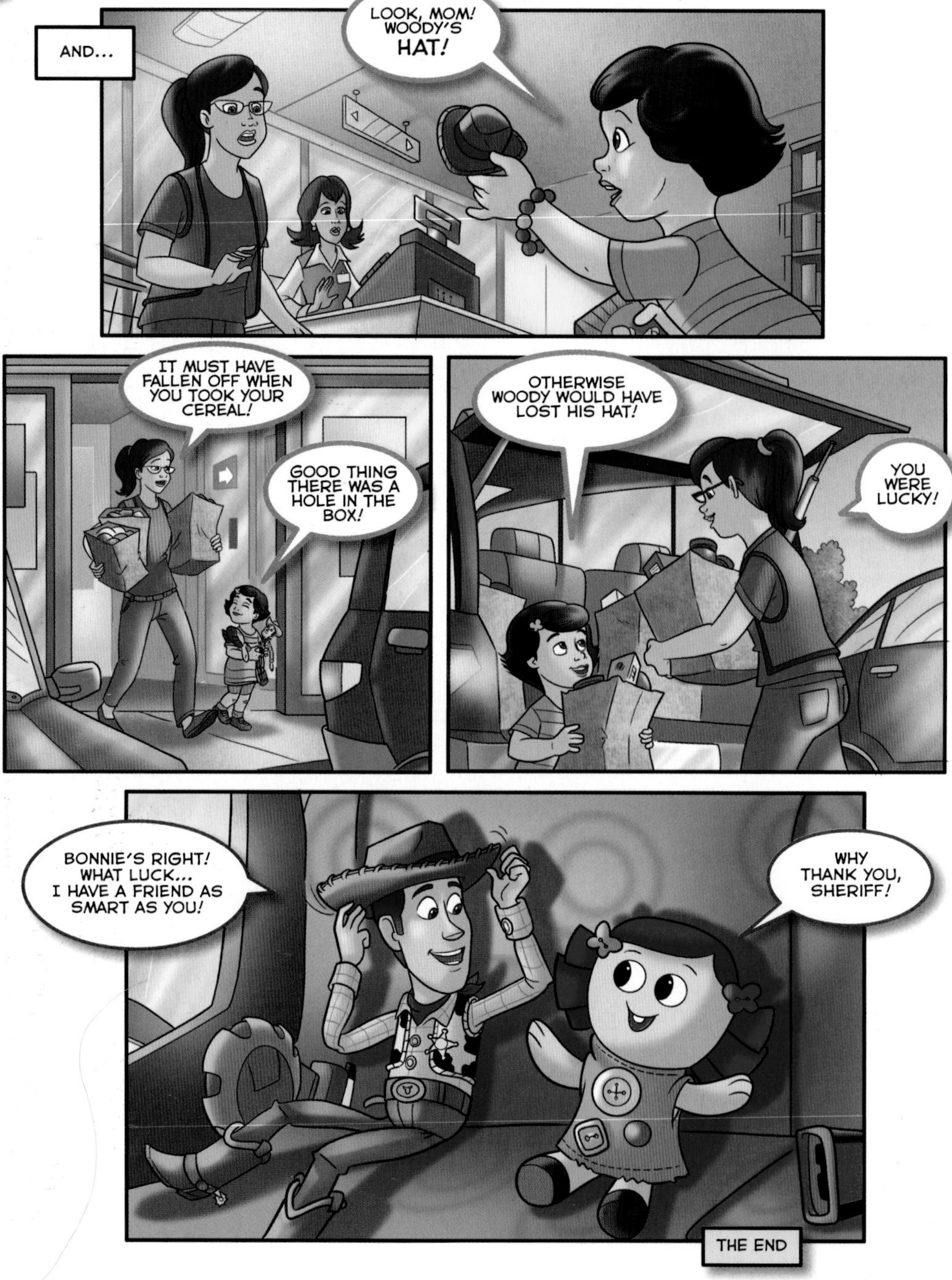
AND...
LOOK, MOM! WOODY'S HAT!
IT MUST HAVE FALLEN OFF WHEN YOU TOOK YOUR CEREAL!
GOOD THING THERE WAS A HOLE IN THE BOX!
OTHERWISE WOODY WOULD HAVE LOST HIS HAT!
YOU WERE LUCKY!
BONNIE'S RIGHT! WHAT LUCK... I HAVE A FRIEND AS SMART AS YOU!
WHY THANK YOU, SHERIFF!
THE END

PARTY-STOPPING PIG

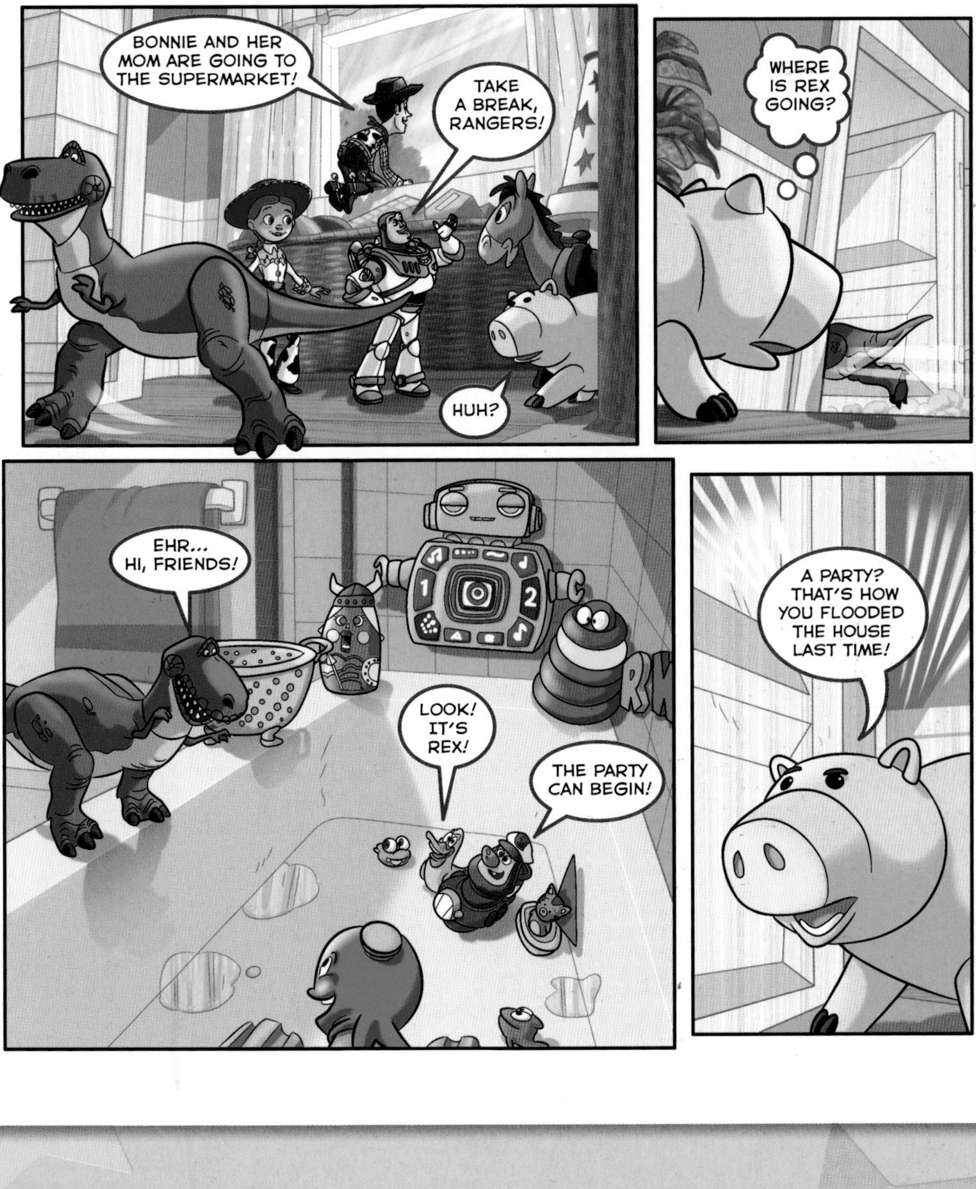

BONNIE AND HER MOM ARE GOING TO THE SUPERMARKET!
TAKE A BREAK, RANGERS!
HUH?
WHERE IS REX GOING?
EHR... HI, FRIENDS!
LOOK! IT'S REX!
THE PARTY CAN BEGIN!
A PARTY? THAT'S HOW YOU FLOODED THE HOUSE LAST TIME!

SCRIPT: ALESSANDRO SISTI, PENCIL: LUCA USAI, INK: MICHELA FRARE, COLOR: LUCIO DE GIUSEPPE

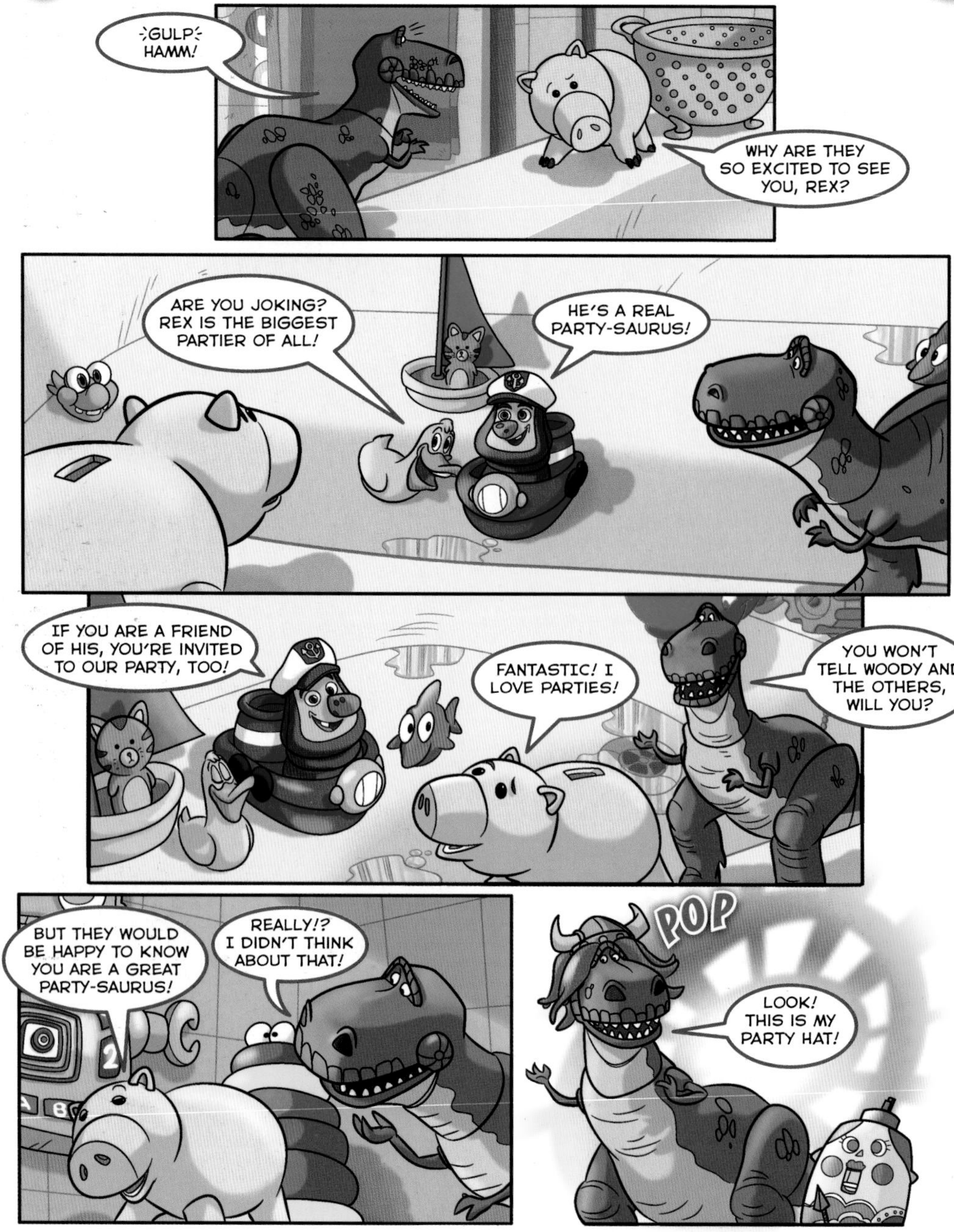
GULP HAMM!
WHY ARE THEY SO EXCITED TO SEE YOU, REX?
ARE YOU JOKING? REX IS THE BIGGEST PARTIER OF ALL!
HE'S A REAL PARTY-SAURUS!
IF YOU ARE A FRIEND OF HIS, YOU'RE INVITED TO OUR PARTY, TOO!
FANTASTIC! I LOVE PARTIES!
YOU WON'T TELL WOODY AND THE OTHERS, WILL YOU?
BUT THEY WOULD BE HAPPY TO KNOW YOU ARE A GREAT PARTY-SAURUS!
REALLY!? I DIDN'T THINK ABOUT THAT!
POP
LOOK! THIS IS MY PARTY HAT!

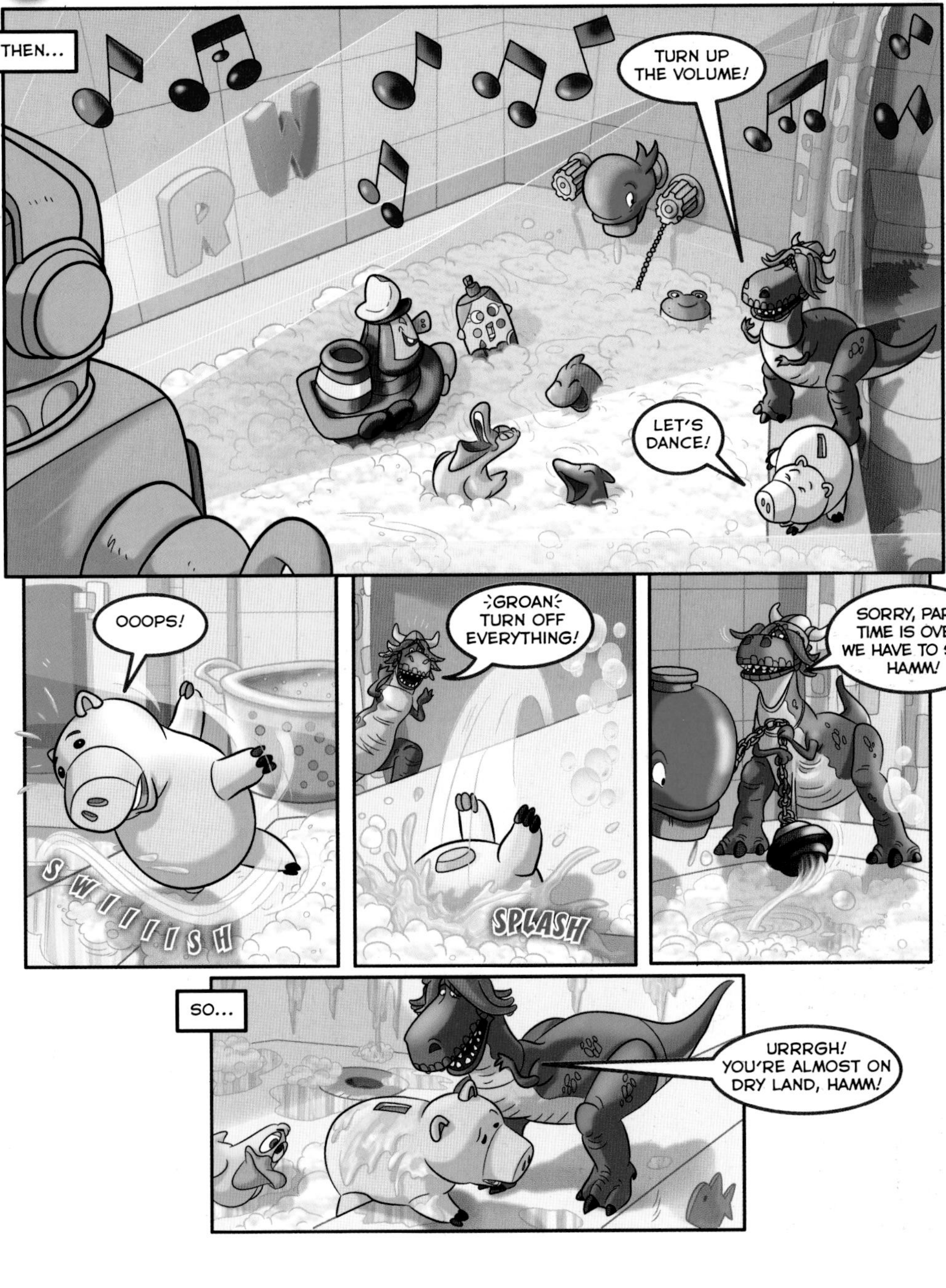
THEN...
TURN UP THE VOLUME!
LET'S DANCE!
OOOPS!
SWIIIISH
GROAN
TURN OFF EVERYTHING!
SPLASH
SORRY, PARTY TIME IS OVER! WE HAVE TO SAVE HAMM!
SO...
URRRGH! YOU'RE ALMOST ON DRY LAND, HAMM!

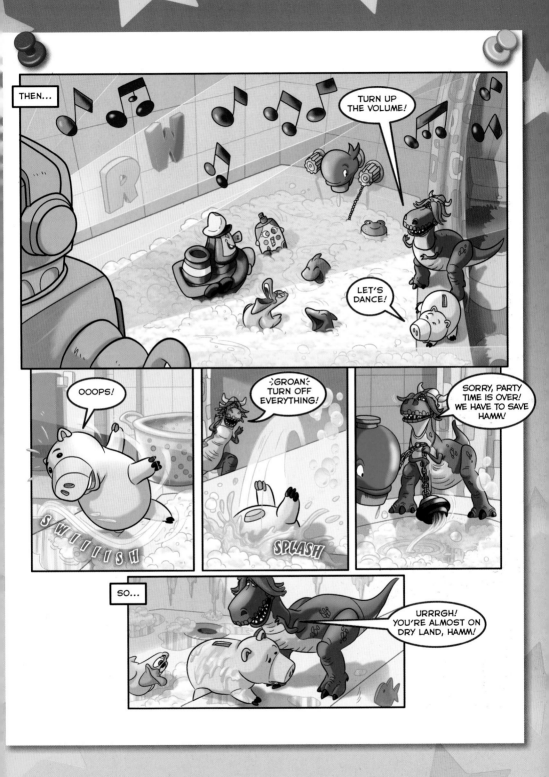

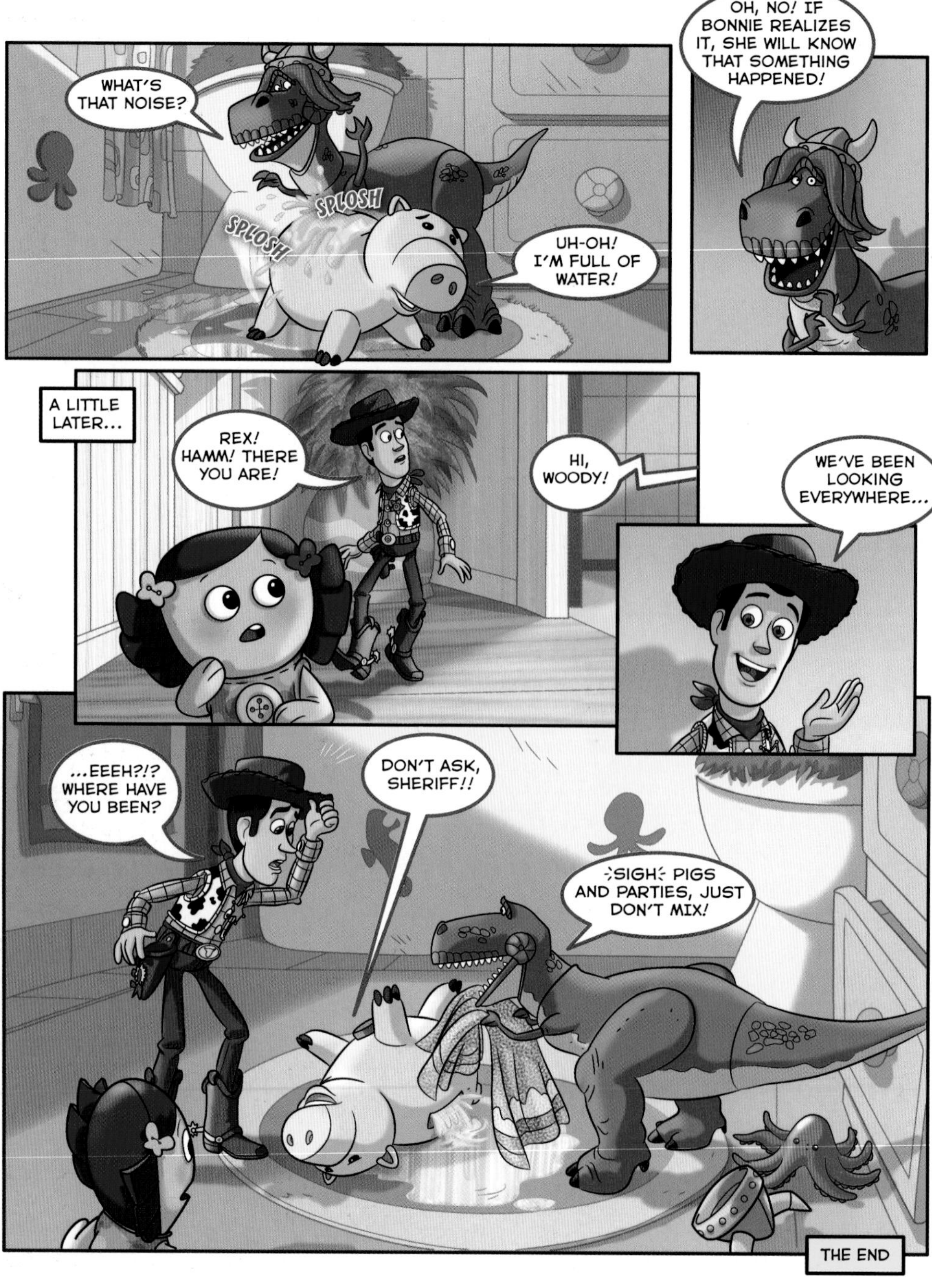
WHAT'S THAT NOISE?
SPLOSH
SPLOSH
UH-OH! I'M FULL OF WATER!
OH, NO! IF BONNIE REALIZES IT, SHE WILL KNOW THAT SOMETHING HAPPENED!
A LITTLE LATER...
REX! HAMM! THERE YOU ARE!
HI, WOODY!
WE'VE BEEN LOOKING EVERYWHERE...
...EEEH?!? WHERE HAVE YOU BEEN?
DON'T ASK, SHERIFF!!
SIGH PIGS AND PARTIES, JUST DON'T MIX!
THE END

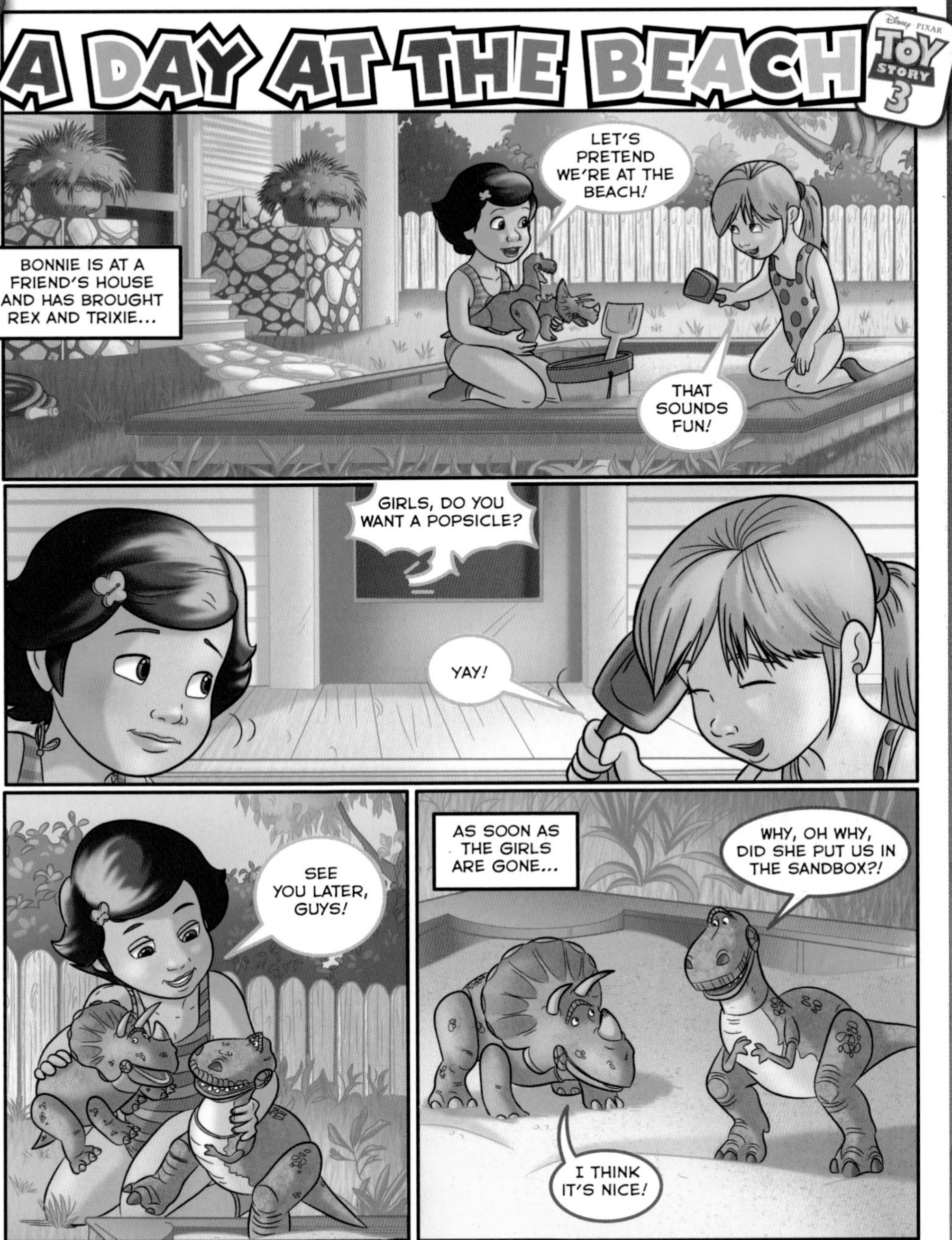
A DAY AT THE BEACH
DISNEY PIXAR TOY STORY 3
BONNIE IS AT A FRIEND'S HOUSE AND HAS BROUGHT REX AND TRIXIE...
LET'S PRETEND WE'RE AT THE BEACH!
THAT SOUNDS FUN!
GIRLS, DO YOU WANT A POPSICLE?
YAY!
SEE YOU LATER, GUYS!
AS SOON AS THE GIRLS ARE GONE...
WHY, OH WHY, DID SHE PUT US IN THE SANDBOX?!
I THINK IT'S NICE!

SCRIPT: TEA ORSI, PENCIL: GIANFRANCO FLORIO, INK: MICHELA FRARE, COLOR: ANGELA CAPOLUPO

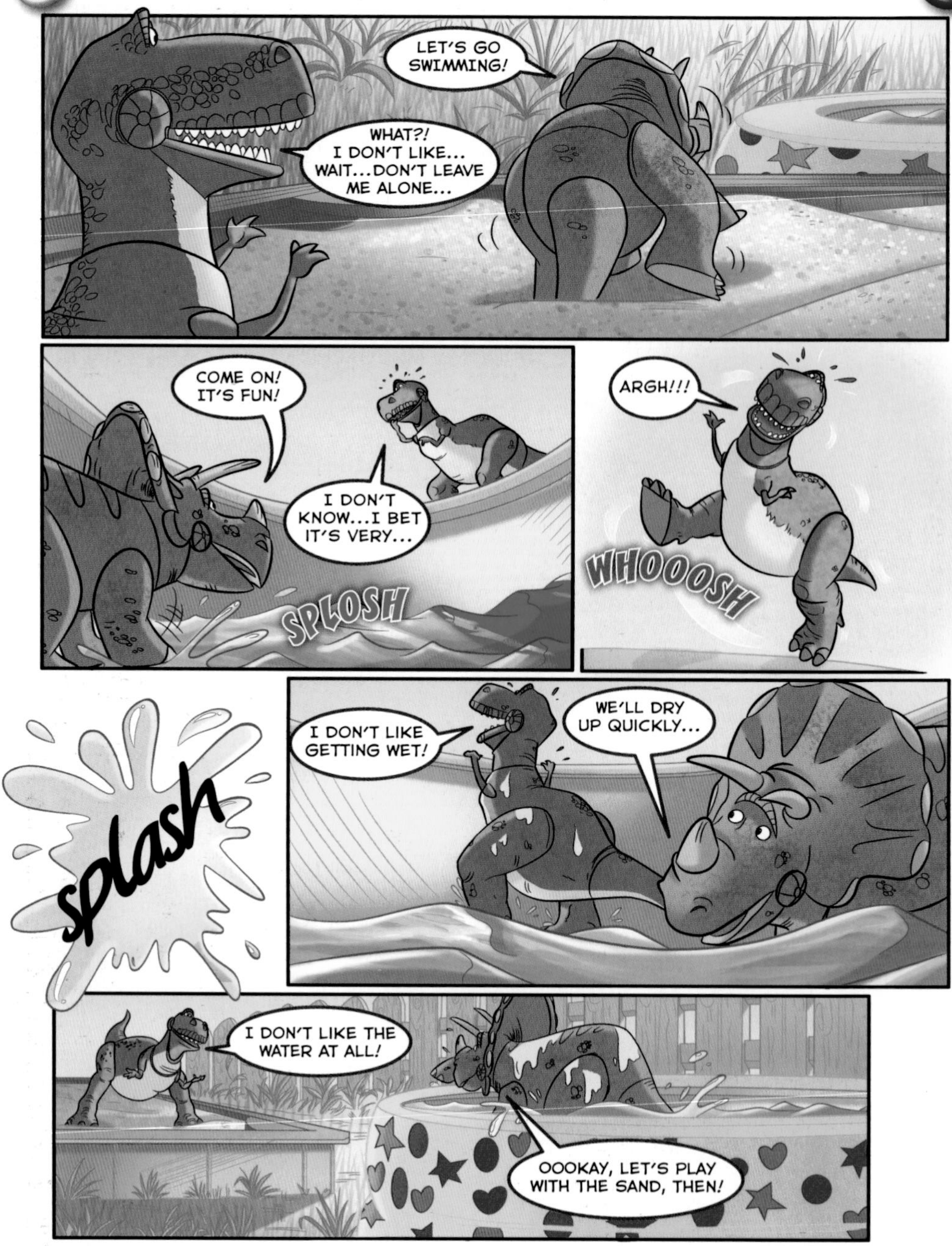
LET'S GO SWIMMING!
WHAT?! I DON'T LIKE... WAIT...DON'T LEAVE ME ALONE...
COME ON! IT'S FUN!
I DON'T KNOW...I BET IT'S VERY...
SPLOSH
ARGH!!!
WHOOOSH
splash
I DON'T LIKE GETTING WET!
WE'LL DRY UP QUICKLY...
I DON'T LIKE THE WATER AT ALL!
OOOKAY, LET'S PLAY WITH THE SAND, THEN!

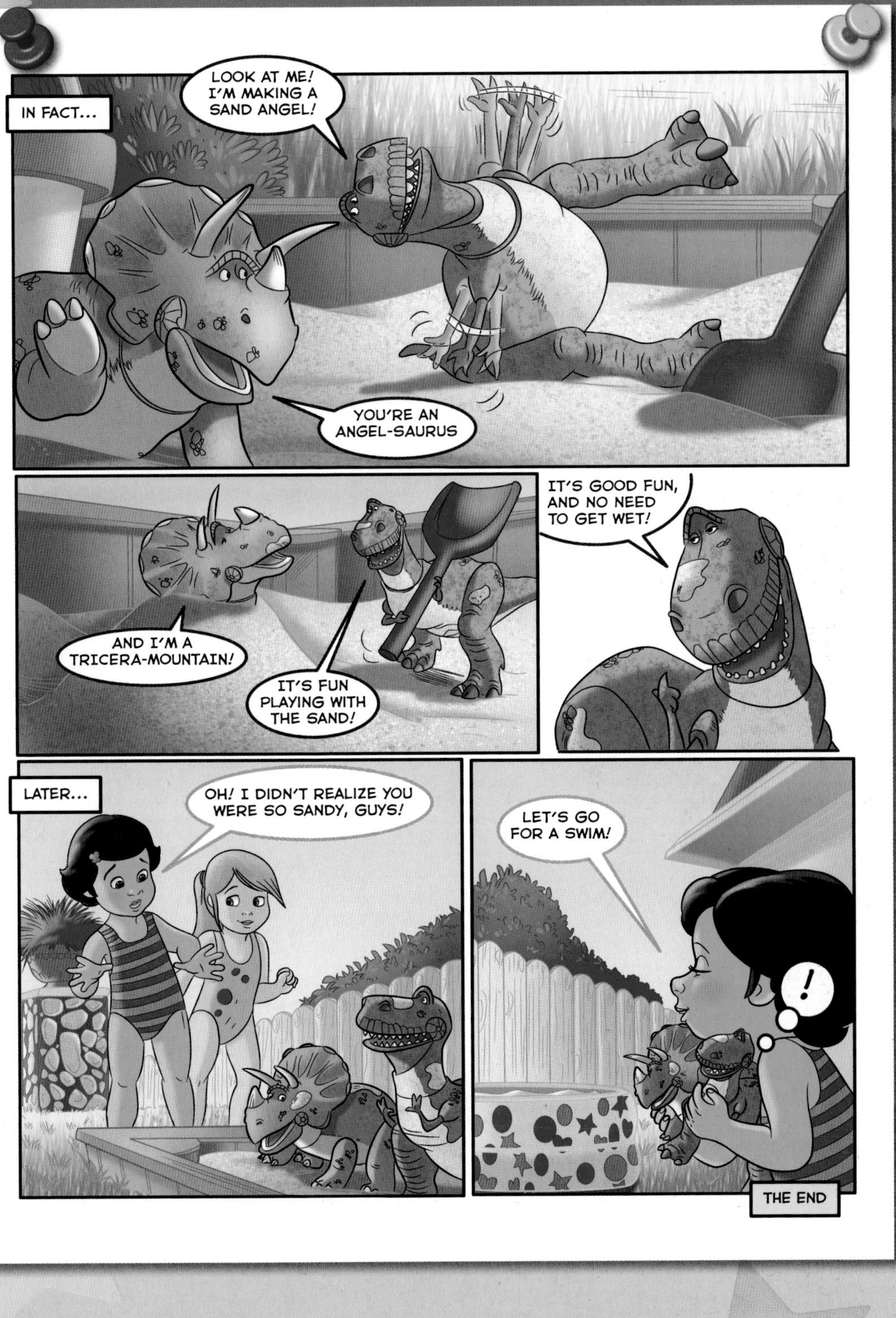
IN FACT...
LOOK AT ME! I'M MAKING A SAND ANGEL!
YOU'RE AN ANGEL-SAURUS
AND I'M A TRICERA-MOUNTAIN!
IT'S FUN PLAYING WITH THE SAND!
IT'S GOOD FUN, AND NO NEED TO GET WET!
LATER...
OH! I DIDN'T REALIZE YOU WERE SO SANDY, GUYS!
LET'S GO FOR A SWIM!
!
THE END

A SLEEPLESS SLEEPOVER

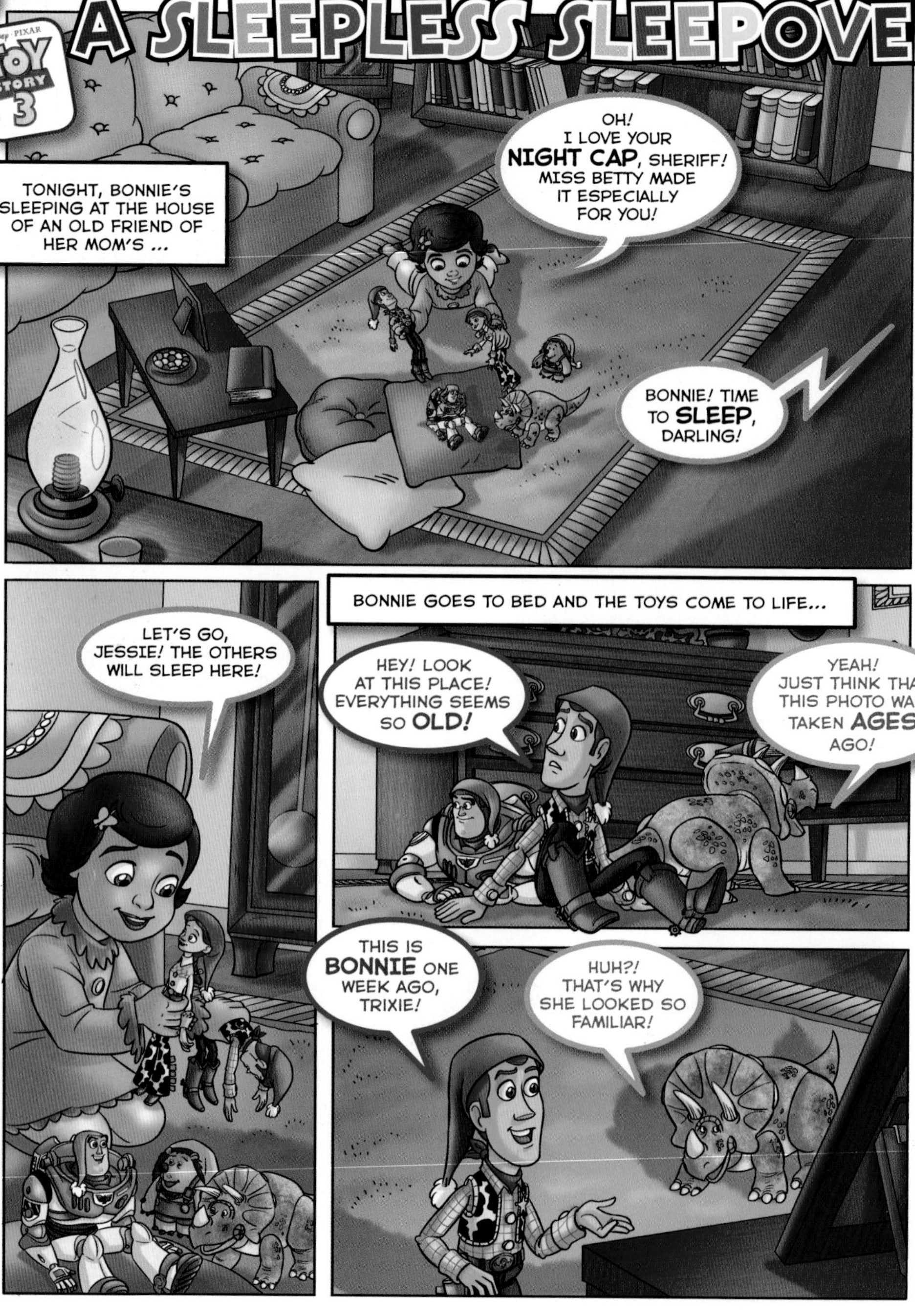

TOY STORY 3
TONIGHT, BONNIE'S SLEEPING AT THE HOUSE OF AN OLD FRIEND OF HER MOM'S ...
OH! I LOVE YOUR NIGHT CAP, SHERIFF! MISS BETTY MADE IT ESPECIALLY FOR YOU!
BONNIE! TIME TO SLEEP, DARLING!
LET'S GO, JESSIE! THE OTHERS WILL SLEEP HERE!
BONNIE GOES TO BED AND THE TOYS COME TO LIFE...
HEY! LOOK AT THIS PLACE! EVERYTHING SEEMS SO OLD!
YEAH! JUST THINK THAT THIS PHOTO WAS TAKEN AGES AGO!
THIS IS BONNIE ONE WEEK AGO, TRIXIE!
HUH?! THAT'S WHY SHE LOOKED SO FAMILIAR!

SCRIPT: TEA ORSI; LAYOUT & INK: VALENTINO FORLINI; COLOUR: ANGELA CAPOLUPO

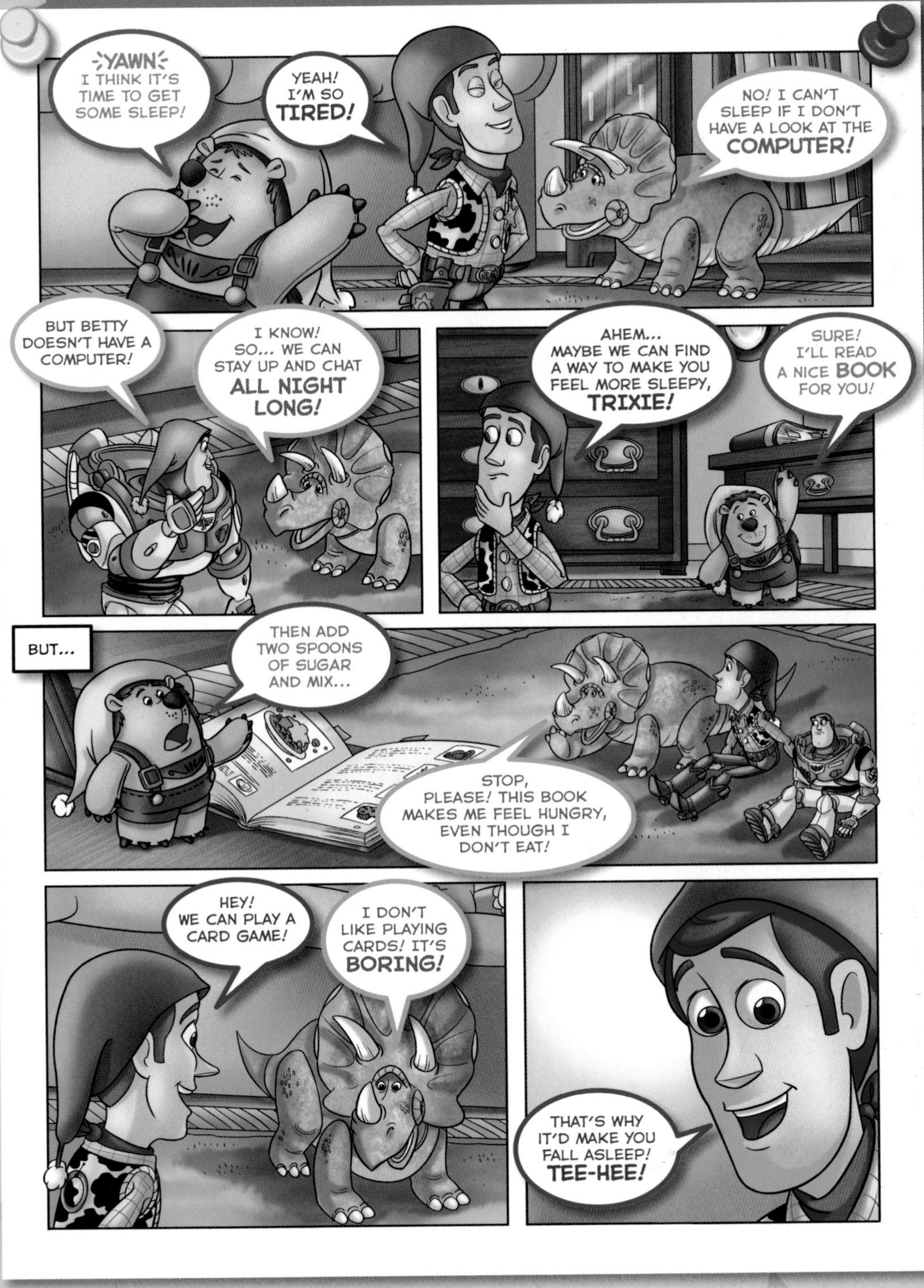

YAWN! I THINK IT'S TIME TO GET SOME SLEEP!
YEAH! I'M SO TIRED!
NO! I CAN'T SLEEP IF I DON'T HAVE A LOOK AT THE COMPUTER!
BUT BETTY DOESN'T HAVE A COMPUTER!
I KNOW! SO... WE CAN STAY UP AND CHAT ALL NIGHT LONG!
AHEM... MAYBE WE CAN FIND A WAY TO MAKE YOU FEEL MORE SLEEPY, TRIXIE!
SURE! I'LL READ A NICE BOOK FOR YOU!
BUT...
THEN ADD TWO SPOONS OF SUGAR AND MIX...
STOP, PLEASE! THIS BOOK MAKES ME FEEL HUNGRY, EVEN THOUGH I DON'T EAT!
HEY! WE CAN PLAY A CARD GAME!
I DON'T LIKE PLAYING CARDS! IT'S BORING!
THAT'S WHY IT'D MAKE YOU FALL ASLEEP! TEE-HEE!

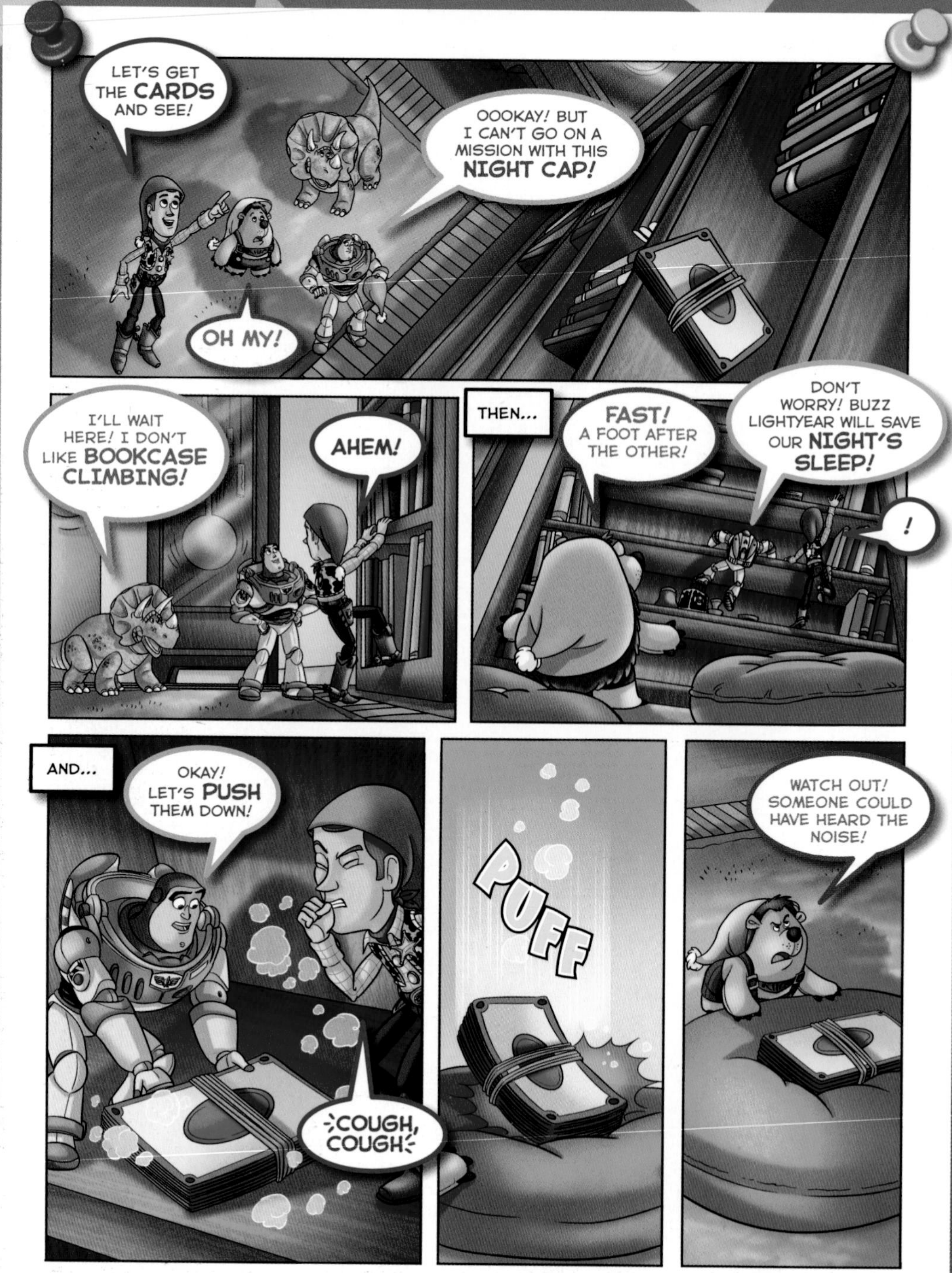
LET'S GET THE CARDS AND SEE!
OOOKAY! BUT I CAN'T GO ON A MISSION WITH THIS NIGHT CAP!
OH MY!
I'LL WAIT HERE! I DON'T LIKE BOOKCASE CLIMBING!
AHEM!
THEN...
FAST! A FOOT AFTER THE OTHER!
DON'T WORRY! BUZZ LIGHTYEAR WILL SAVE OUR NIGHT'S SLEEP!
!
AND...
OKAY! LET'S PUSH THEM DOWN!
COUGH, COUGH
PUFF
WATCH OUT! SOMEONE COULD HAVE HEARD THE NOISE!

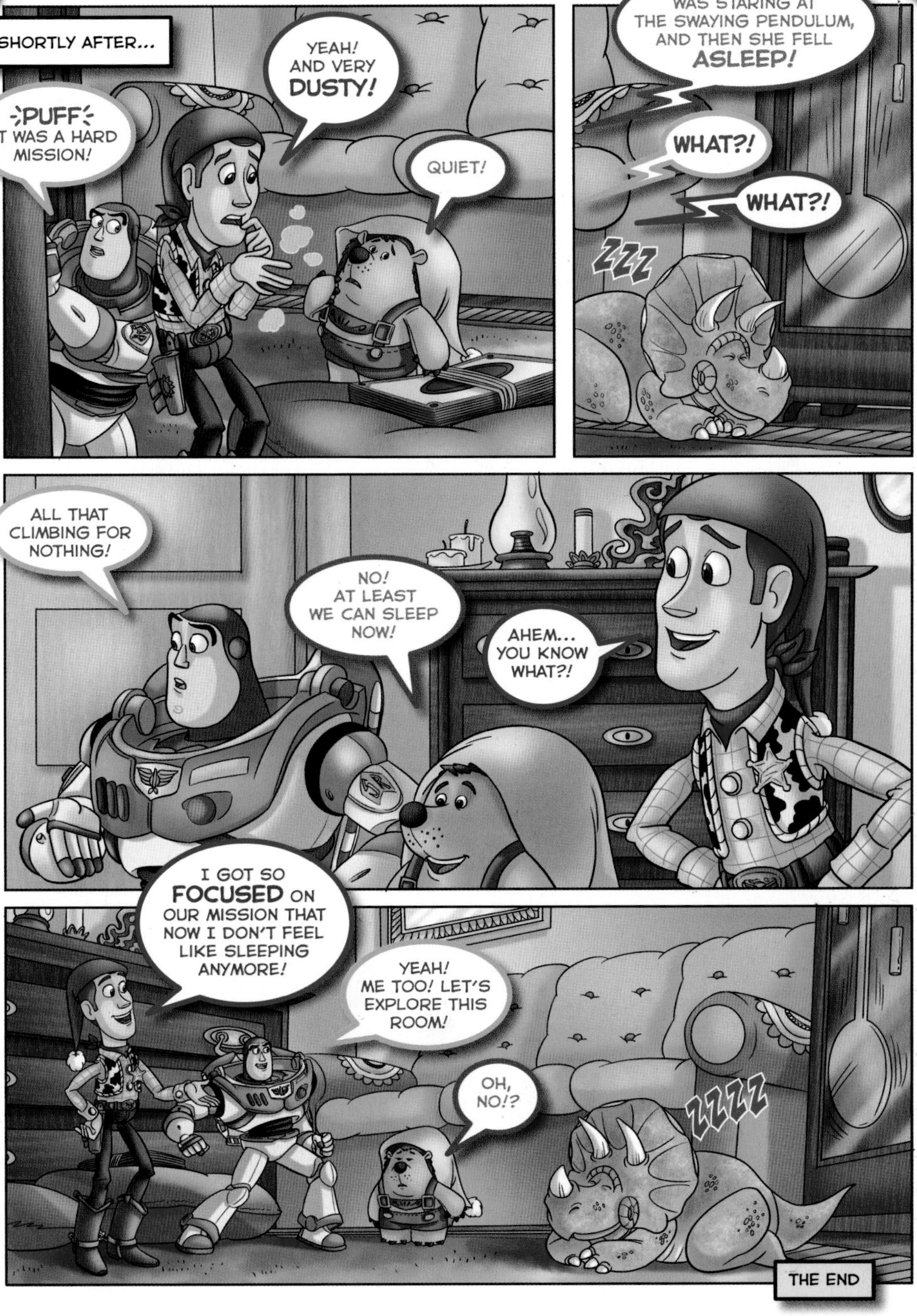
SHORTLY AFTER...
PUFF IT WAS A HARD MISSION!
YEAH! AND VERY DUSTY!
QUIET!
TRIXIE WAS STARING AT THE SWAYING PENDULUM, AND THEN SHE FELL ASLEEP!
WHAT?!
WHAT?!
ZZZ
ALL THAT CLIMBING FOR NOTHING!
NO! AT LEAST WE CAN SLEEP NOW!
AHEM... YOU KNOW WHAT?!
I GOT SO FOCUSED ON OUR MISSION THAT NOW I DON'T FEEL LIKE SLEEPING ANYMORE!
YEAH! ME TOO! LET'S EXPLORE THIS ROOM!
OH, NO!?
ZZZZ
THE END

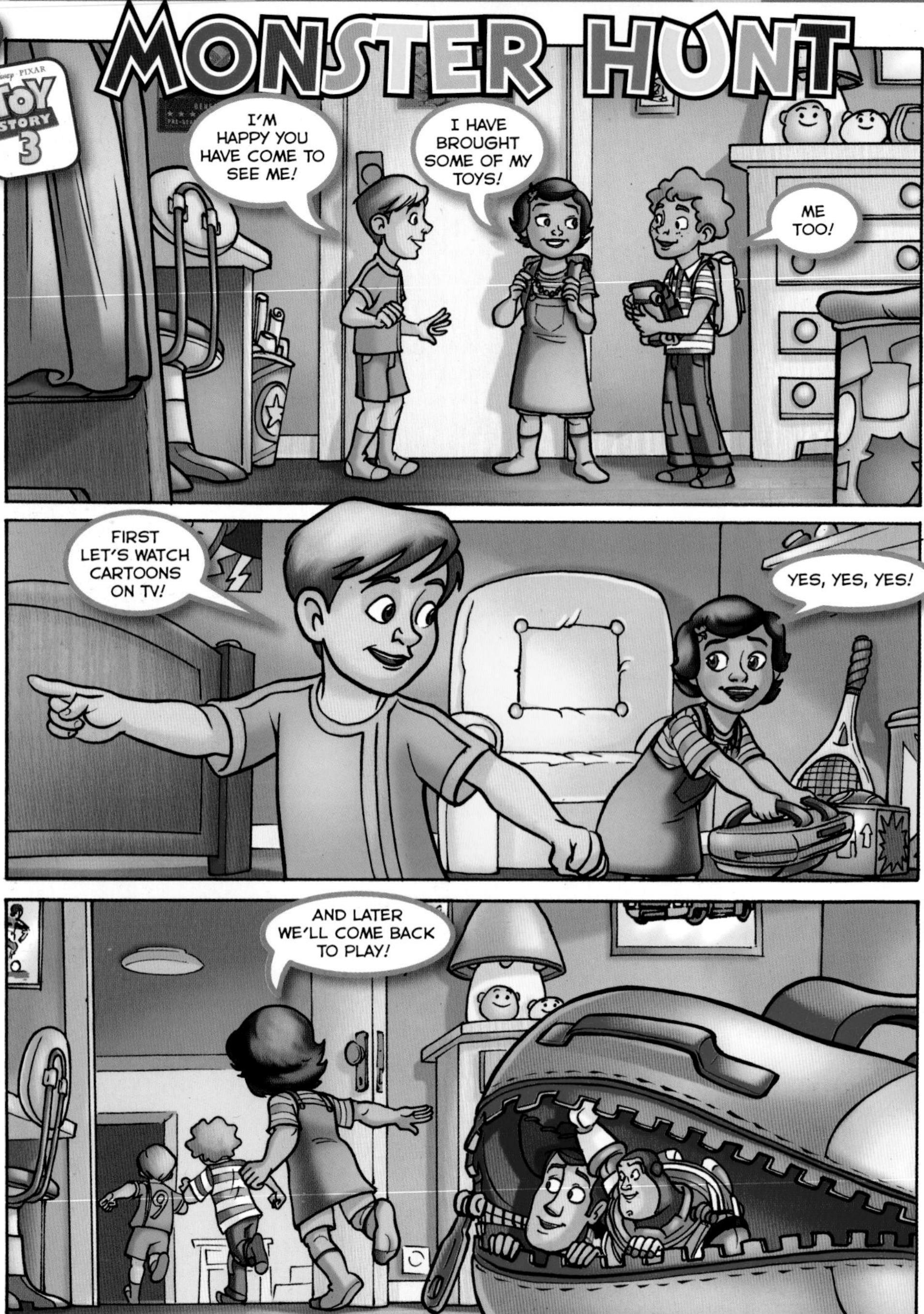
MONSTER HUNT
DISNEY PIXAR TOY STORY 3
I'M HAPPY YOU HAVE COME TO SEE ME!
I HAVE BROUGHT SOME OF MY TOYS!
ME TOO!
FIRST LET'S WATCH CARTOONS ON TV!
YES, YES, YES!
AND LATER WE'LL COME BACK TO PLAY!

SCRIPT: ALESSANDRO SISTI; LAYOUT & INK: VALENTINO FORLINI; COLOUR: ANGELA CAPOLUPO

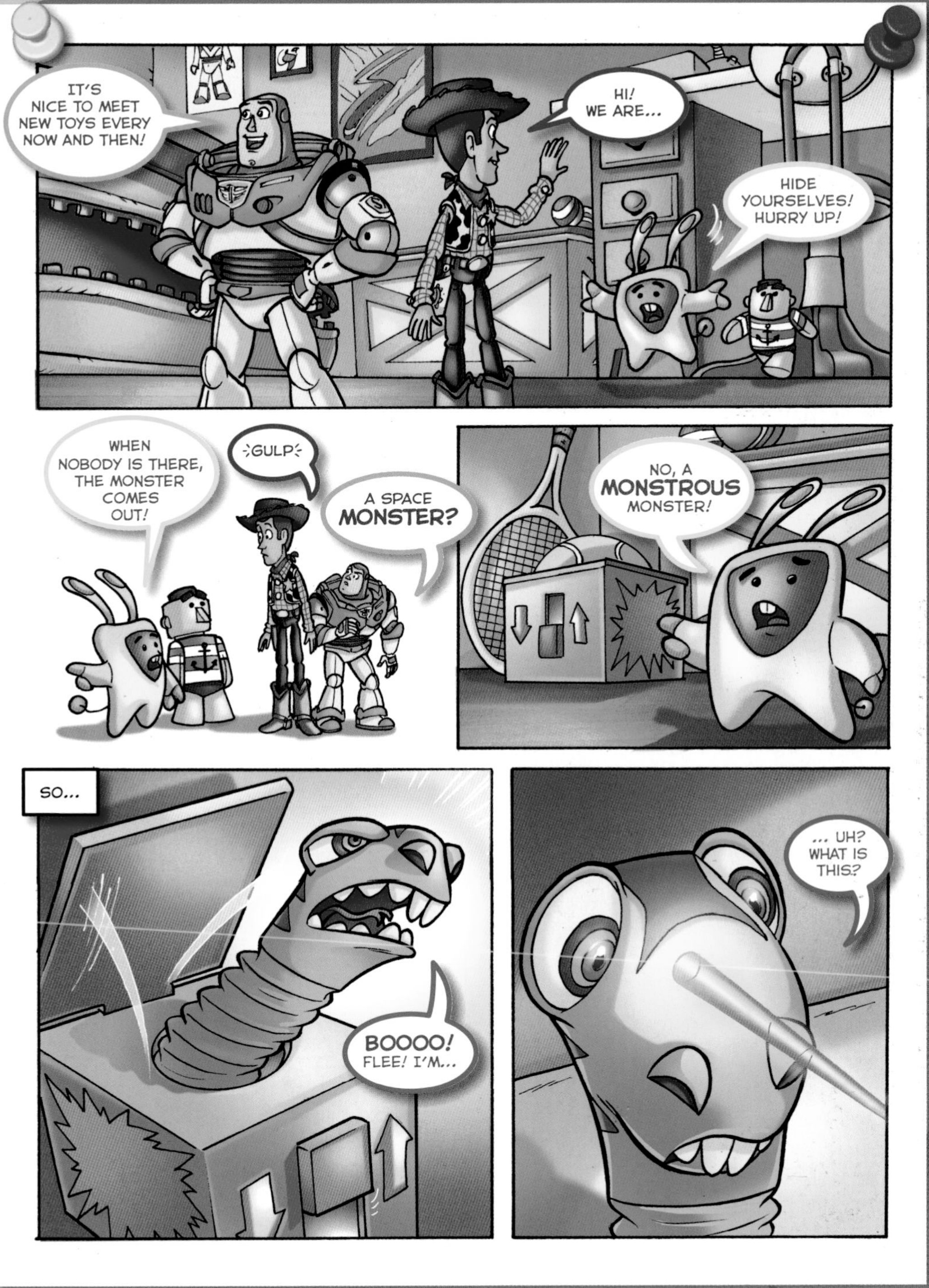

IT'S NICE TO MEET NEW TOYS EVERY NOW AND THEN!
HI! WE ARE...
HIDE YOURSELVES! HURRY UP!
WHEN NOBODY IS THERE, THE MONSTER COMES OUT!
GULP
A SPACE MONSTER?
NO, A MONSTROUS MONSTER!
SO...
BOOOO! FLEE! I'M...
... UH? WHAT IS THIS?

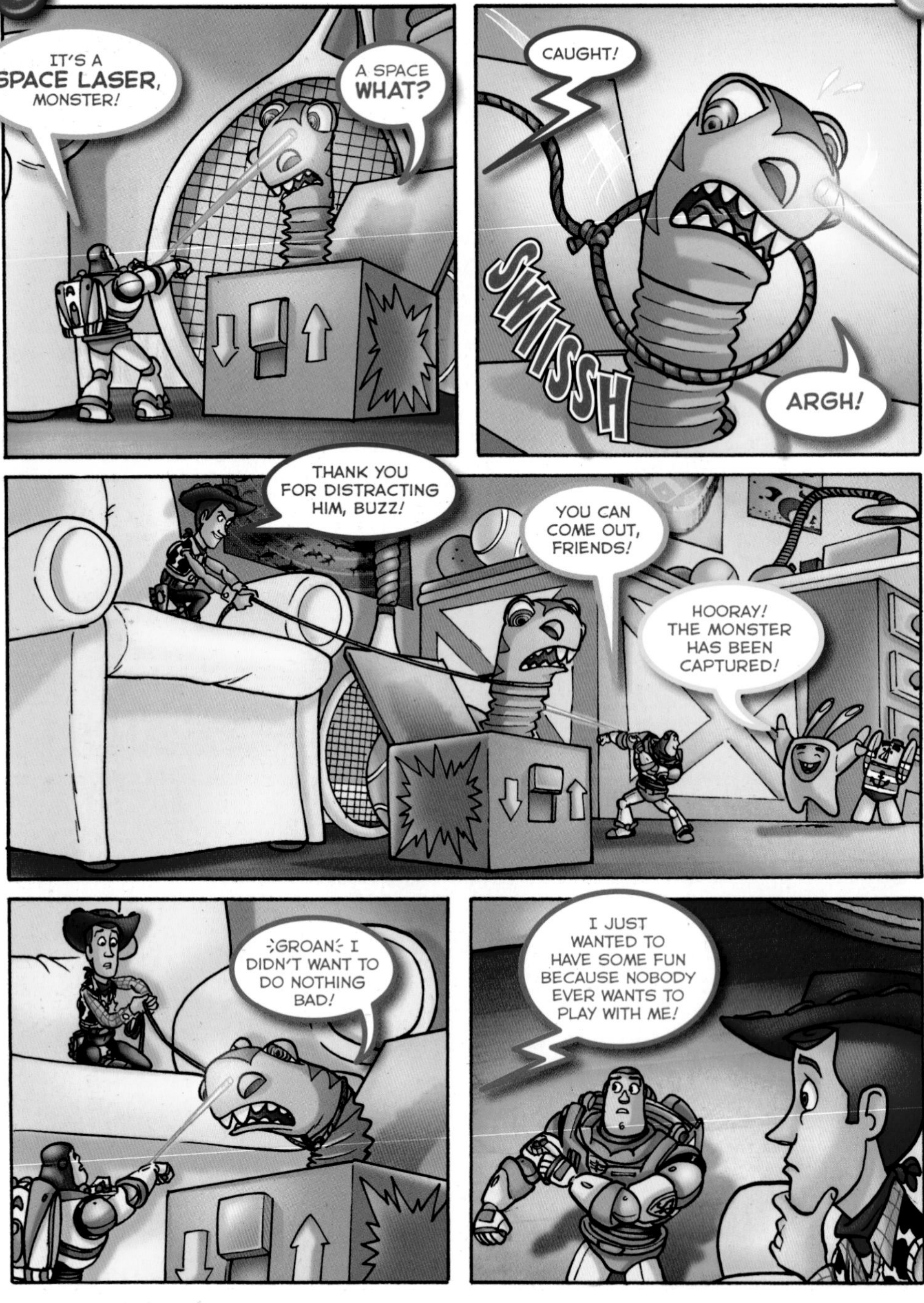
IT'S A SPACE LASER, MONSTER!
A SPACE WHAT?
CAUGHT!
SWISSH
ARGH!
THANK YOU FOR DISTRACTING HIM, BUZZ!
YOU CAN COME OUT, FRIENDS!
HOORAY! THE MONSTER HAS BEEN CAPTURED!
GROAN I DIDN'T WANT TO DO NOTHING BAD!
I JUST WANTED TO HAVE SOME FUN BECAUSE NOBODY EVER WANTS TO PLAY WITH ME!

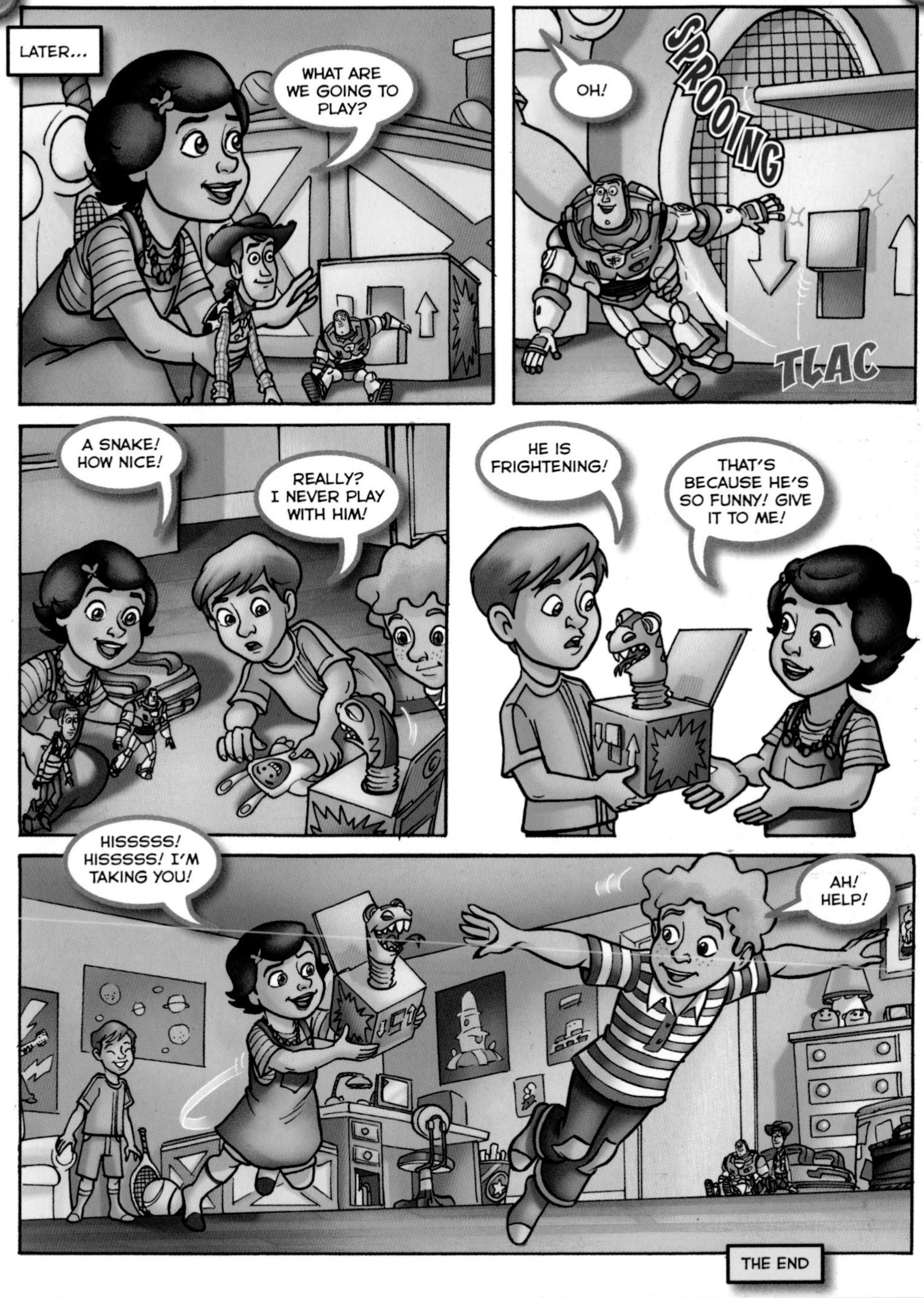
LATER...
WHAT ARE WE GOING TO PLAY?
OH!
SPROOING
TLAC
A SNAKE! HOW NICE!
REALLY? I NEVER PLAY WITH HIM!
HE IS FRIGHTENING!
THAT'S BECAUSE HE'S SO FUNNY! GIVE IT TO ME!
HISSSSS! HISSSSS! I'M TAKING YOU!
AH! HELP!
THE END

BEWARE OF THE DOG

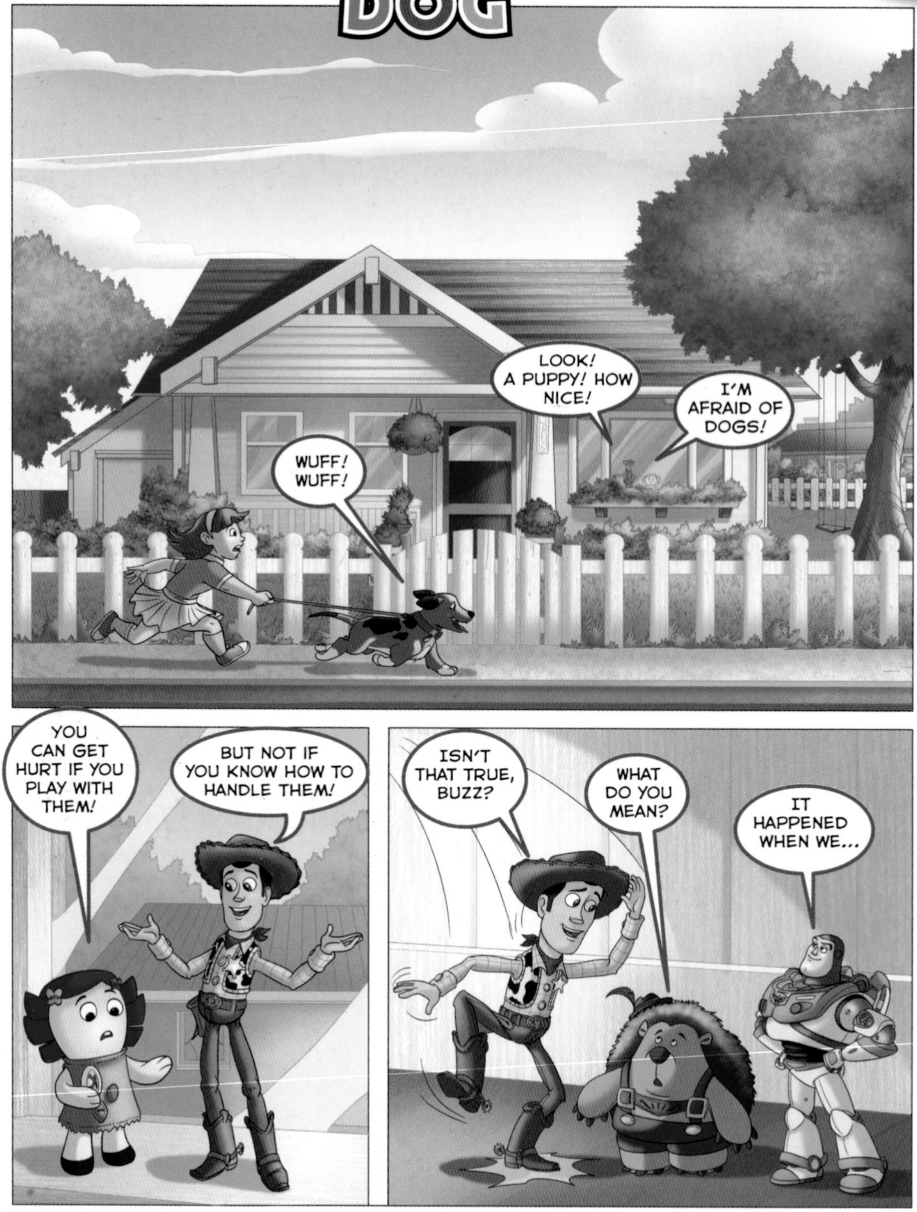

WUFF! WUFF!
LOOK! A PUPPY! HOW NICE!
I'M AFRAID OF DOGS!
YOU CAN GET HURT IF YOU PLAY WITH THEM!
BUT NOT IF YOU KNOW HOW TO HANDLE THEM!
ISN'T THAT TRUE, BUZZ?
WHAT DO YOU MEAN?
IT HAPPENED WHEN WE...

SCRIPT: ALESSANDRO SISTI, PENCIL & INK: VALENTINO FORLINI, COLOR: ANGELA CAPOLUPO

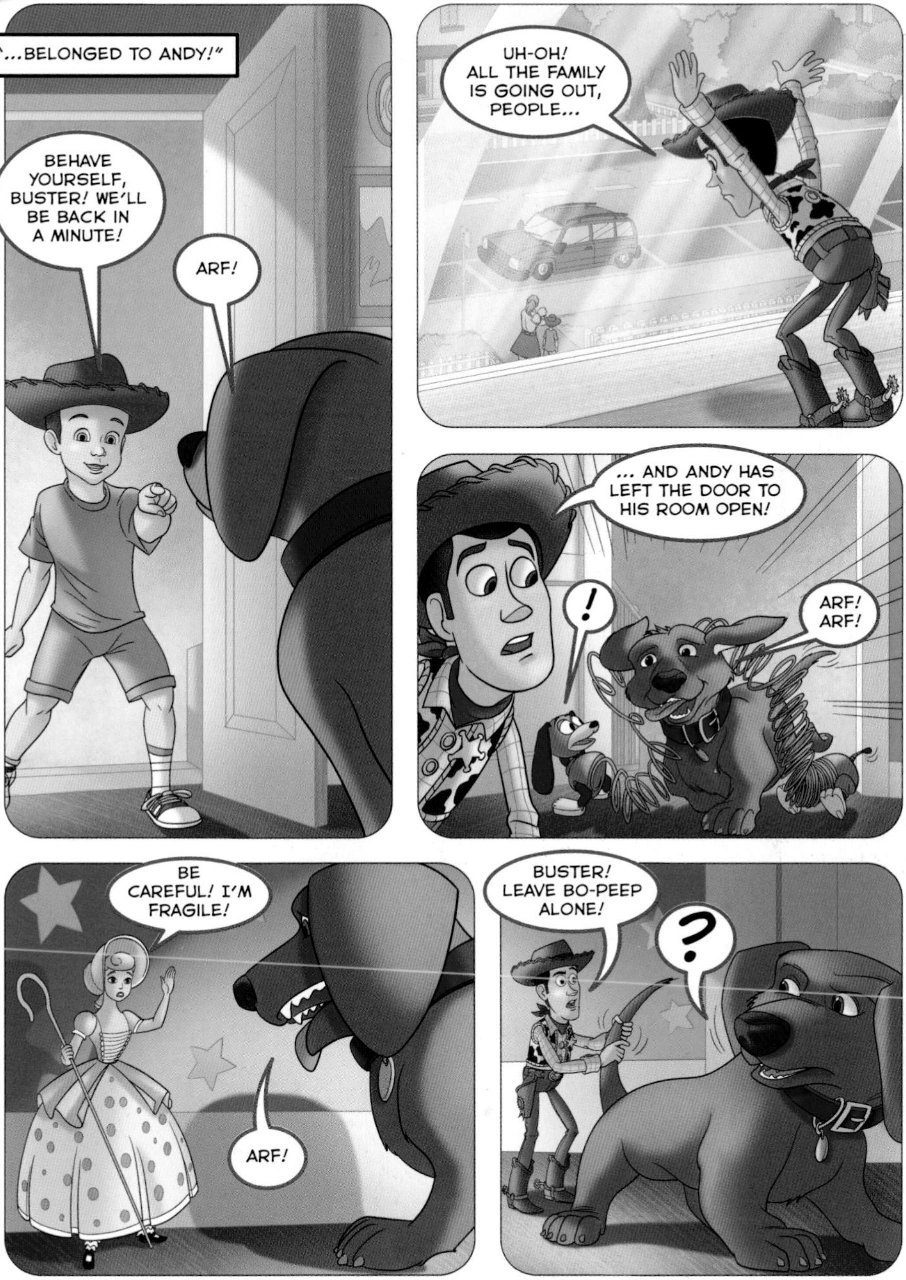
"...BELONGED TO ANDY!"
BEHAVE YOURSELF, BUSTER! WE'LL BE BACK IN A MINUTE!
ARF!
UH-OH! ALL THE FAMILY IS GOING OUT, PEOPLE...
... AND ANDY HAS LEFT THE DOOR TO HIS ROOM OPEN!
!
ARF! ARF!
BE CAREFUL! I'M FRAGILE!
ARF!
BUSTER! LEAVE BO-PEEP ALONE!
?

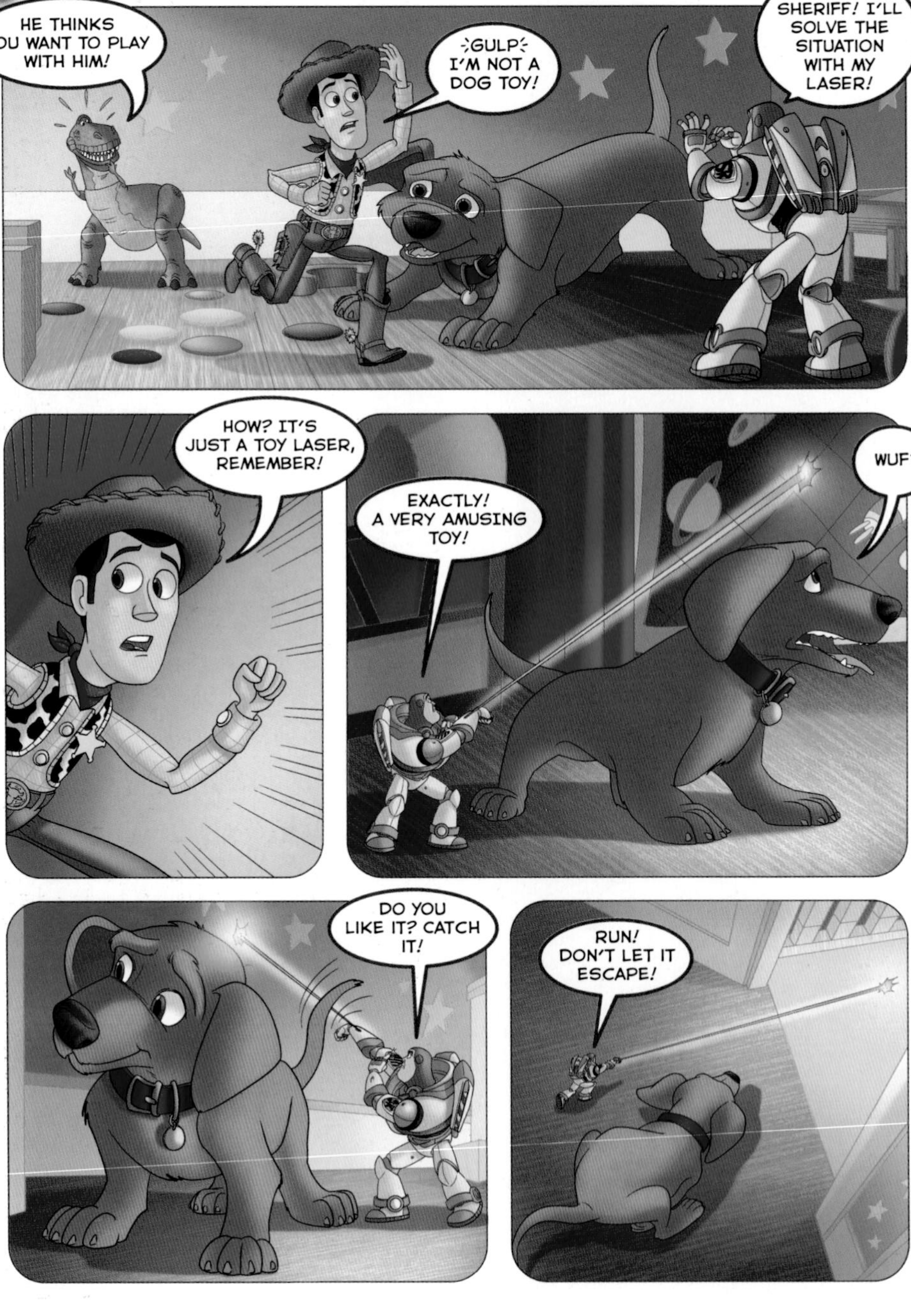
HE THINKS YOU WANT TO PLAY WITH HIM!
GULP I'M NOT A DOG TOY!
HANG ON, SHERIFF! I'LL SOLVE THE SITUATION WITH MY LASER!
HOW? IT'S JUST A TOY LASER, REMEMBER!
EXACTLY! A VERY AMUSING TOY!
WUF?
DO YOU LIKE IT? CATCH IT!
RUN! DON'T LET IT ESCAPE!

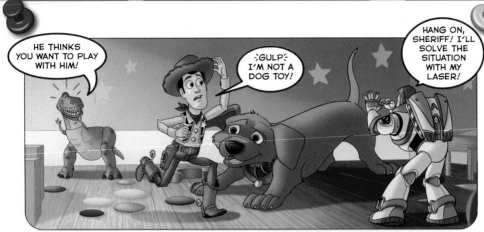

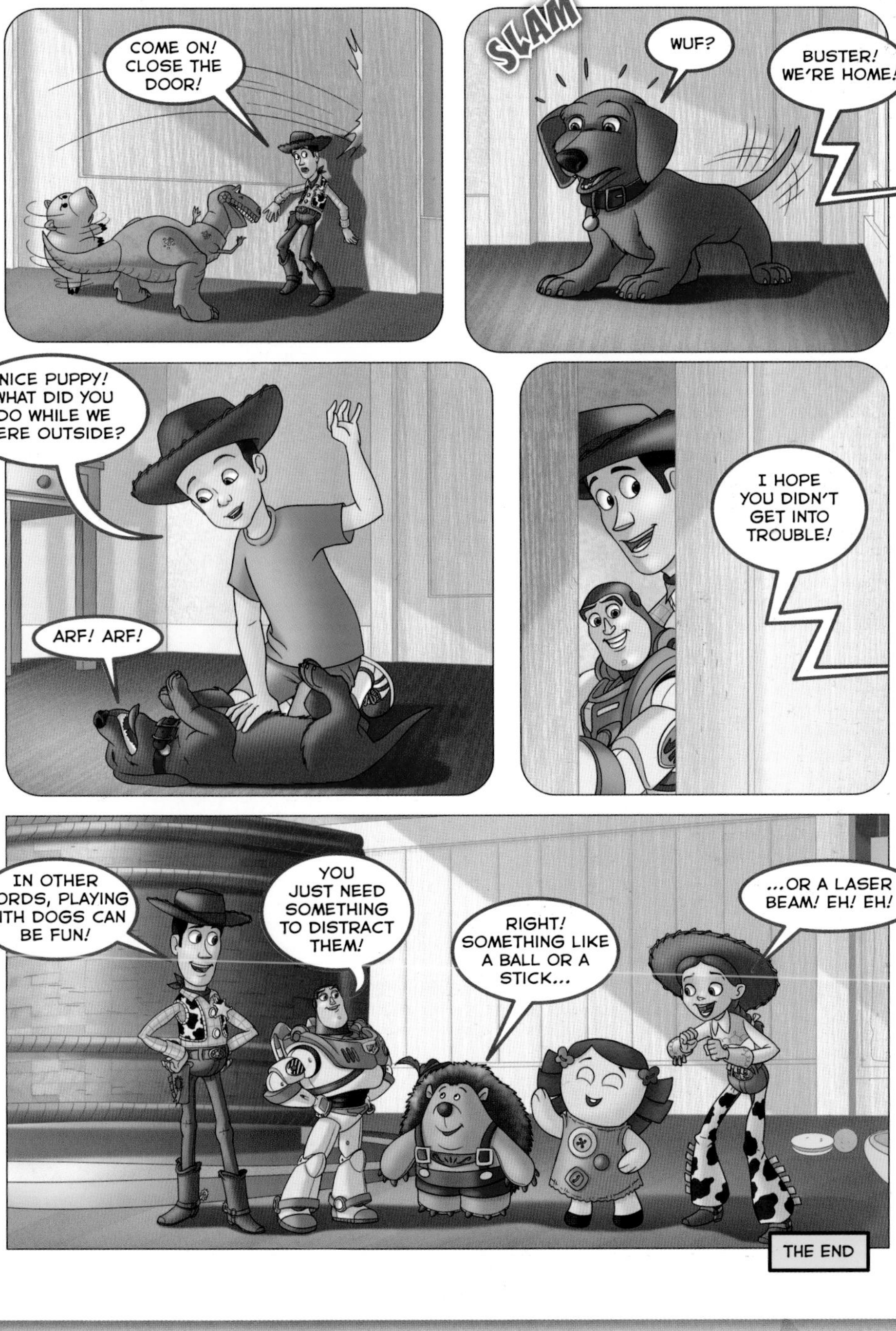
COME ON! CLOSE THE DOOR!
SLAM
WUF?
BUSTER! WE'RE HOME!
NICE PUPPY! WHAT DID YOU DO WHILE WE WERE OUTSIDE?
ARF! ARF!
I HOPE YOU DIDN'T GET INTO TROUBLE!
IN OTHER WORDS, PLAYING WITH DOGS CAN BE FUN!
YOU JUST NEED SOMETHING TO DISTRACT THEM!
RIGHT! SOMETHING LIKE A BALL OR A STICK...
...OR A LASER BEAM! EH! EH!
THE END

SUSPICIOUS GIFT

SCRIPT: TEA ORSI; LAYOUT: LUCA USAI; INK: MICHELA FRARE; COLOUR: ANGELA CAPOLUPO

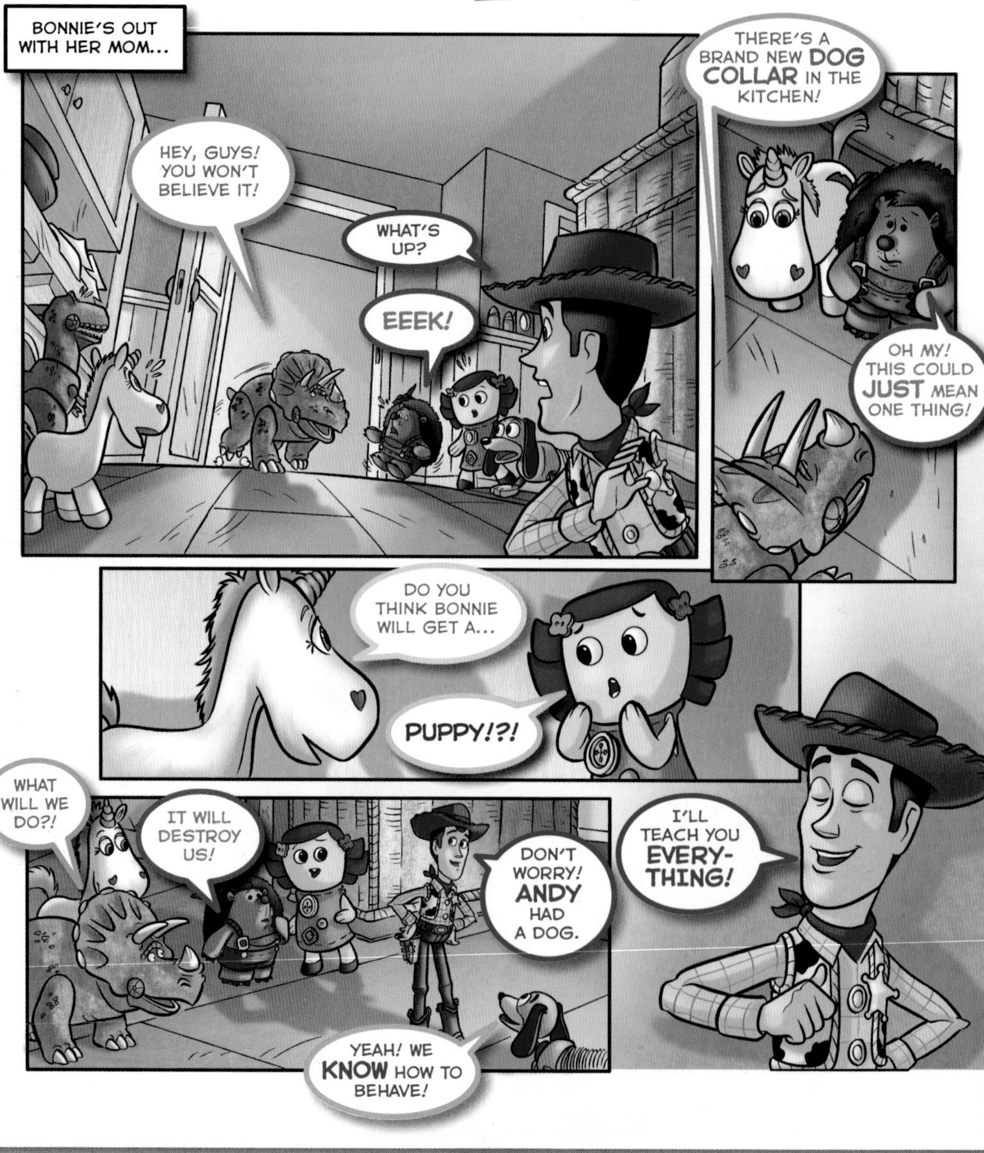

BONNIE'S OUT WITH HER MOM...
HEY, GUYS! YOU WON'T BELIEVE IT!
WHAT'S UP?
EEEK!
THERE'S A BRAND NEW DOG COLLAR IN THE KITCHEN!
OH MY! THIS COULD JUST MEAN ONE THING!
DO YOU THINK BONNIE WILL GET A...
PUPPY!?!
WHAT WILL WE DO?!
IT WILL DESTROY US!
DON'T WORRY! ANDY HAD A DOG.
YEAH! WE KNOW HOW TO BEHAVE!
I'LL TEACH YOU EVERY-THING!

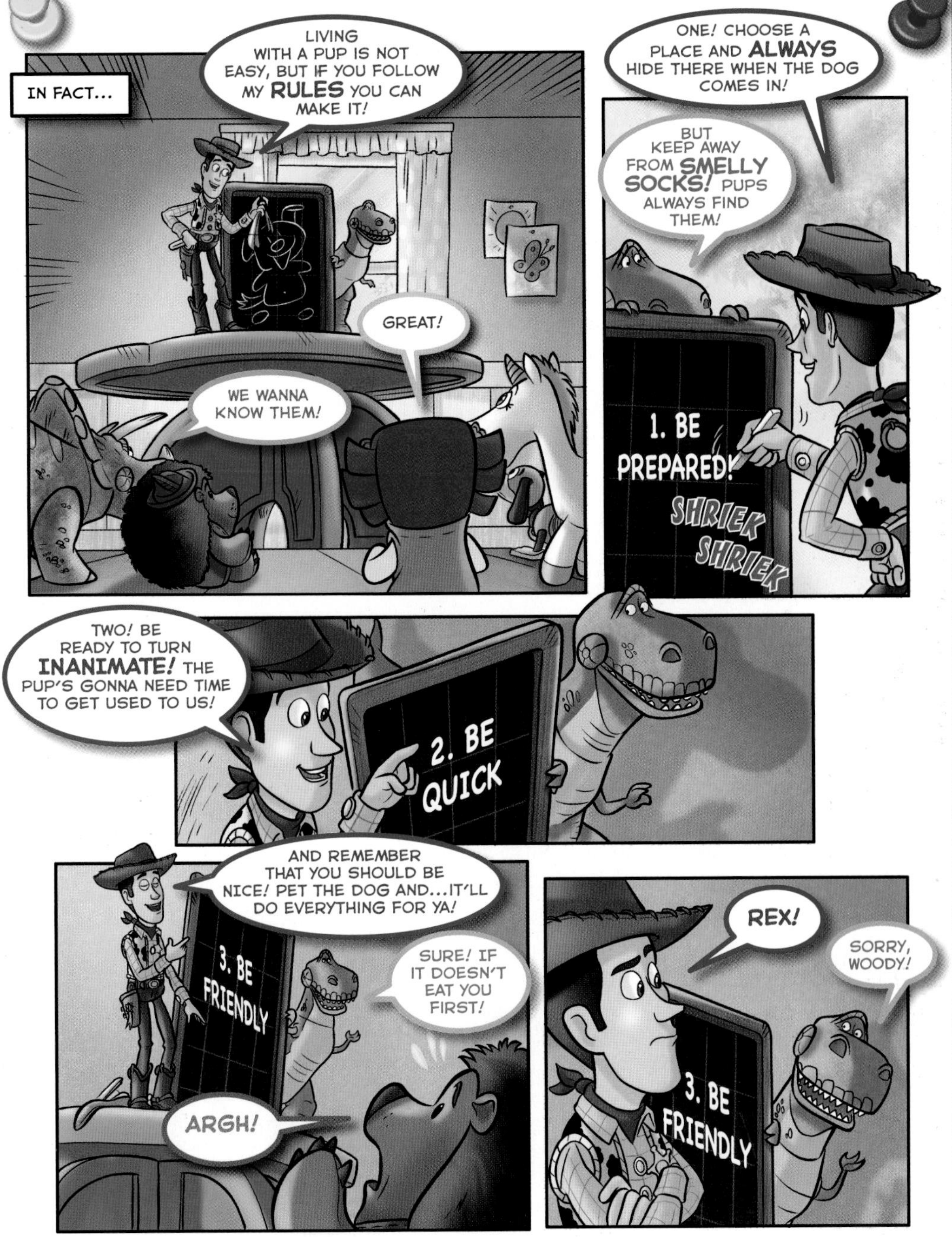
IN FACT...
LIVING WITH A PUP IS NOT EASY, BUT IF YOU FOLLOW MY RULES YOU CAN MAKE IT!
GREAT!
WE WANNA KNOW THEM!
ONE! CHOOSE A PLACE AND ALWAYS HIDE THERE WHEN THE DOG COMES IN!
BUT KEEP AWAY FROM SMELLY SOCKS! PUPS ALWAYS FIND THEM!
1. BE PREPARED!
SHRIEK SHRIEK
TWO! BE READY TO TURN INANIMATE! THE PUP'S GONNA NEED TIME TO GET USED TO US!
2. BE QUICK
AND REMEMBER THAT YOU SHOULD BE NICE! PET THE DOG AND...IT'LL DO EVERYTHING FOR YA!
3. BE FRIENDLY
SURE! IF IT DOESN'T EAT YOU FIRST!
ARGH!
REX!
SORRY, WOODY!
3. BE FRIENDLY

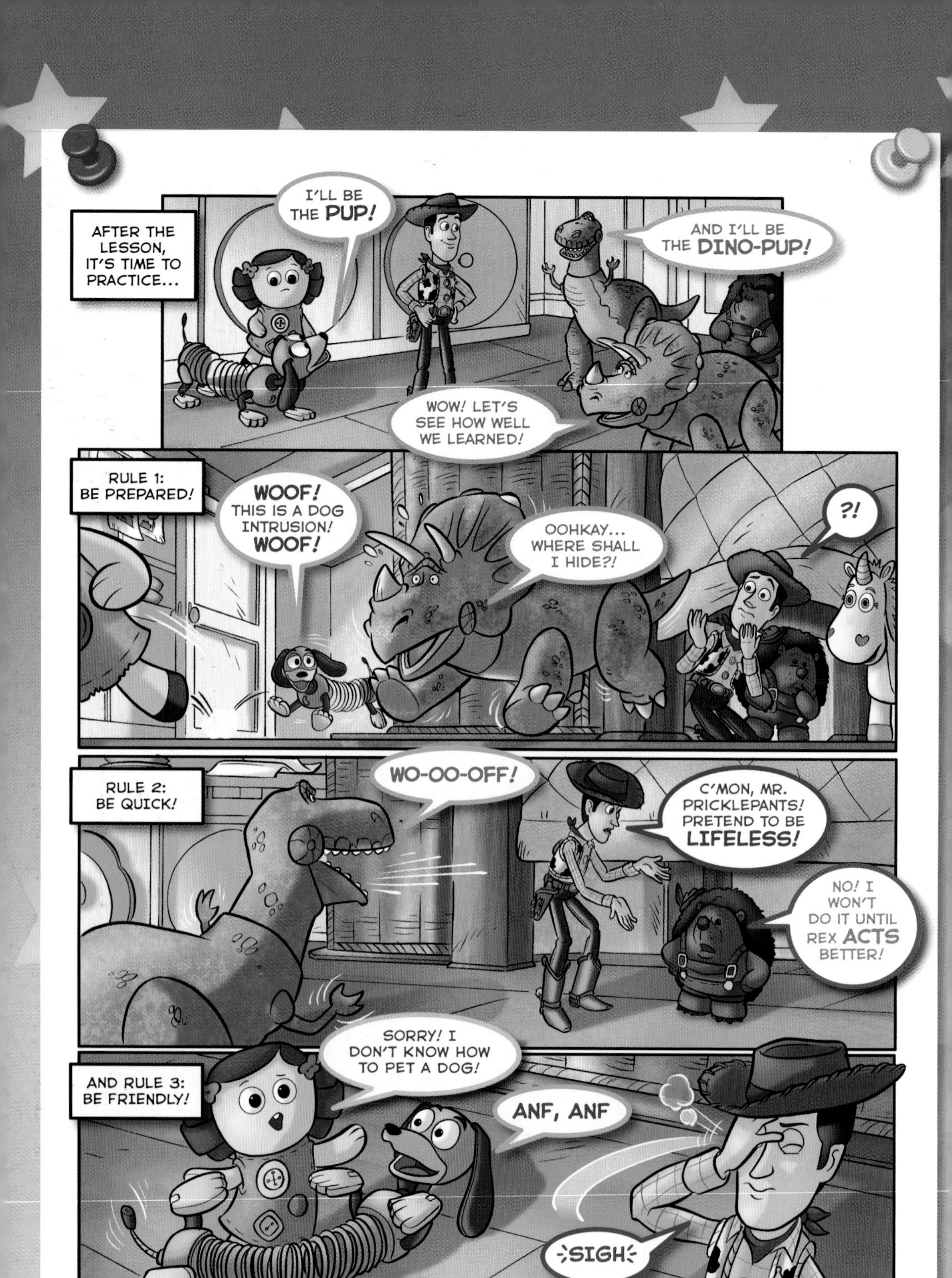

AFTER THE LESSON, IT'S TIME TO PRACTICE...
I'LL BE THE PUP!
AND I'LL BE THE DINO-PUP!
WOW! LET'S SEE HOW WELL WE LEARNED!
RULE 1: BE PREPARED!
WOOF! THIS IS A DOG INTRUSION! WOOF!
OOHKAY... WHERE SHALL I HIDE?!
?!
RULE 2: BE QUICK!
WO-OO-OFF!
C'MON, MR. PRICKLEPANTS! PRETEND TO BE LIFELESS!
NO! I WON'T DO IT UNTIL REX ACTS BETTER!
AND RULE 3: BE FRIENDLY!
SORRY! I DON'T KNOW HOW TO PET A DOG!
ANF, ANF
SIGH

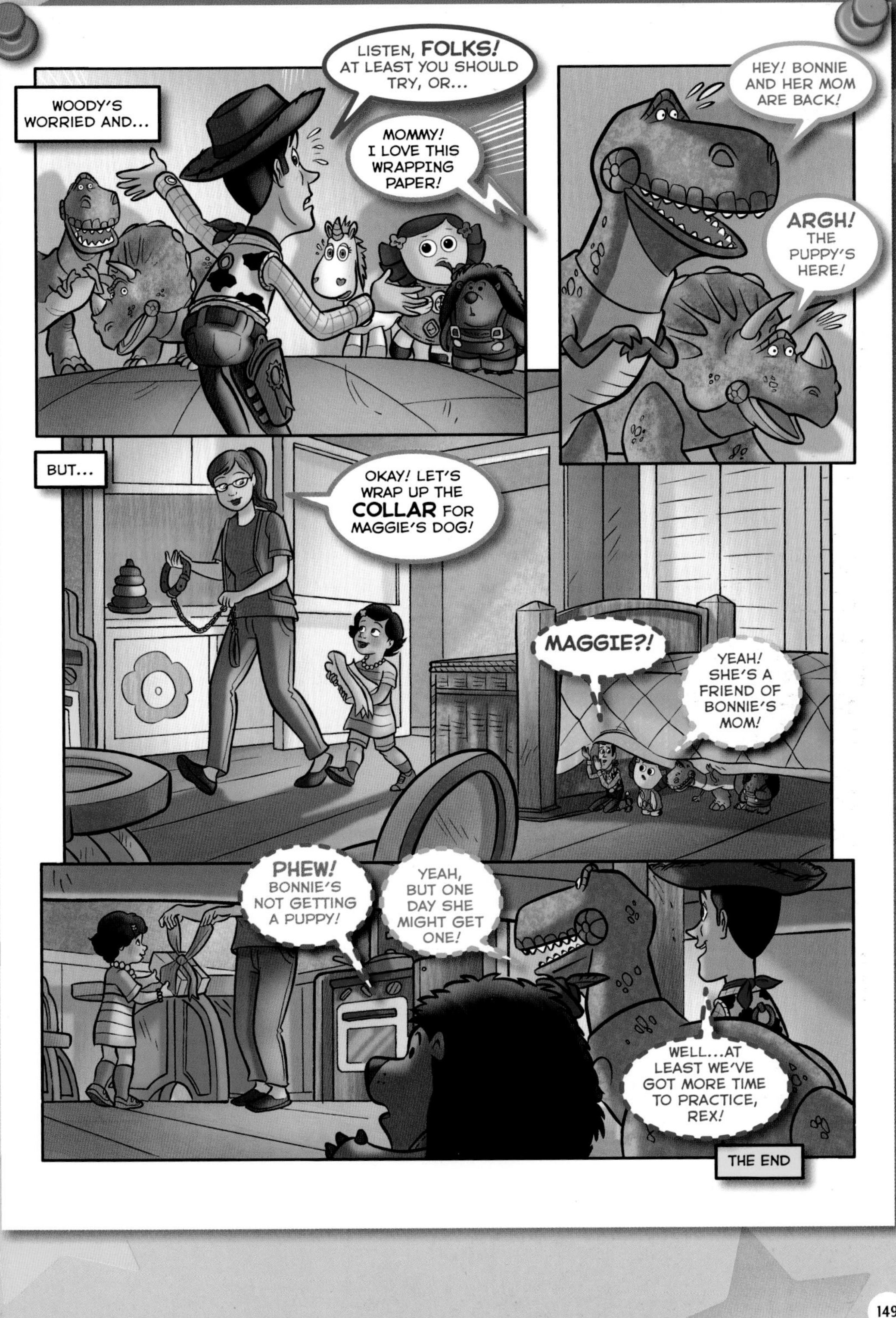
WOODY'S WORRIED AND...
LISTEN, FOLKS! AT LEAST YOU SHOULD TRY, OR...
MOMMY! I LOVE THIS WRAPPING PAPER!
HEY! BONNIE AND HER MOM ARE BACK!
ARGH! THE PUPPY'S HERE!
BUT...
OKAY! LET'S WRAP UP THE COLLAR FOR MAGGIE'S DOG!
MAGGIE?!
YEAH! SHE'S A FRIEND OF BONNIE'S MOM!
PHEW! BONNIE'S NOT GETTING A PUPPY!
YEAH, BUT ONE DAY SHE MIGHT GET ONE!
WELL...AT LEAST WE'VE GOT MORE TIME TO PRACTICE, REX!
THE END

A SMILE FOR CHUCKLES

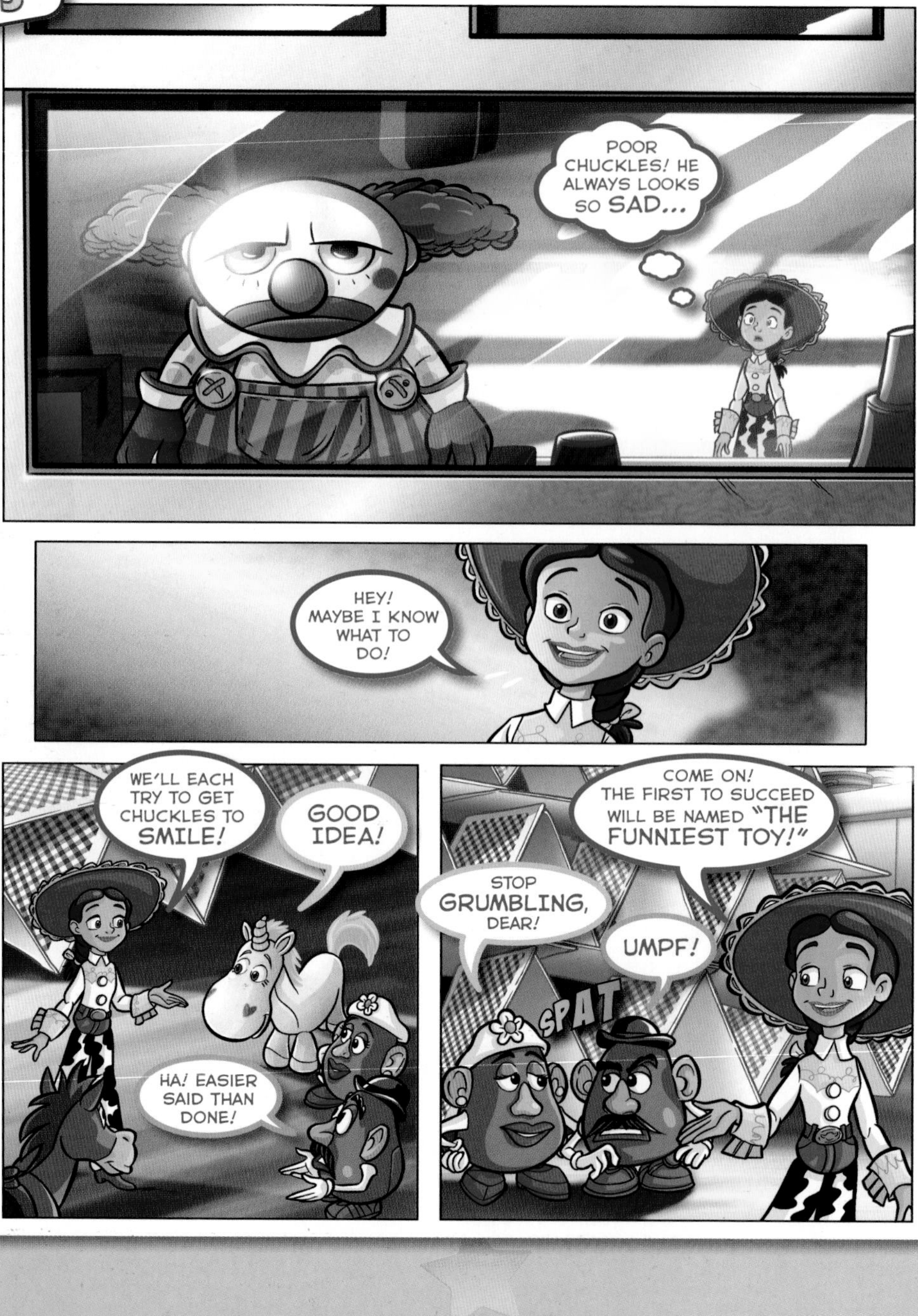

TOY STORY 3
POOR CHUCKLES! HE ALWAYS LOOKS SO SAD...
HEY! MAYBE I KNOW WHAT TO DO!
WE'LL EACH TRY TO GET CHUCKLES TO SMILE!
GOOD IDEA!
HA! EASIER SAID THAN DONE!
COME ON! THE FIRST TO SUCCEED WILL BE NAMED "THE FUNNIEST TOY!"
STOP GRUMBLING, DEAR!
UMPF!
SPAT

SCRIPT: TEA ORSI; PENCILS & INK: VALENTINO FORLINI; COLOUR: DARIO CALABRIA

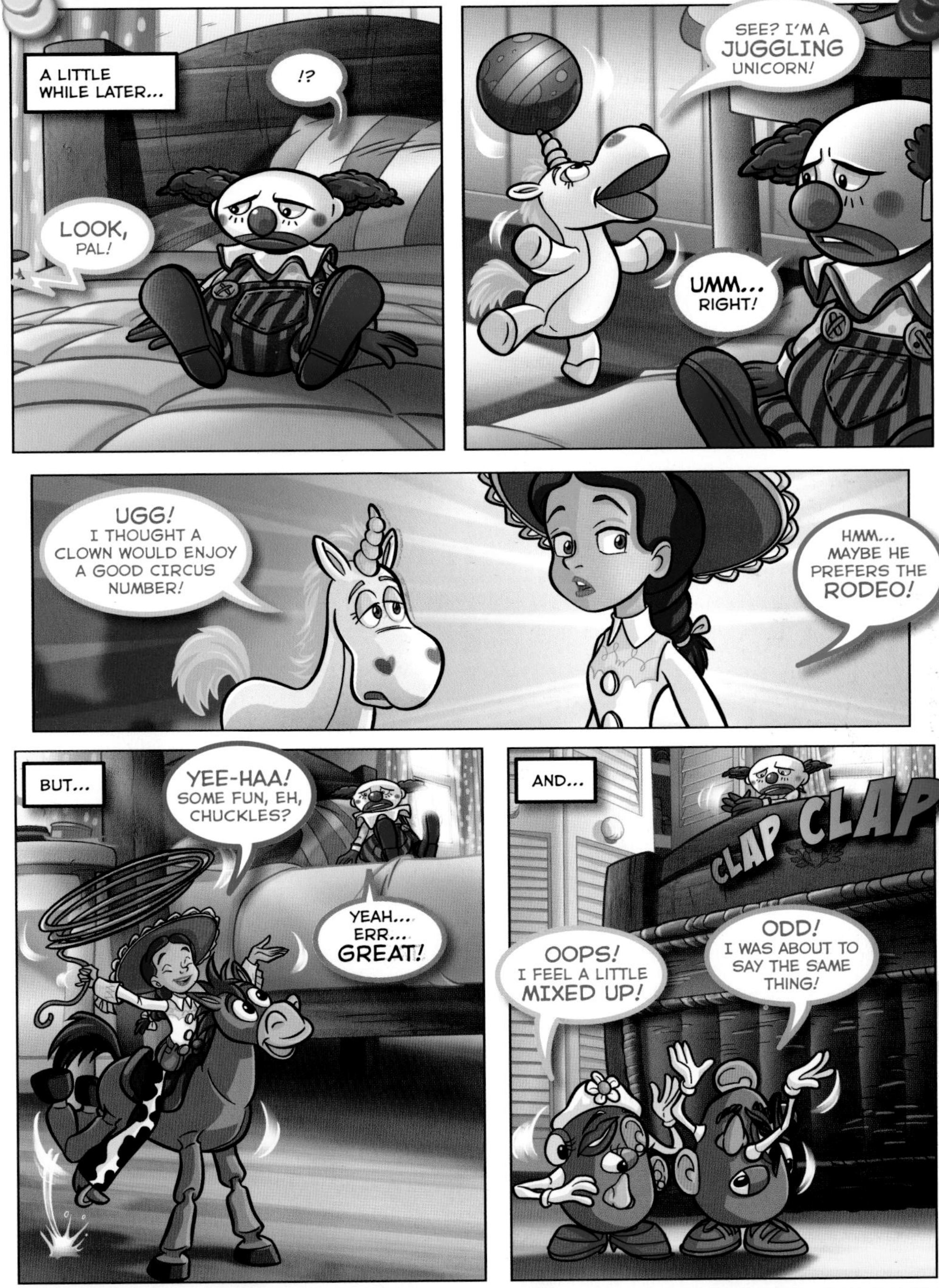
A LITTLE WHILE LATER...
!?
LOOK, PAL!
SEE? I'M A JUGGLING UNICORN!
UMM... RIGHT!
UGG! I THOUGHT A CLOWN WOULD ENJOY A GOOD CIRCUS NUMBER!
HMM... MAYBE HE PREFERS THE RODEO!
BUT...
YEE-HAA! SOME FUN, EH, CHUCKLES?
YEAH... ERR... GREAT!
AND...
CLAP CLAP
OOPS! I FEEL A LITTLE MIXED UP!
ODD! I WAS ABOUT TO SAY THE SAME THING!

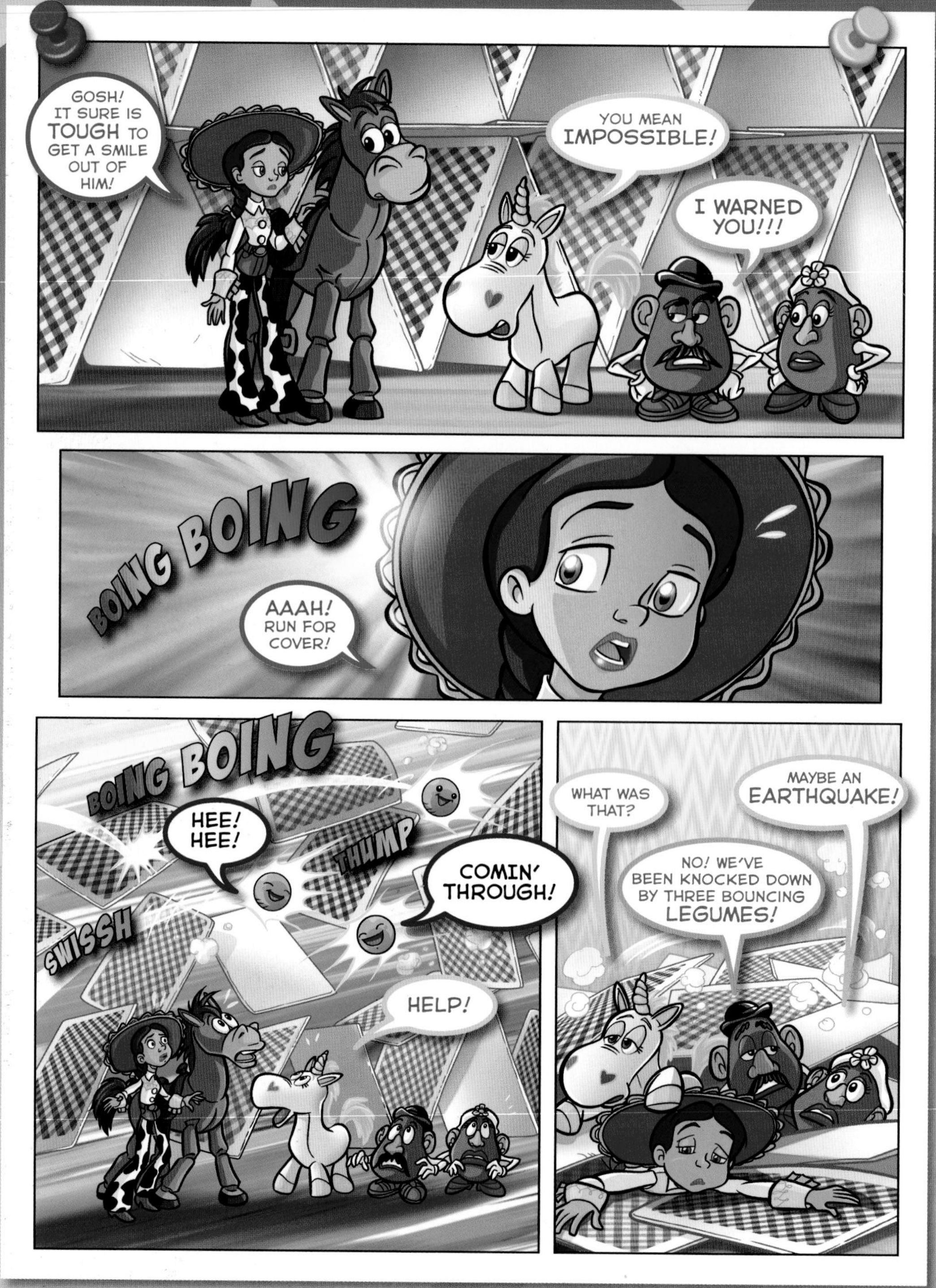

GOSH! IT SURE IS TOUGH TO GET A SMILE OUT OF HIM!
YOU MEAN IMPOSSIBLE!
I WARNED YOU!!!
BOING BOING
AAAH! RUN FOR COVER!
BOING BOING
HEE! HEE!
THUMP
SWISSH
COMIN' THROUGH!
HELP!
WHAT WAS THAT?
MAYBE AN EARTHQUAKE!
NO! WE'VE BEEN KNOCKED DOWN BY THREE BOUNCING LEGUMES!

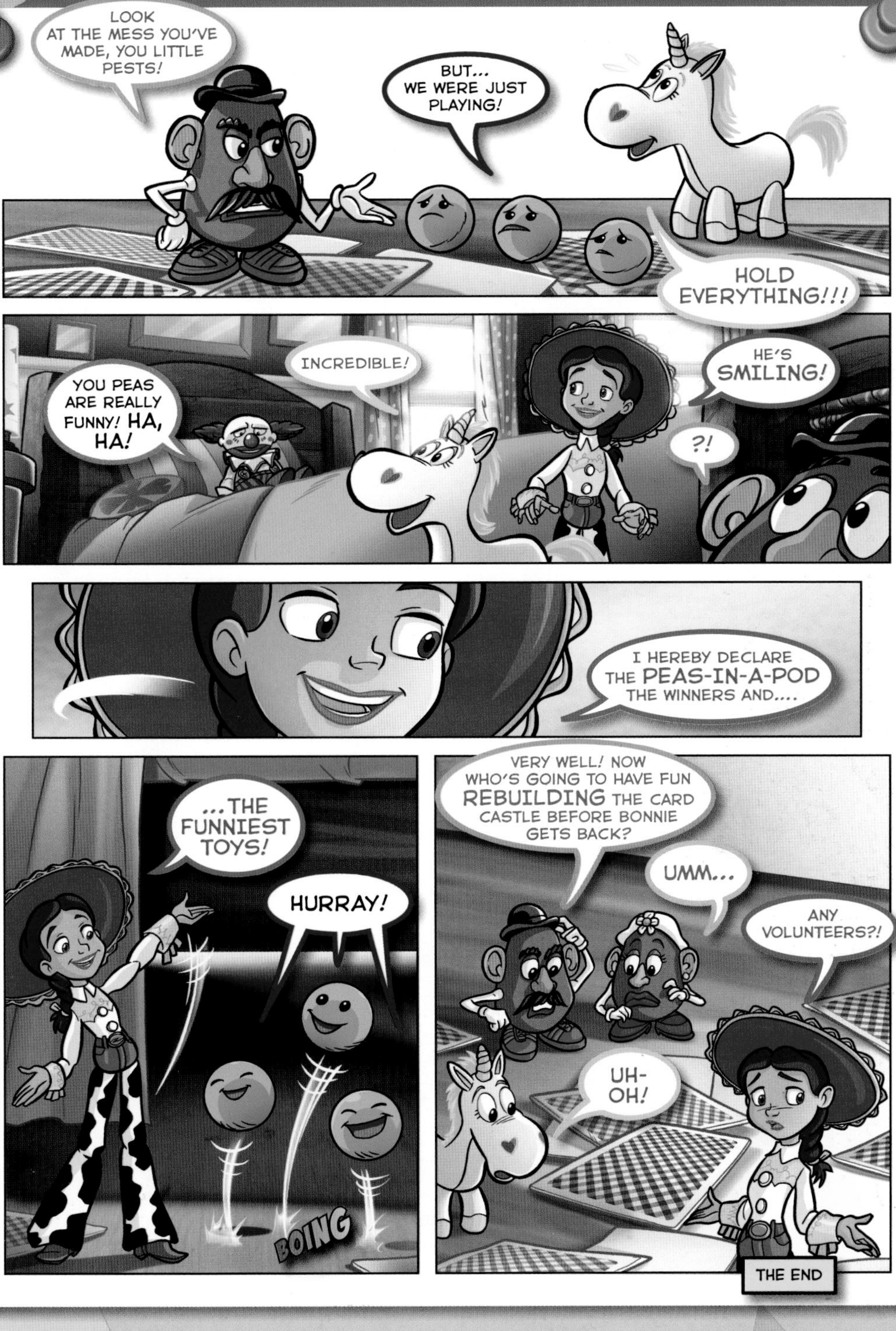

LOOK AT THE MESS YOU'VE MADE, YOU LITTLE PESTS!
BUT... WE WERE JUST PLAYING!
HOLD EVERYTHING!!!
YOU PEAS ARE REALLY FUNNY! HA, HA!
INCREDIBLE!
HE'S SMILING!
?!
I HEREBY DECLARE THE PEAS-IN-A-POD THE WINNERS AND....
...THE FUNNIEST TOYS!
HURRAY!
BOING
VERY WELL! NOW WHO'S GOING TO HAVE FUN REBUILDING THE CARD CASTLE BEFORE BONNIE GETS BACK?
UMM...
ANY VOLUNTEERS?!
UH-OH!
THE END

WHO LAUGHS FIRST?

HEY, WHAT ARE THEY DOING?

THEY'RE PLAYING WHO LAUGHS FIRST!

HMM...

THE FIRST ONE TO LAUGH LOSES.

HA, HA, HA!

I WON!

IT LOOKS FUN! LET'S PLAY TOO!

SHH! DON'T TELL CHUCKLES.

IF HE PLAYS, HE'LL BE WINNING ALL THE TIME!

THE END

SCRIPT: TEA ORSI, PENCILS & INK: VALENTINO FORLINI, COLOUR: ANGELA CAPOLUPO

FEARFULLY FUNNY

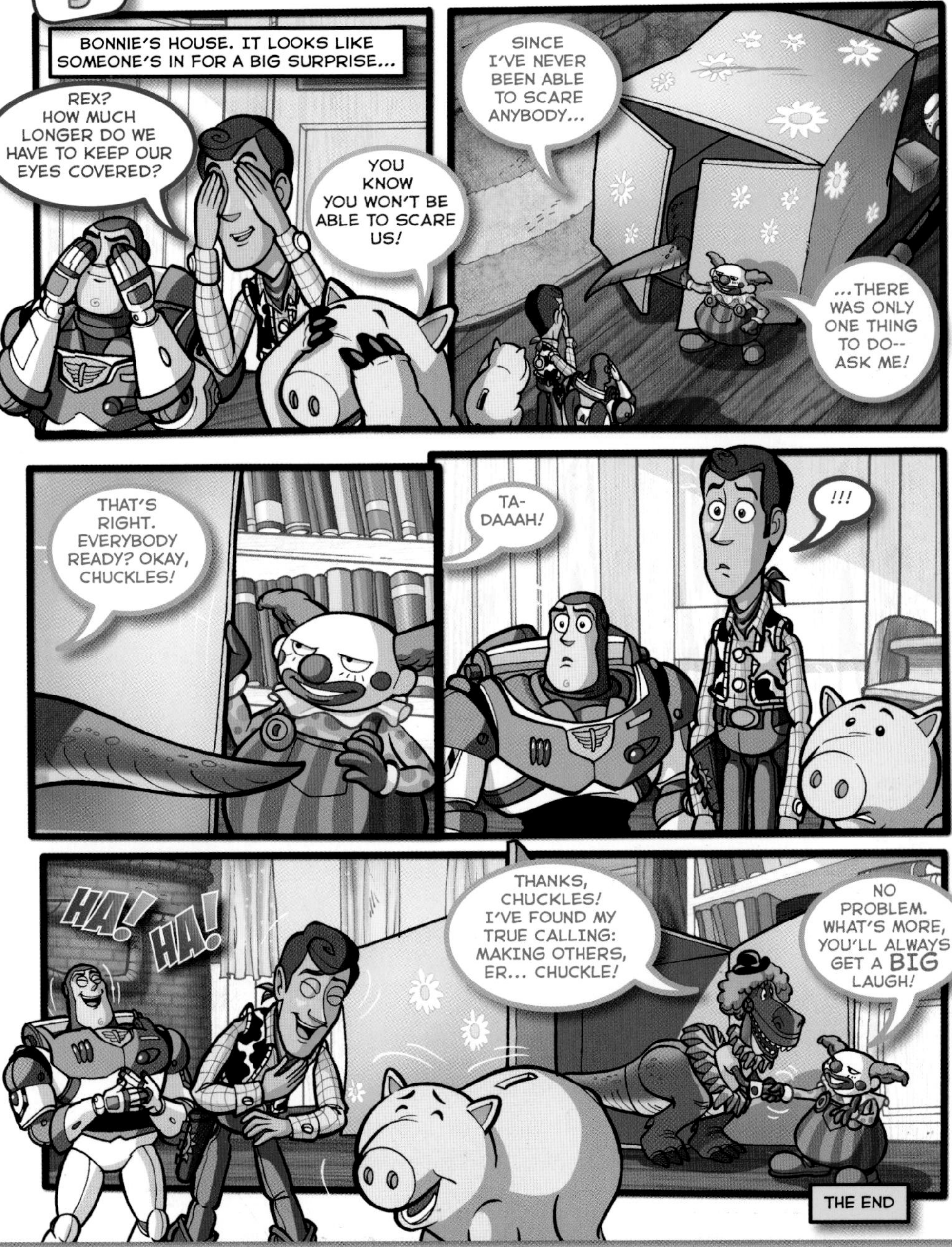

BONNIE'S HOUSE. IT LOOKS LIKE SOMEONE'S IN FOR A BIG SURPRISE...
REX? HOW MUCH LONGER DO WE HAVE TO KEEP OUR EYES COVERED?
YOU KNOW YOU WON'T BE ABLE TO SCARE US!
SINCE I'VE NEVER BEEN ABLE TO SCARE ANYBODY...
...THERE WAS ONLY ONE THING TO DO-- ASK ME!
THAT'S RIGHT. EVERYBODY READY? OKAY, CHUCKLES!
TA-DAAAH!
!!!
HA! HA!
THANKS, CHUCKLES! I'VE FOUND MY TRUE CALLING: MAKING OTHERS, ER... CHUCKLE!
NO PROBLEM. WHAT'S MORE, YOU'LL ALWAYS GET A BIG LAUGH!
THE END

SCRIPT: ALESSANDRO FERRARI; PENCILS: VALENTINO FORLINI; INK: FEDERICA SALFO; COLOUR: GIANLUCA BARONE

THE LOST BUTTON

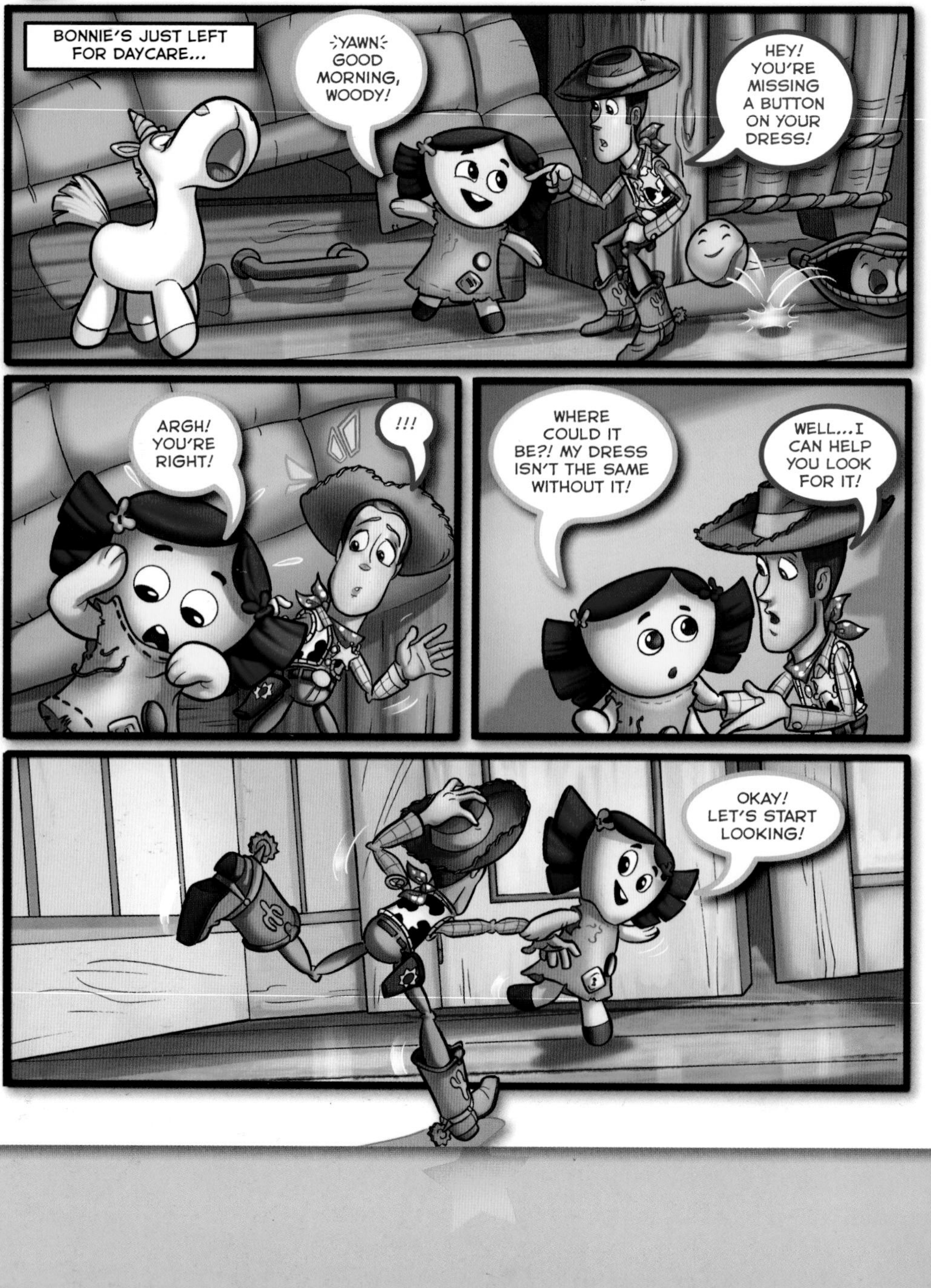
BONNIE'S JUST LEFT FOR DAYCARE...
-YAWN- GOOD MORNING, WOODY!
HEY! YOU'RE MISSING A BUTTON ON YOUR DRESS!
ARGH! YOU'RE RIGHT!
!!!
WHERE COULD IT BE?! MY DRESS ISN'T THE SAME WITHOUT IT!
WELL...I CAN HELP YOU LOOK FOR IT!
OKAY! LET'S START LOOKING!

SCRIPT: TEA ORSI; PENCILS: GIANLUCA BARONE; INK: MICHELA FRARE; COLOUR: KAWAII CREATIVE STUDIO

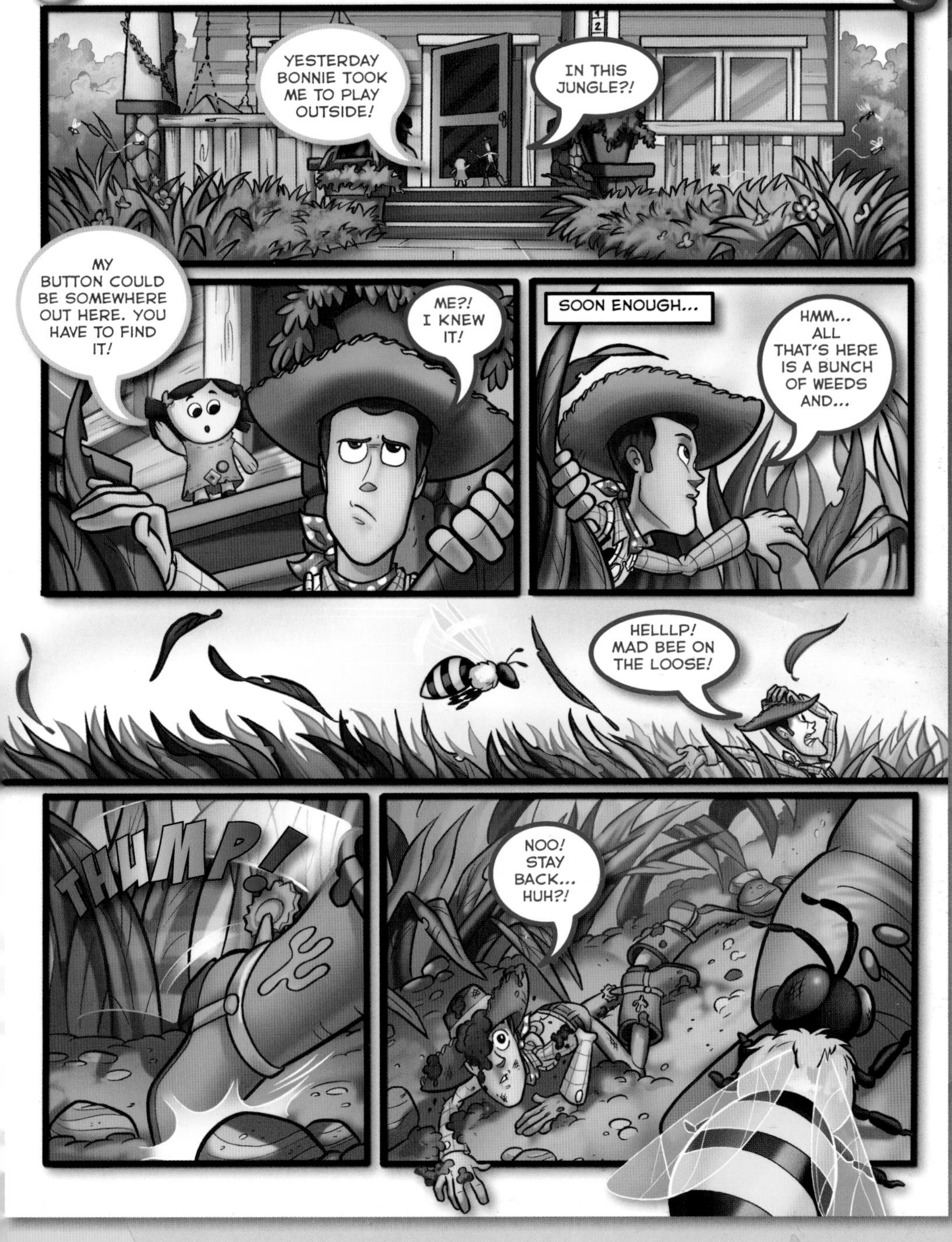
YESTERDAY BONNIE TOOK ME TO PLAY OUTSIDE!
IN THIS JUNGLE?!
MY BUTTON COULD BE SOMEWHERE OUT HERE. YOU HAVE TO FIND IT!
ME?! I KNEW IT!
SOON ENOUGH...
HMM... ALL THAT'S HERE IS A BUNCH OF WEEDS AND...
HELLLP! MAD BEE ON THE LOOSE!
THUMP!
NOO! STAY BACK... HUH?!

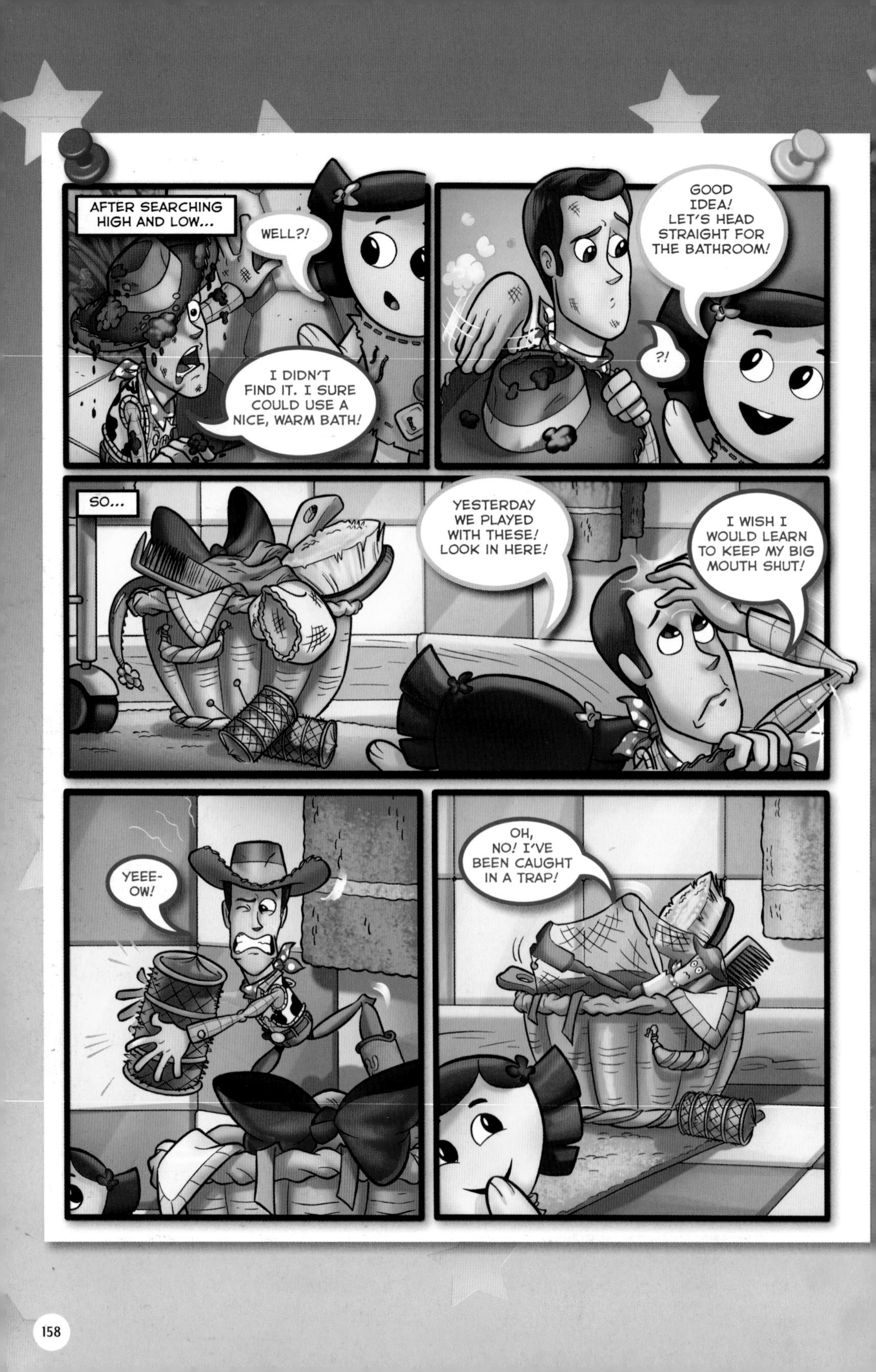
AFTER SEARCHING HIGH AND LOW...
WELL?!
I DIDN'T FIND IT. I SURE COULD USE A NICE, WARM BATH!
GOOD IDEA! LET'S HEAD STRAIGHT FOR THE BATHROOM!
?!
SO...
YESTERDAY WE PLAYED WITH THESE! LOOK IN HERE!
I WISH I WOULD LEARN TO KEEP MY BIG MOUTH SHUT!
YEEE-OW!
OH, NO! I'VE BEEN CAUGHT IN A TRAP!

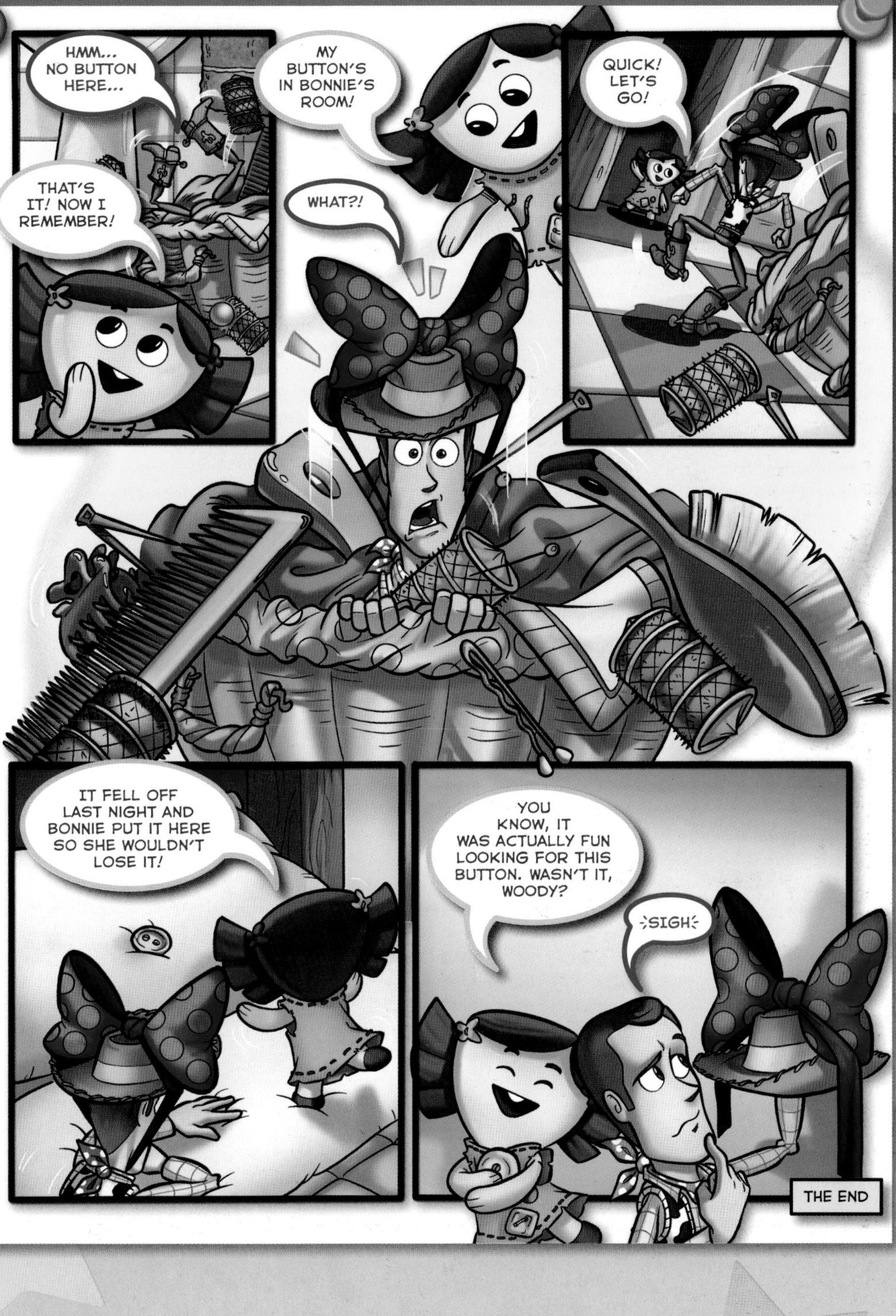
HMM... NO BUTTON HERE...
THAT'S IT! NOW I REMEMBER!
MY BUTTON'S IN BONNIE'S ROOM!
WHAT?!
QUICK! LET'S GO!
IT FELL OFF LAST NIGHT AND BONNIE PUT IT HERE SO SHE WOULDN'T LOSE IT!
YOU KNOW, IT WAS ACTUALLY FUN LOOKING FOR THIS BUTTON. WASN'T IT, WOODY?
SIGH
THE END

A DINOSAUR SECRET

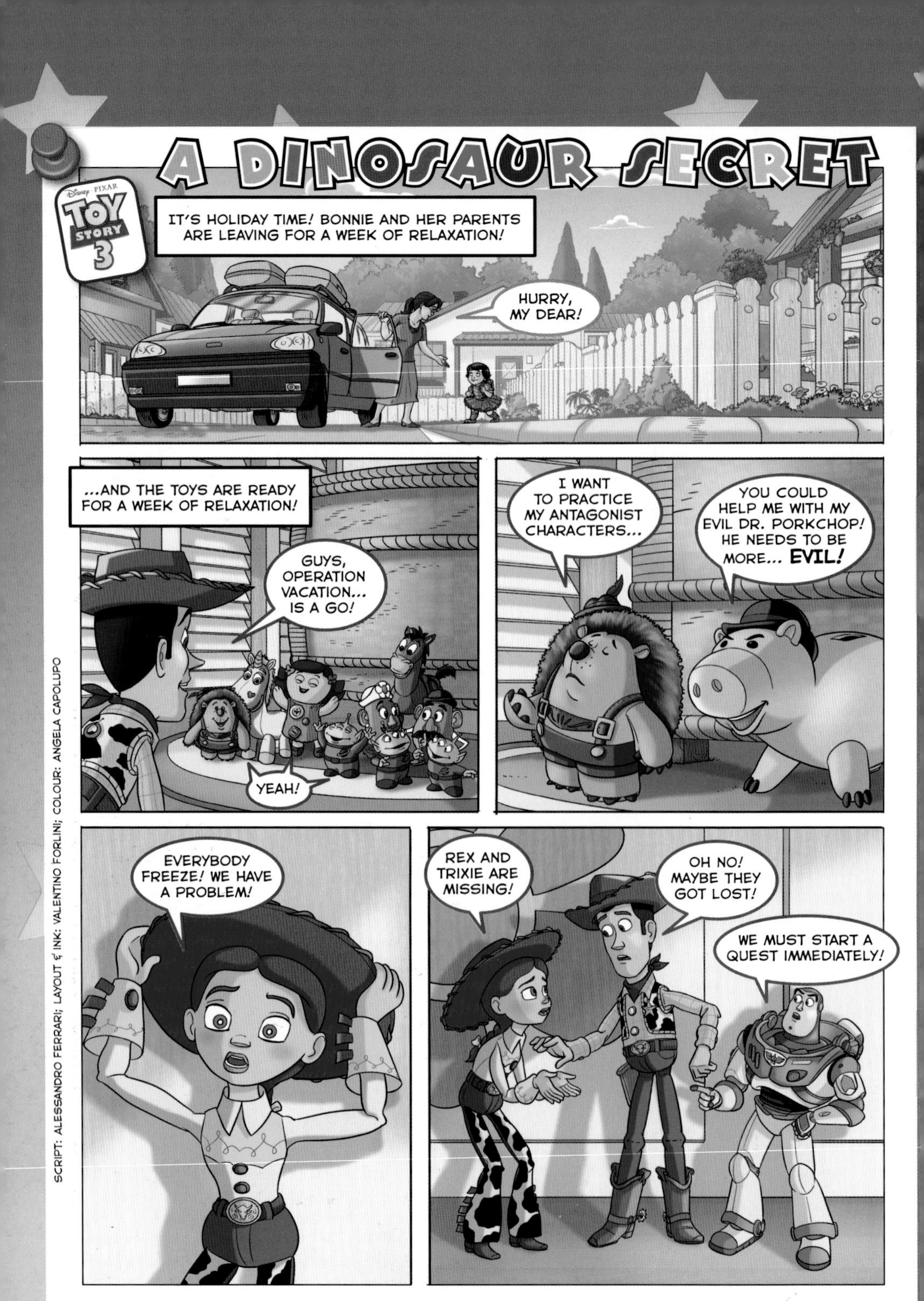
Disney · PIXAR
TOY STORY 3
IT'S HOLIDAY TIME! BONNIE AND HER PARENTS ARE LEAVING FOR A WEEK OF RELAXATION!
HURRY, MY DEAR!
...AND THE TOYS ARE READY FOR A WEEK OF RELAXATION!
GUYS, OPERATION VACATION... IS A GO!
YEAH!
I WANT TO PRACTICE MY ANTAGONIST CHARACTERS...
YOU COULD HELP ME WITH MY EVIL DR. PORKCHOP! HE NEEDS TO BE MORE... EVIL!
EVERYBODY FREEZE! WE HAVE A PROBLEM!
REX AND TRIXIE ARE MISSING!
OH NO! MAYBE THEY GOT LOST!
WE MUST START A QUEST IMMEDIATELY!

SCRIPT: ALESSANDRO FERRARI; LAYOUT & INK: VALENTINO FORLINI; COLOUR: ANGELA CAPOLUPO

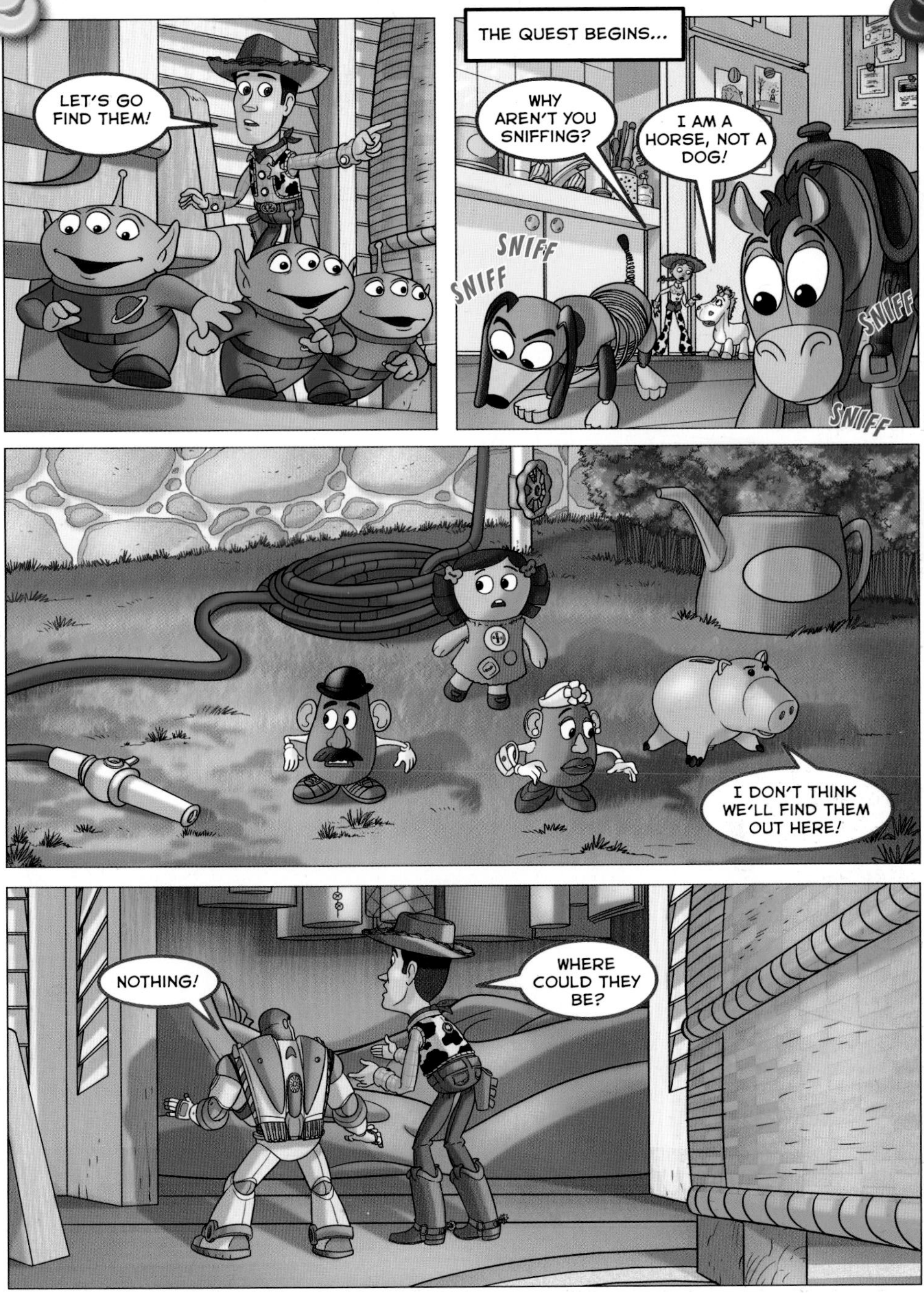
LET'S GO FIND THEM!
THE QUEST BEGINS...
WHY AREN'T YOU SNIFFING?
I AM A HORSE, NOT A DOG!
SNIFF
SNIFF
SNIFF
SNIFF
I DON'T THINK WE'LL FIND THEM OUT HERE!
NOTHING!
WHERE COULD THEY BE?

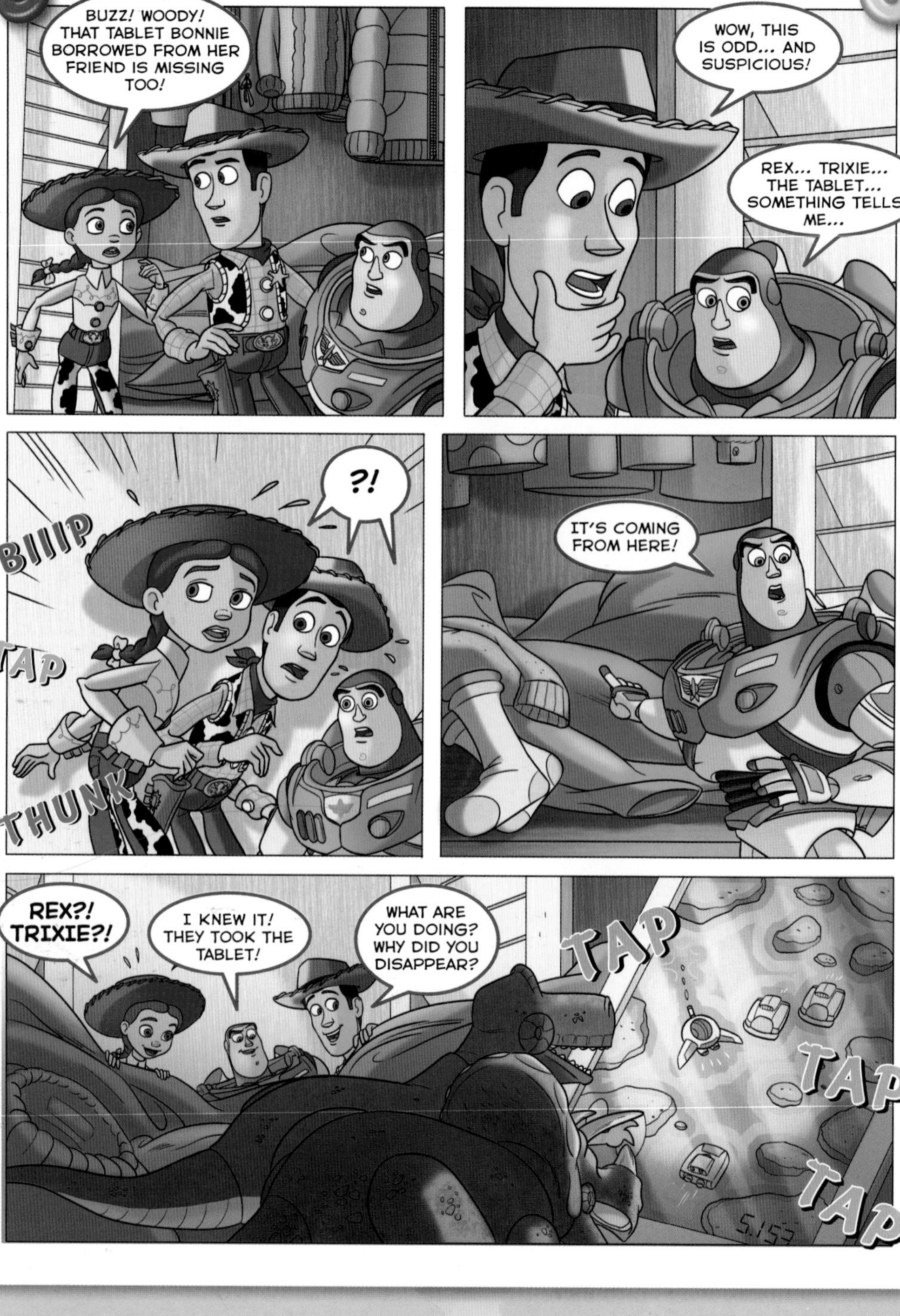
BUZZ! WOODY! THAT TABLET BONNIE BORROWED FROM HER FRIEND IS MISSING TOO!
WOW, THIS IS ODD... AND SUSPICIOUS!
REX... TRIXIE... THE TABLET... SOMETHING TELLS ME...
BIIIP
TAP
THUNK
?!
IT'S COMING FROM HERE!
REX?! TRIXIE?!
I KNEW IT! THEY TOOK THE TABLET!
WHAT ARE YOU DOING? WHY DID YOU DISAPPEAR?
TAP
TAP
TAP

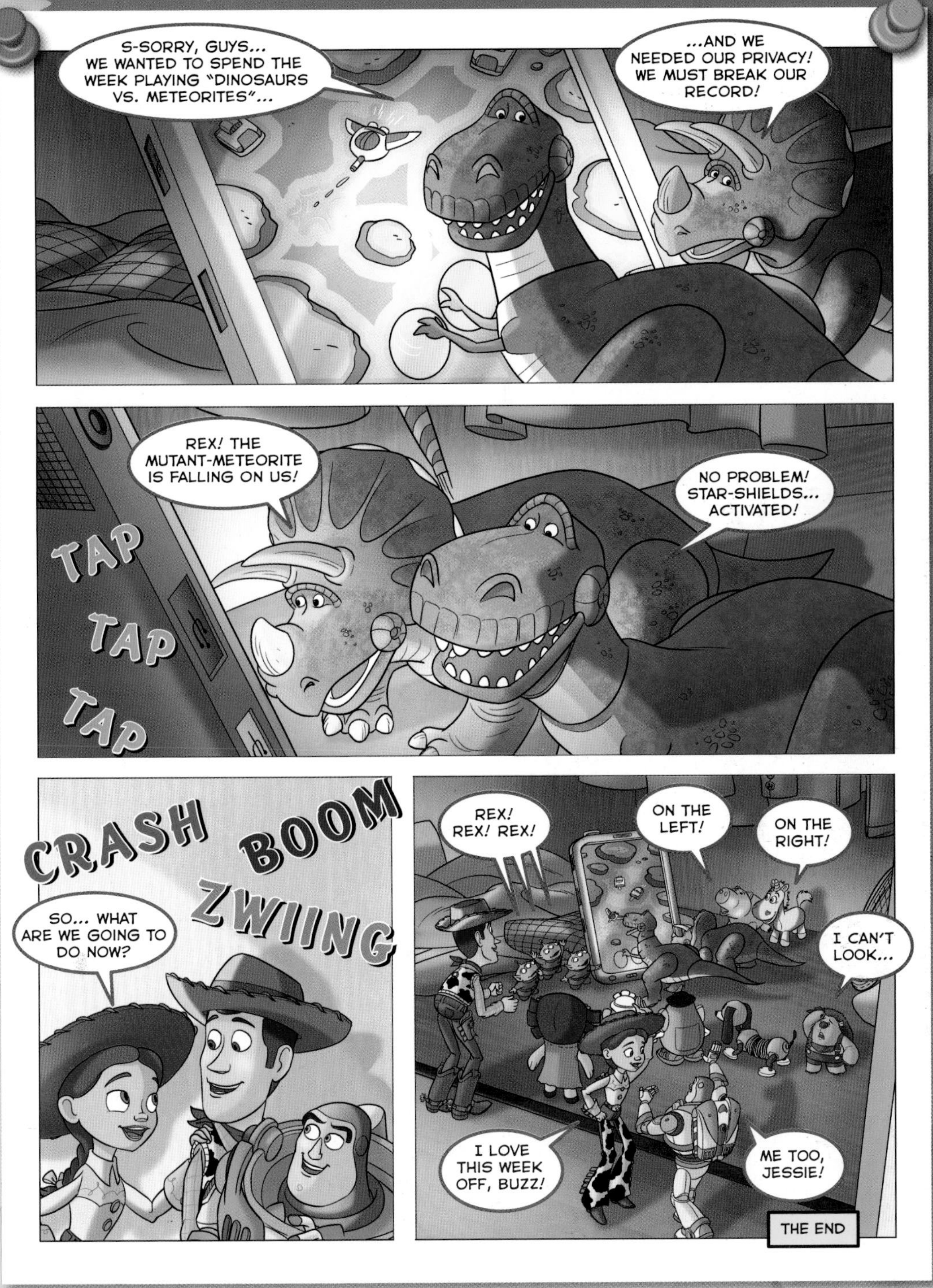

S-SORRY, GUYS... WE WANTED TO SPEND THE WEEK PLAYING "DINOSAURS VS. METEORITES"...
...AND WE NEEDED OUR PRIVACY! WE MUST BREAK OUR RECORD!
REX! THE MUTANT-METEORITE IS FALLING ON US!
NO PROBLEM! STAR-SHIELDS... ACTIVATED!
TAP
TAP
TAP
CRASH
BOOM
ZWIING
SO... WHAT ARE WE GOING TO DO NOW?
REX! REX! REX!
ON THE LEFT!
ON THE RIGHT!
I CAN'T LOOK...
I LOVE THIS WEEK OFF, BUZZ!
ME TOO, JESSIE!
THE END

DINO CHANGES

SCRIPT: ALESSANDRO FERRARI; LAYOUT: ANDREA GREPPI; INK: MICHELA FRARE; COLOUR: ANGELA CAPOLUPO

LOOK, REX! AN ONLINE COURSE IN PALEONTOLOGY!

I-IS IT A-ABOUT US, TRIXIE?

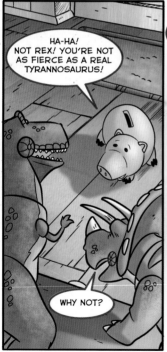

HA-HA! NOT REX! YOU'RE NOT AS FIERCE AS A REAL TYRANNOSAURUS!

WHY NOT?

YOU'RE TOO SCARED OF EVERYTHING!

SO TRUE... -:SIGH:-

YOU COULD TRY!

HOW?

LET'S TRAIN HIM!

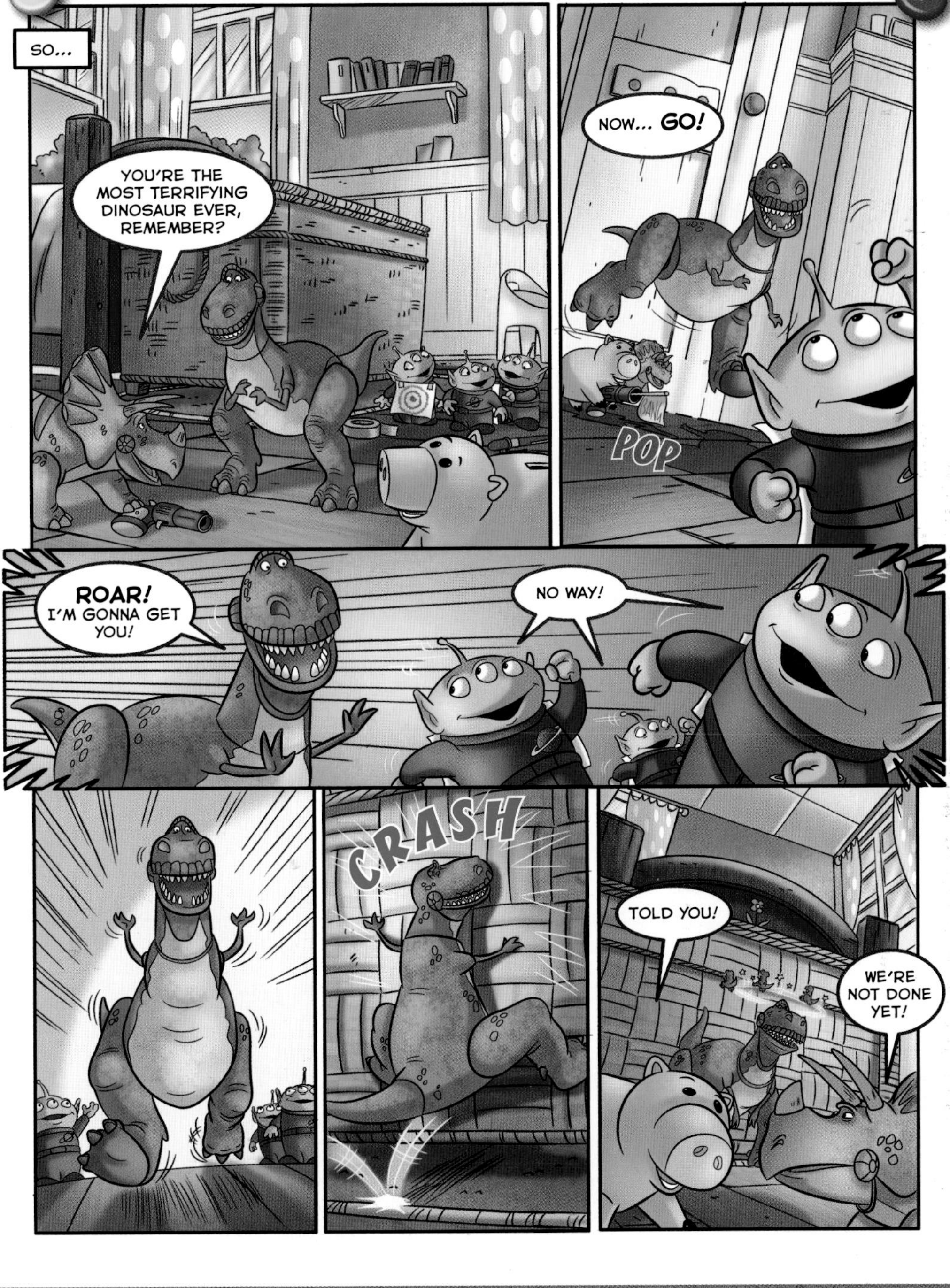
SO...
YOU'RE THE MOST TERRIFYING DINOSAUR EVER, REMEMBER?
NOW... GO!
BANG
POP
ROAR! I'M GONNA GET YOU!
NO WAY!
CRASH
TOLD YOU!
WE'RE NOT DONE YET!

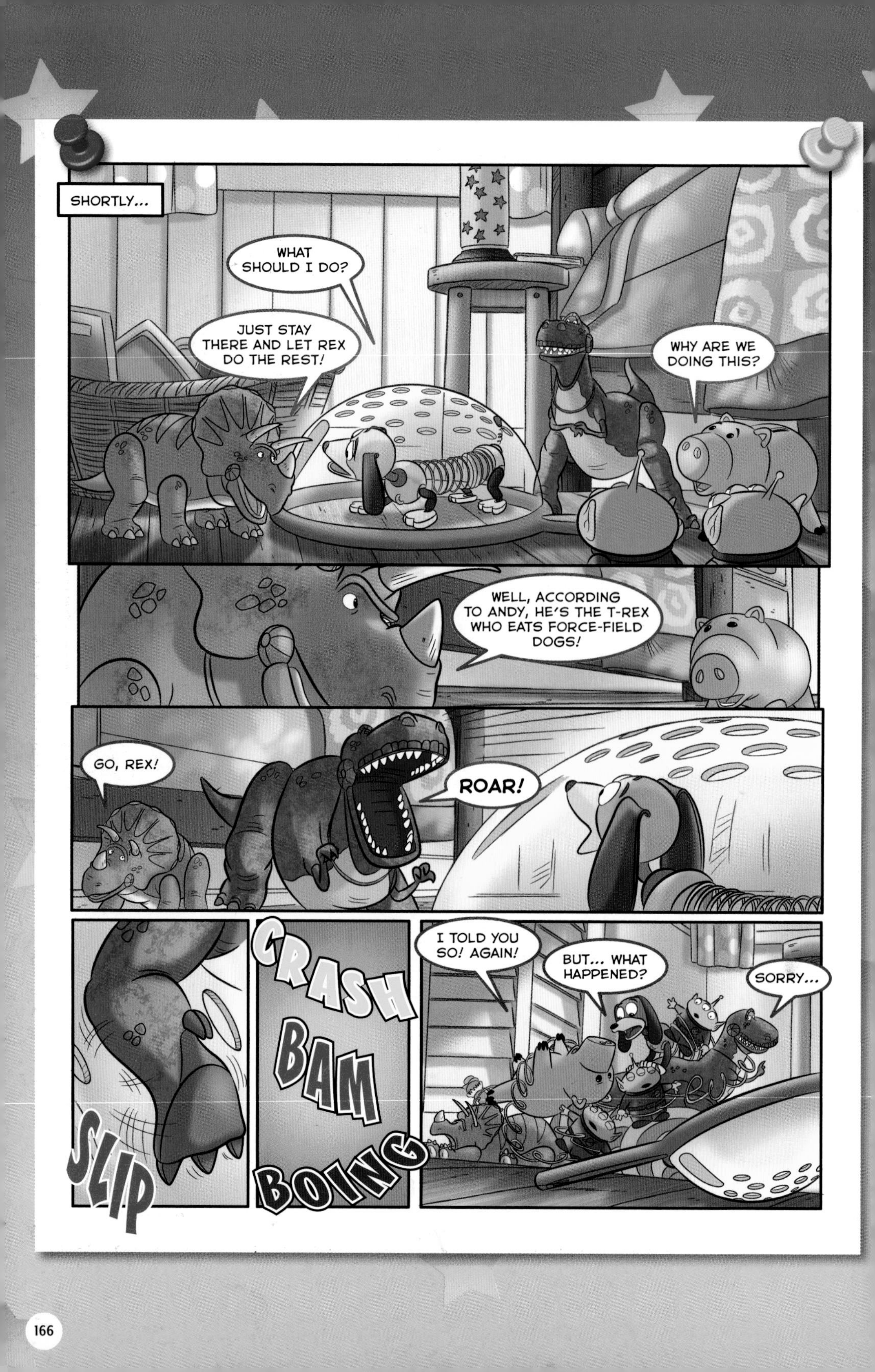
SHORTLY...
WHAT SHOULD I DO?
JUST STAY THERE AND LET REX DO THE REST!
WHY ARE WE DOING THIS?
WELL, ACCORDING TO ANDY, HE'S THE T-REX WHO EATS FORCE-FIELD DOGS!
GO, REX!
ROAR!
SLIP
CRASH
BAM
BOING
I TOLD YOU SO! AGAIN!
BUT... WHAT HAPPENED?
SORRY...

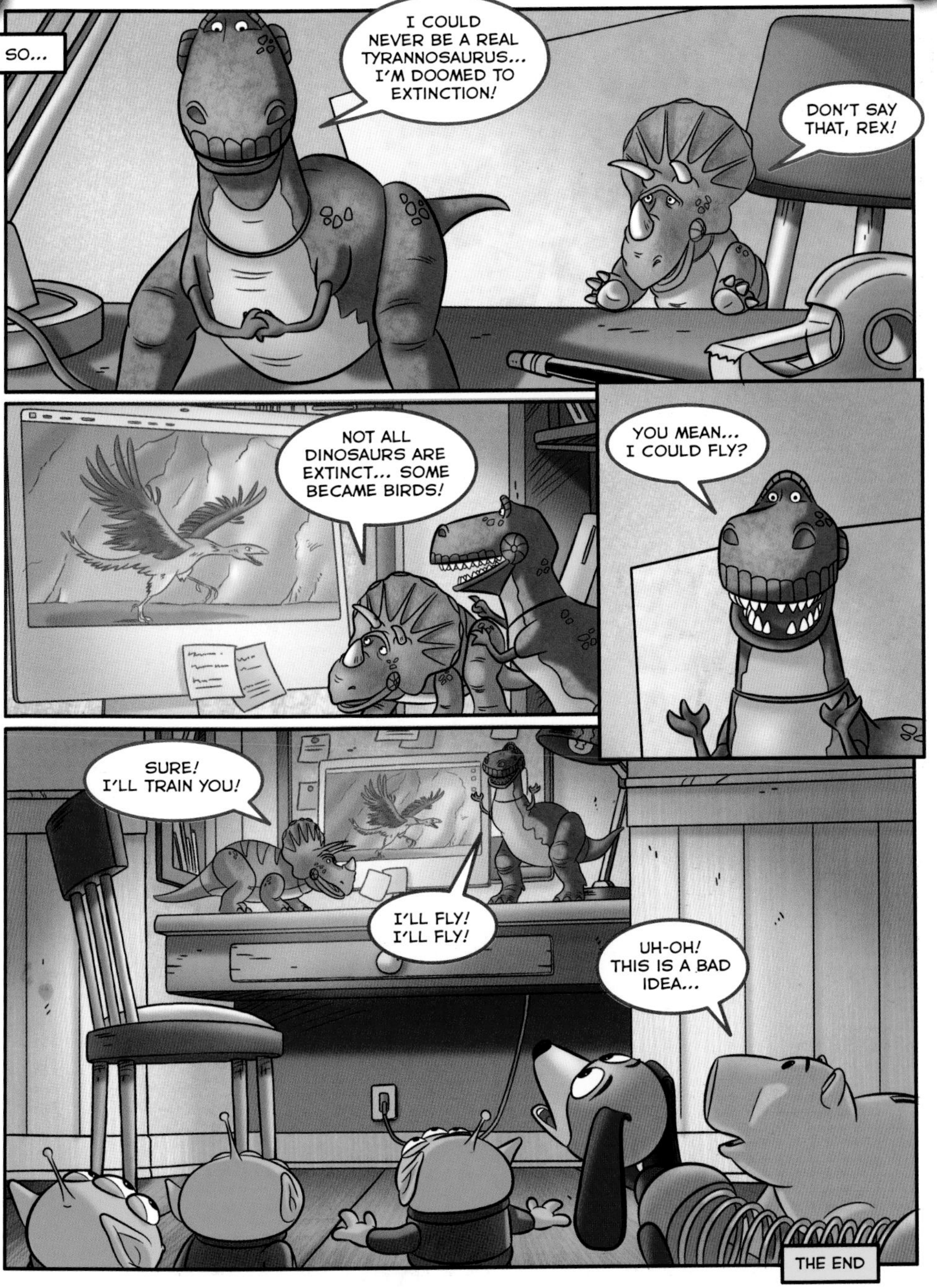
SO...
I COULD NEVER BE A REAL TYRANNOSAURUS... I'M DOOMED TO EXTINCTION!
DON'T SAY THAT, REX!
NOT ALL DINOSAURS ARE EXTINCT... SOME BECAME BIRDS!
YOU MEAN... I COULD FLY?
SURE! I'LL TRAIN YOU!
I'LL FLY! I'LL FLY!
UH-OH! THIS IS A BAD IDEA...
THE END

BUZZ'S BEST

ONE MORNING, IN BONNIE'S ROOM...

DOLLY! I NEED **ADVICE!**

ZAC ZAC

SURE!

TELL ME... **UH!** WHAT'S THAT **WORRIED** FACE?!

I'D LIKE TO DO SOMETHING **GALACTIC** FOR JESSIE, SOMETHING TO MAKE HER HAPPY!

WOW! THAT'S NICE!

YEAH! THE PROBLEM IS THAT I **DON'T** KNOW WHAT TO DO!

MMM... JUST LET ME THINK ABOUT IT...

DONE! LET'S CALL THE **OTHERS** AND FIND SOME IDEAS!

UH!

SCRIPT: TEA ORSI; LAYOUT: LUCA USAI; INK: MICHELA FRARE; COLOUR: ANGELA CAPOLUPO

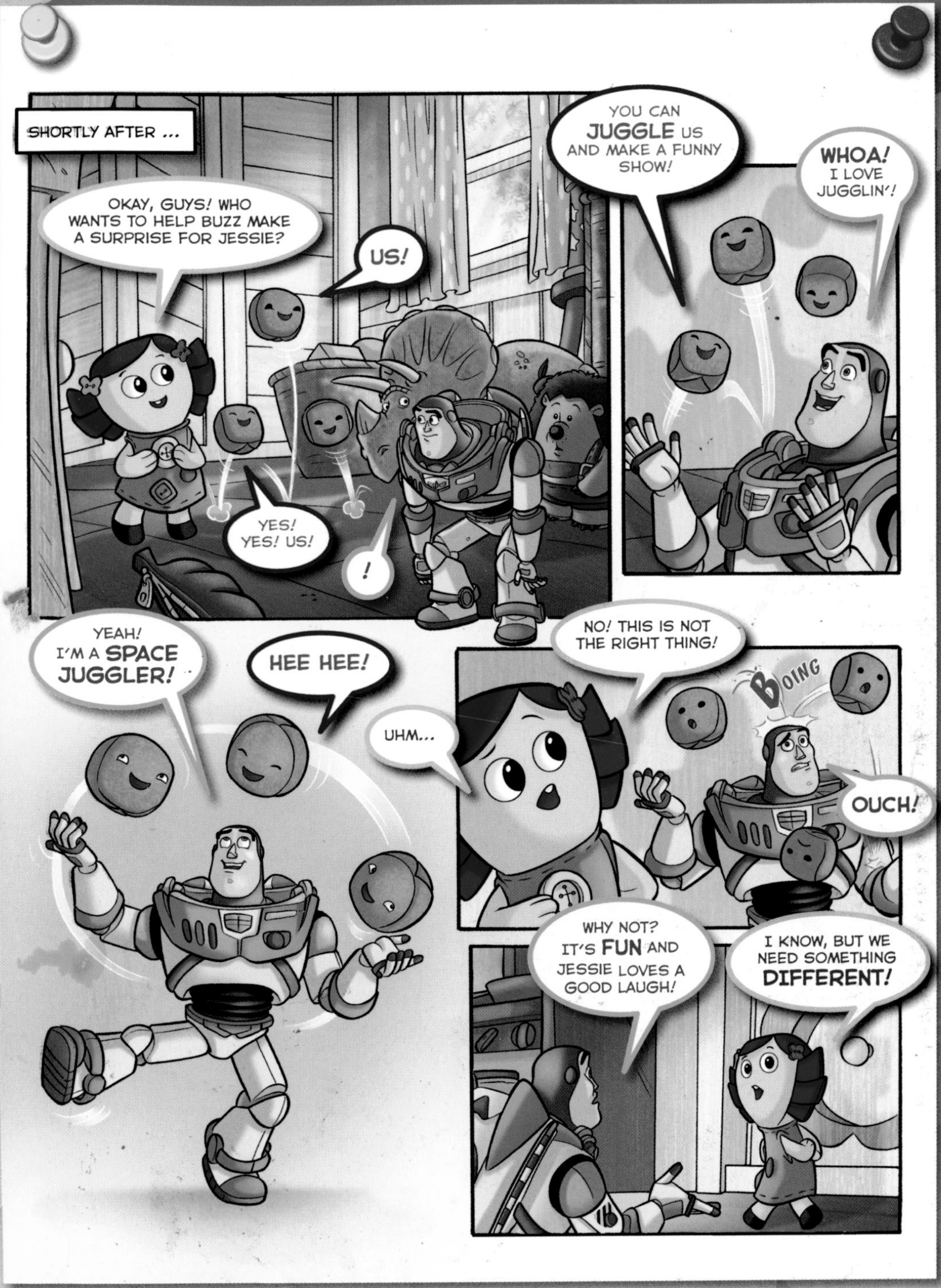
SHORTLY AFTER ...
OKAY, GUYS! WHO WANTS TO HELP BUZZ MAKE A SURPRISE FOR JESSIE?
US!
YES! YES! US!
!
YOU CAN JUGGLE US AND MAKE A FUNNY SHOW!
WHOA! I LOVE JUGGLIN'!
YEAH! I'M A SPACE JUGGLER!
HEE HEE!
UHM...
NO! THIS IS NOT THE RIGHT THING!
BOING
OUCH!
WHY NOT? IT'S FUN AND JESSIE LOVES A GOOD LAUGH!
I KNOW, BUT WE NEED SOMETHING DIFFERENT!

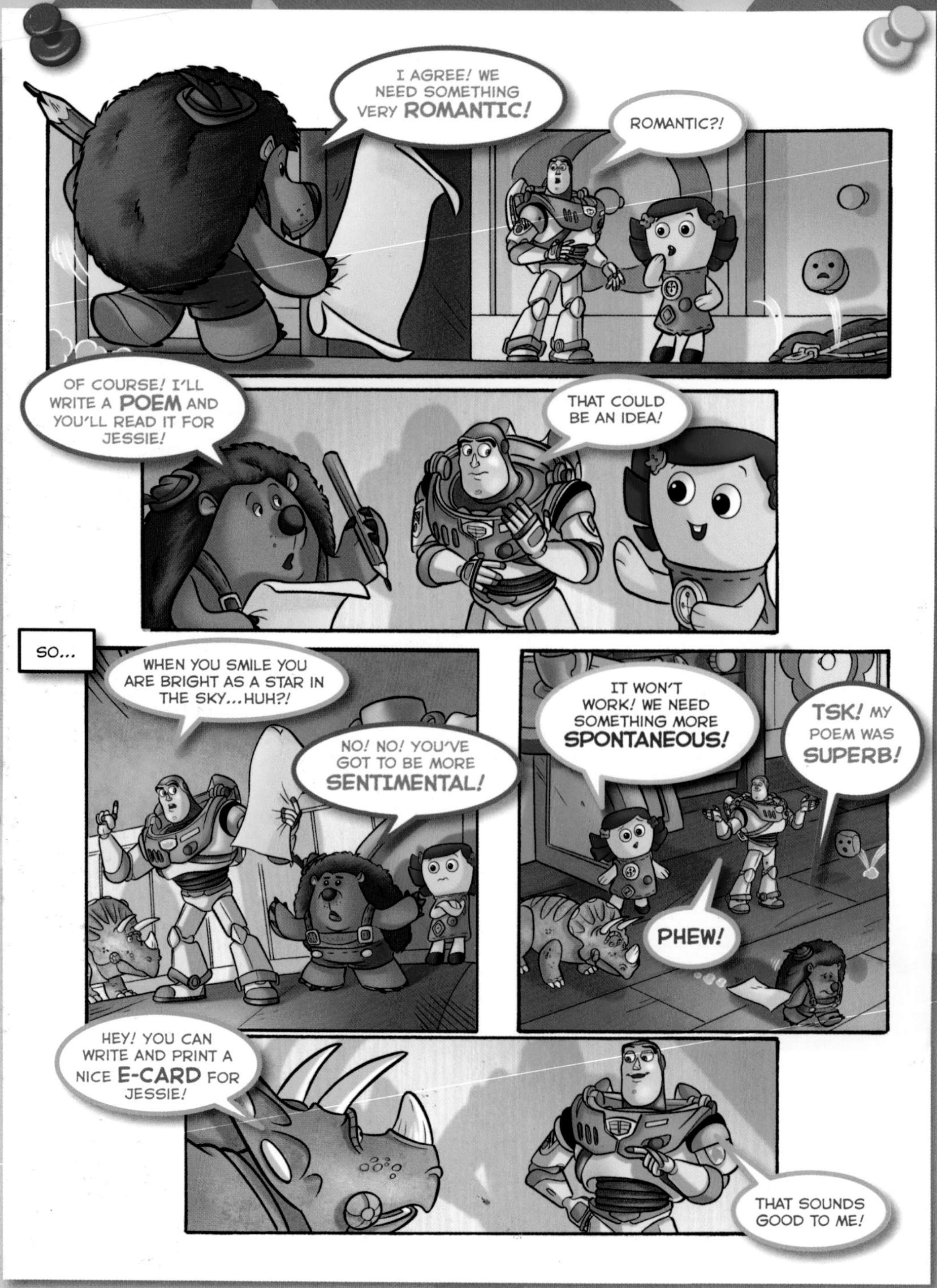
I AGREE! WE NEED SOMETHING VERY ROMANTIC!
ROMANTIC?!
OF COURSE! I'LL WRITE A POEM AND YOU'LL READ IT FOR JESSIE!
THAT COULD BE AN IDEA!
SO...
WHEN YOU SMILE YOU ARE BRIGHT AS A STAR IN THE SKY... HUH?!
NO! NO! YOU'VE GOT TO BE MORE SENTIMENTAL!
IT WON'T WORK! WE NEED SOMETHING MORE SPONTANEOUS!
TSK! MY POEM WAS SUPERB!
PHEW!
HEY! YOU CAN WRITE AND PRINT A NICE E-CARD FOR JESSIE!
THAT SOUNDS GOOD TO ME!

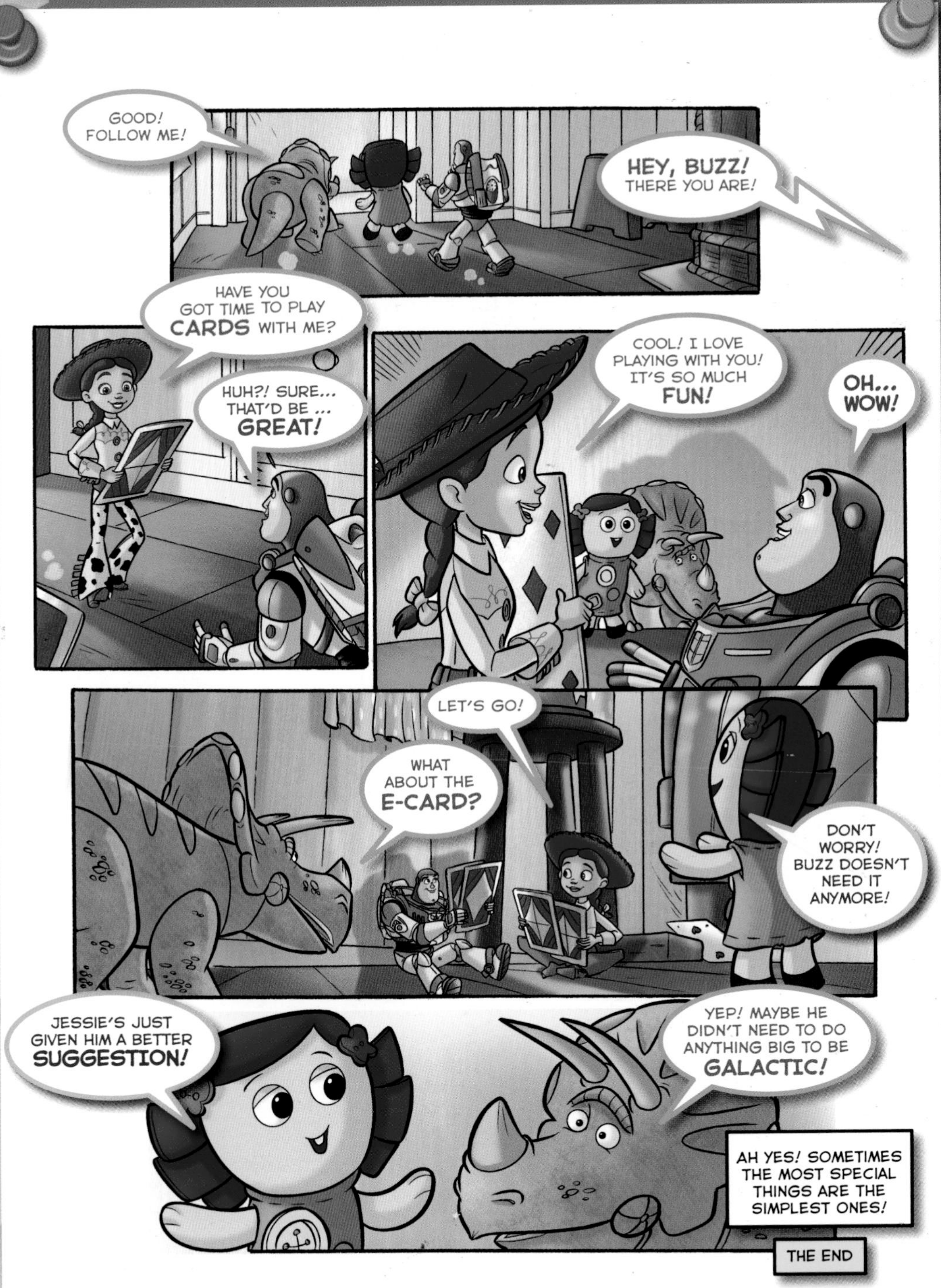

GOOD! FOLLOW ME!
HEY, BUZZ! THERE YOU ARE!
HAVE YOU GOT TIME TO PLAY CARDS WITH ME?
HUH?! SURE... THAT'D BE ... GREAT!
COOL! I LOVE PLAYING WITH YOU! IT'S SO MUCH FUN!
OH... WOW!
LET'S GO!
WHAT ABOUT THE E-CARD?
DON'T WORRY! BUZZ DOESN'T NEED IT ANYMORE!
JESSIE'S JUST GIVEN HIM A BETTER SUGGESTION!
YEP! MAYBE HE DIDN'T NEED TO DO ANYTHING BIG TO BE GALACTIC!
AH YES! SOMETIMES THE MOST SPECIAL THINGS ARE THE SIMPLEST ONES!
THE END

UNEXPECTED TRIP

I CAN'T WAIT TO BE AT THE MOUNTAIN RESORT!

I'M SO GLAD I'M NOT GOING!

WHY?

BECAUSE YOU GET WET AND COLD SKIING WITH BONNIE! IT'LL BE TERRIBLE!

BESIDES, YOUR SCARVES LOOK RIDICULOUS!

!

YEAH, I'M LUCKY TO BE STAYING HERE!

BUT...

YOU'D BETTER COME TOO, HAMM! I MIGHT NEED SOME CASH FOR COCOA!

ARGH!

THE END

SCRIPT: TEA ORSI, LAYOUT: VALENTINO FORLINI, INK: VALENTINO FORLINI, COLOUR: ANGELA CAPOLUPO

MR. POTATO HEAD, THE SNOWMAN

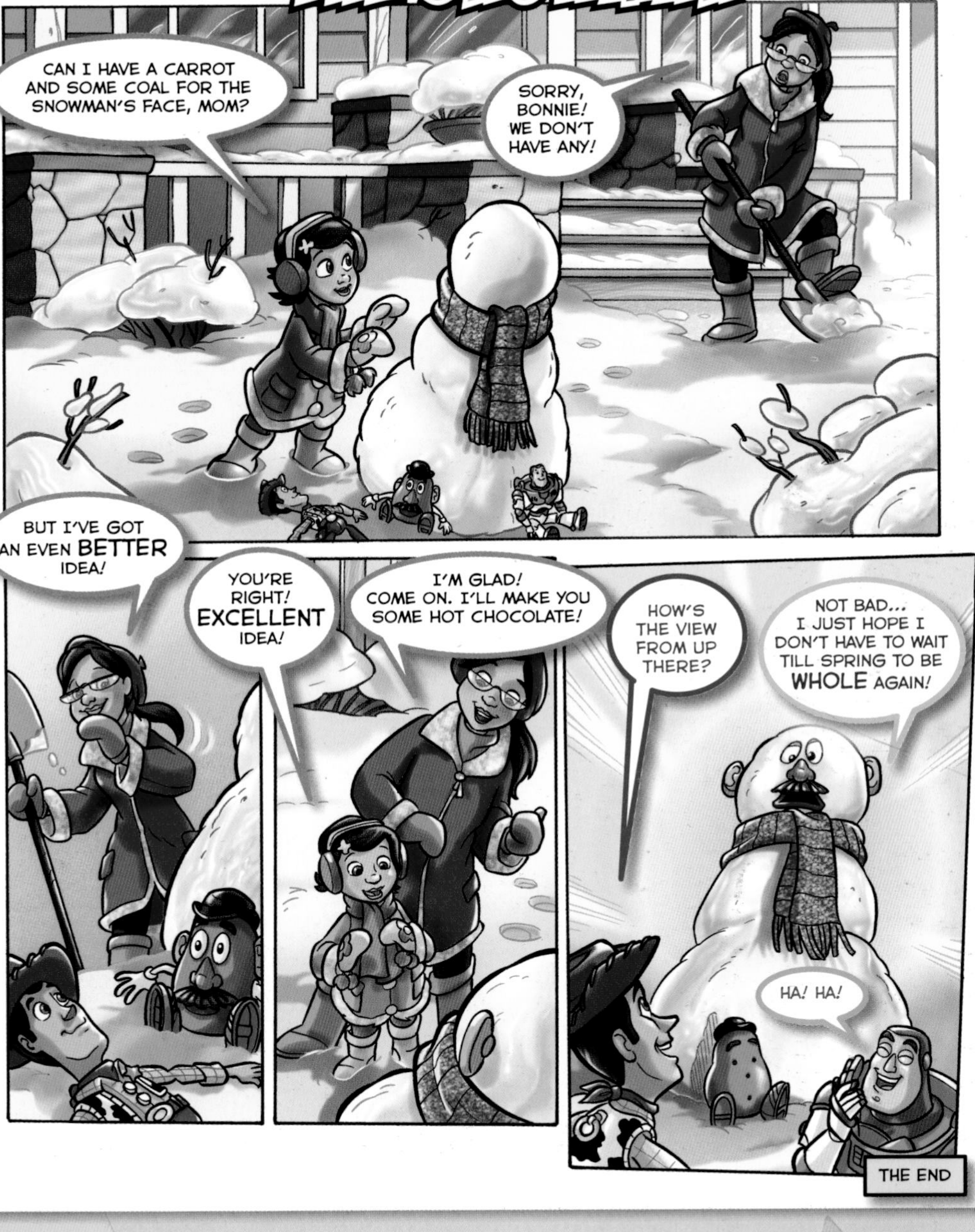

CAN I HAVE A CARROT AND SOME COAL FOR THE SNOWMAN'S FACE, MOM?
SORRY, BONNIE! WE DON'T HAVE ANY!
BUT I'VE GOT AN EVEN BETTER IDEA!
YOU'RE RIGHT! EXCELLENT IDEA!
I'M GLAD! COME ON. I'LL MAKE YOU SOME HOT CHOCOLATE!
HOW'S THE VIEW FROM UP THERE?
NOT BAD... I JUST HOPE I DON'T HAVE TO WAIT TILL SPRING TO BE WHOLE AGAIN!
HA! HA!
THE END

SCRIPT: ALESSANDRO SISTI; LAYOUT: LUCA USAI; INK: MICHELA FRARE; COLOUR: LUCIO DE GIUSEPPE

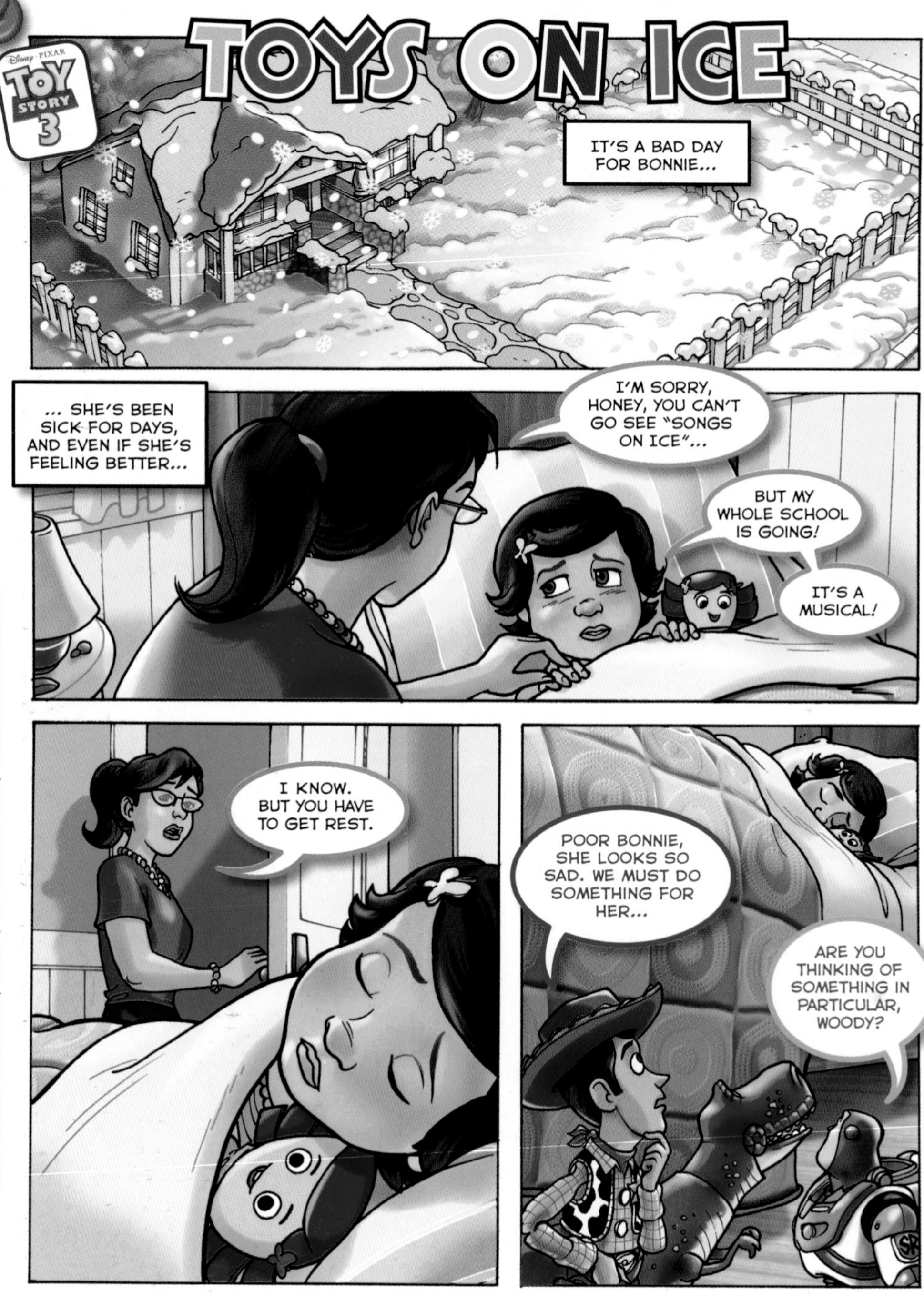
TOYS ON ICE
DISNEY · PIXAR TOY STORY 3
IT'S A BAD DAY FOR BONNIE...
... SHE'S BEEN SICK FOR DAYS, AND EVEN IF SHE'S FEELING BETTER...
I'M SORRY, HONEY, YOU CAN'T GO SEE "SONGS ON ICE"...
BUT MY WHOLE SCHOOL IS GOING!
IT'S A MUSICAL!
I KNOW. BUT YOU HAVE TO GET REST.
POOR BONNIE, SHE LOOKS SO SAD. WE MUST DO SOMETHING FOR HER...
ARE YOU THINKING OF SOMETHING IN PARTICULAR, WOODY?

SCRIPT: ALESSANDRO FERRARI; LAYOUT & INK: VALENTINO FORLINI; COLOUR: LUCIO DE GIUSEPPE

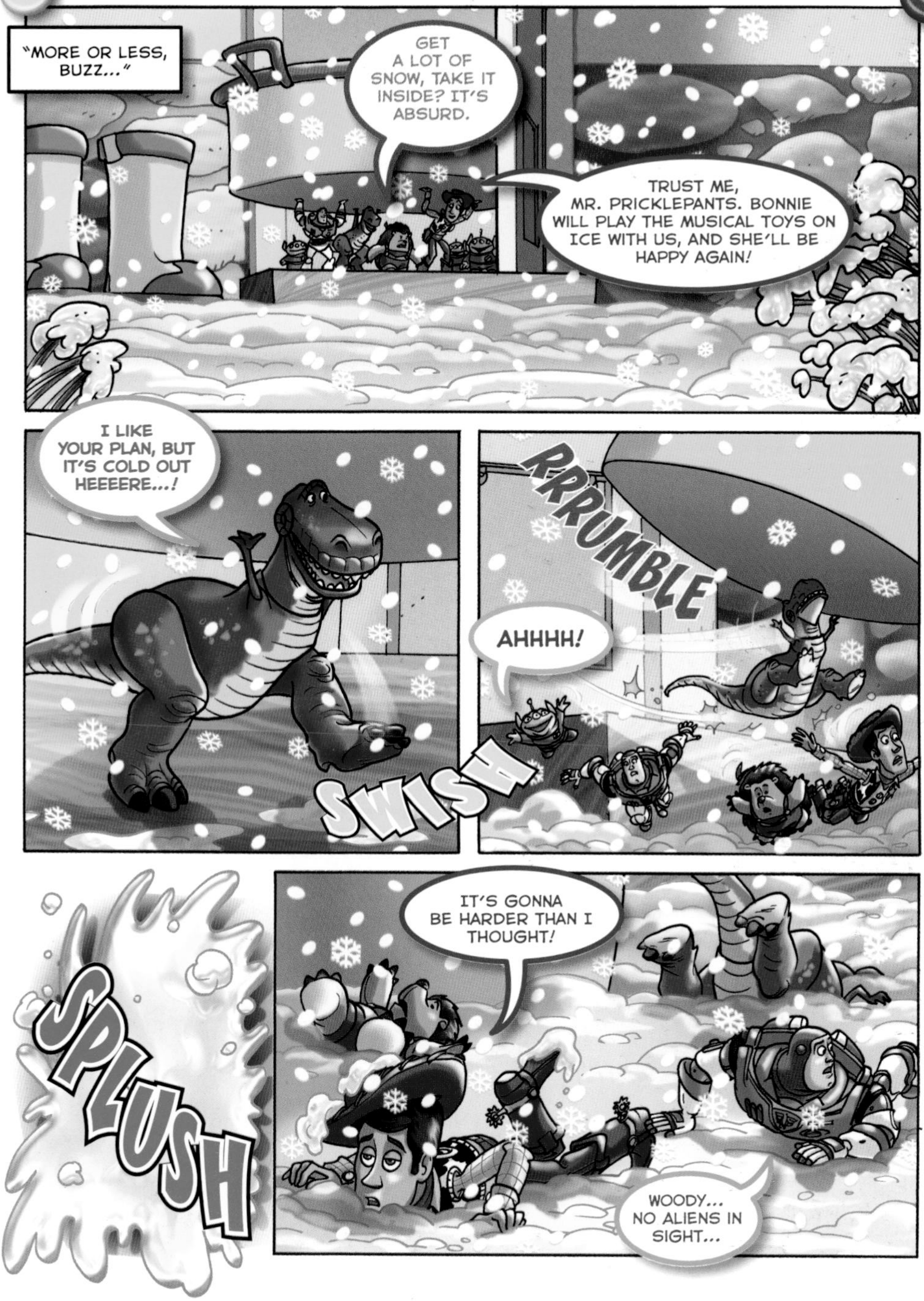
"MORE OR LESS, BUZZ..."
GET A LOT OF SNOW, TAKE IT INSIDE? IT'S ABSURD.
TRUST ME, MR. PRICKLEPANTS. BONNIE WILL PLAY THE MUSICAL TOYS ON ICE WITH US, AND SHE'LL BE HAPPY AGAIN!
I LIKE YOUR PLAN, BUT IT'S COLD OUT HEEEERE...!
RRRUMBLE
AHHHH!
SWISH
SPLUSH
IT'S GONNA BE HARDER THAN I THOUGHT!
WOODY... NO ALIENS IN SIGHT...

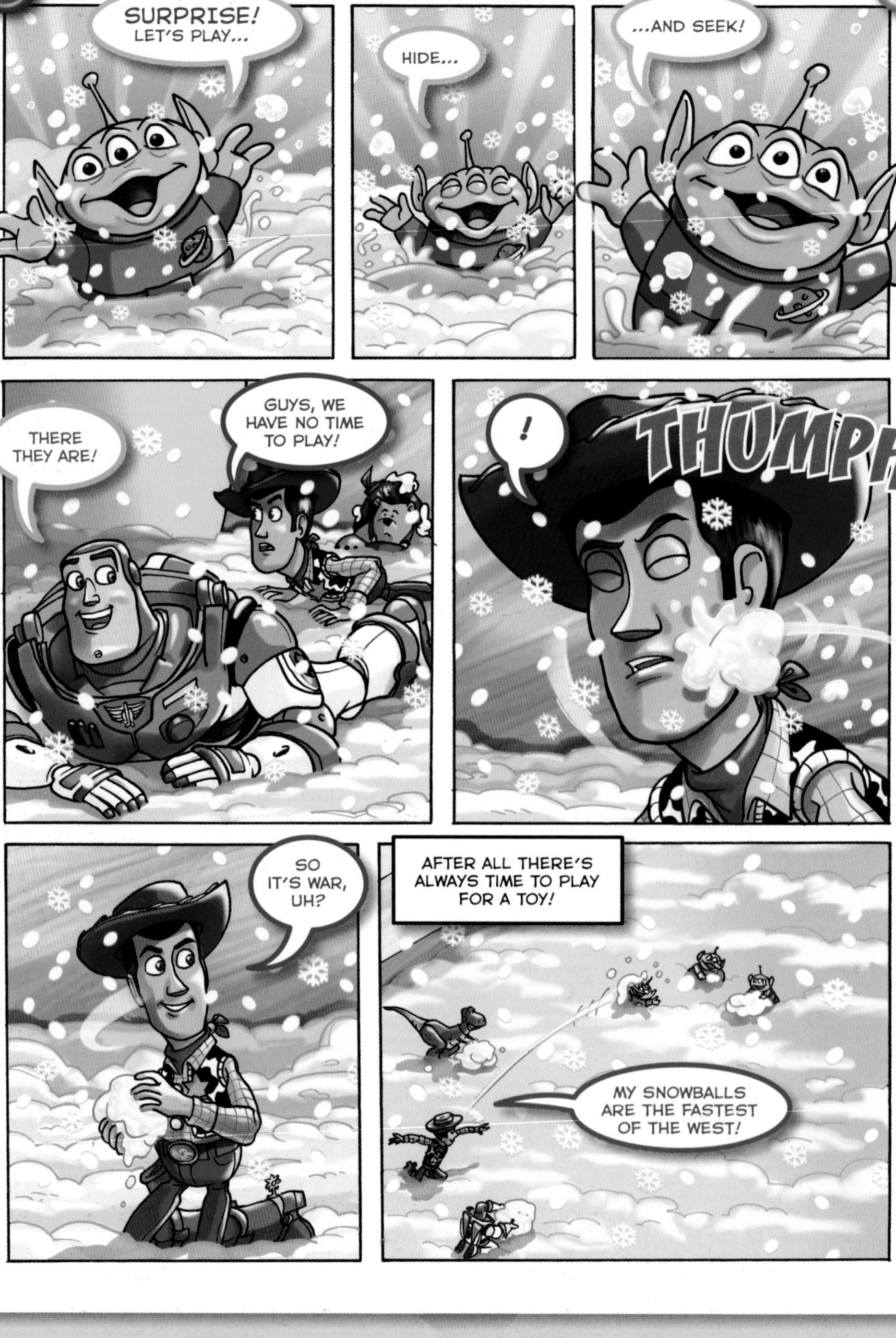
SURPRISE! LET'S PLAY...
HIDE...
...AND SEEK!
THERE THEY ARE!
GUYS, WE HAVE NO TIME TO PLAY!
!
THUMPH
SO IT'S WAR, UH?
AFTER ALL THERE'S ALWAYS TIME TO PLAY FOR A TOY!
MY SNOWBALLS ARE THE FASTEST OF THE WEST!

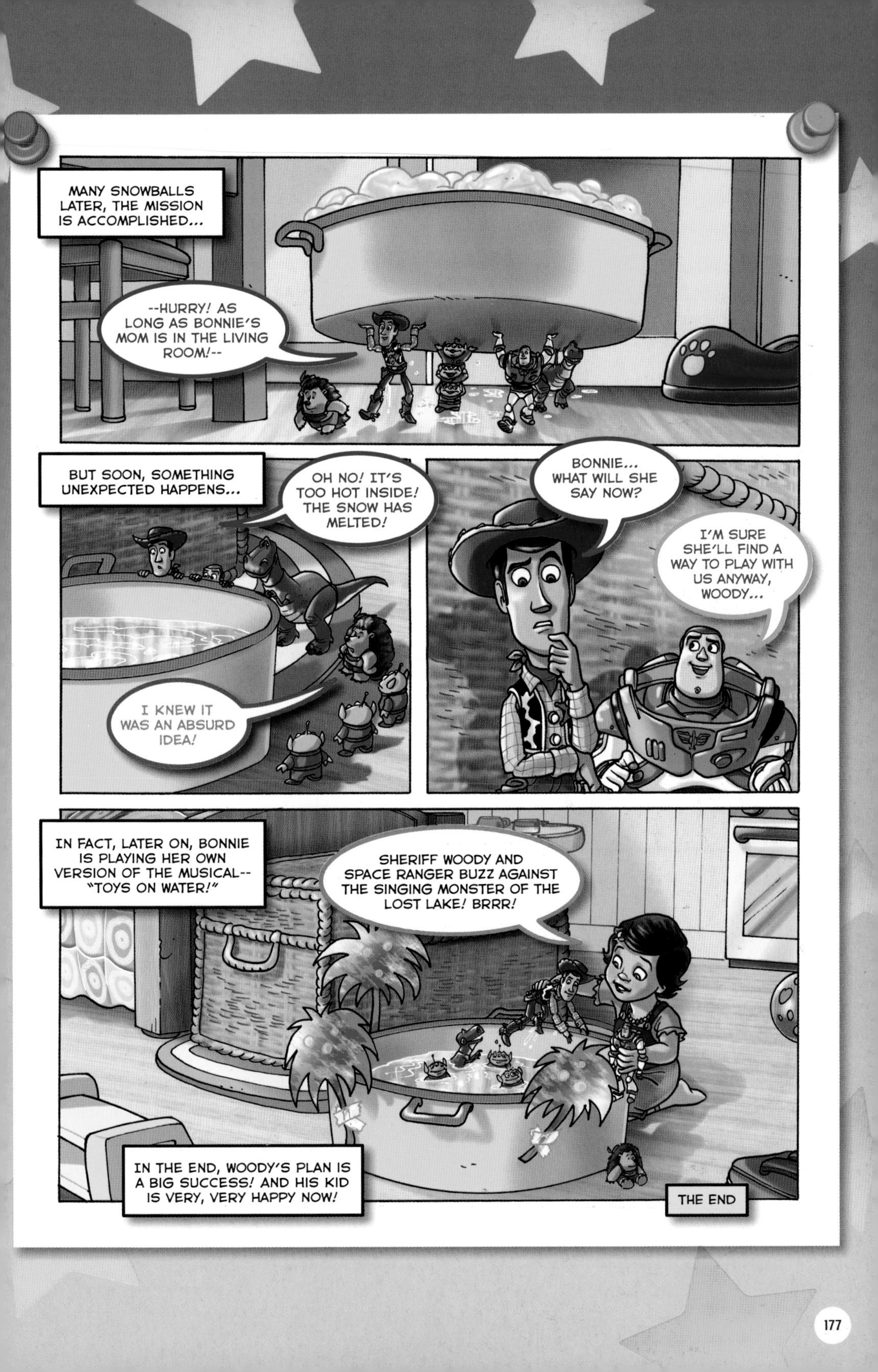

MANY SNOWBALLS LATER, THE MISSION IS ACCOMPLISHED...
--HURRY! AS LONG AS BONNIE'S MOM IS IN THE LIVING ROOM!--
BUT SOON, SOMETHING UNEXPECTED HAPPENS...
OH NO! IT'S TOO HOT INSIDE! THE SNOW HAS MELTED!
I KNEW IT WAS AN ABSURD IDEA!
BONNIE... WHAT WILL SHE SAY NOW?
I'M SURE SHE'LL FIND A WAY TO PLAY WITH US ANYWAY, WOODY...
IN FACT, LATER ON, BONNIE IS PLAYING HER OWN VERSION OF THE MUSICAL-- "TOYS ON WATER!"
SHERIFF WOODY AND SPACE RANGER BUZZ AGAINST THE SINGING MONSTER OF THE LOST LAKE! BRRR!
IN THE END, WOODY'S PLAN IS A BIG SUCCESS! AND HIS KID IS VERY, VERY HAPPY NOW!
THE END

GAMES OLD AND NEW

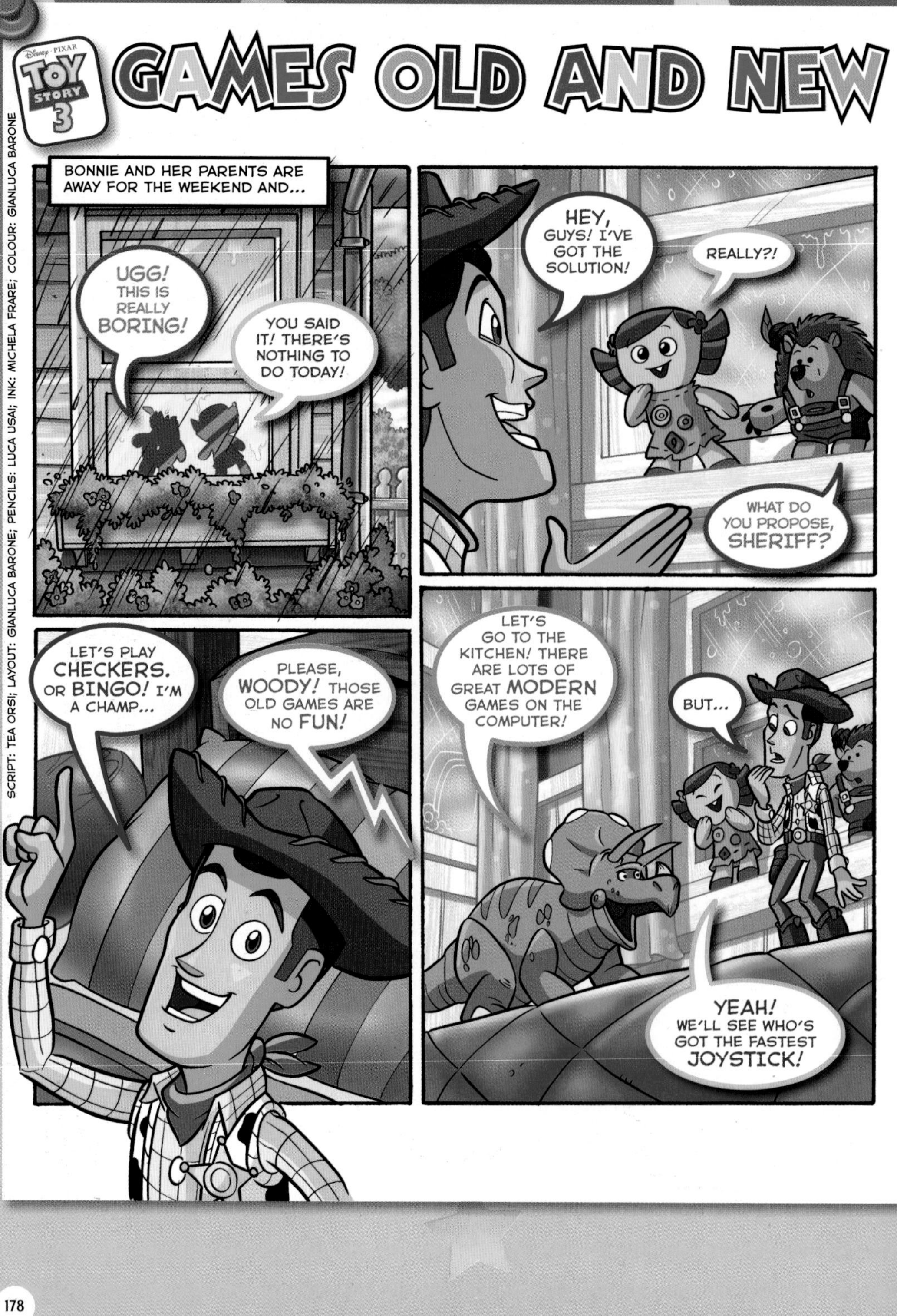

Disney PIXAR TOY STORY 3
SCRIPT: TEA ORSI; LAYOUT: GIANLUCA BARONE; PENCILS: LUCA USAI; INK: MICHELA FRARE; COLOUR: GIANLUCA BARONE
BONNIE AND HER PARENTS ARE AWAY FOR THE WEEKEND AND...
UGG! THIS IS REALLY BORING!
YOU SAID IT! THERE'S NOTHING TO DO TODAY!
HEY, GUYS! I'VE GOT THE SOLUTION!
REALLY?!
WHAT DO YOU PROPOSE, SHERIFF?
LET'S PLAY CHECKERS. OR BINGO! I'M A CHAMP...
PLEASE, WOODY! THOSE OLD GAMES ARE NO FUN!
LET'S GO TO THE KITCHEN! THERE ARE LOTS OF GREAT MODERN GAMES ON THE COMPUTER!
BUT...
YEAH! WE'LL SEE WHO'S GOT THE FASTEST JOYSTICK!

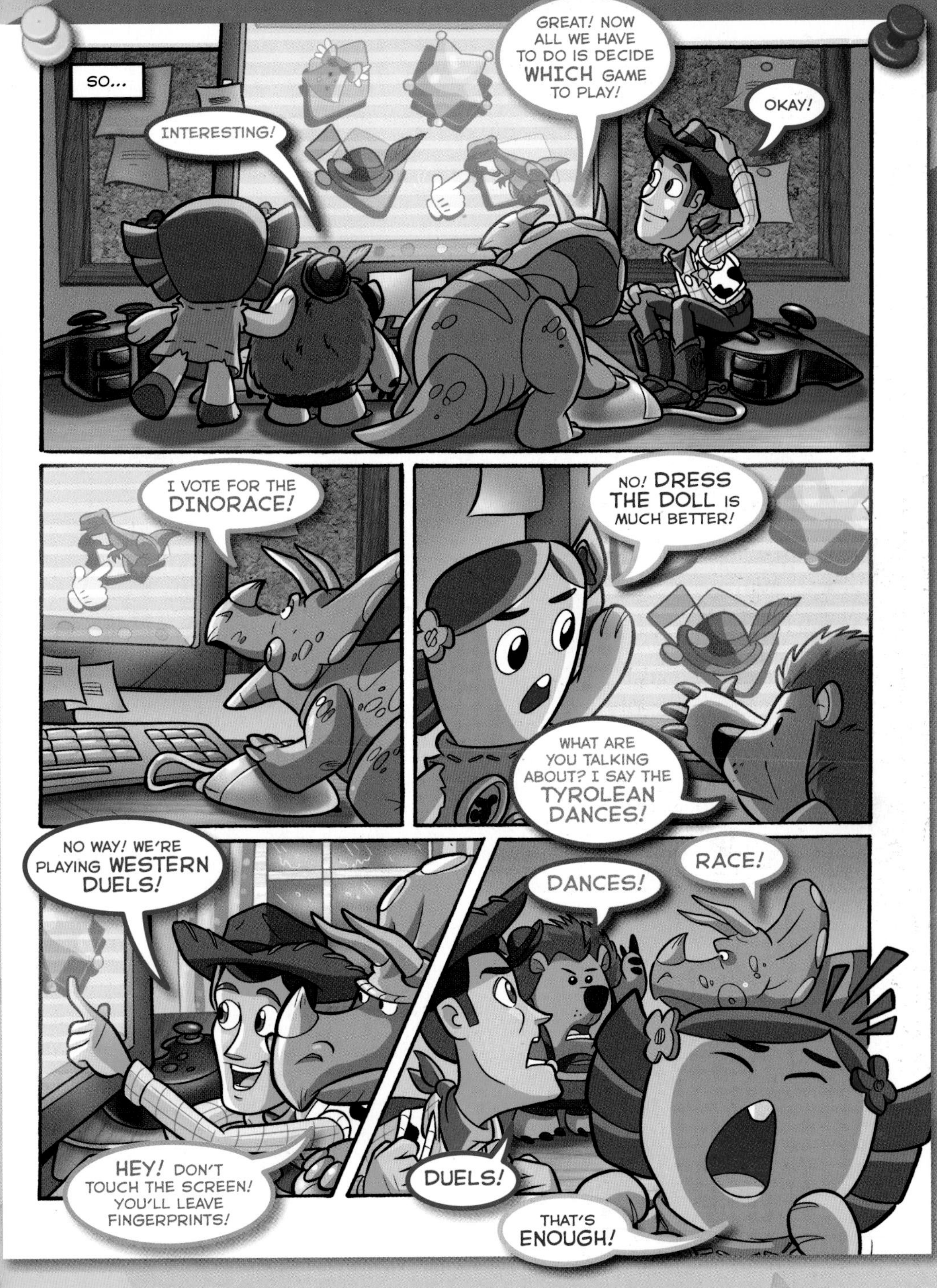
SO...
INTERESTING!
GREAT! NOW ALL WE HAVE TO DO IS DECIDE WHICH GAME TO PLAY!
OKAY!
I VOTE FOR THE DINORACE!
NO! DRESS THE DOLL IS MUCH BETTER!
WHAT ARE YOU TALKING ABOUT? I SAY THE TYROLEAN DANCES!
NO WAY! WE'RE PLAYING WESTERN DUELS!
HEY! DON'T TOUCH THE SCREEN! YOU'LL LEAVE FINGERPRINTS!
DANCES!
RACE!
DUELS!
THAT'S ENOUGH!

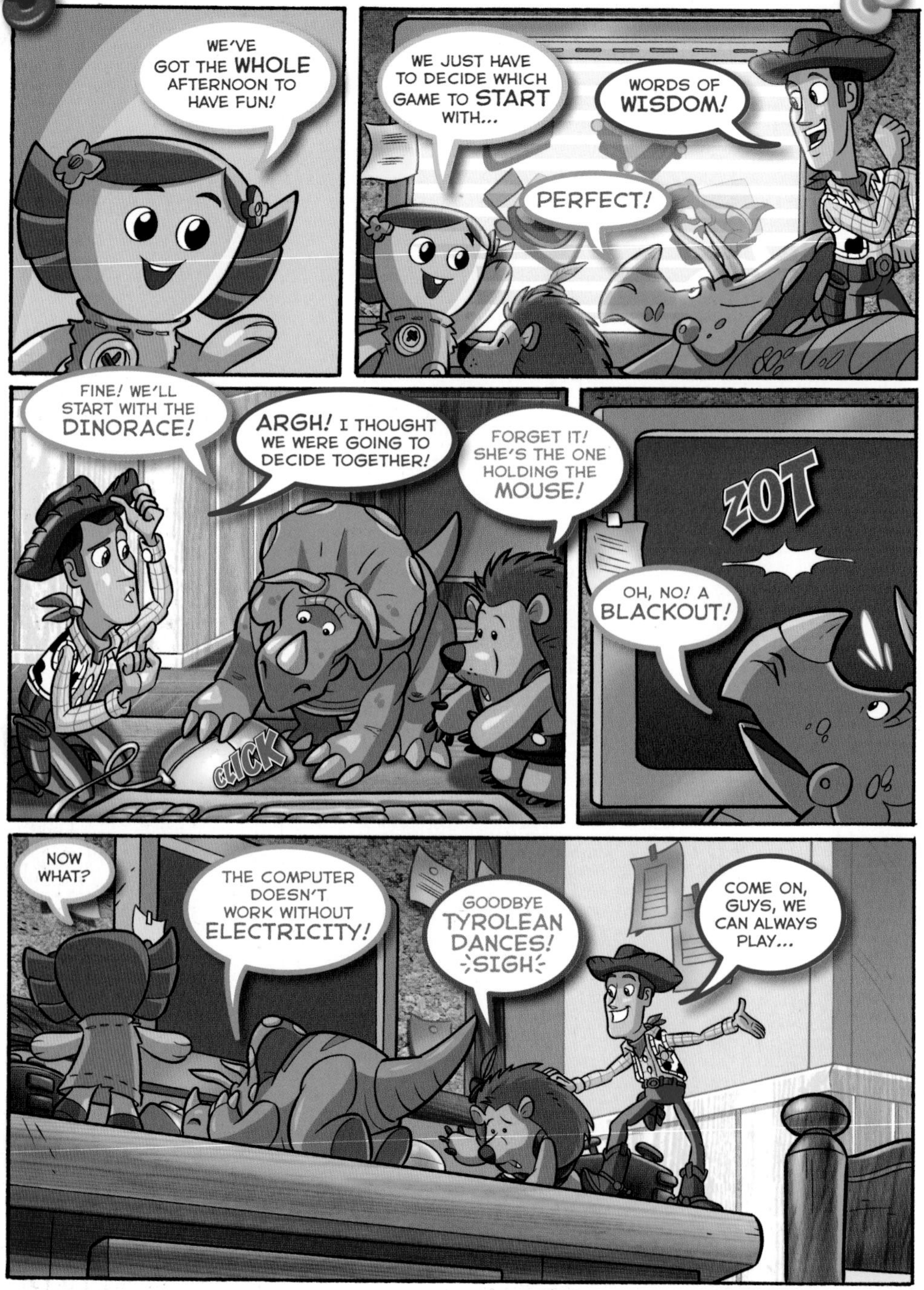
WE'VE GOT THE WHOLE AFTERNOON TO HAVE FUN!
WE JUST HAVE TO DECIDE WHICH GAME TO START WITH...
WORDS OF WISDOM!
PERFECT!
FINE! WE'LL START WITH THE DINORACE!
ARGH! I THOUGHT WE WERE GOING TO DECIDE TOGETHER!
FORGET IT! SHE'S THE ONE HOLDING THE MOUSE!
CLICK
ZOT
OH, NO! A BLACKOUT!
NOW WHAT?
THE COMPUTER DOESN'T WORK WITHOUT ELECTRICITY!
GOODBYE TYROLEAN DANCES! SIGH
COME ON, GUYS, WE CAN ALWAYS PLAY...

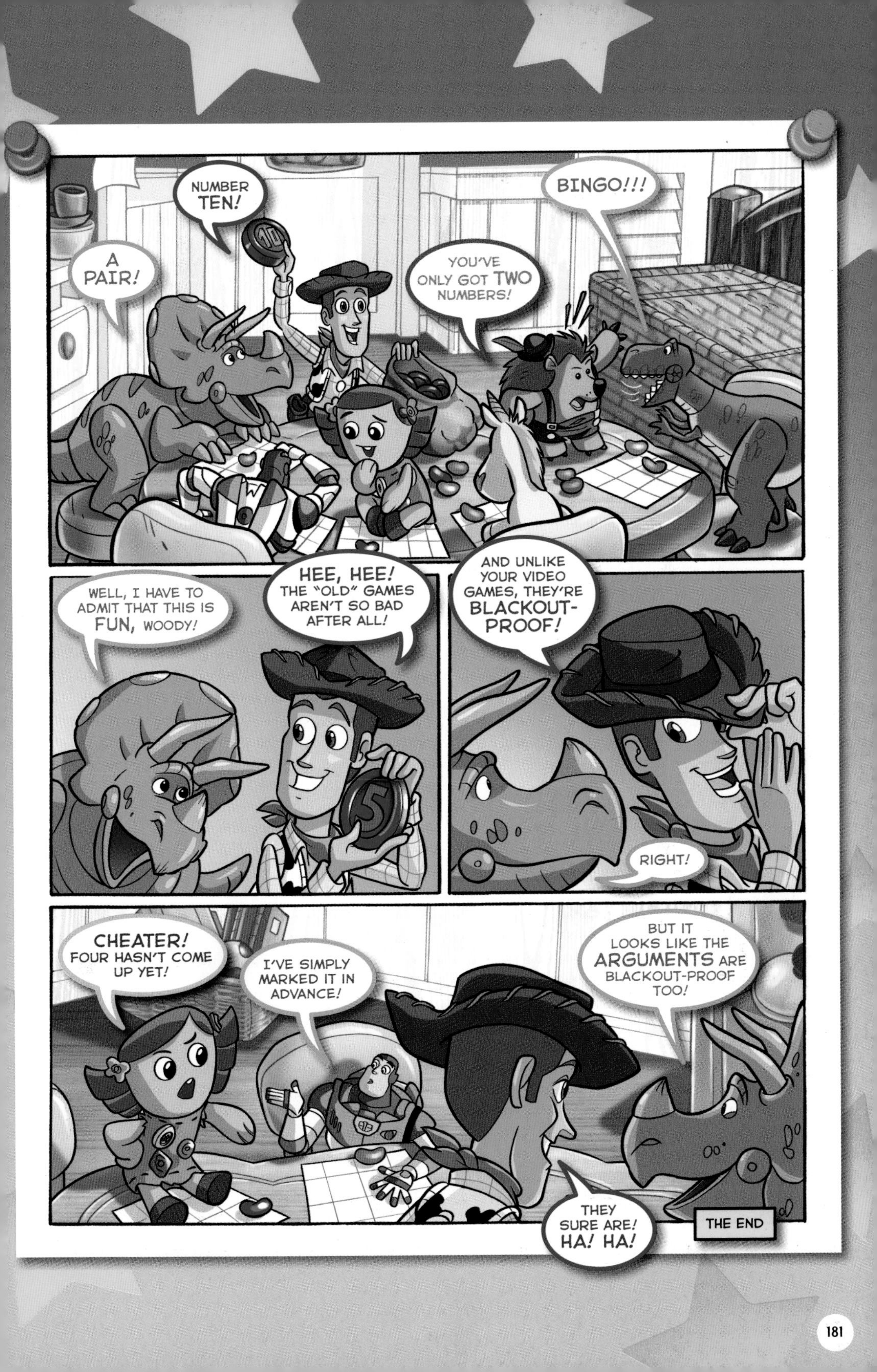
A PAIR!
NUMBER TEN!
YOU'VE ONLY GOT TWO NUMBERS!
BINGO!!!
WELL, I HAVE TO ADMIT THAT THIS IS FUN, WOODY!
HEE, HEE! THE "OLD" GAMES AREN'T SO BAD AFTER ALL!
AND UNLIKE YOUR VIDEO GAMES, THEY'RE BLACKOUT-PROOF!
RIGHT!
CHEATER! FOUR HASN'T COME UP YET!
I'VE SIMPLY MARKED IT IN ADVANCE!
BUT IT LOOKS LIKE THE ARGUMENTS ARE BLACKOUT-PROOF TOO!
THEY SURE ARE! HA! HA!
THE END

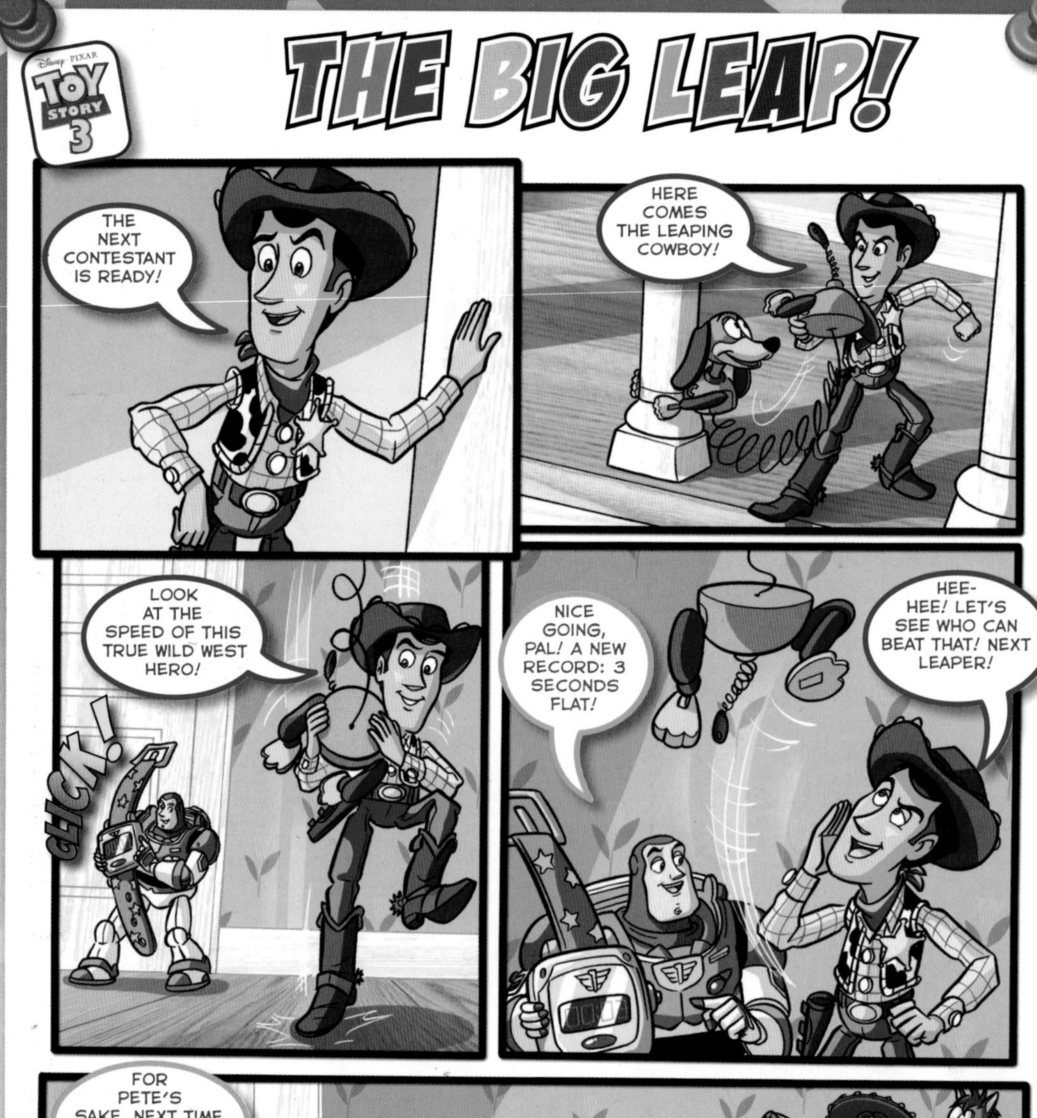
DISNEY · PIXAR TOY STORY 3
THE BIG LEAP!
THE NEXT CONTESTANT IS READY!
HERE COMES THE LEAPING COWBOY!
LOOK AT THE SPEED OF THIS TRUE WILD WEST HERO!
CLICK!
NICE GOING, PAL! A NEW RECORD: 3 SECONDS FLAT!
HEE-HEE! LET'S SEE WHO CAN BEAT THAT! NEXT LEAPER!
FOR PETE'S SAKE, NEXT TIME WE'LL PLAY HIDE-AND-SEEK!
THE END

SCRIPT: SIMONA GRANDI; PENCILS: VALENTINO FORLINI; INK: MICHELA FRARE; COLOUR: GIANLUCA BARONE

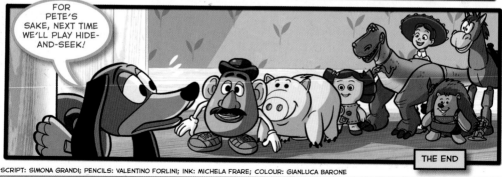

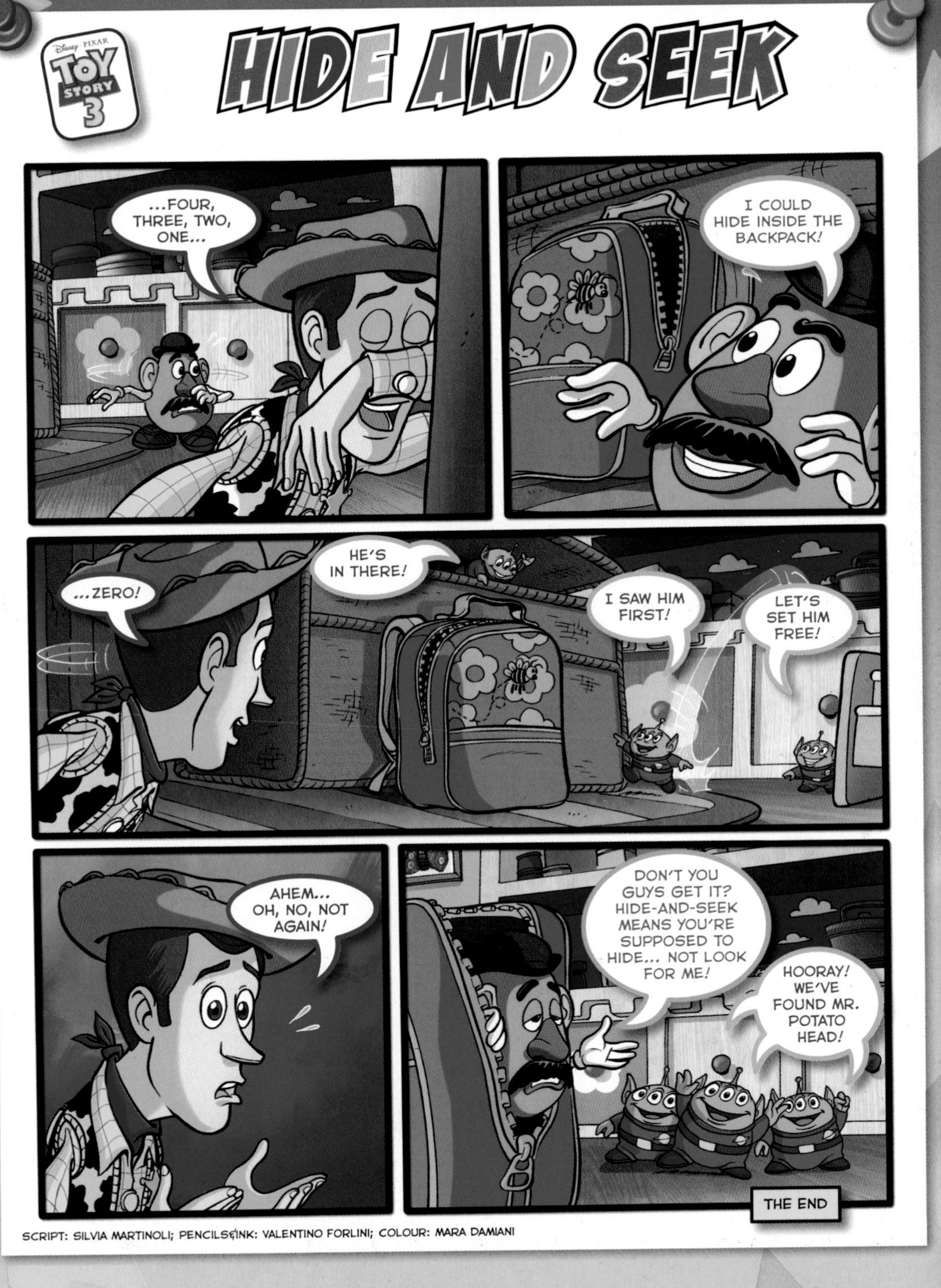
HIDE AND SEEK
TOY STORY 3
...FOUR, THREE, TWO, ONE...
I COULD HIDE INSIDE THE BACKPACK!
...ZERO!
HE'S IN THERE!
I SAW HIM FIRST!
LET'S SET HIM FREE!
AHEM... OH, NO, NOT AGAIN!
DON'T YOU GUYS GET IT? HIDE-AND-SEEK MEANS YOU'RE SUPPOSED TO HIDE... NOT LOOK FOR ME!
HOORAY! WE'VE FOUND MR. POTATO HEAD!
THE END

SCRIPT: SILVIA MARTINOLI; PENCILS&INK: VALENTINO FORLINI; COLOUR: MARA DAMIANI

QUIET, MOUTH!

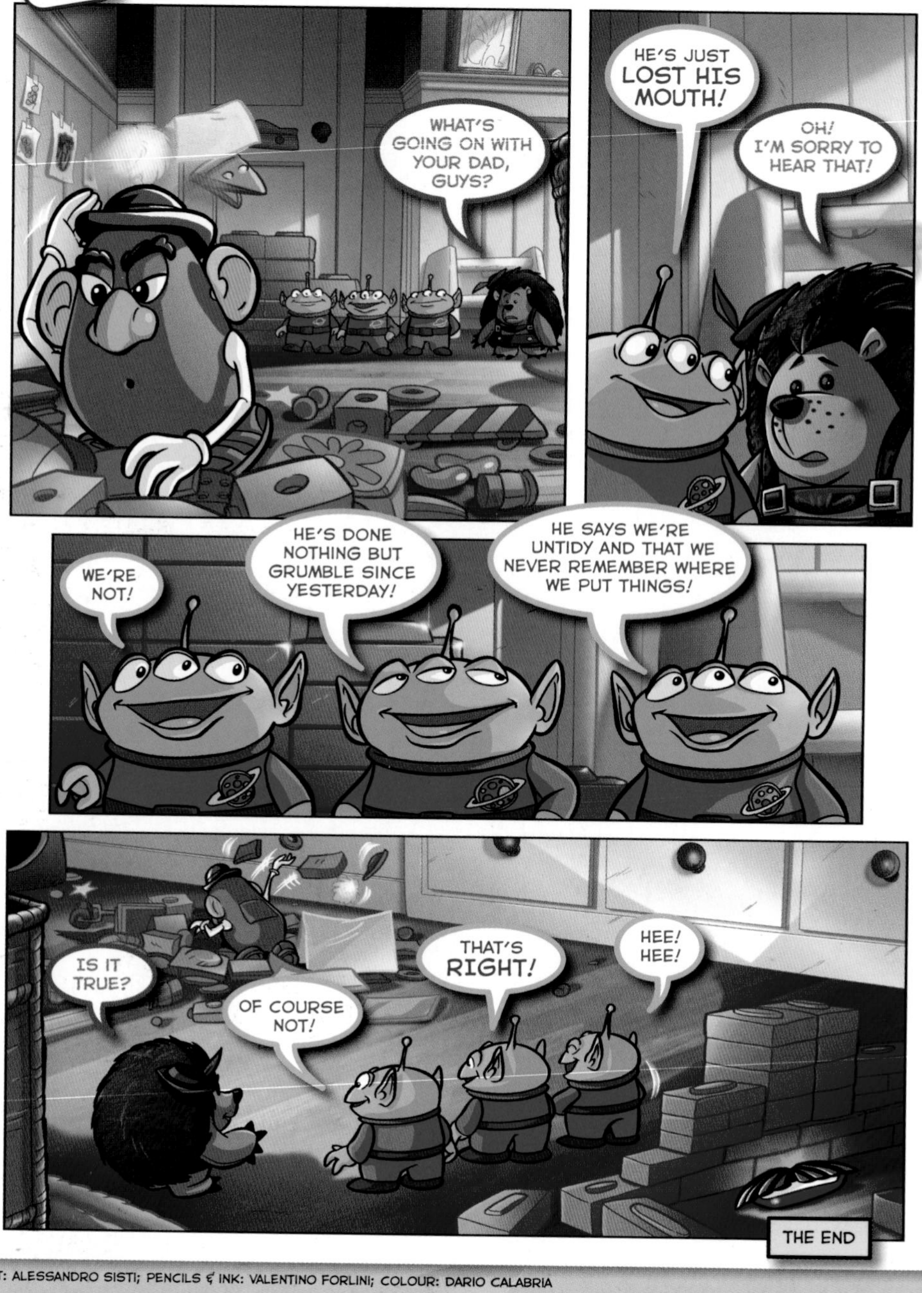

WHAT'S GOING ON WITH YOUR DAD, GUYS?
HE'S JUST LOST HIS MOUTH!
OH! I'M SORRY TO HEAR THAT!
WE'RE NOT!
HE'S DONE NOTHING BUT GRUMBLE SINCE YESTERDAY!
HE SAYS WE'RE UNTIDY AND THAT WE NEVER REMEMBER WHERE WE PUT THINGS!
IS IT TRUE?
OF COURSE NOT!
THAT'S RIGHT!
HEE! HEE!
THE END

SCRIPT: ALESSANDRO SISTI; PENCILS & INK: VALENTINO FORLINI; COLOUR: DARIO CALABRIA

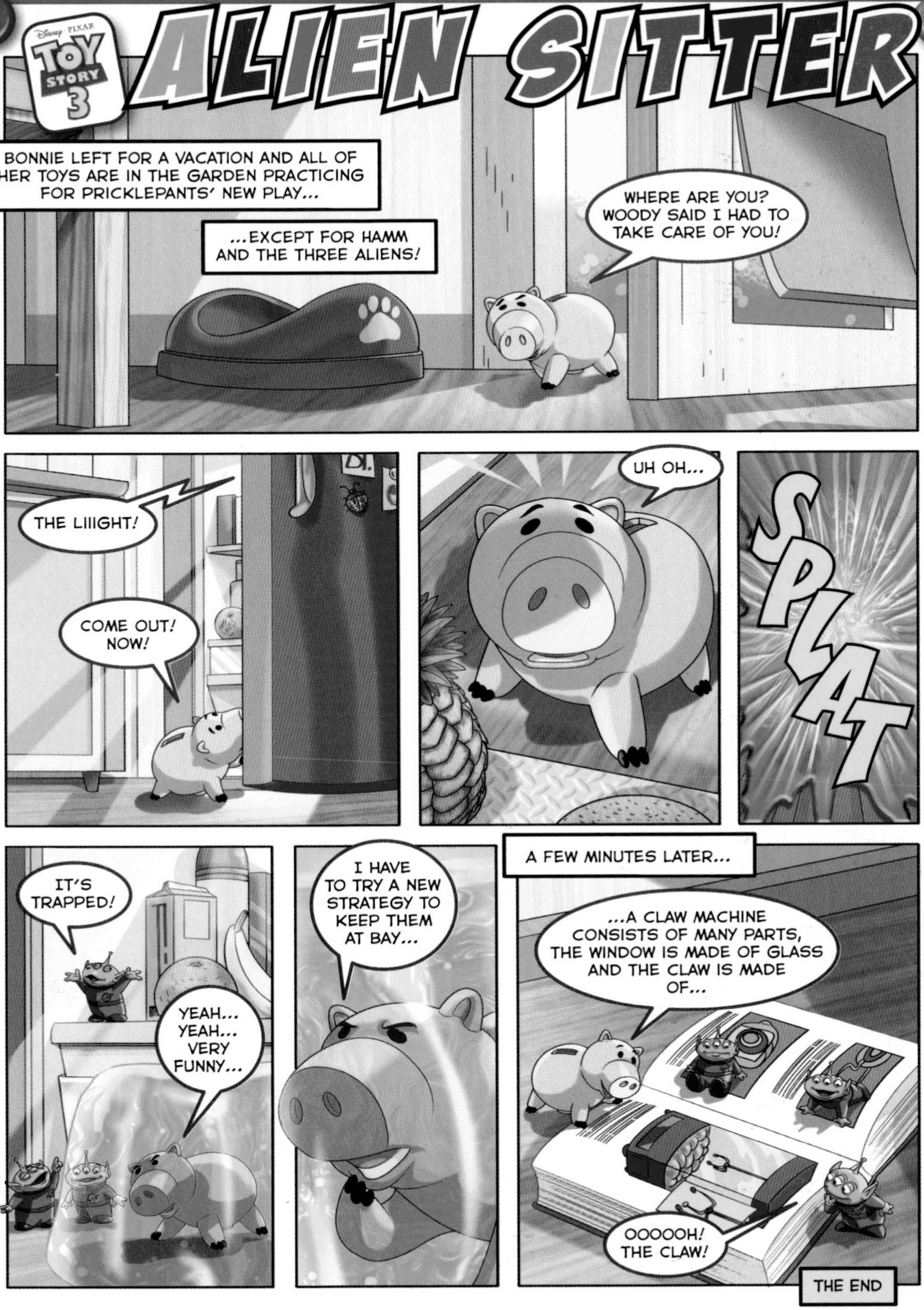
Disney · PIXAR
TOY STORY 3
ALIEN SITTER
BONNIE LEFT FOR A VACATION AND ALL OF HER TOYS ARE IN THE GARDEN PRACTICING FOR PRICKLEPANTS' NEW PLAY...
...EXCEPT FOR HAMM AND THE THREE ALIENS!
WHERE ARE YOU? WOODY SAID I HAD TO TAKE CARE OF YOU!
THE LIIIGHT!
COME OUT! NOW!
UH OH...
SPLAT
IT'S TRAPPED!
YEAH... YEAH... VERY FUNNY...
I HAVE TO TRY A NEW STRATEGY TO KEEP THEM AT BAY...
A FEW MINUTES LATER...
...A CLAW MACHINE CONSISTS OF MANY PARTS, THE WINDOW IS MADE OF GLASS AND THE CLAW IS MADE OF...
OOOOOH! THE CLAW!
THE END

SCRIPT: ALESSANDRO FERRARI; LAYOUT: VALENTINO FORLINI; INK: VALENTINO FORLINI; COLOUR: LUCIO DE GIUSEPPE

KING OF THE RODEO

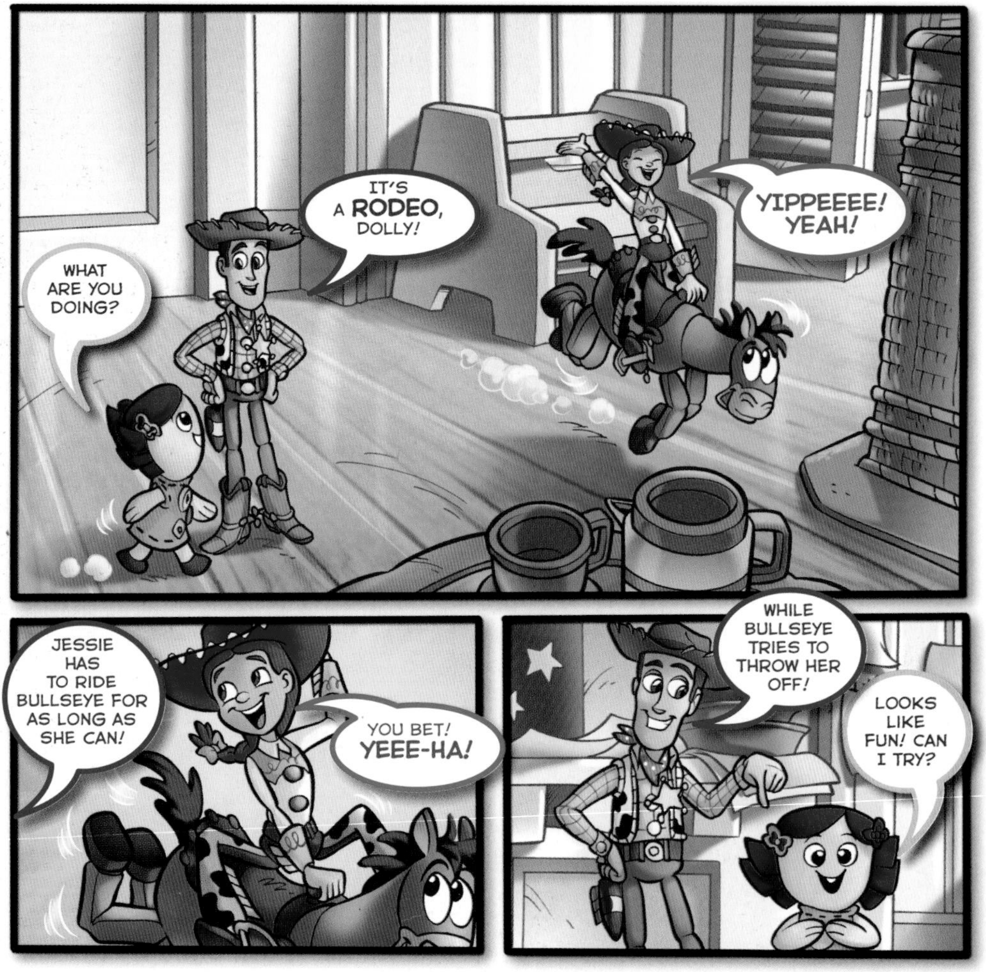
WHAT ARE YOU DOING?
IT'S A **RODEO,** DOLLY!
YIPPEEEE! YEAH!
JESSIE HAS TO RIDE BULLSEYE FOR AS LONG AS SHE CAN!
YOU BET! **YEEE-HA!**
WHILE BULLSEYE TRIES TO THROW HER OFF!
LOOKS LIKE FUN! CAN I TRY?

SCRIPT: ALESSANDRO SISTI; PENCILS & INK: LUCA USAI; COLOUR: KAWAII CREATIVE STUDIO

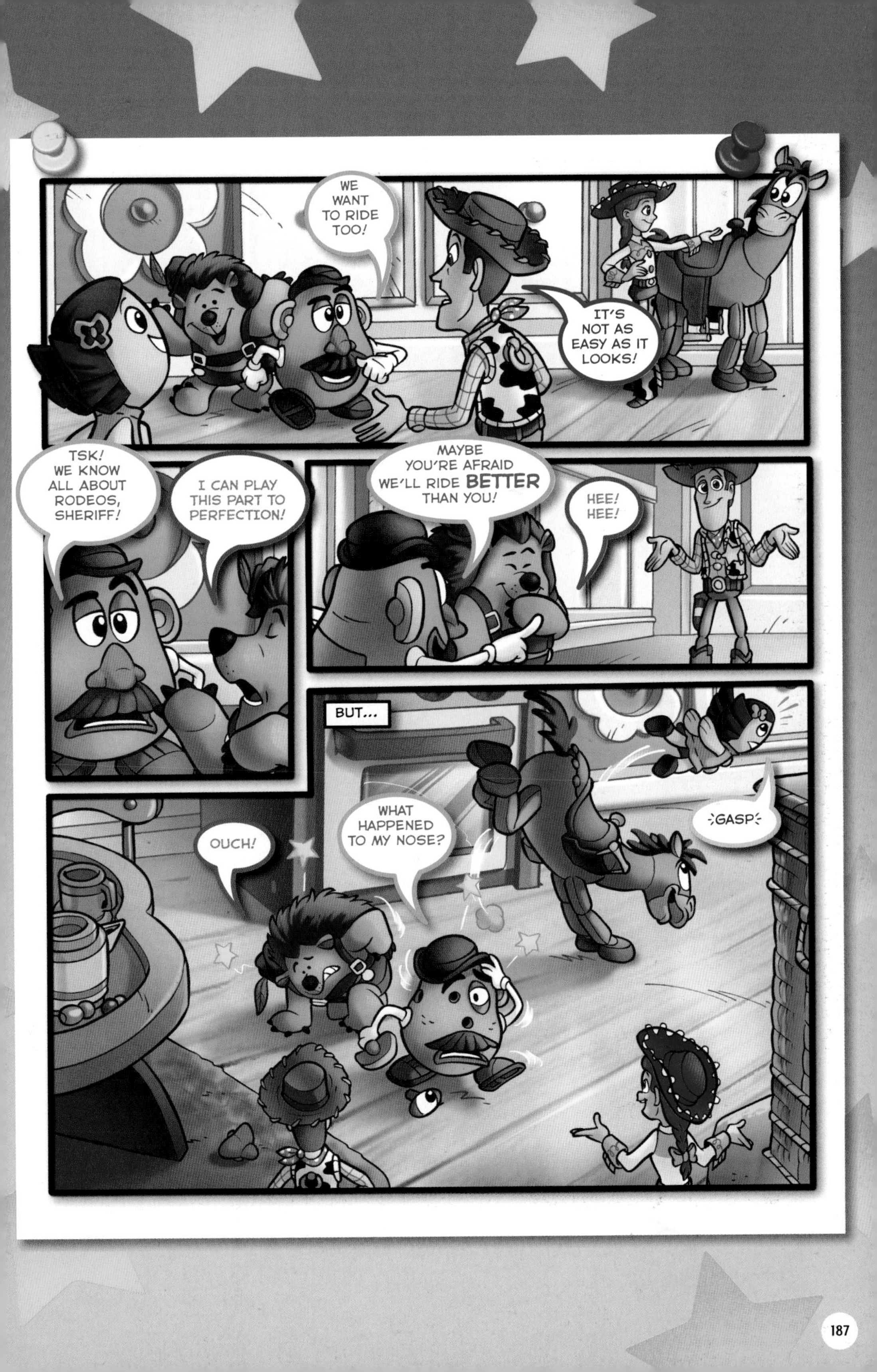
WE WANT TO RIDE TOO!
IT'S NOT AS EASY AS IT LOOKS!
TSK! WE KNOW ALL ABOUT RODEOS, SHERIFF!
I CAN PLAY THIS PART TO PERFECTION!
MAYBE YOU'RE AFRAID WE'LL RIDE BETTER THAN YOU!
HEE! HEE!
BUT...
-GASP-
WHAT HAPPENED TO MY NOSE?
OUCH!

NOT EVERYBODY'S CUT OUT TO BE A COWBOY!
I GUESS YOU'RE RIGHT, JESSIE!
CAN I TRY TOO, WOODY?
HUH?
DACHSHUNDS CAN'T RIDE HORSES!
THAT'S NOT QUITE WHAT I HAD IN MIND!
I WANT TO TAKE BULLSEYE'S PLACE!
WHII-I-INNY?
CLIMB ON, JESSIE! THERE'S ROOM FOR BOTH OF YOU!

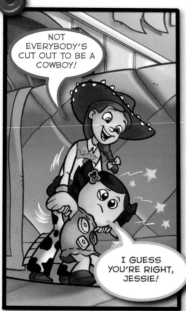

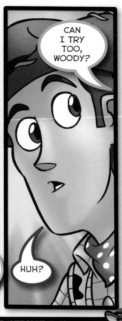

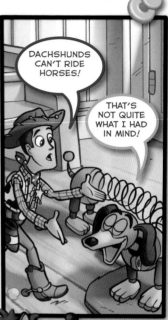

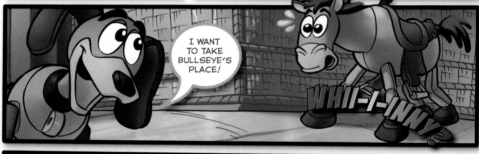

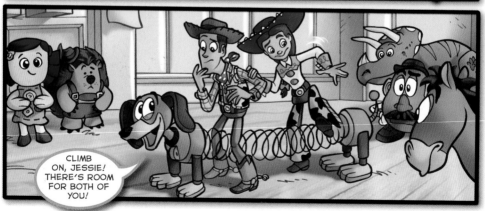

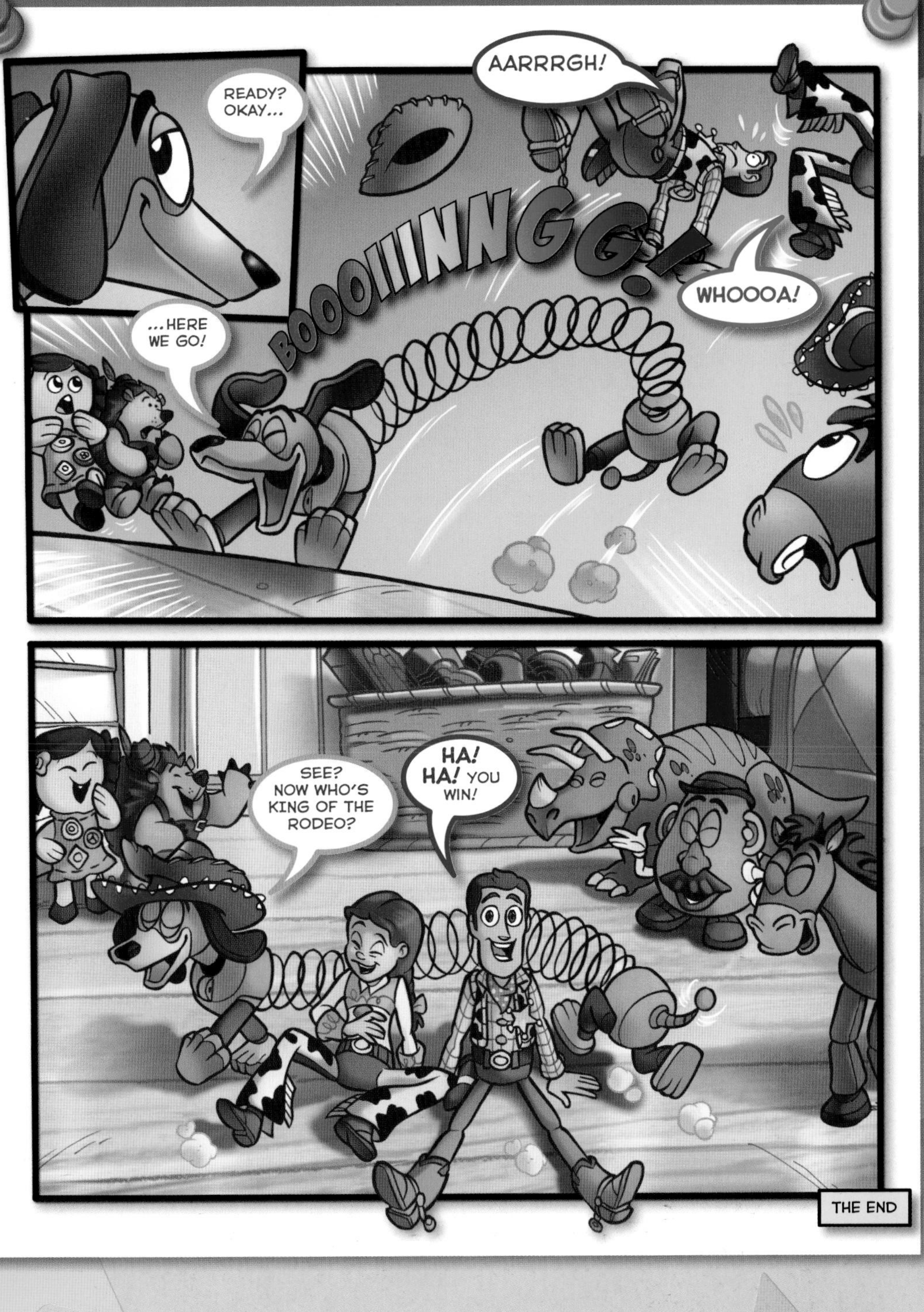
READY? OKAY...
...HERE WE GO!
BOOOIIIINNGG!
AARRRGH!
WHOOOA!
SEE? NOW WHO'S KING OF THE RODEO?
HA! HA! YOU WIN!
THE END

THE RACE

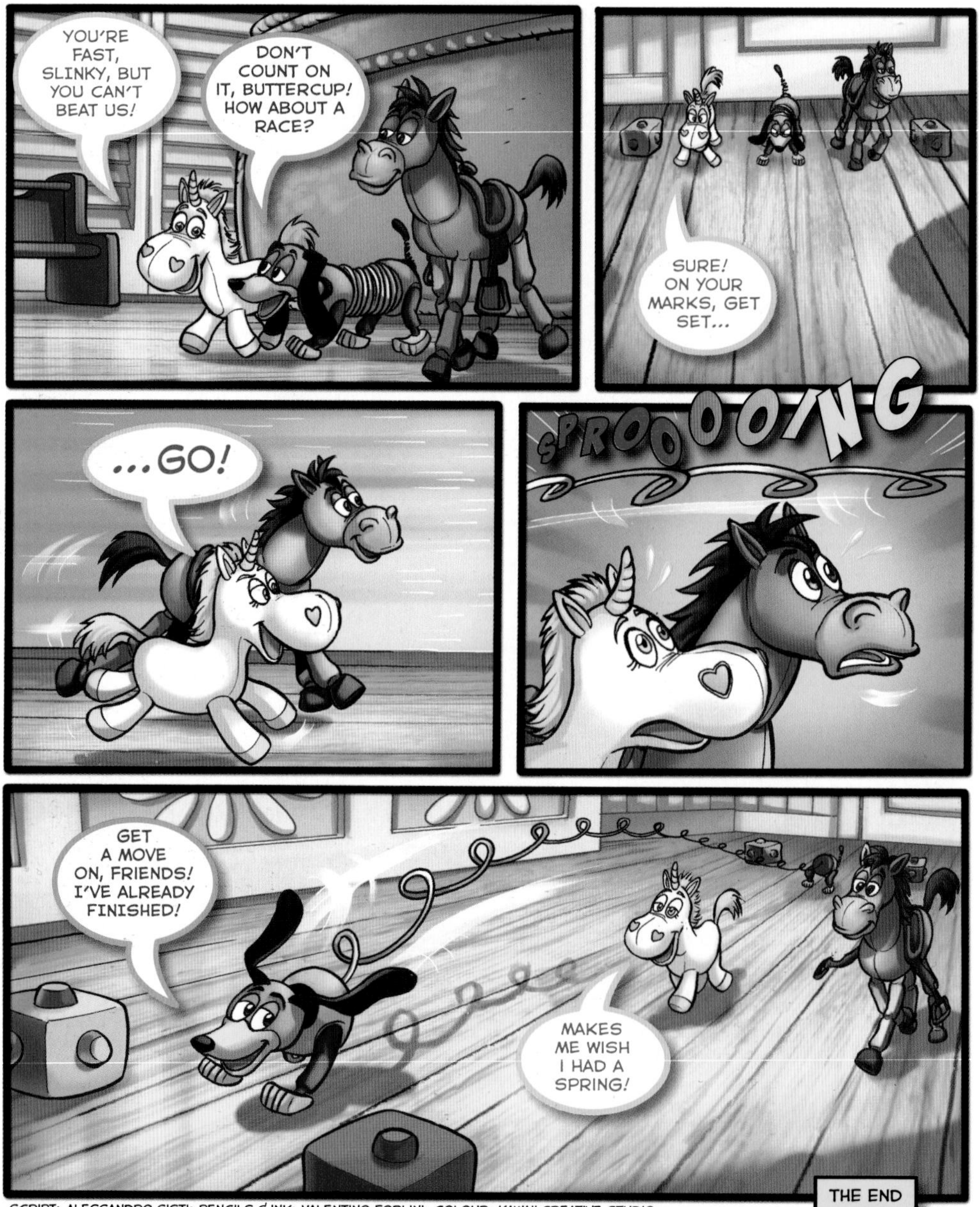
YOU'RE FAST, SLINKY, BUT YOU CAN'T BEAT US!
DON'T COUNT ON IT, BUTTERCUP! HOW ABOUT A RACE?
SURE! ON YOUR MARKS, GET SET...
...GO!
SPROOOOING
GET A MOVE ON, FRIENDS! I'VE ALREADY FINISHED!
MAKES ME WISH I HAD A SPRING!
THE END

SCRIPT: ALESSANDRO SISTI; PENCILS & INK: VALENTINO FORLINI; COLOUR: KAWAII CREATIVE STUDIO

THE BEST RODEO-DINO HORSE

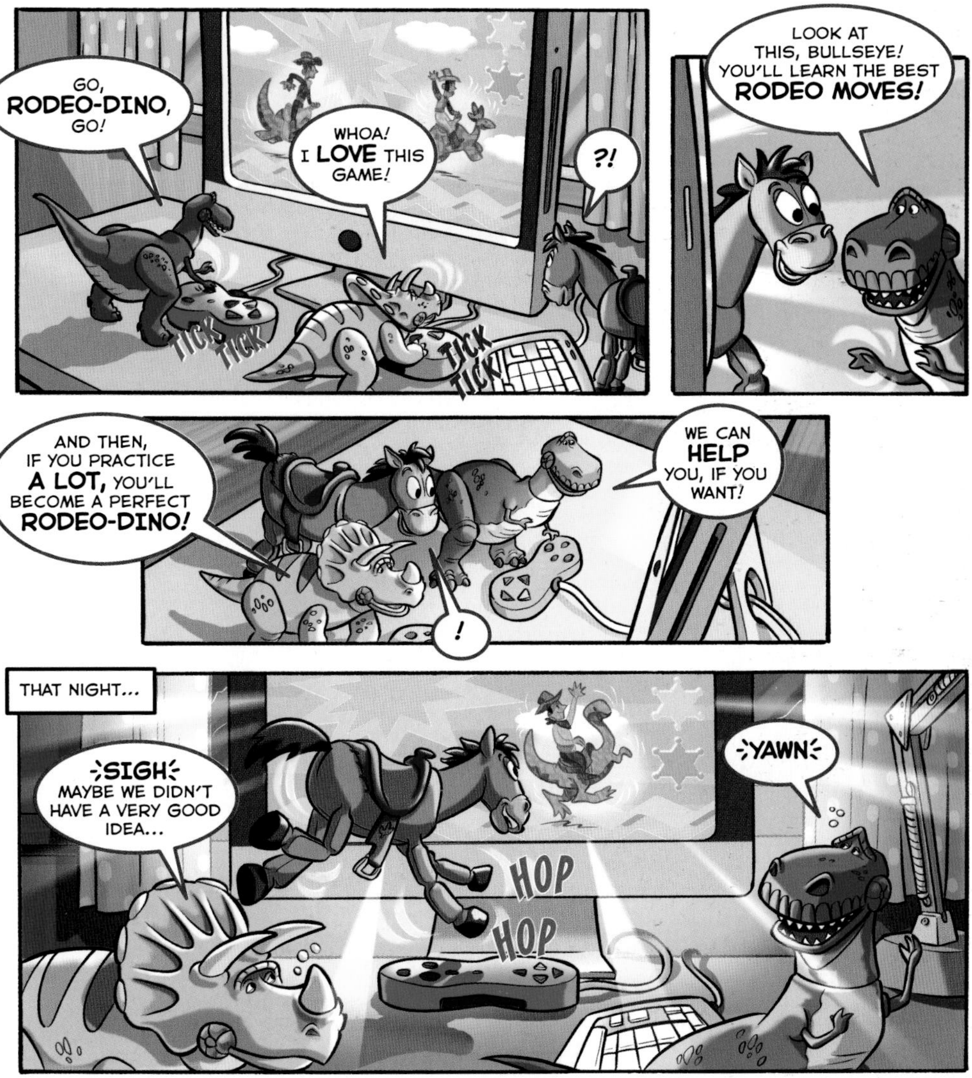
GO, RODEO-DINO, GO!
WHOA! I LOVE THIS GAME!
?!
TICK TICK
TICK TICK
LOOK AT THIS, BULLSEYE! YOU'LL LEARN THE BEST RODEO MOVES!
AND THEN, IF YOU PRACTICE A LOT, YOU'LL BECOME A PERFECT RODEO-DINO!
WE CAN HELP YOU, IF YOU WANT!
!
THAT NIGHT...
SIGH MAYBE WE DIDN'T HAVE A VERY GOOD IDEA...
HOP
HOP
YAWN

SCRIPT: TEA ORSI; LAYOUT: LUCA USAI; INK: MICHELA FRARE; COLOUR: LUCIO DE GIUSEPPE

THE END

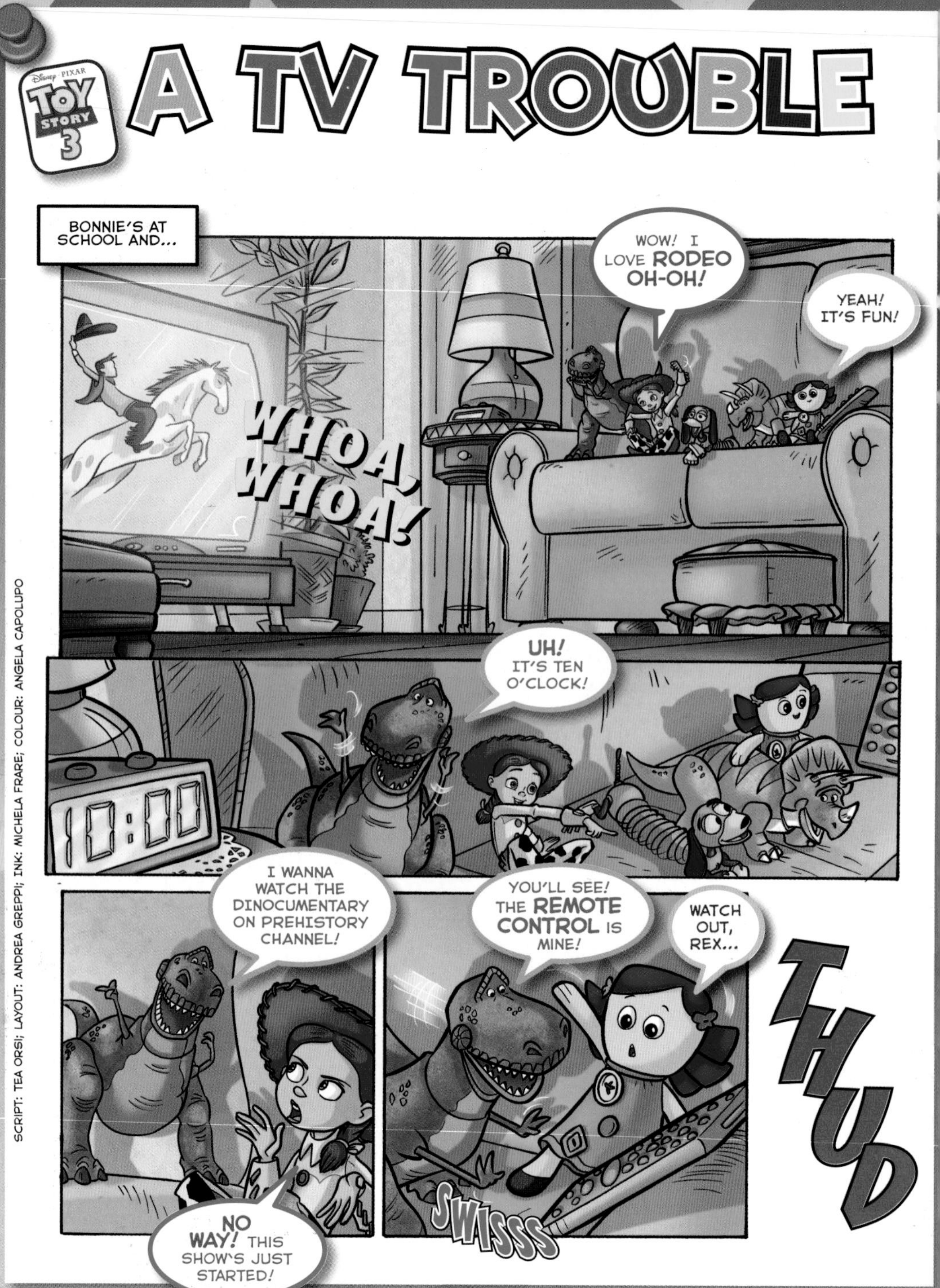

TOY STORY 3
A TV TROUBLE
BONNIE'S AT SCHOOL AND...
WOW! I LOVE RODEO OH-OH!
YEAH! IT'S FUN!
WHOA, WHOA!
UH! IT'S TEN O'CLOCK!
10:00
I WANNA WATCH THE DINOCUMENTARY ON PREHISTORY CHANNEL!
NO WAY! THIS SHOW'S JUST STARTED!
YOU'LL SEE! THE REMOTE CONTROL IS MINE!
WATCH OUT, REX...
SWISSS
THUD
SCRIPT: TEA ORSI; LAYOUT: ANDREA GREPPI; INK: MICHELA FRARE; COLOUR: ANGELA CAPOLUPO

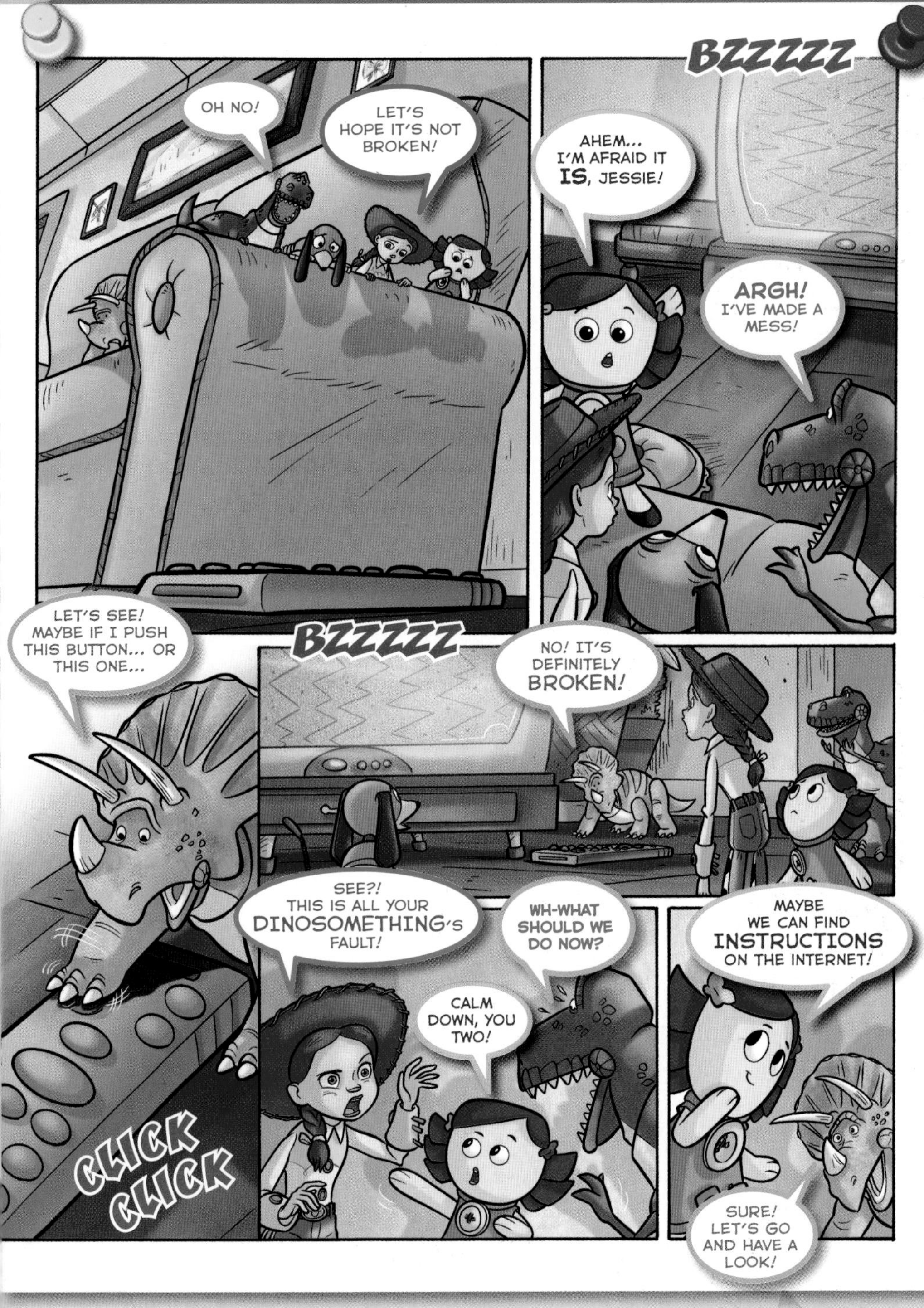
OH NO!
LET'S HOPE IT'S NOT BROKEN!
BZZZZZ
AHEM... I'M AFRAID IT IS, JESSIE!
ARGH! I'VE MADE A MESS!
LET'S SEE! MAYBE IF I PUSH THIS BUTTON... OR THIS ONE...
CLICK CLICK
BZZZZZ
NO! IT'S DEFINITELY BROKEN!
SEE?! THIS IS ALL YOUR DINOSOMETHING's FAULT!
WH-WHAT SHOULD WE DO NOW?
CALM DOWN, YOU TWO!
MAYBE WE CAN FIND INSTRUCTIONS ON THE INTERNET!
SURE! LET'S GO AND HAVE A LOOK!

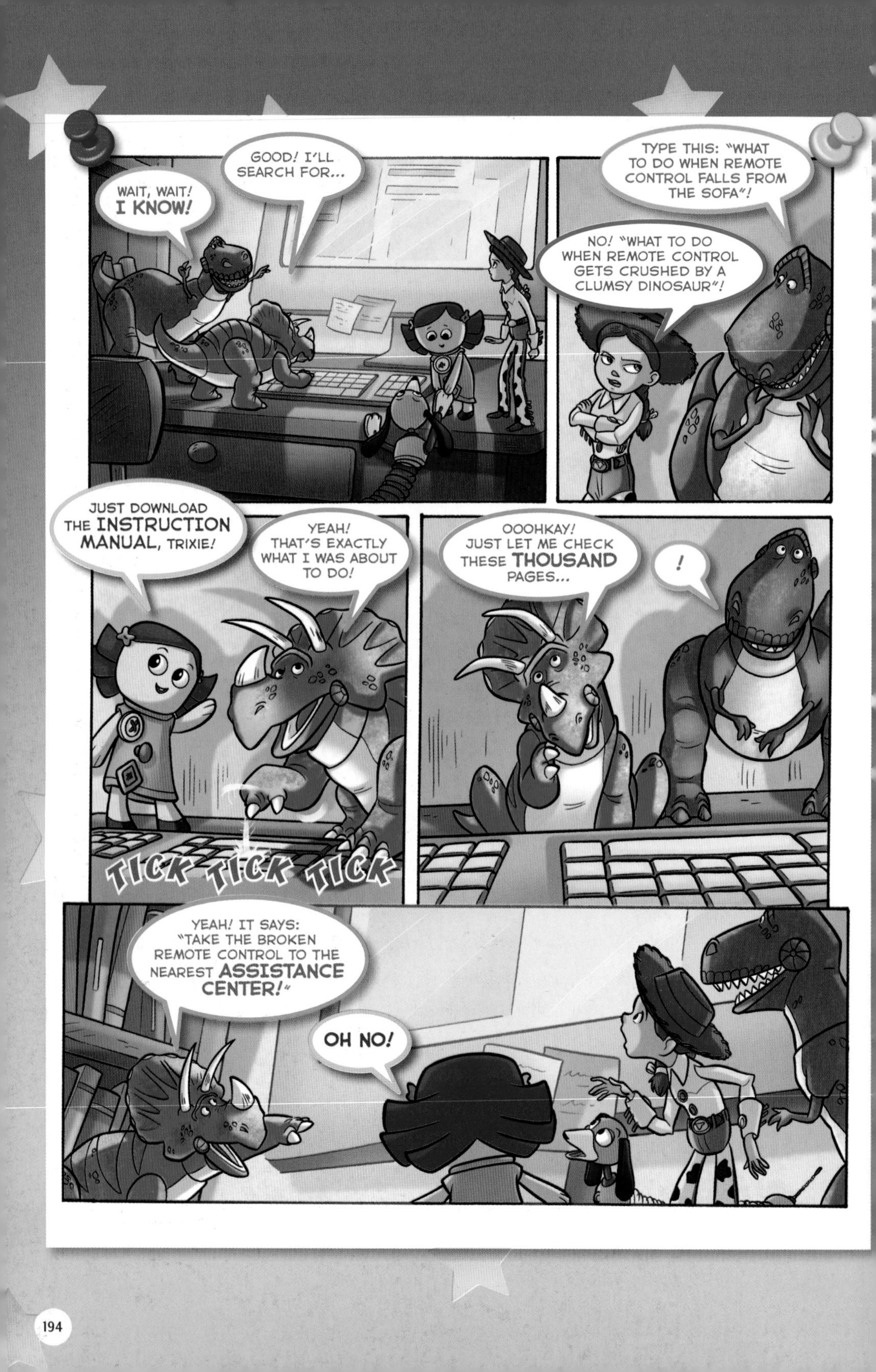

WAIT, WAIT! I KNOW!
GOOD! I'LL SEARCH FOR...
TYPE THIS: "WHAT TO DO WHEN REMOTE CONTROL FALLS FROM THE SOFA"!
NO! "WHAT TO DO WHEN REMOTE CONTROL GETS CRUSHED BY A CLUMSY DINOSAUR"!
JUST DOWNLOAD THE INSTRUCTION MANUAL, TRIXIE!
YEAH! THAT'S EXACTLY WHAT I WAS ABOUT TO DO!
TICK TICK TICK
OOOHKAY! JUST LET ME CHECK THESE THOUSAND PAGES...
!
YEAH! IT SAYS: "TAKE THE BROKEN REMOTE CONTROL TO THE NEAREST ASSISTANCE CENTER!"
OH NO!

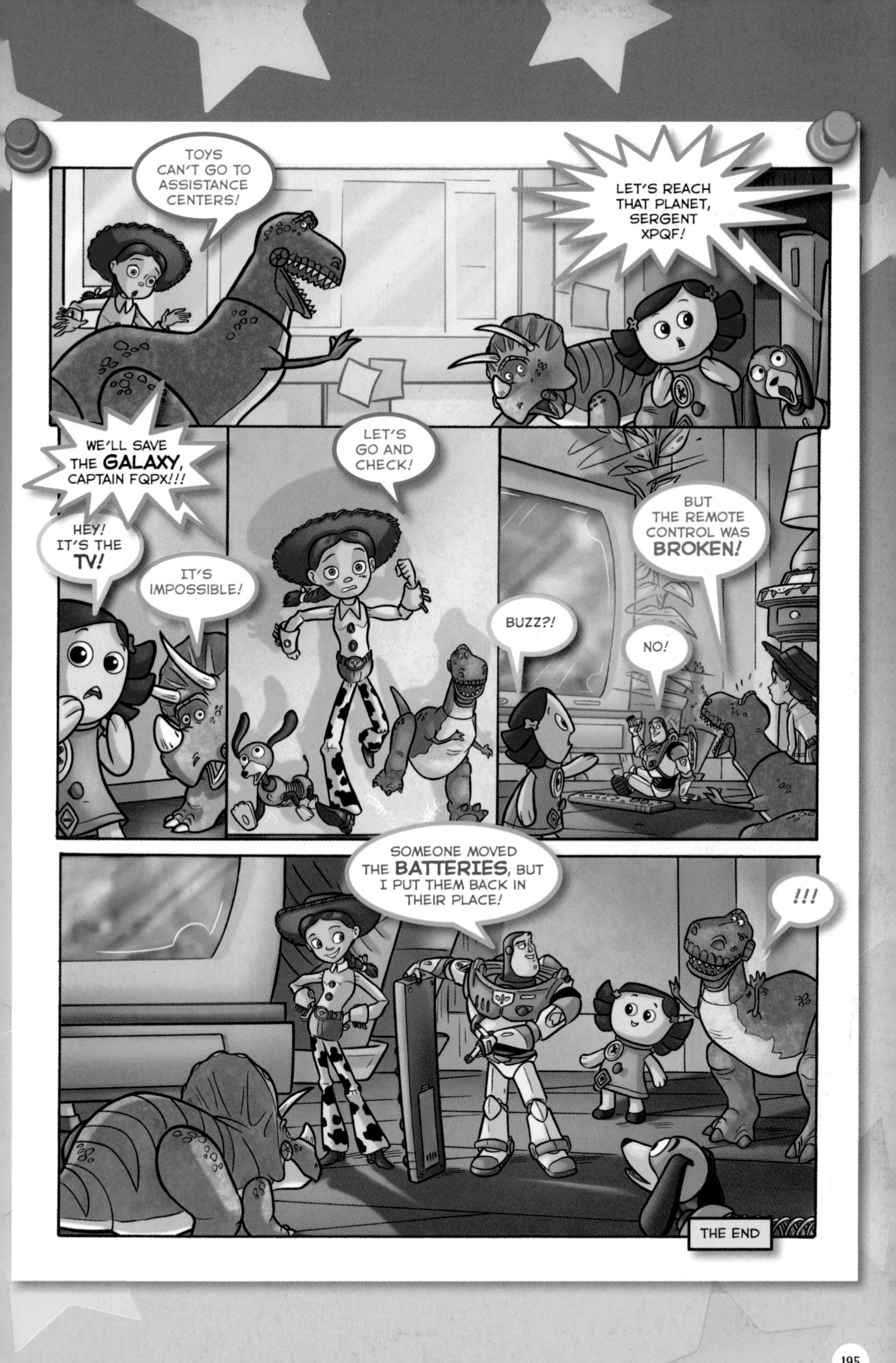
TOYS CAN'T GO TO ASSISTANCE CENTERS!
LET'S REACH THAT PLANET, SERGENT XPQF!
WE'LL SAVE THE **GALAXY**, CAPTAIN FQPX!!!
HEY! IT'S THE **TV!**
IT'S IMPOSSIBLE!
LET'S GO AND CHECK!
BUZZ?!
NO!
BUT THE REMOTE CONTROL WAS **BROKEN!**
SOMEONE MOVED THE **BATTERIES**, BUT I PUT THEM BACK IN THEIR PLACE!
!!!
THE END

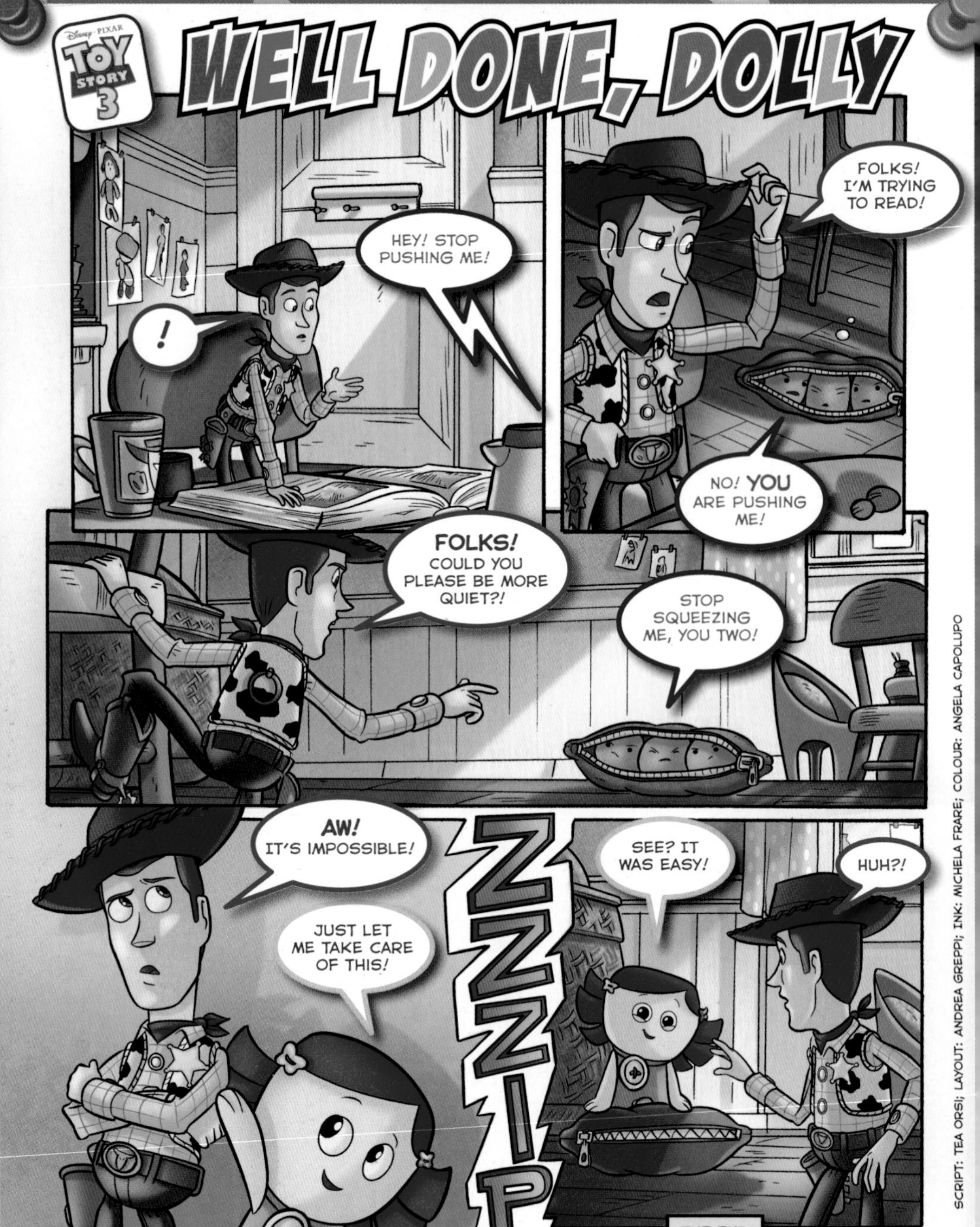
DISNEY · PIXAR
TOY STORY 3
WELL DONE, DOLLY
!
HEY! STOP PUSHING ME!
FOLKS! I'M TRYING TO READ!
NO! YOU ARE PUSHING ME!
FOLKS! COULD YOU PLEASE BE MORE QUIET?!
STOP SQUEEZING ME, YOU TWO!
AW! IT'S IMPOSSIBLE!
JUST LET ME TAKE CARE OF THIS!
ZZZIP
SEE? IT WAS EASY!
HUH?!
THE END
SCRIPT: TEA ORSI; LAYOUT: ANDREA GREPPI; INK: MICHELA FRARE; COLOUR: ANGELA CAPOLUPO

REX'S FAVORITE SHOW

TOY STORY 3

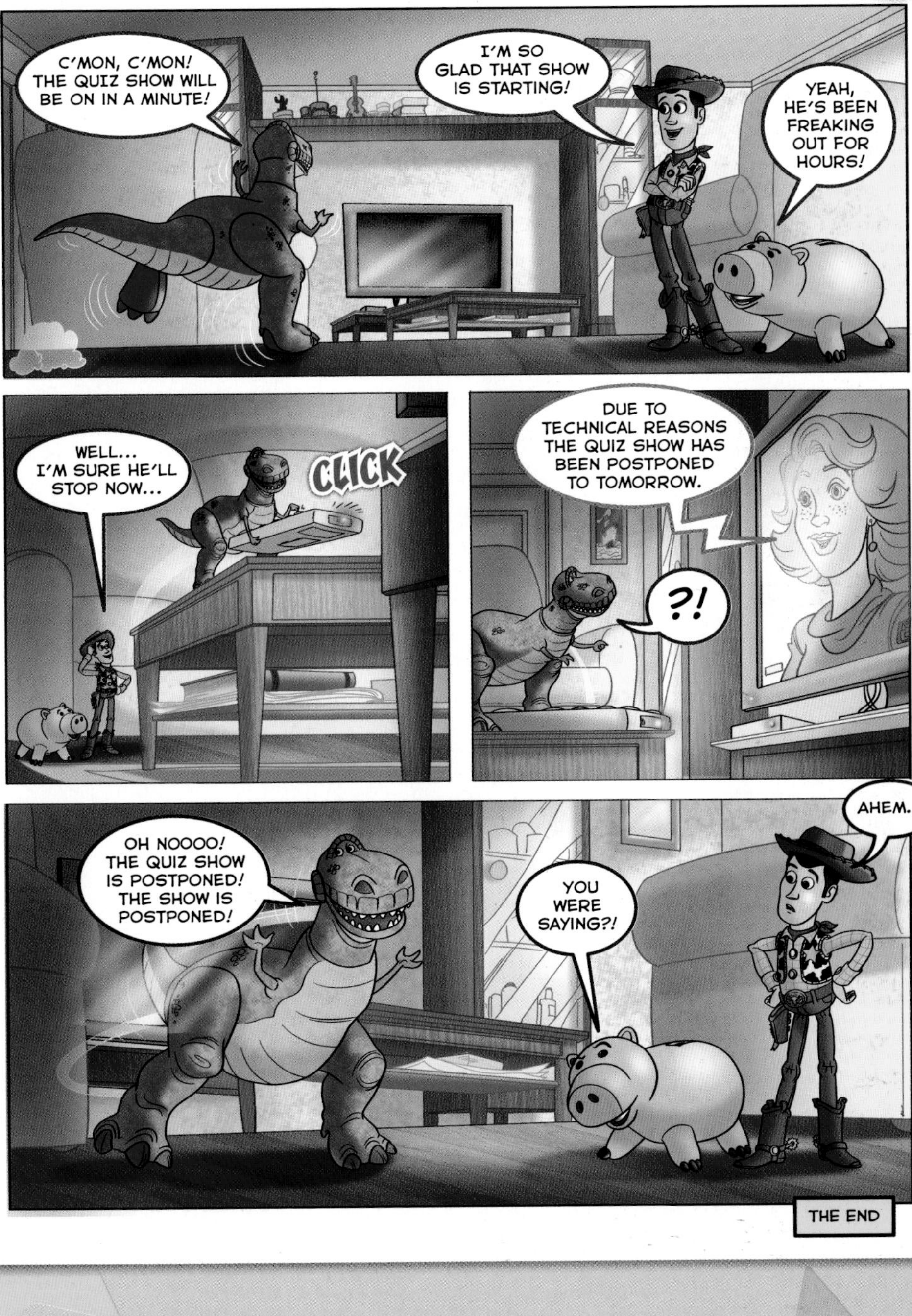
C'MON, C'MON! THE QUIZ SHOW WILL BE ON IN A MINUTE!
I'M SO GLAD THAT SHOW IS STARTING!
YEAH, HE'S BEEN FREAKING OUT FOR HOURS!
WELL... I'M SURE HE'LL STOP NOW...
CLICK
DUE TO TECHNICAL REASONS THE QUIZ SHOW HAS BEEN POSTPONED TO TOMORROW.
?!
OH NOOOO! THE QUIZ SHOW IS POSTPONED! THE SHOW IS POSTPONED!
YOU WERE SAYING?!
AHEM...
THE END

SCRIPT: TEO ORSI, PENCIL & INK: VALENTINO FORLINI, COLOR: ANGELA CAPOLUPO

COMPUTER CRAZY!

SCRIPT: ALESSANDRO SISTI; PENCILS: GIANLUCA BARONE; INK: MICHELA FRARE; COLOUR: KAWAII CREATIVE STUDIO

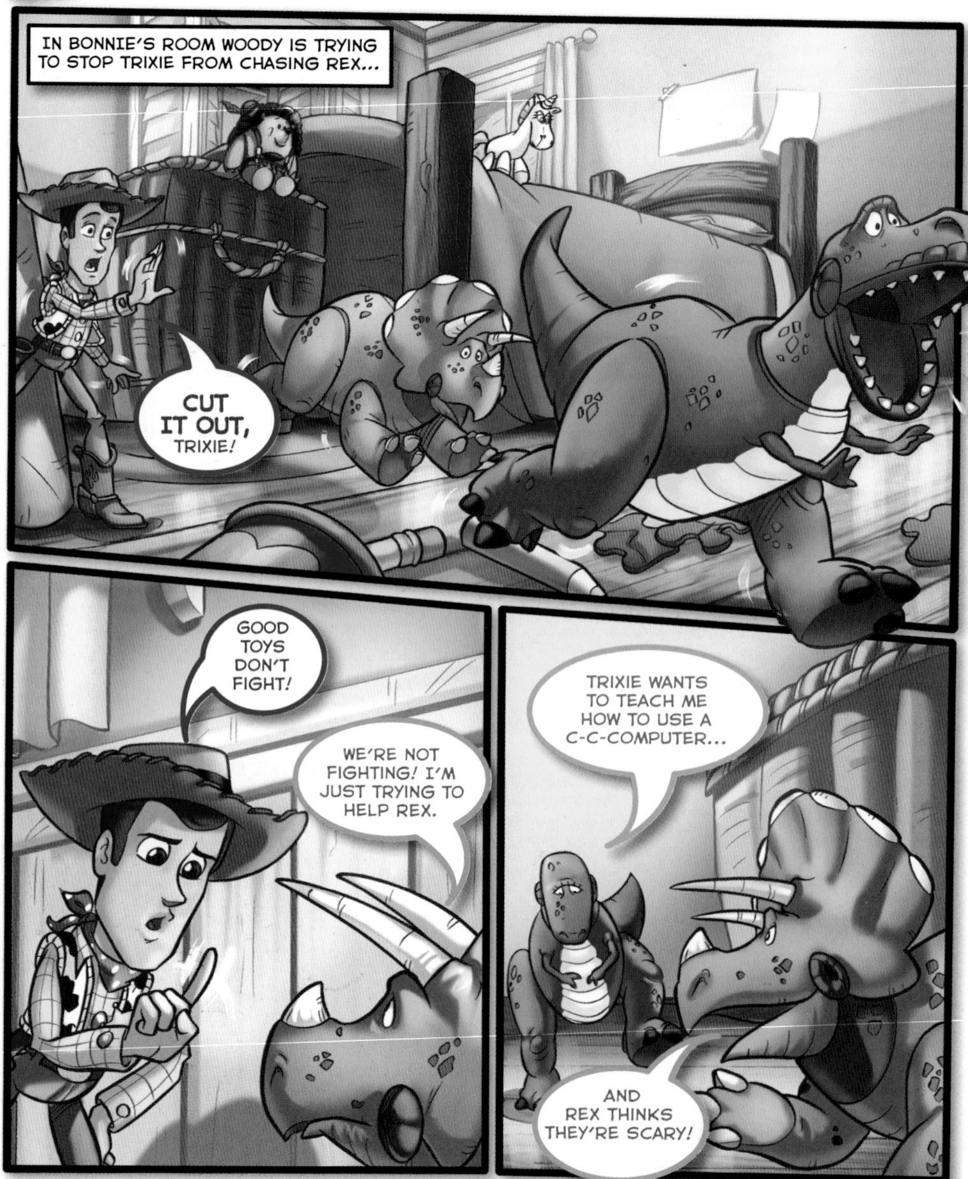
IN BONNIE'S ROOM WOODY IS TRYING TO STOP TRIXIE FROM CHASING REX...
CUT IT OUT, TRIXIE!
GOOD TOYS DON'T FIGHT!
WE'RE NOT FIGHTING! I'M JUST TRYING TO HELP REX.
TRIXIE WANTS TO TEACH ME HOW TO USE A C-C-COMPUTER...
AND REX THINKS THEY'RE SCARY!

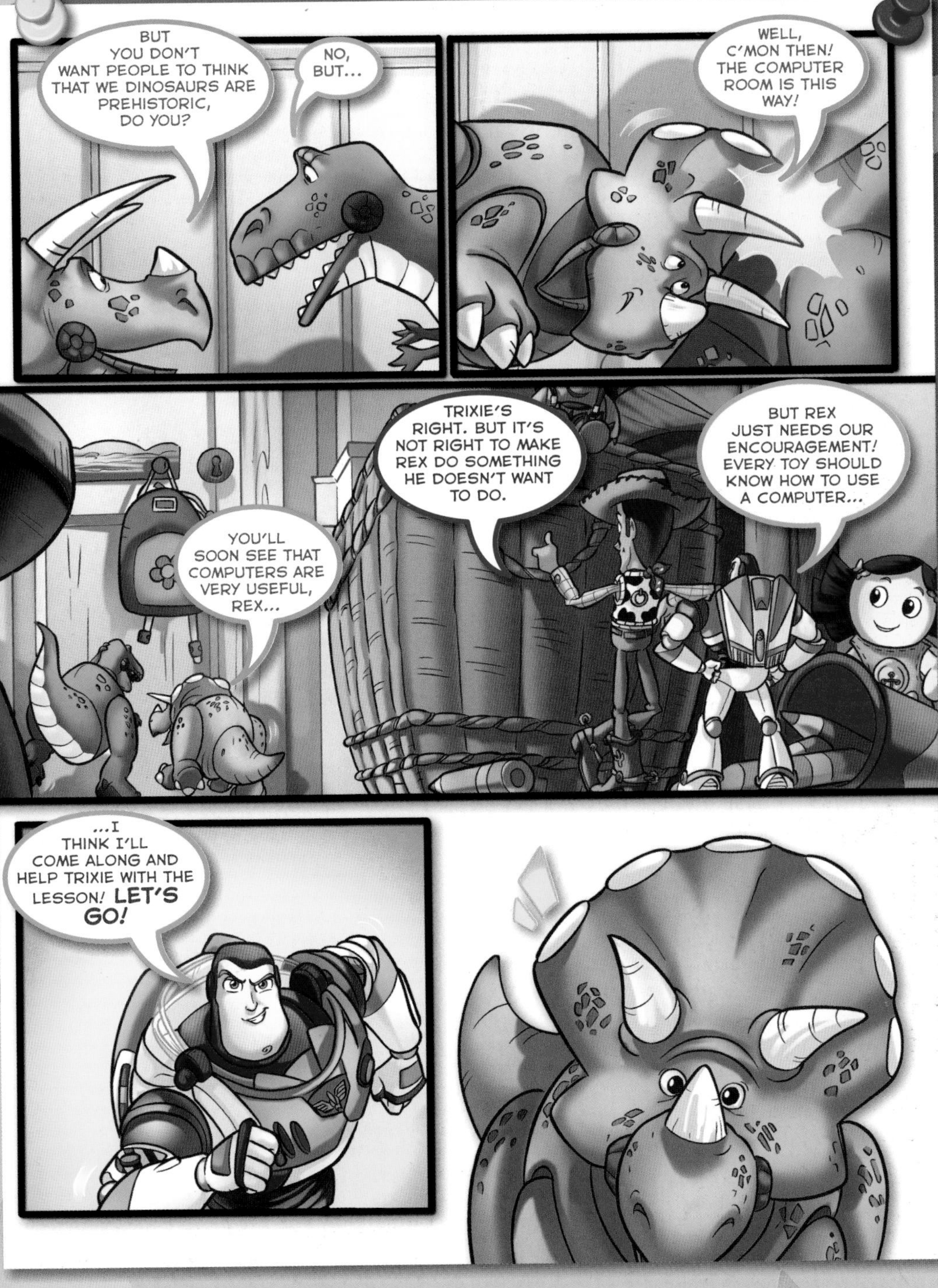
BUT YOU DON'T WANT PEOPLE TO THINK THAT WE DINOSAURS ARE PREHISTORIC, DO YOU?
NO, BUT...
WELL, C'MON THEN! THE COMPUTER ROOM IS THIS WAY!
YOU'LL SOON SEE THAT COMPUTERS ARE VERY USEFUL, REX...
TRIXIE'S RIGHT. BUT IT'S NOT RIGHT TO MAKE REX DO SOMETHING HE DOESN'T WANT TO DO.
BUT REX JUST NEEDS OUR ENCOURAGEMENT! EVERY TOY SHOULD KNOW HOW TO USE A COMPUTER...
...I THINK I'LL COME ALONG AND HELP TRIXIE WITH THE LESSON! LET'S GO!

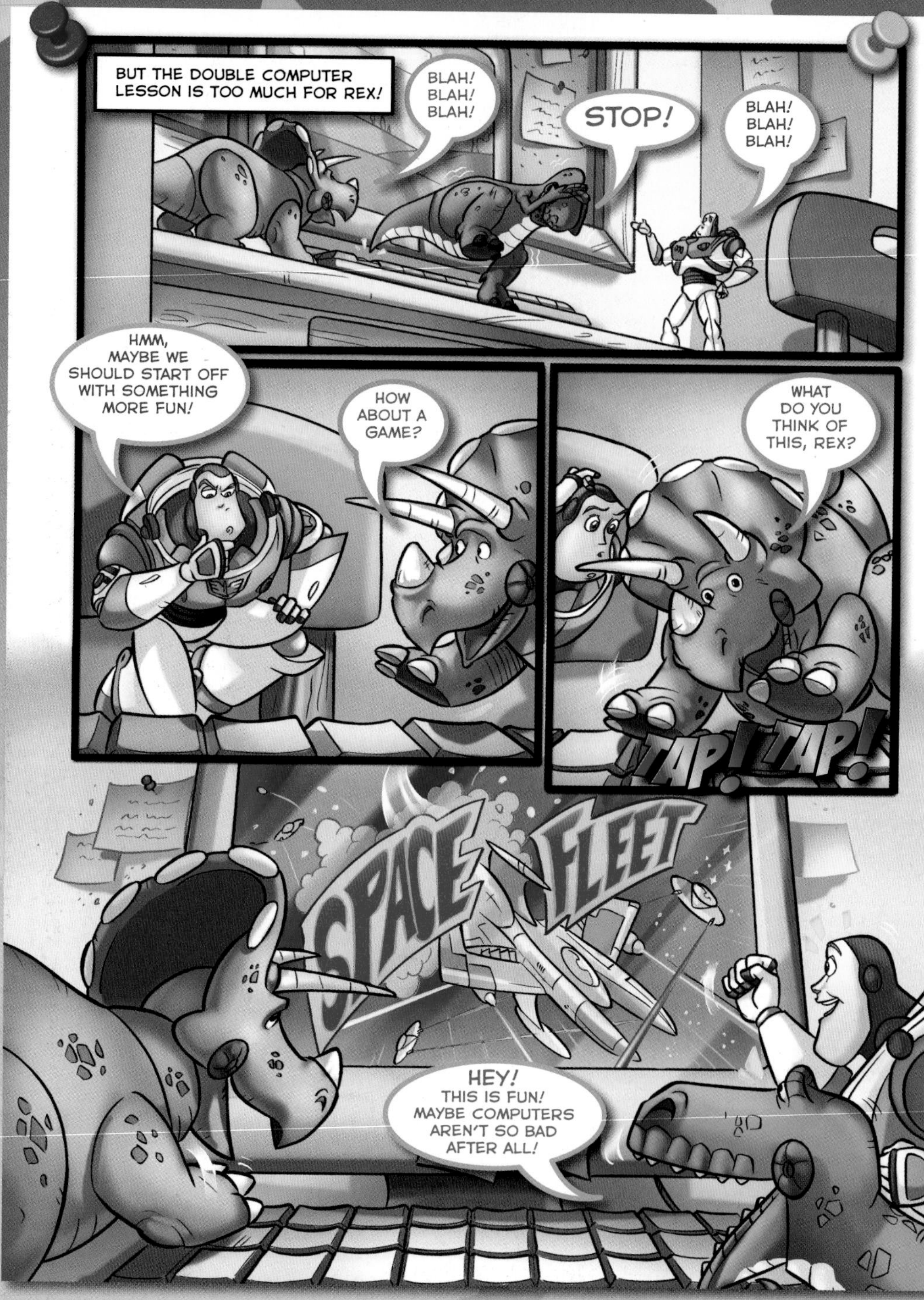

BUT THE DOUBLE COMPUTER LESSON IS TOO MUCH FOR REX!
BLAH! BLAH! BLAH!
STOP!
BLAH! BLAH! BLAH!
HMM, MAYBE WE SHOULD START OFF WITH SOMETHING MORE FUN!
HOW ABOUT A GAME?
WHAT DO YOU THINK OF THIS, REX?
TAP! TAP!
SPACE FLEET
HEY! THIS IS FUN! MAYBE COMPUTERS AREN'T SO BAD AFTER ALL!

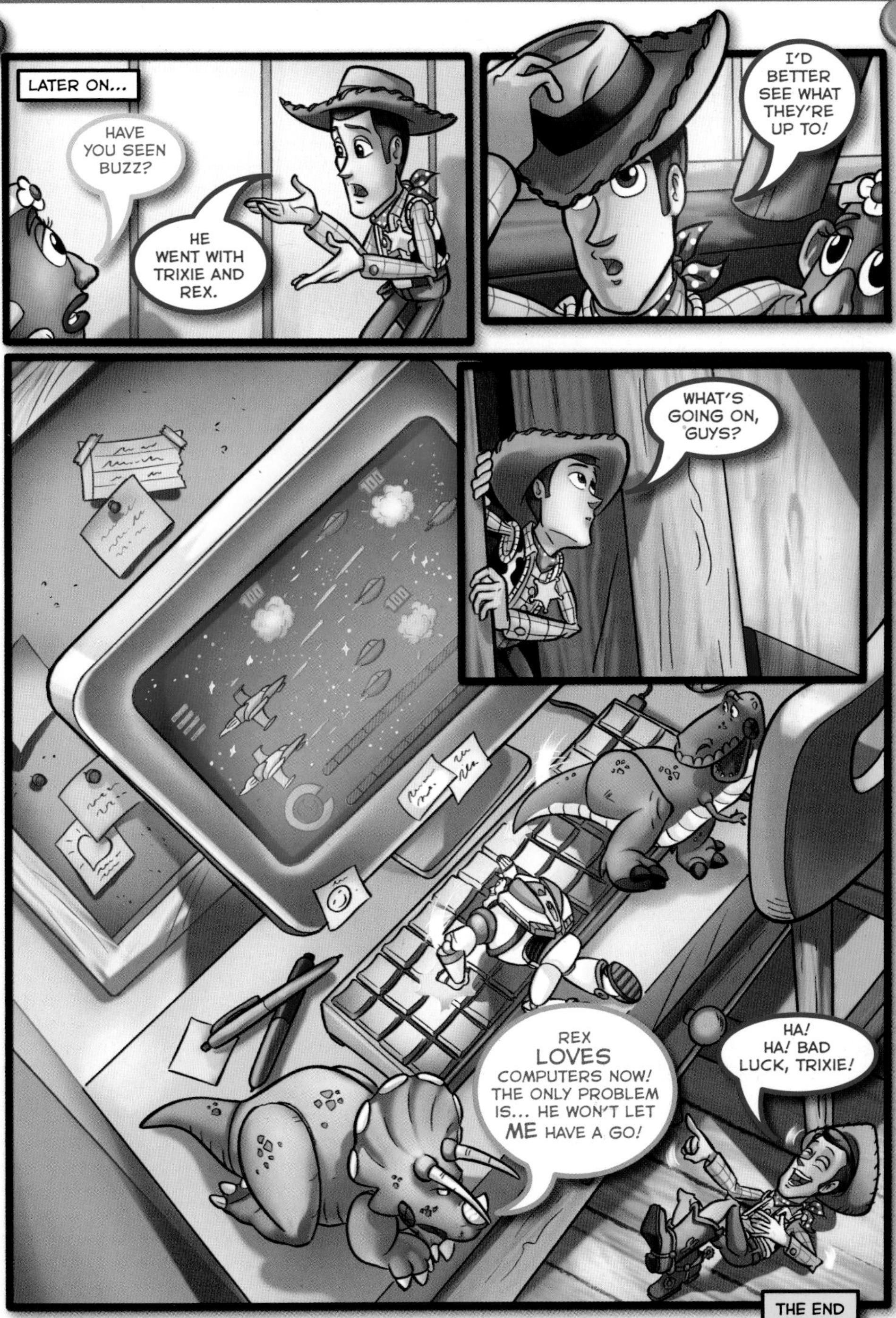

LATER ON...
HAVE YOU SEEN BUZZ?
HE WENT WITH TRIXIE AND REX.
I'D BETTER SEE WHAT THEY'RE UP TO!
WHAT'S GOING ON, GUYS?
REX LOVES COMPUTERS NOW! THE ONLY PROBLEM IS... HE WON'T LET ME HAVE A GO!
HA! HA! BAD LUCK, TRIXIE!
THE END

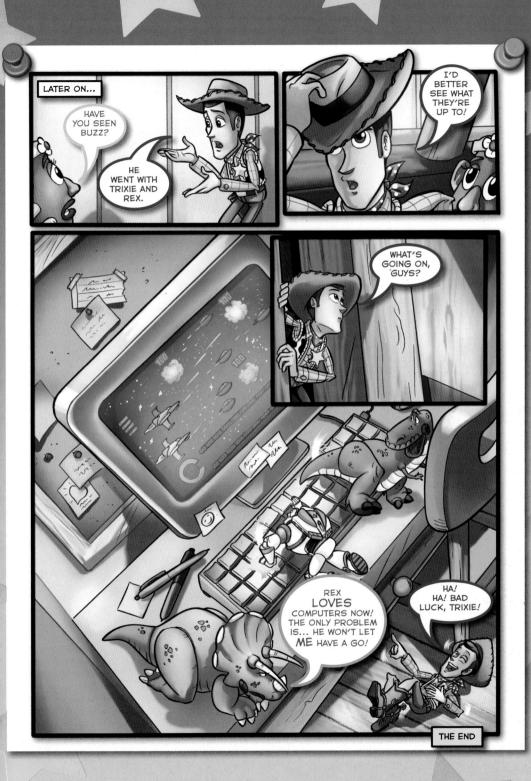

WAYS OF COMMUNICATION

LOOK, WOODY! I'VE JUST CREATED MY SUPERCHAT ACCOUNT!

SHORTARMS123! NICE!

SHORTARMS123

ISN'T IT GREAT? NOW I CAN CHAT WITH TRIXIE WHENEVER I WANT!

BUT... WHAT'S THE POINT? YOU'RE IN THE SAME HOUSE!

SHORTARMS123

WHAT DO YOU MEAN?!

I'M SAYING THAT--

PLOING

HEY! HEY! TRIXIE HAS JUST SENT ME A MESSAGE!

WHERE ARE YOU?

GOOD! ANSWER HER!

I'M **HERE!** IN THE **LIVING ROOM!**

AHEM... THIS IS EXACTLY WHAT I MEANT!

THE END

SCRIPT: TEA ORSI; LAYOUT: LUCA USAI; INK: MICHELA FRARE; COLOUR: ANGELA CAPOLUPO

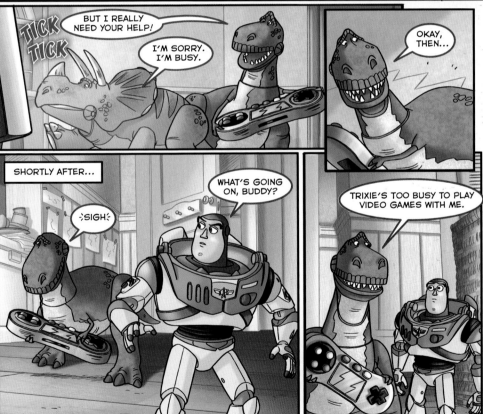

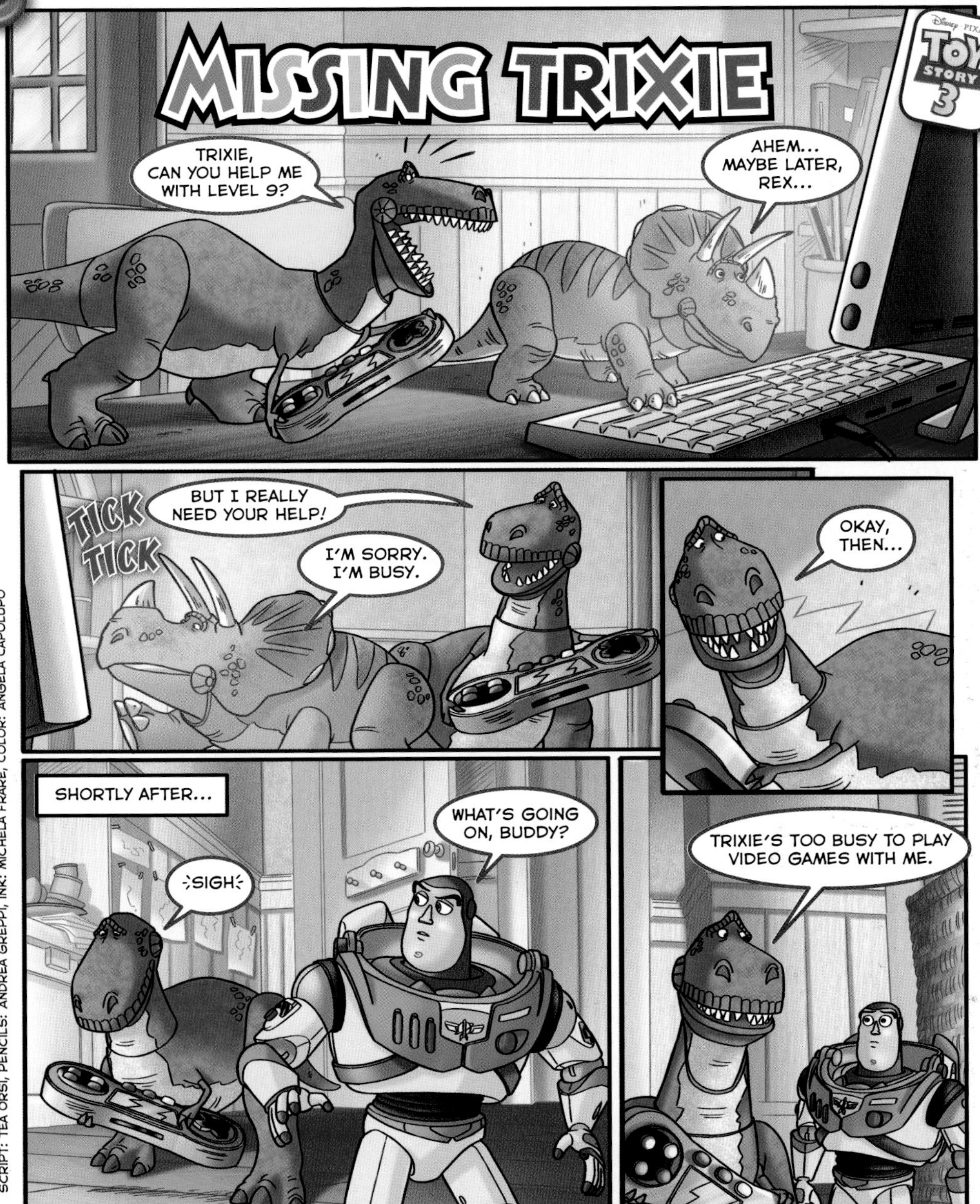

MISSING TRIXIE

TRIXIE, CAN YOU HELP ME WITH LEVEL 9?

AHEM... MAYBE LATER, REX...

TICK TICK

BUT I REALLY NEED YOUR HELP!

I'M SORRY. I'M BUSY.

OKAY, THEN...

SHORTLY AFTER...

:SIGH:

WHAT'S GOING ON, BUDDY?

TRIXIE'S TOO BUSY TO PLAY VIDEO GAMES WITH ME.

SCRIPT: TEA ORSI, PENCILS: ANDREA GREPPI, INK: MICHELA FRARE, COLOR: ANGELA CAPOLUPO

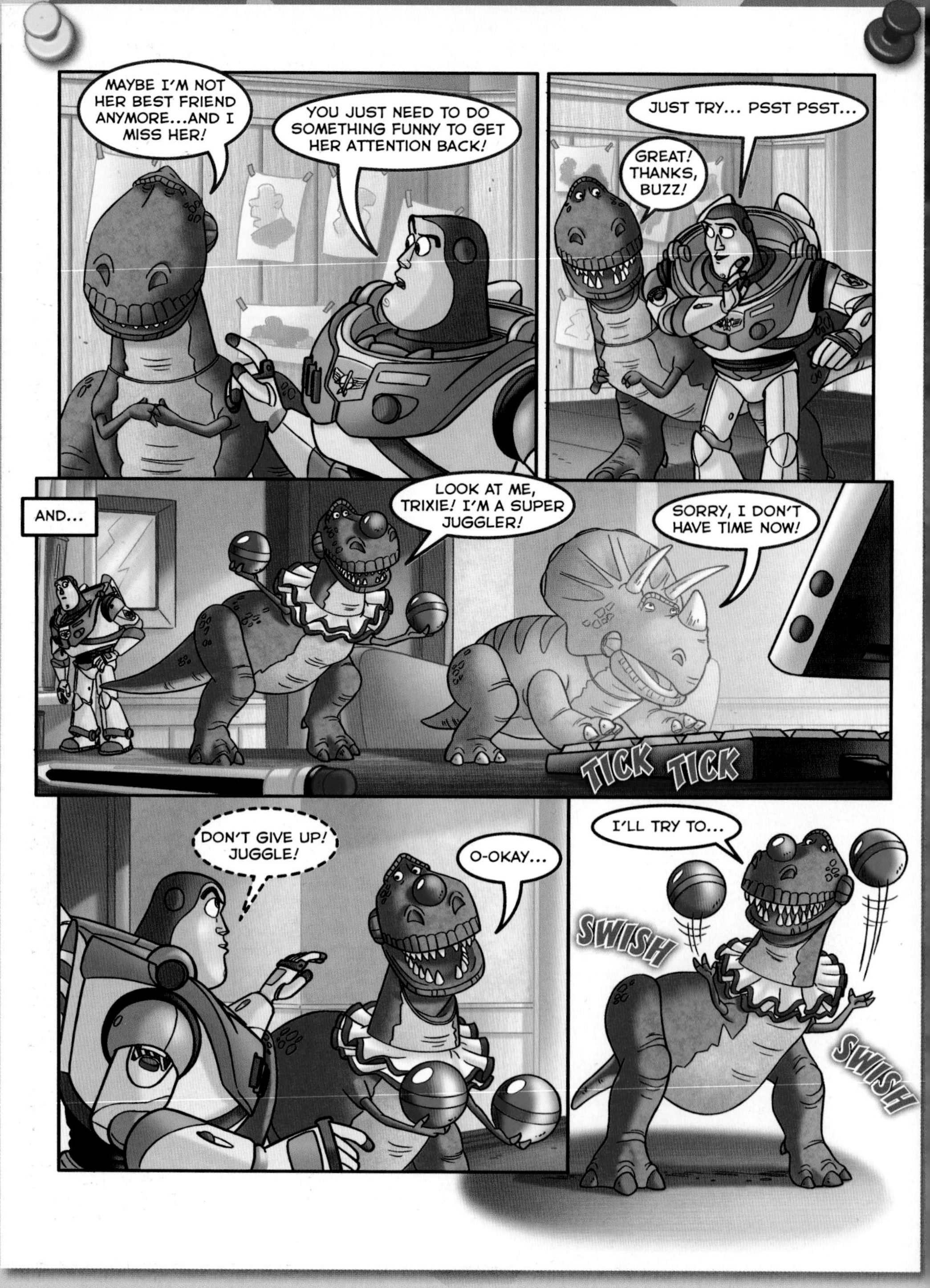
MAYBE I'M NOT HER BEST FRIEND ANYMORE...AND I MISS HER!
YOU JUST NEED TO DO SOMETHING FUNNY TO GET HER ATTENTION BACK!
JUST TRY... PSST PSST...
GREAT! THANKS, BUZZ!
AND...
LOOK AT ME, TRIXIE! I'M A SUPER JUGGLER!
SORRY, I DON'T HAVE TIME NOW!
TICK TICK
DON'T GIVE UP! JUGGLE!
O-OKAY...
I'LL TRY TO...
SWISH
SWISH

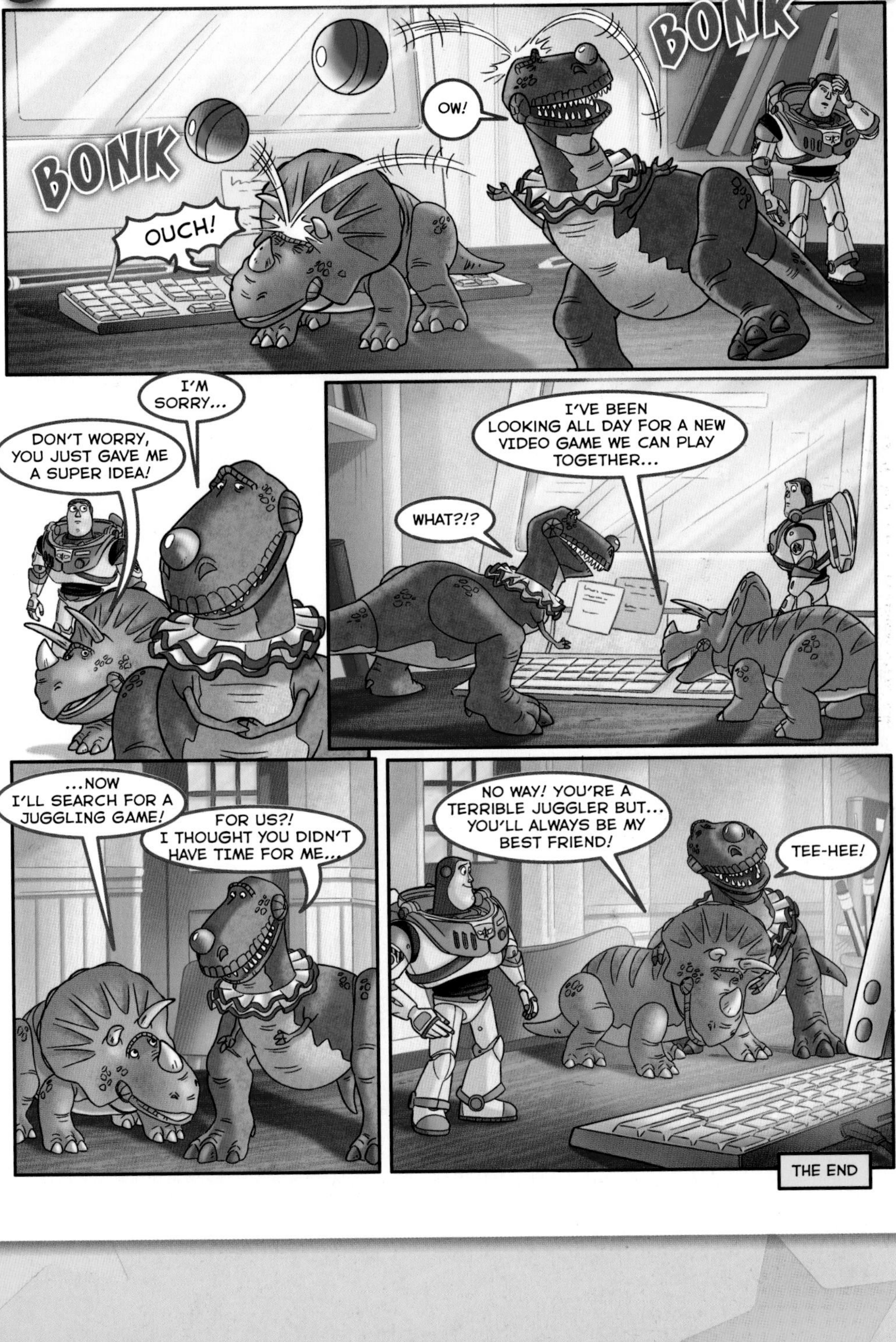
BONK
OUCH!
OW!
BONK
I'M SORRY...
DON'T WORRY, YOU JUST GAVE ME A SUPER IDEA!
I'VE BEEN LOOKING ALL DAY FOR A NEW VIDEO GAME WE CAN PLAY TOGETHER...
WHAT?!?
...NOW I'LL SEARCH FOR A JUGGLING GAME!
FOR US?! I THOUGHT YOU DIDN'T HAVE TIME FOR ME...
NO WAY! YOU'RE A TERRIBLE JUGGLER BUT... YOU'LL ALWAYS BE MY BEST FRIEND!
TEE-HEE!
THE END

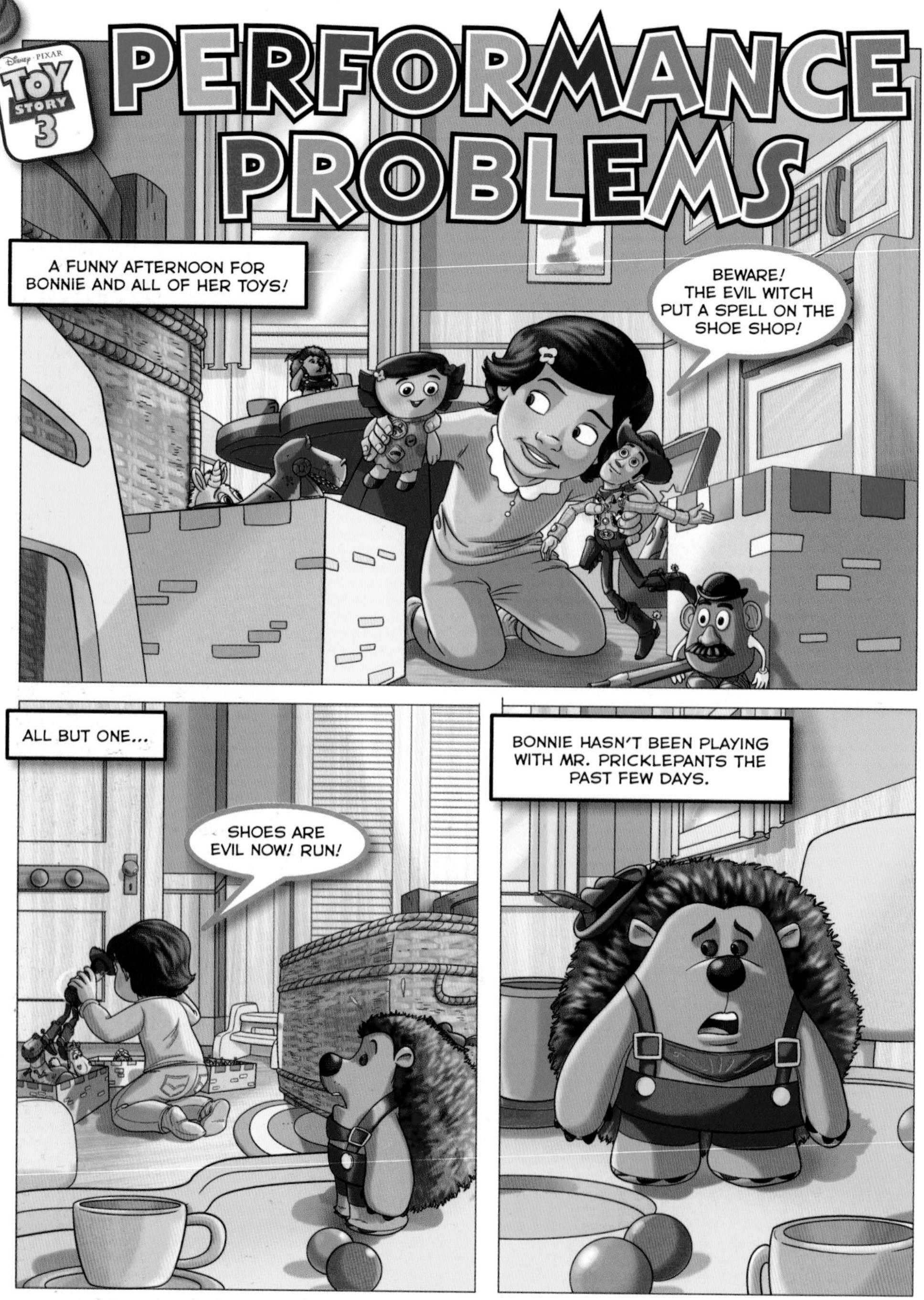
TOY STORY 3
PERFORMANCE PROBLEMS
A FUNNY AFTERNOON FOR BONNIE AND ALL OF HER TOYS!
BEWARE! THE EVIL WITCH PUT A SPELL ON THE SHOE SHOP!
ALL BUT ONE...
SHOES ARE EVIL NOW! RUN!
BONNIE HASN'T BEEN PLAYING WITH MR. PRICKLEPANTS THE PAST FEW DAYS.

SCRIPT: ALESSANDRO FERRARI; LAYOUT & INK: VALENTINO FORLINI; COLOUR: LUCIO DE GIUSEPPE

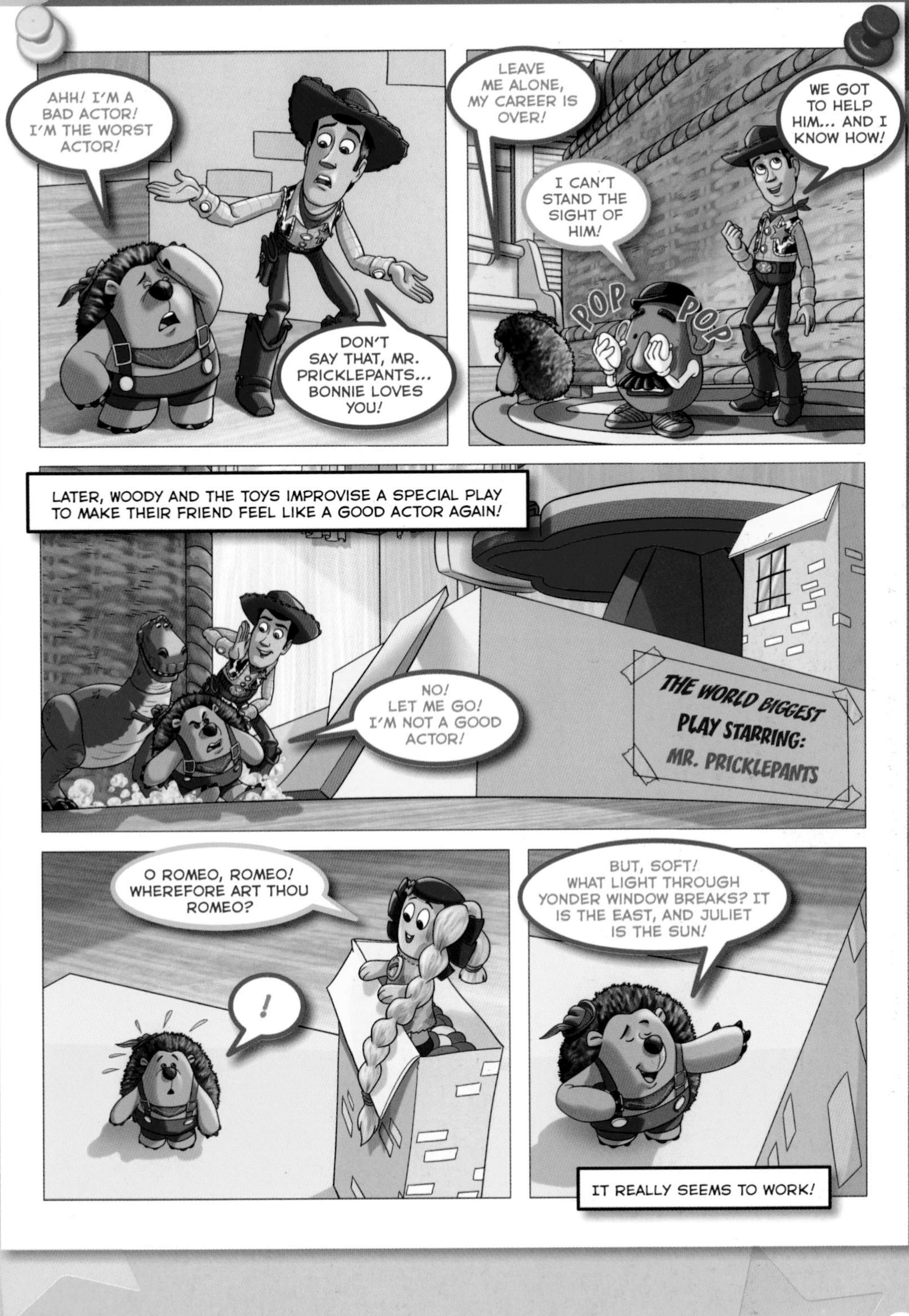
AHH! I'M A BAD ACTOR! I'M THE WORST ACTOR!
DON'T SAY THAT, MR. PRICKLEPANTS... BONNIE LOVES YOU!
LEAVE ME ALONE, MY CAREER IS OVER!
I CAN'T STAND THE SIGHT OF HIM!
POP
POP
WE GOT TO HELP HIM... AND I KNOW HOW!
LATER, WOODY AND THE TOYS IMPROVISE A SPECIAL PLAY TO MAKE THEIR FRIEND FEEL LIKE A GOOD ACTOR AGAIN!
NO! LET ME GO! I'M NOT A GOOD ACTOR!
THE WORLD BIGGEST PLAY STARRING: MR. PRICKLEPANTS
O ROMEO, ROMEO! WHEREFORE ART THOU ROMEO?
!
BUT, SOFT! WHAT LIGHT THROUGH YONDER WINDOW BREAKS? IT IS THE EAST, AND JULIET IS THE SUN!
IT REALLY SEEMS TO WORK!

HERE'S EXCALIBUR! AND I'M THE KING!
IF I DID, WOULD YOU LET HIM GO?
YES, BELLE. BUT YOU MUST PROMISE TO STAY HERE FOREVER!
MR. PRICKLEPANTS IS HAPPY AGAIN!
BUT THAT AFTERNOON, WHEN IT'S BONNIE'S PLAYTIME...
SHERIFF WOODY CATCHES THE WITCH!
...EVERYTHING IS BACK AS IT WAS!
THE SHOE SHOP IS SAVED! HURRAY FOR THE SHERIFF!

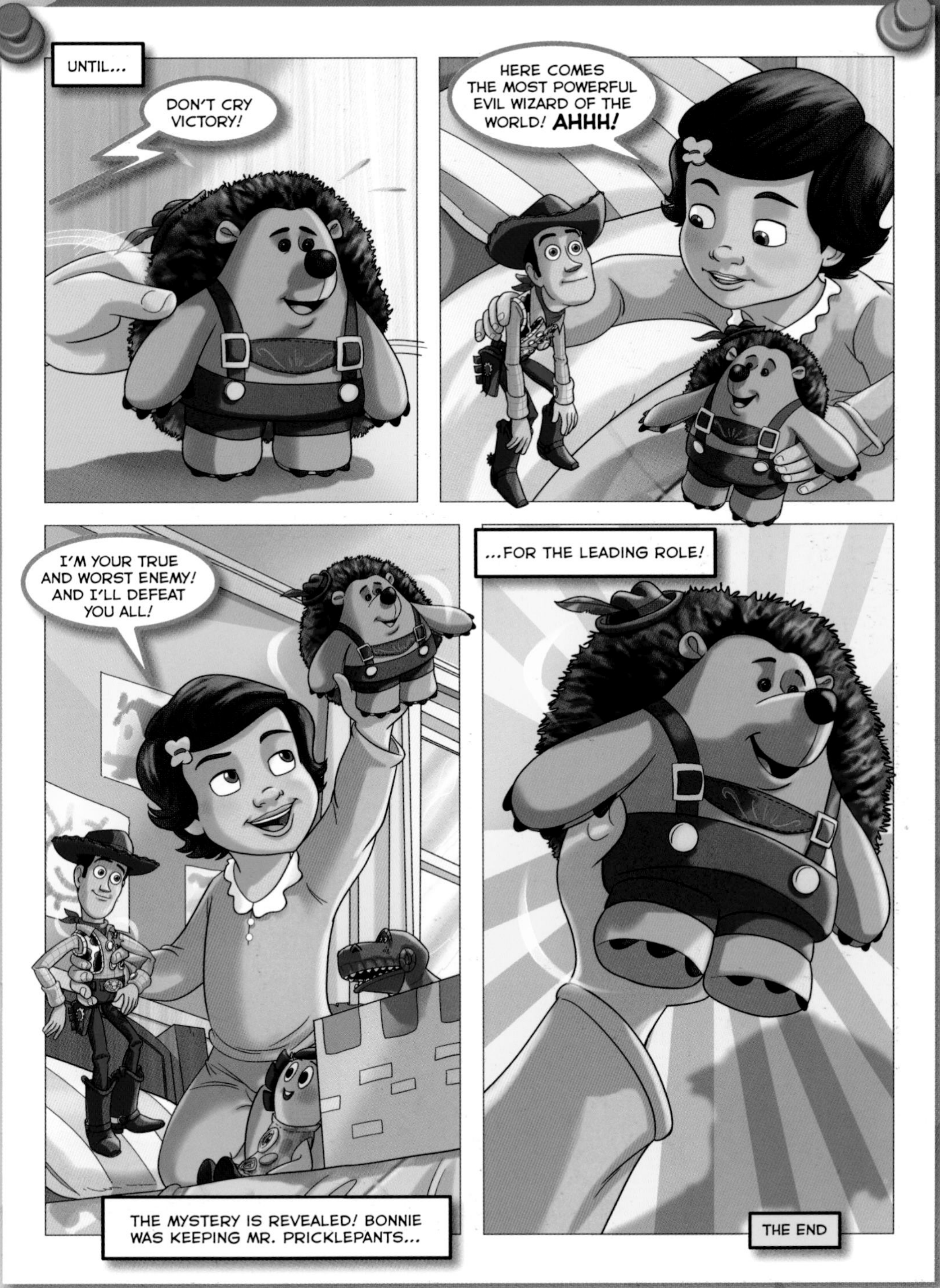

UNTIL...
DON'T CRY VICTORY!
HERE COMES THE MOST POWERFUL EVIL WIZARD OF THE WORLD! AHHH!
I'M YOUR TRUE AND WORST ENEMY! AND I'LL DEFEAT YOU ALL!
THE MYSTERY IS REVEALED! BONNIE WAS KEEPING MR. PRICKLEPANTS...
...FOR THE LEADING ROLE!
THE END

THE ACTING LESSON

Disney PIXAR TOY STORY 3

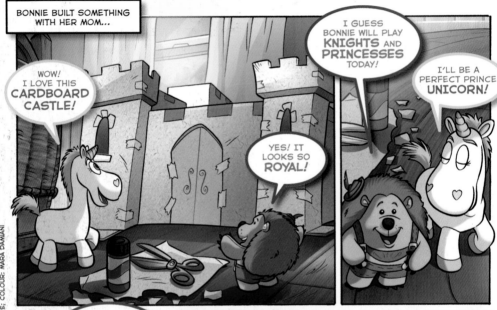

BONNIE BUILT SOMETHING WITH HER MOM...

WOW! I LOVE THIS CARDBOARD CASTLE!

I GUESS BONNIE WILL PLAY KNIGHTS AND PRINCESSES TODAY!

I'LL BE A PERFECT PRINCE UNICORN!

YES! IT LOOKS SO ROYAL!

SCRIPT: TEA ORSI; LAYOUT: LUCA USAI; INK: MICHELA FRARE; COLOUR: MARA DAMIANI

YEAH! YOU'LL BE GREAT IN THAT ROLE BUT...

I'M NOT SO SURE ABOUT THEM!

EWW!

YAY!

AND SUPER GALAXY ACTIVATED HIS LASER!

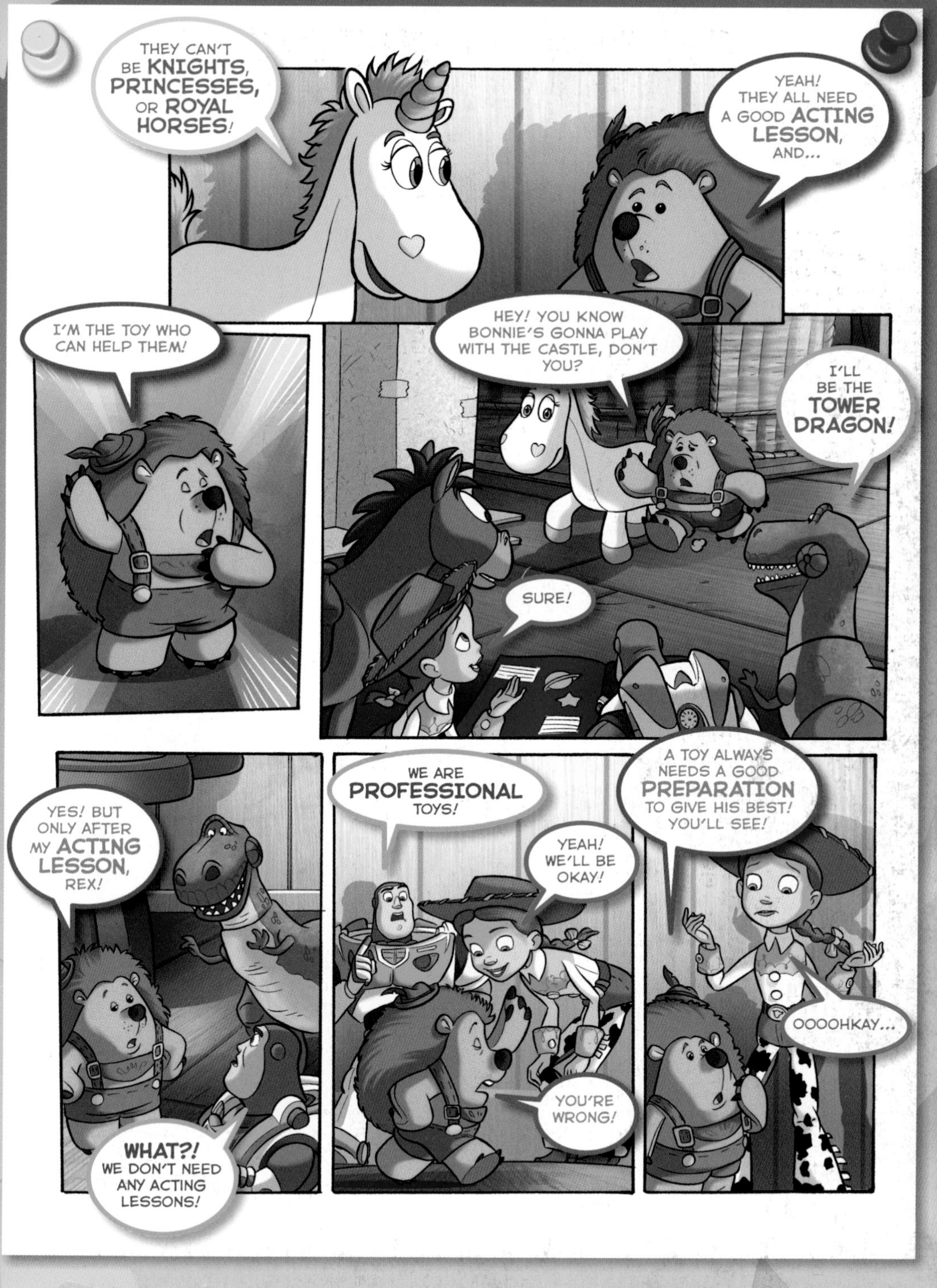
THEY CAN'T BE KNIGHTS, PRINCESSES, OR ROYAL HORSES!
YEAH! THEY ALL NEED A GOOD ACTING LESSON, AND...
I'M THE TOY WHO CAN HELP THEM!
HEY! YOU KNOW BONNIE'S GONNA PLAY WITH THE CASTLE, DON'T YOU?
I'LL BE THE TOWER DRAGON!
SURE!
YES! BUT ONLY AFTER MY ACTING LESSON, REX!
WHAT?! WE DON'T NEED ANY ACTING LESSONS!
WE ARE PROFESSIONAL TOYS!
YEAH! WE'LL BE OKAY!
YOU'RE WRONG!
A TOY ALWAYS NEEDS A GOOD PREPARATION TO GIVE HIS BEST! YOU'LL SEE!
OOOOHKAY...

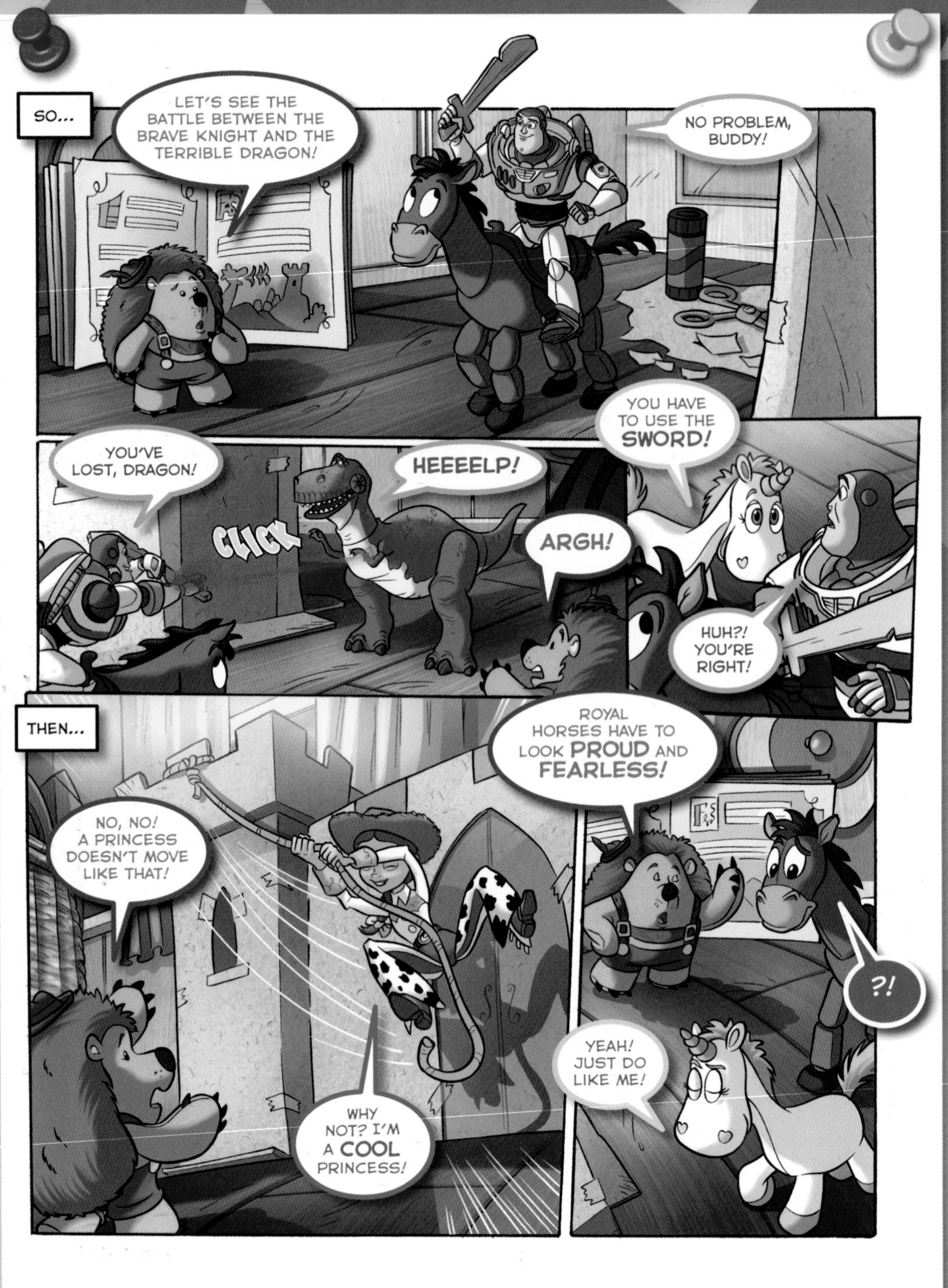
SO...
LET'S SEE THE BATTLE BETWEEN THE BRAVE KNIGHT AND THE TERRIBLE DRAGON!
NO PROBLEM, BUDDY!
YOU'VE LOST, DRAGON!
CLICK
HEEEELP!
ARGH!
YOU HAVE TO USE THE SWORD!
HUH?! YOU'RE RIGHT!
THEN...
NO, NO! A PRINCESS DOESN'T MOVE LIKE THAT!
WHY NOT? I'M A COOL PRINCESS!
ROYAL HORSES HAVE TO LOOK PROUD AND FEARLESS!
?!
YEAH! JUST DO LIKE ME!

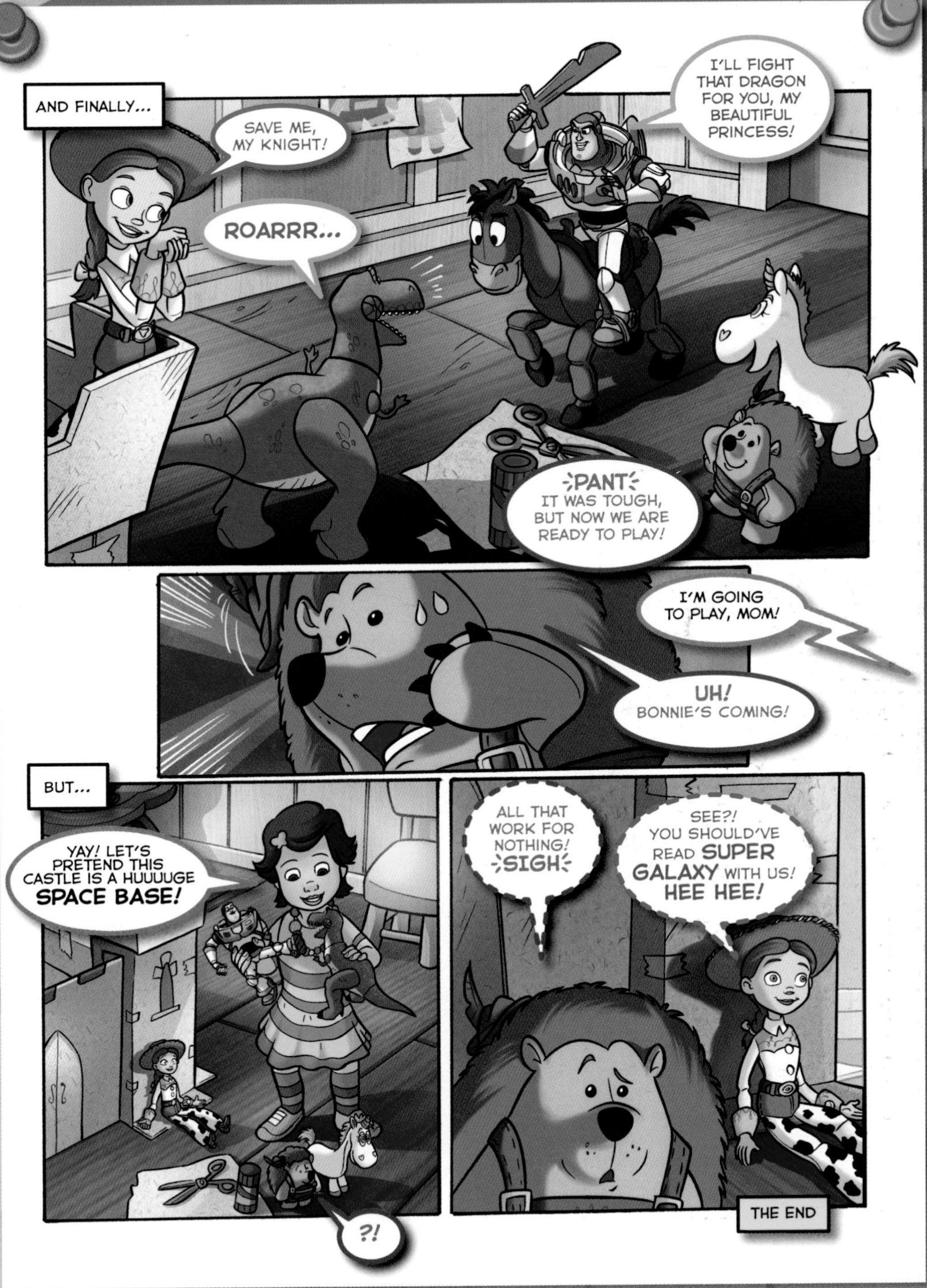
AND FINALLY...
SAVE ME, MY KNIGHT!
I'LL FIGHT THAT DRAGON FOR YOU, MY BEAUTIFUL PRINCESS!
ROARRR...
PANT
IT WAS TOUGH, BUT NOW WE ARE READY TO PLAY!
I'M GOING TO PLAY, MOM!
UH! BONNIE'S COMING!
BUT...
YAY! LET'S PRETEND THIS CASTLE IS A HUUUUGE SPACE BASE!
?!
ALL THAT WORK FOR NOTHING! SIGH
SEE?! YOU SHOULD'VE READ SUPER GALAXY WITH US! HEE HEE!
THE END

DON'T MESS WITH ROMEO

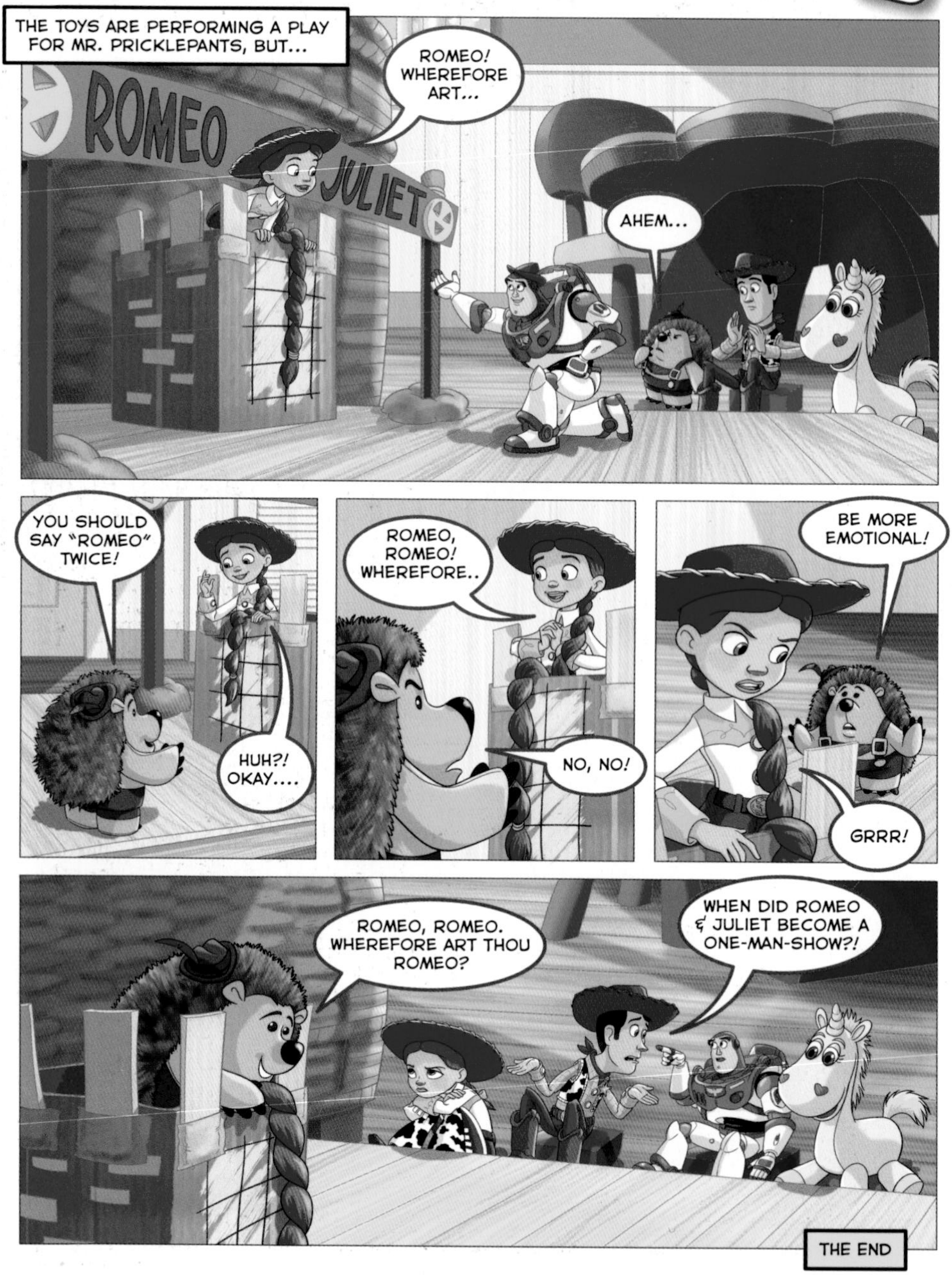

THE TOYS ARE PERFORMING A PLAY FOR MR. PRICKLEPANTS, BUT...
ROMEO
JULIET
ROMEO! WHEREFORE ART...
AHEM...
YOU SHOULD SAY "ROMEO" TWICE!
HUH?! OKAY....
ROMEO, ROMEO! WHEREFORE..
NO, NO!
BE MORE EMOTIONAL!
GRRR!
ROMEO, ROMEO. WHEREFORE ART THOU ROMEO?
WHEN DID ROMEO & JULIET BECOME A ONE-MAN-SHOW?!
THE END

SCRIPT: TEA ORSI, PENCIL & INK: VALENTINO FORLINI, COLOR: LUCIO DE GIUSEPPE

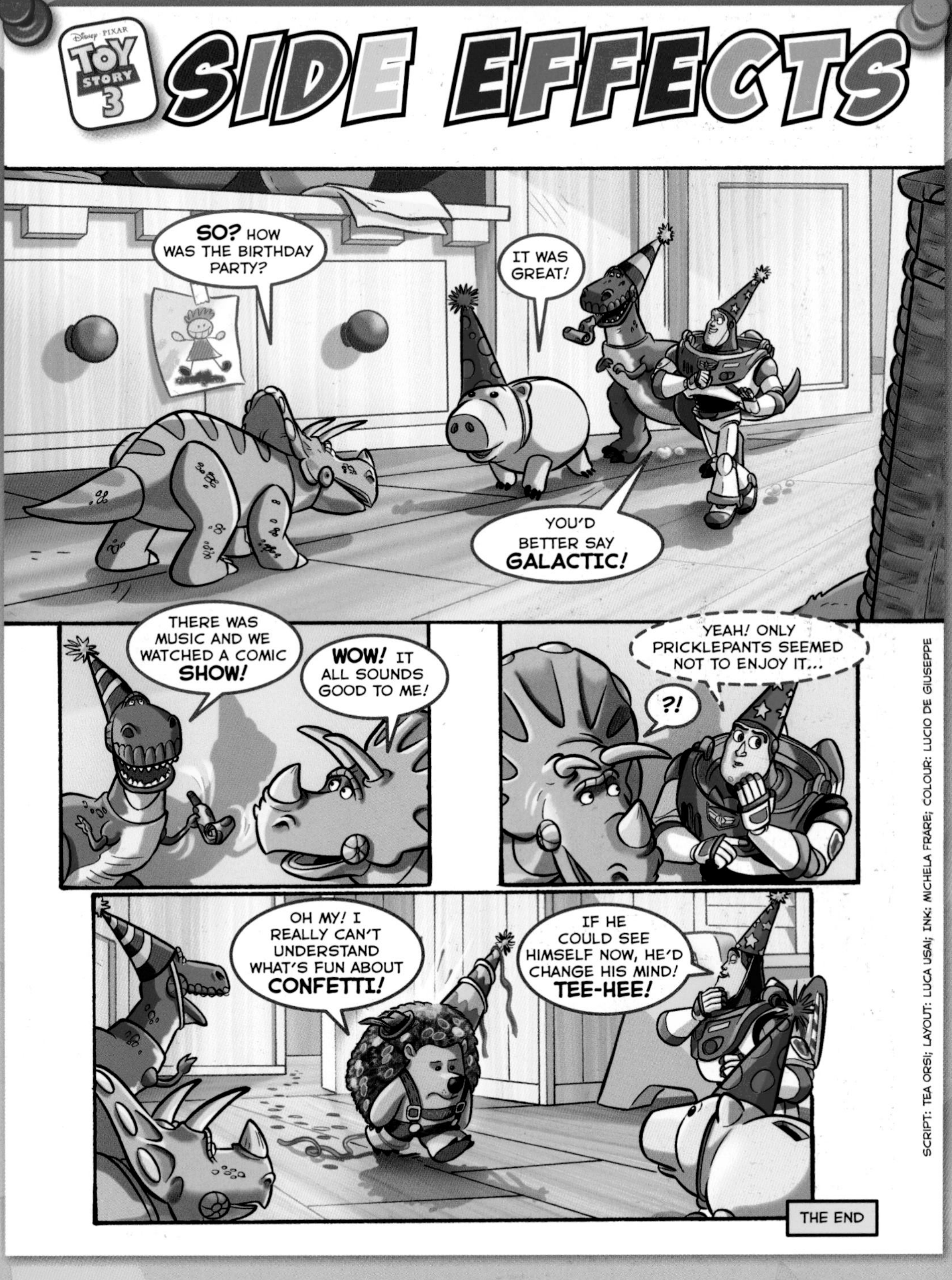
Disney · PIXAR
TOY STORY 3
SIDE EFFECTS
SO? HOW WAS THE BIRTHDAY PARTY?
IT WAS GREAT!
YOU'D BETTER SAY GALACTIC!
THERE WAS MUSIC AND WE WATCHED A COMIC SHOW!
WOW! IT ALL SOUNDS GOOD TO ME!
YEAH! ONLY PRICKLEPANTS SEEMED NOT TO ENJOY IT...
?!
OH MY! I REALLY CAN'T UNDERSTAND WHAT'S FUN ABOUT CONFETTI!
IF HE COULD SEE HIMSELF NOW, HE'D CHANGE HIS MIND! TEE-HEE!
THE END
SCRIPT: TEA ORSI; LAYOUT: LUCA USAI; INK: MICHELA FRARE; COLOUR: LUCIO DE GIUSEPPE

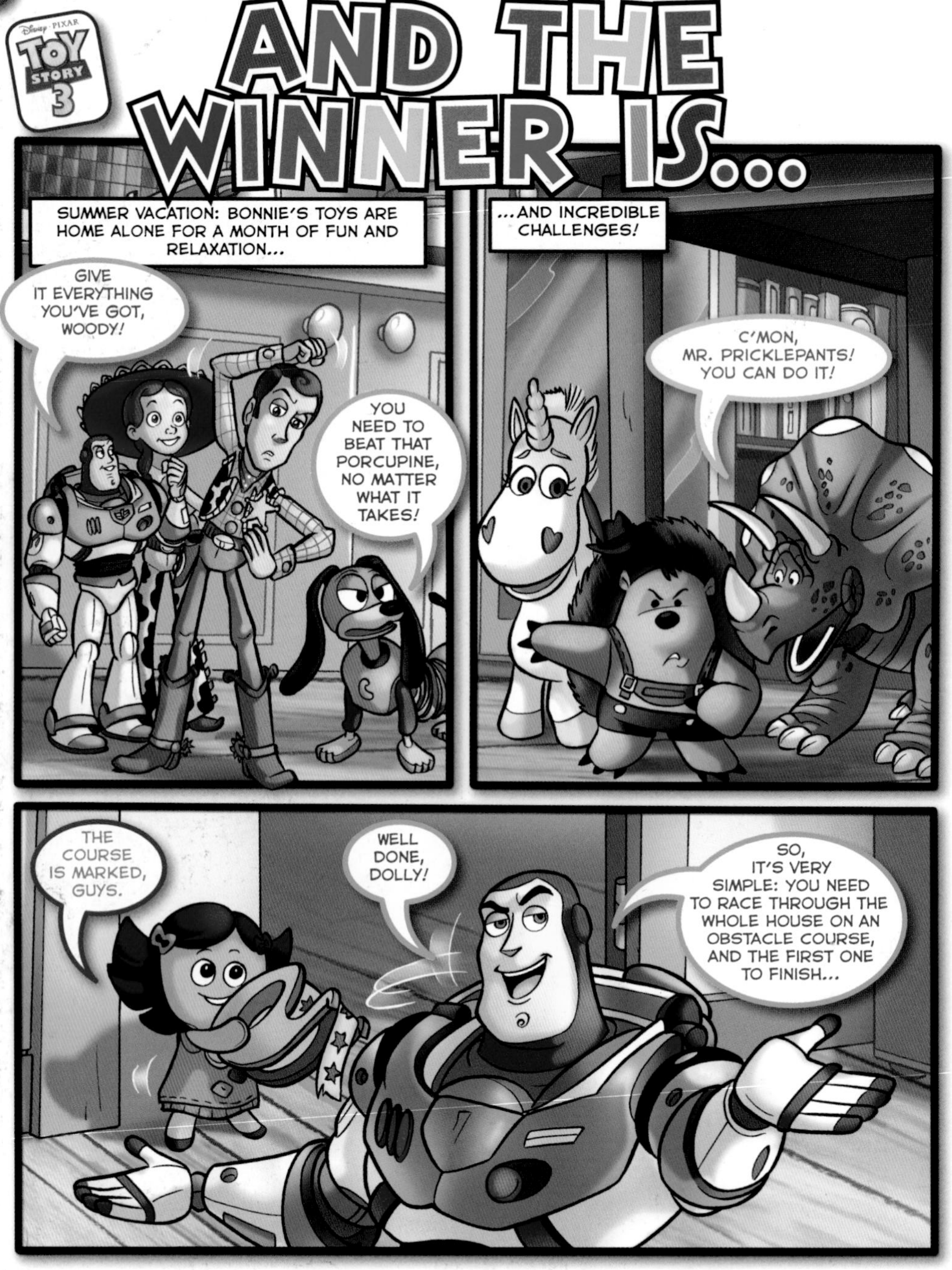
TOY STORY 3
AND THE WINNER IS...
SUMMER VACATION: BONNIE'S TOYS ARE HOME ALONE FOR A MONTH OF FUN AND RELAXATION...
GIVE IT EVERYTHING YOU'VE GOT, WOODY!
YOU NEED TO BEAT THAT PORCUPINE, NO MATTER WHAT IT TAKES!
...AND INCREDIBLE CHALLENGES!
C'MON, MR. PRICKLEPANTS! YOU CAN DO IT!
THE COURSE IS MARKED, GUYS.
WELL DONE, DOLLY!
SO, IT'S VERY SIMPLE: YOU NEED TO RACE THROUGH THE WHOLE HOUSE ON AN OBSTACLE COURSE, AND THE FIRST ONE TO FINISH...

SCRIPT: ALESSANDRO FERRARI; PENCILS: VALENTINO FORLINI; INK: MICHELA FRARE; COLOUR: KAWAII CREATIVE STUDIO

...IS THE WINNER!
READY... SET...
GO!
YOU'LL NEVER BEAT ME, COWBOY!
WE'LL SEE ABOUT THAT, PRICKLEPANTS!
!
HA HA! OBSTACLES ARE MY SPECIALTY, PARTNER!

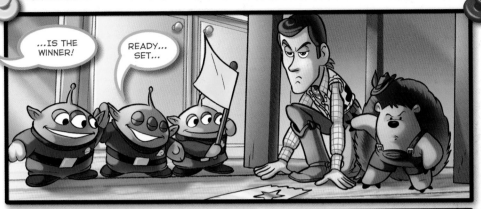

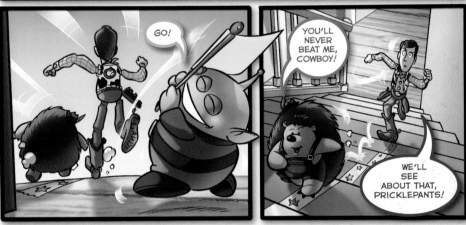

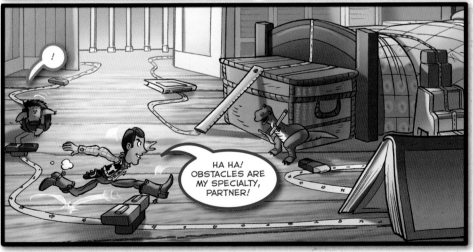

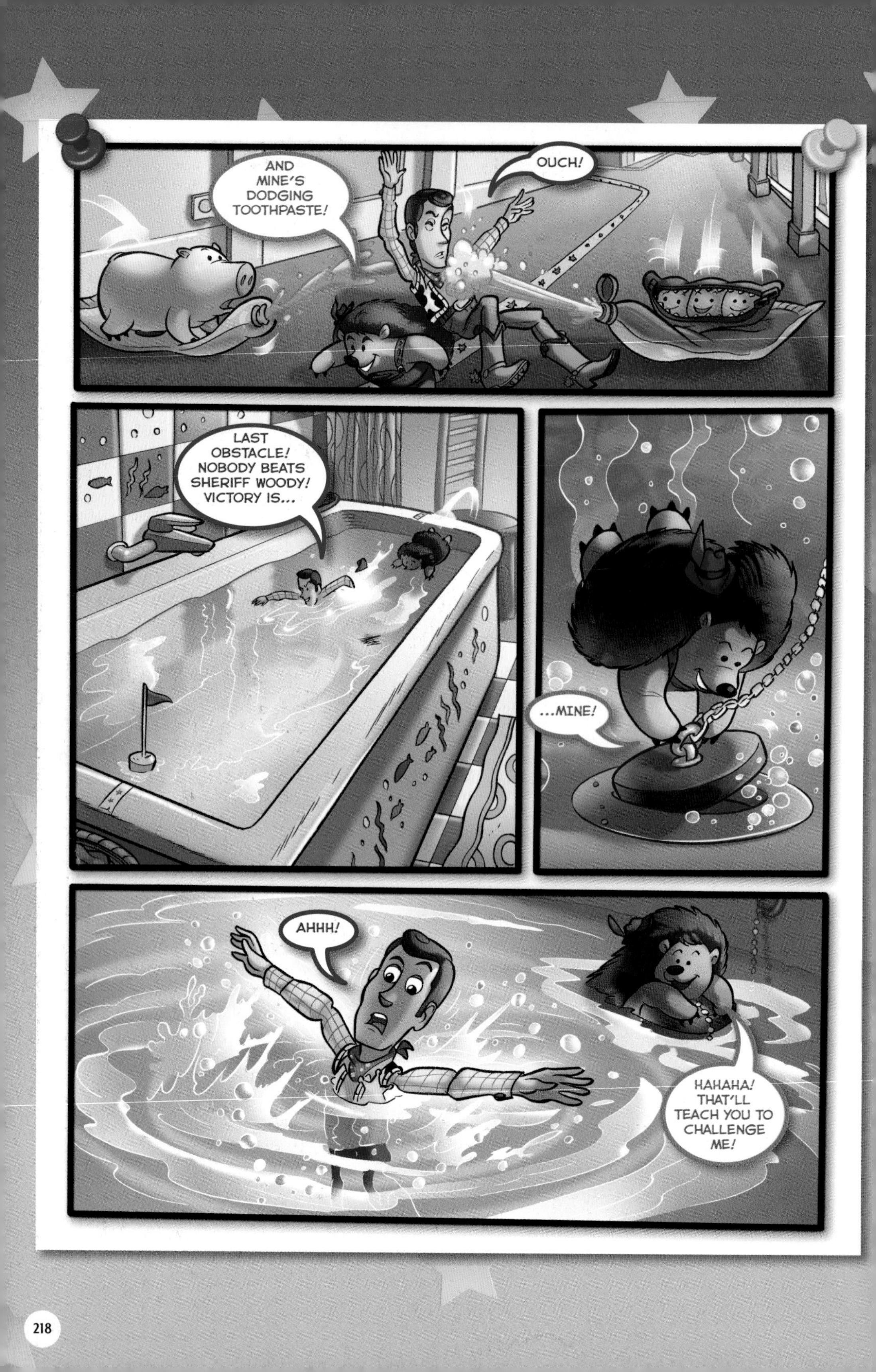
AND MINE'S DODGING TOOTHPASTE!
OUCH!
LAST OBSTACLE! NOBODY BEATS SHERIFF WOODY! VICTORY IS...
...MINE!
AHHH!
HAHAHA! THAT'LL TEACH YOU TO CHALLENGE ME!

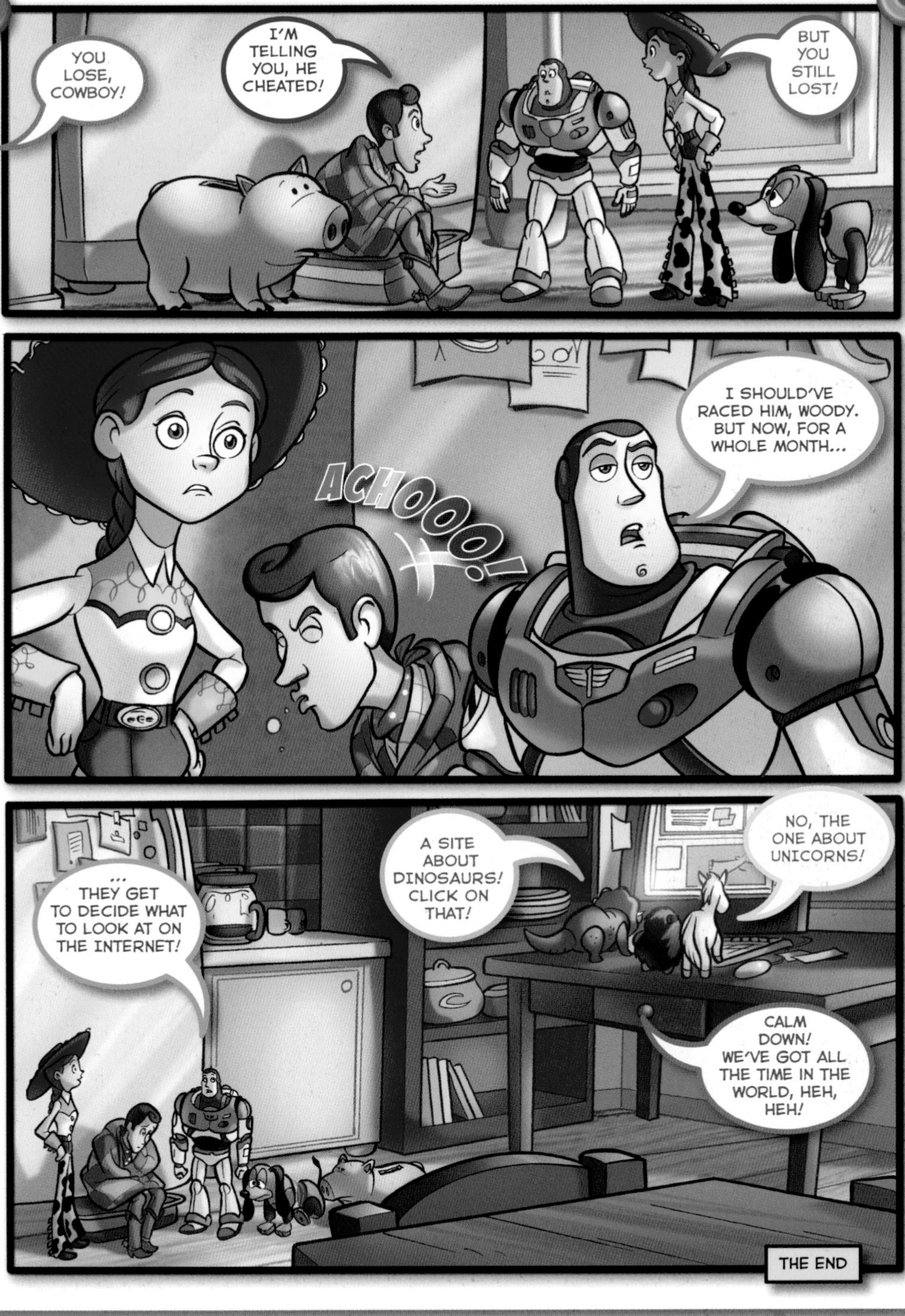
YOU LOSE, COWBOY!
I'M TELLING YOU, HE CHEATED!
BUT YOU STILL LOST!
I SHOULD'VE RACED HIM, WOODY. BUT NOW, FOR A WHOLE MONTH...
ACHOOOO!
... THEY GET TO DECIDE WHAT TO LOOK AT ON THE INTERNET!
A SITE ABOUT DINOSAURS! CLICK ON THAT!
NO, THE ONE ABOUT UNICORNS!
CALM DOWN! WE'VE GOT ALL THE TIME IN THE WORLD, HEH, HEH!
THE END

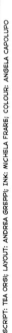

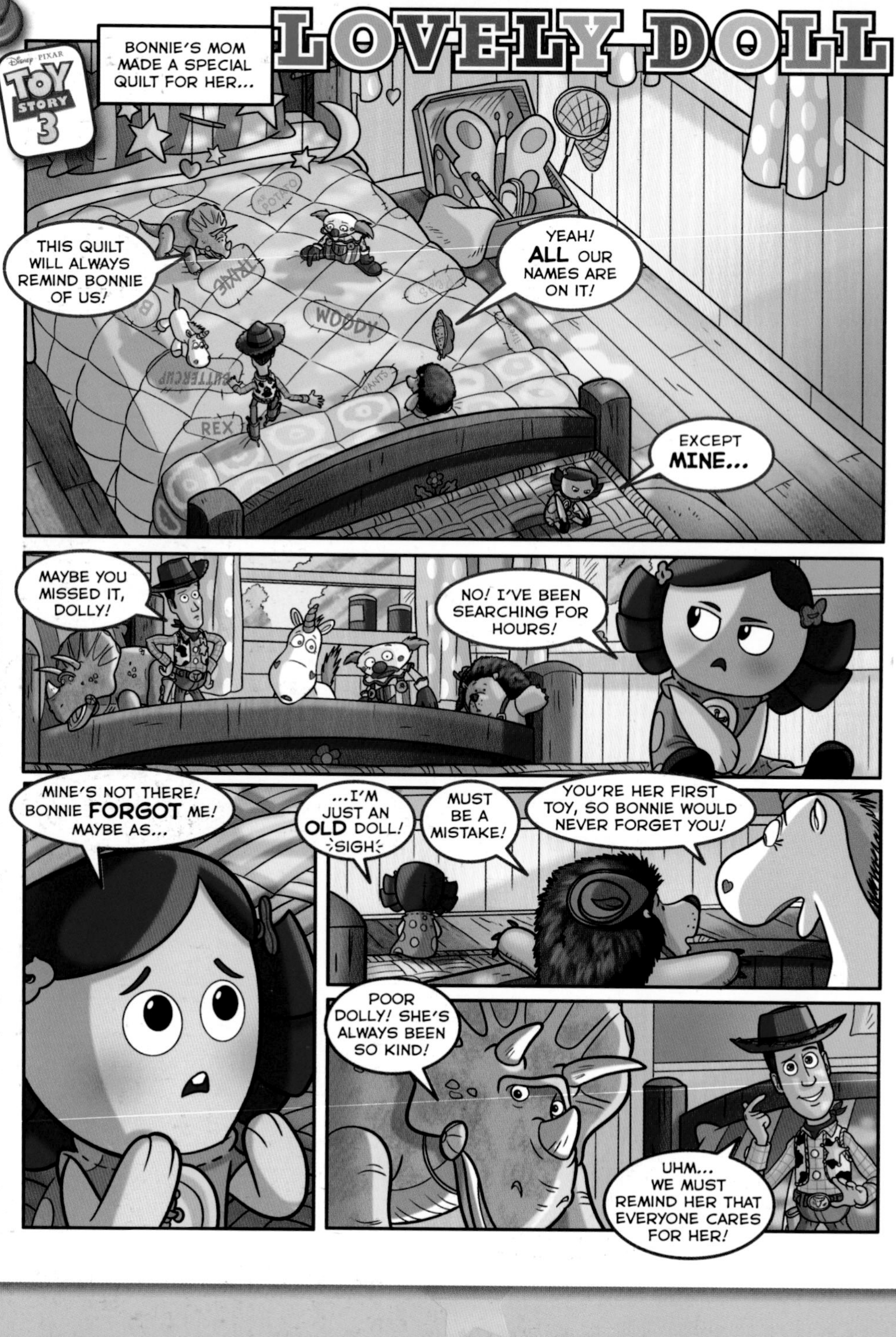
LOVELY DOLL
BONNIE'S MOM MADE A SPECIAL QUILT FOR HER...
THIS QUILT WILL ALWAYS REMIND BONNIE OF US!
YEAH! ALL OUR NAMES ARE ON IT!
EXCEPT MINE...
MAYBE YOU MISSED IT, DOLLY!
NO! I'VE BEEN SEARCHING FOR HOURS!
MINE'S NOT THERE! BONNIE FORGOT ME! MAYBE AS...
...I'M JUST AN OLD DOLL! SIGH
MUST BE A MISTAKE!
YOU'RE HER FIRST TOY, SO BONNIE WOULD NEVER FORGET YOU!
POOR DOLLY! SHE'S ALWAYS BEEN SO KIND!
UHM... WE MUST REMIND HER THAT EVERYONE CARES FOR HER!

SCRIPT: TEA ORSI; LAYOUT: ANDREA GREPPI; INK: MICHELA FRARE; COLOUR: ANGELA CAPOLUPO

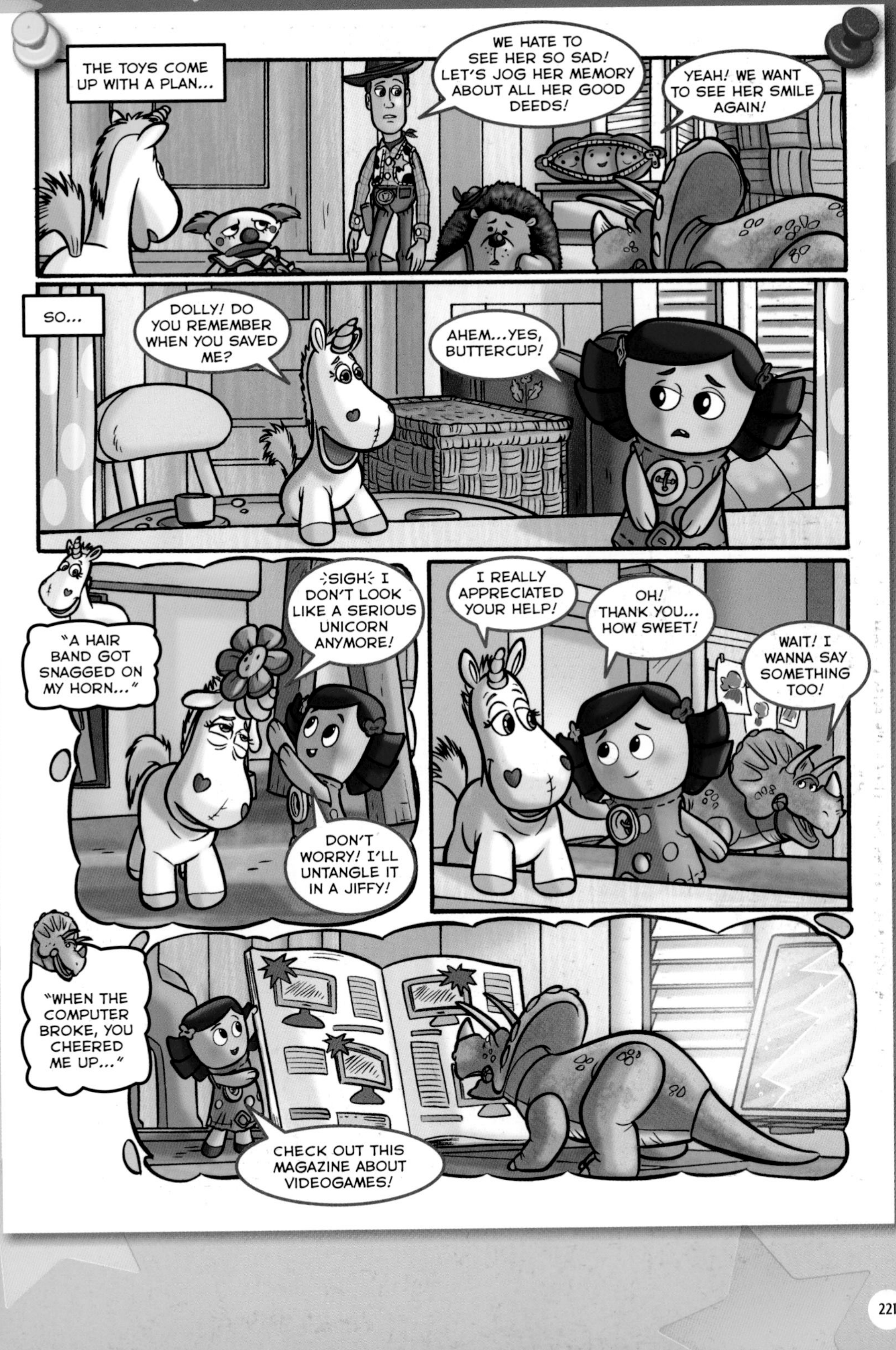
THE TOYS COME UP WITH A PLAN...
WE HATE TO SEE HER SO SAD! LET'S JOG HER MEMORY ABOUT ALL HER GOOD DEEDS!
YEAH! WE WANT TO SEE HER SMILE AGAIN!
SO...
DOLLY! DO YOU REMEMBER WHEN YOU SAVED ME?
AHEM...YES, BUTTERCUP!
"A HAIR BAND GOT SNAGGED ON MY HORN..."
SIGH I DON'T LOOK LIKE A SERIOUS UNICORN ANYMORE!
DON'T WORRY! I'LL UNTANGLE IT IN A JIFFY!
I REALLY APPRECIATED YOUR HELP!
OH! THANK YOU... HOW SWEET!
WAIT! I WANNA SAY SOMETHING TOO!
"WHEN THE COMPUTER BROKE, YOU CHEERED ME UP..."
CHECK OUT THIS MAGAZINE ABOUT VIDEOGAMES!

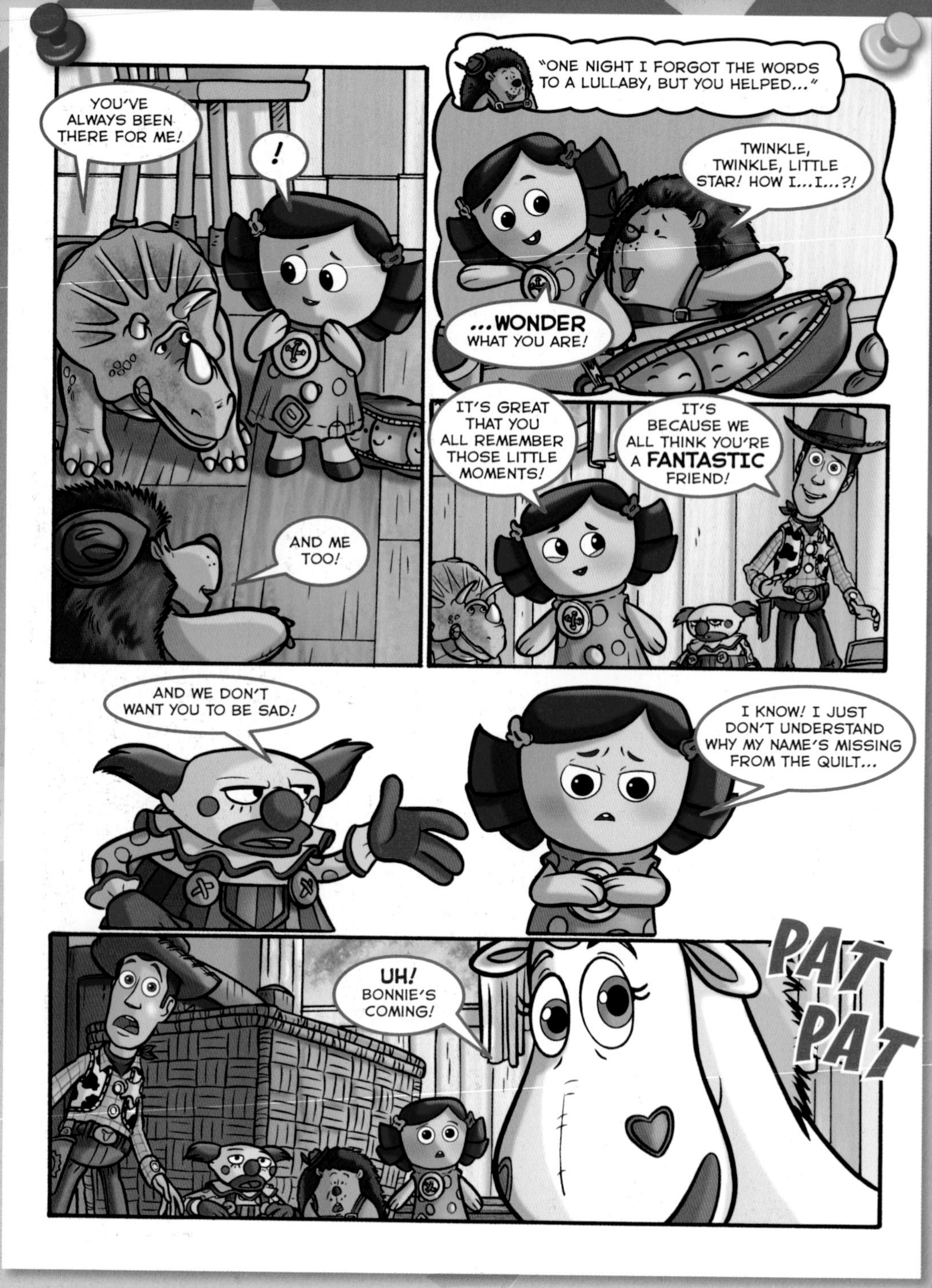

YOU'VE ALWAYS BEEN THERE FOR ME!
!
AND ME TOO!
"ONE NIGHT I FORGOT THE WORDS TO A LULLABY, BUT YOU HELPED..."
TWINKLE, TWINKLE, LITTLE STAR! HOW I...I...?!
...WONDER WHAT YOU ARE!
IT'S GREAT THAT YOU ALL REMEMBER THOSE LITTLE MOMENTS!
IT'S BECAUSE WE ALL THINK YOU'RE A FANTASTIC FRIEND!
AND WE DON'T WANT YOU TO BE SAD!
I KNOW! I JUST DON'T UNDERSTAND WHY MY NAME'S MISSING FROM THE QUILT...
UH! BONNIE'S COMING!
PAT PAT

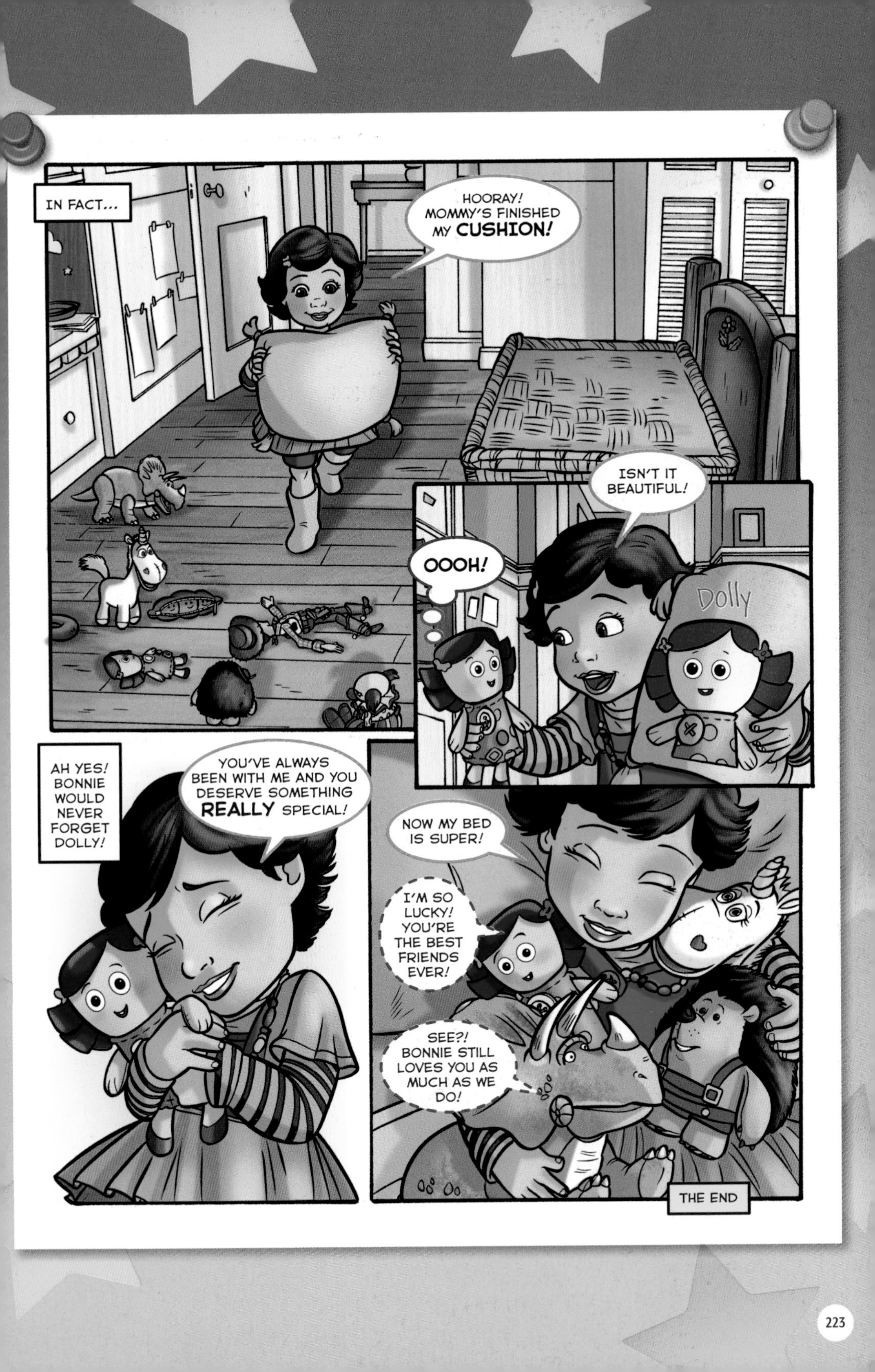

IN FACT...
HOORAY! MOMMY'S FINISHED MY CUSHION!
ISN'T IT BEAUTIFUL!
OOOH!
Dolly
AH YES! BONNIE WOULD NEVER FORGET DOLLY!
YOU'VE ALWAYS BEEN WITH ME AND YOU DESERVE SOMETHING REALLY SPECIAL!
NOW MY BED IS SUPER!
I'M SO LUCKY! YOU'RE THE BEST FRIENDS EVER!
SEE?! BONNIE STILL LOVES YOU AS MUCH AS WE DO!
THE END

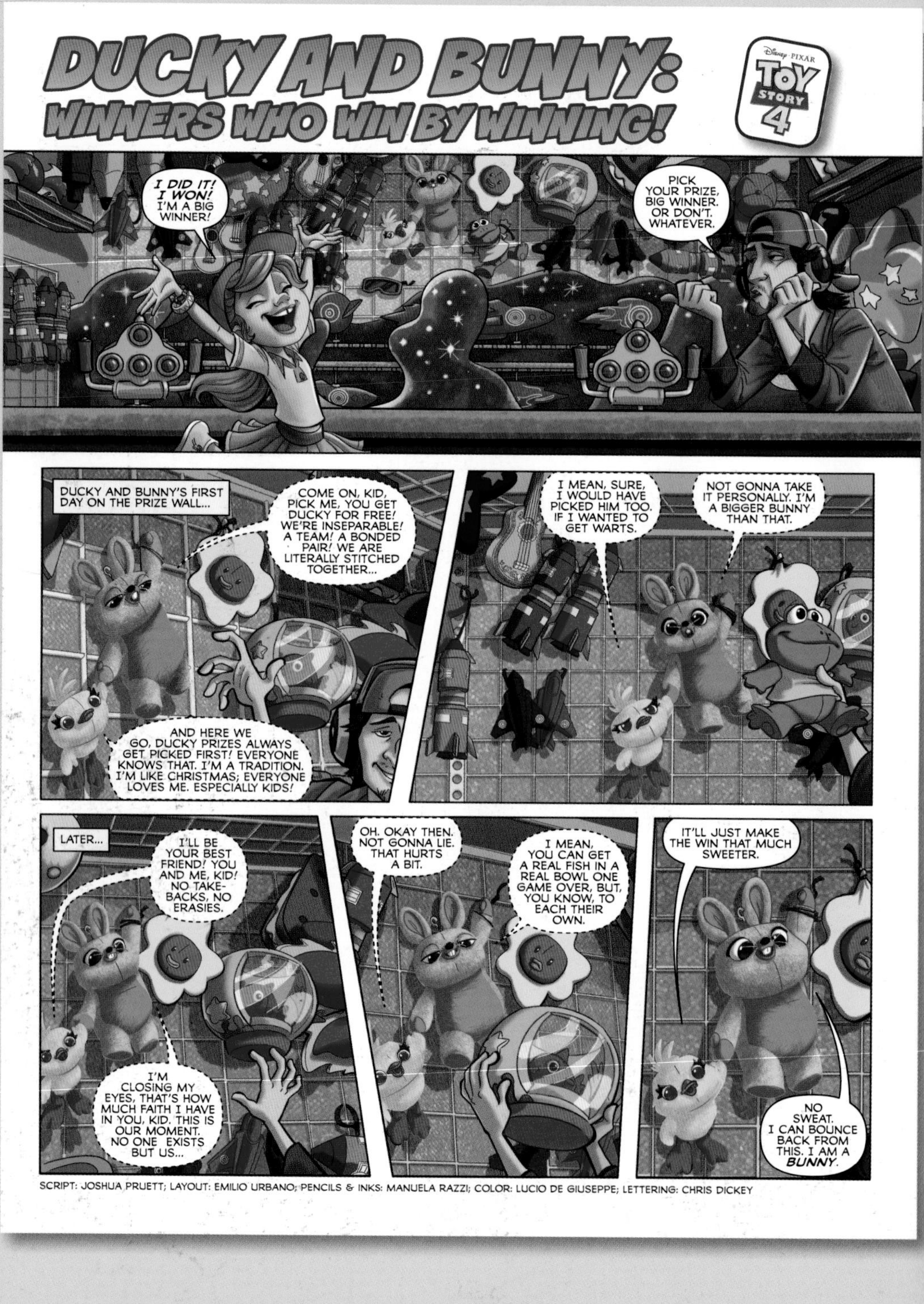

DUCKY AND BUNNY: WINNERS WHO WIN BY WINNING!
DISNEY · PIXAR TOY STORY 4
I DID IT! I WON! I'M A BIG WINNER!
PICK YOUR PRIZE, BIG WINNER. OR DON'T. WHATEVER.
DUCKY AND BUNNY'S FIRST DAY ON THE PRIZE WALL...
COME ON, KID, PICK ME, YOU GET DUCKY FOR FREE! WE'RE INSEPARABLE! A TEAM! A BONDED PAIR! WE ARE LITERALLY STITCHED TOGETHER...
AND HERE WE GO, DUCKY PRIZES ALWAYS GET PICKED FIRST! EVERYONE KNOWS THAT. I'M A TRADITION. I'M LIKE CHRISTMAS; EVERYONE LOVES ME. ESPECIALLY KIDS!
I MEAN, SURE, I WOULD HAVE PICKED HIM TOO. IF I WANTED TO GET WARTS.
NOT GONNA TAKE IT PERSONALLY. I'M A BIGGER BUNNY THAN THAT.
LATER...
I'LL BE YOUR BEST FRIEND! YOU AND ME, KID! NO TAKE-BACKS, NO ERASIES.
I'M CLOSING MY EYES, THAT'S HOW MUCH FAITH I HAVE IN YOU, KID. THIS IS OUR MOMENT. NO ONE EXISTS BUT US...
OH. OKAY THEN. NOT GONNA LIE. THAT HURTS A BIT.
I MEAN, YOU CAN GET A REAL FISH IN A REAL BOWL ONE GAME OVER, BUT, YOU KNOW, TO EACH THEIR OWN.
IT'LL JUST MAKE THE WIN THAT MUCH SWEETER.
NO SWEAT. I CAN BOUNCE BACK FROM THIS. I AM A *BUNNY*.
SCRIPT: JOSHUA PRUETT; LAYOUT: EMILIO URBANO; PENCILS & INKS: MANUELA RAZZI; COLOR: LUCIO DE GIUSEPPE; LETTERING: CHRIS DICKEY

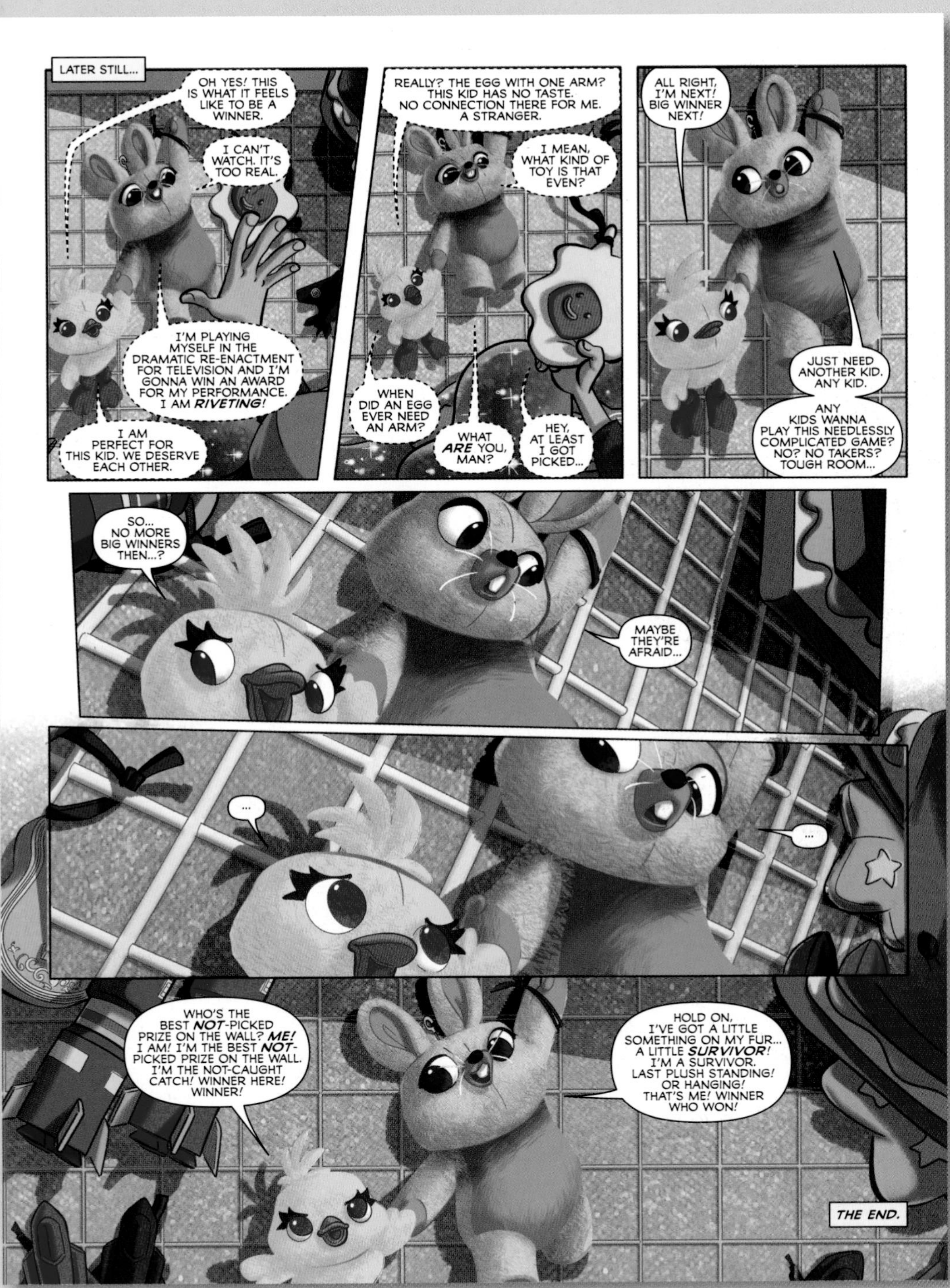

LATER STILL...
OH YES! THIS IS WHAT IT FEELS LIKE TO BE A WINNER.
I CAN'T WATCH. IT'S TOO REAL.
I'M PLAYING MYSELF IN THE DRAMATIC RE-ENACTMENT FOR TELEVISION AND I'M GONNA WIN AN AWARD FOR MY PERFORMANCE. I AM RIVETING!
I AM PERFECT FOR THIS KID. WE DESERVE EACH OTHER.
REALLY? THE EGG WITH ONE ARM? THIS KID HAS NO TASTE. NO CONNECTION THERE FOR ME. A STRANGER.
I MEAN, WHAT KIND OF TOY IS THAT EVEN?
WHEN DID AN EGG EVER NEED AN ARM?
WHAT ARE YOU, MAN?
HEY, AT LEAST I GOT PICKED...
ALL RIGHT, I'M NEXT! BIG WINNER NEXT!
JUST NEED ANOTHER KID. ANY KID.
ANY KIDS WANNA PLAY THIS NEEDLESSLY COMPLICATED GAME? NO? NO TAKERS? TOUGH ROOM...
SO... NO MORE BIG WINNERS THEN...?
MAYBE THEY'RE AFRAID...
...
...
WHO'S THE BEST NOT-PICKED PRIZE ON THE WALL? ME! I AM! I'M THE BEST NOT-PICKED PRIZE ON THE WALL. I'M THE NOT-CAUGHT CATCH! WINNER HERE! WINNER!
HOLD ON, I'VE GOT A LITTLE SOMETHING ON MY FUR... A LITTLE SURVIVOR! I'M A SURVIVOR. LAST PLUSH STANDING! OR HANGING! THAT'S ME! WINNER WHO WON!
THE END.

MORNING ROUTINE

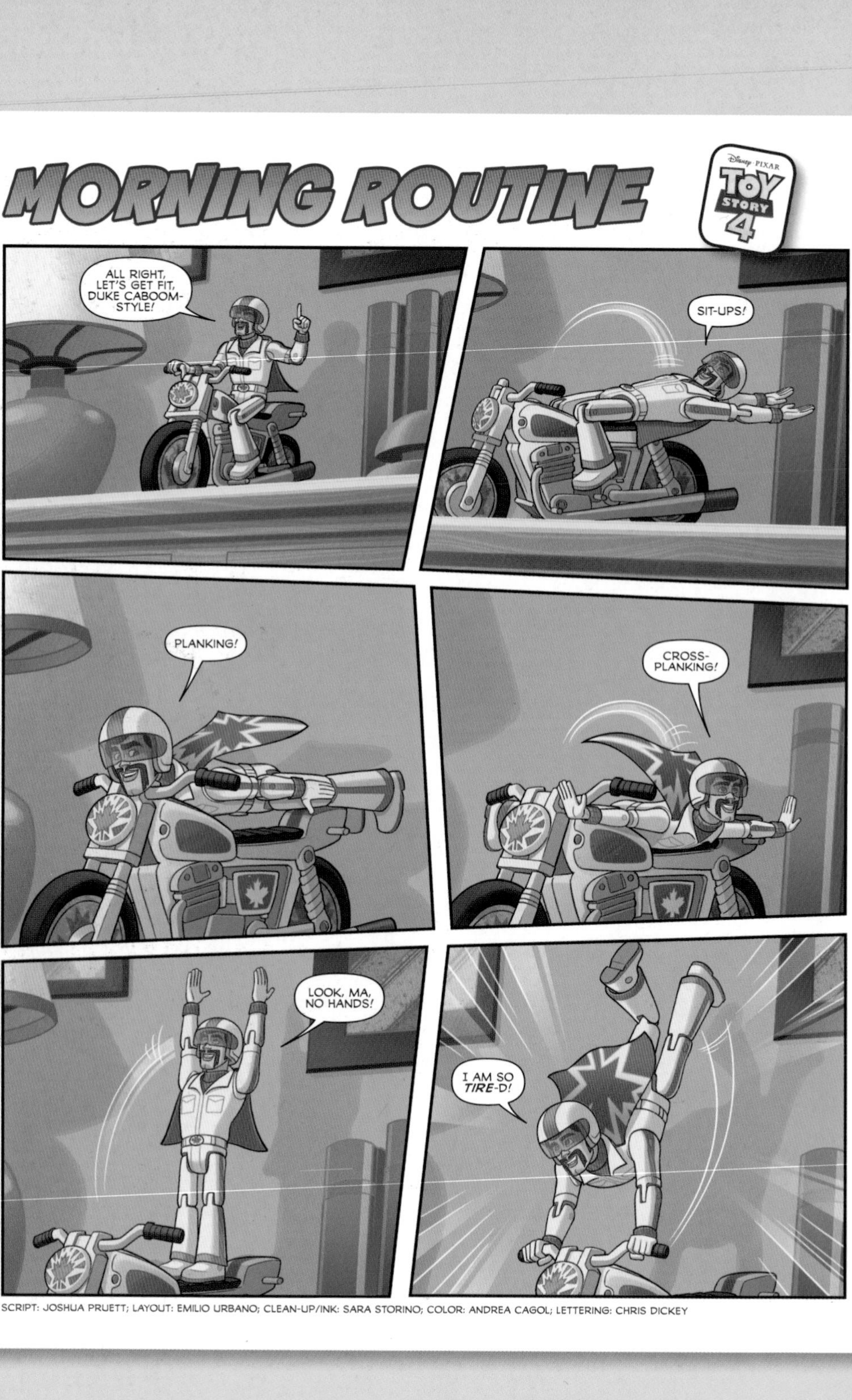

DISNEY·PIXAR TOY STORY 4
ALL RIGHT, LET'S GET FIT, DUKE CABOOM-STYLE!
SIT-UPS!
PLANKING!
CROSS-PLANKING!
LOOK, MA, NO HANDS!
I AM SO *TIRE*-D!

SCRIPT: JOSHUA PRUETT; LAYOUT: EMILIO URBANO; CLEAN-UP/INK: SARA STORINO; COLOR: ANDREA CAGOL; LETTERING: CHRIS DICKEY

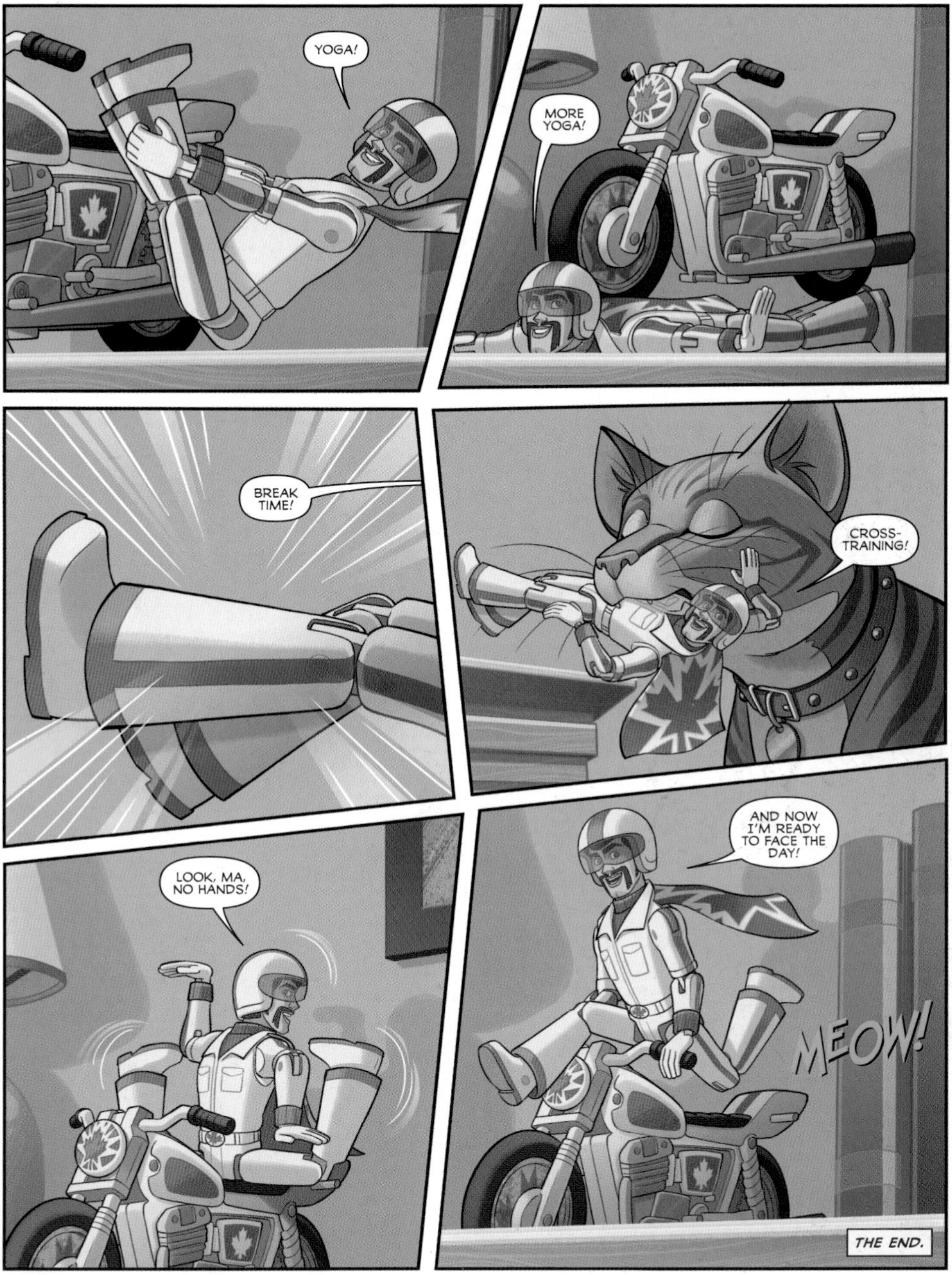
YOGA!
MORE YOGA!
BREAK TIME!
CROSS-TRAINING!
LOOK, MA, NO HANDS!
AND NOW I'M READY TO FACE THE DAY!
MEOW!
THE END.

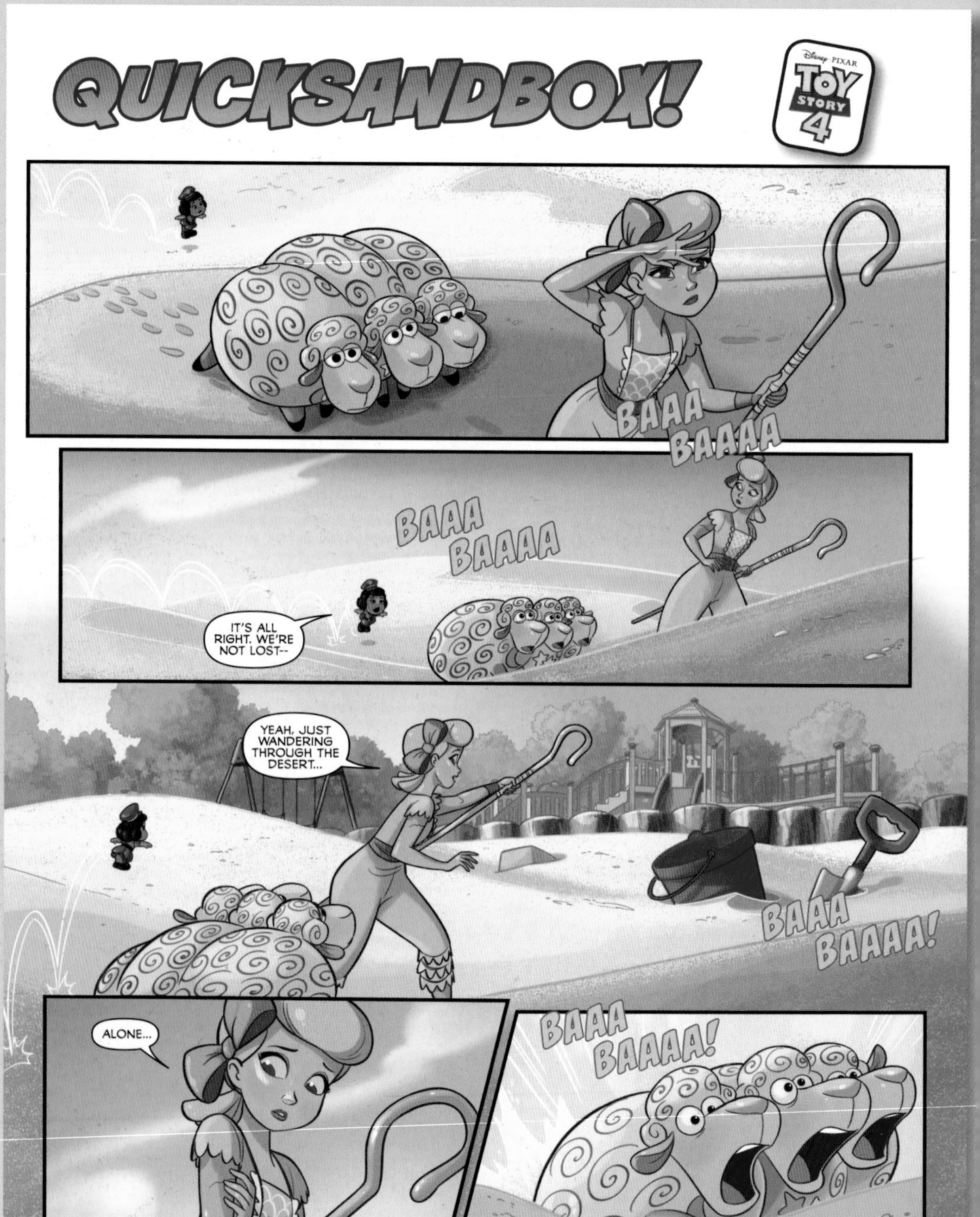
QUICKSANDBOX!
DISNEY · PIXAR TOY STORY 4
BAAA BAAAA
BAAA BAAAA
IT'S ALL RIGHT. WE'RE NOT LOST--
YEAH, JUST WANDERING THROUGH THE DESERT...
BAAA BAAAA!
ALONE...
BAAA BAAAA!
SCRIPT: JOSHUA PRUETT; LAYOUT: EMILIO URBANO; PENCILS & INKS: SARA STORINO; COLOR: MARIA CLAUDIA DI GENOVA; LETTERING: CHRIS DICKEY

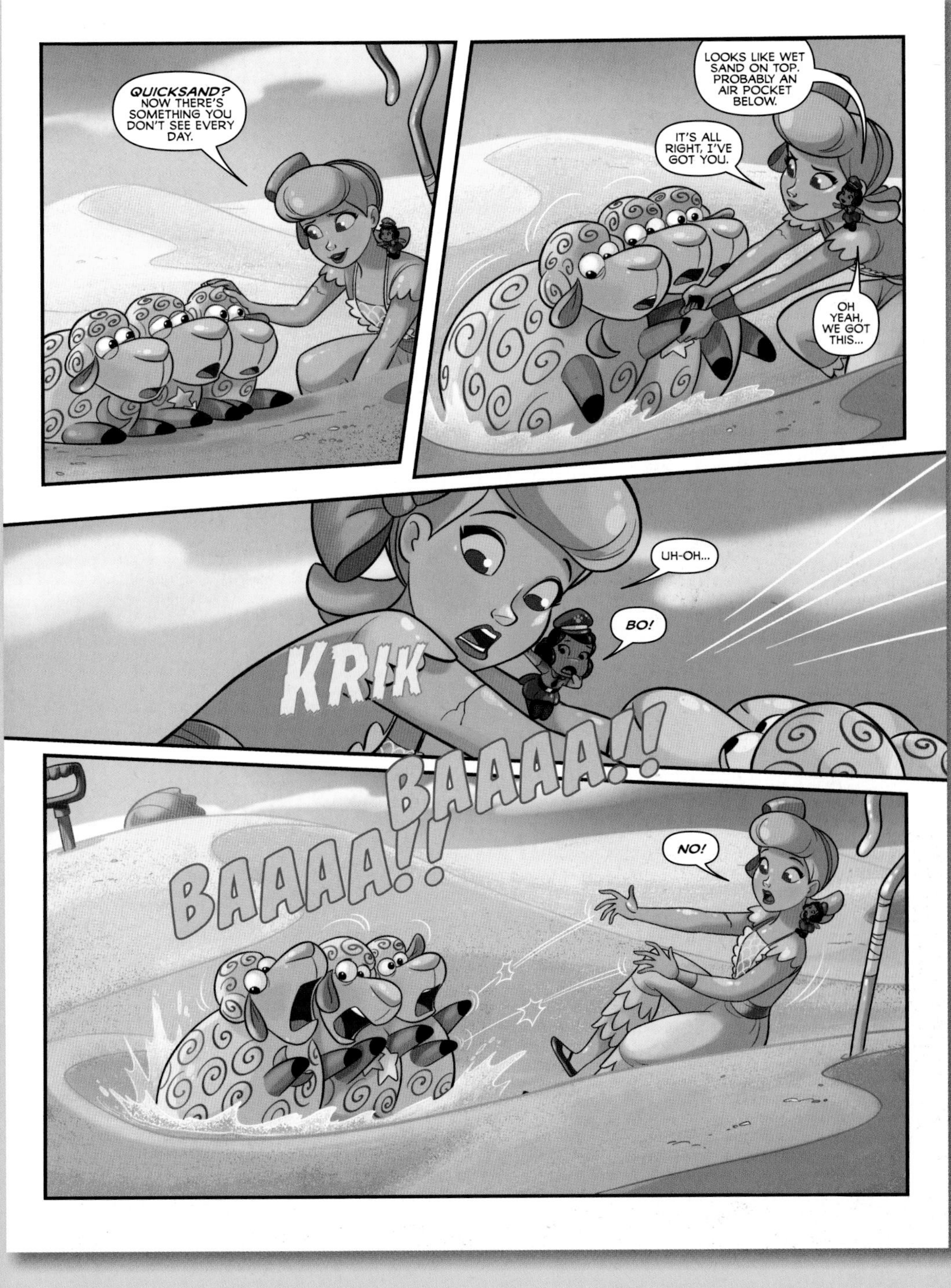
QUICKSAND? NOW THERE'S SOMETHING YOU DON'T SEE EVERY DAY.
LOOKS LIKE WET SAND ON TOP. PROBABLY AN AIR POCKET BELOW.
IT'S ALL RIGHT, I'VE GOT YOU.
OH YEAH, WE GOT THIS...
UH-OH...
BO!
KRIK
BAAAA!!
BAAAA!!
NO!

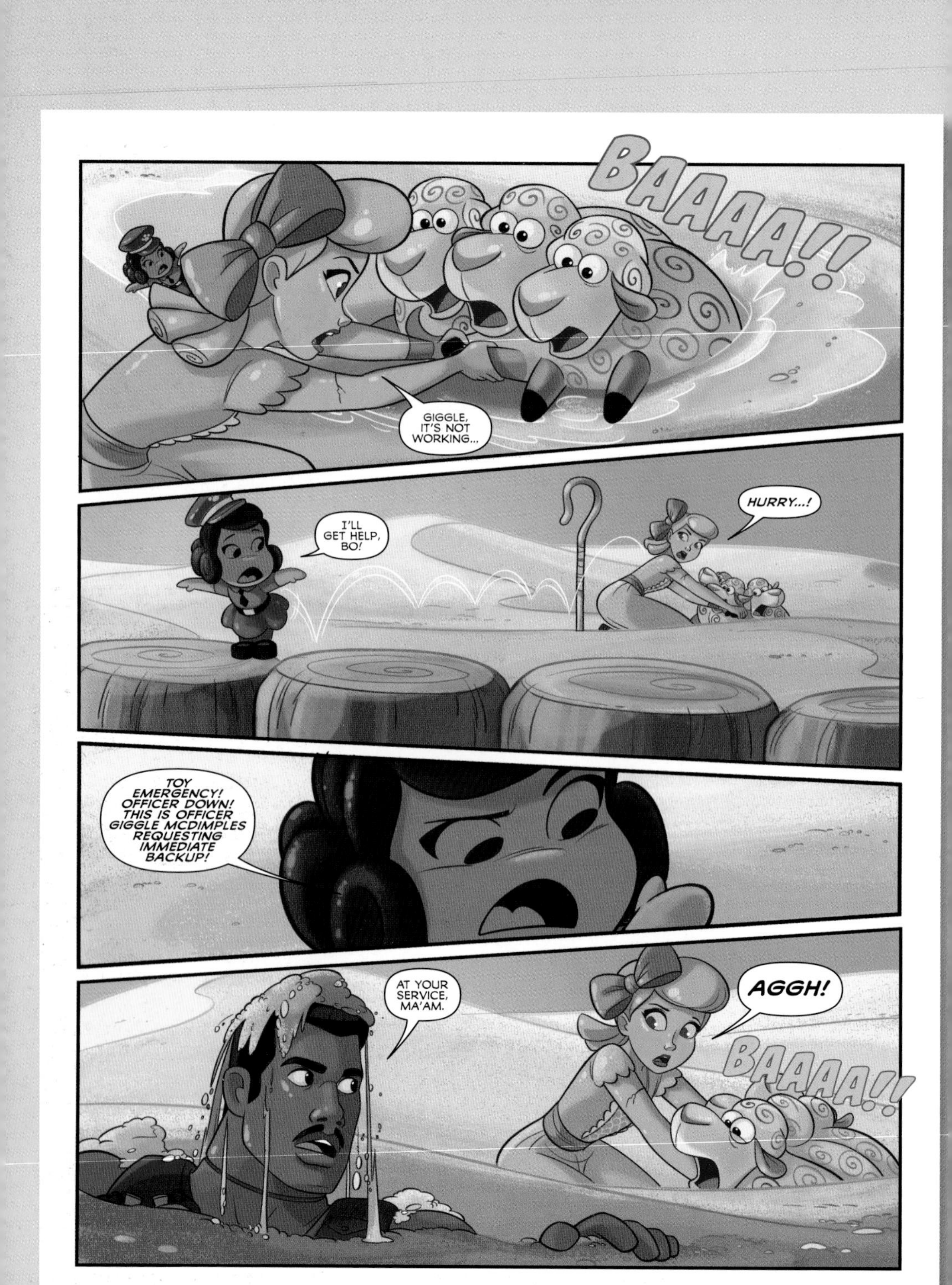
BAAAAA!!
GIGGLE, IT'S NOT WORKING...
I'LL GET HELP, BO!
HURRY...!
TOY EMERGENCY! OFFICER DOWN! THIS IS OFFICER GIGGLE MCDIMPLES REQUESTING IMMEDIATE BACKUP!
AT YOUR SERVICE, MA'AM.
AGGH!
BAAAAA!!

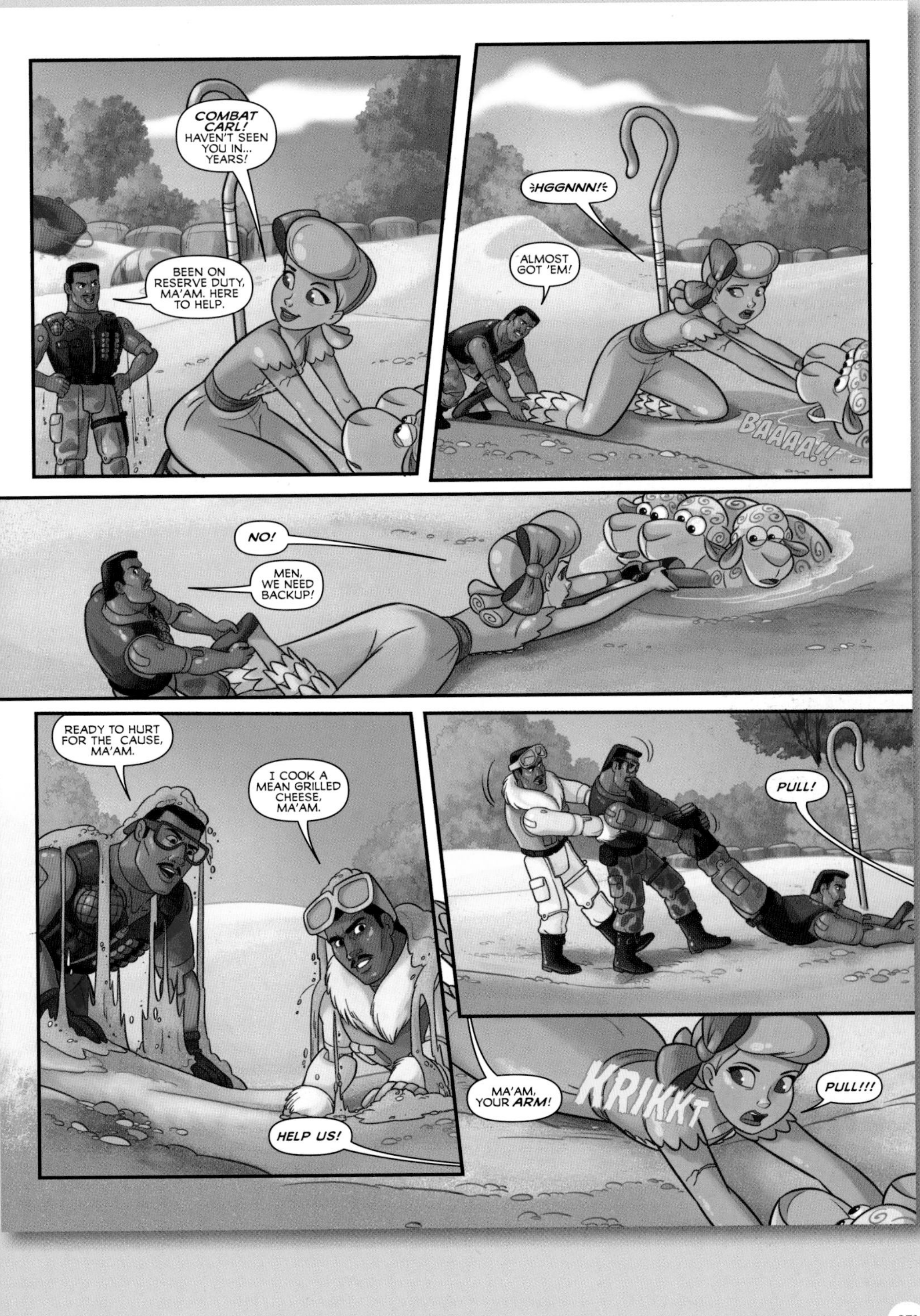
COMBAT CARL! HAVEN'T SEEN YOU IN... YEARS!
BEEN ON RESERVE DUTY, MA'AM. HERE TO HELP.
HGGNNN!
ALMOST GOT 'EM!
BAAAA!!
NO!
MEN, WE NEED BACKUP!
READY TO HURT FOR THE CAUSE, MA'AM.
I COOK A MEAN GRILLED CHEESE, MA'AM.
HELP US!
PULL!
MA'AM, YOUR ARM!
KRIKKT
PULL!!!

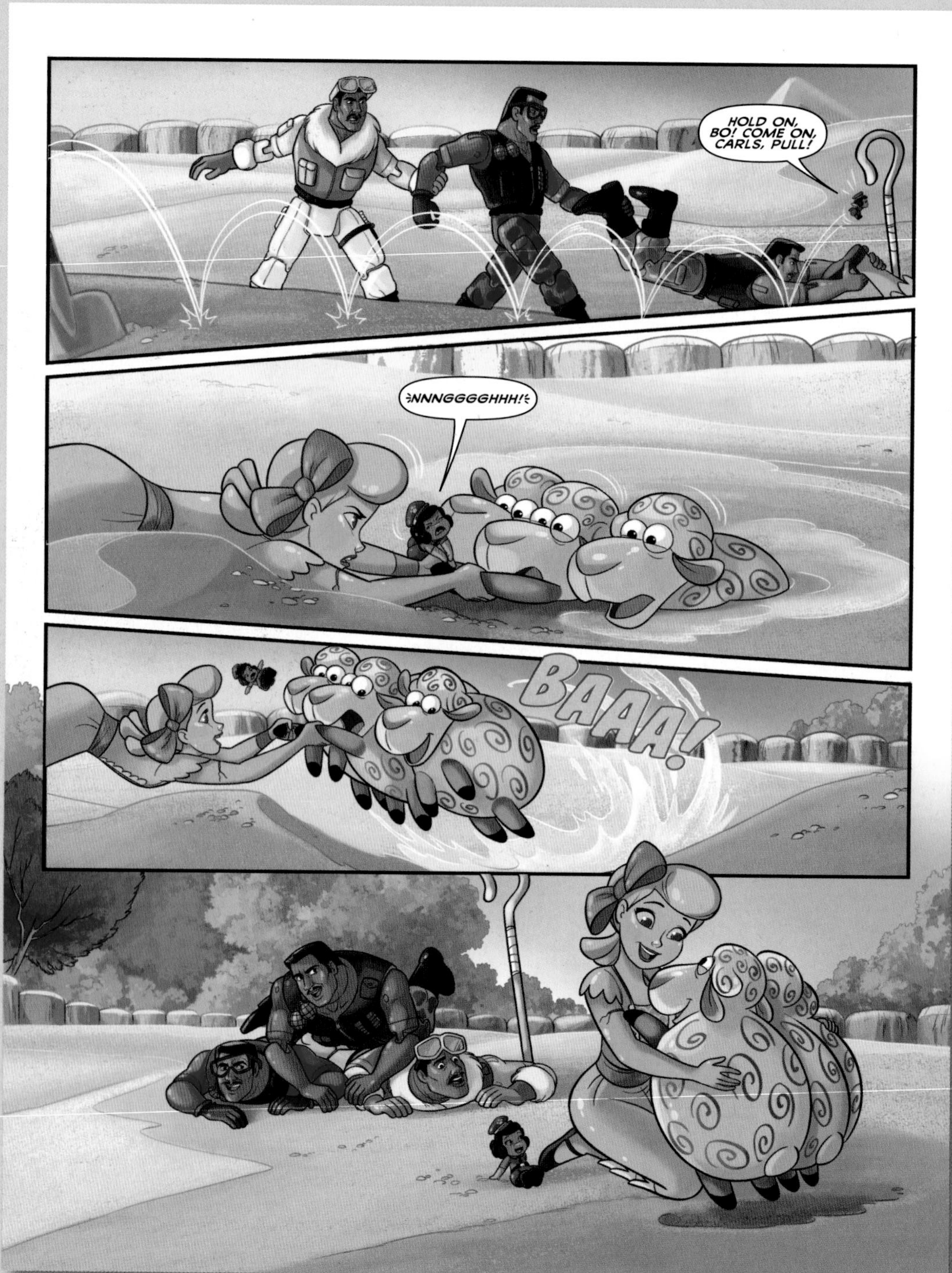
HOLD ON, BO! COME ON, CARLS, PULL!
NNNGGGGHHH!
BAAA!

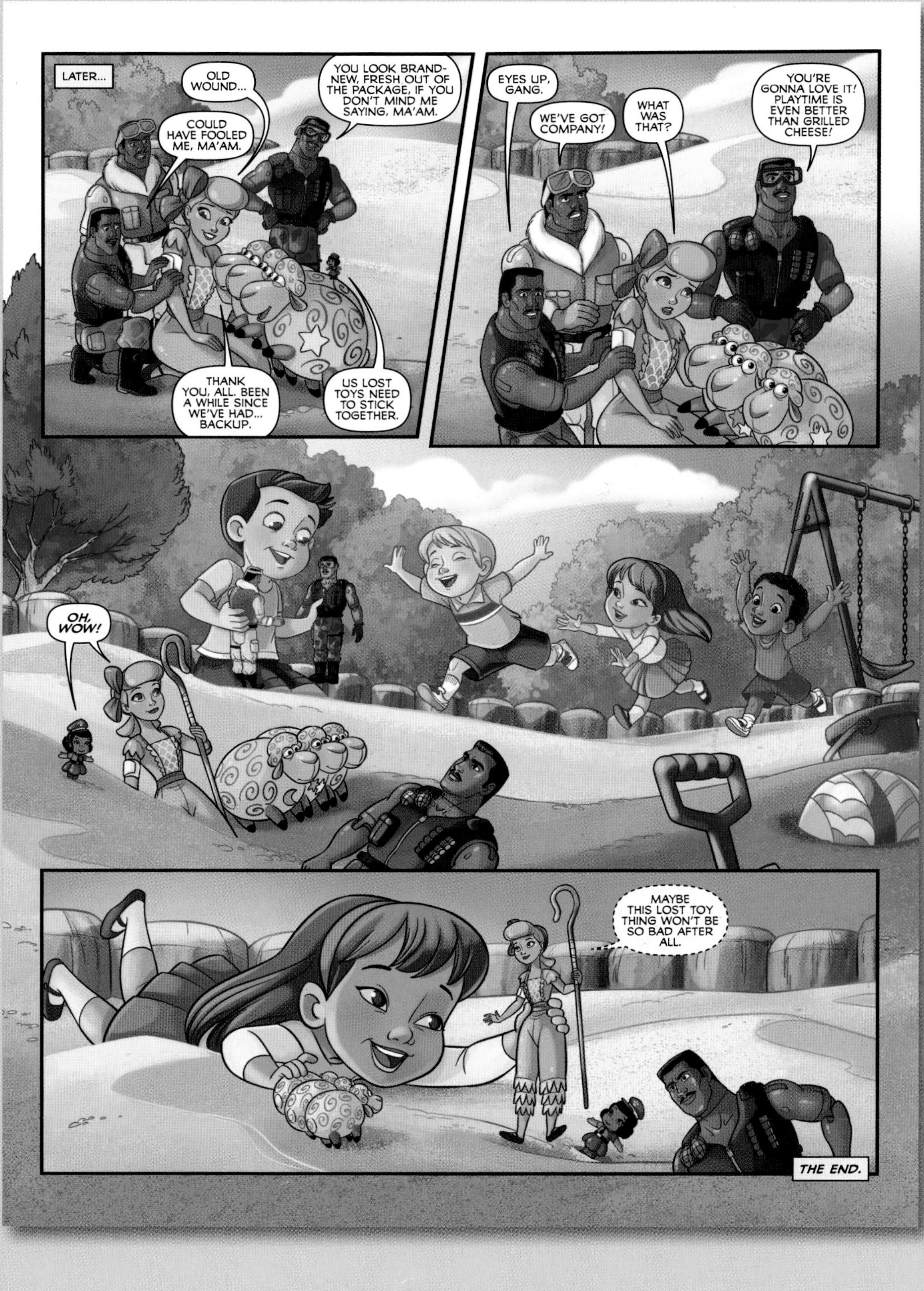

LATER...
OLD WOUND...
COULD HAVE FOOLED ME, MA'AM.
YOU LOOK BRAND-NEW, FRESH OUT OF THE PACKAGE, IF YOU DON'T MIND ME SAYING, MA'AM.
THANK YOU, ALL. BEEN A WHILE SINCE WE'VE HAD... BACKUP.
US LOST TOYS NEED TO STICK TOGETHER.
EYES UP, GANG.
WE'VE GOT COMPANY!
WHAT WAS THAT?
YOU'RE GONNA LOVE IT! PLAYTIME IS EVEN BETTER THAN GRILLED CHEESE!
OH, WOW!
MAYBE THIS LOST TOY THING WON'T BE SO BAD AFTER ALL.
THE END.

THE LONG ROAD

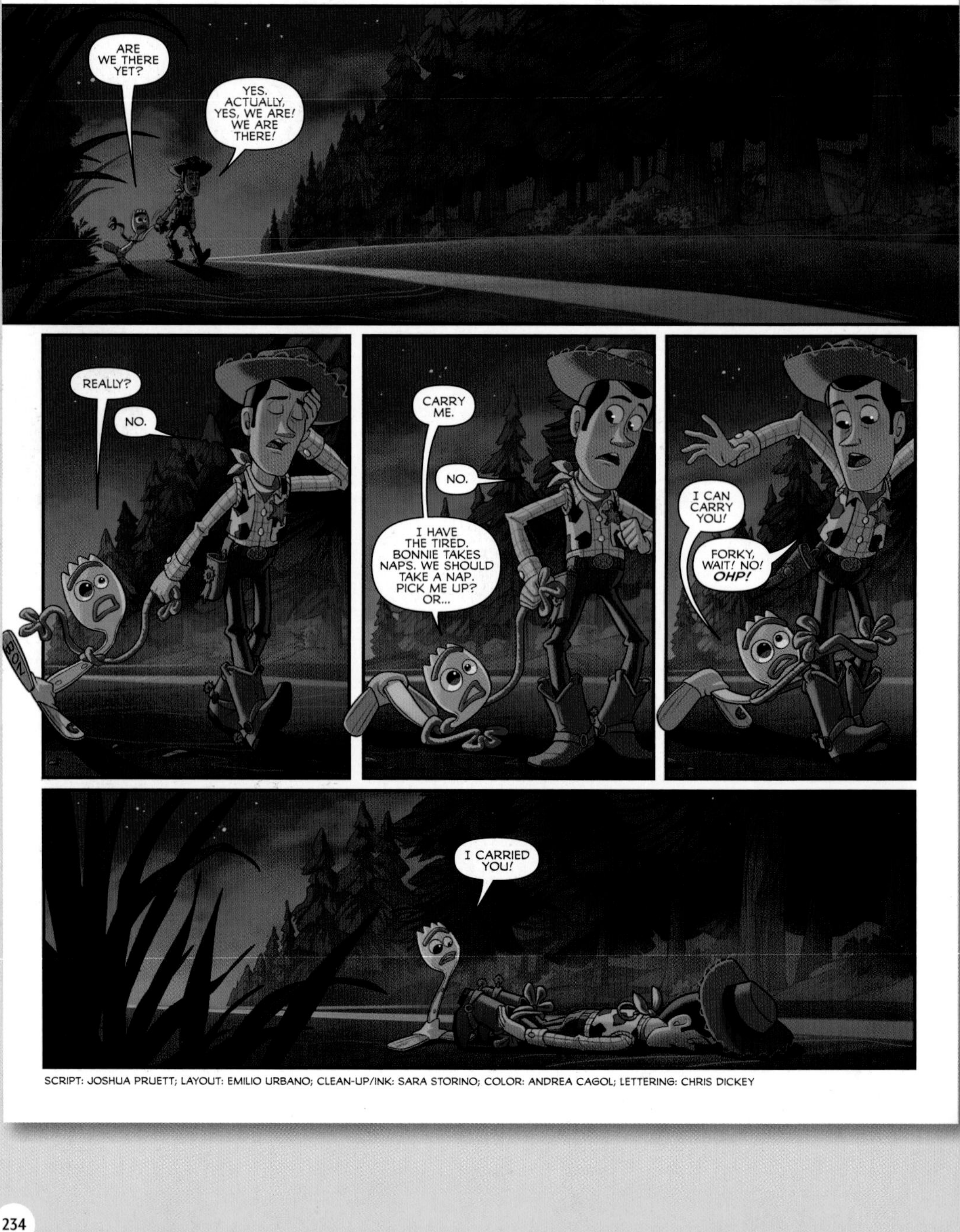
ARE WE THERE YET?
YES. ACTUALLY, YES, WE ARE! WE ARE THERE!
REALLY?
NO.
CARRY ME.
NO.
I HAVE THE TIRED. BONNIE TAKES NAPS. WE SHOULD TAKE A NAP. PICK ME UP? OR...
I CAN CARRY YOU!
FORKY, WAIT! NO! *OHP!*
I CARRIED YOU!

SCRIPT: JOSHUA PRUETT; LAYOUT: EMILIO URBANO; CLEAN-UP/INK: SARA STORINO; COLOR: ANDREA CAGOL; LETTERING: CHRIS DICKEY

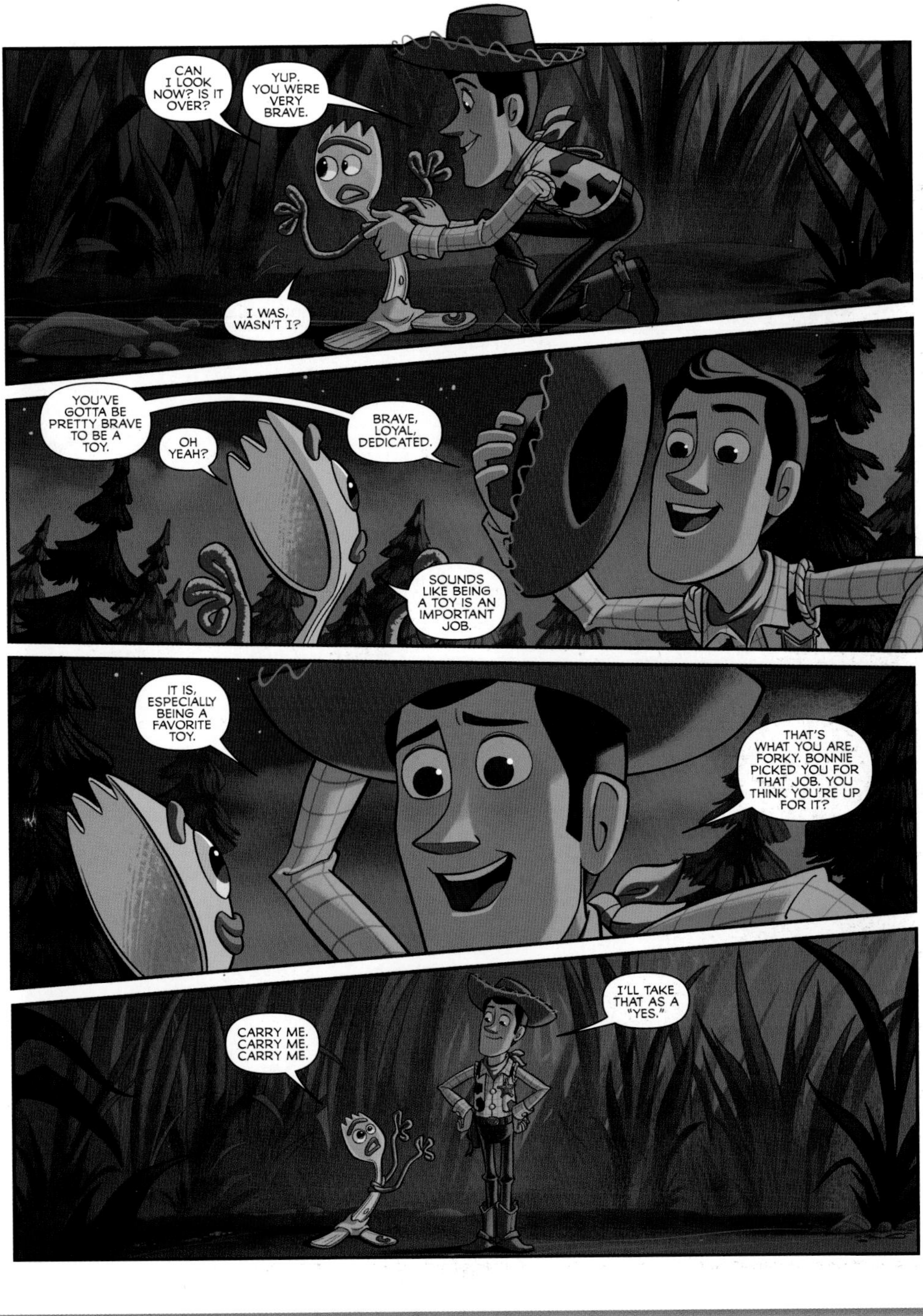
CAN I LOOK NOW? IS IT OVER?
YUP. YOU WERE VERY BRAVE.
I WAS, WASN'T I?
YOU'VE GOTTA BE PRETTY BRAVE TO BE A TOY.
OH YEAH?
BRAVE, LOYAL, DEDICATED.
SOUNDS LIKE BEING A TOY IS AN IMPORTANT JOB.
IT IS, ESPECIALLY BEING A FAVORITE TOY.
THAT'S WHAT YOU ARE, FORKY. BONNIE PICKED YOU FOR THAT JOB. YOU THINK YOU'RE UP FOR IT?
CARRY ME. CARRY ME. CARRY ME.
I'LL TAKE THAT AS A "YES."

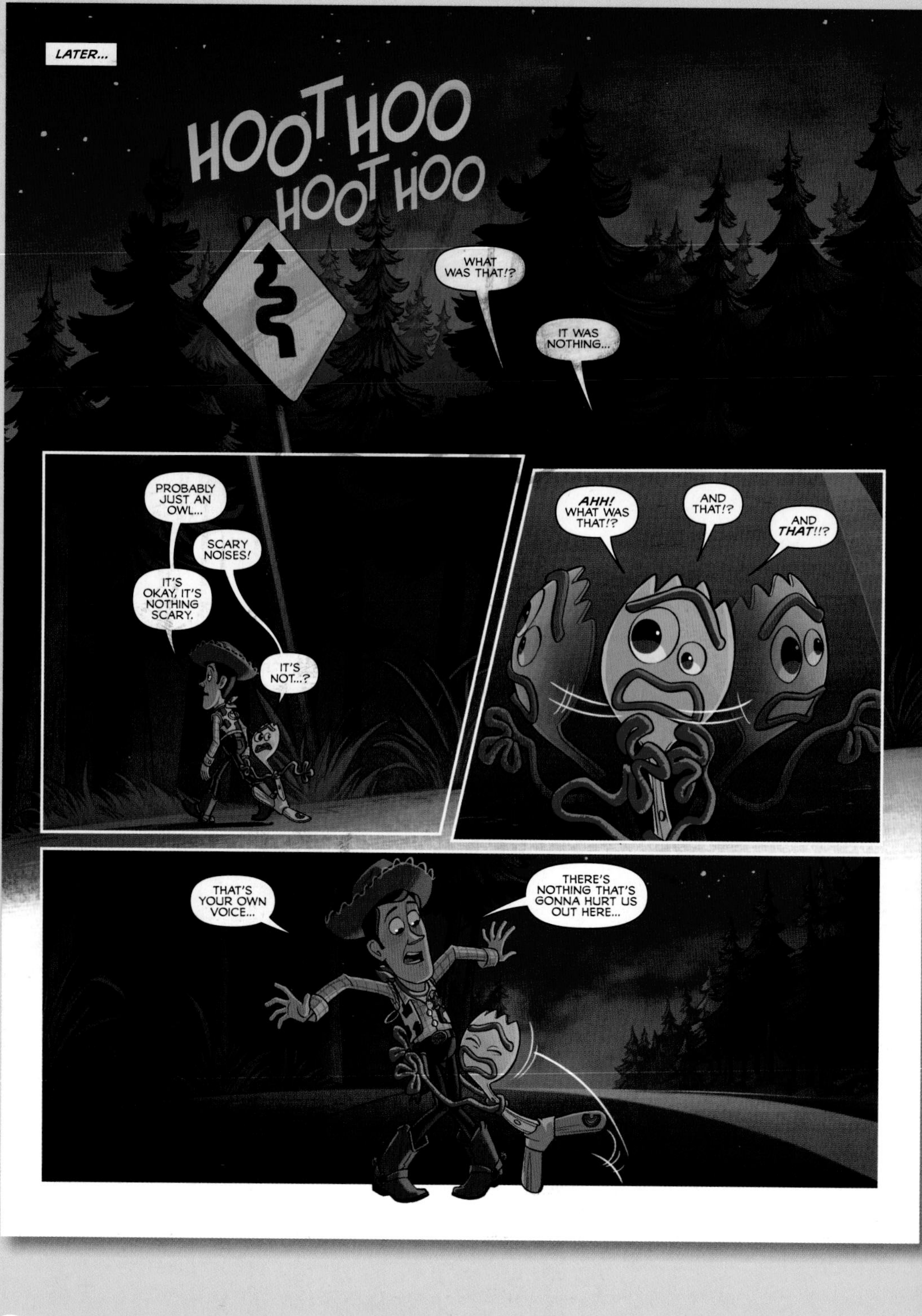
LATER...
HOOT HOO
HOOT HOO
WHAT WAS THAT!?
IT WAS NOTHING...
PROBABLY JUST AN OWL...
SCARY NOISES!
IT'S OKAY, IT'S NOTHING SCARY.
IT'S NOT...?
AHH! WHAT WAS THAT!?
AND THAT!?
AND THAT!!?
THAT'S YOUR OWN VOICE...
THERE'S NOTHING THAT'S GONNA HURT US OUT HERE...

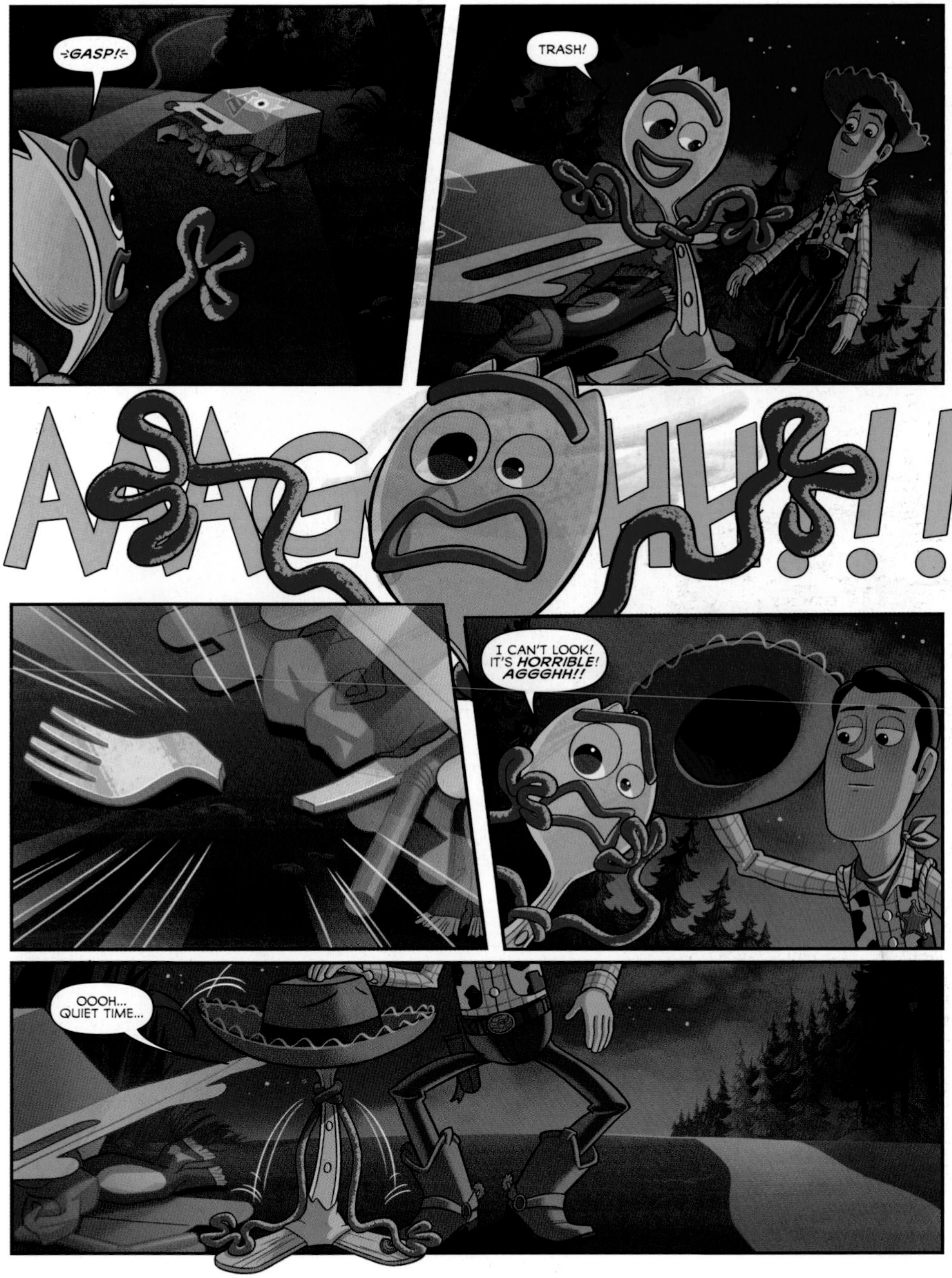
⁼GASP!⁼
TRASH!
AAAGGHHH!!
I CAN'T LOOK! IT'S *HORRIBLE!* *AGGGHH!!*
OOOH... QUIET TIME...

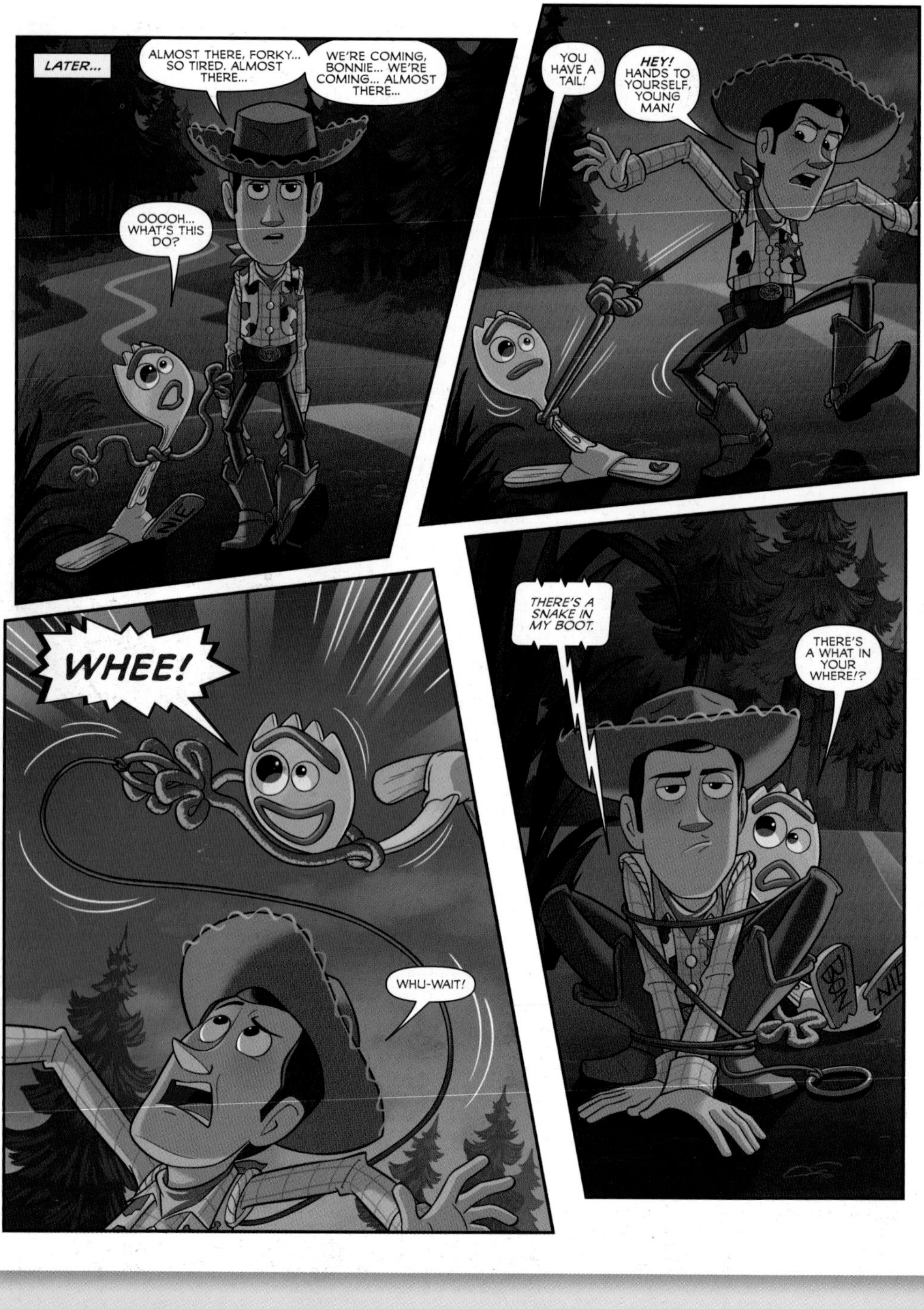
LATER...
ALMOST THERE, FORKY... SO TIRED. ALMOST THERE...
WE'RE COMING, BONNIE... WE'RE COMING... ALMOST THERE...
OOOOH... WHAT'S THIS DO?
YOU HAVE A TAIL!
HEY! HANDS TO YOURSELF, YOUNG MAN!
WHEE!
WHU-WAIT!
THERE'S A SNAKE IN MY BOOT.
THERE'S A WHAT IN YOUR WHERE!?

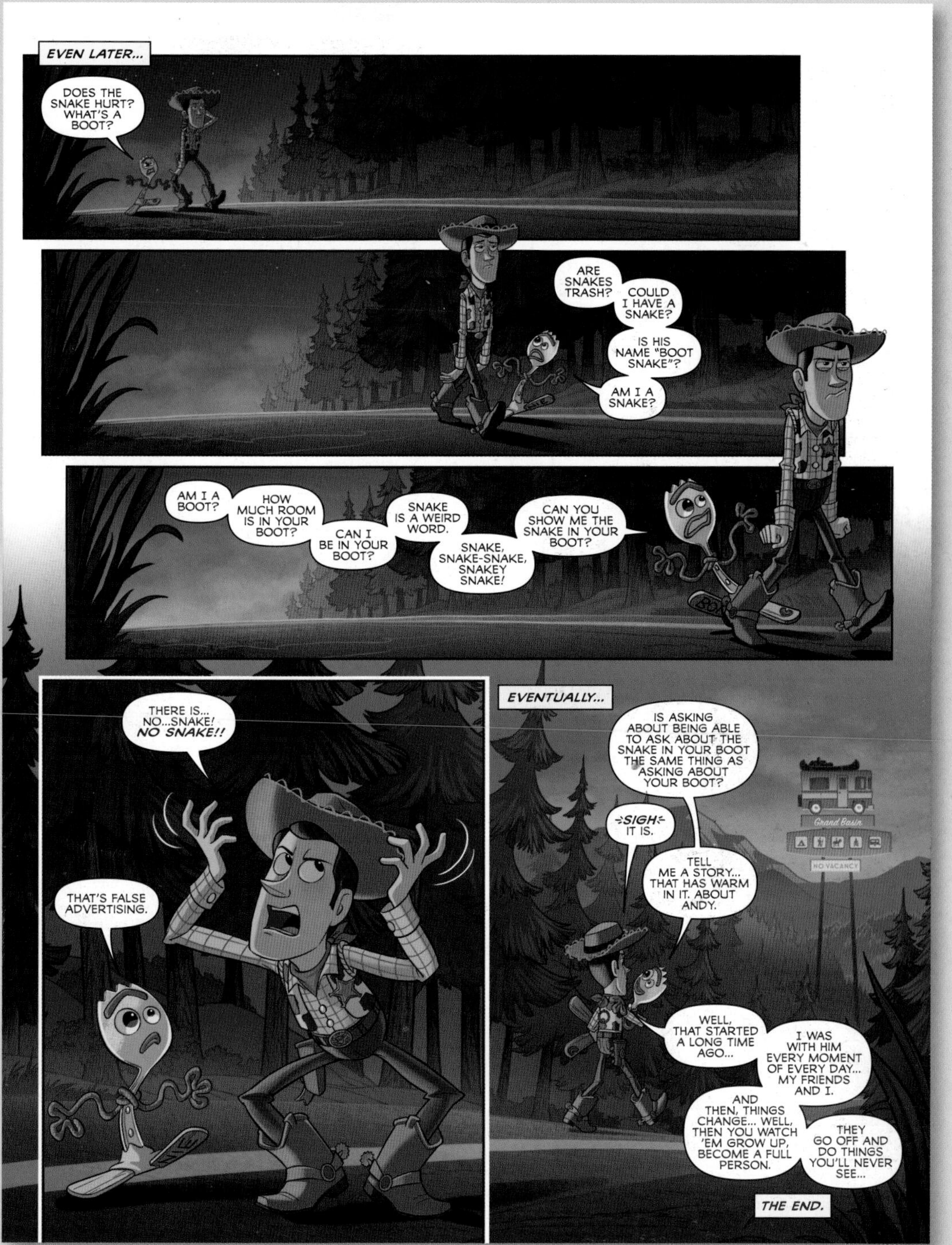
EVEN LATER...
DOES THE SNAKE HURT? WHAT'S A BOOT?
ARE SNAKES TRASH?
COULD I HAVE A SNAKE?
IS HIS NAME "BOOT SNAKE"?
AM I A SNAKE?
AM I A BOOT?
HOW MUCH ROOM IS IN YOUR BOOT?
CAN I BE IN YOUR BOOT?
SNAKE IS A WEIRD WORD.
SNAKE, SNAKE-SNAKE, SNAKEY SNAKE!
CAN YOU SHOW ME THE SNAKE IN YOUR BOOT?
THERE IS... NO...SNAKE! NO SNAKE!!
THAT'S FALSE ADVERTISING.
EVENTUALLY...
IS ASKING ABOUT BEING ABLE TO ASK ABOUT THE SNAKE IN YOUR BOOT THE SAME THING AS ASKING ABOUT YOUR BOOT?
SIGH IT IS.
TELL ME A STORY... THAT HAS WARM IN IT. ABOUT ANDY.
Grand Basin
NO VACANCY
WELL, THAT STARTED A LONG TIME AGO...
I WAS WITH HIM EVERY MOMENT OF EVERY DAY... MY FRIENDS AND I.
AND THEN, THINGS CHANGE... WELL, THEN YOU WATCH 'EM GROW UP, BECOME A FULL PERSON.
THEY GO OFF AND DO THINGS YOU'LL NEVER SEE...
THE END.

Disney · PIXAR

TOY STORY

ADVENTURES
VOLUME 1

CATCH UP WITH WOODY AND FRIENDS FROM DISNEY·PIXAR'S *TOY STORY*!

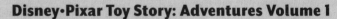

Disney·Pixar Toy Story: Adventures Volume 1

A collection of short comic stories based on the animated films Disney·Pixar *Toy Story 1*, *Toy Story 2*, and *Toy Story 3*!

Set your jets for adventure. Join Woody, Buzz, and all of your *Toy Story* favorites in a variety of fun and exciting comic stories. Get ready to play with your favorite toys along with Andy and Bonnie, join the toys as they take more journeys to the outside, play make-believe in a world of infinite possibilities, meet new friends, have a party or two—experience all of this and more in this collection of *Toy Story Adventures* Volume 1! **978-1-50671-266-6 $10.99**

AVAILABLE AT YOUR LOCAL COMICS SHOP OR BOOKSTORE!
To find a comics shop in your area, visit **comicshoplocator.com** For more information or to order direct: On the web: **DarkHorse.com**
Email: **mailorder@darkhorse.com** Phone: **1-800-862-0052** Mon.–Fri. 9 a.m. to 5 p.m. Pacific Time

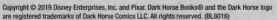